DUTY ROSTER

David Sherman

Keith R.A. DeCandido

D1453967

THE 18th RACE — OMNIBUS

DAVID SHERMAN
with
KEITH R.A. DeCANDIDO

Pennsville, NJ

PUBLISHED BY
eSpec Books LLC
Danielle McPhail, Publisher
PO Box 242,
Pennsville, New Jersey 08070
www.especbooks.com

Copyediting: Keith R.A. DeCandido and Greg Schauer
Design: Mike and Danielle McPhail
Cover Art: Mike McPhail, McP Digital Graphics

CONTENTS

– ISSUE IN –
DOUBT

DAVID SHERMAN

"Enemy on island. Issue in doubt."
Commander Winfield S. Cunningham, U.S. Navy,
the Battle of Wake Island

This book is dedicated to the memory of:

Corporal John F. Mackie

The first US Marine to earn
The Medal of Honor;
At the Battle of Drewry's Bluff
May 15, 1862

PROLOG: FIRST CONTACT

McKinzie Elevator Base, Outside Millerton,
Semi-Autonomous World Troy

SAMUEL ROGERS JERKED WHEN HE HEARD THE BEEPING OF THE PROXIMITY alert. HE spun in his chair to look at the approach displays and his jaw dropped. With one hand he toggled the space-comm to hail the incoming ship, with the other he reached for the local comm to call Frederick Franklin, his boss.

Franklin sounded groggy when he answered. "This better be good, Rogers. I just got to sleep."

"Sorry, Chief, but are we expecting any starships? One just popped up half an AU north. Uh oh."

"No, we aren't expecting anyone. And what do you mean, 'uh oh'?"

"Chief—" Rodgers' voice broke and he had to start again. "Chief, data coming in says the incoming starship is three klicks wide."

"Bullshit," Franklin snapped. "There aren't any starships that big!"

"I know. It's got to be an asteroid. And it's on an intercept vector."

"There aren't any asteroids north." Franklin's voice dropped to a barely intelligible mumble. "North, that would explain how it 'just popped up.'" Indistinct noises sounded to Rogers like his boss was getting dressed. "Have you tried to hail her?"

"The same time I called you. But half an AU..."

"Yeah, yeah, I know. Stand by, I'm on my way."

"Standing by." Rogers sounded relieved.

Franklin burst into the spaceport's operations room and headed straight for the approach displays. In seconds he absorbed the data, and let out a grunt.

"Any reply yet?" he asked.

Rogers shook his head. "Too soon, Chief."

Franklin grimaced; he should have realized that and not have asked such a dumb question. The starship—asteroid, whatever—was half an Astronomical Unit out, half the distance from old Earth to Sol. It would take about four minutes for the hail to reach the incoming object, and another four minutes for a reply to come back. Plus however much time it would take for whoever it was to decide to answer the hail. The two men watched the data display as time ticked by.

After watching for another fifteen minutes, with no reply, and nothing but confirmation as to its velocity, vector, and probable impact time, Franklin decided to kick the problem upstairs.

"Office of the President." James Merton's voice was thick when he answered the president's comm; the night duty officer must have been dozing.

"Jim, Fred here. We've got a situation that requires some attention from the boss."

"Can it wait until morning? Bill's had a long day, and he's dead to the world."

"Come morning, it might be too late to do anything."

"Come on, Fred," Merton said. "No offense intended, but you're an elevator operator. What kind of earth-shattering problem can you possibly have?"

"Exactly that: a literally earth-shattering problem. There's a large object on an intercept course. That's large, as in planet-buster. It'll be here in less than a standard day."

There was a momentary silence before Merton asked, "You aren't kidding, are you?"

"I wish. Stand by for the data." Franklin nodded to Rogers, who transmitted a data set to the president's office. A minute later, Franklin and Rogers heard Merton swear under his breath.

"You called it, something that big really is a planet buster, isn't it?" the duty officer asked.

"Unfortunately," Franklin answered.

"Now, according to the data you sent me, the object is metallic, and it seems to have the density of a starship rather than the density of an asteroid. Am I reading those figures right?"

"You're reading right," Franklin said. "But nobody makes starships that big."

"At least nobody we know of," Rogers murmured. "Have you tried to contact it, I mean, in case it *is* a starship?"

"Yes, we did." Franklin looked at Rogers, who held up four fingers. "Four times. No response."

"And you're sure it's on a collision course?"

Franklin shivered. "Absolutely."

"Keep trying to make contact. I'll wake the president."

An hour and a half later, a three-man Navy rescue team under the command of Lieutenant (j.g.) Cyrus Hayden, rode the elevator up to Base 1, in geosynchronous orbit, where they boarded the tender *John Andrews* to take a closer look at the rapidly approaching object. If it was a starship their orders were to again attempt radio contact. If she did not reply, to attempt to board her. If the object was an unusual asteroid, Hayden and his men were to plant a nuclear device on its side, then back off to a safe distance before detonating the bomb. It was hoped that the explosion would deflect the object's course enough to avoid the collision that was looking more certain with each passing minute.

The North American Union Navy tender *John Andrews* was still 100,000 kilometers from the object when laser beams lanced out from it and shredded the tender.

Twenty shocked minutes later, the orbital lasers of Troy's defensive batteries shot beams of coherent light. The only effect the lasers seemed to have on the object, which was now obviously a warship from some unknown people, was to provide the enemy with the location of the defensive weapons. Within minutes, all of Troy's orbital laser batteries were knocked out by counter-battery fire from the enemy starship. It had committed an act of war when it vaporized the *John Andrews*, hadn't it? Didn't that make it the enemy?

When the enemy starship was a quarter million kilometers out, it fired braking rockets, which slowed its speed and altered its vector enough to reach high orbit rather than colliding with the planet. Small objects began flicking off it and heading toward the surface.

Ground-based laser and missile batteries began firing at the small vessels. The mother-ship killed those batteries as easily as she had killed the orbital batteries.

Shortly after that the first landers made planetfall, and reports of wholesale slaughter began coming in, William F. Lukes, President of Troy, ordered all the data they had on the invasion uploaded onto drones and the drones launched: Destination Earth.

The unidentified enemy killed the first several drones, but stopped shooting them when it became obvious that they were running away rather than attacking.

Two days later, four of the drones reached the Sol System via wormhole. It took ten more days for a North American Union Navy frigate to pick one of them up and carry it to Garroway Base on Mars, from where its coded message was transmitted to the NAU's Supreme Military Headquarters on Earth.

Supreme Military Headquarters, Bellevue,
Sarpy County, Federal Zone, North American Union

MAJOR GENERAL JOSEPH H. DE CASTRO SWEPT PAST THE GUARDS STANDING OUTSIDE the entrance to the offices of the Chairman of the Joint Chiefs of Staff and marched through the cavernous, darkly paneled outer office directly to the desk of Colonel Nicholas Fox, which sat below the colors of all the military services of the NAU.

"Nick," de Castro said, "I need to see the Chairman, right now. I don't care who he's meeting with."

Fox leaned back in his chair and looked up at de Castro with mild curiosity. "Joe, you know I can't let people just barge in on the Chairman." He shook his head. "His schedule today is packed tighter than a constipated jarhead. Maybe if he stops by the Flag Club later on, you can get a minute or two with him. Can't help you, Joe." Fox then looked intently at his console, as though he had pressing business to attend to. His behavior was insubordinate, but in this office, acting in his official capacity as gatekeeper to the Chairman, he effectively outranked anybody with fewer than four stars, and de Castro had only two.

"If you knew what I have here," de Castro tapped the right breast pocket of his uniform jacket, "you wouldn't be wasting my time. I'd already be telling the Chairman what I've got."

"So tell me what you've got. I'll decide if it's important enough to disrupt the Chairman's schedule."

De Castro glowered at Fox for a few seconds, then said, steely-voiced, "Have it your way, Nick. You can explain to the Chairman why I had to jump the chain." He about-faced to march out, but Fox stopped him before he'd taken more than two steps.

"Wait a minute, Joe. What do you mean, 'jump the chain'?"

De Castro half turned back. "I'm going fifty paces. This can't wait." Fifty paces was the distance from where he was to the offices of the Secretary of War.

"You wouldn't!" Fox said, shocked.

"I will."

Colonel Fox opened his mouth to say something more, but thought for a couple of seconds before he spoke. "Wait one," he said, and tapped his desk comm, the direct line to the Chairman's inner sanctum.

"Sir," he said apologetically when the Chairman came on, "Major General de Castro is here. He says he has something that requires the Secretary's immediate attention." He paused to listen, answered, "No Sir, he won't tell me what it is." Another pause to listen. "I'll tell him, Sir." He looked at de Castro. "He'll see you in a minute or so."

De Castro faced the door leading deeper into the Chairman's offices, and stood at ease, patiently waiting. A moment later, the door opened and de Castro snapped to attention. Fleet Admiral Ira Clinton Welborn, Chairman of the Joint Chiefs of Staff, ushered out a man de Castro recognized as Field Marshal Carl Ludwig, Welborn's counterpart in the European Union's military. Welborn was making placating noises, and assuring Ludwig that he would have dinner with him at the Flag Club that evening.

As soon as the EU's military chief was gone, Welborn turned on de Castro and snarled. "This better be good. I've been getting close to a diplomatic breakthrough with that martinet, and you might have just bollixed it!"

"It is, Sir," de Castro said in a strong voice.

"Follow." Welborn headed back to his inner sanctum. De Castro followed a pace behind and slightly to Welborn's left. The two marched along a darkly wainscoted corridor with offices branching off to both sides, toward a wider space at the end, where a navy petty officer sat at a desk working on a comp. Two Marines in dress blues, a first lieutenant and a gunnery sergeant, both armed with holstered sidearms, stood at parade rest flanking the doorway to the inner sanctum. The two came to attention at Welborn's approach. De Castro couldn't help but notice that the gunnery sergeant had several more rows of ribbons on his chest than he himself did, and the lieutenant had nearly as many as the gunny. It was obvious that the Marines were from the combat arms.

"Siddown," Welborn snapped as the petty officer began to stand. She did and returned to her work. "Close it," he snarled at the Marines. The door to the inner sanctum closed silently behind de Castro when the two swept past.

Inside was an office only slightly less opulent than that of the Secretary of War himself. Its walls were covered with pictures of warships: paintings, engravings, lithographs, photographs, and holograms. Wooden ships: with rams and oars; with sails; with sails and cannon; iron clad with sails; iron clad with sails and steam engines. Steel ships: with guns in turrets, aircraft carriers with and without turrets and missiles. Space-going warships.

Welborn headed for his massive desk and dropped into the leather-upholstered executive chair behind it. "All right, de Castro, what do you have?" He didn't offer a seat.

"This came in ten minutes ago, Sir," de Castro said as he fingered a crystal out of his right breast pocket. "By your leave, Sir?" He made to insert the crystal in the comp to the side of the desk. Welborn grunted assent, and de Castro completed the action. In a second, a report appeared on the console. Welborn quickly read through it.

"Images?"

"They're garbled, Sir. The cryptographer who decoded the message and the watch officer who delivered it from her to me are attempting to clean them up now."

"Is anybody helping them?"

"Only if they're disobeying my orders. I instructed them to keep this between themselves, and to discuss it with nobody but me."

"Good. Instruct your security personnel to quarantine them as soon as they're done. And I want the images zipped to me the instant they're intelligible, no matter where I am. Right now, you and I are going to see the Secretary."

De Castro called in the orders to isolate the cryptographer and the watch officer as he followed the Chairman out of the office. He didn't even glance at Colonel Fox as he passed through the outer office. Four minutes later, the two were face to face with Richmond P. Hobson, the Secretary of War himself, one of the three most important and powerful people in the entire North American Union.

Hobson seated them in a conversational group of chairs around a small table, and made small talk while a Navy steward poured coffee. De Castro, who had never before been in this office, glanced around. Portraits were hung above dark blond wainscoting that looked like it might be real oak. De Castro recognized enough of the faces in the paintings to know that they were previous NAU Secretaries of War, and the Secretaries of Defense of the old United States, the Canadian Ministers of Defence, and the Mexican Ministers of Defense going back to the beginning of the twentieth century free-trade agreement among the three countries—the precursor of the North American Union.

Hobson took a sip of coffee as the steward exited, then asked, "Well, Ira, what does J2 have that's so important that you have to bring its director to me on such short notice?"

"Show him," Welborn said.

"Yes, Sir." De Castro looked around for a comp. Hobson pressed a button on the side of his chair and one arose from the side of the coffee table. "Thank you, Sir." De Castro inserted the crystal. He angled the display so the Secretary could read the report without leaning to the side.

After a moment, Hobson sat back. "How firm is this?"

"We haven't had time to verify, Sir," de Castro said. "This only came in about fifteen minutes ago."

"What about images?"

Welborn told him that the garbled images were being worked on, but he expected to have something shortly. De Castro nodded agreement.

"We have to tell the President instantly," Hobson said. "And get State in on it." He pressed another button on the side of his chair, and a Navy lieutenant commander appeared inside the door.

"Tom," Hobson addressed him, "kindly contact your counterparts at the President's office and SecState, and inform them that I request a meeting at the earliest possible moment. Emphasize that it's of the gravest importance."

"Aye aye, Sir." The lieutenant commander about-faced and exited.

"Tom Irving," Hobson told Welborn and de Castro, "good man." He looked directly at Welborn. "When his tour with me is over, he deserves to have three full stripes, and be given a command."

Welborn nodded. "Sir, with a recommendation like that, I think a promotion and command assignment will be expedited."

"Do you think we should send a reconnaissance mission to Troy?" Hobson asked Welborn, getting back to the topic at hand.

"Yes, Sir, I do."

"I hoped you'd say that. Who do you recommend?"

"Marine Force Recon."

"Oh?" Hobson cocked his head. "Not SEALs or Rangers?"

"No, Sir. Force Recon. While both SEALs and Rangers are adept at intelligence gathering, they spend as much time training in commando strikes. Force Recon spends almost all of its time and energy 'snooping and pooping,' as they call it, gathering intelligence. They fight only *in extremis*, and believe their mission has failed if they have to fight. I don't want anybody fighting until we know who—or what—we're up against."

"Very good. How soon can Force Recon deploy a sufficient number of teams?"

"Within three days after an operation order is drawn up, Sir. Possibly sooner. *Probably* sooner."

"Very good. Get started on the op order as soon as you can. I'll authorize deploying the Marines as soon as the President gives his permission."

"Aye aye, Sir," the Chairman said.

De Castro jerked; his comm had vibrated. He looked at it. "Excuse me, Sirs, I think I should take this."

Hobson gestured for him to rise and take the call. De Castro stepped away a few feet before answering his comm. He listened for a moment, said something, listened again, gave an order, broke the connection, and resumed his seat.

"Sirs, three more drones from Troy have been brought in. They all have the same message as the one you've seen. One of them had a few usable images. They are being sent to all three of us."

"Good!" Hobson rubbed his hands briskly and looked at the comp. In seconds, it signaled incoming traffic from J2. "I'll put them up on the big screen." He pressed another button on his chair, and a two-by-three-meter display screen rose on the wall behind the grouping where they sat. After a few touches on his comp controls, a slide show began on the display.

The three men watched in stunned silence as little more than half a dozen images, some stills and some vids, rotated through. None of the pictures were fully in focus, and some had scrambled—or completely missing—portions. But they all showed the attackers, and the slaughter they wrought.

The third time through, Hobson cleared his throat and said softly, "We always suspected they were still out there." He pressed the button that summoned his aide.

"Tom, have you heard back from the President or State yet?" he asked.

"Sir," Irving said, "they're coordinating a time, and will let us know instantly."

Hobson stood, Welborn and de Castro jumped to their feet as well.

"Instantly isn't fast enough. Get my car, and tell the President's office and State that we're on our way to the Prairie Palace."

"Aren't you meeting with Marshal Ludwig today?" Hobson asked Welborn as the three headed for the Secretary's vehicle.

"Yes, Sir. I broke off my meeting with him to bring this to you. I'm having dinner with him at the Flag Club later."

"Whatever you do, unless the President orders otherwise, *don't* let him know about this until I tell you to."

"Ludwig's sharp, Sir. He'll know there's something important I'm not telling him." Welborn flexed his shoulders. "But I'm sharp, too. I'll manage to avoid offending him."

The Prairie Palace, Omaha,
Douglas County, Federal Zone, NAU

When the United States of America, Canada, and Mexico merged into the NAU, none of the three would accept either of the other's national capital for the capital of the new Union. They settled on Omaha, Nebraska because it was situated roughly in the middle of the continent. Moreover, Omaha was cold enough in the winter to satisfy Canadians' yen for the Great White North, and hot enough in the summer for the Mexicans to fondly remember the deserts of Sonora and Chihuahua—or so it was said. As for the USA, Omaha was a major part of the Great American Heartland, being an established city of the second tier. It and Douglas County were fully adequate for a capital city. Sarpy County, directly to the south, was the home of Offutt Air Force Base, one-time headquarters of the Strategic Air Command, an ideal location for the new Supreme Military Headquarters. And Pottawatomie County, Iowa, directly across the Missouri River from Omaha, provided more than ample space for the buildings needed to house what was sure to be a massive central bureaucracy. Some in Nebraska strenuously objected to losing Douglas and Sarpy, and Iowa to losing Pottawatomie to the new Federal Zone. They were reminded of the benefits previously enjoyed by the parts of Maryland and Virginia adjacent to the District of Columbia—not to mention the additional taxes garnered by those states from the increased population of government workers who lived in adjacent counties—and graciously agreed to losing those population centers.

Competitions were held to design the new Union's legislative capitol and the presidential residence and office. Nobody other than the bureaucrats who selected it was happy with the monumental faux sod-house design of the president's residence and office, christened "The Prairie Palace," although nearly everybody outside government came to agree that it was appropriate that the legislative Capitol was erected on what had once been the stock yards for the South Omaha slaughter houses.

It was to the Prairie Palace, located on the site of what had once been Central High School, that Secretary Hobson, Chairman Welborn, and Deputy Director de Castro went to see the President of the NAU.

The Round Office, The Prairie Palace

Albert Leopold Mills, tall and lean, in his late fifties, was a distinguished, mild-mannered gentleman. Until he got behind closed doors.

"What the fuck is the meaning of this!" he demanded as soon as the door to the Round Office closed behind his visitors from military headquarters. "I have more important things to do than sit around in a circle jerk with you. I should have all of your resignations on my desk within the hour!"

"Sir, if you don't agree that what's on this," Hobson held up a crystal, "is worth disrupting your schedule, you'll have my resignation as soon as I can scribble it out."

"We'll see about that." Mills snatched the crystal from Hobson's fingers. He popped it into his comp and scanned the text report. Then reread it more slowly. "Who did it?"

"Sir, we don't know for certain who they are, but there are images," Hobson said.

"Show me."

Hobson nodded to de Castro, who stepped to the President's desk and took control of the console to show the images.

"They aren't all of the best quality, Sir," de Castro said as he activated the first image. It was an eleven-second vid, bouncy as though the person shooting it was trembling and had forgotten to stabilize the view. It showed armed—*creatures*—racing along a street. Heavily muscled legs ending in taloned feet propelled them faster than a human could run, even a human augmented with military armor. They were bent at the hips, their torsos held parallel to the ground. Sinuous necks, triple the length of a human's, held their heads up, and whipped them side to side. The faces jutted forward, with long jaws that seemed to be filled with sharp, conical teeth. Arms little more than half the length of their legs held weapons that could have been some kind of rifle. A crest of feathery structures ran from the tops of their faces all the way down their spines, where fans of long, feathery structures jutted backward providing a counterbalance to their forward-thrusting torsos. Their knees bent backward, like birds'. They appeared to be naked except for straps and pouches arrayed around their bodies. Packs of smaller creatures that might have been juveniles of their kind sped among them.

Mills was expressionless looking at the vid to the end. "Next."

De Castro activated the second image. This one was a grainy still shot, showing one of the creatures rising up slightly from horizontal to put its rifle-like weapon to its shoulder.

The third image was another vid, seventeen seconds long this time. It had been garbled along the way, and parts of the image were so badly pixilated they couldn't be made out. But it showed enough to make clear what was happening. Packs of the smaller creatures were leaping onto people, shredding them with their talons, ripping into them with their toothy jaws.

Two more stills showed one of the creatures biting chunks out of a downed woman.

A thirty-three-second vid, taken from behind defensive works from which the human soldiers of the battalion assigned to Troy's defense were fighting, showed the creatures and their packs of small companions assaulting the position. They ran zigging and zagging randomly, almost too fast for the eye to follow. Some of the creatures were hit, and tumbled to the ground, presumably dead or severely wounded. But those hits were by chance; the creatures moved too fast to be hit by aimed fire. The last few seconds of the vid showed the creatures and their packs bounding over the defensive works to land among the soldiers and begin ripping them apart.

"That's enough," Mills said softly; he could see that there was another image or two that hadn't been run. He took a moment to compose himself, then said to Hobson, "You were right to bring this to my attention immediately. It was worth disrupting my schedule." He tapped his inter-office comm. "Where's State?" he barked into it.

"She's entering the building now, Sir," came the reply.

"Well, get her tail in here instantly!"

Mills turned to Welborn. "What's our first step?"

"Sir, I've already given orders to draw up an operation order for a Force Recon platoon to head for Troy and get usable intelligence on the situation."

"How soon will it be ready?"

"By morning."

"And how soon after that can the Marines go?"

"As soon as you give authorization, Sir."

"You've got it. I want to know what's happened out there."

There was a discrete knock and the door of the Round Office eased open.

"About time you got here, Walker," Mills snapped.

Mary E. Walker, NAU Secretary of State, stopped flat-footed and glared at the President. "Sir, I was in the middle of delicate negotiations with the EU Foreign Minister when I received Richmond's message. He failed to say what was so grave about the matter. I *couldn't* walk out without an explanation. As it is, when I told him about your summons, he gave the distinct impression that by the time I get back, he might be on his way back to Luxembourg."

"Then good riddance! We just got word of something much more important than the feelings of an overly sensitive Euro. Take a look." He angled his comp's display toward her and activated the image of the vid showing the assault on the defense battalion.

"What?" the Secretary of State gasped when the vid had run its course. "Where?" She looked distinctly green.

"Troy," Hobson said softly. "This came in..." He looked at de Castro.

"About forty-five minutes ago, Ma'am," the J2 director said.

"Is it *them*?" she asked. "The ruins?"

The President looked at the other men for an answer to the question he'd wondered himself.

Welborn replied, "We have no way of knowing. But, yeah, I imagine so. Or if not whoever it was that destroyed those other civilizations, then somebody maybe just as bad." In its spread through space, humanity had discovered ruins left by seventeen non-human civilizations. One of them was on the level of the pyramid builders of ancient Earth, while most of them had technologically developed far enough to be on the threshold of interstellar travel—one actually seemed to have achieved it.

"They had no word? No ultimatum? No warning?" Walker asked.

"Not that we know of, Ma'am," de Castro said when the President looked at him. "We have a text message saying they were under attack by an unknown enemy, and a few images. You just saw one of them; it isn't necessarily the worst."

"We need to alert everybody," Walker said. "If you'll excuse me, Sir, I'll notify Minister Neahr right now." She turned away, reaching for her comm.

"You'll do no such thing!" Mills snapped.

"Sir?" She spun back to him, shocked by both his tone and the words.

"Until we know exactly what's happening on Troy, this is strictly need-to-know—and Zachariah C. Neahr doesn't need to know."

"But—"

"No buts," Mills cut her off. "I'd rather present all the worlds that humanity is on with a *fait accompli* than unnecessarily cause a panic. Your job in this, Madam Secretary, is to keep the rest of the world in the dark about NAU's upcoming offworld troop movements."

"You're going to send our soldiers into, into *that*?" she asked, appalled.

Mills curled his lip at her. "As you would know if you hadn't been so tardy getting here, we're sending Force Recon to gather intelligence. Then we'll send a counter-invasion force in to clear out those...those *creatures*." He turned to Hobson and Welborn. "I want you to stand up a counter-invasion force, and ready Navy shipping to get them there once we know what we're up against."

"Right away, Sir," Hobson said.

"Aye aye, Sir." Welborn grinned. What was the point of having a Navy that traveled the stars, and command of one of the largest and most powerful militaries in all of human history if he never got to give the orders to attack an entire world?

"I'll notify Congress once the counter-invasion force is on its way," Mills said. "Now get everything moving."

De Castro didn't say anything, but he wondered how the President was going to justify taking military action without an Act of Congress authorizing it, or without even consulting with the Congressional leadership.

First Lieutenant Mitchell Paige gave the twenty Marines of his section a final look over—he'd already inspected them—before saying a few words prior to them entering their landing craft. His Marines weren't exactly invisible, but he'd have had a hard time picking them out in the dim light if they hadn't had their helmets and gloves off. The patterning of the utilities worn by Force Recon tricked the eye into looking *beyond* them instead of registering *on* them.

"Marines, we don't know what you're going to find on Troy." Paige ignored the quiet chuckles that statement brought from the Marines. "That's why Force Recon is going in, to find out."

Some of the Marines exchanged glances: *No shit Sherlock. That's what Force Recon does; we go in to find out when nobody knows dick.*

"The Monticello been listening on all frequencies since exiting the wormhole, but as of—" Paige checked his watch. "—three minutes ago, no transmissions have been picked up, nor has anything registered on any of the ship's sensors. So we know no more than we did when we left Earth." He gave a wolfish grin. "That's why the Union called on us. We're going to find out, and then some alien ass is going to get kicked!"

"OOH-RAH!" the twenty Marines roared. None of them said, or even thought, anything about the fact that their commander wasn't going planetside with them. Everyone understood an officer going along with a Force Recon squad on a mission would only be in the way.

"Mount up!" Paige bellowed over the cheers. The Force Recon Marines pulled on their helmets and gloves as they filed into the landing craft and the waiting Squad Pods. One Marine in each squad carried a rifle. The other Marines were armed only with sidearms and knives—purely defensive weapons.

Paige watched until the landing craft's ramp closed, then gruffly said, "Let's go," and ducked through the hatch from the launch bay. Gunnery Sergeant Robert H. McCard, the first section chief, followed. The two Marines headed for the Command and Communications Center, where Captain Jefferson J. DeBlanc, 2nd Force Recon Company's executive officer, and the company's First Sergeant John H. Leims waited for them. Along the way, they had to press against the side of the narrow passageway to let the platoon's second section pass on its way to the launch bay.

It wasn't long before the officers, senior non-commissioned officers, and communications men of 2nd Force Recon Company (B) were gathered in C&C, and eight Force Recon squads were on their way to the surface of Troy.

The *Cayuga* Class frigate *Monticello* was a stealth vessel, specially configured to support Marine Force Recon and small raiding parties. To that end, she had a compartment equipped with comm gear to allow a command element to communicate with its planetside elements via burst microwaves, and give it directions as needed. Her external shape had odd, unexpected angles designed to reflect radar signals in directions other than back at a radar receiver. A coating over the entire hull except for the exhausts was designed to absorb and/or deflect other detection methods. Strategically placed vanes and trailing stringers dispersed heat from the exhausts, giving the starship a faint, easily overlooked heat signature. She was not designed for offensive fighting; her weapons and counter-weapon systems were strictly defensive.

Two hours earlier, the Monticello had exited a wormhole two light minutes northeast of Troy and slowly drifted planetward while using all of her passive sensors to search for spacecraft loitering in the area of her destination world. The warship also constantly scanned the planet's surface for signs of life, human or alien. When no signs of any presence, human or alien, were detected either in space or on the surface, the order was given for the landing party to prepare to head planetside.

The *Monticello's* equally stealthed landing craft were each capable of landing up to fifty fully armed infantrymen on the surface of a planet, or launching four "Squad Pods" into the upper atmosphere for scattered planetfall. They were called "Spirits," both because they were as visible to standard detection methods as ethereal spirits and because they could spirit troops to or away from a planet's surface. The Squad Pods were intended to be mistaken for meteorites during their transit through an atmosphere: an ablative coating was designed to stop burning as soon as the antigrav drive kicked in when the pod was close to the ground, giving the impression that the meteorite had burned up. The Squad Pods normally landed away from populated areas, and flew nape-of-the-earth to their final destinations.

The eight Force Recon squads landed on Troy at widely separated locations so they could cover as much territory as possible. Upon completion of their missions, the Marines would return to their Squad Pods and rendezvous with the landing craft for return to the *Monticello*, where she maintained station near the collapsed entrance to the wormhole.

The *Monticello* stood ready to reopen the wormhole on fifteen minutes notice, either to return to Earth with the Marines, or to flee from an approaching enemy starship.

Planetfall, Semi-Autonomous World Troy

Squad Pod Alpha-1, with First squad aboard, plunged to the ground near the McKinzie Elevator Base. Its meteorite-mimicking track blinked out two and a half kilometers above the surface when its antigrav engine cut in to bring the small craft down twenty-seven kilometers distant, gently enough to avoid injuring its passengers, then scooted along, barely above the ground, to its final destination. Squad Pod Alpha-4, carrying Fourth squad, made planetfall on the opposite side of Millerton from the elevator base. Pods Alpha-2 and 3, and Bravo-1, 2, and 3 made planetfall in other locations on East Shapland, the primary settled continent on Troy. Squad Pod Bravo-4 was the only one to visit the continent called West Shapland, which only had one settlement; some twelve thousand souls resided in and around the coastal fishing town of Pikestown. There was less than two minutes from the time the first pod reached its landing zone until the final one touched down on its.

Foot of the McKinzie Elevator Base,
Millerton, Semi-Autonomous World Troy

Staff Sergeant Jack Lummus, leader of the First squad, didn't give any orders when his Marines dashed off Alpha-1; touchdown was a well-rehearsed maneuver, and everyone knew what to do. The five Marines darted off in five different directions and went to ground fifty meters away from the pod, facing away from it. Each Marine had his motion detector, air sniffer, and infrared receiver operating before he took cover in one of the many craters that pocked the tarmac. Lummus didn't even say anything when his four men all reported they were in position and searching. Not that he was concerned about being overheard by whatever possible enemy that might be lurking nearby. Force Recon helmets were well enough muffled that any sounds that escaped them were unintelligible up close, and totally inaudible beyond a meter or two. Anyway, communication was via radio burst-transmissions that faded out within two hundred meters—it simply wasn't necessary for him to say anything.

The Marines lay waiting, and watching their surroundings and various detectors for sign of anybody in the vicinity.

After half an hour, Lummus transmitted, "Report."

The four reports came in. Corporal Tony Stein had seen a skinny dog that seemed to be scrounging for something to eat, but none of the Marines had seen, heard, or detected anything human, or even remotely resembling the aliens they'd seen in the images they'd studied on Earth and on the ship. Nobody had seen a body, or anything that looked like part of a body, human or otherwise.

"One and two," Lummus ordered, the command for his Marines to check their first and second objectives. "Record."

"Recording," Sergeant Elbert L. Kinser said as he and and Stein headed for the elevator station's control building.

"Recording." Corporal Anthony P. Damato and Lance Corporal Frank P. Witek headed to the elevator.

After the two teams searched their first objectives, the squad would reassemble and move on.

Lummus remained where he was so he could coordinate the two pairs. One Marine in each pair had a vidcam on his helmet, keyed to his eye movements; the vidcams would record everything the Marine looked at. As a just-in-case, the vidcams had a "deadman switch" arrangement that would automatically transmit their contents to the starship loitering above if the Marine was killed or incapacitated.

The Elevator

Damato and Witek were closer to their objective and reached it first. An executive elevator cab was in its docking cradle. Scorching around the open hatch gave evidence of fighting. The two Marines checked their surroundings and didn't detect anybody nearby except for the other Marines.

"Go," Damato sent. He and Witek went around the cab-dock in opposite directions to meet at its rear. Neither saw or otherwise detected anybody either along the way or once they rejoined. The elevator cab was an oblate spheroid, with three observation ports equally spaced around its circumference, and the airlock in the position of a fourth port.

"Cover." Damato climbed an access ladder to the top of the docking cradle as he gave the order, while Witek remained on the ground watching their surroundings. Another ladder looked to Damato like it went up the elevator's pylon at least as far as the anchoring stays. But he was only going up it far enough to look into the port on that side of the cab.

The cab's interior lights were off, and little ambient light reached inside, so Damato used his infrared scope. All he could make out was the passenger seating and the refreshment console next to the attendant's station, or rather their remains. The interior of the cab was wrecked. He removed his feet from the ladder rung they were on and slid down the ladder the same way he would going from level to level in a starship. That saved his life.

The Control Building

Sergeant Kinser and Corporal Stein reached the control building a minute after Damato and Witek reached the elevator's foot. The building was small. They knew from mission prep that it had two rooms, an administration room and a control room. The former had front and rear entrances, as well as a window on each exterior wall and another into the control room. The latter was windowless, climate controlled, and had no direct access to the outside. The main door, off center on the front wall, was off its hinges, blown into the building. The front window was broken.

"With me," Kinser said. He led Stein in a circuit of the building. They trod on shattered glass going past the administration room; the windows on the side and rear were broken out from the inside. The broken back door was on the ground, also knocked out from the inside. On the way around, Kinser looked in through the windows while Stein checked the area with his eyes, ears, and all of his detectors.

Back at the open entrance, Kinser said, "Inside." The two Marines held their weapons the way a police officer would; finger outside the trigger guard, muzzle pointed up. An infantryman entering a building like this would have his finger on the trigger and the muzzle pointed where his eyes were looking.

The interior of the admin room was a shambles. Everything—desks, chairs, cabinets, office machines—was overturned and broken. Files, hardcopy and crystal both, littered the floor. Using infrared, Kinser and Stein saw stains on the floor, walls, and furniture that experience told them was most likely blood. They saw no bodies or body parts. Looking through the broken door and shattered window to the control room, they could see that the computers and other equipment in it had been smashed.

Kinser and Stein had just turned to enter the control room when they heard the first shot.

Downtown Millerton, Fifteen Kilometers
From the McKinzie Elevator Base

Fourth squad's pod touched down on what looked like a junkyard, but had actually been a parking lot. Corporal James L. Day began recording the instant the Squad Pod dropped its ramp to let the Marines out. PFC Joseph W. Ozbourn began recording as soon as his feet hit the pavement. Land vehicles of all manner were in the lot, every one of them smashed, tumbled, leaning on or piled on others. The Marines headed rapidly for the nearest unblocked exit from the lot to take positions. Day and PFC James D. La Belle went fifty meters left, to the far edge of the parking lot. Lance Corporal William R. Caddy and PFC James D. La Belle headed the other way. They didn't have to go quite as far to reach that end of the lot. Sergeant Grant F. Timmerman remained where they'd exited and watched into the lot.

Fourth squad was on a narrow street, with the lot on one side and the backs of buildings, mostly one story, none more than three, on the other. Doors and windows all along the block had their doors and windows knocked out from the inside. Timmerman was nervous about being so close to so many buildings he and his Marines hadn't cleared, so he only kept his squad in place for ten minutes before calling his men in and leading them into the middle-most building.

The interior was a cavernous space, with only three doorways to smaller rooms; the wall next to two of the rooms was marked with the universal symbols for male and female restrooms, the third with the word "office" next to it. The doors were all broken in. Stains on the floor showed that water had flowed out of the restrooms, though it no longer was. Day and Ozbourn checked inside the rooms while the others covered them. All the fixtures were broken, which explained the water stains on the floor outside them.

A more-than-waist-high counter separated a kitchen area from the larger area; the space had obviously been a restaurant. That was confirmed when the Marines examined the broken chairs and tables—and broken crockery—that littered the floor. The front door and windows had been blown in.

The Marines didn't linger in the restaurant, but began methodically searching the buildings to the right of it. Timmerman always had someone watching the buildings on the other side of the street. Everywhere they went they found destruction; nothing inside the buildings had been left unshattered. There were no bodies or body parts.

They had almost completed a circuit back to their starting point when there was a burst of fire, and La Belle, who was watching the street, pitched to the ground, bleeding profusely.

Jordan, East Shapland

Fifth squad landed a klick away from Jordan, a farming town a thousand kilometers from Millerton and the McKinzie Elevator Base, located on a river of the same name. Like First squad at Millerton, the five Marines dashed away from their pod toward the points of an imaginary star and settled in place to watch and wait. But they didn't spend as much time in observation before moving.

"Up, move out," Staff Sergeant William G. Harrell ordered after twenty minutes in place. He didn't have to tell his Marines what direction they to head in, or in what order to go. Corporal Hershel W. Williams led off, followed by Harrell, Lance Corporal Douglas T. Jacobson, and Sergeant Ross F. Gray. Corporal Anthony Casamento had rear point. Williams and Jacobson recorded. Their first objective was a small cluster of farm buildings about three hundred meters off, on the way to Jordan. They went through a field of chest-high corn. The Marines went at a normal walking pace. They weren't concerned about being seen; they knew how effectively the camouflage pattern on their uniforms tricked the eye, and the rows of corn were far enough apart that they didn't give away their movement by pushing through them.

The first thing the Marines encountered was some kind of native avians that rose complaining to fly away from dead animals they'd been feeding on. The Marines guessed the corpses were dogs, but it was hard to tell; the carcasses had been thoroughly scavenged and the bones scattered.

"Be sharp," Harrell said. He wondered how the crow-like avians had detected him and his men, and knew that their noisy flight would alert anybody in the area to the Marines' presence.

The first of the farm buildings they examined was the barn. It had large double doors. One side of the door was down, the other was hanging on one hinge. Inside, whatever stalls the barn may have held were buried under the debris of what had been the floor of the barn's hay loft. The Marines carefully made their way through the debris, but didn't see anything that looked like human remains, though there were obvious cattle skulls. Elsewhere, a grain silo had been torn open to spill its contents. A shed was broken apart, as were the vehicles it had sheltered before the farm was attacked. The remains of a smaller building and its contents appeared to have been a small smithy.

Harrell saved the farmhouse for last. The porch roof sagged—two of the pillars that held it up had been broken away. The door was blown in, as were the windows on the front of the house. The squad headed for the porch.

The *Monticello* had withdrawn after launching the *Spirits*, and was more than one and a half light minutes from Troy by this time, resulting in a five minute time lag between when Staff Sergeant Lummus at the foot of the McKinzie elevator sent the message that the squads in Millerton were under attack and the message was received by Fifth squad.

"Hold," Harrell ordered when he received the message. The Marines lowered themselves to the ground in a five pointed star, facing outward. "Someone's hitting First squad," Harrell told his men. After a couple of minutes with no further message, and no sign of unwelcome company, he ordered, "Inside, on the double."

The Marines jumped up and dashed into the farmhouse. The interior of the house was as thoroughly trashed as the barn and other out buildings had been. The only differences were that the farmhouse's second floor hadn't been collapsed into the first, and there were no bones. The windows on the side and rear walls were all blown outward, as was the back door.

After a few minutes search, with no additional reports on what was happening elsewhere, Harrell gave the order to resume the movement to Jordan. The Marines kept to the field, walking between the rows of corn, bent low enough that only their heads were above the corn stalks.

Edge of Alberville, Thirty-Five Kilometers West of Millerton

With plenty of space for its relatively small population, the people of Troy revived a lifestyle that began in the middle of the twentieth century, but died out in the first half of the twenty-first: the bedroom community. Alberville had a large enough shopping district to tend to the basic needs of its population of 18,000, and schools from pre-elementary to pre-college for its children. But other than shopkeepers and teachers, people went to Millerton or other locations for work. Commuting was via a network of high speed maglev trains, which people also used to go elsewhere for entertainment, dining, and recreation.

Sixth squad found that the alien invaders had demolished the train system as thoroughly as they had everything else. The guideways were broken and collapsed. The train cars were broken and their parts scattered about. The train station was gutted, and its roof was sagging.

Half an hour after landing, having ascertained that there was nobody nearby, Staff Sergeant William J. Bordelon ordered his squad into Alberville proper. The five Marines spot-checked houses on their way to the shopping district. Everywhere it was the same: front doors and windows had been broken in, those on the sides and rear blown out, the entire contents of the houses reduced to scrap. No sign of a body or body part.

The Marines were confident in the ability of their camouflage to keep them unseen to any observers. Still, they spread out and moved stealthily, flitting from shadow to shadow.

Bordelon called a halt when the squad reached a park that marked the transition from housing to shopping. Again, the Marines examined their surroundings and checked their sensors. Again, they saw and detected nothing.

Until Bordelon gave the order to move out.

"I have movement," Corporal Louis J. Hauge, Jr. suddenly said from the squad's rear point. "Seventy-five, five o'clock."

Bordelon slowly swiveled to his right rear. Seventy-five meters away was a house he recognized as one he'd checked himself.

"They're following us," Bordelon said out loud, while silently cursing himself—how could anybody be coming up from behind? Where did they come from? His motion detector was set to check three-sixty, but it hadn't shown any movement. "Down." He set action to words by lowering himself to the ground. "Show me."

Hauge aimed a pulse of ultraviolet light at the empty window frame where he'd detected movement.

Bordelon looked where Hauge indicated, but the only thing he saw inside the window was the strobing flash of an automatic rifle firing at him. In an instant, he had his handgun drawn and fired at a point behind the muzzle flash. He never knew if he'd hit anything—just as he fired, a burst of automatic fire tore into his right side, shattering his ribs and shredding internal organs.

Less than a minute after Hauge reported motion, all five Marines of Sixth squad were dead.

McKinzie Elevator Base, Millerton

By chance, Staff Sergeant Lummus had been looking in the right direction to see the flash of the weapon that fired at Corporal Damato.

"Sixty-five degrees!" he shouted into his helmet comm. *That shot just missed Damato. How the hell did anybody see him?* he wondered. *I know where he is, and I can hardly see him!*

Damato and Lance Corporal Witek took cover behind the elevator pylon. Sergeant Kinser and Corporal Stein took vantage points inside the control building, Kinser facing the direction the shot had come from, and Stein watching the rear. No more shots came for almost a minute.

Abruptly, shrill shouts rang out from all directions around the elevator. Most of them sounded like they were more than two hundred meters distant.

Well within range of our detectors, Lummus thought. *Why didn't we pick up anything?*

No point in worrying about it, it was time for the squad to get out. Lummus looked to his rear. He was fifty meters from the Squad Pod, but his men were three times as far. If he could make it to the pod, he could pilot it in two short hops to pick them up. If the aliens didn't have something to knock it out before he could get to them. In a few words, he told his Marines what he was going to do. They all said they'd be ready to pile in as soon as he reached them.

"I'll cover you," Kinser said—he had the only rifle in the squad.

Lummus braced himself, then lunged out of his crater like a sprinter leaving the blocks. He heard the loud cracks of Kinser's rifle firing, and the less-loud cracks of the other Marines' handguns. Lummus zigged and zagged to spoil the aim of anyone shooting at him. He was more than halfway to the Squad Pod when he looked beyond it and saw a mass of aliens racing toward him. The speed with which they jinked side to side startled him so badly he stutter-stepped. That was just enough to allow bullets from two directions to hit him. He crashed to the tarmac, dying.

At the rear of the control building, Stein shouted, "I hope he gets here in a hurry!" as he fired his handgun at rushing aliens. "There must be a hundred of them coming at us."

Kinser swore. "He's not coming, they got him." He turned and ran to the back of the building to help Stein try to fight off the aliens. The two fired as fast as they could, but most of their shots missed. The attackers reached the building and dove through the door and windows, dropping their weapons in favor of using their long, vicious claws to rend the Marines.

Damato and Witek fired into the mass of charging aliens from opposite sides of the pylon, but to little effect.

"He better get here soon, or we're screwed," Witek shouted.

"We're screwed." Damato swore softly. He hadn't looked in the direction of the Squad Pod, but he knew that Lummus should have reached it and been on the way by then. But he didn't hear the pod's engine—he knew it wasn't coming.

Downtown Millerton

Corporal Day was the closest to PFC La Belle. He pulled the wounded Marine away from the door where he'd been shot and grimaced at the blood coming from several holes in his shirt. He glanced at La Belle's face; it was pale, and his eyes were rolled up—shock was setting in.

"Stay with me, Jim." Day wrenched La Belle's first aid kit from his belt and reached into it for the self-sealing bandages. He tore La Belle's shirt open and grimaced again when he saw the wounds. Working feverishly, he did his best to cover all of the punctures. Blood welled up around the edges of the bandages. Day guessed at exactly where the holes were, and poked a finger into the bandages in those spots. He got three out of five on the first attempt; the synthetic material of the bandages sank into the wounds and began to do their job, speeding a coagulation agent. By the time Day found the other two holes, blood had stopped welling out and La Belle wasn't breathing.

"I told you to stay with me, man!" Day slapped La Belle.

"Let's go," Sergeant Timmerman snapped, gripping Day's shoulder.

For the first time since he began tending to La Belle, Day was aware of the sound of gunfire from inside the building; the other Marines had been firing at whoever had shot La Belle.

"We're going back to the Squad Pod," Timmerman said.

"Right." Day stood and bent to lift La Belle over his shoulders in a fireman's carry.

"Move it, people!" Timmerman shouted at his squad.

Lance Corporal Caddy and PFC Ozbourn stopped firing out of the windows and followed Day at a sprint to the rear of the building. Timmerman brought up the rear.

Outside, they were almost to the Squad Pod before they ran into trouble. Fire erupted from the building they'd just exited, and the one they'd first entered. The first shots were wild and missed. Day reached the pod and dove in, hauling La Belle as far from the hatch as he could get.

Caddy fell through the hatch, shot in the back of his neck. Day turned back to pull him inside. Then had to reach outside to help Timmerman get Ozbourn, who also was shot, inside. Timmerman suddenly pitched forward with his legs dangling outside the pod. Day dragged him in the rest of the way, then slapped the "close" button to shut the hatch. He crawled over his squad mates to the front of the pod and took the controls.

It was several minutes later, when the Squad Pod was arrowing to orbital altitude to rendezvous with the *Spirit*, before Day was able to turn his attention from piloting the pod to checking the other Marines.

They were all dead.

How did they spot us?

Nearing Jordan, East Shapland

"I have movement, two o'clock, one seventy-five," Corporal Williams said from the point position.

"Hold." Staff Sergeant Harrell's order held his Marines in place, facing outward, weapons drawn. "Moving where?"

There was a pause before Williams answered. "Whoever it is seems to have stopped, my motion detector isn't showing anything now."

"I have movement, nine o'clock, one fifty," Corporal Casamento said a few seconds later. "Approaching at a slow walk."

Harrell thought about it: Someone stationary was 175 meters to the right front, someone else 150 meters away was approaching from the left, through the rows of corn rather than between them. They could be aliens, or they might be survivors. For that matter, they could be farm animals, starving or well on the way to turning feral. He checked his own motion detector to see exactly where the object to the left was. He stood. Using his magnifying face shield, he could make out movement in the tops of the corn in the right direction and distance. A cow? A pig? It wasn't tall enough to show above the stalks. It could be a child.

"Increase interval," he ordered. "We'll take the one coming from the left. Stay alert to everything else. Let me know if you detect anything." He listened for the string of "Aye ayes" that told him his Marines heard and understood. A barely audible rustling told him his men were shifting their positions from ten meters apart to fifteen.

In just under two minutes, the approacher reached them. It passed through the last row of corn three meters from Sergeant Gray. It was bent at the hips, its torso parallel to the ground. It had a short snout that gaped open slightly, showing many dagger-like teeth. Feathery structures protruded from the backs of its arms and legs, ran down its long neck and spine, and formed a jutting tail. It wore leather webbing studded with pouches. It was armed.

Gray and Casamento moved reflexively as soon as they saw it; they dove at the alien to tackle and restrain it. It saw them almost as soon as they saw it, and let out a loud screech as it dropped its weapon and slashed at Gray with talons that hadn't seemed to be on its hands seconds before. Gray screamed in agony, and fell onto his side, clutching the intestines that boiled out of his abdomen.

Before the creature could do anything else, Casamento slammed into it, bearing it to the ground. Lance Corporal Jacobson dashed up and jumped over Gray to get to the alien. He grabbed an arm that was swinging at Casamento, talons extended to rip the Marine's face from his head. The alien was strong, its arm swing sent Jacobson tumbling—but its bones were fragile, and one snapped. It shrieked in pain, and the broken arm flopped.

Harrell dove in. He grabbed the alien's head, twisted it and pulled its neck straight so it couldn't get to Casamento to bite him. Jacobson recovered from his tumble and pinned the alien's thrashing legs. In an instant, he had a tie-down wrapped around the creature's lower legs, preventing it from kicking out. Casamento managed to wrestle both of its arms behind its back and bound its wrists. Then he wrapped another tie-down around its muzzle to keep it from biting.

"The one at two o'clock is running this way," Williams shouted.

"Jacobson, check Gray," Harrell ordered. "Williams, Casamento, get ready." He checked his motion detector, and drew his sidearm, aiming it in the direction his detector showed the rapidly approaching jinking movement.

The second alien burst through the last row of corn and staggered to an abrupt stop, shrieking as it saw the other, bound alien.

And just that fast, the three Marines fired at it.

Two pistol and one rifle bullet struck it. It reared up, stretching its neck high, mouth wide as though to scream. But only a weak caw came out. The alien toppled to the ground. Harrell put another bullet in the thing's head.

"I want its weapon and gear," the squad leader said. "Be careful, it might have post mortem spasms." Then to Jacobson: "How's Gray?"

"I think he's dead." Jacobson's voice was thick.

Harrell knelt next to his assistant squad leader. Blood flowed slowly around the loops of intestine that had fallen through the deep gashes in Gray's belly. His eyes were open and glazed. Harrell checked for breathing and a pulse and found neither. He sighed.

"Put bandages on him to seal his gut," he told Jacobson. "Then we gotta get out of here." He looked at the alien that was now bound with more tie-downs, the alien that had killed a friend of his. "Bring the prisoner," he said, gritting his teeth. He didn't say he'd rather kill the monster. But he thought it. He didn't need to say to bring Gray's body; that was automatic.

Aboard the NAUS Monticello, Leaving Troy Space

The Force Recon mission was a disaster. Eight squads, forty highly skilled Marines, had made planetfall. Close to thirty of them had died. Two squads had been completely wiped out, and their bodies not recovered. Most of the other squads only had one or two survivors; all except one squad that had a survivor had managed to bring back their dead. Only

Fifth squad had lost but one Marine. The mission would have been a failure as well as a disaster if Fifth squad hadn't captured one of the aliens.

Who *were* these aliens?

The War Room, Supreme Military Headquarters,
Bellevue, Sarpy County, Federal Zone, NAU

Secretary of War Hobson's eyes swept the room as he strode in. Everyone he had called for was already gathered around the conference table: Chairman Welborn and Major General de Castro, as well as Army Chief of Staff General John C. Robinson, Chief of Naval Operations Admiral James J. Madison, Commandant of the Marine Corps General Ralph Talbot, Force Recon Commander Colonel Aquilla J. Dyess. Simultaneously least and not nearly least on the military side was Staff Sergeant Harrell, whose squad had captured the alien on Troy.

The civilian contingent was much smaller: Secretary of State Walker sat to Hobson's right. Next to her was Secretary of Extraterrestrial Affairs Orlando E. Caruana. Jacob F. Raub represented both the medical and exobiology communities. Special Assistant to the President Ignatz Gresser rounded out the gathering.

Harrell was the only one who rose to his feet when Hobson entered.

"Seats!" Hobson barked.

Harrell dropped into his chair at the foot of the table and sat at attention, looking nervously down its length at the Secretary of War. He was comfortable enough with the flag officers, but found the high-ranking civilians intimidating.

"Before we begin," Hobson said in a gravelly voice, "I want you all to understand that everything said here is classified Top Secret, and is not to be discussed with anybody not here without specific permission from me or the President. Violation of that will land you in a federal prison so fast your head won't have time to spin. If any of you don't find that acceptable, you can leave now and submit your resignation." He stopped to fix the civilians with a glare. "By authorization of the President, that applies to you as well."

The civilians looked shocked, and Walker opened her mouth to protest.

Ignatz Gresser's adam's apple bobbed as he cleared his throat to interrupt her, and said, "That is what the President said, Mary. He told me himself right before I left the Prairie Palace to come here."

"He can't do that!" Caruana of Extraterrestrial Affairs objected. His normally fair complexion seemed to turn whiter. "That's not—"

"He most certainly can," Hobson cut him off. "He's invoked the Alien Threat clause of the War Powers Act. To refresh your memories in case it's slipped your minds, basically what that means is that Albert Leopold Mills can do just about anything he pleases so long as it has something to do with the alien threat."

"But..." Walker objected weakly, her fingers fluttering at her throat. She shook her head and said more firmly, "I'll take this up with the President when I see him next."

"You do that," Hobson told her. To the group; "Does anybody want to resign?"

They all shook their heads, murmured negatives.

"Good, the President and I would hate to lose any of you." He neither looked nor sounded relieved. "Now to the business of this meeting." He turned to the sole enlisted Marine in the room.

"Staff Sergeant, I've already heard about it from the Commandant and J2, as I imagine everybody else here has. Now I want to hear about it from a man who was there. *What the hell happened on Troy?* How did more than two dozen Force Recon Marines get killed on one quick in-and-out mission?" He didn't sound angry, just baffled.

Harrell cleared his throat, then spoke in a firm voice befitting a Marine non-commissioned officer. "Sir, it was like they were expecting us. They hit us from ambush, except for my squad..."

The basic telling only took a few minutes, then the questions began. Hobson was the first.

"Have you seen the after-action reports from the other squads?"

"Yes, Sir. And I've talked to the other survivors."

"All of them?" Robinson asked, incredulously.

"Yes, Sir. Every one of them." Harrell repressed a shudder at how few of the Force Marines had survived what should have been a simple in-and-out.

"And you didn't see any people?" Walker wanted to know. "Any of the citizens of Troy?"

"Yes, Ma'am. Ah, I mean no, Ma'am. We didn't see any people."

"You're absolutely positive that you didn't see any people?"

Harrell looked at her sharply, but his voice was level when he answered. "Ma'am, neither I nor any of the other sur—" He paused to swallow. "Any of the other Marines saw any people." He took a deep breath before continuing. "We didn't see any body parts, either. Although we did find old marks that were probably blood stains." He was gratified to see the Secretary of State flinch—he'd been offended that she'd seemed to doubt his word.

"What about alien corpses?" Welborn asked.

"Sir, the only aliens we saw were alive. Except for the ones we killed," he finished harshly.

"Different topic." Madison's fleshy cheeks and jowls testified to the many years he'd spent skippering a desk. "What did you see of enemy aircraft or space vehicles?"

"Sir, you'd have to ask Commander Schonland about spacecraft. On the ground, we didn't see any aircraft." Harrell saw a question in the eyes of a couple of the civilians, and added, "The captain of the *Monticello*."

"I know who Schonland is," Madison growled.

"I know you do, Sir. I wasn't telling you."

A corner of Talbot's mouth twitched, as close as he'd allow himself to a smile at how smoothly the Marine staff sergeant put that overbearing squid in his place. Talbot looked every bit the former recruiting poster Marine he had been.

Madison glared at Harrell, but went stone-faced when his eyes flicked to Talbot and he recognized that he wasn't going to get any satisfaction from the Marines over that enlisted man's impertinence.

Neither Madison's question nor Harrell's answer meant anything at this point; Schonland had already been debriefed by Hobson and the Joint Chiefs. There had been no sign of spacecraft—or atmospheric craft either—in Troy's space. So far as the *Monticello*'s sensors could tell, Troy was a dead world, not home to any sentient life, and its space was empty of anything not to be found in any similarly lifeless planetary system.

"Did you see any structures?" Raub, the exobiology representative, asked Harrell. "I mean alien structures, that is."

"No, Sir. Only what was left of the human structures built by the colonists. Damage ranged from severe all the way to totally demolished."

"And you're speaking for all the survivors when you say that?"

"Yes, Sir. Force Recon Marines take careful note of our surroundings. Nobody saw anything that wasn't obviously human-construction. We have the vids from all eight squads. None of them show anything that could be an alien structure."

"So where did the aliens that attacked you come from?" Raub's Ichabod Crane-like face jutted forward on his thin neck, obviously hoping for something that would give him a clue about the aliens. "Did they have any, what do you call them, dug-in fighting positions?"

"Sir, every alien any of us saw was on his feet and running at us." Harrell shook his head in wonderment. "We have no idea where they came from. None of our detectors picked them up, either, until right before they attacked." He held up his hand. "Excuse me, Sir. There were two snipers that fired from inside human buildings. Otherwise, all of them that we saw were in the open."

Raub shook his head, but in disappointment rather than disbelief.

De Castro cleared his throat and asked, "Your squad was the only one that was able to secure any alien artifacts and bring them back?"

"That's right, Sir." Harrell took a deep breath to quell the tremble that suddenly threatened to overcome him. "The others had to withdraw under heavy fire." He hung his head for a brief moment, then continued in a strong voice. "The only other Marines who got close enough to an alien to get their weapons or equipment died in hand-to-hand combat."

De Castro nodded in sympathy. "I understand, Sergeant—Staff Sergeant." He corrected himself, remembering that to Marines a "sergeant" had three stripes and no rockers, a sergeant with a rocker under his chevrons was properly addressed as "Staff Sergeant." "You have my most profound sympathy."

"Thank you, Sir."

Secretary Hobson looked around the room. "Does anybody else have any questions?"

In murmur or strong voice, they all answered, "No."

"Then you are dismissed, Staff Sergeant."

"Aye-aye, Sir." Harrell stood, came to attention, said, "Thank you Sirs, Ma'am," and marched out of the room.

Hobson looked at Colonel Dyess and nodded—the Force Recon commander wouldn't be needed for the rest of the meeting, either.

Dyess stood. "Thank you, Sirs and Ma'am." He followed Harrell out.

When the door closed behind the two Marines, Hobson turned to Raub. "What do we know about the aliens, and what were you able to learn from the items that brave Marine brought back?"

Jacob Raub, the NAU's top expert on extraterrestrial lifeforms, made a face. "Not a lot. At least not much of interest to anybody who isn't an exobiologist. The harness is made from leather from an animal that we can't identify, although we're fairly certain it's native to the aliens' homeworld."

"What about the weapons?" Commandant Talbot interrupted.

Leave it to a Marine to want to know about small arms right off, Madison silently groused.

"Ah yes," Raub said with a sigh. "Weapons aren't organic, so they aren't a strong suit of mine." He looked Talbot in the eye, then at Army CoS Robinson. "But the engineering people I gave them to tell me they're not anything like what we have. Their caliber is smaller than 5.56mm and bigger than flechette, partly powered by something resembling a low-power railgun." He shook his head. "Whatever that means."

"Back to the gear," Hobson said. "We can return to the weapons later."

Raub shook his head again. "The harness is stitched together with a vegetable fiber of unknown origin. The same for the pouches attached to it. The vegetable fiber is also presumably from the aliens' homeworld. The stitching is of a type that could have been done in a human factory." He looked at Hobson and shrugged. "Without more artifacts, or knowledge of the place of origin of the harness, there really isn't anything more I can say."

Ignatz Gresser asked, "What can you surmise about the biology of the animal the leather comes from?"

"There I'm on slightly firmer ground." Raub straightened in his chair and leaned his angular body forward. "We were able to secure tissue and fluid samples of the prisoner—non-destructively, let me assure you," he rapidly added when Walker looked like she was about to protest. "We went to lengths to avoid injuring him."

"Are you sure the alien is a 'he'?" Walker asked. "I've seen the pictures. The creature is naked, and it has what looks like a vaginal slit between its legs."

"Yes, Ma'am," Raub said, "but body waste comes from that slit, and there is no evident anus. We believe it is more analogous to a cloaca."

Walker nodded. "So the sex organs are interior. Have you seen anything like a penis come out of the cloaca?"

"No we haven't," Raub admitted.

"Then it just as well could be female?"

Raub spread his hands. "It could, yes. But in most life forms that we've encountered, both on Earth and on the explored planets, the males, or male analogs, of most species are the more aggressive, more combative, of their species. Granted, there are a large number of insectoids and piscine species in which the female is the more aggressive, but the larger animals—reptilians, avians, mammalians and their analogs, it's the male that's combative. For all we know, these aliens have more than two sexes or genders. But it's a convenient convention to call the alien a 'he' rather than an 'it'."

Walker turned over a hand, indicating that she was willing to accept Raub's explanation for now.

Raub nodded at the Secretary of State, and continued. "The alien's DNA is, of course, totally different from that of humans. But analysis of the leather of his harness showed that the animal its leather came from is closely related to the alien itself, strongly indicating that it evolved on the same world. The same goes for the threads of the stitching. Naturally, we don't know what the alien eats. However, his amino acids are comprised of the same elements ours are: carbon, hydrogen, oxygen, and nitrogen. Not, of course, in exactly the same ratios. And there are only twenty pairs of chromosomes, instead of the twenty-three that we have. We don't yet know which are the aliens' essential acids, so we don't know what to feed him."

"What *are* you feeding him then?" Caruana asked.

Raub nodded at the question. "We're offering him a variety of foods, both animal and vegetable, cooked and raw. He wouldn't take any at first, but we ate samples to show him that they weren't poison. It's too early in the process to determine which he can hold down, and whether any of them provide him actual nutrition. He seems to prefer semi-cooked meat to other foodstuffs." He looked around, noticing the expression of boredom on the faces of some of the military and non-scientists and decided to wrap up his presentation. "Otherwise, we surmise that he comes from a world with a similar gravity and atmosphere to Earth normal, although his lack of clothing suggests the world might be somewhat warmer, perhaps it orbits closer to its primary." He paused and asked, "Are there any other questions for right now?"

"How has he behaved toward you and your people?" Talbot asked.

"He's been largely threatening, but we have him in a cage and feed him through a one-way drawer so that he can't get to us."

"What about his talons, are they always out?"

Raub shook his head. "Our vid surveillance shows that his talons are folded away when he thinks he's alone, but are extended when he can see one of us."

"Wait a minute," Caruana said. "Where do his talons go when they aren't extended?"

"They fold back along the sides of his fingers."

"That's curious," Caruana murmured. Then louder, "If his talons are folded against his fingers, how manipulative are his fingers? I mean, how could his kind build anything?"

"We believe that when his talons are, ah, retracted you might say, they become flexible. We will have to sedate him and perform a close examination, perhaps even surgery, in order to be certain of that, and to learn the mechanism if they do become flexible."

"When do you think you'll do that?" Robinson asked.

"In the next few days, Sir. I can't be more specific. We don't know which sedative will put him under for long enough. Or which might kill him, for that matter."

"The big question I have," Chairman Welborn asked, "is, could this alien, his species, be the ones responsible for the destruction of those seventeen dead civilizations we've discovered?"

Raub hesitated before answering. "Sir, I have no way of knowing. Is it possible? Yes. Is it fact?" He shrugged and spread his hands. "Without considerably more data, I can't say."

"Then it's also possible that they aren't the ones?" Walker asked.

"That's right, Ma'am."

"I'd like to get back to the weapons," Talbot said when it seemed neither Walker nor Raub had anything else to say.

"As I said, General, I'm not an engineer or a soldier, I don't really know anything about them."

"I'm aware of that, Mr. Raub. But surely the engineers told you something beyond the caliber and propulsion system?"

"Well..." Raub didn't know what to say.

"Do the engineers think they can replicate the weapons?" the Marine prompted.

"Oh, yes Sir! They've already disassembled them and are figuring them out."

Talbot nodded. "Would you be so good as to have them forward their findings to me? And if they do replicate them, I want to see the weapons." He noticed the sour expression on Madison's face and added, without looking directly at the CNO, "We might want to modify our body armor, depending on what the weapons do to our existing armor."

"Certainly, General," Raub said, relieved that he didn't have to say anything more about a topic on which he was as ignorant as he was about the weapons. Yes, let the engineers deal with the Marines.

After that, Hobson looked around. Nobody else seemed to have anything to add, or have an informed question to ask.

"All right, then. The President has already given his go-ahead to launch a military operation to Troy. We don't know a damn thing about what might be waiting for us there. It could be a small force that the recon elements had the bad fortune to chance upon. It could be a major army of occupation. It could be the beginning of a colony." He paused before continuing portentously, "Or we could find a staging operation for the invasion of another human world, even Earth itself." He looked at Welborn. "Prepare a force strong enough to meet any of those contingencies. You are authorized to tell your top staffs as much as they have to know in order to plan the operation—that much and no more, and with the same resignation option and penalty as presented at the beginning of this meeting. If nobody else has anything to add, this meeting is over."

He stood to leave, but paused when Walker asked,

"But where are the *people*, where are their *bodies*?"

"Maybe we'll find out once we get there." Hobson left without another word.

The Joint Chiefs began their planning, but the rest of the military continued in their normal training regimens.

The Central Pacific and Oahu, Hawaii, North American Union.

"ALL RIGHT, PEOPLE, YOU KNOW THE DRILL." STAFF SERGEANT AMBROSIO GUILLEN shouted loudly enough to be heard over the whine of the landing craft motors and sloshing of water in the welldeck of the Landing Ship Infantry NAUS *Oenida*. "Keep it by squads."

"As if we can do anything else," PFC Harry W. Orndoff grumbled.

Lance Corporal John F. Mackie half turned back and grinned at Orndoff; the junior man was right, the way the Marines of Third platoon were lined up to board the landing skids it was almost impossible for anybody to get separated from his squad.

"Eyes front!" Sergeant James Martin snarled from his position behind his First fire team.

Mackie snapped back to his front, his eyes fixed on the back of his fire team leader's helmet, and continued shuffling forward.

First squad reached its skid and Corporal Harry C. Adriance, the First fire team leader, dropped to his belly to slide in, pushing his rifle ahead of himself. Mackie followed, and found his position to the right of Adriance. Orndoff slid in to Mackie's right, and PFC William Zion to the corporal's left. Martin squeezed in next to Zion. Second and Third fire teams followed under Guillen's watchful eye. The rest of the platoon quickly boarded their skids.

Then all that was left of India Company, 3rd Battalion, 1st Marines to board was the company command group. Minutes later, the *Oenida*'s bow opened like a giant clamshell set on edge, and the skids slid out, into the warm waters of the Central Pacific Ocean, sixty kilometers off the east coast of Oahu. The skids maneuvered to get in line abreast a few hundred meters shoreward of the ship. There they waited, slowly bobbing in the gentle swells, while Kilo, Lima, and Weapons Companies boarded skids and formed waves behind India Company.

On board the *Oenida*, the landing launch officer keyed the final command that transferred control of the landing force to the ground commander, and the four waves of skids, looking like nothing so much as manic, oversized sea turtles, shot toward land at close to 100 KPH. The skids' periscopes, all that showed above the waves, threw up rooster tails of spray. At ten kilometers off shore, the skids cut their speed in half, reducing the height of their rooster tails. At five kilometers, most of the skids dropped their periscopes, making them almost impossible to spot from the beach.

Nearly an hour after starting toward shore, the first wave of skids surged through the surf and up the beach to the edge of the trees of Bellows Field Park, and the Marines jumped up through the suddenly opened tops of the skids and raced into the trees, rifles at the ready.

"Go, go, go!" Guillen and Second Lieutenant Henry A. Commiskey both shouted on the platoon net.

"Move, move, move!" the squad and fire team leaders shouted on the squad nets.

As he ran, Mackie glanced to his right to make sure Orndoff was with him and saw, twenty meters away, the famous trid actor Amos Weaver and the equally famous director Ulysses G. Buzzard. The two were intently talking as they watched the wakes of the oncoming skids as they rose above the surface of the bay. An assistant standing behind Buzzard was taking notes. Beyond them, Mackie saw trid-cam crews setting up their equipment. He curled his lip at the sight, but didn't break pace in his charge across the beach.

Ten meters into the trees, Sergeant Martin called for First squad to hit the deck and take up firing positions. As one, the thirteen Marines thudded to the ground under the weight of their combat loads and put their rifles to their shoulders, looking along the barrels farther into the trees, looking for anything that would indicate an aggressor was there.

"First squad, report!" Martin ordered.

"First fire team, sound off," Adriance snapped.

"Mackie!" Mackie called back.

"Orndoff!"

"Zion!"

"First fire team, all present," Martin reported.

In seconds, all three fire teams of First squad had reported everybody present, and Martin reported to Commiskey. So did second and third squads, along with the gun squad attached to the platoon.

"Third platoon, stand fast and look alert," Commiskey barked.

"What was that back on the beach?" Orndoff asked Mackie as soon as it became evident that they'd be in position for at least a few minutes. "That looked like Amos Weaver."

"Where have you been, Orndoff? That *was* Amos Weaver. And Ulysses G. Buzzard next to him."

"No shit?"

"No shit."

"Wow, I was almost close enough to Amos Weaver to touch him!"

Mackie shook his head. How could Orndoff be so dense he didn't realize Buzzard and Weaver were there setting cam-lines to shoot 2nd Battalion when it made a landing in obsolete armored amphibious vehicles in the wake of 3rd Battalion's landing? How could anybody in the 1st Marines not know they were making an epic trid of one of the major sea battles of the twenty-second century European Union War, and had hired 2nd Battalion as extras? Mackie grimaced; he thought Buzzard should have hired 3rd Battalion instead of 2nd. Hell, everybody in the First Marine Division knew 3rd Battalion was the best in the 1st Marines, probably the best battalion in the entire division. Maybe the best battalion in the entire Marine Corps.

Mackie's reverie was interrupted by Martin's order: "First squad, on your feet. We're going in column. First fire team, Second, and Third. I'm between First and Second. Third, maintain contact with First gun team. Move out."

"Mackie, take point," Adriance ordered. "Me, then Zion. Orndoff, maintain contact with Sergeant Martin. Do you have the route, Mackie?"

Mackie turned on his heads-up-display. A map showing the terrain a kilometer in each direction appeared. Red dots, many of them slowly moving, showed the last known positions of other members of the company. The dot in the middle blinked, indicating his position. A small cluster of purple dots to his right rear had to be Buzzard, Weaver and their aides. A red line showed the route Mackie was to follow in leading the squad. There were none of the blinking yellow lights that would show suspected positions of aggressor forces. Mackie didn't attach any importance to the lack of yellow, he'd been in the Marines long enough to know that the aggressors wouldn't necessarily show up anyway.

"Got it," Mackie reported.

"Go," Adriance told him.

Mackie oriented himself on the HUD map, picked a faintly seen landmark through the trees, turned his HUD off, and stepped out on a meter-wide trail, headed for his aiming point. From here on, Adriance would direct him.

The trees weren't particularly high or very thick, which made for a spotty canopy that allowed plenty of sunlight through for dense undergrowth to sprout. Numerous narrow paths wove through the area. Some were worn by small game and other animals, others by the many civilians who came to Bellows Field Park for recreation—it was common for Marines practicing wet landings to charge up the beach through crowds of startled sunbathers. Because Bellows Field was a state park as well as a military training area, the Marines stayed on paths instead of breaking their way through the brush as they would in other training areas in order to protect the environment.

A hundred meters along, Mackie toggled his helmet net to the fire team circuit. "See anything on your HUD?"

"I'll let you know if anything pops," Adriance answered. "Just keep your eyes peeled."

"Aye aye." Mackie kept swiveling his head side to side, looking into the trees in all directions, the muzzle of his rifle constantly swinging to point where his eyes went. He swallowed. Something wasn't right. He couldn't remember another training exercise where the platoon hadn't made contact within a hundred meters of the waterline.

Then he saw a flash up ahead and froze, with his left hand dropped down and out from his side, palm facing the rear, signaling Adriance to stop.

"What do you have?" Adriance asked.

"I don't know. Movement off the trail about thirty meters ahead." Mackie lowered himself to one knee, looking to where he'd seen the motion, pointing his rifle at it.

In a few seconds, Martin dropped to a knee next to him. "Tell me."

Mackie pointed. "See that double-trunked tree on the left and the mound next to it?"

"'Bout a meter high?" When Mackie nodded, Martin said, "Got it."

"I couldn't see for sure what it was, but something moved there."

"Did you see it?" Martin asked Adriance.

"No. My HUD doesn't show anybody, either."

"You sure you saw somebody, Mackie?"

"I saw *something*. It was too fast, I couldn't tell if it was a person. But it might be."

Martin thought for a moment, looking where Mackie said he saw motion. "All right, Mackie, you saw it, you go. Adriance, send somebody with him."

"Orndoff," Adriance called softly, "you go."

Mackie looked back and signaled Orndoff to join him. "I'm going up the right side of the trail. You go up the left. When I reach that mound, I'm going over it. You hit it from the flank, and be ready to blow away anybody you see who isn't me. Got it?"

"Got it." Orndoff sounded like he had a frog in his throat.

Padding rapidly, Mackie headed for the low mound, keeping his eyes and rifle sweeping over and around its sides. There was no movement and no sound. As soon as he was alongside the mound, he spun to his left and dashed up it, angling his rifle to shoot anybody who might be hiding behind it. There was. Mackie instantly recognized the white band around the Marine's hat and jerked his muzzle up before he shot him in the face.

"Don't shoot!" Mackie shouted at Orndoff.

An enlisted referee was on his knees in front of Mackie. A major with a similar white band on his camouflage cover crouched behind him.

"Damn, but you scared me!" the enlisted referee gasped. Sweat popped out on his face. Mackie knew the Marine had to be scared. Even though the Marines were firing blanks on this exercise, at the range he'd nearly shot the referee, the Marine would have been injured, possibly even blinded.

"How'd you know we were here?" the major asked in a shaky voice.

"I saw movement, Sir," Mackie replied.

The major stood up and shook his head. "I was positive we were hidden before you got close enough to see us."

Mackie grinned. "India Three/One, Sir. We're the best." He turned to look at where the rest of the squad was moving up. "Referees, Sergeant Martin."

"Referees, huh?" Martin reached the mound and looked at the major. "Sorry to have disturbed you, Sir. Mackie, good job. Continue as you were."

"Aye aye, Sergeant." Mackie returned to the trail to resume his advance.

A couple of minutes later, Lieutenant Commiskey's voice came over the platoon net. "The point just flushed a couple of referees, so you know bad guys have to be close. Everybody, look alert." Primary functions of the "referees" were to determine who were "casualties", which casualties were wounded, which killed, and to free up the "casualties" once it was proper for them to move.

Commiskey was right; less than fifty meters beyond where he'd discovered the referees, Mackie, taking a slow step, felt a tug on his boot. He eased his foot back and looked down, but couldn't see what he'd felt. He took a careful step backward, and lowered himself to examine the path close up.

There! He caught the faint glimmer of a monofilament tripwire about ten centimeters above the ground. He followed it with his eyes in one direction and saw where it was secured to the base of a sapling. In the other it was attached to a flash-bang, a simulated antipersonnel mine. The wire was taut, holding the fuse's striker out. If the tension on the wire was released by the wire being broken, the striker would slam home, setting off the mine.

"Damn," Adriance murmured just behind Mackie's shoulder.

"Got that right," Mackie murmured back. He carefully examined the area around the flash-bang without touching anything. He was looking for the safety pin; if he could find it he could insert it to prevent the striker from going home when the tripwire broke. He didn't expect to find the pin.

"Pull back," Adriance said, and duck-walked backward himself. Mackie followed.

Sergeant Martin joined them. "Talk to me," he said. Mackie told the squad leader what he'd found. Martin toggled his helmet comm to the platoon's command circuit and reported the finding of the booby trap to Commiskey. He didn't look happy when he'd gotten his instructions.

"Mark the booby trap, then move off the trail to the right and wait for instructions. Second squad's going to the left and Third's in reserve. We're going to sweep the area to the front, looking for an ambush. Do it while I tell the rest of the squad."

"Aye aye." Adriance's expression said he didn't like it either. "You heard the man. Mark that booby trap."

"Right. Mark it with what?"

"Come on, Mackie, you're smart."

"Yeah," Mackie said sourly. "Field expedient. Hold this for me." He extended his rifle for his fire team leader to take. As he returned the few meters to the booby trap, he reached into the first aid kit hanging from his belt and withdrew a field dressing. He stopped far enough away from where he remembered the tripwire was that he wouldn't accidentally hit it, and knelt. While he looked for anchor points that wouldn't interfere with the wire, he opened the field dressing and unwound its straps. He tied the end of one strap to a sapling a few centimeters from the one the tripwire was attached to, then tied the end of the other strap to a similar place near the flash-bang. When the field dressing was in place a few centimeters higher than the wire, he withdrew his bayonet and drew a series of "X"s in the path under the marking, with two arrows pointing at the explosive. Finished, he backed off.

"Here." Adriance handed his rifle to him. "Let's go." Adriance pointed into the brush next to the trail. "You know where it is. Take a position two meters in from it and wait."

"Are you sure?" Mackie asked. "That close to the trail?"

Adriance shrugged. "That's what the man said."

"What about protecting the environment?"

"Just do it, Mackie."

Mackie shook his head. He didn't think two meters from the path was deep enough, and he'd let higher-higher worry about trampling the environment. He went where Adriance sent him and lowered to one knee, pointing his rifle to his front, ready to open fire. Sounds to his right told him that Adriance was positioning the rest of the fire team. More sounds, faintly-heard, were Sergeant Martin positioning the rest of the squad.

Commiskey's voice came over the platoon net. "First and Second squads, move out. Maintain your interval and dress."

The two squads started advancing slowly, the twenty-six Marines walking as quietly as they could through the brush, which wasn't as quiet as any of them wanted. They watched their front for the "enemy," and looked to their sides to check their intervals and dress—made sure they didn't bunch up and that they stayed approximately on line.

PFC Zion, on the fire team's extreme right, eight meters from the path, was the first to spot the ambush. Unfortunately for him, the ambush had heard the squad's approach, and shifted position to face its flank. The detectors on Zion's chest registered the fire aimed at him and his armor froze him in mid-step before he could get off a shot. Off balance, he toppled to the ground.

At the sound of the first shot, Mackie dove for the ground. But before he got there, a flash-bang went off close to his right front. His armor froze and he hit the ground in the attitude he'd been diving; his rifle pushing forward to go into his shoulder, his left arm extending along the rifle's forestock, right arm bending to the side, his legs spreading, his torso curving. He slapped into the ground and the blank-fire-adapter on the muzzle of his rifle skidded into the leaves and dirt in front of him. For an instant, Mackie's toes and the adapter on his rifle held him off the ground, then the weight of his load toppled him onto his right side; momentum carried him over onto his left. After a second, he rocked back to his right side, then left again. It took several rocks before he reached an uncomfortable equilibrium.

Adriance and Orndoff were diving and were hit at the same time as Mackie. They also froze and rocked as Mackie had, until the three of them looked like nothing so much as three upended tortoises.

Before Second squad managed to realign itself and charge across the path into the flank of the ambush, First squad suffered five more simulated casualties. Third squad rushed up from behind and added its fire to the fight.

In the end, none of the bad guys got away, but Third platoon had suffered eight "dead" and seven more "badly wounded," including Commiskey. That left Guillen in command of a platoon of twenty-seven Marines, the strength of two squads plus someone in command. Everyone in First squad was out of action.

The referees Mackie had discovered followed behind Third squad and closely observed the fire fight, noting where all the casualties were. When the shooting was over, the major unfroze them one at a time, noting each casualty's name, and handed the "dead" over to the enlisted referee to escort to the "morgue," where they would remain until the end of this phase of the exercise. Third platoon and the company corpsmen were responsible for moving the "wounded" to the battalion aid station.

A few hours later, phase one of the exercise was finished. All the dead were resurrected, and the seriously wounded were healed. Captain Carl L. Sitter, the India Company commanding officer, assembled his Marines for a debriefing during the hour they had before the next phase of the exercise began. The enlisted Marines gathered in a semi-circle in front of him, the officers and platoon sergeants grouped to his rear.

"Did I tell you to unass your gear?" Sitter snarled. Nearly all of the Marines had removed their packs and load-bearing webbing to ease the strain of carrying the nearly one hundred kilos of weaponry, ammunition, and other items in their basic combat loads. Sitter and the senior Marines behind him were all wearing their packs and gear.

"We didn't do too well out there today," Sitter said after giving his Marines a moment to re-don their gear and start to squirm under his glare. "Things started off well when First platoon found two referees," he looked at Mackie, who looked back without expression, "but went to hell from there. When a company starts off by losing more than a third of a platoon, it doesn't bode well for accomplishing the company's objective.

"And we barely did." Sitter looked slowly over the company again. "As a matter of fact, if we'd been up against a real enemy instead of an aggressor force that was supposed to let us win, I don't think we would have accomplished our mission.

"All right, break into platoons and chow down on field rats. Keep your packs and other gear on, so you don't forget how we screwed up today.

Maybe it'll have you doing better on tonight's evolution. And clean your weapons!"

"Hey, what did we do wrong?" PFC Orndoff demanded as First squad settled in the shade of a tree to eat their rations. "The aggressors got us fair and square!"

"Explain it to him, Adriance," Sergeant Martin said.

"You're supposed to be smart, Mackie," Corporal Adriance said. "Tell him what we did wrong."

Lance Corporal Mackie cleared his throat. "We didn't exactly do anything wrong," he said slowly. "It's, well, it's just that we aren't supposed to give the bad guys a fair and square chance to do anything to us. We're supposed to kill them before they can do anything."

"See? I said Mackie's supposed to be smart," Adriance said.

"Yeah he is," Martin agreed. "Keep it up, Mackie, and maybe you'll make corporal one of these years."

"Hey, how should we have approached that ambush?" Orndoff demanded.

Martin looked at him, then at the rest of the squad. "I'll bet that right now Lieutenant Commiskey is hearing all about what he should have had the platoon do so that we didn't walk into that ambush. But I didn't say that, and you didn't hear it from anybody. Right?"

Mackie shrugged. "I didn't hear nobody say nothing."

PFC Zion gave his fire team leader a startled look. "What, did somebody say something?"

Orndoff shook his head. "I didn't hear nobody say nothing." He grinned at Adriance, who nodded back.

"Remember that, Marine," Adriance said.

Orndoff grinned, then his expression reverted to confused. "But what *should* we have done?"

Adriance sighed. "Tell him, Mackie. What would you have done?"

Mackie was startled by Adriance again dropping the ball onto him, but recovered quickly. "What I would have done was take us deeper into the trees. That way we would have come in behind the ambush, instead of walking straight into it."

"Oh," Orndoff said, awed.

EVERY MARINE, NO MATTER HIS RANK, OR POSITION IN A UNIT, IS EXPECTED TO BE ABLE to step into the position of his immediate commander or leader, sometimes even a higher position, and perform well. Unknown to everybody below the platoon command level, one element of the night phase of the training exercise was to test that ability among the junior NCOs and junior enlisted Marines of 3rd Battalion, 1st Marines.

Third platoon was in column in Bellows's Exercise Area Bravo—a less environmentally sensitive area of the park, one that had few civilian visitors—moving toward their objective. The Marines had their night vision screens in place to allow them to see in the dark forest. Occasional flash-bangs went off in seemingly random locations—simulated enemy harassment-and-interdiction artillery fire.

Halfway to the objective, Commiskey called a halt. "Squad leaders up," he ordered on his helmet comm. "Assign your men defensive positions."

While nearly all instructions and data could be conveyed over the net, there was always a chance of enemy intercept. Besides, sometimes a face-to-face meeting was better than remote communications, so nobody thought there was anything unusual about Commiskey calling a squad leaders' meeting. Commiskey led Guillen and platoon right guide Sergeant Richard Bender twenty meters off the path. Sergeant James E. Johnson, the Second squad leader, being closest to the command group, was the first to join Commiskey. Commiskey withdrew a flash-bang from a cargo pocket and tossed it to the side, away from the platoon. It went off before the other squad leaders made it through the trees to join the command group.

"Oh, shit!" Sergeant Martin shouted, hitting the dirt at the flash and the bang. A few meters to his left, Third squad leader Sergeant Frederick W. Mausert also swore and hit the deck. So did the gun squad leader, Sergeant Matej Kocak.

When a few seconds passed without another simulated artillery strike, or any word from the command group, the squad leaders pushed themselves up into crouches and dashed to where they believed the platoon command group was. They found the four Marines gently rocking on their backs in their frozen body armor. Using a few words to coordinate their actions, the two squad leaders checked the downed Marines and their comps.

"Damn, damn, damn," Martin swore under his breath. Then into the platoon net, "Where's comm?"

"I'm here," Corporal John H. Pruitt said as he scrambled to the scene.

"Get me company," Martin told him.

"Right." Pruitt got on the net and contacted Captain Sitter. He gave the handset to Martin.

"Six Actual, this is India-three-one," Martin said in a voice steadier than he felt, "India-three-six, three-five, three-four, and three-two are all down." India-three, Third platoon, three-six, -five, -four, the ancient designations for the platoon commander, platoon sergeant, and right guide. Three-one, -two and -three, the designators for First, Second, and Third squad leaders.

"All seniors in India-three are down except for three-one and three-three, is that right?" Sitter asked.

"And guns. What do you want us to do with the casualties?"

"I've got a GPS lock on your position. I'll forward it to battalion, and they'll pick them up. All right, three-one, you still have an objective to take. You're now acting six. Three-three is now acting five. Assign the senior fire team leader in each squad to acting squad leader. You've got three minutes to reorganize and get moving again. India-six-actual out."

Martin returned the handset to Pruitt and looked at Mausert and Kocak. "It's on us," he said. "I'm acting six, and Fred's five. We've got three minutes to reorganize the platoon and move out."

Mausert shook his head. "I always figured I'd make platoon sergeant some day. But, damn, I expected to have the rank when I did."

"You gonna give your squad to Phillips?" Martin asked.

"Yeah," Mausert answered. "He's got seniority, and he's pretty good."

"Do you have any problem with Glowin taking over second squad?"

Mausert shook his head. "I think he can do it."

"Good. Let's give them the news. I'm giving my squad to Adriance." He turned to Pruitt. "Looks like we've got a new command group. You and me will be between First and Second. Fred," back to Mausert, "you're between Second and Third. No sense in being where one round can get both of us. Matej, keep your guns where they are in the column."

"Sounds good to me," Mausert said. Kocak nodded.

"All right, time's wasting. Let's do it."

"What do you think the lieutenant wanted us for?" Mausert asked.

Martin shook his head. "Maybe we'll find out after this phase. Unless this was a set up."

"Could be," Mausert agreed.

"Let's go."

The four headed back to the rest of the platoon and made the new assignments.

"Mackie," Martin said after making Adriance the acting squad leader, "this makes you acting fire team leader. Put one of your men up front, and move out."

"Aye aye," Mackie replied. He turned to his two men. "Zion, take point. Me, then Orndoff."

"Why me?" Zion objected. "I already got killed once today."

"So did all of us," Mackie snapped. "Move out. I'll guide you."

Zion stepped out, and the rest of Third platoon followed. As soon as the platoon was beyond the place where they'd stopped and lost the command group, an umpire appeared out of the shadows and unlocked the armor of the downed Marines.

"Wait here for battalion," he instructed the four, then resumed trailing Third platoon.

An hour later, not much more than half a kilometer from the position that was the platoon's objective, but still in forest, Sergeant Martin called a halt and reformed the platoon into squad columns twenty-five meters apart, with First squad in the middle, flanked by the other two rifle squads. The gun teams were on the flanks. He went ahead of First squad and called on the net, "Squad leaders up." The three corporals who were acting as squad leaders quickly joined him and Mausert.

"Going for a repeat performance, Sergeant Martin?" Adriance asked with a soft laugh, thinking of what happened when Commiskey called for a squad leaders' meeting.

"Just for that, your ass is mine later," Martin said. After making sure everyone he wanted was present, he said, "Follow me," and stepped out in the direction of the platoon's objective.

A hundred meters farther, the forest petered out into a terrain spottily covered with shrubs about half human-height. In most places, there was sufficient space between bushes for a man to pass without brushing one. Fifty meters beyond where Martin stopped his command group, the ground started slanting upward at a modest angle until it formed a ridge more than three hundred meters distant. The last fifty meters looked to be cleared of shrubs. They could faintly make out bunkers on the military crest of the ridgeline.

"I wanted you to get a good look at what we're facing. Now, most of us have been here before," Martin told the others, "so you'll remember those bushes are thorny. But not all of our Marines have had to make this kind of movement at night. The trick is going to be to use those bushes for concealment as we advance, while not getting hung up in them. The closer we can get to that ridge without being detected, the better our chances of taking the objective. Any suggestions or questions?"

"Stay low, that's all I can think of," Corporal Glowin said. "The trees behind us should hide any silhouettes until we get fairly close."

"Unless they've got good night vision," Adriance added.

"That's why we keep low," Glowin said.

Martin studied the landscape to the front for a few moments, deciding how to proceed. Finally he said, "Go back, get your squads and bring them up. Put your people in columns of fire teams with ten meter intervals. The lead man in each fire team has to find a way between the thorny bushes, so be careful about who you put where. We'll get as close as we can before I give the signal to open up. Depending on how close we are, we'll either advance by fire and maneuver, or we'll get on line and charge. Questions?"

Nobody had any questions.

"So get your squads."

Fifteen minutes later, nine fire teams and the guns were on line parallel to the ridge. Martin gave the signal to move out.

Lance Corporal Mackie looked at his two men and decided he'd take the lead between the bushes.

"Stay low," he said. "Try not to rise up above the tops of the bushes." The same thing Adriance had just told the fire team leaders. "Stay close to me, and go exactly where I go. If you see me flinch, or back up, don't go where I did, because that'll mean I just got stuck by thorns. Got it?"

PFCs Orndoff and Zion said they did.

"Let's go." Mackie crouched, almost doubled over and stepped out. While he looked mostly at the bushes close in front of himself to avoid the thorns, he also looked forward to make sure he had bushes in his line of sight, between himself and the ridgeline. He also checked his HUD to see where the red dots of his fire team were relative to the dots of the others. A few times Sergeant Martin called on the net for most of the platoon to hold in place while someone caught up, or for a fire team to stop because it had gotten too far ahead of the rest.

The weight of his combat load made it difficult to walk bent over below the height of the bushes, and Mackie was feeling the strain in his back after a couple of hundred meters. He knew Orndoff and Zion had to be feeling at least as much back strain, probably more—they hadn't been Marines for as long as he had. He was just grateful that so far nobody in the platoon had gotten hung up on thorns and given them away.

But it couldn't last. Still more than seventy-five meters from the top of the ridge somebody, Mackie couldn't tell who, yelped out loud. The aggressor force on the ridge must have been alert, because the entire line erupted with fire.

"Squads," Martin shouted into the platoon net, "advance by fire and maneuver! Guns, lay down supporting fire!"

Seconds later, randomly spaced flash-bangs started going off on the slope, simulating mortar fire.

"First and Third fire teams, advance twenty meters!" Adriance shouted.

"First fire team, let's go! Spread to my flanks." Mackie lurched ahead, still hunched over. Orndoff and Zion ran to his sides. Zion stumbled into a thorn bush and yelled. Mackie had to dodge a bush himself. "Disconnect and catch up!" About twenty meters ahead of where he'd been when the order to advance came, he hit the dirt and began firing up the slope toward the ridge. But he was shooting blind, he couldn't see anything through the bushes. Over the fire, he heard Adriance order Second fire team to advance. The platoon's fire didn't sound as heavy as it should have, he thought the enemy fire must be effective if that many of the Marines were down, frozen in their armor.

"First fire team, go!" Adriance shouted. "Second and Third, lay down fire!"

Good! Mackie thought. The textbook method of two fire teams advancing while one covered them didn't provide enough covering fire, so Adriance was moving the fire teams up one at a time to provide a heavier base of fire. *Just what I'd do.*

And then he broke out of the bushes onto ground that had been cleared as a killing zone.

"First fire team, down!" Mackie said. He heard Zion drop down on his right and begin firing up slope. He didn't hear Orndoff on his left.

"Orndoff, report!" No answer. Damn! Mackie didn't have time to worry about Orndoff now, he had to place heavy, accurate fire on the positions on the ridge top.

In moments, it sounded like most of Third platoon had reached the cleared area. Even the gun teams had moved up to add their heavier fire. The return fire wasn't as heavy as it had been; the Marines' fire must have had an effect on the aggressor force. But the flash-bangs showing mortar strikes were coming closer.

"Fire and maneuver individually within fire teams, twenty meters!" Martin ordered.

"Fire team leaders, advance your men one at a time!" was the order from the squad leaders.

"Zion, go ten meters," Mackie said. As soon as Zion dropped into a firing position ten meters farther up the slope, Mackie called out, "Orndoff!" but got no reply. He jumped up himself and sprinted a zigzag to drop down a few meters from Zion, and resume firing. "Zion, go ten!" This time, when Zion hit the deck, Mackie didn't call for Orndoff, but jumped up and ran forward. In seconds, everyone in Third platoon who was still combat effective was on line, about thirty meters away from the ridgeline positions.

Martin gave the order. "Third platoon, charge!"

The Marines surged to their feet and sped uphill, firing as they went.

There was a bunker almost directly in front of Mackie. He angled his run to reach the bunker just at the side of its embrasure, firing his automatic rifle at the opening. He reached the bunker, slammed his back against its front next to the embrasure, and jerked a flash-bang simulated grenade from his webbing. He held it for a couple of seconds after pulling its pin, then threw the flash-bang inside as hard as he could. After the simulated grenade went off, Mackie spun around the side of the bunker and jumped into a communications trench behind it. He quickly looked to both sides, but only saw other Marines from Third platoon in it.

He looked at the bunker he'd just passed with surprise—fire was still coming out of its front. He readied another flash-bang grenade and threw it hard into the bunker's entrance.

"With me!" he shouted at Zion, and followed the flash-bang as soon as it went off.

"What the...?" Mackie expected to find bodies, frozen in their body armor. Instead, he found a rifle set on a robotic shooter-mount, still firing downslope. Two other rifles had been knocked off their robots. There were no bodies. He knocked the firing rifle off its mount, and the bunker went quiet. He reported what he'd found to Adriance, who reported to Martin what Mackie had found.

"Third platoon, cease fire!" Martin's voice came over the platoon net. "Cease fire!"

The platoon stopped firing, but most of the defensive positions continued firing downslope.

"Squad leaders, have your fire teams check those bunkers."

In moments, the firing stopped all along the line as the Marines disconnected the weapons inside the bunkers from their robot mounts.

"Does anybody see an aggressor anywhere?" Martin asked. Nobody answered that they did. "Everybody, hold your position. And don't fire unless you actually see somebody. Squad leaders, put your people in defensive positions. And report!"

"First squad, report," Corporal Adriance said.

"First fire team, I'm missing Orndoff."

"Second fire team, all present."

"Third fire team, Kuchneister's down," Corporal Button reported.

"First squad, we have one down and one missing," Adriance reported to Martin.

"Who's missing?" Martin asked after second and third squads gave their reports.

"Orndoff."

"Where's Orndoff? Has anybody seen Orndoff?" Martin asked over the platoon net.

"He's over here," Corporal Thompson of Third squad answered.

"What the hell's he doing with you?" Martin asked, then without waiting for an answer, "Orndoff, get over where you belong!"

"Where's that?" PFC Orndoff asked.

Mackie stood and waved. "Over here, numbnuts."

Martin considered the situation. The platoon had lost four of its top leaders to a simulated artillery strike; he felt they were lucky to have lost only five more in the assault on the ridgeline. "Everybody, maintain your positions and watch outboard—not you, Orndoff," he added when he saw Orndoff drop into the trench, "return to your squad. Everybody, be ready for a counterattack."

"What happened to you?" Adriance demanded when Orndoff rejoined his fire team.

"I got hung up in a thorn bush," Orndoff said defensively. "By the time I got loose, I didn't know where Mackie and Zion were. So I went upslope until I found some Marines."

"Third squad," Mackie said, shaking his head.

Orndoff shrugged. "It was still the platoon."

Adriance shook his head. "Well, you're back. That's better than some." He looked down the slope to where PFC Thompson and four other members of the platoon lay frozen in their armor, awaiting release by the referees.

"Every squad, send a fire team to collect our casualties," Martin said on the platoon net. "This was an automated position. There's gotta be bad guys around here somewhere, so everybody be alert."

It took five minutes to locate all the casualties and lug them, frozen in awkward positions, up to the trench line. During that time, Martin and Mausert discussed what to do next. When everybody was back in position, Martin spoke into the platoon net.

"Listen up! I don't have any instructions on what we're supposed to do after taking this position, but I don't like where we are. The aggressors have to know that we've taken the ridge, and they know how it's laid out. That gives them a hell of an advantage in a counterattack. So we aren't going to be here when they come for us. I'm sending the squad leaders a map, showing where we're going. We move out in four minutes. Bring our casualties. Get ready."

"Fire team leaders up," Adriance ordered. He was studying the new map by the time First squad's three fire team leaders joined him. He projected the map onto their HUDs.

Mackie studied the map while Adriance explained Martin's plan. "We're setting an ambush to hit the counterattack from the flank." A thick clump of trees a hundred meters to the northwest was highlighted, and squad positions were marked in it.

✪

"Unless the aggressors come through the trees behind us," Lance Corporal Mackie murmured.

"We do the best we can with what we've got," Corporal Adriance said. "You got a problem with that?"

"No, Corporal. Just making an observation."

Less than fifteen minutes later, Third platoon was in position in the clump of trees. Adriance had passed on Mackie's concern, and Martin adjusted his plan to have one fire team from each squad positioned to watch the rear approaches to the trees. The platoon sat in ambush for two hours before the call to stand down came from battalion headquarters. A referee came by to unlock the armor of the casualties, and lead the platoon back to India Company's bivouac area.

The exercise wrapped up two days later, and the battalion forced marched along a winding, twenty kilometer route to the Marine base at Kanehoe Bay, where the Marines of Three/One were given temporary billeting.

Marine Corps Base Kaneohe Bay,
Oahu, Hawaii, North American Union.
Early morning

The forced march from Bellows had ended about 0230 hours, and the Marines had immediately set to cleaning their weapons and gear, including the blank fire adapters and hit detectors. After they returned the training gear to the supply sergeants, they showered, shaved, and dressed in clean uniforms for morning formation, after which they were marched to a dining facility for their first hot meal since they left the *Oenida* to make the landing at Bellows.

Back in formation after chowing down, a very welcome liberty call was sounded—most of the Marines in the battalion had never been to Hawaii before, and were looking forward to visiting the beach at Waikiki, and the famed fleshpots of Hotel Street in Honolulu.

"Come on, Mackie, we've got liberty!" Lance Corporal Garcia said. He was dressed in civvies. So was Lance Corporal Cafferata; First squad's three lance corporals usually pulled liberty together. Everybody had brought along a seabag with a dress uniform and civilian clothes. The seabags had been stored in the ship's hold, and brought ashore to the temporary billets during the exercise.

Mackie shook his head. "Nah, I've got a paper due for my Marine Corps Institute course a couple of days after we get back to Pendleton. I should work on it."

"What, more of that Napoleonic Wars crap?" Garcia asked.

"Little tin soldiers all in a row," Cafferata said. "That's all you need to put in a paper about the Napoleonic Wars."

Garcia poked Cafferata's shoulder. "Got that right, Marine! Stand in rows and bang away at each other." He shook his head. "What a damn dumb way to fight a war."

"Come on, man," Mackie protested. "Infantry weapons back then were so inaccurate that you couldn't count on hitting anything at more than fifty meters. Besides, the gunpowder they used kicked out so much smoke that you couldn't see anything after two or three volleys. Standing in rows and banging away was the only way you had a chance of hitting anything."

"Maybe so, but the Royal Marines used rifles," Garcia said. "So did the U.S. Marines. No tin soldiers all in a row for the Marines!"

Mackie looked at Garcia. "Did you ever look at a parade formation? What's that if not little tin soldiers all in a row?"

Cafferata guffawed at that, while Garcia said,

"Point to you."

Cafferata slapped Mackie's shoulder. "Come on, man. Let's go have a few brews, check out some hula hula girls."

Mackie looked at the books he'd packed in his hold-seabag, and the pad he was taking notes on. The paper only had to be a thousand words. He decided that he knew enough about the Napoleonic Wars to knock that out in a couple of hours. He stood.

"Give me a couple minutes to change. I want to try a real Hawaiian mai tai."

Mackie never got the chance to write that paper. And it was a very long time before any of the survivors got to see that Amos Weaver movie.

THE JOINT CHIEFS OF STAFF ASSEMBLED VII CORPS (REINFORCED) FOR THE TROY mission, dubbed Operation Menelaus, and assigned Lieutenant General Joel H. Lyman to command it. The main body of the corps consisted of four Army divisions: combined infantry, armor, artillery, and air. The "reinforced" part was the First Marine Combat Force, which consisted of the First Marine Division, Second Marine Air Wing, and supporting elements. The First MCF's commander was Lieutenant General Harold W. Bauer. The Marines were there to "kick in the door," as such assaults are called, with the Army to follow close behind to do the bulk of whatever fighting there might be. The Navy's transport vessels, designated Amphibious Ready Group 17, were to be escorted by the warships of Task Force 8, under the command of Rear Admiral James Avery. TF8 was built around two carriers, one with four atmospheric combat and support squadrons, and two space fighter squadrons, the other a fast attack carrier with two space fighter squadrons. Ten other warships; two cruisers, five destroyers, and three frigates provided the task force's major firepower.

While the entire force was in space, Rear Admiral Avery was in command. Planetside, Lieutenant General Bauer was in command until VII Corps landed, at which time Lieutenant General Lyman would assume overall ground and air command.

Considering what the *Monticello* had found, or more importantly *not* found, in the vicinity of Troy, and what the Force Recon Marines had encountered planetside, the combined force was considered to be more than sufficient to deal with whatever might be there, the monstrously large ship that carried the original alien invasion force not withstanding. After all, the *Monticello* hadn't seen that ship.

It was possible to covertly assign units to Operation Menelaus, but impossible to assemble and send off that large a force in secret. So as soon as the order to begin assembling the task force elements was issued, President Mills initiated a conference call to his counterparts in the European Union, the South Asian Cooperative, Greater Eurasia, Pacific America, the East Asian Cooperation Sphere, and Man-Home Origin. The first two because, along with the NAU, they were the richest, most powerful supra-nationals; the third because its major component was Russia, a historic trouble-maker that always needed to be appeased; the latter three because they were the locations of three of the four space elevators, all of which would be needed to lift the entire task force into orbit. Simultaneously, the Secretaries of State and War paid personal visits to the capitals of the supra-nationals with the space elevators.

Austro-Pacifica, the Caliphate, and the Junta were considered irrelevant to the current situation, and formal notification of their leadership could wait.

There rose, of course, a furor, with the loudest voices sounding off from Moscow.

Then the dickering started. Pacific America, the East Asian Cooperation Sphere, and Man-Home Origin naturally understood the necessity of the NAU using all of the elevators to put their force in orbit. Just as naturally, they each saw an opportunity to make a massive profit. Accordingly, they almost instantly demanded quadruple their normal fees for use of their elevators. The elevator located on Jarvis Island just below the equator in the mid-Pacific was the only one that didn't require negotiation: the island had been a territory of the old United States of America before the founding of the North American Union, and remained an NAU territory.

It took nearly two weeks of hard negotiating, but everybody eventually settled for double the normal fees. Both the European Union and the South Asian Cooperative felt it was in their interest to aid the NAU in paying the higher fees. After all, whoever those aliens were, they probably had EU or SAC colonies in their sights—possibly even Earth.

Greater Eurasia broke the news publicly, so President Mills hastily convened a press conference to inform the world at large of what was known about the invasion, and what the NAU was doing about it.

Austro-Pacifica, the Caliphate, and the Junta were considerably put off by not having been notified earlier. But they got over it. Then everybody settled back to watch developments.

Military staffs require constant work. If they aren't planning or running an actual mission, they are making contingency plans. So after standing up the VII Corps (Reinforced), the Joint Chiefs' staff began planning to stand up the Second Army, which would be the largest military force to be assembled under one commander in centuries. Second Army would consist of four Army corps, each with three combined arms divisions. Two Marine Combat Forces were designated to fill out the Second Army. In addition to transport ships, the Navy would provide a battle group with three carriers, each with four atmospheric combat squadrons and two space combat squadrons; a mix of thirty combat ships; cruisers, destroyers, frigates, and—perhaps most important—three dreadnoughts. The Navy didn't have enough transport shipping to carry Second Army with all of its heavy weapons, and other equipment and supplies, so they assumed that they'd have to commandeer a full quarter, perhaps more, of the NAU's civilian space fleets. Not an eventuality anybody looked forward to.

They issued a training order: Stand up the Third Marine Combat Force and XII Corps. After all, there was a possibility, no matter how remote, that the VII Corps (Reinforced) might run into more than it could handle on its own. Together, the Third MCF and XII Corps would form the core of Second Army.

Second-level navy staffers began back channel negotiations with their counterparts in the major supra-nationals that had navies to possibly enlist their aid in transporting a larger force should it prove to be necessary. All hypothetically, of course.

Marine Corps Base Camp Pendleton, California,
North American Union

The Marines of the First Marine Division, the ground combat element of the First Marine Combat Force, were resplendent in their dress blues as they marched, battalion by battalion, onto the parade ground and formed into three infantry regiments, each with three independent battalions; a light armored infantry regiment; an artillery regiment with three medium gun battalions and one heavy; another regiment included three armored amphibious battalions, one armored, one reconnaissance, and the division's headquarters battalion. The division band followed, its drummers beating a tattoo as the regiments and battalions marched in. Twenty-two thousand, five hundred and seventy-five Marines in all. All were armed save the musicians; most with rifles carried at right shoulder arms, the others with sidearms holstered on their belts. As each battalion reached its designated position in the formation, their commanding officers called out, "Order, *arms!*" and as one, the rifles flashed off the Marines' shoulders to be positioned alongside their right trouser seams. Sunlight glinted off the brass of the Marines' buttons and emblems. The splashes of color on the left chest of their stock-collared jackets were the ribbons that told a Marine's history.

Major General Hugh Purvis, the division's commanding general, stepped onto the reviewing stand and stopped front and center to face his Marines. He took a moment to look them over. More than a quarter of them had no decoration on their uniform jackets other than rank insignia and marksmanship badges. Half or more of the Marines had one or more medals; the Good Conduct Medal, perhaps one or two deployment medals, indicating whatever peacekeeping or humanitarian aid deployments they'd been on. Fewer than a quarter of them had the expeditionary or campaign medals that showed they'd gone in harm's way. Not all of those wore the Combat Action Ribbon on their right chests, to demonstrate that they'd come under enemy fire. Fewer than one in ten of the Marines who'd gone in harm's way wore the decorations awarded for heroism in the face of the enemy.

Internally, Purvis sighed. Not one in five of his Marines had looked into the mouth of the cat. He and his officers and senior NCOs had done their best to train the Marines. But had they done enough? Finished scanning his division, Purvis looked directly at the division chief-of-staff, Brigadier General James Dougherty, who stood on the parade ground before the reviewing stand.

Dougherty raised his right hand to the gleaming black bill of his barracks cover. "Sir," his amplified voice boomed out loudly enough to be heard even in the rear ranks of the division, "First Marine Division, all present and accounted for!"

Purvis brought his right hand up sharply in salute, held it for a beat, and cut sharply. Dougherty cut his, then marched to the side of the reviewing stand and mounted it to stand to the left and rear of his commander.

"Marines!" Purvis said, his amplified voice easily reaching everyone in the formation before him. "You have heard on the news, a colony world allied with the North American Union has been attacked." He paused a beat, then continued. "It's true. And it is true that the attackers were an alien sentience—that is, not human. It's also true that it appears that the entire population of Semi-Autonomous World Troy has been killed or taken prisoner. All attempts to contact the authorities, or anybody else, on Troy since the initial alert of an attack have met with failure. We do not know who attacked Troy, or in what force. Nor do we know the strength of any force presently occupying the planet.

"The First Marine Division has been selected to establish a planethead on Troy, to kick in the door to allow the Army to land and retake the planet. We will be supported in this endeavor by the First Combat Support Brigade, and, once we secure space for their operations, the Second Marine Air Wing will fly cover for us.

"We will take this planethead against a foe of unknown strength, with unknown defensive capabilities. We are Marines. We will do it. No enemy has ever successfully withstood us when we attempted to establish a beachhead—or planethead.

"When you return to your barracks, you will be briefed on everything we know about the alien enemy. We are going to respond with full force, and defeat them.

"We begin embarking on Navy shipping in three days.

"We are *Marines!* We always win. Semper Fi!"

As one, the men and women of the First Marine Division roared out, "*Ooh-rah!*"

As the last echoes finished reverberating across the parade ground, he said, "That is all."

Dougherty stepped forward and called out, "Pass in review!"

The division band began playing, its drums, brasses, and skirting bagpipes sounding the chords of *The Marine Corps Hymn*. Battalion by battalion, the 22,575 Marines raised their rifles to right shoulder arms, columned to the right, marched to the end of the parade ground, turned left and left again, to pass before the reviewing stand, their arms and legs flashing metronomically.

Fort Bragg, North Carolina, North American Union

Lieutenant General Joel H. Lyman's chest swelled with pride as he watched the VII Corps assemble. His VII Corps! Four divisions strong; the 2nd, the 9th, the 25th, and the 106th. Three of the divisions each had three brigades, the 25th Division had four. Each brigade had one infantry battalion, leg or mounted, one armored battalion, heavy or light, and an artillery battalion. One brigade in each division had a fourth battalion, three of the extra battalions were aviation, the fourth was rocket. And there were the brigades directly under the Corps: engineers, signals, Rangers, military police, and medical. Eighty-five thousand soldiers, his to lead into combat.

Lyman had great confidence in his troops. He knew that he, his generals, their officers and senior noncoms had done an exemplary job of training the soldiers of the VII Corps. He and his corps were ready to take on and defeat anybody who dared oppose them!

He watched his eighty-five thousand soldiers take to the parade ground in their camouflaged war dress. The camouflage pattern was designed to trick the eye into not making out details, or even forms. As he looked out over his corps, except for the faces, he was unable to distinguish individual soldiers; the camouflage pattern blurred them together. Indeed, at the farther edges of the mass formation, the soldiers effectively disappeared from his sight—save for their bare faces.

"Soldiers!" Lyman said in a firm voice, picked up by repeating amplifiers so that every soldier could hear it no matter where in the formation he stood, and never boomed out. "Your time for training is over, now it is time to put your training to work in war. You've heard by now that Troy has been invaded by aliens! We don't know who these aliens are, where they came from, or why they attacked without warning. But that lack of knowledge won't stop us, won't slow us down in our mission to kick them off a human world, and teach them that when they decided to tangle with *homo sapiens*, they bit off more than they can chew!

"You, the officers and men of the VII Corps, are beyond doubt the best led, best trained, most prepared, and best armed military force in history. You are going to perform splendidly, and wipe those aliens off all human worlds!

"When you are dismissed, you will spend the next week learning everything we know about the aliens, what they've done, and how we are going to deal with them when we reach Troy." He paused and, with a chuckle, added, "The Marines are going in first, to be our doormen."

Then more firmly, almost solemnly, "That is all."

Battalion by battalion, regiment by regiment, division by division, with the division and brigade bands playing *When the Caissons Go Rolling Along*, the soldiers of VII Corps passed in review. Lieutenant General Lyman saluted each division's, each regiment's, each independent battalion's colors as it passed in front of the reviewing stand.

Barracks, Company I, 3rd Battalion, 1st Marines,
MCB Camp Pendleton, California, NAU

"JESUS H...." LANCE CORPORAL MACKIE WHISPERED.

"No screaming shit," Corporal Adriance whispered back.

Master Sergeant Thomas W. Kates from 3rd Battalion's S2 section, intelligence, had just shown them the vids of the attack on Troy, and was now standing next to the projector on the company classroom's small stage, silently looking at the Marines as they digested what they'd just seen. The company's officers and senior NCOs stood stone-faced at the rear of the classroom—they'd already seen the vids and been briefed. Some of the Marines sitting on the benches facing the stage were likewise stone faced—they were mostly squad leaders, although some were fire team leaders, or even junior enlisted. Many, including a couple of the squad leaders, looked appalled, or even frightened. The eyes of a few glowed with the excitement of facing a new and horrible enemy, eager to test themselves.

After a moment Kates spoke calmly. "Nobody knows who they are, where they came from, or why they attacked." That was a statement that had been made many times, at every command level since the word of the attack on Troy was first given by Fleet Admiral Welborn and Commandant Talbot to Lieutenant General Bauer and his top staff. The same statement Jacob Raub had given to the group assembled by Secretary of War Richmond Hobson. The same given by Lieutenant General Lyman to his staff and subordinate commanders. And that statement would be repeated many more times, by officer and enlisted, Marine to Marine, soldier to soldier, sailor to sailor, until nearly all were sick of hearing it.

"All we know for certain," Kates continued, "is they attacked without warning. The defenders of Troy managed to send off these vids and some text messages via hyperspace drone." He paused for a beat before saying, "We haven't heard anything more from them."

A soft buzz broke out as Marines whispered to each other.

"As you were, people!" Kates shouted over the susurration. The Marines quieted and returned their attention to him. "I'm sure most of you are aware of the fact that in human exploration of the galaxy we have discovered evidence of at least seventeen civilizations that have been destroyed by someone, or something. Totally wiped out. And I'm sure you're wondering if the aliens who attacked Troy are the same aliens responsible for those destructions." He took a deep breath before shaking his head. "We don't know. Actually, there's very little we do know that isn't in the vids I just showed you.

"But there is something more." He popped out the crystal that held the vids he'd shown them and inserted another one. "Shortly after the initial data came in from Troy, the Combined Chiefs sent a Force Recon mission to Troy to find out what the situation was. An entire Force Recon Platoon, forty Marines, made planetfall in eight different locations. These are the recordings they returned. Not the entire recordings, mostly just the parts that show the aliens. I've left out the audio on these recordings." He pressed the "play" button and stepped aside so he wouldn't obstruct anybody's view.

The first images that flickered across the screen showed the cityscape of Millerton in the middle- and background, with the idle McKinzie Elevator Base in the foreground.

"Where is everybody?" someone asked, just loudly enough to be heard by most of the Marines in the classroom.

They watched as four Marines in hard-to-focus-on cammies headed for the base of the elevator and the control building. The picture abruptly jumped to show feathery, beaked creatures jinking and jagging toward the cams, firing weapons as they ran. A Marine watching the vid gasped. On the screen, some of the aliens dropped, shot by the Marines recording their charge. Then the aliens were on the Marines, and the vid cut off, to be replaced by the view of a similar attack somewhere else.

By now most of the Marines were shouting, and many were on their feet, leaning forward, hands clenching as though grasping weapons, looking like they were about to charge the aliens. Someone vomited when a cam's pickup was spattered with blood.

"You're cleaning that up, Marine!" First Sergeant Robinson barked. He let everyone react to the vids of the Force Recon Marines losing their fights for a moment or two longer, than ordered, "Seats! And shut up! Pay attention so you can learn what we're going up against."

Less quickly than they had quieted when Kates had ordered them to when they learned that there hadn't been any other reports from the people on Troy, the Marines settled back onto their benches and resumed intently watching the scenes unfolding in front of them.

The intelligence NCO let the vids run their course, from all eight of the squads, ending with the capture of the alien. When Kates resumed his position on the stage and looked at them, he saw something different from what he had before. This time some were angry, others stunned. Then he hit them with what he knew would be a real shocker.

"Eight Force Recon squads landed on Troy. Only one made it offworld with only one dead. Two didn't make it off at all, because all five Marines in each of those squads were killed." That drew gasps; Force Recon hardly ever lost anyone, they were too good at snooping and pooping.

"Now you have a good idea of what we're up against, so I'll give you back to your officers and senior NCOs. Captain Sitter?"

"Thank you, Master Sergeant," the company commander said as he marched to the front of the classroom and mounted the stage.

"Thank *you*, Sir," Kates said, and left the classroom. He had to give the same presentation to another company.

"Now you know everything that I know about the aliens." Sitter looked over his company. "Make no mistake, we're likely going to be in the toughest fight any of us has ever seen, maybe the toughest since the world wars of the twentieth century."

Alpha Troop Barracks, 1st of the 7th Mounted Infantry,
Fort Bragg, North Carolina, NAU

Second Lieutenant Theodore W. Greig carefully watched his men from his position at the side of the classroom while they watched the vids of the attack on Troy. He and the other officers of Alpha Troop had already seen them at an officers' call at Tenth Brigade's headquarters. He didn't know whether the troops would also be shown the vids from the Marine Force Recon mission. He hoped that collection of vids wouldn't be shown until the troops were aboard the Navy transports and on their way to Troy. Not that he thought any of the soldiers would desert if they saw those vids, but he thought it was better if they saw them on the way, psych them up for the coming mission when there's no possibility of finding a way to get out of it.

The vids of the attack stopped and Captain Henry C. Meyer, Alpha Troop's commanding officer, took the stage.

"Men," he said, "as you just saw, we are going up against a manic alien enemy. Nobody knows who they are, where they came from, or why they attacked without warning." He didn't know how many times that sentence had been said by officers and noncoms throughout VII Corps, and wouldn't have cared if he did—it bore repetition, and he was certain he'd say it many times more.

"It doesn't matter how manic these aliens are. The Marines are going in first to secure a planethead for us. Let me guarantee you, after those aliens chew up the Marines and spit out their bones, they're going to find out what a *real* fighting force is like. We will make them regret they ever attacked Troy.

There were hoots and catcalls at mention of the Marines. "Hey diddle-diddle, straight up the middle!" one soldier called out. "Show offs!" another shouted. "Marines!" someone cried, and gave a Bronx cheer. "Better them than us," a more thoughtful soldier said quietly.

Captain Meyer let them go for a moment, barely repressing a smile. "All right, all right," he said at last, "quiet down and listen up. Now, all intelligence services, both military and civilian, are working hard and fast to learn everything they can about this enemy. As we learn more, you will be told everything you need to know to help us defeat them. When you are dismissed, you will return to your quarters and prepare to move out. We will be heading into space via the elevators in Kenya."

He looked over his men, seeming to look each of the one hundred and twenty-five of them in the eye, and stepped off the stage.

"Troop, a-ten-*shun!*" troop First Sergeant Powhatan Beaty shouted as Meyer marched out of the classroom, followed by the other officers. When the captain was gone, he said, "Platoon sergeants, when I dismiss you take your men to their quarters and take care of last minute preparations. There will be an inspection in two hours. We will board transportation for the first leg of our trip to Kenya in the morning. Dismissed!"

Barracks, India/3/1, MCB Camp Pendleton, California, NAU

"First squad, on me," Sergeant Martin called when Third platoon reached its squadbay. The Marines who had already entered their rooms came back out to the corridor and gathered with the others in front of their squad leaders. Elsewhere along the corridor, Third platoon's other squad leaders were gathering their men as well.

"Listen up, and listen carefully," Martin said seriously. "You saw the Force Recon vids. An important question that wasn't answered was, how did the aliens spot those Marines? The camouflage of our utilities makes us damn hard to see in the field. You've seen Force Recon in action. Their utes are even harder to spot. Maybe the aliens see in a different part of the spectrum, or maybe they have some other sense that makes them less reliant on their eyes. I hope we find some way of knowing before we make planetfall, because right now we can't rely on our cammies to be invisible to the aliens. Keep that in mind when you're going for cover and concealment—they might still be able to see you.

"Now get into your rooms and finish getting your shit together. I'm going to inspect in half an hour, and I want everything ready to go the minute we get the word to move out. Go."

Back in their room, First squad's First fire team didn't start getting ready for the inspection. Instead, Corporal Adriance and Lance Corporal Mackie dropped into the chairs at their tiny desks and stared wide-eyed at each other. PFCs Orndoff and Zion collapsed on their racks and turned their faces to the wall.

"This is real," Mackie whispered, half to himself.

"No shit, Sherlock," Adriance whispered back. When he noticed that Mackie was trembling, he realized that he was trembling himself, and that the trembling was in danger of overwhelming him. He straightened up and took a deep breath. He looked at his dress blues tunic and saw the Combat Action Ribbon on its right breast, and the two campaign medals and Marine Expeditionary Medal that followed the Good Conduct Medal on the left breast. He didn't have to look at the tunics of his men to know that none of them had the CAR or any campaign medals. He'd been there before, they hadn't. It was up to him to set the example, to keep his men from falling apart before they'd even heard a shot fired in anger.

"Listen up," he snapped. "We're Marines, this is what we signed up for. When you walked into that recruiting office and signed up, you knew that some day you might have to fight a war, might have to kill—or even be wounded or killed yourself.

"Well, we're Marines. We have a long history behind us, Marine ancestors who were always the toughest, most winning warriors of their times. And we're the toughest, most winning warriors of our time. We aren't going out there to get wounded or killed. We're going out there to put a serious hurting on whoever or whatever it was that slaughtered the people on Troy." He carefully didn't mention what happened to the Force Recon Marines.

"We're Marines. We fight. And when we fight, we win. So stop pissing and moaning about what's coming up, and start thinking about how we're going to kick some alien ass!"

"What about what happened to Force Recon?" Zion asked.

"What about it?" Adriance asked back. "Force Recon went in expecting to snoop and poop and gather intelligence. They weren't prepared to fight.

We'll go in expecting to kick ass. Now we've got an inspection to prepare for. Get busy!"

Not only did the squad pass Martin's inspection, the whole platoon passed Second Lieutenant Commiskey's inspection which followed minutes later, and Captain Sitter's inspection. Everything they weren't taking, which included their dress blues and most of their personal belongings, went into the company supply room for storage during their absence. Then it was time to fall in behind the barracks and head for the dining facility for evening chow.

The next morning the First Marine Regiment boarded C215 transport aircraft from VMGR 352, Marine Air Group 11, and flew to the space elevator base near Quito, Ecuador, Pacific America.

Transit to Semi-Autonomous World Troy

Even with four elevators operating round the clock, it took time to ferry the twenty-two and a half thousand Marines of the 1st Marine Division the nearly 36,000 kilometers to the geosync station where they boarded Navy shipping. It was a full week before the entire division was boarded and the Amphibious Ready Group in formation to head for the wormhole that would take the Marines to Troy. As soon as the ARG moved off, the 2nd Marine Air Wing, with its aircraft, munitions, fuel supplies, parts, and the rest of its impedimenta began rotating onto the elevators to mate with their waiting flotilla.

From orbit, it took three days at flank speed to reach the wormhole through which they would travel the sixty-two light years to their destination. The sixty-two light years was the quickest part of the journey.

The gator task force was preceded into the wormhole by Task Force 8, built around the carrier NAUS *Rear Admiral Norman Scott*. The five destroyers went in first, followed closely by two cruisers, the battleship that was the flagship, and the fast attack carrier. The TF's three frigates tailgated the *Scott*. Both carriers launched their spacecraft squadrons as soon as they exited the wormhole in Troy's space. The twelve warships *pinged* Troy-space, searching for other spacecraft, but found nothing other than planets, moons, asteroids, and miscellaneous space junk, certainly nothing that remotely resembled spacecraft. Rear Admiral Avery ordered a drone dispatched to the ARG, which then flowed through the wormhole.

ARG17, fifteen gator ships—"gator," an archaic term from when humanity was only on one world, and Marines were landed from water seas to land—centered around Landing Platform Shuttle-1 NAUS *Iwo Jima*. LPS-1 was the fifth ship to carry that name. The 1st Marine Regiment was embarked on her. Traveling at three-quarter speed, it took five days for the

ARG to take station off Troy and prepare to land the landing force. While the gator ships were moving into position, the warships of TF-8 took defensive positions around the planet, covering all approaches, and guarding against ground-based attacks.

Land the Landing Force, Semi-Autonomous World Troy

"ALL RIGHT, MARINES, LINE IT UP!" STAFF SERGEANT GUILLEN ROARED.

"Get out there and get in line!" the squad leaders shouted.

"Move, move, *move!*" the fire team leaders cried.

There was a pounding of boots on the deck and a clatter of loose gear jerking about. Here an "Oof." There a grunt. Elsewhere a curse as the Marines of Third platoon scrambled out of the squad compartments in which they'd billeted for the trip. They scrambled into a double line in the passageway, one line on each side, jostling one another in their haste, and trying not to bump into their squad leaders or the platoon sergeant.

"Squad leaders, report!" Guillen ordered as the thirty-nine Marines settled into position.

"Fire team leaders, report!" the squad leaders echoed.

"First fire team, all present and accounted for!"

"Second fire team, all present and accounted for!"

"Third fire team, all present and accounted for!" came the replies, one of each for each of the three squads.

"First squad, all present and accounted for!" And the same for Second and Third squads.

Guillen clasped his hands behind his back and strode the length of the platoon, looking at each Marine as he passed, his experienced eye looking to make certain every man had everything he needed to carry for the landing. None failed his inspection—all possible failures had already been dealt with by the squad leaders inside the compartments before they fell out.

"You know the drill," Guillen said when he reached the far end of the platoon. "As many times as we've done this, you damn well *better* know it." He looked past the platoon to where Second Lieutenant Commiskey stood just beyond the end of the formation.

"Sir, Third platoon is all present and accounted for, and ready to move out."

"Thank you, Staff Sergeant," the platoon commander replied. "You may take the platoon to its boarding point."

"Aye aye, Sir. Third platoon, face aft!"

The Marines pivoted, those on one side of the passageway facing to their right, those on the other to their left.

"Third platoon, route step, march!"

They moved out, not marching in step, turning this way and that as they wended their way through the passageways, up ladders and down, until they linked up with the rest of India Company at a closed hatch outside the hanger deck. Elsewhere on the *Iwo Jima* other platoons and companies were assembling at equally closed hatches leading to the hanger deck until all of 3rd Battalion, 1st Marines was ready. 1st and 2nd Battalions followed in trace.

A clanging from the other side of the hatches announced bosons mates undogging them. In a moment the hatches were flung open, and the Marines surged through, urged on by the "Move move *move!*" of platoon sergeants and squad leaders.

"Follow the yellow lines!" the bosons mates shouted at the Marines racing past them. As if the Marines needed the reminder—they'd rehearsed going through the hanger deck to their assigned shuttles so many times during the past five days they could have found their way in their sleep. Or so many of them claimed. Nonetheless, "Follow the yellow lines!" the bosons mates shouted again and again. They *had* to keep shouting the instruction—sailors think Marines are dumb. Hey, you aren't going to catch squid-boy landing on a hostile planet where he can get his sweet ass shot off. Nossiree!

"Now what do we do?" PFC Zion groused a couple of minutes after Third platoon crammed itself into a shuttle.

"Now we wait for what comes next," Corporal Adriance said.

Lance Corporal Mackie didn't say anything, just squinched his shoulders, trying to make himself as comfortable as he could, jammed shoulder to shoulder against Adriance and Zion, with his pack pressed against his back, the items on his combat-loaded belt poking into his hips and thighs and midriff.

It was long minutes of uncomfortable waiting before they heard faintly through the armor of the shuttle, "Land the landing force!"

Rumbles announced the suctioning of the atmosphere from the hangar deck, followed by the opening of the bay doors. More rumbles and jerks told of tractors moving the shuttles to the launch ramp. With a final shove, the shuttles lost the gravity generated within the starship, and they began drifting away to a distance where it was safe to light their engines. Minutes later, more than fifty shuttles were in formation and began the plunge planetward.

Inside the windowless shuttles the Marines couldn't see the flashes of the barrage the destroyers of TF-8 were laying on the landing zone, nor could they see the atmospheric aircraft off the carrier *Admiral Scott* orbiting to begin their strafing runs when the barrage stopped.

Planetfall, Semi-Autonomous World Troy

The shuttles touched down at hundred and fifty meter intervals five klicks from Millerton. Not all of them touched the ground; some hovered two or three meters above the scrub-covered dirt. The Marines scrambled off, some running straight from the ramps, others having to jump a meter or two from the ramp's lip to the ground. They raced a hundred meters from the shuttles, spreading out and getting on line in squads and platoons and companies. Fifteen seconds after touching down, the shuttles launched, jumping straight up on the downward-facing jets on their undersides. Their combined roars would have burst the eardrums of the Marines, had they not been wearing full-head helmets insulated to block exterior sounds. Still, some noise got through, momentarily deafening the Marines. At five hundred meters altitude the shuttles angled their noses upward and fired their main engines, shooting up into the atmosphere and back to orbit.

By then, more than three thousand Marines were on the ground, in prone shooting positions, scanning the surrounding landscape, ready to repel an assault. In addition to their personal weapons, one fire team leader in each squad used a motion detector, one used an infrared scanner, and the third had a sniffer checking for chemical signs of animal life wafting on the breeze. The Marines watched through the spotty fires set off by the shuttles' jets.

"Ears!" the command came down from Regiment to the battalions when the shuttles' roar was sufficiently muted by distance.

"Ears!" the command went from battalions to companies.

"Ears!" the command went from companies to each Marine on the defensive line.

"Turn on your ears," Sergeant Martin ordered First squad.

"Unplug your ears," Corporal Adriance told his men.

Now they listened, as well as watching with their eyes and their detectors. At first all they heard was the faint crackling of the fires that were quickly dying down, the minor noises made by the Marines to their sides, and the buzzing of flying insectoids. After a few moments, the cries of avians picked up, as did the rustling of small animals skittering through the scrub.

The Marines waited and watched for an hour and then some, while regimental and battalion headquarters launched a dozen and a half Unmanned Aerial Vehicles disguised as local flying animals to circle in ever-widening orbits, seeking enemy positions or movement. Three of the UAVs went directly to Millerton, where two made swooping orbits and the other perched on one of the pylons anchoring the space elevator.

All any of the UAVs saw was a landscape or cityscape devoid of animate life.

1st Marines HQ, Five Klicks West of Millerton

Colonel Justice M. Chambers, the commanding officer of the 1st Marines, listened to the report of Major Reginald R. Myers, the regiment's S2, intelligence officer, regarding the total lack of human or vaguely humanoid forms seen anywhere within a ten kilometer radius of the landing zone. Chambers comm-linked with his battalion commanders.

"1st Battalion, I want you to secure this landing zone until the next wave lands. Once a battalion of the Fifth Marines is here to relieve you, move forward to positions west of Millerton. 2nd Battalion, secure the space elevator to prepare a landing field for the airedales. 3rd Battalion, have two companies sweep through the city to make sure nobody's home, and have one company send platoon-size patrols ten klicks beyond the city. Headquarters Company, move to the elevator and set up in its buildings.

"Questions?"

There were no questions, all the battalion commanders understood the commander's intent. And they all knew that "airedale" was the derogatory term ground-combat Marines used for Marine air units and their personnel.

On the Move, South of Millerton

"Third platoon, saddle up!" Staff Sergeant Guillen shouted. "We're moving out."

"Ah, just when we were getting settled in," Lance Corporal Mackie quipped.

"That's Mother Corps for you, Mackie," Corporal Adriance said. "As soon as you relax, she's got work for you to do." Then to Sergeant Martin, "Where we going, honcho?"

"You know as much as I do," the squad leader replied. "Is everybody up and ready?" He looked along the line of his squad and, by focusing hard, was able to make out that everyone was on his feet. It was a long time since he'd last been discomfited by how hard it was to see Marines in their cammies. He turned to look where he thought the platoon's command group stood and waited for the next order.

"Squads in line," came the order from Second Lieutenant Commiskey. "First squad on the left, Second in the middle, Third on the right. First squad link with Kilo Company on your left, Third squad link Second platoon with on your right. Wait for my signal."

"First fire team, me, Second, Third," Martin gave his squad their marching order. The Marines quickly got in order.

"Orndoff, me, Mackie, Zion," Adriance told his men. "Zion, make sure you don't lose Sergeant Martin."

"As if," PFC Zion snorted. "I don't think it's possible for the honcho to lose touch with the man in front of him even if that man's *trying* to break contact."

"I heard that, Zion," Martin said. "And you better believe it."

A moment later the command to move out came down. 3rd Battalion, which had been on the right side of the regiment's defensive line, hardly had to veer to go past the right side of the area where isolated flames still licked. They skirted the south side of the small city, where the houses and other buildings petered out and gave way to fields and thin woods. India Company, on the left of the battalion formation, filtered through the structures.

On the Southern Outskirts of Millerton

"India Company, check inside the buildings," Lieutenant Colonel Ray Davis, the battalion commander, ordered. "I don't want anybody popping up behind us. Kilo, Lima, slow your pace so India doesn't fall behind."

India Company's First and Second platoons encountered and quickly searched structures before Third platoon finally did.

"First fire team, check it out," Martin ordered as First squad approached a two story, white-painted clapboard house with gabled roof and a porch that wrapped around the near side of the building.

"Aye aye," Adriance answered.

"Orndoff, Zion, look in the windows. Mackie, go around and get ready to go through the front door when I tell you to."

There were two windows on the first floor of the side facing them. They climbed over the porch railing, and the two junior men headed to the windows to cautiously look into them. Mackie went around the corner to the front door, and Adriance took position at the corner where he could cover all three of his men.

"All I see is an empty room," Orndoff said.

"What about furniture?" Martin asked.

"Yeah, it's got furniture. And what looks like an entertainment center. But no people, no animals, no aliens."

"Same thing here," Zion reported. "It's a bedroom. At least, it's got a bed."

"Can either of you see through a door into the rest of the house?"

"The bedroom door's ajar, but I can't really see anything beyond it," Zion said.

"I see a door. It's wide open," Orndoff reported. "Beyond it there's just another room with furniture, and a window on its far side. No curtains or drapes on the window. Not closed curtains, anyway."

"All right, hold your positions, and let me know if anything changes. And keep watch behind yourselves."

"Aye aye," they said.

"Mackie, wait for me, then we go in."

A large hole had been broken out in the lower part of the front door, but the hole's top was too low for a human to duck through without doubling over. The door's bottom scraped along the floor when Mackie, standing to its side, shoved it open. Adriance stood on the doorway's other side. Both Marines had their rifles ready and their helmets' ears turned up. There was no sound from inside the house.

"Go!" Adriance said.

In well practiced movements, Mackie darted through the doorway and to his right, looking everywhere, with his rifle muzzle pointing where he looked. Adriance followed on Mackie's heels and to the left, likewise looking everywhere, muzzle sweeping along with his eyes.

Dust motes dancing in the sunlight streaming through the window on the room's left provided the only movement. There was no sound except for the blood pounding in their ears, and the breath in their helmets.

On the right wall was the open door to the room Orndoff was looking into. Another open door on the left of the back wall led into another room. A stairwell leading up was on the rear wall's right. Another door, ajar, was on the side wall near the stairs.

"Cover me," Adriance said. "I'm going to check that back room."

"Right." Mackie moved to his left front, to where he could see into the back room. It was a large kitchen.

Adriance went behind Mackie to reach the kitchen, staying out of his line of fire, then ducked low to enter the room.

After a moment, he called, "Mackie, get in here."

Mackie didn't run getting into the kitchen—there hadn't been any urgency in Adriance's voice—but still went in quickly. It only took him a second to locate his fire team leader; the camouflage pattern wasn't as effective indoors as out.

"Check it out," Adriance said, pointing at the stove and a table set for six. A pot of something long gone to rot and mold was on the stove. The same was true of three of the six bowls on the table. It was as though the residents had been interrupted halfway through serving dinner, but not so suddenly that whoever was serving didn't have time to put the pot back on the stove.

"Damn," Mackie murmured.

"Cover me," Adriance said, and headed for two doors on the far side of the kitchen. One door was open; it was a slope-ceilinged pantry with a cold-storage unit. Adriance opened the storage unit, flinched away, and slammed it shut again. "It's loaded with organics that've gone bad," he said, and shuddered. There was nothing else in the pantry that could conceal a body, living or dead. He went to the closed door. It opened to a small water closet. Again, no one was in it.

"You know what's weird?" Mackie asked.

"Tell me," Adriance said absently as he headed out of the kitchen and to the stairs leading up.

"There's no blood, no sign of a fight except for the broken front door, and nothing seems out of place."

"You noticed," Adriance said dryly. Let's check out the second deck, and then get out of here." Second deck, not second floor. The Marine Corps was born in Navy ports and on Navy ships, so Marines use many Navy terms.

"Aye aye." Mackie took the lead going to the second floor. Again, he didn't race but still went rapidly, stepping along the side of the stairs so they wouldn't creak. Halfway up the stairs took a turn to the left, over the pantry. At the top, he looked left before turning to the right and stepping out of Adriance's way.

The second floor was smaller than the first, and had three bedrooms. One, larger than the others, had its own bathroom. A second bathroom was between the other two bedrooms, and was obviously shared by their occupants. One bedroom had bunk beds.

"Parents' room, kids' rooms," Adriance said.

"Three kids had to share one bathroom," Mackie said with a shake of his head, relegating the former occupants of the house to the past tense. "I hope they weren't all girls."

Adriance grunted.

They were checking inside the last of the closets when Sergeant Martin's voice came over the comm. "First fire team, get a move on in there, we need to move."

"Just finishing up," Adriance reported back. "We'll be out in a couple of minutes."

That first two story, white-painted clapboard house was typical of what India Company found on the south side of Millerton. No bodies, no sign of struggle, very little out of place, hardly any blood. The southern fringe was like the *Mary Celeste*, a nineteenth century ship found abandoned off Portugal, seaworthy and fully provisioned, with no sign of foul play to explain the disappearance of her crew and passengers.

The heart of the city was very different. It was obvious that a fierce battle had been fought there. Structures were severely damaged, some burned to their foundations. Broken vehicles littered the streets. Unpaved ground was gouged. Blood stains were everywhere.

But there wasn't a single person, human or alien, to be found. Not even a body part. Not even a dog or a cat turned feral.

That feral dog Force Recon saw must have died, Mackie thought.

As ordered, India Company sent out three platoon-size patrols ten klicks east of Millerton. None of them found any sign of human or alien life, or domestic animals gone feral.

A battalion from the Fifth Marines landed in the second wave, escorting Marine Tactical Air Command Squadron 28, and Marine Attack Squadron 214 from Marine Air Group 14; the squadrons took off for the McKenzie Elevator Base as soon as they were off-loaded from the shuttles. The battalion relieved 1st Battalion, 1st Marines and secured the landing zone while the rest of the First Marine Combat Force made planetfall.

LIEUTENANT GENERAL HAROLD W. BAUER, COMMANDER OF THE 1ST MARINE COMBAT Force, studied his situation board. The 1st Marine Division was all present. Sixteen battalions—infantry, light armor, armor—all ranging out far from Millerton on search-and-destroy missions, seeking the aliens who had invaded the world, and hoping to find survivors. The division's reconnaissance battalion roamed in platoons and squads farther out. The rest of the division was in defensive positions surrounding Millerton and the planethead, formerly called the landing zone, five klicks to the west of Millerton. The 2nd Marine Air Wing was all planetside. Sixteen of the fighter and ground attack squadrons flew cover for the battalions; the other three flew search patterns where the ground forces didn't go. Two of the atmospheric squadrons off the carrier *Rear Admiral Norman Scott* had been deployed planetside and joined the Marine air in searching for humans and aliens in areas not being patrolled by the ground forces. The rest of the MAW's units were assigned to building, securing, and maintaining its base, and maintaining, refueling, and rearming the squadrons' aircraft when they returned from their patrols. The First Marine Logistics Group was busy building Camp Puller, which would be the division's home base on Troy, and in preparing ground for the VII Corps to establish its base when it made planetfall.

The level of the force's activities satisfied Bauer—except for one detail. They had yet to find one bit of activity that they wouldn't find on any habitable world that didn't have human or other sentient occupants. For all he, or anybody else, could tell, Troy was an uninhabited world of ruins, or human structures that would someday decay into ruins.

The report from the Navy in orbit seconded what the Marines on the ground and in the air found: No vessels other than Task Force 8's warships were anywhere in or near Troy's system; Amphibious Ready Group 17 had already returned to Earth to pick up VII Corps. The satellites ringing the planet found nothing but a few gravitational anomalies on the world, not all that unusual for extraterrestrial planets—gravitational anomalies had long been known on Earth and its moon. Troy's two moons had similar gravity irregularities.

The situation was such that Bauer and Rear Admiral James Avery considered sending a message to Earth calling off the deployment of VII Corps. In the end they decided that, in the interest of training for the Army and the ARG, not to send the message.

Wormhole, Troy Space

TF8's two cruisers, the *Coral Sea* and *Ramsey Strait*, two of its destroyers, the *Lance Corporal Keith Lopez* and *Chief Gunners Mate Oscar Schmit, Jr.*, and the fast attack carrier *Rear Admiral Isaac C. Kidd* took up station where the wormhole was about to open. Avery thought, there being no threat in Troy's system, that this was simply a training opportunity for his warships.

An area of empty space, some 400,000 kilometers north of the ecliptic, seemed to somehow shimmer and waver in a manner difficult to see and focus on. Indeed, anyone who stared at it for more than a few seconds was in danger of developing a severe headache. Then, with a *pop* that was somehow felt but not heard, a vacancy that could be called neither black nor a hole in space, abruptly took the place of the shimmering waver and a wormhole opened. A convoy of Navy transports exited single file from the rent in the fabric of space-time; Amphibious Ready Group 17 was returning to Troy space. As the ships exited, they maneuvered into an open formation. The waiting warships took station around the ARG as it formed up. ARG17 now had a quarter more ships than it had before. While there were more than twice as many soldiers in VII Corps as there had been Marines in the initial landing, the Marine aircraft had taken considerable space. That worked out to, man per man, a one-division-one-wing MCF needed nearly as much shipping as a four division Army Corps.

Once the ARG was fully exited and deployed into its new formation, with its five warship escort in place, it began its five-day-long cruise to orbit around Troy where it would land its landing force. When it was three quarters of the way there, a gravitational anomaly on Troy's lesser moon, called "Mini Mouse," which at the time was on the far side of the planet from the warships orbiting in geosync, and out of sight of any Navy assets in the Troy system, gave up its secret.

Sections of the moon's surface rolled aside and missiles shot out. Less than a kilometer above the moon's surface they turned onto a parabolic path on course to intercept the oncoming ARG and its escort.

Combat Action Center, NAUS Durango,
Task Force 8's Flagship, in geosync orbit around Troy

The CAC was quiet and dimly lit, the only light was from the screens of the displays at the various stations in the room, and the dim lights that showed where the hatches were. The compartment felt cavernous, but that was only because the stations were spaced sufficiently far apart that the glow from one screen wouldn't distract the techs at the next. The soft voices of the sailors watching the displays as they occasionally made reports were the only sounds. There weren't even the *pings* that normally would have been heard to indicate radar signals; the *Durango's* radar wasn't on.

"Chief, do we have an exercise going?" Radarman 3 John F. Bickford asked, staring at his display, speaking more loudly than he had when making routine reports.

"Not that anybody told me," Chief Petty Officer James W. Verney answered. He took the two steps from his station to Bickford's and stood over him to look at the display.

After a brief moment Verney called to Lieutenant Thomas J. Hudner, the radar division head, "Mr. Hudner, it looks like we've got possible hostiles heading our way!" His voice cracked. The soft murmurs silenced, and everyone turned to look at Verney.

"Say what?" Hudner asked, startled from his reverie; he'd been think-ing of the homecoming he was going to get from his fiancée when this cruise was over. He glanced at the chief to see which display he was looking at, then dialed his screen to show that view seen at his station. It was a second or two before he fully absorbed the sight that met his eyes. Then he got on the comm to the bridge.

"Bridge, CAC."

"CAC, Bridge. What do you have?" came back the bored voice of the watch officer, Lieutenant Commander Allen Buchanan.

"We've got a lot of bogeys approaching from Mini Mouse. They look on course to intercept the ARG."

"What?" Buchanan squawked, his boredom abruptly vanished. He leaned forward and ordered, "Show me." He quickly examined the display from the CAC that popped up on the bridge's main board. "God," he murmured as he slapped the comm button to the captain's quarters.

Captain Harry M. P. Huse awoke instantly and sat up on his bed before hitting the comm button. "Speak," he rumbled.

"Sir, we have bogeys moving at speed from Mini Mouse toward the ARG."

"Sound general quarters and notify Admiral Avery. I'll be with you momentarily." Huse took two minutes to slap water on his face to dredge the sleep from his eyes, and to get dressed.

Bridge, NAUS Durango

"Captain on deck!" Petty Officer 2 Henry Nickerson shouted as the *Durango's* commanding officer stepped into the bridge.

The bridge wasn't kept dark like the CAC, and routine voices spoke in normal volume. But all went silent when Lieutenant Commander Buchanan reported to Captain Huse, and everybody appeared to be very intent on their duties.

"Carry on," Huse ordered, ignoring the fact that none of the officers or sailors on the bridge had stopped what they were doing following Nickerson's announcement. He strapped himself into his chair, which had just been vacated by Buchanan. As soon as he saw the display showing the bogeys headed toward the ARG, he called to the fast attack carrier *Kidd* and told them, "Bogeys are en route from Mini Mouse to the ARG. Suggest you ready fighters to intercept." He simultaneously transmitted location data on the bogeys and buzzed Admiral Avery.

"Talk to me," the admiral said on his command link with Huse.

"Sir, several dozen, perhaps sixty, bogeys are headed toward the ARG. I have alerted the ARG and the *Kidd*."

There was a pause before Avery said, "I've ordered the *Kidd* to plot intercepts and launch their squadrons. Stand by to protect the Marines on the ground if the enemy launches anything at them. For your information, I have deployed the three remaining destroyers to intercept and destroy the bogeys. That leaves you, *Scott*, and the three frigates to guard the planet. Avery out."

Now all that Huse or anybody else in the *Durango's* crew could do was wait and watch, ready to move into action the instant they saw any sign of threat to themselves or the Marines planetside.

Fleet CAC, NAUS Durango

"I want to know where they came from," Rear Admiral James Avery snapped, glaring at the display showing the bogeys that were headed for ARG 17 as though his very look could turn them aside, if not actually destroy them.

"Aye aye, Sir," Lieutenant Commander R. Z. Johnston replied. "On it."

"Comm," Avery said.

"Sir!" Lieutenant Commander George Davis responded.

"Earth needs to know about this, ASAP. Prepare drones. Launch when ready. Use the wormhole ARG 17 just exited from"

"Prepare drones, aye." Davis began murmuring orders to his section.

Moments later, a barely felt thump signaled the launch of the first drone to Earth. For as long as the wormhole stayed open, more drones followed the first one as the action developed, so that Earth would have the most complete picture of what was happening in Troy space. But Avery knew the picture wouldn't be complete enough, that the wormhole would close long before the action was resolved.

Ready Room, Fast Attack Carrier
NAUS Rear Admiral Isaac C. Kidd

The pilots of VSF 114 "Catfish" squadron were startled by the klaxon that suddenly blared, followed by a voice that commanded, "Ready squadron, stand by for orders!" The pilots glanced at each other; they all caught that the command was to "stand by for orders," not "stand by for briefing."

Captain John P. Cromwell, the *Kidd's* Commander Air Group, strode into the ready room and stepped onto the small stage at its front. All eyes fixed on him. He looked like he'd just been awoken and couldn't quite believe what he was about to say.

"We don't have time for a proper briefing," Cromwell said as soon as he faced the pilots. "At least sixty bogeys have been detected on an intercept vector from Mini Mouse to the ARG. You are to go out there and keep them from reaching their targets. All available data on the bogeys will be fed into your Meteors' comps by the time you reach them. Lionfish squadron will follow you as soon as they can scramble. This is not a drill. Now get out there and seriously kick some ass!"

"Catfish, let's go!" Lieutenant Adolphus Staton, VSF 114's commander, shouted as he jumped to his feet and raced out of the ready room.

The ready room was adjacent to the launch deck, where thirty-two SF6 Meteor interceptors waited. Sixteen of the Meteors stood with their crew hatches open.

"She's as ready as I can make her, Lieutenant," Chief Petty Officer John W. Finn calmly said as Staton reached his Meteor.

"Is she ready enough that I don't have to run a pre-flight myself?" Staton asked, echoing Finn's calmness.

"If you trust me, she is, Sir."

"You don't get to be a chief if you aren't trustworthy," Staton said, climbing into his Meteor.

"I've never lost a pilot yet," Finn told him as he dogged the hatch closed.

"*Yet?*" Staton asked, but the hatch was closed and he hadn't hooked into his comm yet. Well, he did trust Finn. He quickly went through his instrument check; everything seemed to be ready and working properly.

"Catfish, are you ready?" Staton said, testing his comm link. "Sound off."

"Catfish Three and Four, ready for launch," came the voice of Lieutenant (jg) Donna A. Gary, the assistant squadron commander.

"Catfish Five and Six, ready," was Lieutenant (jg) William E. Hall.

The rest of VSF 114's two-spacecraft teams reported in as the spacecraft were trundled to the launch tube.

"Victor Sierra Foxtrot One-one-four, ready for launch," Staton reported to launch operations.

"Victor Sierra Foxtrot One-one-four," replied launch officer Lieutenant Commander Alexander G. Lyle, "launch in five, four, three, two, one, *go!*"

Two by two, flight leader and wingman, the Meteors lunched at ten second intervals. Less than a minute and a half after Staton was slammed back into his seat by the force of launching, VSF 114 was in formation and heading on an intercept vector toward the oncoming bogeys.

VSF 218 "Lionfish" began launching three minutes later.

VSF 114, "Catfish" squadron, off NAUS Kidd,
En Route to Intercept Bogeys

"Talk about your target rich environments!" Ensign Paula Foster shouted.

"Restrain your enthusiasm, Pinball," Lieutenant Adolphus Staton said to his wingman.

"Right, boss. But there's still a lot of them!"

The squadron was closing with the oncoming missiles at more than a thousand klicks per second.

"All Catfish, listen up," Staton said on the squadron's circuit. "We might only get one pass here, and there's many more of them than there are of us. On my mark, give them everything you've got. Remember, every one of them that gets through will kill a bunch of doggies and some of our shipmates. So kill them all!"

Everything you've got was Beanbags and Zappers. "Beanbags" were canisters loaded with sand and fine gravel that would spread out when the canisters burst open, creating a screen that would blast through anything man made in its path. "Zappers" were missiles with proximity fuses; they emitted powerful electromagnetic bursts designed to fry all electronics within a five klick range.

Staton didn't fret over what he knew to be true: that even if the Catfish and the Lionfish killed every one of their targets, at least some enemy missiles would still get through, and there was nothing he could do about it. In a corner of his mind he hoped that the destroyers and cruisers screening the ARG, and the destroyers coming out from the planet, could get everything the Meteors didn't.

Staton checked that his computer had calculated the times of notification so that each of his squadron's spacecraft would fire simultaneously—the squadron was spread wide enough that there would be a time lag before the most distant fighters would get his fire order. Then he paid attention to the rapidly closing distance between his squadron and the oncoming missiles, and noted the vectors each of his pilots would follow after they fired their loads. He was so intent on studying those vectors that he didn't notice that the enemy missiles had launched smaller missiles of their own—aimed at the Meteors of Catfish Squadron—until his ship's warning system set off its proximity alert.

Staton looked at the front display and almost screamed in horror at what his display showed. Each of the sixty oncoming missiles had split into six; instead of nearly four targets per Meteor, there were now more than twenty.

But he was disciplined enough to squeeze his emergency fire lever and send a fire-and-evade message to his pilots. Then he fired off his port and ventral jets to jink up and to the right to get out of the way of the rapidly approaching threat. The sudden change of direction slammed him down to his left; if it wasn't for his harness, it would have smashed his shoulder into the corner of his acceleration couch, dislocating it if not fracturing bones. "Evade," he verbalized to his computer—the closing speed between the oncoming missiles and his Meteor was too fast for merely human reflexes to successfully maneuver out of harm's way. The Meteor's maneuver jets fired: now port, now starboard, now ventral, now dorsal, often in concert or rapid succession. For the next several moments he was flung about inside his crew pod as the Meteor dodged the enemy counter fire, unable to see where his spacecraft's fire went, much less that of his pilots. Or even if his pilots were surviving.

When the jinking finally stopped and he was able to look, he only found five of the other fifteen of his squadron on his first pass. And far more than half of the enemy missiles were still inbound for the ARG.

"Catfish, on me!" he calmly said into the squadron circuit, and aimed his Meteor at the missiles.

"What are we going to do, boss?" asked Lieutenant (jg) John K. Koelsch as he aligned his fighter to Staton's left rear.

"I'll tell you when I figure it out. All Catfish, sound off!" *Who made it through?* he wanted to know. He tried not to think of who was lost.

He got eight replies, better than he had feared although still too few; one was from a Meteor he hadn't seen on his first look, two were from badly damaged fightercraft that could only limp behind. Counting him, only nine of the sixteen fighters of VSF 114 Catfish had survived the initial contact. He hoped that at least some of the other pilots were still alive in the cockpit pods that were designed to keep pilots alive when their spacecraft were killed.

When Staton saw his remaining Meteors were all close enough, he ordered, "Echelon left." The six lined up to his left, angling back from his position. He had no idea what his truncated, nearly out of ammunition squadron could do to stop the enemy missiles.

They weren't closing; the enemy missiles were faster than the Meteors. He gave the order for the Catfish to fire off the rest of their ordnance. Surely the beanbags and zappers were faster than the enemy.

Destroyer Lance Corporal Keith Lopez,
Approaching the Enemy Missiles at Flank Speed

COMMANDER ERNEST E. EVANS, CAPTAIN OF THE LOPEZ, STUDIED HIS SIT-BOARD. IT clearly showed three dozen bogeys coming on, with VSF 114 turning to chase them, and VSF 218 closing with the bogeys head on. The range to the bogeys was short enough that the *Lopez* could open fire now and get most of them. But VSF 218 was in the line of fire; no matter how good the firing solution was, some of the 218's spacecraft were sure to get killed by a salvo from the *Lopez*.

"Radar, Captain," Evans said into his comm, "How long before 218 clears our LoF?"

"Captain, Radar," came back Lieutenant (jg) Frederick V. McNair. "At current velocities, 218 will pass through the bogeys and clear our line of fire in twenty-seven seconds."

"Weapons, Captain. Did you copy that?"

"Yes, Sir," Lieutenant Guy Wilkinson Castle answered. "Firing solution being calculated. We will be ready to fire the new solution as soon as two-one-eight clears."

As soon as two-one-eight clears wasn't exact; at the distances involved there was relativity to factor in, and VSF 218 was already through the formation of bogeys by the time Radar gave its estimate. What it did was give the fighters a margin of error to clear out of the way of the Lopez's fire.

"Weapons, fire when ready," Evans ordered.

"Fire when ready, aye, Sir."

That was before the alien missiles split.

Destroyer Commander Herald F. Stout,
Pursuing the Enemy Missiles at Flank Speed

"They're getting away from us, Ma'am," Lieutenant Edouard V.M. Izac said shrilly, shocked at how the enemy weapons had suddenly multiplied.

"I'm well aware of that, Mr. Izac," Lieutenant Commander Jane D. Bulkeley, *Stout's* captain, replied.

The *Stout* was on an intercept vector, but the missiles she was chasing were going faster than she was, and there was no maneuver scheme that would close the distance to optimal range for a firing solution. The enemy missiles would be past wherever the *Stout's* weapons intercepted their paths no matter how the ship maneuvered.

"Weapons," Bulkeley said into the comm, "do you have a solution for hitting those bogeys?"

"Affirmative, skipper," answered Lieutenant Edward H. O'Hare. "It's at extreme range, but I think we can hit a few of them."

"'I think' isn't good enough, Mr. O'Hare. Can we hit them?"

"Ma'am, I'm sure we can hit some of them."

"But not all."

"No, Ma'am, I don't think we can hit all."

"Try for all."

"Aye aye, Ma'am. I already have the firing solution programmed in."

"Do it."

Seconds later, the *Stout* shuddered as her tubes ejected Beanbags, Zappers, and rockets at the enemy missiles. None of the *Stout's* missiles could accelerate faster than the enemy's, but they could reach a point in space within a fraction of a second of when their targets did. It wasn't likely that the weapons would physically destroy any of the enemy missiles, but the beanbags might damage some of them enough to slow them down, or deflect their courses; the same went for the rockets with proximity or timed fuses. The better chance was that the zappers would fry some of the missiles' electronics, possibly with shock enough to explode their hydrox— or whatever they used for fuel.

Then the tension on the destroyer was palpable as everyone who could see a display watched their ship's weapons heading toward the enemy.

Several hundred kilometers to port, the destroyers *HM3 Edward C. Benfold* and *First Lieutenant George H. Cannon* also loosed their weapons at the enemy missiles.

Destroyer Chief Gunners Mate Oscar Schmit, Jr., Approaching Enemy Missiles at Flank Speed

Commander Eugene B. Fluckey, the Schmit's captain, gritted his teeth at the view he saw on his situation display. The Meteors of VSF 114 and 218 were doing their best to knock out the oncoming enemy missiles, but already 114 was down to less than half strength, and 218 was being severely punished as well. Fluckey wished he knew the names of the squadrons, so he could pay them proper respect. But he didn't, so their numbers would have to do. It was a pity that there weren't enough of the interceptors to stop the attack on the ARG. Far to the rear of the approaching furball, he saw the missiles fired by the *Stout*, the *Cannon*, and the *Benfold* chasing the attackers. He could tell that many, perhaps most, of the their weapons wouldn't catch up with the enemy.

The defensive weapons being launched by the *Schmit*, and the *Lopez* to starboard and ahead, were taking their toll on the oncoming missiles. But not nearly high enough a price. Many of the missiles speeding toward the two destroyers, he knew, would strike them. Probably enough to kill both warships. Then others would batter the following cruisers, *Coral Sea* and *Ramsey Strait*.

Which would leave the transports of ARG17 defenseless, except for the carrier *Kidd*. And the *Kidd* had virtually no weapons other than her two space squadrons, which were already fighting the enemy.

It didn't matter that the wormhole the ARG had come through had closed; the starships were too far away from where it had been to reach its safety before the attacking missiles arrived even if it had still been open.

NAUS Durango, Flagship Task Force 8, Admiral's Bridge

Admiral Avery helplessly watched the action taking place more than two light minutes distant. At this remove, there was nothing he could do or say to affect the battle. Anything he saw had already happened, any orders he gave to the warships protecting the ARG would arrive more than four minutes after whatever he responded to had happened.

Four minutes in a close-fought space battle might as well be an eternity.

Avery forced his jaw to unclench, his shoulder muscles to unknot. He did it without thought, it was a skill he had developed during the course of nearly four decades of standing watch and commanding ships.

Bright lights that sparked soundlessly in the visual spectrum told of enemy missiles being destroyed by fighter fire. Brighter flashes showed the deaths of interceptors from VSF 114 and VSF 218.

The section of sky short of the approaching convoy suddenly speckled with sparks, the sparks of missiles being killed by fire from the destroyers Avery had sent to aid the defenders of the convoy. But they couldn't kill all of the missiles; there were too many of them.

There weren't enough bright flashes; there were too many of the brighter flashes.

Then came a light that blossomed far larger than any of the missile or fighter deaths he'd already seen—an escort warship exploded, her spine broken by strikes from multiple missiles that had gotten through the screen of defensive fire and interceptors. Then another bright blossom. The *Lopez* and the *Schmit*, the two destroyers in the van of the ARG, were gone.

An even brighter flash heralded the death of one of the cruisers, followed immediately by the brilliant death of the other. Now there was nothing but a few out-classed interceptors left to shield the transports of Amphibious Ready Group 17—and they were chasing the missiles.

Avery didn't allow himself to hang his head; he continued to watch the displays. In another place and time, a fleet commander in his situation would retire to his cabin and commit ritual suicide. But in the here and now, he remained alive and in command, doing whatever he could to salvage the situation, until another admiral arrived from Earth to relieve him.

"Fleet CAC," he demanded into his comm, "have you found where they come from yet?"

"Sir, we know they came from behind Mini Mouse. We're analyzing their trajectory to determine exactly where. We should have the location shortly."

"Keep me informed."

"Aye aye, Sir."

NAUS Durango, Fleet Combat Action Center

Lieutenant Commander R. Z. Johnston scowled, visibly upset that the enemy had sneaked an attack past him. He already had his people back-tracking the trajectory of the missiles to determine exactly where they originated. They came from the far side of Mini Mouse, that much was obvious. The small moon wasn't tidally locked to Troy, so the launch site had moved since the missiles went up. That meant the launch site—sites?— had moved, relative to where the moon's "far side" was now. Elementary to calculate. And they had a complete map of the surface of the small moon. Two analysts were examining the maps, and one of them was plotting the possible site/sites against known gravitational anomalies.

Johnston suspected the launch site was on or just below, the surface put in place after the initial attack. He didn't see any way they could have brought in the heavy equipment they'd need to dig in deeply without being noticed from the planet's surface—or the digging operations noticed by approaching starships even if they were able to shield the operation from surface-based observers on Troy—before the original attack. *Ergo*, Johnston concluded, *the site must be on or near the surface, and camouflaged.*

It was just too bad Mini Mouse hadn't been thoroughly mapped earlier. Then it would have been an easy job to compare that against the navy's maps that showed what was there now.

"Sir," Senior Chief John C. McCloy interrupted Johnston's thoughts, "I think we've hit paydirt."

"Show me."

McCloy toggled one of the analyst's displays to the CAC head's display. It showed four surface soft spots with something with variable density immediately below.

"Bingo," Johnston murmured. "Admiral's bridge, CAC."

Avery was waiting for the call. "Speak to me."

"Sir, we've got four probable targets. Each shows distinct features of camouflaged artillery positions."

"Can their locations be hit by the *Scott* or the *Durango*?"

"Negative, Sir." He looked at McCloy.

"Working on it," McCloy said softly, and turned to the analysts to get them to work on initial plots to move the two warships into position to strike the enemy sites.

"Sir, we are working on vectors for *Scott* and *Durango* to take to be able to strike at the Mini Mouse sites."

"Keep doing it. Let me know when you have the vectors. I'll order them to follow them, and have their CACs coordinate with you. Avery out."

NAUS Peleliu, Flagship of Amphibious Ready Group 17, Commodore's Bridge

Rear Admiral Daniel J. Callaghan, commanding ARG 17, and Lieutenant General Joel H. Lyman, commanding VII Corps, stood at the control bar separating the commodore's station from the officers overseeing the fleet's operations. The main display that hovered before them showed a ninety-light-second-diameter, three dimensional sphere to their front. Callaghan was in his crisp khaki duty uniform. Lyman, who a short time earlier had expected to be making planetfall in his corps' second wave, was in his eye-fooling camouflage field uniform. Where their arms almost touched, Lyman's nearly blended visually into Callaghan's.

Callaghan's mouth was dry. It didn't take any understanding of orbital mechanics to see that Catfish and Lionfish squadrons— what was left of them—had virtually no chance of destroying any of the fifty-eight missiles still homing in on the nineteen transports and supply ships of ARG17, and that most if not all of the starships of ARG17 were going to be hit, possibly—probably—killed. Even a six-year-old playing "Deep Space Fleet" on a child-size HUD could see that.

His only consolation was that he probably wouldn't survive to face a board of inquiry.

He'd long since given the order for his starships to take evasive action, maneuvering in patterns of random movement; he knew it was a feeble attempt to trick the oncoming missiles into missing them, but it was better than nothing. Starships, particularly the transports and support vessels of a gator navy, don't maneuver very nimbly. Feeble or not, the maneuvering might save some of his ships—and the troops they carried.

His mouth was dry, but he stood erect, hands clasped in the small of his back, head held high, expression neutral. He didn't look like a man facing imminent death. Next to him, he barely heard General Lyman murmuring; likely prayers to whatever god he might believe in.

On the main display two icons, representing Landing Platform, Shuttle, LPS8 *Phillips Head* and the logistics support ship *Richmond* merged, then shattered into pieces scattering away.

There goes several hundred sailors and an army brigade, Callaghan thought grimly.

The *Phillips Head* and the *Richmond* hadn't been hit by enemy fire; they'd collided with each other.

Lyman emitted a groan and squeezed his eyes shut.

Seconds later, the oncoming enemy weapons began impacting the starships of his flotilla. Callaghan didn't look away from the main display; he owed the officers and men of ARG17 and VII Corps that much respect. He saw four missiles strike the amphibious landing ferry *Yorktown*, breaking her in two. He watched two missiles hit the amphibious landing dock *Saratoga*, not death-dealing hits, but certainly crippling. The *Grandar Bay* was staggered by one hit. The escort carrier *Kidd* was pummeled by three missiles; Callaghan wondered if she would be able to retrieve her Meteor pilots—if any of them had survived. He only saw one missile strike the *Kandahar*, but she exploded—the missile must have found its way to the power plant.

There were hits on more of the starships of ARG 17, but Callaghan didn't see them. He spent his last seconds standing at attention as he watched five missiles close on the *Peleliu*.

Rear Admiral Callaghan died with his eyes open. Lieutenant General Lyman opened his eyes in time to die the same way.

Troop Compartment A-43-P, NAUS Juno Beach, ARG 17

Before the now-hear-this message even finished its first go-through, Second Lieutenant Theodore W. Greig bolted from the officers mess and raced, twisting side to side to avoid collisions with sailors and soldiers going in the opposite direction in the narrow passageways, to the compartment where his platoon was quartered on the amphibious assault ship.

"Sergeant Quinn," he huffed into his comm unit, "where are you? I'm heading for the platoon."

"I'm almost there, LT. I already put out a call for everyone to report in."

"Thanks, Sergeant."

"Hey, it's what a platoon sergeant does."

"The good ones, anyway." Greig snapped his comm off and twisted past a last few sailors before he reached the door to his platoon's compartment and headed in. A glance showed him that Quinn had just arrived, and only two or three of his soldiers weren't present.

"'Toon, a-ten-*hut*!" Quinn bellowed when the officer entered.

Greig gave his men a few seconds to come to their feet and begin moving into the posture of attention before shouting, "At ease!" He turned and stepped aside at the sound of thudding footsteps in the passageway behind himself, just in time to dodge two soldiers who grabbed the doorway combing and spun into the compartment.

"Is that everybody?" he asked.

Quinn had already called for a squad leaders' report. In seconds, he had it. "Second platoon, all present and accounted for," he barked.

Greig nodded. "Good," he said, then took a couple of seconds to organize his thoughts. "As you just heard on the *Juno Beach's* PA system, the fleet is under attack. That's this fleet, including the ship we're on. There are two fleets, the troop transfer fleet we're in, and a warship fleet. The warships are fighting off the attackers. But, if history's any indication, some of the attackers are going to be successful." He paused to let that sink in. "What this means in practical terms, is the *Juno Beach* might get hit, maybe even destroyed." He had to raise his hands and voice to quell the tumult that rose.

Quinn's roars of "Knock it off and listen up!" probably had more to do with the sudden silence than the lieutenant's shout.

"Yes," Greig snapped. "That means we could all get killed before we even make planetfall. But—" He again had to call for quiet. "But it doesn't mean that we *will* get killed. First, because the enemy might not hit this ship. Second, because there are stasis stations available. We are going to one. All of Second platoon. If the *Juno Beach* gets hit, even destroyed, we'll be safe until we get rescued and brought out of stasis. If we don't get hit at all, we're still safe and alive until someone releases us from stasis.

Sergeant Quinn and I know where the nearest stasis station is. We are going to take you there now and we are all going into stasis. We'll be out of the way of the ship's crew, and we'll be safe in case the *Juno Beach* gets hit. You've all been through a stasis drill, so you know how it's done. Squad leaders, get your troops together, and follow Sergeant Quinn." He nodded at his platoon sergeant. "Lead the way."

Second platoon of Alpha Troop, First of the Seventh Mounted Infantry, 10th Brigade, headed to the nearest stasis station, which was close enough that the lead soldier entered it before the last soldier left the platoon's compartment.

It took less than fifteen minutes for the twenty-four troops of the platoon to get into the individual units, hooked up, and checked by their squad leaders. Greig and Quinn checked the squad leaders.

Before they got into their units, Quinn asked, "LT., did the captain tell all the platoon commanders to head for stasis?"

Greig looked his platoon sergeant in the eye and said quietly, "You can't get in trouble for what you don't know. Remember that, just in case I'm wrong."

NAUS Durango, Admiral's Bridge

"If it pleases Captain Huse, I would like to speak with him," Rear Admiral James Avery said into his comm. Task Force 8 belonged to Avery, but the *Durango* belonged to Huse, and his position must be acknowledged.

"Huse here, Admiral," the captain's voice came back seconds later.

"Captain," Avery said, calling him by his rank rather than his given name as he normally would to make totally clear that he was giving orders, "thanks for getting back to me so quickly." As if there was any doubt that a captain wouldn't answer an admiral's call as fast as possible. "Those bogeys attacking the ARG came from Mini Mouse. Fleet CAC has identified their points of origin. I want you to maneuver into a position where you can continue giving cover to the planetside Marines, and simultaneously fire on the moon. Have your CAC coordinate with mine." The Durango's Combat Action Center directed the ship's fight; the Fleet CAC coordinated the fight of two or more of the fleet's ships. "I'm sending the Scott to attack the identified locations from where the enemy launched its missiles. When you are in position, I will send further orders to *Durango* and *Scott* to coordinate your attacks.

"Questions?"

"Negative, Sir. I will inform the admiral the instant I am in position."

"Thank you, Captain." Avery broke the connection, and settled back to watch developments.

NAUS Durango, Bridge

"Comm," Huse said to Lieutenant Commander George F. Davis, his communications officer, "get me CAC."

"CAC, aye, Sir," Davis answered.

Seconds later; "CAC, Lieutenant Hudner, Sir."

"Mr. Hudner, has Fleet CAC given you the locations on Mini Mouse the enemy fired from?"

"Yes, Sir. They are coming in now."

"Good man. The admiral is about to order a counterattack. Make a priority list with coordinates for bombardment, and send it to me instantly. Remember, we have to maintain cover for the Marines planetside."

"Aye aye. Sir, you will have it immediately."

NAUS Durango, Admiral's Bridge

While Huse was giving orders to his CAC, Avery was in communication with Captain William R. Rush, skipper of the *Scott*. The *Scott* and the *Durango* were two of the most powerful warships in the NAU Navy, and the most powerful in TF8.

It took several seconds longer for Rush to answer Avery's call than it had Huse, during which time the plot arrived from the CAC. But Huse was on the same starship as Avery, while Rush on the *Scott* was more than 100,000 kilometers distant; in space, distance equals time.

"*Scott* Actual here, Sir." Rush's voice when it came was clear and crisp. Identifying himself by position rather than name indicated that he anticipated that he was about to receive action orders.

"*Scott* Actual, I believe that you are in a position from which you can launch Kestrel strikes on Mini Mouse."

Seconds later Rush replied, "That's affirmative, Sir."

"Be advised, the *Durango* is maneuvering into position to strike targets on Mini Mouse. When she is in position, I will give orders to the two of you to coordinate your attacks. In the meantime, launch your squadrons and have them take up parking orbits on the limb of Mini Mouse, where they will wait for orders to strike at these targets which have been identified by Fleet CAC." He pressed a "transmit" button to send the plot to the *Scott*.

"Sir, *Scott* maneuvering to launch Kestrels.

"Launch as soon as you are ready, *Scott*."

MINI MOUSE'S ROTATION HAD MOVED THE LIKELY LAUNCH SITES IDENTIFIED BY FLEET CAC from opposite Troy to halfway to its limb. Troy had likewise rotated but, with a longer rotation period, not as far around its axis. The *Durango* moved far enough to fire on the moon that was still out of sight beyond the edge of Troy, while staying where she could give the Marines on the ground fire support should they need it.

Lieutenant Thomas Hudner and his crew in the *Durango*'s CAC watched over their computers while they calculated firing solutions for the ship's weapons to hit the probable locations of the alien launch sites. It would be nearly impossible for ballistic weapons to make the strikes, but simple for the *Durango*'s—once it was in position. Right now, it was covering the Marines planetside.

"Got it!" Senior Chief Petty Officer Francis Edward Ormsbee exclaimed.

"Show me, Francis Edward," Hudner said, stepping to the man everybody from petty officer first class on up called "Francis Edward."

"Ya see, Mr. T—" Ormsbee called everybody except Captain Huse and the admiral whatever he wanted to. "—we got the jarheads covered right there," he pointed at a group of lines on the schematic he'd just put together, "an' the mizzuls came from there. We can hit 'em from where we are." He looked at his division commander. "Don'cha think ya oughtta tell the skipper?"

"Well now, Francis Edward, I think that might be a good idea. A very good idea indeed."

Hudner notified Captain Huse, who in turn informed Admiral Avery, and two minutes later, the *Durango* fired a barrage of missiles programmed to loop around the side of the side of the planet and then swing past the limb of Mini Mouse, to impact at four locations on the moon's far side.

Four AV16(E) Kestrels followed behind to get visual confirmation of the strikes.

VSFA 132, "Piranha" squadron off NAUS Scott, En Route from Parking Orbit to Target

"Nibblers, Nibblers, all Nibblers, this is Big Teeth. Answer up," Lieutenant Commander Georgia Street said into her squadron circuit. "Verify that you have your strike coordinates and path programmed into your comps."

She watched as her board lit up with replies. All four of the squadron's four fighter-attack craft divisions were properly aligned to bombard their assigned targets, each division coming in from a different direction. Scatter-Blast cluster bombs fired by sixteen craft from two thousand meters altitude. The divisions would loose their loads at ten-second intervals. The Blasters were set to go off one hundred meters above the surface, scattering their munitions over a ten-by-ten-kilometer area, shredding the camouflage coverings to confetti, churning the regolith all the way to the bedrock like a brutally plowed field. If anything was still under the camouflage, it would be obliterated. As soon as their bombs dropped, the AV16C Kestrels' flight paths called for them to shoot into a vertical arabesques, designed to allow them to avoid both each other and the debris blasting up from the surface with margins of safety.

"We aren't going to have much time on our approach," Street continued in a pep-talk tone, "but Piranha squadron is the best in the Navy, and that means nobody can do this job better. So let's get this thing done!"

Not much time indeed. They were speeding around Mini Mouse at close to Mach 4—not that "Mach" meant much of anything in the moon's almost non-existent atmosphere, but it was a convenient term to use to measure velocity—at two thousand meters altitude. When the target came in sight they'd have sixty-three seconds to the fire-and-climb point; sixty-three seconds to lock onto the target and blast it. Nobody, of course, knew what—if any—defenses the launch sites had. But those defenses, if they existed, would have very little time to realize they were under attack, aim, and fire. Unless they had an early warning system, in which case they'd be ready before the Piranhas crossed the visual horizon. If they had an early warning system, Piranha squadron would have to go to Plan B—and would surely have losses.

Mini Mouse had begun life as a dwarf planet, captured by Troy during the system's early childhood. As such it had an iron core, unlike Dumbo, Troy's other moon, that had been torn from the planet's crust during system formation. Even though it was smaller than Earth's moon, the iron core gave Mini Mouse a slightly higher gravity, about .2 G. The gravity aided the *Scott*'s squadrons in approaching their targets from below the horizon. Despite possible problems, the approach looked like it was going to be a milk run.

Then the first division was visible over the target's horizon.

VSFA 132, "Piranha" Squadron, Approaching Target

Defensive weapons, similar to the Beanbags used by the NAUS for missile defense, began throwing up a wall of tiny pellets for the Kestrels to run into. But by the time they did, the range-to-target was so short, and the Kestrels' velocities so great, that the munitions didn't have enough time to fully deploy before the attacking craft were past them. Other weapons opened up, rapidly firing off slugs that could pulverize a fighter if one ran into enough of them. Again, the First division was too close, and the slugs missed, allowing all four Kestrels to fire their munitions, some of which knocked out some of the defensive weapons.

But the other three divisions were ten, twenty, and thirty seconds behind, and the surviving alien defenses were now alerted.

"Big Mouth, Piranha Seven, something hit me!" That was Ensign Charles H. Hammann, the third pilot in the Second division.

Street's display showed Hammann's fighter craft climbing, but flashing red in a sequence that told her that it was not only damaged but out of its carefully calculated arabesque as well.

Another icon began flashing red and stopped moving. It was Piranha 14, piloted by Third division's Ensign Daniel Sullivan. It was down, and Street wasn't receiving vitals—that indicated that Sullivan was likely dead.

Two icons from division Four turned red, but Street didn't bother checking to see who they were, she was too busy doing a damage assessment of the target.

The defensive weapons had ceased fire. Street had no way of knowing whether that was because they were all destroyed, because they were out of munitions, or because the weapons couldn't fire that close to vertical. As seen in the view from her tail camera, even with the clouds of debris from division Four's Scatter Blasts still expanding, the target area looked like it was thoroughly chewed up. There was no satellite image to check against.

It didn't matter either way; VSFA 132 didn't have any Scatter-Blasts for a second run.

"Nibblers, Nibblers, all Nibblers, this is Big Teeth," Street said into her squadron circuit. "We've done all we can for now. Let's head for home." She cleared her throat before adding, "Downed Nibblers, hang in there. Rescue will be on its way as soon as possible. Maybe they're on their way even now. I've noted and sent in your positions, so SAR will be able to head for your location even before they have a lock on you. Big Teeth out."

She checked Piranha Seven's icon. It still displayed a wobbly path, but the Kestrel was still rising, and was keeping up with the rest of the squadron. Her squadron still had three Kestrels down and out of communication; she didn't know if the pilots were alive and well—except for Piranha Seven, whose lack of vitals indicated he was dead—or if they were in imminent danger of being captured.

Command Center, 1st Marine Combat Force, Outside Millerton

"Admiral," Lieutenant General Harold Bauer said to the image on his comm once Avery had described the situation and said what he wanted from the Marines, "you get your SAR craft to me and I'll give you the security you need."

"Your assistance is greatly appreciated, General." Rear Admiral Avery's reply came seconds later. He was in his CAC on board the *Durango* in orbit. "Just remember, the SAR Pegasus craft can't carry a large force."

"I'm well aware of the space limitations of the Pegasus. One squad should be more than adequate for each mission, and won't overly tax the crafts' systems."

"Give me the coordinates of the platoon you're assigning to the mission, I'll have the Pegasuses land at its location."

Bauer shook his head. "I'm not assigning one platoon to the mission, but one squad from each regiment.

Avery arched an eyebrow at that. "Are you trying to prevent one platoon from absorbing too many casualties?"

"I'd rather say I'm spreading the experience throughout my division." Bauer even almost believed what he said.

India Company, Fifteen Kilometers East of Millerton

3rd Battalion had stopped on a rough line some distance east of Millerton, in an area that on Earth would be called a scrub forest; widely spaced trees that looked stunted, and thin undergrowth. The plain was scoured flat except for the boulders, some sitting higher than a human, some small enough for someone unobservant to trip over, and every size in between, that dotted the plain. The extensive boulder field gave clear evidence that

Troy had suffered through at least one ice age; the boulders looked like they'd been carried here by ice sheets from distant locations and dropped in place when the glaciers withdrew. The Marines settled behind boulders and thicker tree trunks. None of them bothered to dig a fighting hole, or even scrape a shallow hollow to lie in. They waited for word of what to do next. When it came, it wasn't anything they expected.

"First squad, on me," Staff Sergeant Guillen shouted.

Lance Corporal Mackie looked around from his position on the platoon's defensive line and saw the platoon sergeant standing erect about twenty meters behind the position. He gave a quick glance to his front, then at Adriance, who was already rising to his feet.

"Move it, people!" Sergeant Martin shouted.

"First fire team, up and at 'em," Corporal Adriance ordered.

Mackie stood and reached for his pack.

"Weapons only, leave your packs in place," Guillen shouted. "Get over here now!"

In less than a minute, the thirteen Marines of the squad were gathered in a semi-circle in front of the platoon sergeant. Second Lieutenant Commiskey joined him.

"By now you've probably heard about the missile strike on ARG17. They came from launch sites on Mini Mouse." Commiskey paused for a few seconds while some of the Marines snickered at the small moon's name. "The carrier *Scott* launched four squadrons to kill those launch sites before they could fire more missiles. The sites had defensive systems, and knocked down some of the Kestrels.

"There are Navy pilots on the surface of Mini Mouse. Some of them might still be alive. At the request of Rear Admiral Avery, Lieutenant General Bauer has tasked the 1st Marines with providing a squad as security for one of the Navy search and rescue teams going in to retrieve the downed pilots. You're the squad."

Mackie blinked at "retrieve." You *rescue* live people, but you *retrieve* corpses.

He must not have been the only one who reacted to the word, because Commiskey quickly added, "'Retrieve' is the word the Admiral used. But as far as anybody knows, most—maybe all—of the downed pilots are still alive. Four squadrons attacked the launch sites, all four had losses. One squad from each regiment and one from the division recon company will go with the SAR craft on the rescue mission. Third platoon has been chosen as the 1st Marines' SAR team. We don't know what kind of ground defenses the enemy has for the sites, so we'll essentially be going in blind. For this mission, we'll be in armored vacuum suits."

He paused for a moment before saying, "Remember, that even though armored vacuum suits give protection from all small arms in the NAUS arsenal, fragments from conventional explosive munitions, and limited protection from both stellar radiation and weapon radiation, they aren't impervious to everything. We don't know what kind of weapons the enemy will throw at us, or if they even have defenses against ground forces. Mini Mouse has an atmosphere so thin it's virtually a hard vacuum. So whatever else you do, don't let your suit get punctured.

"That is all. Staff Sergeant Guillen will take over now. Staff Sergeant, the platoon is yours."

"Yes, Sir." Guillen briefly came to attention, but didn't salute. They were in presumably hostile territory. A salute could attract sniper fire if any enemy were in the area, so Marines didn't salute in the field.

Guillen watched Commiskey head toward the jumble of boulders where Captain Sitter had established the company headquarters, then turned to the men.

"When I dismiss you, return to your positions and resume your watch. When the word comes down, I'll take the squad leaders to get the armored vacuum suits from supply. Any questions? Yes, Zion."

"Ah, Staff Sergeant, when we go, is anybody going to relieve us here?" PFC Zion gave a nervous look over his shoulder at the ground the platoon hadn't secured.

Guillen curled his lip before answering. "Zion, that's above your pay grade to worry about. But, yes, somebody will relieve us in this position. Don't ask who. 'Who' is above *my* pay grade."

He looked from Marine to Marine with an expression that asked, *Does anybody else have a dumb question?* but nobody else seemed anxious to ask anything. "If there are no other questions, Sergeant Martin, get your people back in position and wait for further orders. Dismissed."

Leaning close as they started back toward their positions, Adriance murmured, "Stand by for a head smack, Zion."

"In stereo," Mackie added from Zion's other side.

"What'd I do?" Zion demanded indignantly.

"That's two," said PFC Orndoff.

"Two what? And how come you're all ganging up on me?"

"Dumb questions, peon," Adriance said. "And that makes three. Keep it up, and I'll have to let Orndoff give you a head smack, too, because head-smacking you will be more than a two-man job."

Then they were back at their position. Adriance sat with his back against a tree trunk. Mackie stayed on his feet, leaning over a chest high boulder. Orndoff climbed a tree, and Zion went prone next to a waist high boulder.

They appeared relaxed and casual—to anyone who could make them out in their camouflage utilities—but appearances were deceptive. Their eyes were in constant motion, alertly searching the landscape to their front, checking their sides. Every few minutes Adriance slid his infrared viewer into place before his eyes to search for warm bodies that might not be noticed in visual light. And Mackie frequently checked the fire team's motion detector, looking for movement that wasn't vegetation shifting in the moving air—and was bigger than a mid-sized dog.

So situated, they quietly, alertly, waited for an hour. Then the word came: "Chow down. We go in thirty."

En Route to Mini Mouse

A Navy chief petty officer met the Marines when the McKinzie elevator reached geosync; a squad from the 6th Marines, one from the 7th, and another from 1st Recon filled out the rescue security teams. The CPO was slender, dressed in greasy khakis, and had a headset perched behind his ears. Something that looked suspiciously like a half-smoked cigar but couldn't possibly be—it couldn't *really* be a cigar, could it?—stuck out of the corner of his mouth.

"Ah right, ever'body here?" he drawled. The question must have been rhetorical because he didn't wait for an answer. "I'm Chief Petty Officer Othniel Tripp, and I'm in charge of this here boardin' station. Squadron VSFA 132 lost four fighter craft on their bombing run on one of the alien launch sites. We've got four Pegasus birds—that's what we call our search an' rescue birds, Pegasuses, after the flyin' horses in the Grik stories—going in after 'em. Youse going along to protect the crews in case the aliens have infantry there what needs to be fought off. Our Pegasus crews are better'n anybody else's at searchin' and rescuin', but they ain't so great at rifle fightin'. That's why you're going along. I got four birds out here, you got four squads. That works out jes perfect, one squad one bird. That's a lot better'n four squads an' one bird. You're gonna be pretty cramped as is in them suits youse wearin'."

The Marines were very bulky in the armored vacuum suits that had been waiting for them at the foot of McKinzie —it turned out that they hadn't been delivered to India Company's supply sergeant. The armor's weight—armor, no matter how light, is always heavy—was offset by servos in the main joints that not only allowed the Marines to move as easily as they would unarmored, but added to their strength.

"When your bird lands, the flight commander will tell you if he wants you outside or to stay in. If he tells you outside, be ready to fight right off.

Now, you outta know, the flight commander is an officer, the pilot is a first class, the crew chief is a third class, and the—."

Tripp suddenly looked away from the Marines, pulled his headset's earpieces forward and rotated the mike to his mouth. He listened for a moment, murmured a reply, then looked back up.

"Ah right, who's first? Pegasus One is docked and waiting for you." His drawl disappeared and he became all business. He stepped to the airlock's hatch, which was closed.

"First Marines, that's you. Come with me." Chief Tripp led them to the entrance to the docking chute.

"Line up by fire teams," Sergeant Martin ordered his squad, and took a position on the other side of the airlock from the chief.

Corporal Adriance stood between them facing the hatch. Lance Corporal Mackie took position behind him, and glanced back to make sure PFCs Orndoff and Zion were in place.

"We're ready, Chief," Martin told Tripp as soon as the squad was in line.

Tripp tapped a three touch code on the hatch's lock, and it slid aside. "Go!" he barked. Adriance stepped forward, and the rest of the squad followed. Martin brought up the rear.

Inside the Pegasus a crewman, anonymous in a vacuum suit with a reflective faceplate, directed the Marines to narrow benches along the sides of the cabin.

"No space between you," he said. "We're so tight some of you might have to sit on the deck. Close it up and keep it close!"

Mackie reflexively shook his head when he saw the interior of the cabin. It looked barely big enough to hold an armored vacuum suited fire team, much less an entire squad. "Are we really going to be sitting on each other's laps?" he asked nobody in particular, then when nobody answered: "That's what I thought."

The Marines jammed themselves in. Six squeezed onto the bench along each side. They weren't able to sit straight with their backs against the bulkhead, but twisted their torsos so they overlapped, one man's shoulder in front of the next one's. There was little space between their knees and the knees of the Marines on the opposite side. Martin and Private Frank Hill, the squad's newest and most junior man, managed to find space on the floor amid the feet and knees.

"Hold on, we're about to move," the anonymous crewman alerted them from his station, which was out of sight from the main cabin. "Hold on tight so you don't get banged around."

"Hold onto what?" Orndoff muttered over the fire team circuit.

"Your ass, that's what," Mackie answered.

Adriance snorted, then ordered, "Shitcan the grabass, people. This is serious."

But Orndoff was right; there wasn't anything to grab hold of.

The search and rescue craft lurched, separating from the elevator airlock, throwing the Marines against each other. But they were already tight enough that nobody built enough momentum to injure himself or the Marine he bumped into. Slow acceleration eased Pegasus One away from the geosync station. There were no ports to look through, no display panels to show what was outside; no way to tell where they were, what direction they were headed, how fast they were going, how much time was passing. All the Marines could do was wait, with greater or lesser degrees of patience.

After an indeterminate length of time the anonymous crewman announced from his unseen station, "Halfway there."

Wherever *there* was, and however far *halfway* might be.

Eventually a different voice came to the Marines. "We're going down," the voice—the flight commander?—said. "When we hit, the rear hatch will drop, and I need you to get out there instantly. It looks like bad guys are closing on Piranha 14's position."

When the voice—the pilot? the SAR commander?—didn't say anything more, Sergeant Martin demanded, "How many of them are there? What direction are they coming from? Do they have armor or are they on foot or what? Come on, man, we need more data or we're stepping into an ambush!"

"No time!" the voice said. "We're down." There was a jolt of impact as the Pegasus hit the ground. The hatch in the compartment's rear dropped and became a ramp.

The major joints of the armored vacuum suits had servo motors, made necessary by the mass of the suits. The Marines had been sitting in cramped positions without being able to move. Third platoon's First squad looked clumsy scrambling down the ramp, but without the servos, they couldn't have even stood to shamble off until full circulation returned to their limbs.

"Where are they?" Sergeant Martin demanded as he looked around in attempt to find the foe.

"I'm sending you our feed now," the unidentified voice said.

Martin put it on his HUD for a quick study, and swore. He began shouting orders.

Mini Mouse, LZ 1

"FIRST FIRE TEAM, GET TO THAT KESTREL!" SERGEANT MARTIN SHOUTED. "SECOND and Third, lay down fire on those vehicles!"

The downed Kestrel was a hundred meters away to the northeast. To the north-northeast, two vehicles of an alien design were bouncing toward them at a high rate of speed from less than two kilometers away.

"First fire team, let's go!" Corporal Adriance shouted, and began the shuffling low-gravity walk men had used since Neil Armstrong first stepped on Earth's moon centuries earlier.

Three crewmen from the Pegasus were already on their way, driving a motorized litter to carry the pilot back.

Second and Third fire teams began firing on the approaching vehicles. The Marines' rifles were loaded with alternating armor piercing and explosive rounds. The armor piercing bullets bounced off the armored fronts of the vehicles, the explosive ones barely pitted the surface. The enemy didn't give immediate return fire; maybe they didn't have a mechanism that would compensate for the bouncing.

First fire team reached the Kestrel just as the rescue men were loading the unmoving pilot onto the litter; the Marines couldn't tell if he was conscious or not, or even if he was still alive.

Adriance saw how ineffective the fire from the rest of the squad was, and knew that adding fire from four more rifles on their fronts wouldn't do anything to stop the alien vehicles. He decided to do something else.

"First fire team, try to ricochet your rounds to the undercarriage of the one on the left," he ordered, and began firing into the regolith in front of the vehicle, sending fragments of stone bouncing into its lower front and underneath it. In an instant, the other three Marines began firing the same.

"Our armored vehicles have their strongest armor on their fronts," Adriance explained absently as he maintained steady fire, "and the weakest on the bottom. If these bad guys build theirs the same way, we might be able to break through."

Maybe, maybe not, but it was worth a try—and it was. Something broke in the vehicle. Gases began venting from its bottom. It slewed to a stop, turning its side to the Marines. The vehicle on the right had to swerve violently to its left to avoid running into its damaged mate, throwing up a curtain of dust and gravel before pointing back toward the humans.

Sergeant Martin saw what First fire team did. "Second and Third fire teams," he shouted, "did you see what they did? Do the same thing—bounce your rounds underneath the one that's still coming at us."

By then, the occupants of the first vehicle, a dozen of them, had scrambled out of it and were charging in high, jinking bounds at the Marines by the Kestrel. The shape of their vacuum suits would have stunned the Marines had they not already seen the vids and stills brought back by Force Recon, and sent during the original alien attack on Troy. The legs were long, and bent the wrong way; the arms were too short; forward-jutting heads stuck out on very long necks. A large bulge on the rear of the suits counterbalanced the heads. They ran bent at the hips almost parallel to the ground.

The charging aliens were firing rifles, but their shots were wild and none seemed to come near the Marines. They were closing fast, their run was much faster than the Marines' shuffle, but they didn't seem to be as well trained at low gravity movement. Or maybe their jinking wasn't suitable for rapid movement in low gravity. They kept stumbling and tripping.

The Marines of First fire team took advantage of the stumbles and trips to take aim during the brief seconds their targets were relatively motionless. The armor piercing bullets mostly glanced off the aliens' armor, but some of the explosive bullets punctured them, venting air.

"First fire team, get back here," Martin ordered when the litter was halfway back to the Pegasus.

"Let's go!" Adriance repeated the order to his men. He looked to see that they were obeying. "That includes you, Zion."

But Zion didn't move; he was half sitting, folded over his rifle.

Adriance swore. "Mackie, check Zion!"

Mackie had already began the shuffle-run back to the Pegasus and had to turn back. Adriance didn't wait for him, he was already kneeling over Zion when Mackie reached him.

Adriance's face was barely visible through his faceplate when he looked at Mackie, but his expression was grim. Not all of the aliens' shots had gone wild.

"Marines don't leave their dead," the fire team leader said, thick-voiced. "Give me a hand."

When the two of them raised Zion, Mackie saw where a hole had been punched through the neck of the other's armor where it was jointed to his chest plate. Air had vented explosively, blowing the hole much larger. Blood had vented as well from a wound in Zion's throat, staining the edges of the hole red. They draped his arms over their shoulders and ran, with Adriance carrying Zion's rifle.

By then, fire from the rest of the squad had crippled the second vehicle, and the Marines were firing at the bounding, jinking, stumbling aliens. Only a dozen were still making the mad charge. But not all of the dozen who were down had been hit; at least four of them had gone prone to give aimed return fire.

"Let's move it, First fire team!" Martin shouted. "This bird is almost ready to fly away. The squids'll leave you if you aren't here when they're ready to go!" He looked at the prone aliens giving return fire, and ordered, "Second fire team, take him out." He fired a shot himself at one of the shooters to show who he meant. In seconds, four more bullets struck that one, and he stopped shooting.

"Now get the other shooters!"

The lead running aliens reached the Pegasus at the same time as Adriance and Mackie, and one of them barreled into the two of them and their burden, knocking them down.

Mackie kicked out as he fell, smashing an armored foot into the alien's backward-bending knee, felling him. The Marine jumped up and stomped on the alien's helmet, then grasped his rifle with one hand behind the receiver and the other in the middle of the forestock. He saw another alien rushing at him with his weapon pointed like a spear. Mackie pirouetted out of the way of the lunge, and slammed the butt of his rifle at his assailant's head. But the momentum of his spin carried him around and off balance, so his blow barely staggered the alien. But that slight stagger was enough to allow Adriance to swing his rifle around in a wicked blow that shattered the alien's facemask.

With two down at their feet, Mackie and Adriance had a few seconds to take in the entire fight. It was one-on-one, man-to-man close combat—man to alien; they had to be aliens, there was no way a human being could jam into one of their vacuum suits without breaking bones and disjointing limbs.

No one was shooting in the melee; the combatants faced too much danger of hitting their own if they did. They were all using their weapons as clubs, quarterstaffs, or thrusting spears.

Just a couple of meters away, Orndoff was being forced backward by an alien jabbing and thrusting at him. Mackie and Adriance both stepped toward the two. Adriance swung the butt of his rifle in a golf club stroke at the alien's low-slung head while Mackie reversed his weapon and slammed its butt into the alien's side. Orndoff's attacker fell away in an uncontrolled tumble, and came to rest twisted in ways that couldn't be natural for its kind.

Corporal Button, the Third fire team leader, went down clutching his abdomen. The alien who had knocked him down jumped on his helmet, but in the low gravity lacked the force necessary to break anything. Button rolled away but wasn't able to regain his feet as the alien pursued him with repeated, rapid kicks. Adriance leaped in Button's direction to help him.

Mackie shuffled to the aid of Second fire team's PFC Harry Harvey, who was closer and parrying off rapid blows from another alien.

Orndoff screamed a war cry, heard only by the Marines through their helmet comms. He leaped at the back of one of two aliens attacking Lance Corporal Fernando L. Garcia. He misjudged in the low gravity and sailed over the alien, but managed to slam his rifle's butt downward onto the alien's neck, jarring him. The alien whipped his head around to see what had hit him and saw Orndoff, off balance from hitting him, thud onto the regolith and tumble. The alien leaped at the Marine, freeing Garcia to concentrate on his other attacker.

Orndoff twisted to turn his tumble into a controlled roll, so he was facing up when the alien pounced at him. The alien's jump was better than Orndoff's had been, but he still flew high and came down slowly in the low gravity. The Marine had time to twist his body to the side to miss the worst of the alien's jump, and brace himself to lunge upward with his rifle. The alien already realized that swinging his rifle club-like would throw him off balance; he came down with his rifle pointed straight down, to spear his opponent. He missed Orndoff's twisting body, but the Marine connected with his target when he lunged up and plunged the muzzle of his rifle into the joint where the elongated helmet met the top plate of the neck armor. The alien's limbs shot out away from its body, then it jerked its hands to its throat and clutched at Orndoff's rifle barrel. He crashed onto his side, yanking the rifle out of the Marine's grip. Orndoff jumped to his feet and tried to retrieve his rifle, but it was jammed too tightly into the alien's armor.

Orndoff spun around in a hands-extended crouch, ready to grab or parry any weapon coming at him. The closest alien he saw was the second one attacking Garcia. Garcia had that alien down and was slamming the butt of his rifle repeatedly into his helmet.

A few meters beyond, Mackie had also lost his rifle. He ducked past a thrust from an alien and grabbed its neck just behind its head. Bracing himself, Mackie twisted, spinning around and flinging the alien's body off the ground like a whip. Halfway through a twirl, he fell backward, but didn't release the alien's neck. The alien thudded to the ground and sprawled limply. Mackie hopped upward and kicked the alien's head. It flopped at the end of its long neck. He looked around and saw Adriance down with an alien grabbing at his facemask, looking like it was prying it open. Mackie dove at the alien, hitting him full force on his side. The alien bounced along the ground almost like a flat rock skipping across a pond. Mackie raced after it to grab its neck before it could recover, and fling it the same way he'd killed the other one.

This alien was faster, and was on his feet facing Mackie before the Marine reached him. The two, both without rifles, crashed together. The human was heavier than the alien, and drove him back. The alien flipped, so his head was toward Mackie's feet. Unable to grab the alien's neck the way he had the other one, Mackie wrapped his arms around his torso and stood erect, squeezing as tightly as his augmented arm strength could. It wasn't enough to crush the armor, or even dent it.

The alien struggled, but his arms were too short to wrap around Mackie's legs to pull him off his feet. His legs, though, were big and powerful. He kicked them wildly, and threw Mackie off balance. They crashed on their sides to the regolith. The alien slammed his head against Mackie's legs, and Mackie kicked back at his neck and the underside of his head before letting go and rolling away and bounding up into a crouch.

The alien was already up and leaping at the Marine. Mackie threw himself backward and thrust out with his feet, catching the alien on the upper part of his chest. The alien's momentum rolled Mackie into a reverse somersault, and the Marine's legs were a lever that threw the alien over him and away.

This time Mackie was on his feet first, and reached the alien in time to grab its upper neck. He jerked upward, lifting the alien off the ground, and slammed him onto the regolith hard enough to make him bounce. He grabbed the alien's neck with his hands almost half a meter apart, and brought it down sharply across his knee. He thought he felt something break inside the armor. The alien went into uncontrollable spasms. Mackie gave its head an extra kick, and looked around for another alien.

The fight was ending. Eight Marines and no aliens were standing.

"Fire team leaders, report!" Sergeant Martin's voice was hoarse over the comm.

"I'm here," Mackie reported. "Adriance?" he asked when his fire team leader didn't reply. Instantly, he took over. "Orndoff, are you all right?"

"I'm five by," Orndoff answered, breathing heavily. "Where's Adriance?"

The fire team leaders' reports took longer than they should have because both Corporals Adriance and Button were down. So was Third fire team's PFC Hermann Kuchneister. PFCs Zion and David Porter were both dead.

Corpsmen from the Pegasus were checking the wounded before the fire team leaders' report was finished.

"All right, Marines, get everybody loaded," a voice—the pilot? the SAR commander?—ordered. "Leave the aliens, we don't have room to take any of them. Maybe we can come back later to deal with them."

Two minutes later, the Pegasus took off with a short rolling start. The two dead were propped in corners, the wounded laid out on the deck between the benches.

The Aftermath of the Mini Mouse Missions

In retrospect, it was a good thing that the squads assigned to security duty for the Pegasuses on the Search and Rescue missions were from different regiments. Three of the four squads had contact on the ground, and all three of those suffered casualties. India Company's squad hadn't suffered the most, nor had it suffered the least. Among them, the four squads lost a total of five Marines, with ten more wounded. Most of the latter were expected to recover and return to duty. That would have been very heavy losses for one platoon; forty percent of its strength.

All of the aliens who fought the Marines were killed.

This was the first combat experience for most of the Marines involved, the first time they'd had to kill in order to live, the first time they'd had to deal with buddies getting wounded or killed.

And they still didn't have a clue who these aliens were who they'd had to kill, or why those aliens attacked had Troy and the fleet.

WITH THE OPERATION ON MINI MOUSE UNDERWAY, REAR ADMIRAL AVERY turned his attention back to Amphibious Ready Group 17. The attack was over, all the enemy missiles had been destroyed by the squadrons sent after them, or by fire from the warships—or they'd hit their targets. The wormhole had closed before more than two of the drones he'd sent made it through; all they'd tell Earth was that a missile attack on ARG17 was under way.

Too many alien missiles had made it through the defenses to their targets.

A debris cloud marked where the Amphibious Assault Ship *Peleliu*, ARG 17's flagship, had been. Likewise the AAS *Kandahar* and *Juno Beach*. A single cloud marked the death site of the Landing Platform Shuttle *Phillips Head* and the Logistics Supply Ship *Richmond*. Another showed where the Amphibious Landing Ferry *Yorktown* had been destroyed. The Dry Cargo Ship *Columbus* was dead.

The Amphibious Assault Ships *Grandar Bay,* and *Fallujah* were wounded, as were the Landing Platform Shuttle *Iwo Jima* and the Amphibious Landing Dock *Saratoga*. The DCS *Amundsen* was wounded.

Three other ships of ARG17 were dead; only four of the nineteen had made it through without serious injury.

Task Force 8 had also suffered severely. Four of the five warships Avery had sent to meet and escort ARG17 to Troy from the wormhole were gone. The destroyers *Lance Corporal Keith Lopez* and *Chief Gunners Mate Oscar Schmit Jr.* were dead, and both of TF8's cruisers, the *Coral Sea* and the

Ramsey Strait. Only the fast attack carrier *Rear Admiral Isaac C. Kidd* survived, and she was severely damaged. Damaged or not, she was trying to recover those of her Meteors that had survived the fight with the alien missiles.

Avery spent a long time looking at the results of the enemy attack on the ARG. Fourteen of the nineteen starships in the ARG were troop transports. Six of the fourteen were dead, probably lost with all hands. Five of the others were damaged, with an as yet unknown number of casualties. Only three had come through without significant battle damage or casualties. Three of the five support ships were dead, and one other was wounded.

Perhaps the worst loss was that of the *Peleliu* with the ARG's admiral, and the commanding general of VII Corps and his primary staff.

Finally Avery said in a formal voice, "Comm, get me commander, Marine Combat Force, Troy."

"Aye aye, Sir," Lieutenant Commander Davis said softly; he'd been following the aftermath of ARG17's encounter with the missiles along with the admiral.

While waiting for the Marine commander, Avery called to his aide, Lieutenant Julius Townsend. "Kindly arrange for my transportation planetside, to Lieutenant General Bauer's headquarters." He hesitated, then added, "Tell Chief Jones I want to take the fast way down."

"Aye aye, Sir." Townsend, understanding why his boss needed to meet with Bauer in person and as soon as possible, put a call in to Chief Boatswain's Mate Andrew Jones, who ran the admiral's ship-to-ship, orbit-to-ground shuttles, and told him to be ready to take off on either at a moment's notice. "The Admiral wants to fly down fastest."

"No problem, Lieutenant. My bird will be ready by the time the admiral gets here. Even if he starts right now."

"Thanks, Chief." To Avery: "Chief Jones says he's ready, Sir."

"Thank you, Mr. Townsend. Comm, belay that last. Inform Lieutenant General Bauer I am en route to his location and will provide him with an ETA shortly."

Near the McKinzie Elevator Base,
Outside Millerton, Marine Headquarters

"Admiral," Lieutenant General Bauer said, rising and stepping from behind his small field desk. "Come in, please. Have a seat." He gestured at two camp chairs sitting at a small folding table. A coffee set-up was already on the table.

"Thank you, Sir," Avery replied. He nervously stepped to one of the camp chairs but didn't sit; Bauer out-ranked him, and protocol said the senior man sits first. That's what he told himself.

"Don't stand on ceremony, Jim," Bauer said, smiling. "We're in the field, not the Flag Club. When a man wearing more stars than you tells you to have a seat, you sit your ass down."

"Whatever you say, Harry." Avery plopped into the chair facing into the room. He fidgeted.

"Rough ride down?" Bauer asked as he sat in the other camp chair.

Avery nodded. "'Fast ride on a rocky road,' as you Marines call that plunge." He grimaced, than picked up his coffee mug and took a sip. "I thought I should get down here ASAP." He shook his head. "The way my arthritic joints feel, maybe I should have ridden the elevator instead of taking the shuttle all the way."

Bauer snorted. "Arthritic my ass. There's a lot of negative things that a Marine can say about the Navy—some of them are even true—but complaints about medical care aren't among them. If you have arthritis, it's because you want it."

Avery chuckled. "Yeah. Maybe it's just age getting to me." He looked into a corner of Bauer's Spartan office. "Or maybe it's thinking about our losses."

Bauer sucked in a deep breath. "Tell me all about it. Starting with why you thought it important to pay me a personal visit rather than use your comms when you should be in your CAC directing rescue and recover operations on ARG 17."

Avery flinched at the mild criticism. "It's serious, Harry. Damn serious. I don't want any bad guys who might be listening in to hear me say just how bad things suddenly got."

"I can buy that." Bauer glanced at a random part of the ceiling. "That was quite a light show we were treated to shortly before you announced your impending visit. What the hell happened up there?"

Avery looked at Bauer, and his expression was bleak. "I lost a third of my fighting power. Ships and men. Gone. Dead." He shuddered. "But that's not the worst of it. VII Corps basically no longer exists. ARG 17 got slaughtered, despite the best efforts of my people. We just weren't prepared for an attack like that." He shook his head, and shuddered again. "Two of VII Corps' divisions are gone completely—unless some of the troops managed to get into stasis. If any did, it wasn't many; there weren't enough stasis stations on the ships to handle that many people. One of the other two divisions was hurt so badly I don't think it can function as a division again until it's withdrawn and reconstituted." He stopped talking and looked into a place that only he could see.

"I must be relieved of command, I don't deserve command," Avery said so softly the Marine barely heard him, then was silent again.

After a moment of waiting for him to say more, Bauer asked, "What about the Fourth division? What about General Lyman and his staff?"

Avery shook himself, then spoke more firmly and briskly than he had before. "I believe the 25th Infantry Division lost half a brigade but is otherwise intact." He paused again, swallowed, and continued in a firm voice. "General Lyman and his staff, unfortunately, were on the *Peleliu* when she was killed. I don't believe there were any survivors."

Bauer stared at Avery. What he had just described had to be the worst military disaster in centuries.

He didn't say that, though. Instead he asked, "Have you sent word back to Earth yet?"

Avery shook his head. "I wanted to make sure you assumed command before I send word."

"Jim, if what you said about Lyman being killed is accurate, I'm now the senior officer on or near Troy. Of course I'm in command." Bauer switched to another topic.

"I lost some Marines in the rescue mission to Mini Mouse. What is the Navy's assessment of the lunar operations?"

Now on firmer ground, not thinking directly about his lost ships and sailors, Avery calmed down. "I'm sorry about your Marines, but the mission was a success on multiple levels. First, they brought back all of my downed fliers. Second, the enemy didn't use any defensive fire. Did you know I had drones out there to mimic attacking spacecraft, to attract fire? Well, I did, and the enemy didn't fire on them. The drones over-flew all four sites to assess damage. It didn't look like anything could have survived in the bombed areas."

"Then where did those ground counter-attacks come from?"

Avery shook his head apologetically. "The drones didn't see anything that might have been their bases." He shrugged. "But they weren't looking for them, either."

"Those bases, if they exist, need to be found and neutralized," Bauer said firmly.

"Agreed." Avery bobbed his head, and mentally kicked himself for not ordering a search for ground bases on Mini Mouse before he headed planetside. "I'll order a search as soon as we are through here."

"What is your assessment of the survivability of the people on the starships that were killed?"

"I'm sure some are still alive, in compartments that weren't breached. More than that I can't say at this time. Crews from the uninjured ships are conducting searches. I won't know until I get their reports. The surviving Meteors off the *Kidd* are searching the damaged and killed Meteors for surviving pilots." His shoulders jerked in a half-shrug. "The Meteors' cockpits are survival capsules. If they didn't get holed, the pilots can last up to twelve hours before their life support starts to fail." He looked again into a dark corner of his mind and murmured, "Some of them might still make it back alive."

"Admiral Avery!" Bauer said sharply. "Time enough for that later. Right now we need to rescue everybody who can be rescued and recover those who can't. We need to fully assess the damage to our forces, and prepare to fend off the next alien attack. There *will* be another attack."

Avery flinched as though slapped, but pulled himself out of the depression he'd been sinking into. "You're right, General. You're in command, what are your orders?"

"All you have left for planet defense is your flagship, the big carrier, and three frigates. Is that right?"

"Yes."

"What about the two destroyers you had pursuing the missiles?"

"They are still en route to what remains of ARG 17."

"Good. They can aid in the search and recovery."

"Yes they can."

"Next, you have inter-stel comms, I don't. So I need for you to send a preliminary report to the Joint Chiefs."

"I will pass my message by you before transmission."

Bauer waved that away. "I trust your judgment, and you're better able than I am to tell the Chiefs the status of the Navy forces here, and request what you need. Tell them to start feeding Second Army here."

Avery nodded his acceptance of Bauer's instruction.

"And I want you to find the aliens' ground bases on Mini Mouse. Also, commence satellite reconnaissance of Dumbo. If the aliens had bases on the smaller moon, they probably have installations of some sort on the larger one as well."

"I'll give the orders as soon as I leave your command post."

"Excellent!" Bauer exclaimed, rising to his feet. "Can you think of anything else that needs to be done at this time?"

"No, Sir. I think we covered everything."

"Good. Keep me up to date on what's happening with the search and recovery operations, and what you're finding on the moons."

"Aye aye, General."

Bauer held out his hand, and was relieved at the firmness of Avery's grip. If Avery's grip had been weak, Bauer would have relieved him of command and passed it to the senior surviving captain in either fleet.

Now to prepare his Marines for the next ground attack by the aliens. One thing that wasn't mentioned in his meeting with Avery, but that Bauer knew full well: the engagement on Mini Mouse demonstrated that, in close combat, his Marines were the superior fighters, and they could beat greater numbers.

Remembering the vids he'd seen of the original attack on Troy, and the little from Force Recon, Bauer knew it would be a very tough fight when it came. It would be a fight that might well be decided by numbers.

Unknown was how many soldiers of VII Corps survived the attack on ARG 17, and the state of their morale. High morale and belief in yourself and your comrades was of incalculable value in battle. They were what doctrine and field manuals called "force magnifiers," the intangibles that increased a military unit's ability to fight and win without increasing its size or weapons.

"Sir." A firm knock came on the frame of Bauer's office door. He looked toward it and saw Lieutenant Upshur.

"Come."

Upshur stepped inside the room. "Sir, satellite observation reports a wormhole opening twenty degrees above ecliptic, one point starboard of galactic east. Half a light minute distance."

Galactic east was almost opposite the direction to Earth, and no other human colonized worlds were in that direction.

Damn Navy. Why do they have to use "points" to give direction? Bauer thought but didn't say. He, like most Marines—and just about everybody else for that matter—had to translate points to degrees. A compass point was one thirty-second of a compass rose, slightly more than five and a half degrees. It was good that this wormhole was only one point off galactic east; figuring seven points would have taken more time.

Bauer waited for more.

"So far, nothing has exited the wormhole," Upshur said.

"I need to know instantly when something does."

"Yes, Sir. I will inform you immediately when something exits."

"And get me Brigadier General Porter, ASAP."

"Aye aye, Sir!" Upshur wasn't at all surprised by the "ASAP" rather than the more common, "At his earliest convenience." The just-opened wormhole could only mean the aliens were about to make an appearance.

Less than a minute had passed since Bauer told Upshur he wanted his chief of staff, and the man was already there.

"You must have been waiting for my call."

"As soon as I heard about the wormhole, I knew you'd need me."

"You found out about it before I did? Upshur is my aide, he should report to me first."

Porter shook his head. "He didn't tell me. I was in the comm shack when the message came in from orbit."

"Where do we need to aim to hit a target one point to starboard of galactic east?"

Porter shrugged. "Sometimes it seems the Navy thinks they're still at sea in wooden ships with canvas sails."

Bauer grunted. "Well, defending against starships coming from one point to starboard is going to be their job. We have to defend the ground from both land and air attack. Assemble the staff."

"Aye aye, Sir."

Briefing room, 1st Marine Combat Force Headquarters, Near Millerton

Word of the new wormhole traveled fast, and it was only minutes before every member of the 1st Marine Combat Force's primary staff and their seconds were assembled, along with the commanders of all the major subordinate units.

"Gentlemen," Bauer began, "we don't know when the aliens are going to exit the wormhole or in what force. What we do know is, when they do come we can expect a most serious fight. Using only missiles launched from Mini Mouse, they killed or severely injured three quarters of ARG 17, and a third of TF 8. Along with the ships of ARG 17, the aliens killed or damaged more than half of VII Corps before those poor soldiers could even see the world they were on their way to. The surviving ships of the ARG, reinforced by some of the warships of TF 8, are currently undertaking a massive search and recovery mission where the ships or ARG 17 were killed or wounded.

"The Navy believes that the aliens no longer present a threat to their shipping from Mini Mouse. Perhaps they're right, at least in terms of the aliens having attack-capable warships there. But their ground attack on the squads we sent as security on the SAR missions to Mini Mouse suggests that they have an unknown but possibly substantial ground force still present on the small moon. The Navy is currently investigating, via satellite, both moons, looking for anomalies that could indicate alien installations.

"The Navy, incidentally, refers to them as 'the enemy,' almost as though they are in denial that they aren't human. We've all seen the vids, we know they aren't human.

"For all we know, the aliens are still right here on Troy, hidden in underground facilities. Many times in the past, the ancestors of our Corps went up against enemies who lived and fought in caves. And died in them when Marines went in to dig them out. We have seen nothing to rule out the possibility that the aliens are underground.

"To that end, I want 3rd MAW to apply all possible resources to locating anomalies that could indicate caves or other sub-surface structures." That he directed at Major General Reginald Myers, the commander of 3rd Marine Air Wing. "G-2, use local geological studies and reports to locate possibly usable caves within one hundred klicks of Millerton." That was to Lieutenant Colonel Wendell Neville, his intelligence chief.

"In light of the fact that the remnants of ARG 17 and VII Corps are still in planetary space and not about to make planetfall, we will be on our own for the foreseeable future. So the rest of you, prepare your units to defend against attacks such as we saw in the vids of the initial invasion, and to attack when the aliens show themselves. At a time to be chosen by the enemy, we will be engaged with a foe of unknown strength and capabilities. I intend that the First Marine Combat Force will win.

"Brigadier General Porter, take over."

With that, Bauer marched out of the briefing room. Everybody rose to their feet and stood at attention until Porter called out,

"Seats!" and began giving his instructions.

Stasis Station A-1-53/S, NAUS Juno Beach

SECOND LIEUTENANT TED GREIG AWOKE; THE COMMANDER'S STASIS UNIT IN THE STATION Greig had led his platoon to automatically wake its occupant after two hours, unless ordered to do so at an earlier time.

As with the other two times he'd been in stasis, Greig needed a minute to clear his mind before he could move, or do anything other than groan. He pried his eyes open and sat up. A look around that wasn't as quick as he would have liked told him nobody else was awake yet. He levered himself out of the coffin-like stasis unit and stood on legs that quickly remembered how to stand and, eventually, walk.

Stasis can be a life-saver, he thought, *as long as you don't have to wake up fighting.*

He stretched, twisted left and right, and did a couple of deep knee bends to get himself moving again. Then he checked the time. Two hours since he'd locked his platoon down.

Two hours. The automatic commander's wake-up.

Where was the company commander, why hadn't he roused him, or the rest of the platoon? Or was that the responsibility of one of the ship's officers?

He tried his comm, but all he got was static. Things couldn't be *that* bad though—the ship's gravity was still on.

Greig looked to his left. Sergeant First Class Quinn's stasis unit was still closed; the platoon sergeant was still out. That needed to change, right now.

Whatever Greig did, he was going to need help, and Quinn was the best help available.

In two steps, he was at the control panel for Quinn's unit. Waking him would be child's play: there were two pads on the panel, a green one with the word "UP" blazoned on it, and a red one labeled "DOWN." If "UP" didn't mean, "Rise up from stasis," whoever designed the panel didn't have a very good working knowledge of English. He tapped the green pad and was rewarded by the faint sounds of machinery from within the unit. After a moment the lid rose and he saw Quinn begin struggling to sit up.

"Take it easy, Sergeant," he said, putting a hand on Quinn's shoulder to keep him down. "Let it come naturally." He felt the sergeant's muscles relax.

Quinn worked his jaw, building saliva so he could speak. "Who's up?" he croaked.

"I don't know. Nobody answered my comm."

"Maybe your comm's broken?"

"Yeah, maybe." Greig didn't think so; the comm units were field hardened, supposed to stand up to the rigors of combat. His hadn't had any rough treatment at all.

"I don't think so either." Quinn took Greig's silence as disbelief of the comm being broken. His voice was stronger now, and he managed to sit up with little difficulty. "Gimme a hand." He reached, and Greig grasped his wrist and pulled him out of the unit. "You want me to wake the troops?"

Greig shook his head. "Not until we have a better idea of the situation. As soon as you're ready, let's go exploring."

"How much exploring can we do by ourselves? The ship has what, ten levels?"

"All we really have to explore is this deck, this is where our battalion is billeted. Only three decks are troops, the rest of the ship is ship operations and crew, or cargo."

"You're sure of that, LT?"

Greig nodded. "The *Juno Beach's* layout was covered in an officers call a couple of days before we left Earth. So like I said, we only need to look at this deck."

"Where are the vacuum suits?"

Greig looked a question at his platoon sergeant.

"We were under attack, LT, and nobody answered your comm. At the very least, the ship might have been holed and the atmosphere in the passage has gotten very thin."

When Greig didn't say anything, Quinn went on, "At worst, the ship's been destroyed and this station is drifting in vacuum.

Greig flinched. "Is that what you think happened? That the ship was destroyed, I mean?"

Quinn shrugged. "One thing I've learned in almost twenty years in this army is, when it comes to troop transports, anything's possible."

Greig gave a nervous chuckle. "I'm sure you're right. Let's find the vacuum suits."

The vacuum suits were right where they should be. The station had four rows of "coffins" with a locker at the ends of each row. The lockers held six vacuum suits apiece. The suits were intended for emergency use only, and were strictly intended for short time use. They came in four sizes that almost guaranteed that nobody could find one that fit properly. The one that Quinn got into was a marginally better fit than the one that sagged on Greig. The suits didn't look like the ones he'd seen sailors wearing when they went on EVA missions. They were far less form-fitting, and, instead of helmets, had hood arrangements with broad face plates that allowed the wearer's face to be clearly seen from outside.

"Are you ready, Sarge?" Greig asked over the suit's short-range comm once the two had attached the breathers to their backs.

"As ready as I'll ever be, LT." Quinn was less than two steps from the compartment's hatch. He ignored the display next to it and braced himself against the possible outrush of air if there was vacuum outside. He was staggered only slightly when he hit the "open" button and the air-tight slid into a recess on the bulkhead: the atmosphere outside the compartment was thin enough that they needed the breathers, but far from vacuum.

Greig started to say, "I'll lead," but stopped when Quinn put out a hand to stop him and stepped into the doorway. Leaning so only his head and shoulders were outside, he looked both in both directions along the passageway.

"The emergency lights are on, but that's all I can see." He looked over his shoulder. "Which way, Sir?"

Thinking quickly, remembering the basic plan of the ship, he said, "Go right." Right was forward, toward the front of the ship. The troop command compartments were forward of the troop compartments, the stasis compartments were aft, toward the rear. "There's another stasis compartment on the other side of this passage. Let's check it out first."

"Yes, Sir."

Greig noticed that he had gone from being "LT" to "Sir." Evidently Quinn had decided to let the officer take full responsibility for what they were doing. That was fine by him. If he needed the platoon sergeant's advice at any point, he could ask for it.

The passageway was less than Spartan. It was painted battleship gray, top, bottom, and sides. Conduits and ducts ran the length of the overhead, tunneling through the bulkheads with airtight doors that divided the passageway into twenty-meter segments. Most of them were the same battleship gray as the walls. More anonymous gray conduits ran along the walls.

Stasis Station A-1-53/P was unoccupied; the lids on all the units were ajar. Just to be certain, Greig and Quinn quickly went through the compartment, looking inside each unit. Either nobody had reached the station, or they'd already gotten up and moved out. But if they had, why hadn't they woken him, or at least replied to his comm?

Back in the passageway, Greig tried his comm again.

"Static, nothing but static." Neither man commented on the lack of response, but it seemed possible that their platoon was the only survivors on board the *Juno Beach*.

The second hatch beyond the stasis compartment in which they'd ridden out the battle didn't open when Quinn hit the "open" button.

Greig swore under his breath—that probably meant there was vacuum on the other side of it. "Step back and grab hold of something," he said.

"Are you sure you want to do that, Sir?"

"Got to be done. Now do what I said."

Greig watched Quinn take a few steps back and firmly grip a side duct and an overhead conduit. The sergeant fumbled shoving his gloved fingers behind the duct and conduit so he could get hold of them.

A small hatch was set into the bulkhead next to the airtight. A red lever was set in its middle, blazoned with the message, "Pulling this lever will sound alarms throughout this area of the starship and in all command and control compartments."

Greig braced himself into the corner where the passageway and hatch walls met, and pulled the red lever.

No alarm sounded, but the small hatch swung open, exposing manual controls for the airtight.

Greig took a steadying deep breath and flexed his fingers before slipping them onto the control dial. He twisted it.

And jerked back.

A voice boomed in the passageway: *"Warning! Warning! Opening this airtight is potentially dangerous! Make sure everything is secured before proceeding!"*

Greig looked back at Quinn. He could see his platoon sergeant had his eyes closed and his fingers twitched on the conduit and duct he held onto. He looked back at the manual controls and took another steadying deep breath.

"Here goes," he said softly, and turned the dial all the way to the "open" position. A *clunk* in the airtight told him it was unlocked and ready to be opened. He shoved a hand into the control box, reached the other to the "open" plate, and slapped it. The airtight made a grinding noise as it started sliding into its recess, but the noise quickly died out to silence, although Greig still felt the grinding through the metal. Evacuating air buffeted him as it rushed out of the short passageway into the void beyond.

The lieutenant waited until the air was no longer buffeting him, then, keeping a firm grip in the control box, leaned to the side to see though the now-open airtight.

Straight ahead was solid blackness, but to the left he saw stars. Some of the stars were moving; he thought they must be SAR craft looking for survivors. He hoped they weren't whoever had attacked the troop fleet. None seemed to be close to the Juno Beach. On the right, he faintly made out in starlight reflection the caved in bulkhead of the continuing passageway.

Miraculously, he was still being held to the deck by the ship's artificial gravity.

"Do you have a light, Sarge?" he asked, turning around to look at Quinn.

Quinn patted at his vacuum suit. "Can't find one," he said; his voice was weak. "What's there?"

"A big chunk of the ship's simply missing. But there might be a way forward. If I had a light I could find out."

Quinn's voice was suddenly more confident; the LT sounded like he knew what he was doing. "I think I saw lanterns in that empty compartment we checked out. I'll take a look, Sir."

"I'll be here." Then he had to hold tight again as the air in the next stretch of passageway evacuated past him.

When the buffeting of escaping atmosphere stopped, Greig tried his comm again. This time he thought he heard fragments of voices in the static. That encouraged him to try to raise somebody.

"Anyone who can hear, there are survivors on the Juno Beach. I'm Lieutenant Theodore W. Greig, Alpha Troop, First of the Seventh Mounted Infantry. My platoon is intact. I haven't been able to make contact with anybody else on board the ship, but my platoon sergeant and I are attempting to find other survivors. Any station, do you receive me? Over." He listened as intently as he could, but didn't hear anything that sounded like an attempt to reply to his transmission, not even when he repeated his message.

A bright beam of light suddenly flashed past Greig, illuminating the darkness beyond. He turned to see a grinning Quinn hustling toward him, a headlamp on his helmet and another in his hand. The one he wore was lit.

"I found two of these, Sir!" Quinn stopped in front of the lieutenant and handed him the other lamp.

"Thanks, Sarge." Greig took the offered lamp and put it on before turning back to the void beyond the hatch, careful not to step through the opened door.

Whatever had been to the port side of the passageway was completely gone. The lantern showed jagged, bent edges of metal around the massive..."hole in the hull" seemed an inadequate description of the vacancy where just a couple of hours earlier compartments had existed, keeping the emptiness of space at bay. The gap extended to high above and halfway down, the strike must have come in from above the level of the passageway. It extended a full hundred meters beyond where Greig stood. A narrow ledge ran sporadically along the right side of what had been the passageway. Bits of the overhead were still there, similar to the remaining pieces of decking. Chunks of conduits and ductwork still hung onto the right side wall, but what had been on the ceiling was gone. The right side of the passageway wasn't intact; it was bowed away from the blast in places, and frequently holed. The wall on the far side of the gap was the same, deeply dented and holed.

Greig swallowed to moisten a suddenly dry throat, he doubted that anyone who might have been in the holed compartments had survived, not unless they were in stasis units. Even vacuum suits might not have saved them when the atmosphere blew out and slammed them through the holes, maybe shredding their suits on the jagged metal edges.

"What do you think, Sir?"

"I think we can make it across there."

"Are you sure?" Quinn sounded doubtful.

"It looks like there's enough of the decking left, and we can hold onto the conduits to keep from falling away. So, yes, I think we can make it."

"Ah, LT? I'm surprised we've still got gravity here. You think there's gravity out there?"

Greig hesitated, then admitted, "I hadn't thought of that."

"We better find out before we go walking along."

"Right." Greig pulled himself fully into the doorway and extended a foot to the nearest piece of left over decking on the right wall.

He had to push his foot down to make contact, there was no gravity to pull him to it.

"It's pretty much free fall out here," he told Quinn. "Navy engineering is even more unbelievable than I imagined. How on earth do they manage to have artificial gravity in intact spaces, when it's missing in the next, holed space?"

"Got me on that one, Sir." Quinn sounded like he thought Navy engineering was irrelevant to their situation.

Keeping hold of the frame over his head with his left hand, Greig reached for a conduit with his right and gave it a tug. It held. "I'm going to try. Watch me. Follow if it seems safe."

"Shouldn't we have a rope of some sort, tie ourselves together?"

"That's a great idea, Sarge. But I haven't seen anything that looks like a rope. Have you?"

"Sorry. No I haven't. Be careful, Sir."

Greig glanced out through the gap. Lights still moved around in the distance; what he thought were SAR teams rescuing survivors, just like before. And, the same as before, none were moving in the direction of the *Juno Beach*.

Making sure his right hand grip was firm, Greig reached with his left. He wanted to shuffle along, hands at shoulder level, feet on the remains of the deck, but the lack of gravity forced his legs to drift outward so he was angled away from the bulkhead rather than flush against it. He'd have to travel only using his hands. Unless he could find footholds along the way.

Ten meters along, he reached a punched hole that looked big enough for him to get though without catching himself on a jagged edge. It was.

Before entering, he looked at a sign on the wall. It read, "A-43-P." It was the troop compartment his platoon had been in. If he hadn't moved them to the stasis station, they'd all be dead now.

He decided not to mention that to Quinn. Bunks, lockers, cabinets, and other minor furnishings were jumbled about, funneling toward the opening. Everything was slowly settling to the deck. Personal belongings that had been left behind unsecured during the rapid abandonment of the compartment were mixed in with everything else. Greig felt a slight downward tugging, as of a very weak gravity field. *Amazing*, he thought.

"What do you have in there, Sir?" Quinn asked, sounding worried.

He realized he had to tell his platoon sergeant. "This used to be our platoon's compartment." He hurried on before Quinn could react to the news. "I'm going to search, there might be something we can use. Maybe a stronger comm than the one I have." He didn't find a comm unit, but he did find a spool of electrical cable.

"Sarge, I've got something we can tie off with." He kept looking, now for something to use as a hook on the conduits, but came up dry.

A minute later, Quinn gingerly pulled himself through the opening in the bulkhead. They tied the cable around their waists with a ten meter length between them.

"Now if one of us goes, we both go," Quinn said.

"You're so encouraging, Sarge."

Quinn barked a short laugh.

Greig was surprised to find that he felt more secure tied to Quinn. If he lost his grip and drifted away the other could pull him back. Just as he could pull Quinn back if he lost his. But if they *both* somehow let go at the same time, or if something violently shook the ship and broke their grips, then they'd drift until someone picked them up. If someone picked them up. And if they were still alive.

Feeling more secure, he crawled faster along the wall, and it was only a few minutes before they reached the far side of the gap. The first hatch was broken, pushed in from its frame. It didn't take much effort to push it farther to admit them.

"The strike must have come from aft as well as above," Greig said. "That would explain why this wall and door are battered, but they're intact from the other side."

Quinn grunted. The direction the missile had come from was obvious enough it didn't need commenting on.

Twenty meters farther on they came to the end—the entire forward portion of the *Juno Beach* was missing, blown away by missiles that had zeroed in on the ship's bow.

"I've got a feeling we won't find anybody up ahead," Greig said to himself. He did his best not to show his dismay to Quinn, who was silent himself. He gathered himself and tried his comm again, beginning with identifying himself.

This time, he got an answer.

"Lieutenant Greig, this is Captain McMahan, Foxtrot, Second of the Tenth. Where are you?"

"Sir, I can't tell you how glad I am to hear your voice!"

"That's nice, Lieutenant, now where the fuck are you?"

"Yes, Sir. We're on, on—. I don't know what deck this is, it's the one First Battalion was on. We're at what is now the forward edge of the *Juno Beach*..." His voice caught on that. "The wh-whole front end of the ship is missing."

"All right, I know where you're at. Now, you say 'we.' Who's we?"

"That's my platoon sergeant and me. The rest of the platoon is still in the stasis chamber. I left them in stasis while Sergeant Quinn and I try to find out what's happening."

"Have you located anybody else from your troop?"

"No, Sir. We haven't seen anybody, and you're the first person to answer any of my comms."

"What stasis station is your platoon in?"

"We're in Alpha one dash fifty-three slash Sierra."

"You must have that wrong. Either that or you aren't as far forward as you said. Dash fifty-three is farther to the rear."

"Sir, we're as far forward as we can get—there's no ship in front of us."

"Wait one, I'm almost at the forward edge of what's left of the ship." A moment later Captain McMahan said, "I'm there. Go to the edge and look down. If you're all the way forward, you should see me two decks below you."

Greig took two steps to reach the end of the ship, grabbed something, and leaned out to look down.

"I see you, Sir," he said and waved at the figure he saw leaning out two decks below.

"I see you too, Lieutenant," McMahan said. "Not far aft of here there's a big chunk blown out of the port side of the ship. The stasis station you said you came from is on the other side of it. Care to give me a different station number?"

"Sir, I know about the missing area. We were able to negotiate our way along a narrow strip of decking. Well, mostly we went hand over hand along conduits."

Greig could make out McMahan shake his head. "You're either very brave, or incredibly stupid," the captain said. "You think you can make it back to your station without killing yourselves?"

Greig looked at Quinn, who nodded.

"Yes, Sir, we can do it."

"Then go there and wake your platoon. Right before I heard you, I made contact with SAR. They have us on their list and will be here in a couple of hours. So be ready to be rescued."

Greig and Quinn grinned at each other, relieved to know that someone knew where they were, and was coming for them.

Jordan, Eastern Shapland

During the SAR mission to Mini Mouse, 3rd Battalion, 1st Marines, moved to Jordan, one of the areas where Force Recon had encountered the aliens. India Company's Third platoon was held in reserve pending the return of its First squad. With the squad suffering two dead and three wounded out of its thirteen-man strength, Third platoon remained in reserve for the time being. Kilo Company was in positions on the north and west sides of Jordan, Lima Company on the south and east. Their lines were punctuated and backed up by the heavy weapons of Weapons Company. India Company was billeted inside the small city.

"Mackie, Cafferata," Sergeant Martin called out when he rejoined his squad after the squad leaders' debriefing that was held immediately after the return from Mini Mouse, "on me."

The two lance corporals heaved themselves to their feet from where they had been resting in the shade of a building on the south side of the town, and joined their squad leader. Neither was feeling very enthusiastic about anything, they didn't even feel relieved to be out of anything remotely resembling a defensive position.

"What's up, honcho?" Mackie asked flat-voiced when he reached Martin.

Cafferata didn't say anything, he just gave his squad leader a blank stare. The fight on Mini Mouse had been the first combat for either of them, the first time they'd lost men they knew. The experience was preying on them.

If Martin was depressed or upset by the casualties in his squad, it didn't show on his face or in his voice. "Both of your fire team leaders are out for a while with their wounds, but I guess you figured that."

Mackie mumbled an indistinct "I know," and Cafferata nodded dumbly.

"That means the two of you are acting fire team leaders, until Corporals Adriance and Button return to duty."

This time Mackie nodded dumbly, and Cafferata mumbled, "Yeah, I figured."

Martin looked closely at them, but neither looked back—or even at each other. Their eyes were down and to the side, not looking at anything in particular. He had to break them out of their funk before it got worse and paralyzed them.

"A-ten-*hut*!"

Startled by the unexpected command, the two came to attention, though not as sharply as they would have in garrison—or even before the fight on Mini Mouse.

"What i—?" Mackie started to say.

"Did I tell you to speak, Lance Corporal?" Martin snarled, thrusting his face into Mackie's. He shot a glare at Cafferata, warning him to keep quiet. "Well?" he demanded when Mackie didn't say anything.

"No, Sergeant," Mackie said, clench jawed. His eyes were fixed straight ahead.

Martin took a step back and looked from one to the other before saying, "Listen up, you two, and listen up good. Do you think you're the 1st Marines to lose buddies in combat? *Every* Marine who's gone in harm's way has lost buddies. I have, Sergeant Johnson has, and Sergeant Mausert has. And you better believe Staff Sergeant Guillen has! Some of the corporals in this platoon have lost buddies in combat. I know it's shitty, but shit happens, particularly in war."

He stopped and looked aside for a moment. When he began again, his voice was thick. "I just lost two more Marines, men I was responsible for." His voice harshened. "If you feel like hell, how do you think I feel? Zion and Porter were my men, my responsibility. That weighs, that weighs heavily. Heavier than what's got you down, believe me.

"But if I let it weigh me down too much, it'll make me screw up somehow the next time we meet those aliens, and more Marines will get killed. Then it won't just be because shit happens, it'll be because I screwed up. Their deaths will my fault. I can't allow that to happen. And I can't allow you to feel so sorry for yourselves that you screw up and get good Marines killed. So shape up! Do you understand? *Do you?*"

Mackie swallowed rather than say anything. Cafferata mumbled, "Yes, Sergeant."

Martin again shoved his face to Mackie's. "Do you hate me, Mackie? Is that why you aren't getting with the program?"

Mackie worked up a mouthful of nervous saliva, then swallowed it. "No, Sergeant, I don't hate you. I'm thinking about the squad, how we can function when we're short so many men." His voice was clear, although not as strong as he would have liked.

"Oh?" Martin said, taking a step back. "Do you have a suggestion, Lance Corporal?"

"Ah..." Mackie looked around, thinking.

"I'm waiting, Lance Corporal."

"Well, we're down five men. That leaves us—you—with seven men. Wouldn't reorganizing the squad into two fire teams be better?"

"You mean with me as one fire team leader and Corporal Vittori as the other?"

"Yes, Sergeant, sort of like that."

Martin slowly shook his head. "No, for a couple of reasons. First, our wounded will be coming back fairly soon, and I don't want to have to keep reorganizing the squad. Second, I want to give my lance corporals a bit of experience as fire team leaders—."

"But First fire team is only me and Orndoff! Third fire team is Cafferata and Hill. And what about experience for Garcia, he's a lance corporal, too."

Martin nodded. "That's true, all of what you said. But you and Cafferata only having one man each limits how much you can screw up. And getting Garcia some experience is my problem, not yours, so don't worry about it. Do you remember that exercise in Hawaii, when you wound up being an acting fire team leader when I was a simulated casualty?"

"Yes, Sergeant." Mackie swallowed again.

"That was training. This is real. It's different. Do you understand?"

Mackie's eyes widened. "Yes, Sergeant."

"That's better. Now, are you ready to take on a little responsibility?"

"Yes, Sergeant!"

"What about you, Cafferata?"

"Yes, Sergeant, I am." Cafferata beamed.

Satisfied that the two had no further questions, Martin called out, "First squad, on me!" In a moment the other five members of the squad were standing in front of him. He briefly updated them on the condition of their three wounded Marines and told them how he was reorganizing the squad.

"It's only temporary," he finished. "Corporal Vittori is the senior man, both in rank and experience, so make no mistake, he's second to me in the squad's chain of command regardless of who's First fire team leader. Any questions?"

The question was almost always rhetorical, and was so this time as well—nobody had any questions.

"All right, then. The situation remains the same; India Company is in reserve for the battalion, Second platoon is reserve for the company, and First squad is the platoon's reserve. We'll be the last ones committed if, and I emphasize *if* the aliens attack here."

"I have a question now, Sergeant Martin," Mackie said.

"You couldn't have asked it before?"

Mackie shook his head. "Before was about the squad's reorganization. This is about our reserve status."

"So what's your question?"

"How good is the intelligence that the aliens aren't likely to attack here?"

Martin gave Mackie a hard look, then glanced around to see if any officers or senior NCOs were near by. None were. He motioned everybody to close in.

"All right," he said *sotto voce*, "here's the straight scoop, so far as I know it. Nobody, not recon, Force Recon, air, or satellite, has found the aliens or signs that they were just here.

"But.... Here's where it gets hairy. I've heard scuttlebutt that satellite observation has discovered gravitational anomalies similar to the ones on Mini Mouse, the ones where the aliens came from to attack us when we went in with the SAR birds." He shrugged. "I know, and you probably do too, that all worlds have gravitational anomalies, and they don't necessarily mean squat. But we also know that on Mini Mouse some of the anomalies indicated hiding places for the aliens. What that means is, maybe nobody's here to bother us. Maybe the aliens have us outnumbered and are just waiting for us to let our guards down."

He stepped back and allowed his voice to move back toward normal. "That's everything I know or have heard. What I suspect is, we had best be alert, because those little bad bastards could come at us from anywhere at any time. It doesn't matter that we're in reserve. When they hit, they're just as likely to hit us here as hit anybody at Millerton. And they could even pop up right here inside Jordan, so that India Company would be the First Marines engaged.

"Any more questions? No? Good! So don't give me any shit the next time I tell you to clean your weapons. Now get back to whatever goofing off you were doing. Just keep an eye peeled for trouble, that's all.

"And clean your damn weapons!"

Before the end of the day, the Marines of India Company were moved into the vacant houses in Jordan.

Settling in, Jordan

Over the next three days reports filtered down to the Marines planet-side about elements of VII Corps being located and rescued by Navy Search and Rescue teams. The Army troops were being apportioned to the serviceable transports of ARG17 to continue their voyage to Troy. There were no reports of sightings of the enemy, in space, on Mini Mouse, or planetside.

Three days. That's how long it took for Sergeant Martin to become a prophet.

Number 8, Sugar Clover Place, Jordan, Eastern Shapland

"What the fuck!" Orndoff shouted. He scrabbled across the floor of the house's living room, reaching for his rifle.

"What's the problem?" Mackie asked. He already had his rifle in his hands by the time he looked past Orndoff and saw an alien crouched in the doorway to the dining room, pointing its weapon ahead of itself. The alien looked just like the images they'd studied on their way to Troy—head at the end of a long neck, body horizontal on top of legs that bent the wrong way, feather-like structures ran from its crown down the length of its back until they blossomed into a spray on its tail.

"Oh, shit!" Mackie shouted. He didn't hesitate but began shooting even before he had his rifle trained on the intruder. The alien got off a short, automatic burst from its weapon before bullets from Mackie's rifle blew it out of the doorway.

"First squad, report!" Sergeant Martin shouted from somewhere else in the house. Pounding footsteps said that he was running toward the fire.

"First fire team, we're all right," Mackie shouted after glancing at Orndoff to make sure he hadn't been injured in the brief exchange of fire.

While Vittori and Cafferata were reporting no casualties in their fire teams, Mackie positioned Orndoff.

"Get behind the divan and cover me."

"Where are you going?" Orndoff shouted.

Martin burst into the room and swept it with his eyes. "What happened, Mackie? And where are you going?" Martin demanded.

Mackie paused on his way to the door where the alien had appeared and looked at his squad leader, noticing that Martin hadn't taken the time to grab his helmet. "An alien just came in. I blew him away. Now I'm going to see where he went."

Martin had heard Mackie tell Orndoff what to do. He spared the PFC a glance to judge his angle of covering fire, then said, "I'm coming with you, from the other side. Where's your helmet?"

"The same place as yours."

"Let's do it."

The two approached the doorway at different angles, neither straight ahead. Mackie from the left, looking through the door to the right, Martin from the right looking into the area to the left of the doorway.

"Do you see it?" Martin asked.

"It's not in my field of view."

"Did it come out of the kitchen?" Martin asked. The kitchen was the only other room that entered into the dining room. Martin had reached the door and was against the wall to the right, looking as deep into the room as possible. A china cabinet and a credenza were against the walls, too close for anyone to hide behind. The dining table had a cloth, but it barely overlapped the table top, providing no way to hide underneath. Neither did the chairs placed around the table obstruct the view.

"I don't know. It was already in the doorway by the time I saw it." He was opposite Martin at the doorway. Between them they could see nearly the entire interior of the dining room.

"You ready?" Martin asked. When Mackie nodded, he said, "On three, you then me. One. Two. *Three!*"

Mackie charged through the doorway left to right, spinning to cover the corner he hadn't been able to see into. Martin was right behind him, going right to left and covering the corner he hadn't seen into.

"Clear," Mackie shouted.

"Clear," Martin echoed.

The alien wasn't there. But...

"I have a blood trail," Mackie said.

"And I've got a weapon," Martin said. Turning his head back to the living room, he called, "Orndoff, get in here. Secure that." He pointed to the alien's—rifle, for lack of a better name to call it. Then he got on his comm to report to Second Lieutenant Commiskey.

After reporting the bare bones of what had already happened, he said, "We've secured the weapon and are following the blood trail into the kitchen. There's an exit to the backyard there, maybe it came from outside."

"When you find where it went next," Commiskey said, "don't pursue. Report, then we'll decide what to do next."

"Aye aye, report but don't pursue."

Commiskey signed off, presumably to report to Captain Sitter.

"Orndoff," Martin said, "cover us. Mackie, let's check the kitchen the same way we came in here."

"Roger that, honcho." Mackie answered. He froze a soon as he turned to check the corner.

"The basement door's open," he said softly. "And I found the body."

"Orndoff, get in here and give us some cover," Martin said.

Orndoff came in carrying the alien's rifle in his left hand and his own in his right.

"Put the alien weapon down and hold your rifle like you know how to use it, Orndoff," Mackie snapped.

Martin got on his comm. "Vittori, get your fire team into the dining room, it looks like the alien came through the kitchen from the basement. Cafferata, I want you and your fire team in the living room." He waited for them to "roger," then reported to Commiskey.

When he was through on his comm, he joined Mackie to examine the alien corpse. It was sprawled, both arms reaching toward the open basement door. One leg stretched out behind, the other cocked as though it had been pushing itself forward one leg at a time. Blood, a red similar to human blood but somehow not the same red, was pooled around it, but no more seemed to be leaking out of any of its wounds.

"You got your tie downs on you?" Martin asked.

"Always," Mackie said, handing Martin one of the ties that the Marines used to bind prisoners, or secure anything else that needed to be secured.

Martin looped one end in a hasty knot around the alien's trailing foot, then backed out of the kitchen. Mackie went ahead of him. In the dining room, with a wall between them and the alien, Martin gave the cord a sharp jerk, then a more steady pull, until he was confident the corpse had moved at least a meter.

"I guess he didn't booby-trap himself," Mackie said.

"Always check to make sure," Martin said. He stood to return to the kitchen, and reeled back, shouting, "Aliens!"

There was no place to go for cover, he dropped to a knee and started firing through the kitchen door.

"Everybody, into the living room!" Martin shouted. "Take cover there." He kept firing rapidly into the kitchen. It was enough to keep the aliens he'd seen rushing out of the basement from coming farther.

A chittering voice, commanding even though it was in a higher register than a human's, shouted from out of sight, probably at the head of the basement stairs. Several high-pitched voices answered it, they sounded like protests, enlisted who didn't want to go into a fire storm.

"Somebody, throw a grenade in there!"

"I got it!" Mackie shouted. He armed a grenade, and bowled it along the floor so that it ricocheted off the jam and spun behind the wall toward the basement door.

The voices in the kitchen erupted in high-pitched jabbering, accompanied by the scrabbling of something hard—claws?—on the floor. The grenade exploded, setting off shrill cries, and more commanding shouts.

Martin took advantage of the aliens' momentary confusion to dash out of the dining room, into the living room. He got on his comm to report, and only then heard the reports from the rest of the platoon; all three of the houses the platoon was divided into were under attack from aliens that came up from the basements.

"Cafferata," Martin shouted, "look out the windows, watch for aliens. Mackie, take Orndoff and check the bedrooms, then get back in here."

Shouts and scrabbling from beyond the dining room announced that the aliens in the kitchen were about to charge into sight.

"Get ready!" Vittori shouted to his men.

"Orndoff, let's go!" Mackie shouted as he raced for the bedroom hallway. There were three bedrooms along a hallway behind the living room. The first one's door was halfway open. Mackie slammed into the door to smash anyone hiding behind it into the wall and spun away into the middle of the room, looking all around for aliens. Orndoff was close behind him.

"Orndoff, check the closet, I'll cover you."

"Right." Orndoff darted to the closet and slammed its sliding door to the side. He jabbed into its corners with his rifle muzzle, but met only clothing. As soon as he announced the closet was clear, Mackie dropped down and looked under the bed. It was clear except for dust bunnies. After looking out the windows and not seeing anyone, human or alien, they ran into the next bedroom, anxious to finish their search and get back to the living room, where they heard an increasing volume of gunfire.

"The bedrooms are clear," Mackie reported to Martin when he and Orndoff returned. "We looked outside. Didn't see anybody, but it sounds like every occupied house has a fire fight going on inside." He wanted to ask how things were going here, but the four alien bodies in the doorway to the dining room and continued high pitched shouts from just out of sight told him all he needed to know.

"Do you think you can bounce another grenade in there?" Martin asked him.

"I can give it a try."

"Just don't bounce it to someplace it'll hit us."

"No sweat." Mackie moved to his right as he readied a grenade. He judged his angle, then cocked his arm and threw the grenade hard enough to spin wildly out of sight behind the wall where the alien voices came from. Before it went off, three aliens shot through the doorway, faster than the Marines could point their weapons at the rapidly moving forms and fire. In the dining room, voices rose to a new pitch just before the grenade went off. After it exploded, there were far fewer voices.

But three aliens were in the living room with the Marines. One of them leaped on Lance Corporal Fernando Garcia and another attacked Cafferata, trying to get beyond him to the window. The third darted around aimlessly.

Garcia luckily managed to get his rifle up to block the leaping alien that swung talons on the ends of its short arms at him. The Marine's arms were enough longer to keep the talons from ripping into his chest, but they gouged deep furrows in both of his arms, sending blood shooting out. PFC Harry Harvey, a bare meter away, slammed the butt of his rifle into the alien's head, knocking it away from Garcia before it could do any further damage to the wounded Marine. Orndoff was close enough that he could reach Garcia before anybody else. He ran to the wounded Marine and yanked the draperies from the windows to wrap around Garcia's arms to staunch the bleeding.

Dazed, the alien was slow getting back to its feet, but that short delay was all Harvey needed to drop his rifle and get to it to snap its neck over his knee, the way Mackie had killed one of the aliens on Mini Mouse. The alien went into spasms, and its arms and legs flailed about, its head flopping about from the break in its neck. Harvey picked up his rifle, stomped on the alien's neck just below its jaw, and shot it in the head. Its spasms stopped. Harvey turned to Garcia, and found that Orndoff was already stopping the bleeding.

Cafferata was turning to see what was going on inside the room when the alien jumped at him, so it didn't hit him with its full force. It was still enough to knock him away from the window. The alien ignored the Marine now that he wasn't blocking the window; it tried to jump through it, but bounced back—it hadn't realized the clear glass meant the window was closed—right into Hill, who grabbed it high on its neck and whirled around. Something snapped, and the alien let out a distressed *caw*. It ran about chaotically, its head swinging from its high-held neck, until Cafferata swung his rifle at its legs, taking them out from under it. Hill jumped feet first on the alien's chest. Bones snapped loudly.

The third alien suddenly stopped its aimless dashing about and looked at the situation it found itself in. Six Marines were facing it, holding their weapons ready to use one way or another to bring it down.

Martin was the only one who hadn't been involved with the other aliens, and was waiting for the alien to stop long enough for him to get off a shot. He fired just as the alien bolted for the bedroom hallway. He missed.

Mackie heard the shot and turned to look. The alien was jinking side to side as it sped down the hallway, but the hall was narrow enough that it couldn't dodge widely. Mackie began firing after it, as did Martin. They were never later able to tell which of them hit the alien, but it crashed to the floor, bleeding profusely. Mackie ran to it, knocked its weapon out of reach, and put a bullet through its head.

"Cease fire!" Martin ordered. When everybody stopped shooting, he listened very carefully. Gunfire and the shouts of Marines in battle came from other houses, but he didn't hear any noises in his squad's house other than the small noises his squad was making.

"Mackie, give 'em another grenade."

"Aye aye, honcho." Mackie stepped to the side of the dining room door and threw a grenade hard around the jam. No cries, no scrabbling joined the *thunking* of the grenade as it bounced in the room, no cries followed the explosion.

Martin got on his comm to report to Commiskey. It took a moment for the lieutenant to answer his call.

"Report, One," Commiskey said over the background sound of gunfire.

"We seem to have beaten them off, Six. What the hell's going on over there?" Martin replied.

"Same as with you, One. Everybody got hit. We're driving them back."

Martin shuddered. "Do you have any casualties?"

"Only one. Doc's patching him now. How many do you have?"

"Also one WIA." Martin looked at Garcia; the bandages on his wounds seemed to be holding. "I think he'll be all right until a corpsman can get to us."

"It shouldn't be a long wait." It sounded that way to Martin, the fire was slackening off.

"I'll let you know when Doc's on his way. Have you checked the entire house yet?"

"No, Sir, that's my next step."

"Do it, then report back. Six out."

Martin looked at Mackie, nodded toward the dining room and said, "Take a look."

Mackie took a deep, steadying breath, and flung himself through the doorway, to land prone on the floor next to the dining table, facing the kitchen and aiming his rifle at the door.

"Second fire team, collect the weapons," Martin ordered.

Vittori and his two men gathered the aliens' weapons, first the ones in the doorway, then the ones near the dozen dead or dying in the dining room. They piled the weapons in the living room, away from the dining room door, and stacked the bodies at the end of the dining room opposite the kitchen. Two of the aliens were still alive. Martin ordered their hands tied off, and for them to be placed back to back, with their elbows lashed together.

"Think they'll survive?" Vittori asked.

"I don't give a good goddam," Martin said. He glanced at the two, bleeding from multiple wounds. "How's Garcia?" he asked Orndoff.

"He's been better."

"I'll be fine as soon as a corpsman dresses my wounds," Garcia said.

"Sure you will," Martin said, but he didn't believe it. Garcia's voice was weak, and he looked pale from blood loss. "Doc's on his way."

Turning to the rest of the squad, Martin said, "All right, let's check out the kitchen and the basement. If these two are still alive after that, we'll see what we can do about stopping their bleeding."

There were another five bodies in the kitchen and three more on the stairs to the basement.

The basement was one large, bare room.

"All right, where'd they come from?" Martin said. There weren't any exits other than the stairs the Marines had come down. "Nobody was here when we moved in. So how the hell'd they get down here?"

Nobody had an answer.

"We need the engineers to check this place out."

They had killed nearly twenty of the aliens and captured two more. Garcia was the only wounded Marine. They had trouble believing their good luck.

"We had experience from Mini Mouse," Martin told his men. "If it hadn't been for that, we most likely would have lost more men just now." He looked at the stacked corpses. "Maybe none of them had combat experience."

Expeditionary Air Field, Jordan, Eastern Shapland

LIEUTENANT COLONEL RAY DAVIS, COMMANDING OFFICER OF 3RD BATTALION, 1ST Marines, watched from inside the operation center as four speeding dots resolved into four Marine Kestrels that took station orbiting the expeditionary air field a couple of hundred meters above the ground, ready to pounce on any threat. Another division of four Kestrels began orbiting higher up, watching for any threat that might approach on land or in the air. A C126VEC "Bulldog," VIP transport/electronic warfare/command and control aircraft following the Kestrels touched down and came to a stop a hundred meters away from the OpCen. Only then did Davis step outside. He did his best to ignore the buffeting wind, even though the wind was what had kept him inside until nearly the last minute. The hatch on the side of the Bulldog opened just as a short stairway rolled up to it. A Marine appeared in the open hatch, looked around, fixed on Davis, and marched down the stairs. Another Marine, and a third followed him and marched just to his rear and left when they reached the field's decking.

Davis met them halfway, came to attention and raised his right hand in salute. "Welcome to Marine Corps Station Jordan, Sir," he said. The wind almost blew his words away.

Lieutenant General Bauer crisply returned the salute, paused for 1st Marines' commander Colonel Justice Chambers to trade salutes with Davis, then gripped his hand with both of his to shake. Chambers returned the salute of Bauer's aide, Captain Upshur.

"You beat them all off successfully?" Bauer asked without preamble as the three started toward a waiting ground car—they had to lean into the wind.

"My men did, Sir." Davis shook his head. "Most of the action was inside the houses where individual squads were billeted. There was very little I or any other officers could do to affect the fighting—especially as most command elements were also under attack and fighting off the aliens."

Bauer shook his head. Not in disbelief, but in something closer to awe. "It was a squad leader's war."

"It certainly was, Sir. Even when they hit in Officer Country, the command elements had to fight like squads."

"Most of the command elements were attacked?"

"Nearly every one of them, Sir."

"And every attack came from inside the houses?

"From the basements, yes, Sir."

The driver of the ground car stood holding the door firmly with one hand to keep the wind from banging it against the vehicle's side. He didn't stand at attention or salute, and his rifle was in his other hand while he looked around for threats. The three officers entered the car, Davis then Chambers with Bauer last.

When they were seated, Bauer asked, "Is it usually that windy here?"

"No, Sir. It's just that the ground has been so thoroughly cleared around the air field that there's nothing to break the wind."

Bauer nodded his understanding, then got to the reason he was visiting the Marines in Jordan.

"You haven't found any way they could have gotten into the basements before the attacks?"

"That's right, Sir. That's why I requested engineers with ground penetrating radar. There have to be tunnels below the houses, and hidden entrance into the basements. So far, none of my people have been able to find an egress."

"You're going to show me some of the houses." It wasn't a question.

"Our first stop is one of the houses India Company's Third platoon was in. It was one of the most successful at fighting off the aliens."

Bauer thought for a moment. "India's First platoon. One of its squads wiped out a couple of squads worth of the aliens on Mini Mouse, didn't it?"

"Yes, Sir. The very squad we're about to visit, as a matter of fact."

"And they were one of the most successful in repelling the aliens here?"

"That's right, Sir."

Bauer grunted. "Experience makes all the difference in the world."

Number 8, Sugar Clover Place, Jordan, Eastern Shapland

"Attention on deck!" Lance Corporal Mackie shouted when he saw Bauer and the other officers step onto the house's veranda. He raced to the door, threw it open, and stepped aside at attention. Bauer graced him with a curt nod as he walked in.

"Who's in command here?" he asked.

"Second Lieutenant Commiskey, Sir," Davis answered.

"Were you in this house during the fight, Mr. Commiskey?" Bauer asked.

"No, Sir. That was Sergeant Martin," Commiskey said. "He was in command here during the fight."

"You were involved in your own firefight at the time?"

"That's right, Sir."

"We'll get to that later. Right now I want to find out about this one." Bauer looked at the other Marines in the room. "Sergeant Martin?"

"Here, Sir." Martin took a step toward the general.

"Walk me through it, Sergeant."

"Aye aye, Sir. It started when Lance Corporal Mackie, he's the one by the door, saw a Duster in the doorway..."

"Duster?" Bauer interrupted Martin.

"Yes, Sir. Those feather things on their tails make them look like feather dusters. So we're calling them 'Dusters' for short."

"This squad has had more contact with them than any other, you've earned the right to name them. So that's what I'll call the aliens, too. Dusters. Continue, please."

"Yes, Sir. Mackie saw a Duster in the dining room door and blew him away."

"Sir," Mackie said, "by your leave, General, Sir, it was PFC Orndoff who saw the Duster first."

"But you shot it?"

"Yes, Sir, I did."

"Very good." Bauer turned back to Martin. "You were saying, Sergeant."

"Right, Sir. After PFC Orndoff saw the Duster and Lance Corporal Mackie shot it... ." Martin related the battle, showing Bauer the captured weapons, the blood stains on the flooring, and the rooms the action took place in, finishing in the basement. "We can't figure out how they got down here. There has to be a hidden doorway, because we checked this place from top to bottom when we first moved in, and the basement was empty."

"Are you saying you checked because you wanted to make sure there wasn't anybody hiding here?"

"No, Sir," Martin said with an embarrassed laugh. "We were looking to see if there was anything left behind that we could use."

"Of course. Now, where are the bodies?"

"They're in the back, Sir," Commiskey said, "waiting to be picked up."

"Show me."

Behind the house were two rows of bent corpses; legs that wouldn't go straight along the axis of the bodies, long necks that held serpentine curves even in death. There were ten corpses in each row, naked except for leather-like straps with pouches on them.

Bauer looked at Martin. "Now your casualties."

"Lance Corporal Garcia, Sir." Martin indicated a Marine with bandaged arms. "He's the only one."

"And you had two prisoners?"

"*Had* is the right word, Sir. One of them died. That one." He pointed to a corpse at the end of the nearer row. "Battalion S2 collected the live one."

Bauer spent a moment looking at the alien corpses, then at Garcia.

"Mr. Commiskey, how many casualties did your platoon have in total?"

"Sir, we had two KIA and six wounded, including Lance Corporal Garcia."

"Against how many aliens?"

"More than sixty, Sir."

Bauer nodded, as though to himself. "All in confined spaces, rather than in the open."

"That's right, Sir."

The general turned back to Martin. "You have an outstanding squad, Sergeant. He looked at the rest of the squad. "All of you. You performed here today in the highest tradition of the Marine Corps." Back to Martin: "Is there anything you could have used to make your victory more decisive?"

"Yes, Sir, there is." Martin glanced at the bodies. "They move fast, and really jink when they run. Just like in the vids we saw onboard ship coming here, and like we ran into on Mini Mouse. We need scatter guns. Weapons that will hit a rapidly moving target with something other than a lucky shot. If they hadn't been in confined spaces, if they'd been able to move like they can in the open, we might have been in serious trouble."

"I'll see what I can do. Semper Fi, Marines. Let me say again, you did an outstanding job." Bauer turned to walk around the side of the house.

"I want to see a couple more squads, make sure one of them is one that didn't do so well," Bauer said to Davis. "I also want to see a company command element and your headquarters."

He said to Upshur, "Make a note, I am requesting thirty thousand shotguns, and a month's supply of ammunition for them."

Back to Davis, "I understand that your command elements had higher casualty rates than the squads did, is that correct?"

"Yes, Sir, it is," Davis said, sounding distinctly unhappy. "I lost twenty-three officers and seventeen staff NCOs. Most of the elements were smaller than the squads, and none of them were as well armed."

"Do whatever reorganizing you have to in order to rebuild your command structures. I'll see what I can do about replacing officers and senior NCOs." He paused in thought for a second. "Some of the losses can be made up with promotions and brevet commissions from the ranks. Look into who deserves it."

They reached the ground car. Bauer paused before getting in, looking at the sky and surrounding trees. "It's amazing how trees can cut down on the wind."

After Davis gave the driver direction to their next stop, Bauer asked Davis about the rest of the battalion's casualties.

"In addition to the casualties in the various command groups, I lost more than fifty NCOs and junior enlisted, both KIA and wounded badly enough to require evacuation to ship-board medical facilities."

Bauer refrained from asking how many aliens had died. "Let's get on with this show."

Admiral's Cabin, NAUS Durango, in Orbit Around Troy

Ships of the NAU Navy that were configured for flagship designation had marvelous capabilities undreamt of by any other than the most pie-in-the-sky dreamers of earlier naval planners. Among them was the automatic monitoring of all friendly communications in nearby space, including planetary surfaces and atmospheres. And monitor surface communications was exactly what Rear Admiral Avery did during the alien attack on the Marines in Jordan.

"Distraught" was not too strong a word to use in describing Avery's state of mind at the time. He was still extremely upset over the nearly total loss of ARG 17 and still blamed himself for the loss. As distraught as Admiral Avery was, and as intent as he was on listening to the communications among the squads in Jordan, it didn't occur to him to also monitor communications from the Marines in and around Millerton and the McKinzie Elevator Base. If it had occurred to him, and if he had acted on it, he would have realized that the only combat was in Jordan, and only involved one battalion of Marines—a fairly small portion of the Marine strength on Troy.

Being distraught and possessing only limited intelligence is a very bad combination for a commander—it can lead to mistakes.

Avery made a mistake. More than one, as a matter of fact.

His first was continuing to blame himself for the loss of most of ARG17. After paying attention to an entirely too small part of Troy, he blamed himself for the alien attack on the Marines in Jordan, and—without consulting anyone more familiar with ground combat than he was—assumed the results of the battle were worse than they in fact were.

His greatest mistake was concluding that the Marines planetside were being defeated, were about to be driven out of their planethead. Or at least from Jordan and probably all of Eastern Shapland.

He quickly, again without conferring with anyone, prepared a message to be sent via drone to the North American Union's Supreme Military Headquarters on Earth. After drawing a bleak picture of what had happened to ARG17 and was happening planetside the message concluded:

Issue in doubt.

Three words immediately recognizable to anyone familiar with the first days of the old United States of America's involvement in the world-spanning war that took place in the middle of the twentieth century.

First MCF Headquarters, Outside Millerton

"Captain Upshur," Bauer said as he entered his HQ building, "prepare a message to send to Earth via Navy drone. I don't care if they have to open a wormhole for just this purpose."

Upshur positioned his comp to take the information needed for Bauer's message. "Ready, Sir."

"You heard the replacements Chambers and Davis asked for? Double the number. You have my note about shotguns and shells? Add a month's supply of grapeshot for our artillery. Add a company of engineers with lots of ground penetrating radar and tunneling equipment. Say why I want them. Got it all?"

"All of it, Sir."

"Hand deliver it to Townsend on the *Durango*. I don't want to take the chance of it getting misplaced, or put into routine routing."

"Aye aye, Sir. By your leave?"

"Go. Let me know when you get back."

Comm Shack, NAUS Durango, in Orbit

"Captain Upshur!" Lieutenant Townsend exclaimed on seeing Bauer's aide. "What brings you to orbit?"

"Lieutenant," Upshur said, extending a hand to his Navy counterpart. "I heard a rumor, probably false, that the Navy has excellent coffee, and thought I'd come up for a mug of it."

Townsend laughed. "Not false. The NAU Navy has the best coffee in the entire universe. And you're more than welcome to a mug—or more. Let's head for the ward room and you can tell me why else you're here."

"Before we go to the ward room for some of that delicious coffee, I need a favor. Or General Bauer needs it."

"Oh? And what might the distinguished general want?"

Upshur drew a crystal from his jacket pocket. "A message to SecWar and the President."

"Has Admiral Avery seen it?" Townsend said, taken aback.

Upshur shook his head. "Not unless he radioed a copy to him since I left his HQ. He said he doesn't want this to get bogged down in any routine handling. He also said that if necessary I should make you open a wormhole to send it."

Townsend considered the crystal before taking it. "All right. It so happens that a wormhole is opening in a few hours. I just sent a drone to Earth from the admiral. I can send off another drone right now and it should reach the wormhole before it closes again."

"Thanks, Julius. You've just earned the gratitude of a Marine lieutenant general."

"Not something to be taken lightly." Townsend set about getting the crystal into a drone for immediate launch for Earth.

The ward room coffee was just as good as rumored.

The War Room, Supreme Military Headquarters, Bellevue, Sarpy County, Federal Zone, NAU

A day after Admiral Avery's two messages about the attack on ARG17 reached Earth, his "issue in doubt" message arrived.

It took a week for the messages to reach Earth, where they were promptly delivered to NAU President Mills and Secretary of War Hobson. Hobson took no action on receipt of the initial messages; he needed more information. But when he read the third one...

Knowing that the President didn't necessarily read his messages from offworld as soon as he received them, Hobson chose to call him rather than wait for the President to contact him first. He was right, Mills hadn't yet gotten around to reading the message.

"'Issue in doubt,' what does that mean?" Mills asked when he finished reading.

"It means, Sir, that Admiral Avery thinks the Marines on Troy will be defeated by the aliens."

There was silence for a moment before Mills asked somewhat shakily, "When was the last time that happened? That anybody defeated our Marines?"

Hobson didn't have to think about it, he knew. "Not in my lifetime or yours."

"Then how can it happen this time?"

"We went in having no idea of the enemy's strength. If there are enough of them, or if they're heavily enough armed, they could do it."

"So what can we do?

"I don't know yet. Nobody but you and I know about Avery's messages. I am meeting with the Joint Chiefs this afternoon."

"Now, now this message is from the Navy commander. What does the Marine commander have to say about the situation?"

"We haven't heard from General Bauer. For all I know, he was killed in the action Avery describes."

"Gods," Mills murmured, remembering the pics and vids he'd seen of the original alien attack on Troy. He pulled himself together and asked in a firm voice, "Didn't you order a large follow-on force to be stood up?"

"Yes, I did. The Second Army."

"What's its status?"

"Its command structure is in place, and most of its component elements have been identified. The Navy is still working on finding enough shipping to transport that large a force."

"How long will it be before Second Army will be ready to go?"

Hobson stifled a sigh. As knowledgeable as Mills was in political matters, he was quite ignorant about the military.

"That's not the question," he said with more patience than he felt. "The right question is, what are we up against on Troy. Until we hear from General Bauer, or whoever is the ranking remaining Marine on the ground, we simply don't know enough to even make a guess."

Mills took a deep breath. "All right, what are you going to do?"

"As I said, I'm meeting with the Joint Chiefs this afternoon. Then we will begin deciding what to do."

Mills took another deep breath. "Keep me appraised," he said.

"I will do that, Mr. President. I most assuredly will." *And if things go to hell in a handbasket, I'll assuredly find a way to lay the blame on you.*

17

The War Room, Supreme Military Headquarters,
Bellevue, Sarpy County, Federal Zone, NAU

Ignatz Gresser was already waiting in the War Room when the Joint Chiefs of Staff's Director of Intelligence, Major General Joseph de Castro, arrived.

"Mr. Gresser," de Castro greeted the President's special assistant.

"General," Gresser said with a nod. He rose from the seat he was occupying at the foot of the long table and extended his hand to de Castro. It was the kind of handshake exchanged between men who know each other mostly by reputation rather than men who know and respect each other personally.

"You're the intelligence guy, right?" Gresser asked once they were both seated. De Castro, the lowest ranking military man who would attend the meeting was also at the lower end of the table.

"They've been calling me that for most of my career," de Castro said with a chuckle, "but you're the first civilian to use that term on me."

"I hope I didn't offend you."

"Not at, not at all. Intelligence is my game. To demonstrate, I sensed another question behind that one."

Gresser nodded. "Intelligence on more than one sense, eh? You're right, President Mills got the distinct impression from SecWar that the Marines were just about wiped out on Troy. Is that really the situation?"

De Castro held a steady look on Gresser for several seconds, betraying nothing, before saying, "That's about the situation as I first heard it."

Gresser raised an eyebrow. "As you *first* heard it?"

"As you first heard what?" said another voice.

The two turned toward the door and saw Army Chief of Staff General John C. Robinson entering the War Room.

"Mr. Gresser was just trying to get a step up on everybody, that's all," de Castro said blandly. "Don't worry, he probably doesn't know anything that you don't. At least if he does he didn't get it from me."

Gresser blushed.

Robinson moved to the top of the table and took the seat at the left hand of the head chair, opposite where the Chairman would sit. "I hope somebody has a step up. All I've heard is we ran into a shitstorm on Troy, and are in danger of becoming one of those ruins-planets like we've found a few times."

De Castro shook his head. "My analysis suggests it's not that bad. Not quite."

"Your analysis is why you're here, of course," said Commandant of the Marine Corps, General Ralph Talbot as he stepped into the room. He looked grim.

"Keep your seats," Hobson said, striding in directly behind Talbot. The Chairman of the Joint Chiefs, Fleet Admiral Ira Welborn, came in with the Secretary of War.

Hobson glanced around and snarled, "Where the hell's Madison?"

"I'm here, Sir," Madison said, sounding out of breath. His face was flushed; he must have run to get to the meeting.

"Secure the door behind yourself," Hobson ordered. He took his seat at the head of the table while the CNO closed the door, completing the seal that blocked all signals, audible or electronic, from leaving the room.

"You've all read Avery's messages." It wasn't a question; he'd immediately have the resignation of any member of the Joint Chiefs who hadn't read it. "Comments."

"I'm still absorbing the loss of VII Corps," Robinson said. "Admiral Avery wasn't very clear on which ships were killed. We need to find out what elements are still combat capable." He shook his head sadly. "Lyman is a major loss to the Army."

Hobson grunted. "Next."

"I'm embarrassed," Madison said. "I had no idea Callighan was that incompetant."

"Explain yourself," Welborn snapped.

Madison started at being spoken to so sharply. "Why... why, what other excuse could there be for losing an entire ARG?" he sputtered.

"The ships of the ARG were unarmed, and Rear Admiral Callighan had no reason to believe his group would be attacked, much less the way it was."

"But—."

"Next," Hobson cut him off. Not for the first time, he thought he needed a new CNO.

Next was Talbot. "Lieutenant General Bauer is one of the best officers I have ever had the pleasure of knowing. Regardless of what Admiral Avery's message says, it stretches my credulity beyond the willing suspension of disbelief to think that his entire MCF could have been destroyed, or that it could be forced to evacuate the planet after only one action."

"Of course a Marine would think like that," Madison said, having regained his composure. He didn't notice the hard look Hobson directed at him.

"General de Castro, what is your analysis?" Hobson asked.

De Castro held up a finger. "We don't know how much of ARG 17 survived the attack." He raised a second finger. "Therefore, we do not know how much of VII Corps is still combat capable." A third finger went up. "Fully aside from the Marines' well-known propensity for self-aggrandizement, I agree with Commandant Talbot, the First MCF has not been defeated." He glanced at Talbot. "Which isn't to say they won't be. We need more intelligence. The question at this point is, how do we get it?" He looked at Madison. "My analysis suggests that the Navy send a surveillance ship to scan the system from the mouth of a wormhole."

"Sir," Gresser raised his hand. "Before we get to that, please excuse my ignorance, but just what does 'issue in doubt' mean?"

Hobson scowled. "It's a very polite way of saying that the most probable outcome of the situation in question is total failure."

Gresser nodded and looked at his hands folded on the tabletop in front of him. That was what he thought, he'd just wanted confirmation. It was evident to him that President Mills thought so, too.

"If I may, Sir?" Talbot said to SecWar. When Hobson signaled his consent, the Commandant said to the President's assistant, "A Navy officer sent that message early in a twentieth century war. The Marines believed they could have held out until a relief force arrived. But the message convinced higher command not to send relief. So the Marines and others—the ones who weren't killed when they surrendered—spent four years in prisoner of war camps."

"You sound like you think we should send more troops," Gresser said.

"I think the battle's not lost until the last infantryman is rooted out."

"Enough of the sidetalk," Hobson snapped. "Madison, I asked you a question. Can you send a stealth starship to gather intelligence from near the mouth of a wormhole in the Troy system?"

The CNO made a moue. "Yes we can," he said grudgingly. "But it will be risky. We don't know what kind of security the aliens have out there. They might have warships stationed at every possible wormhole entry point and ready to fire as soon as one opens."

"That's why it's called, 'going in harm's way,' Madison." Hobson shook his head disgustedly.

"Robinson, how is Second Army coming along?"

"The major command elements are in place and most of the component elements have been identified," the Army Chief of Staff said. "I'm not sure about the Marines." He looked a question at Talbot.

"Second and Third MCFs are on 96 hour standby for the personnel. Their major equipment can start moving to the elevators as soon as transportation is provided. Does that answer your question about Marine readiness, General?"

Robinson smiled faintly as he nodded at the Marine.

Hobson nodded, satisfied by Talbot's response. "Robinson, start putting the component elements of Second Army on standby. Madison, begin assembling naval transportation. Welborn, I'll leave arranging the civilian auxillary to you. De Castro, coordinate with Madison on your intelligence needs. Unless somebody else has something important, that's it for this meeting."

Nobody else had anything, so they all stood to leave. Hobson was the last out. He turned toward his office, and looked curiously at a man running toward him.

"Sir," Joseph Gion, Hobson's Chief of Staff called out as he hustled along the corridor, "I think you'll want to call everybody back."

"What? Why?" Hobson asked, startled. "All of you," he called to the Chiefs of Staff, "wait one!" He looked at Gion. "What do you have?" he asked and snatched the flimsy Gion held out to him. He quickly scanned it, asked, "When did this come in?" and ordered the Joint Chiefs back into the War Room when told the message had arrived only ten minutes earlier.

Closed back in the War Room, Hobson held the flimsy out. "The Commandant was right. The Marines have not been defeated on Troy. I'll get you all copies of this later, but right now I'll read the most germane sentences. 'Elements of First MCF have twice encountered the alien invaders and decisively defeated them on each occasion.'

"That's one item, the other is a request; he wants 30,000 shotguns and a month's combat load of ammunition for them, and canister for his artillery. He also requests two thousand additional Marines, including a Whiskey Company for each of the regiments in the MCF along with enough additional officers of appropriate ranks to staff a battalion."

"What's a Whiskey Company?" Madison asked.

Hobson nodded at Talbot to answer.

"It's a company-size unit outside the normal compliment of a battalion or regiment, used specifically as either a reserve or be doled out piecemeal to companies as replacements for casualties."

The Round Room, the Prairie Palace, Omaha,
Douglas County, Federal Zone, NAU

"What the hell's the matter with those people?" President Mills roared. "Don't they talk to each other?" He had just read Bauer's message, which thoroughly contradicted the message from Avery, which he'd read scant hours earlier.

"Evidently not in this instance," Hobson said calmly.

"What next?" Mills demanded. "Is someone else going to send a message saying that A R—, A R..., whatever the hell it was called, is fine and landed that Army force?"

"No, Sir, I don't believe we will get any such message. I believe Admiral Avery was right when he said ARG 17 was severely injured. Possibly even as nearly destroyed as he said. What's next, Sir, is the Joint Chiefs have begun mounting a larger force to retake Troy. The Navy is shortly going to request permission to commandeer a large segment of civilian interstellar shipping to augment its own fleet."

"The Navy doesn't have enough shipping of its own?" Mills asked, astounded.

"We've never had this large a force to send at one time."

Mills rapidly looked side to side, twisting from his shoulders, as though seeking something he knew wasn't there. "All right," he finally said, "what do you suggest?"

"Let me give the Chiefs the go-ahead."

"What about Congress?"

Hobson shrugged. "What about Congress? How did the honorables react when you told them about Troy and our response in the first place?"

"They'd already voted me war powers," Mills said softly, almost a murmur.

"There you are. Congress abdicated its war waging responsibility. They gave it to you, Mr. President. Congress can't do anything, not without revoking the war powers. I imagine that would be a lengthy process."

Mills studied Hobson from under lowered brows. "Do you think we'll succeed if we take the next step?"

"Bauer seems confident. And Talbot has the highest confidence in him. The rest of the Chiefs also have confidence in the Marines, at least in their ability to hold out until Second Army reaches them."

Someone had once told Mills that a mark of a great leader was to make snap decisions based on incomplete information. He had tried to follow that dictum during a long and successful political career. So far it had worked well for him.

"Do it," he said. "Send that army to relieve the Marines."

A Wormhole, Troy Space

A non-human fleet began disgorging.

Ends Book I

Issue in Doubt

—IN ALL—
DIRECTIONS

DAVID SHERMAN

On being told that his regiment was surrounded at Koto-ri
during the withdrawal from the Chosin Resevoir,
Colonel Lewis B. "Chesty" Puller,
commander of the 1st Marine Regiment,
is reputed to have said,
"We've got them right where we want them.
Now we can shoot in all directions!"

This book is dedicated to the memory of:

Hospital Apprentice First Class
David E. Hayden

Awarded the Medal of Honor
While serving with 2nd Battalion, 6th Marines
Battle of Saint-Mihiel
September 15, 1918

ACKNOWLEDGEMENTS

I want to thank the members of 17th Street Writers of Fort Lauderdale for their very helpful comments during the writing of *In All Directions*, particularly Anita, Christopher, Fatima, Gregory, Mona, Pat, Roy, and Stu—the irregulars.

PROLOG

A wormhole, 30 AU from
the Semi-Autonomous World Troy

A NON-HUMAN FLEET BEGAN DISGORGING FROM THE WORMHOLE.

Because of its location before the Scattered Disc of Troy's system, and due to the fact that the fleet waited until all of its ships were assembled, it was nearly a month before the human fleets close to the planet noticed it.

Firebase Zion, Company I, Third Battalion,
1st Marines, West Shapland
Semi-Autonomous World Troy

"FIRST SQUAD UP!" SERGEANT JAMES MARTIN CALLED AS HE APPROACHED HIS SQUAD'S area. Two nervous-looking strangers carrying rifles and full field packs followed him. The packs looked new.

It took little more than a minute for the ten Marines of his squad to gather in front of their leader. They cast curious glances at the new men.

"Listen up," Martin said. "We're a skosh bit under strength. Or we were. This is PFC William Horton." He indicated one of the strangers who stood off to one side behind him. "He's the replacement for Zion." A cloud briefly washed across his face at his mention of the Marine who'd been killed in an earlier action. He looked at Corporal William Button, the Second fire team leader. "Can't give him to you, Bill. Two Williams in the same fire team might make for confusion." To Horton, he said, "The William we've already got has been here longer, and he's got stripes on you. So if we use first names, you're Billy. Got that?"

Horton grimaced, but nodded and said, "All right, Sergeant, I'm Billy. But I'd rather just be 'Horton'."

"Good, that's settled. Mackie, he's replacing a man from your fire team, that makes him yours."

"But Sergeant Martin," Corporal John Mackie objected, "Zion was in First fire team, I've got Third."

"Shitcan that, Mackie. What was First fire team is now Third. You and Orndoff are still in the same fire team, and you're short-handed. I already gave you Cafferata, now you get Horton to get back to full strength. No more crap. Got it?"

"Yes, Sergeant," Mackie said. "You," he pointed a finger at Horton, then at his feet, "over here." He ignored the look Martin gave him.

"Continuing," Martin said, "Button, you get PFC Herbert Preston. Go," he told Preston, and gestured toward Corporal William Button, the leader of Second fire team.

Martin looked at his squad, at full strength for the first time since their initial combat on Troy. "You're probably wondering where these replacements came from. No, more Marines haven't joined us. Lieutenant Colonel Davis is reassigning support personnel to keep the rifle companies up to strength. Horton was a clerk in the battalion headquarters company, and Preston was a mechanic in the battalion motor pool."

He raised a hand and patted the air to quell any protests before they were voiced. "As you were, people," he said loudly. "No matter what their duty was yesterday, they're Marines. Remember, every Marine is a rifleman. It's been like that ever since Marines were climbing the rigging of wooden ships on water seas and firing down at the decks of enemy ships, shooting enemy officers and cannoneers. Every Marine goes to the rifle range every year to fire for requalification, so you know that they know how to shoot."

"But do they know how to duck?" Lance Corporal Hermann Kuchneister blurted.

"Don't sweat it, they'll catch on in a hurry," Corporal Joseph Vittori said.

"Duck, hell," Mackie said, looking askance at Horton. "Do they know how to snoop and poop?"

"As you were!" Martin roared. "They're Marines, they've been trained. They know what to do."

"Trained but inexperienced," Lance Corporal Cafferata whispered to Mackie.

Martin ignored that and other quiet remarks from members of the squad. "They're with us now," he said. "We're back up to strength. I want you to return to your positions and get acquainted with the new Marines." His mouth twisted before he added, "Your lives might depend on how well you know the new men."

Their positions were three bunkers, one per fire team, inside the wire of Camp Zion, which was named after the first member of India Company to be killed in action on Troy.

"Inside, Horton," Mackie said when Third fire team reached their bunker.

Horton dropped into the beginning of the entrance tunnel, a meter-deep pit. The tunnel itself went in two sandbags deep before taking a ninety-degree turn for a meter and a half, then another ninety-degree turn to the interior of the bunker.

Mackie followed Horton while Cafferata and PFC Orndoff went around to the front of the bunker and sat on its forward edge, facing the land beyond the perimeter.

"Stow it there," Mackie said, pointing at an unoccupied section of wall. "There's the grenade sump." He pointed at a hole dug in the floor of a corner. Any hand-held explosive thrown into the bunker could be knocked into the hole and its explosion contained. That was the theory; none of the Marines ever wanted the chance to test it.

Horton dutifully dropped his pack where Mackie indicated, then uncertainly stood waiting, hunched over because of the low overhead.

Mackie studied his new man in the dim, uneven light that the bunker's firing aperture offered. "You were a clerk, huh?" he said before the silence became uncomfortable.

"That's right, Corporal Mackie."

"Just Mackie. Unless an officer is nearby. We don't stand much on formality here."

"Right, Corp—, ah, right, Mackie."

"Do you have *any* combat experience?"

Horton shook his head. "No."

"Did you even come under fire anytime?"

Another headshake, another, "No."

Mackie stared at him for a moment. "Pay attention to me, Cafferata, and Orndoff. Do what we do, and obey my orders immediately. That's your best chance of making it through alive and uninjured. I already lost one man. I don't want to lose another."

"Yes, Corp—,ah, yes, Mackie. I'll do my best."

Mackie nodded curtly. "Let's go topside and meet the rest of the fire team."

Horton's meeting of the rest of the fire team was brief, not very in depth, and not in any particular order.

"Where are you from?"

"Illinois."

"Have you ever been in a rifle company before?"

"No."

"Are you married? Do you have a steady girl?"

"I used to, but she broke up with me right before we got orders to Troy."

Nobody remarked on that, but they all thought it was a bad sign. A Marine who just lost his woman might make a serious mistake that could get him or someone else killed. Or maybe it wouldn't be a mistake.

"Who were you with before Three/One?" Mackie asked before Cafferata and Orndoff could dwell on Horton's recent break up.

"I joined Three/One right out of school." They understood the school was Marine administrative training, not Horton's civilian school. And it begged a follow up question:

"How long have you been in?"

"Twenty-one months." Which explained why Three/One was his first duty station; he hadn't been in long enough to complete a tour at one station.

"How do you like getting assigned to the real Marines?" To most infantry Marines, anybody who wasn't a trigger-puller—infantry, recon, artillery, pilots and air crew of armed aircraft, and anybody else whose duties put them in the line of fire—wasn't a real Marine, no matter what uniform they wore or how much rank they had.

"Kind of nervous. It's why I enlisted in the Marines, but now that it's real...."

"Damn skippy, it's real. It doesn't get any realer than this."

"What did you qualify as on the range?"

"High Sharpshooter." That was the second highest marksmanship level.

"You've seen the vids of the Dusters?"

"Yes."

"They move too fast for you to aim at them, but you have to do better than just spray-and-pray," Ordnoff said. "Spray and pray," put out enough rounds fast enough and you're bound to hit something sooner or later.

Then it was time for chow. The sun had almost reached the horizon by the time First squad finished eating and moved into their overnight defensive positions, which were the same bunkers they slept in, the same bunkers facing the perimeter and the cleared ground beyond.

Overnight

"Have you stood much perimeter duty?" Mackie asked Horton once Third fire team was in its bunker; he'd assigned first watch to himself and the new man.

"Not since Infantry School." Horton swallowed to moisten his suddenly dry mouth.

Every new Marine, even cooks and bakers and clerks, went to Infantry School to learn how to be a rifleman before going on to whatever other school might be his destination. The women, many of whom were cooks and bakers and clerks and pilots, also went to Infantry School. If you didn't know how to fight as a rifleman, the Marines didn't want you.

"Then you probably need a refresher course," Mackie said. "The first thing about perimeter duty is knowing what's in front of you, so you can recognize anything that doesn't belong in the middle of the night."

"Right, I remember." Horton looked at Mackie's profile. "Look at all the shapes out there. Watch them as night falls so you know what they look like in the dark, so a shadow doesn't have to move for you to know if it belongs or not."

"That's right. You're doing a good job so far. Or you would be, if you were looking outboard instead of at me."

"Ulp! I—I'm sorry, Corporal Mackie. It's just that it's been...." Flustered, Horton jerked his head to the front and tried to memorize the shapes that were turning into shadows.

"I know, it's just that it's been so long since Infantry School." Mackie looked away from the darkening landscape to his newest man. "That's why I'm giving you a refresher course. Now pay attention and do it right."

Two hours later, Mackie woke Orndoff to take the watch while he and Horton got some sleep. Two more hours, and Orndoff woke Cafferata. After Mackie and Horton had four hours sleep, Cafferata woke them for another watch.

Half an hour into their second watch, Horton tapped Mackie's shoulder, pointed, and whispered, "Does that look right?"

Mackie couldn't tell exactly where Horton pointed, but he'd seen the same shadow jitter. "Wake Cafferata and Orndoff," he whispered back. He toggled his helmet comm to the squad freq and notified everyone awake that something was making movement at his eleven o'clock, distance undetermined.

Cafferata and Orndoff took their positions at the firing aperture. They'd made less noise waking and moving into position than Horton had in moving to wake them.

A couple of minutes later, Sergeant Martin came on the squad freq. "My motion detector shows multiple movements, two hundred and fifty meters out. They're all across the squad's front and lapping onto the rest of the platoon."

Seconds later, Second Lieutenant Henry Commiskey, the platoon commander, spoke on the platoon's all-hands freq. "Everyone is reporting movement all around the firebase, we're surrounded. That also means they're in a circular firing squad formation. Stay low, and they'll be shooting each other. The Skipper is ordering illum. Don't fire until the lights go on. Acknowledge." The other platoon commanders gave the same order.

Then began the ritual: junior men reported to fire team leaders that they heard and understood the company commander's order, fire team leaders reported to squad leaders, squad leaders to platoon commanders, and back to the company commander. It didn't take many seconds for every man in the company to report up the chain of command that he had received and understood the order.

"They're closing slowly," Martin said on the squad freq. "Maybe they don't realize we know they're there."

"Stand by in five," Captain Carl Sitter, India Company's commanding officer, said on the all-hands freq.

Five seconds later, there was a series of muffled booms from the middle of the firebase. Just a couple of seconds later, sharper *bangs* sounded in the sky above, and brilliant light flooded the ground outside the perimeter, exposing hundreds of nightmare forms coming toward the wire.

"*Fire!*" Sitter shouted, and all around Marines began blasting away with rifles, machine guns, and grenade launchers.

The Dusters were caught off guard, unaware that the humans had detected them, so they didn't start moving instantly when the flares turned the pre-dawn night into a flickering noon-day brightness. That cost them casualties. The rate of casualties slackened when they began jinking and dodging, too fast for the Marines to take aim.

"Don't shoot where they are," Mackie shouted over the clatter of his men's firing, "shoot where they're going to be!" He saw the flash of a Duster twisting to change its direction and fired a three-round burst into the space he expected it to head. One bullet clipped the base of the Duster's tail and spun it around. He fired off another three, and the Duster staggered, and tumbled to the ground, dropping its weapon as it fell.

He rapidly shot bursts into spaces he thought Dusters were headed into, but usually missed. In his peripheral vision he saw his men firing three-round bursts the same as he was. Most of their bursts also missed, but a few hit. It didn't seem to have much impact on the numbers coming at the perimeter.

Mackie was vaguely aware of projectile hits on the bunker's face, but the Dusters' aim was far off because of their own rapid movement, and nearly all of their shots missed the bunkers altogether.

"Incoming!" Captain Sitter shouted on the all-hands freq.

Over the cacophony of fire from the Marines and Dusters, Mackie made out the whistle of artillery rounds hurtling toward the ground. "Down!" he shouted, and ducked below the lip of the firing aperture.

"Get down!" he shouted again, and grabbed Horton by the arm and jerked; Horton was still up and firing his rifle.

"What?" Horton looked confused.

"Incoming!" The word was drowned out by the sudden eruption of artillery rounds exploding beyond the perimeter. The noise was so great that the impacts of fragments slamming into the front and top of the bunker were felt rather than heard. Mackie was looking away from the barrage, and was able to see the blur of a chunk of jagged metal that flashed through the aperture, to impact against the bunker's rear wall.

The barrage stopped, bringing the bunker to a stunned silence. The noise had been so great that Mackie felt as though his ears were stuffed with cotton. He yawned wide and worked his jaw side to side to clear his hearing. His body felt like it had just gone several rounds with a boxer from a higher weight class. It took a lot of effort for him to force himself up to look out.

"Up!" he shouted when he saw outside. He threw his rifle into his shoulder and began firing again. Almost instantly, Cafferata was also up and firing. Orndoff took a few seconds to rouse himself and resume fighting. Horton remained curled on the bunker's flooring, his eyes wide and mouth gaping.

The Dusters had closed to less than a hundred meters when the artillery barrage began. The concussions had broken some of their bodies, and shrapnel had scythed through many others. But there were so many to begin with that there were still more of them than there were Marines inside the perimeter. And the closest were almost to the wire.

"Get up!" Mackie shouted, and kicked Horton in the ribs, not sure the new man had yet recovered enough that he could hear. He fired a burst at a Duster that was leaping at the wire.

Horton stirred and looked up vaguely.

"Get up!" Another kick. Another burst hit a leaping Duster.

Horton rolled onto his hands and knees and slowly pushed himself up.

"Your weapon, numbnuts! Where's your rifle?" He knocked a Duster down, but it landed on the wire.

Horton looked dumbly down and spotted his rifle. He bent to pick it up, then moved to his firing position and started putting out unaimed bursts.

The lumination flares that had preceded the barrage were dropping close to the ground and burning out. Another round of flares burst overhead. The fresh light showed Dusters throwing themselves onto the wire, pinioning themselves to it, turning their bodies into bridges for other Dusters to scamper across. As Mackie's hearing began to return he heard the fierce, manic *cawing* of the Dusters. He added his voice to all those crying out, "They're inside the wire!"

A Duster raced to the bunker and flattened itself next to the side of the aperture. It shoved the muzzle of its rifle through the opening and began jerking the trigger. Mackie let go of his rifle with one hand and grabbed the barrel of the Duster's with his other hand. He yanked hard and pulled the alien soldier to the front. Cafferata shot it, and his burst threw the thing away.

More Dusters crossed the wire and closed on the fronts of the bunkers. Most of those Dusters were killed quickly, although they managed to wound or kill some Marines. Worse trouble was caused by Dusters that raced around to the rear of the bunkers, where the entrances were.

"Hector, cover the door," Mackie snapped when he saw Dusters racing too far to the side to be coming at the front; he thought they must be going between the bunkers.

Cafferata turned just in time to hear a scrabbling at the bunker's entrance. He didn't wait, but started shooting at the entrance, trying to angle his shots to ricochet around the first corner. He was rewarded by a warbling caw followed by a thump. He sped to the entrance and poked the muzzle of his rifle into it and fired another burst. An anguished *caw* answered.

In front, Mackie saw bodies piling up in front of the bunker, and fewer Dusters coming at him.

A change in the tempo and echoes of firing in the firebase gave testimony to many Dusters attempting to enter the bunkers from their rears. The *caws* and *skrees* of Dusters rang throughout, as did the cries and shouts of many Marines. An occasional shriek told of human casualties.

Mackie was turning to see if Cafferata needed help at the entrance when a yelp next to him spun him back. Orndoff was falling back with a blade of some sort protruding from his chest. Mackie looked past him just in time to see Horton put a burst into the face of the Duster whose bayonet stabbed Orndoff.

"Are you okay, Hector?" he shouted.

"I'm good, honcho," Cafferata shouted back.

Mackie knelt at Orndoff's side. Orndoff was struggling to breathe with the weight of the weapon pressing on his chest. "Take it easy, Marine," Mackie said. "I've cut myself worse than that shaving."

He grasped the Duster rifle to keep it from flopping over and tearing up the Marine's chest. Orndoff gasped in pain from the movement. A quick look showed Mackie how to detach the bayonet. He disengaged it, and tossed the alien rifle away. Orndoff wasn't wearing his gear belt; none of them were. Mackie scrabbled for one and pulled the field dressing out of it. He packed it around the bayonet where it penetrated Orndoff's chest, pressing down onto the wound, sopping up the blood. He grabbed another dressing and added it, doubling the thickness to stop the bleeding. He tied the bandages off with a third dressing.

"Stay there and don't move," Mackie ordered. "Doc'll be here be here most ricky-tick to take care of you."

Orndoff looked at him wide-eyed, and gave a shallow nod.

"Now I gotta get back to work." Mackie gave Orndoff's shoulder a squeeze, and stood to resume fighting.

"How's it look?" he asked Horton. He could see for himself that almost all of the Dusters in sight to the front of the bunkers were down—which was good, as Horton just shrugged in reply. Many of the Dusters lay twisted in ways that couldn't be comfortable, much less natural. Only a few were moving, and none of them seemed to pose a threat. Not even the still-live Dusters who had given themselves up to be bridges over the wire.

"Kill anyone that looks like a threat, and let me know if they mount another charge," Mackie said, clapping Horton on the back. He turned toward the entrance. "How's it going, Hector?"

"It's quiet for now. At least they don't seem to be trying to come in anymore."

Mackie listened for sounds of battle outside his fire team's bunker. He could hear sporadic gunfire and some shouts from human lungs. There weren't many of the caws and shrieks of the Dusters. He toggled on his helmet comm and called Sergeant Martin.

"What's going on out there?" he asked when he got his squad leader. "It's quiet here now, but Orndoff has a chest wound and needs the doc."

"The reports are that most of the Dusters are down," Martin replied. "Hang tight until a corpsman can get to you. Do you have Orndoff stabilized?"

Mackie looked at his wounded man. Even though he was still grimacing, he seemed to be breathing more easily, and hardly any blood was flowing from around the edges of the field dressings. "I think so. He doesn't look like he's going into shock."

"Good. Keep him that way. Look sharp, the Dusters might decide to hit us with another surprise. Martin out."

"Keep me posted," Mackie said, but he knew Martin was no longer listening.

He joined Cafferata at the entrance and listened to the sporadic sounds of fighting elsewhere in the compound, but none close to their bunker. "Keep alert," he said, then went to the front to look out with Horton.

Mackie studied the bodies littering the ground, some broken and dead, others injured. "Any of them moving toward us?" he asked.

"Maybe. Could be. I don't know."

"You better know. If one of them has an explosive and gets close enough to chuck it in, we're screwed. Got it?"

"Y-Yes, Corporal."

"It's Mackie. Just Mackie out here."

"Right. Sorry about that."

"Don't be sorry, just do it." Mackie thought of something. "Keep watching." He scuttled to the section of flooring where his gear was and rooted through it. In a moment he was back with his shaving mirror. Holding it at an angle, he stuck it through the aperture and looked to see if it showed any Dusters laying against the bunker's wall where they couldn't be seen. There weren't any either under the aperture or at the sides of the front.

He realized he hadn't heard any shooting or caws since he'd left Cafferata's side. "Either of you hear anything out there?" he asked.

"I've got nothing," Cafferata answered.

"I don't hear anything," Horton said.

Lieutenant Commiskey came up on the platoon all-hands freq. "It seems the excitement is over. Each squad, put a fire team out to make a sweep through the platoon's area to make sure we don't have anybody faking it."

While Martin was assigning First fire team to join in the sweep, a welcome voice spoke up outside the bunker's entrance. "It's Doc Hayden. I hear you've got a patient for me."

Camp Zion, Aftermath of the battle

THANKS TO SHARP-EYED WATCHERS, MOTION DETECTORS, THE TIMELY USE OF illumination, and close in artillery, India Company suffered a scant ten casualties, two of them killed, during the night attack. PFC Orndoff was the only injury in Third platoon's First squad.

The Dusters were nearly all killed or wounded. The wounded ones had already been gathered into a makeshift open-air dispensary where the company's corpsmen were tending their wounds. Not that they could do much for them other than bandage bleeding wounds and splint broken limbs. They couldn't use any medications to reduce pain or fend off infection, because they had no idea of how the aliens' systems would react to human medicine. Some of the Dusters didn't get any more than the most rudimentary wound coverings—the Corpsmen thought their injuries were so severe they had no chance of surviving more than a few hours without treatment by their own medical personnel, who would know better how to deal with their wounds.

"They aren't very good fighters, are they?" PFC Horton said in the cold light of dawn, looking at the bodies laying on the ground around and between the bunkers, bodies the Marines were gathering into stacks like cordwood. They were like nothing he had ever seen in life. They were man-sized, bent at the hip almost parallel to the ground, balanced on powerful-looking thighs over spindly lower legs that ended in wickedly taloned feet. Their arms looked to be half the length of their legs, and held rifle-like weapons in long-fingered hands. Feathery crests rose above their heads, and ran down the length of their spines to a fan of feathers at the ends of their tails. Their heads jutted forward on the long necks he'd seen whipping side to side during the attack. They had long jaws, filled with rows of sharp, conical teeth. They were naked other than for leathery straps bearing pouches.

Corporal Mackie shook his head. "Don't fool yourself. They got slowed down by the wire, and the concussion of the artillery barrage must have disoriented them. Besides, they had a damn hard time trying to get to us in our bunkers. They're much better fighters than you think." He looked into someplace only he saw. "We're lucky they only killed two Marines this time. They've killed a lot more before." His head shot at Horton. "Who the hell do you think this firebase is named after? A Marine who was in this fire team and got killed by a Duster, that's who. So don't you say they aren't good fighters. You're dead fucking wrong. They can kill you just as dead as I can!"

Horton abruptly took a step back, shocked by the fury in Mackie's voice and eyes. "I—I'm sorry, C-Corporal M-Mackie. I—I didn't mean anything."

Mackie grunted and turned away. He didn't correct Horton on calling him by his rank instead of by just his name.

"Knock off the grab-assing, people!" Staff Sergeant Ambrosio Guillen, the platoon sergeant, bellowed. He and Second Lieutenant Commiskey were returning from a debriefing at the company headquarters. "Let's get this area policed up. We have a ton of bodies to bury."

Mackie cast a glare at Guillen, he wasn't grab-assing. He snapped at Horton, "This one," and picked up the taloned feet of a nearby Duster. He squeezed the ankles and twisted them hard enough to grind the bones together; if the alien was faking it would react to the pain. It didn't react.

Horton picked the alien up by its shoulders. Ever since he and his fire team leader had first picked up a Duster, he'd been surprised at how light they were compared to a human. "Hollow bones," Mackie had explained. "We think they're some kind of bird analogue."

They were fifteen meters from the nearest collection point. This alien joined the twelve that were already there, stacked two high.

Sergeant Martin came by and counted the baker's dozen. "Start a new stack with that one. The Skipper wants them stacked by the dozen, to make it easier to tally them." He looked around at the few bodies still on the blood-stained ground behind the bunkers. "Go forward and start a new stack with those bodies. I'll have Vittori's fire team finish up here."

"Right, honcho," Mackie said. He jerked his head at Horton and headed to the area between the bunkers and the wire perimeter. "Watch close, Hector," he said to Lance Corporal Cafferata as he passed their bunker. Cafferata sat on top of the bunker keeping watch over the land beyond.

"You're just lucky Orndoff is out of it. If we were full strength, you'd be out here stacking Dusters along with me."

"Hey, sentry's dirty duty, bu they, somebody's got to do it."

"Keep that up, and I'll have you spell me and Horton all by your lonesome."

"Sure thing. Hey, any word yet on how Orndoff's doing?"

Mackie shook his head. "I haven't had a chance to check on him. I don't think Sergeant Martin has either. If Lieutenant Commiskey knows, he's not sharing."

Cafferata grimaced. Not being told how a wounded man was doing generally wasn't good news.

There were more bodies between the bunkers and the wire than there had been behind the bunkers—it had been a Duster slaughterhouse.

"Let's get started," Mackie told Horton. "We'll start with those three," he said, pointing at a trio of corpses that were already almost lined up.

Horton grabbed the shoulders of the nearest one and lifted. Then he looked to see why Mackie wasn't lifting the legs.

Mackie was standing immobile, looking beyond the wire. "We aren't going to be stacking those," he said softly.

Horton blanched when he looked to see what Mackie meant. There were bodies beyond the wire, bent and cast aside the same as the bodies inside it, and hung up on it. There were also bits and pieces of bodies, remnants of bodies that had been blown apart by the artillery barrage; they wouldn't stack.

Cafferata saw what Mackie was looking at. "We're going to need buckets to clean that up," he called.

"Buckets, yeah," Mackie said numbly. He bent to help Horton with the whole bodies inside the wire.

When the stacking of Duster dead was done, including the wounded who had been put aside in the makeshift dispensary and died of their wounds, there were more than three hundred of them. An additional fifty-eight were still alive and receiving rudimentary medical care. The bits and pieces of the Dusters blown apart by the artillery might have amounted to another fifty, or even more.

For centuries, the rule of thumb had been, attackers need to out-number defenders by a margin of three to one in order to take a fortified position.

The Dusters had outnumbered the Marines at Camp Zion by nearly four to one.

"Damn," Mackie whispered when he heard the enemy count.

Heavy equipment came in while the bodies and body parts were being collected. They dug trenches to bury the Dusters, and filled them in once the bodies and parts were deposited. The regimental chaplain said a few words over the grave site, in an attempt to invoke whatever god or gods the Dusters might or might not believe in.

Sick bay, Camp Zion

"Why did you leave the bayonet in him, Corporal?" asked Lieutenant Middleton Elliot, the battalion surgeon.

"Sir," Mackie answered, trying to keep "That's a dumb question" out of his voice and expression, "I didn't know what kind of damage had been done inside him. It's possible that the bayonet was keeping him from serious hemorrhage."

"I see they're making Marine junior NCOs smarter these days," the doctor said, nodding. "That was the right thing to do, even if it wasn't necessary. The bayonet jammed in PFC Orndoff's ribs, all that was cut was surface muscle. No internal organs, no important blood vessels. But if it had gone in two more inches, he could have been in serious trouble and you leaving the bayonet in might have been the only thing that kept him alive.

"Good job, Marine. Now get him out of my sick bay, I need the bed."

"Thank you, Sir, I need him. You can have the bed." *You and that cute nurse I noticed looking at you when I came in,* he thought. To Orndoff, he said, "Come on, Harry. Let's get out of here."

"And just when I was getting comfortable."

First squad, third platoon's area

Neither of the killed Marines were from Third platoon; they were relieved that the platoon had only suffered three wounded, and that all were quickly returned to duty. In addition to Orndoff, Second squad's Lance Corporal James Burns and Third squad's Corporal Thomas Prendergast were wounded. Prendergast's wound was the worst of the three, his left humerus was broken—fortunately, it was a clean fracture. But he'd be on light duty for three or four weeks. He couldn't patrol, but he could stand sentry duty. Which was fine with the members of his fire team, because that meant they didn't have to patrol as often as they would have had his injury healed more quickly.

Prendergast notwithstanding, the rest of the Marines in the platoon had to go on patrols.

Seven kilometers southwest of Camp Zion

"What do you have, Mackie?" Sergeant Martin asked. He headed for his point fire team, which had stopped advancing.

"You tell me, Sergeant," Corporal Mackie answered. "It looks like a hell of a lot of Dusters were here recently."

Martin joined Mackie at the edge of an area cleared of underbrush, the first such they'd seen in the thin forest the squad had been patrolling through. Before examining the ground, he glanced about to see where Mackie's Marines were; they were set out in defensive positions, providing security.

"Vittori, take your fire team fifty meters up and set in," Martin ordered. "Button, watch our rear." He watched while the two fire teams moved into position. Satisfied that security was in place, he told Mackie, "Bring your men. Let's take a closer look." He made sure his helmet cam was running.

"Third fire team, up," Mackie called. "Go twenty or thirty meters in from us and look sharp," he said when they joined him and Martin. "We don't know if any Dusters are still in this area, or if they'll return." He looked at the squad leader.

"This looks like it might be a bivouac area," Martin said. "We're going in. Keep ahead of us. Twenty meter intervals."

"Aye aye," Lance Corporal Cafferata said. He and the two PFCs moved into the clearing.

The ground was barren except for slight traces of green where growth was starting to come back. Sunlight filtering through the treetops dappled the ground, making it more shaded than sunny. Martin examined the canopy and found it denser than he'd supposed, which could explain why this bivouac hadn't been spotted by a visual search. But an infrared search should have found it; it looked large enough to be the staging location for the entire force that had attacked Camp Zion three days earlier.

"Do you think these are scratches?" Mackie asked. "From their claws, I mean."

Martin nodded. "That's what it looks like to me." He took images of the scratches from multiple angles and heights.

"They cook their food." He recorded a rectangular scorch mark. "If this was a human site, I'd say this is where their kitchen was." Off to one side a muddy area bore circular gouges. "Dish washing," he hazarded.

A little farther and they found rows of two centimeter diameter holes, evenly spaced about a meter and a half apart side to side, three meters going deeper.

"Holes for tent posts maybe?" Mackie said.

Martin shrugged. "Could be. Or maybe they sleep on roosts. They are kind of bird-like. Let's see how many there are." He started giving orders immediately. "Cafferata, come here. Mackie, take your other men and find the far end of these holes. Count the rows. Cafferata, you go that way until you run out of holes. Count them, starting with that one." He pointed to the hole he wanted Cafferata to start counting on. "I'll go this way. Questions?"

"No," Mackie said. Cafferata shook his head.

"Let's do it." Martin stepped off

"Orndoff," Mackie said when he reached his men, "see the rows of holes? Count them, beginning with that one." He pointed at the first row beyond where Orndoff stood. "The first number is seventeen. Got it?"

"Start counting there, first number is seventeen. Got it."

"I'll take your flank. Move out."

It didn't take long to count the holes. Multiply the rows by the number in a row, and there were 576 holes. They also found three more scorched rectangles, each accompanied by a muddy area. More kitchens?

"All right," Martin said on the squad freq, "we either have 144 tents or 288 roosts, and four possible kitchens. Mackie, stay in place until Cafferata joins you. Then split in pairs and check the perimeter, see if you find any latrines."

Cafferata and Orndoff went one way, Mackie took Horton the other.

"Whew!" Horton exclaimed before they reached the corner.

"I smell it too," Mackie said. "It's like ammonia." He followed his nose to a stretch of disturbed dirt. There were a pair of holes at each end of it. Did the Dusters have a roost mounted over the latrine, like Humans used a platform with holes in it?

"Looks like they covered it over," Mackie said. "Let's go, this shit is burning my eyes."

"Mine too," Horton said.

They found three more along the side.

"We found four probable latrines," Mackie reported when they rejoined Martin.

"So did we, four of them," Cafferata said. "Real stinkers."

"What about tracks leading in?" Martin asked.

"Nothing like a beaten path, nothing that would indicate several hundred Dusters arriving in a formation. I did see some paths that looked like they'd been used recently."

"There was a bigger one that might be leading to Camp Zion," Cafferata said.

"Come with me," Martin said after a moment's thought. "I want to get vid of one of the latrines. And the bigger path you saw." That last was to Cafferata.

"We don't have to dig one up, do we?" Mackie asked.

"Not without orders from higher-higher. The science people might want to dig one up, though."

After getting vid of the supposed latrine, "Too bad we can't capture the smell," Martin observed. He called in a report describing what the squad had found, and sent the vids and other images he'd taken. His report concluded with, "It looks like they filtered in from multiple directions. There's no sign of whatever was in the postholes."

Captain Sitter took hardly any time to think before he ordered them to follow the bigger path, to see if it led to the Marine base. "I don't want just one squad to investigate the infiltration paths, that's a job for a larger unit, or for Force Recon."

The large path led to within half a kilometer of Camp Zion, where the Dusters appeared to disperse to take positions for their assault.

AMPHIBIOUS READY GROUP 17 WASN'T DEAD; ON LIFE SUPPORT WOULD BE A MORE accurate descriptor of its condition. Five of the fifteen troop ships in the ARG had been destroyed by the Duster missile attack, as had two of the four support ships. Five of the other transports were injured—three would need to be towed to Troy orbit, the other two could limp in on their own. Only five of the transports remained whole after the attack.

Five troop ships whole, five injured, five destroyed. Nobody in the amphibious ready group found solace in the symmetry.

The fast attack carrier NAUS Rear Admiral Isaac C. Kidd was the only remaining warship of the detachment from Task Force 8 that had been deployed to escort ARG 17. Her space fighters had retrieved the surviving pilots of the SF6 Meteor interceptors that had died defending the ARG from the attacking missiles, and recovered the bodies of those pilots who hadn't.

Shuttles from the surviving troop ships were making their way from killed ship to wounded ship to killed ship seeking survivors. On every vessel there were some soldiers or crewmen who'd made it to stasis units in time. In a few cases, entire platoons remained intact. It took several days to locate all the survivors and transfer them to viable quarters on their wounded ship, or onto others that had space. Once everybody was rescued and bodies recovered, the remnants of ARG 17 and its escort would group into a rough formation and began the slow limp to Troy orbit, and the elevator ride planetside. The exception was the undamaged NAUS *Diamunde*, which filled with ready units and headed for Troy.

Company commander's office,
Alpha Troop, First of the Seventh Mounted Infantry,
NAUS Juno Beach

The amphibious assault ship Juno Beach had been sorely injured in the missile attack, and needed to spend months undergoing repairs in a shipyard before she could join another ARG. Still, she was able to make the short trip to Troy under her own power. Returning to the shipyards of Earth would require a tow from an uninjured ship.

Half of the troops who had embarked on the *Juno Beach* and survived the attack were still aboard her; the other survivors had been transferred to other ships that had made it through the one-sided battle. The units transferred included Alpha Troop, First of the Seventh Mounted Infantry, and the battalion's command group, which went to the Landing Platform, Shuttle, NAUS *Diamunde*.

Second Lieutenant Theodore W. Greig, commander of Second platoon, Alpha Troop, and his platoon sergeant, Sergeant First Class Alexander M. Quinn, stood in front of their company commander's desk. They weren't quite at attention.

"You didn't lose a single man?" Captain Henry C. Meyer asked incredulously.

"That's right, Sir." A hint of pride was audible in Greig's voice. "No one was killed, not a single soldier of mine was even injured."

Meyer slowly shook his head. "Amazing," he said softly, and turned his head to look at the company's top dog, First Sergeant Powhatan Beaty.

Beaty's head dipped marginally in nod. "Second was the only platoon to come through intact, Sir," he said. He bestowed a look of approval on Greig and Quinn.

"Lieutenant, Sergeant," Meyer said, turning back to them, "When we make planetfall, I'm going to rely heavily on you—at least until I get replacements for the other platoons' losses." He grimaced. Eight dead and seventeen wounded out of his 150 officers and men, before they could even make contact with the enemy. Before they could see them even. Well, at least most of his officers and men had made it to stasis units before the ship was holed and most of her atmosphere vented into space. He twisted his shoulders to loosen them from the tension that suddenly hit when he thought of his losses.

"The *Diamunde* is taking us to the geosync elevator station. Second platoon will be the first element of the battalion to make planetfall. Once there, you'll be under the command of the senior Army officer planetside.

The *Diamunde* will be in orbit around Troy before ship's dawn tomorrow. I need you to have your platoon at the debarcation station for transit to the elevator at 0530, ship's time. The enlisted mess will begin serving at 0430, so your platoon will have adequate time to eat before you board transfer shuttles. Personal items are to be stowed in containers with each man's name and army ID number. All weapons and field equipment will be carried into the shuttles by each man. That includes company-level crew-served weapons. Right. Did I mention Second platoon will be reinforced by a mixed weapons squad? Well, you are. Sergeant Gumperts is leading it, he'll join the two of you once he finishes organizing his squad.

"For the big picture, Troy has two continents, Shapland and Eastern Shapland." He shook his head. "Not real big on imaginative place names here. Anyway, the Army's area of operations is Shapland. The Marines are on Eastern Shapland. In addition to us, the NAU Forces headquarters is on Shapland, and some Navy fighter squadrons and a couple of Marine squadrons are there to provide close air support for us.

Questions?" he finished with a wry twist to his mouth. If he'd already told them everything he knew about the mission, he couldn't answer any questions.

"Yes, Sir," Greig surprised his company commander. "What are the Marines doing? Do they have the situation under control?"

"The last I heard, and this isn't necessarily the latest intelligence, is that the Marines have beaten off enemy attacks and it's pretty quiet. They're just conducting mop-up operations." He gave the lieutenant a look that said, *Please don't have any more questions.*

"Thank you, Sir."

"If that's all, you're dismissed."

Greig didn't exactly come to attention, but he did salute Meyer before turning about and leading Quinn out of the captain's small office.

"So what do you think, Sir?" Quinn asked when they were far enough that Meyer couldn't overhear.

"If the Marines say all they're doing now is mopping up, it's probably fairly hot planetside."

Well deck, Landing Platform, Shuttle Diamunde

"Close it up," Bo'sun's Mate Thomas Gehegan called out. "Belly to back, back to belly. Keep 'em close and stay between the yellow lines!"

"Right, 'belly to back,'" Third squad's PFC Richard J. Gage said to PFC Nicholas Boquet, the man to his front in Second platoon's line. "Only a swabbie would want men to line up belly to back."

"Just make sure you keep your distance, Gage," Boquet said. "If I feel anything poking me, it better be your gear."

"What kind of gear you talking about?" PFC Jacob Sanford asked from his position behind Gage.

"The hard kind," Boquet said.

"There's hard and then there's hard," Sanford said with a laugh.

"Let's have some quiet in the line," Gehegan called out again. "Pay attention. Back to belly, belly to back, stay between the yellow lines."

"I still say only a swabbie would say that," Gage softly repeated. Boquet and Sanford laughed quietly.

Not all the soldiers were in spirits as high as Gage, Bouquet, and Sanford. They'd breakfasted on steak and eggs. Some in the troop had enough of a sense of history to know that steak and eggs was the traditional breakfast the Navy served to Marines and soldiers about to make a landing against an entrenched enemy.

"Knock off the chatter, troops," Staff Sergeant Albert O'Connor shouted.

There was little more chatter as Second platoon trooped single file between the yellow lines under the watchful eyes of several bo'sun's mates whose job it was to keep anybody from wandering off and getting lost among the plethora of orbit-to-surface and intra-orbit craft that filled the well deck.

"Tighten it up, troops," Sergeant First Class Quinn shouted when the platoon filed into an intra-orbital shuttle. Not that they needed to cram in; the shuttle could accommodate half a company, so there was plenty of elbow room for one reinforced platoon. Quinn's order was more force of habit than necessity.

The shuttle's hatch was closed and sealed when the last soldier was aboard, and it trundled to the sally port that was used when only one shuttle was launching, so that the entire well deck didn't need to be evacuated and then atmosphere pumped back in after the launch. The sally port was an airlock large enough to hold a single shuttle. Seal the sally port's hatch behind the shuttle, pump out the air, open the outer hatch, and a piston ejected the shuttle with enough force to propel it a hundred meters in a few seconds. At that safe distance, the coxswain piloting the shuttle would fire its engine and aim it at the elevator.

The-ship-to-elevator trip took half an hour. Once there, the shuttle docked at the elevator station and station crew sealed the egress tunnel to the shuttle's hatch. Bo'sun's mate James Byrnes "swam" through the egress tunnel to the hatch and opened it to enter the shuttle. Three more sailors followed him.

"Listen up, people," Byrnes said loudly enough to be heard throughout the shuttle. "By now you've probably noticed you're no longer under gravity. So to get you safely from here to the elevator, we're going to clip you to a guide line. I know you've all done this before, so I won't bore you with the standard safety lecture. Let's just get you clipped to the line and haul you aboard." Actually, he didn't know whether or not everybody in second platoon had transited from an intra-orbit shuttle to an elevator station—in fact, most of them hadn't. But he had orders to get them aboard as fast as possible because they were needed planetside.

Nobody suffered more than a minor bruise getting from their seats on the shuttle, to the egress tunnel, to the platform, to the elevator cabin, to their seats. The movement was counted as a major success.

Elevator to Troy

Gravity was restored in the station as soon as the shuttle disconnected and began its return to the Diamunde. It was only a quarter G, but even that small amount of pull was enough to let the soldiers know beyond doubt which way was "up" and which was "down." That prevented enough abdominal distress that nobody lost the hearty breakfast he'd eaten so recently. Second platoon wasn't in the station for long; an elevator cab was already docked and waiting for them. Still linked together, they were escorted into the cab and strapped into seats. Byrnes looked them over to make sure everybody was properly secured, then stood by the cab's entrance.

"Gravity will gradually increase as you approach planetside," he said, "until you'll be under a full G by the time you get there. When you disembark, good hunting." He essayed a salute before backing out of the cab and dogging its hatch. Only when the soldiers could no longer hear him he said softly, "Better you than me doing the hunting."

Nobody actually floated out of their seats as the cab plunged toward the surface of Troy, although several of Second platoon's soldiers later swore they were in free fall on the ride down. Lieutenant Greig took advantage of the period of inactivity to review the orders Captain Meyer had given him before his platoon left the *Juno Beach*.

On landing at the McKinzie Elevator Base, outside Troy's capital city of Millerton, the platoon would board the Marine vehicles waiting for them and be transported to a location two hundred and fifty kilometers northeast of the city where they would establish security for the battalion headquarters company, the first elements of which would follow when the *Diamunde* brought them. Over the ensuing two days, the rest of the First of the Seventh would reach the surface and join second platoon and the lead headquarters elements. In the meanwhile, a compliment from the Navy Construction Battalion would begin building a forward base for the battalion.

What he hadn't been told in that briefing was that a platoon from 10th Brigade's Mobile Intelligence company was also part of the initial complement, and would coordinate its activities with second platoon's.

Greig had yet to meet First Lieutenant Archie Miller, the recon platoon's CO. The Mobile Intel platoon had already made planetfall via Navy shuttles, the same way the Marines had in the initial landing.

McKinzie Elevator Base

"Who's in command there?" a gruff voice shouted as Second platoon disgorged from the elevator cab.

A soldier detached himself from the group and headed toward the Marine who'd called. "I am. Lieutenant Greig. Who're you?"

"I'm Gunnery Sergeant Stewart, Sir. I'm the man responsible for transporting you and your do- uh, sojers to where the squid CBs are building you a base."

If Greig noticed the "do-" he didn't acknowledge the "doggies" it implied, a slur on the Army.

But SFC Quinn, who joined his officer in time to hear Stewart name himself did. He gave the Marine a hostile glare.

Stewart looked blandly back at him.

"How many men you got, Mr. Greig? And crew served weapons?" Stewart asked, glancing toward the elevator base and noticing a machine gun.

"Fifty men, including Sergeant Quinn and myself. The weapons squad has one M-69, two M-40s, and two M-5Cs.

Stewart nodded sagely. "You'll probably need them. Especially the M-69." The M-69 "Scatterer" was a Gatling gun-type weapon, capable of firing two thousand rounds per minute. It had already been used to good effect by the Marines. "Right over there now," he pointed fifty meters away at a line of four skirted, armored vehicles. All of them spouted the barrel of a weapon, but two showed multiple barrels, some much bigger, "that's your transportation. Two Hogs and four Scooters. They're air cushioned, so the ride'll be smooth almost regardless of the terrain."

"I've ridden an amphib before, Sergeant," Greig said.

"Yeah, I imagine you have. But have your men?"

Greig nodded, conceding the point. "Only some of them."

"Now, fifty men you say? That includes your weapons crews?"

"Yes, Sarge. The weapons squad is thirteen men."

"Right. Split them up. I want half of them in one Scooter, the rest in another—the weapons take a lot of space. Your platoon has three squads?" Without waiting for an answer, he continued, "Put one and a half squads in each of the Scooters. Put your platoon sergeant and radioman with half of your weapons squad in the rear Hog. You and the rest of your weapons ride up front with me. That'll give just about everybody room to stretch out a bit. The normal load for Scooters and Hogs is more than that.

Got it?"

"Got it, Sarge."

"With all due respect, Sir, it's Gunny, not 'Sarge'."

4

Midway Between Millerton and
the Forward Base Under Construction

"What was that?" Second Lieutenant Greig yelped when the Hog he was in jolted violently.

"I'd say we just got hit by something," Gunny Stewart said calmly as he reached for the comm link to the convoy commander's compartment and listened as the lieutenant in it gave orders to the vehicles. He could also hear the commander of the lead Hog, the one he and Greig were riding. What he heard gave him warning to grab a handhold to steady himself as the armored vehicle began jinking and jerking violently in evasive maneuvers.

The Hog shuddered as its thirty-millimeter main gun spat a burst of explosive rounds. A lighter tinkling testified that the Hog's fifty-caliber guns were also spraying the surrounding area. He faintly heard firing from the other vehicles in the convoy.

Grieg didn't have the same warning Stewart had, and was thrown from his web seating when the Hog began its violent maneuvering. The gunnery sergeant reached out an arm to grab Greig's jacket collar and jerk him back onto his seat.

"Strap in and hold on, Lieutenant," he said.

"Th-thanks."

Reverberating pings and thuds told of enemy fire hitting the Hog, but nothing penetrated the vehicle's armor—yet.

"Do you have comm with your people?" Stewart had to shout to be heard above the bangs and rattles of incoming and outgoing fire, and the roaring of the maneuvering Hog's engine.

"I ran a comm check as soon as we boarded," Greig shouted back.

"That was then. If you still have comm, tell them we're under attack. But hold tight, we'll get them out of this." He continued listening, unable to see outside—the armored vehicles had no windows or periscopes in the troop cabin. The vehicles had periscopes for the vehicle commanders and drivers, and the Hogs for the gunners, but that was all the visibility anybody had with the hatches closed.

Crew Cabin, Hog 1-3-B

"Damn, but they're fast!" shouted Corporal Donald L. Truesdale as he swiveled his quad-fifty, spraying fifty-caliber rounds at the side of the hill the aliens were scrambling down. The jinking and jerking of the Hog's evasive maneuvers constantly threw his aim off, and most of his bursts went high or wide or plowed into the dirt in front of the aliens.

"Fire shorter bursts, Truesdale," Staff Sergeant William E. Shuck, the vehicle commander, ordered.

"Git me more ammo," Sergeant Phillip Gaughn called to the loader, Lance Corporal Fernando L. Garcia.

"It's in your bin," Garcia shouted back; the automatic-filler bin next to the thirty-millimeter main gun was filled almost to the top with rounds. At Gaughn's current rate of fire, it would be a few more minutes before Garcia needed to top it off.

"Run 'em over?" the driver, Sergeant James I. Poynter shouted at Shuck.

Shuck looked through his periscope and saw, behind a thin screen of slender trees, a knot of about a dozen Dusters fifty meters ahead and slightly to the side of the Hog. Some of the Dusters were firing rifle-like weapons, others were assembling what looked like a crew served weapon that might be big enough to do damage to the Marine armored vehicles.

"Smash 'em!" Shuck snapped.

"Yahoo!" Poynter bellowed. He stomped on the accelerator and yanked the steering yoke to the left, aiming straight at the cluster of aliens, who looked up, startled at the sudden roar coming at them.

The aliens started to scramble out of the way when the Hog was ten meters away, but not all of them made it. Four or five got sucked under the air cushioned vehicle and were shredded by the gravel and debris being flung about by the powerful fans that lifted the Hog off the ground. So did the big weapon they were mounting.

"Turn about," Shuck ordered, and Poynter twisted the yoke, spinning the Hog around on its axis. "Head for those small boulders!" he said when he saw an area covered with stones up to the size of a soccer ball. "Squat on them."

"Aye aye," Poyter shouted gleefully. He sped the Hog to the small field of boulders. There, he vectored the fans to blow straight down and applied enough power for them to lift the Hog an extra dozen centimeters.

Large rocks and small boulders sprayed out in all directions from under the vehicle. Many of them slammed into Dusters unable to dodge them, tearing off limbs, tails, heads, plowing holes through bodies.

"What's happening?" Greig shouted. He let go of a handhold with one hand to grab Stewart's arm to get his attention and shouted his question again.

"It sounds like the Dusters are getting slaughtered," Stewart shouted back.

Moments later the only sounds were the roars of the vehicles' engines and the blasting of their weapons; there wasn't any more incoming fire from the Duster ambush. The convoy didn't stop to deal with the Duster casualties.

"What about the enemy bodies?" Greig asked. "Should we just leave them there like that? Shouldn't we collect their weapons and check the bodies for documents?"

"Let 'em police up after themselves," Stewart said. "Besides, if we unass from these vehicles, any of them still able to shoot will get some of us. And they never seem to have documents. Even if we could read their chicken scratching."

Advance Firebase One, Under Construction

The scene that greeted Greig and Sergeant First Class Quinn when they dismounted from the armored Hogs was one of controlled chaos. Thick lines of dirt berms were piled man-high on the west side of the construction area, opposite the direction the convoy had come from. Ferrocrete cladding had been laid on some of the berms, and a machine was busily laying ferrocrete on another section of dirt berm. Other machines were piling more sections of earthen berm, yet more were digging holes. In the already-finished sections it looked like finishing touches were being put on the entrances to bunkers that were built into the berm. Men in dirty uniforms bustled about, supervising the machines delivering materials from one location to another, or supervising other men. There were the tops of a few more bunkers inboard from the berm. A large tent stood in the middle of the complex. A spindly tower sprouting antennas, with rotating dishes near its top—Greig identified them as radar, infrared, and other detection devices—was twenty meters to one side of the large tent. A more substantial looking tower topped by a basket with a man in it was an equal distance on the other side of the tent. A spike rose from the side of the basket, flying the flag of the North American Union. In all, it looked like the base when finished would cover more than twenty acres.

Greig found the site surprisingly quiet despite all the activity.

"You must be Greig," a middling-big man said, extending a hand to shake. His uniform was as dirty as everybody else's. Given his age, probably mid-fifties; Greig would have taken him for a chief petty officer had it not been for the gold oak leaves on his collar points. "Welcome to Firebase Anonymous."

"Yes, Sir," Greig said. He started to salute, then extended his hand to shake.

Stewart made the introductions. "Mr. Greig, this is Lieutenant Commander William Harrison. He's the engineer in charge of building this base for you."

"Pleased to meet you, Sir. Anonymous?"

Harrison grinned. "I don't know how you do it in the Army, but in the Navy and Marines, we name our forward bases after heroes, usually dead ones. We don't have either yet, so it's up to you to name this place. So unless you brought a name with you, we call this place Firebase Anonymous One."

"Ah, yes, Sir. I'm glad to hear that. I mean, no heroes or dead."

"We've been here for five days," Harrison said, clamping a hand on Greig's shoulder to lead him toward a finished section of berm. "And this is all we've had time to accomplish so far. But now that you're here, I can take my people off security duty and put them to work constructing, and the pace will pick up dramatically. I see that Chief Cronin has your people well in hand. He'll see to getting them settled in and chowed down." He waved a hand at the tent. "That's our temporary mess hall. One table is designated as officers' and chiefs' mess. You and your platoon sergeant will join my top people and me for meals—allowing for who's on duty."

Looking back at his platoon, Greig saw a burly man standing next to SFC Quinn and gesturing, evidently giving information and instructions. Looking around more, he asked, "What about quarters? Where are they?"

"We spent a couple of days roughing it, bedding down on the ground. Since then we've taken to sleeping in the bunkers. Except for the ammo bunkers, that could be damn dangerous. We're still roughing it, the cots we were promised haven't been delivered yet." He shrugged, as though cots were irrelevant. "Defensive positions right now are more important than quarters, so we're concentrating on the berm and fighting positions. Plus ammo bunkers, of course."

They reached a finished section of berm and Harrison ducked into a bunker, drawing Greig along with him. The entryway had an open blast door on the outside, closely followed by two ninety-degree turns, and another blast door, also open, on the inside. An aperture, wide enough to allow three men to fire rifles through it at the same time—or one rifleman plus a machine gun—was in the center of the wall facing outward. Against each side wall, an open bin with dividers served as lockers for the bunker's occupants. A thin mattress lay on top of each of the lockers. A second bunk was half a meter above the lower. The floor sloped toward a corner of the back wall, with a sump hole at the lowest point.

"A grenade sump?" Greig asked.

"You got it. So far the Dusters haven't used grenades, or any other hand-throwable explosives that we've heard of. But you never know. Better to be safe.

"Now, look out here." Harrison guided Greig to the aperture.

Greig stooped slightly to see through the opening in the front of the bunker. He saw scorched ground stretching three hundred meters to a line of scraggly trees, the face of a thin forest. Small boulders, none larger than an athletic ball, speckled the barren ground.

"The day before we got here," Harrison said, "the Marines bombed a square kilometer with Dragon's Breath."

Greig whistled. Dragon's Breath was a fiery weapon so horrendous it was banned for use against people. It was, however, still used sometimes to clear ground, sometimes even enemy-held cropland, although that use was generally frowned upon, especially if there was a civilian population that might starve from loss of the crops.

"Nobody's going to get close to Firebase Anonymous without us knowing they're on their way.

Just then Harrison's comm squawked at him, "Incoming from the west, fifteen klicks."

"Let's see what that's about," Harrison said, heading for the bunker's exit. Outside, he headed at a brisk pace for a bunker that barely showed above ground level. "Command post," he said over his shoulder to Greig, who was scrambling to catch up.

The CP bunker was easily twice the size of the fighting bunker Greig had just seen. A long table along one wall held workstations, not all of which Greig immediately recognized—he thought some of them must have construction or engineering functions that he wasn't familiar with. A man and two women were bent over three of the stations.

"What'cha got for me?" Harrison asked, leaning in to look over the shoulder of one of the techs.

"Three aircraft," she answered. "Unfamiliar design. But they look human."

"Defense?"

"Only one AA is operational," said another tech. "It's locked onto the nearest aircraft."

"They've started orbiting, Sir," the first tech said.

"Comm, any contact?" Harrison asked the third tech.

"Not on any Navy or Marine freq. I'm trying Army now." Seconds later, "Bingo."

"Put it up."

"Aye-aye." She touched something and a voice came out of a speaker.

"...ee Bee base, this is NAUA Mike India Papa dot Nine Bravo, orbiting twelve klicks from your location. Do you hear me? Come on, guys. I know you see me, you've got a lock on my lead aircraft."

Harrison picked up a mike. "Mike India Papa, this is Charlie Bravo Actual. Where the hell'd you come from?"

"Charlie Bravo Actual, been doing our job—reconnoitering. What do you think?"

"Advance to be recognized, Mike India Papa Bravo." Harrison put the mike back down. "I've seen the Dusters and heard their voices. No way one of them could speak good human. Were you expecting a Mobile Intel platoon?"

"Yeah, but I thought they'd follow us on the ground, or already be here when we arrived."

Fifteen minutes later three P-43 Eagles, bristling with sensor antennas and weapons, were settled in the middle of the compound and the twenty enlisted members of the First platoon of the 9th Infantry Division's mobile intelligence company were forming up in front of their aircraft.

A tall soldier with blackened lieutenant's bars on the collars of a cruddy shirt walked to where Harrison and Greig stood in front of the CP bunker. "Sir, I'm First Lieutenant Archie Miller," he said, waving a casual salute at Harrison. "I'm in nominal charge of that band of reprobates you see behind me. We're First platoon, 9th Mobile Intel Company."

"And I'm Lieutenant Commander Bill Harrison. I'm in charge of building this here base. Until it's finished and I turn it over to the Army, I own it. That makes me your landlord. This," he jerked a thumb at Greig, "is Second Lieutenant Ted Greig. He's base personnel, responsible for security here, and for running patrols out there. You and yours are TAD here." Temporary

Additional Duty, on loan, not permanent personnel. Harrison gave a wry smile at his men being labeled as TAD. "That sort of makes him your superior officer, even though you outrank him."

"That so?" Miller stuck a hand out for Greig to shake. "Glad to meet'cha, Louie."

Greig took Miller's hand, and didn't flinch at Miller's crushing grip. He knew his hand would be sore later, but he wasn't going to give the MI officer the satisfaction.

"So, Bossman, Whaddya want us to do first?" He gave Greig's hand a final squeeze before releasing it.

"How about a report on what you found? While you're doing that," he looked at Harrison, "I imagine the commander can have someone show your people where to stow their things."

"Chief Cronin's taking care of that right now." Harrison nodded in the direction of the MI enlisted men, where Chief Petty Officer Cronin was already taking them in hand. He sniffed. "While he's at it, I'm sure he'll also introduce them to the shower point. If you've been out there snooping and pooping, I expect they'd like to sluice off the accumulated crud. After that, it'll be chow call for you and yours.

"In the meantime, let's get you settled in. You can begin briefing Mr. Greig while you're getting your gear stowed and yourself cleaned up."

Lieutenant Commander Harrison billeted First Lieutenant Miller and his platoon sergeant, Master Sergeant James H. Bronson, in a half-finished bunker, then pointed the direction to the officers' and chiefs' shower point. It was smaller and more centrally located than the enlisted shower, but was otherwise the same: a canvas-walled enclosure with water fed from a fuel drum set above it on a scaffold. While Miller was stowing his gear, Lieutenant Grieg got ready for his own shower; he hadn't had a chance to clean since the transfer from the *Juno Beach*. He was finished and dressed by the time Miller arrived.

When both were clean and in fresh uniforms, Miller accompanied Greig to the mess tent. Some of the Mobile Intelligence troops were filtering in after having showered themselves, as was a squad of Greig's platoon. Unlike their officers, the enlisted men didn't sit together, but stayed with their own. In the manner of enlisted men of all armies, they didn't sit close to the officers.

The first thing Miller told Greig was, "We're tied into the satellite net. Everything we found and recorded got uploaded to the Navy intel people as we got it. Now it's your turn to find out." Harrison joined them as he began giving his briefing.

"We flew around for two days," Miller said between chews of his ham steak. "Every couple of klicks one of our birds would make a stop-and-go touchdown. Sometimes a team would drop out." He gave Greig a penetrating look. "You understand why we made a lot of touch-and-goes without letting anybody out, don't you?"

Greig nodded. "If the Dusters were observing your flights, they wouldn't know whether or not you were letting a patrol out. That's a basic tactic for reconnaissance teams."

"Good. Maybe you're not as dumb as most Leg LTs."

"Careful there, Lieutenant. Mounted Infantry is a lot smarter and tougher than Legs."

Miller grinned, and washed down a mouthful of reconstituted mashed potatoes with a drink of strong Navy coffee. "I know that, Ted. Just wanted to make sure you do." He stuck out a hand. "Call me Archie."

Greig took the hand and shook; Miller's grip wasn't as tight as the first time. "Sure thing, Archie. We're on the same team here. So what did you find?"

Miller sighed. "We found a lot of they-wuz-here. We searched in the vicinity of every town, village, farm, or other homestead, as well as a bunch of other likely hiding locations. Almost everywhere we looked, we found signs of Dusters having been there but nary a Duster to be spotted." He grimaced. "We've got what, less than a division and a half left from the entire VII Corps? Plus the Marines who made planetfall first? Worse, most of what's left of VII Corps still hasn't made planetfall. If I can extrapolate continent-wide from what we found, they've got us outnumbered by at least four-to-one, probably more—and that's not until the rest of the corps gets here. We're good fighters, but they know where we are, and we can't even make an educated guess as to where they are. That's tough odds."

Harrison interjected, "What I hear from Task Force 8 is, they aren't having much more luck than planetside assets are in locating the Dusters."

Greig swallowed. "The Navy and Marines have ground attack aircraft, that should go a long way toward evening the odds."

"The same thing applies. They know where our airfields are, we don't know where they are. They could knock out a lot of our aircraft on the ground. Bang, there goes that advantage."

"Navy has limited assets for orbit-to-ground fire support," Harrison said. "So we can't look for much help from that direction."

"You're just a feast of good cheer, aren't you?"

"I'm only telling it the way I see it. Did you get the full briefing about them?" Miller asked.

"If I didn't, I wouldn't know it," Greig answered. "What do you know that maybe I don't?"

"In our interstellar explorations, we've found evidence of seventeen other sentient civilizations. All of them had been destroyed, much like what happened to the colony here. Thinking is, these Dusters are the same bunch that did in those others."

Greig gasped. "I knew there had been a few, but I had no idea it was that many. Seventeen?"

"Seventeen." Miller lowered his voice to where Greig and Harrison had to strain to hear him. "That's what has me quaking in my boots."

Camp Puller, Headquarters of NAU Forces, Troy,
near Millerton, Shapland,
Semi-Autonomous World Troy
Office of Lieutenant General Bauer

"SIR," CAPTAIN WILLIAM UPSHUR SAID, STANDING IN THE DOORWAY OF LIEUTENANT General Bauer's small office, "Navy has sent us the reports from the Army Mounted Infantry platoon. I have it along with an abstract G-2 prepared for you."

Bauer looked up and held out his hand for the flimsy and the crystal his aide offered. "Thanks, Bill. Did Colonel Neville say anything about it?"

"No, Sir. He said it's self explanatory."

"I'll let you know if I need anything more."

"Yes, Sir." Dismissed, Upshur returned to the outer office.

Bauer skimmed the flimsy as he slipped the crystal into his comp. The flimsy provided a brief description, little more than a table of contents, of the MI's report. The crystal proved to be of great interest; it included visuals of Duster presence and the destruction they'd wrought on human settlements and structures, as well as maps showing where the MI platoon had scouted. They'd covered a considerable area.

"Sir," Upshur reappeared in Bauer's doorway.

"Yes, Bill?"

"I have a follow up report from India Three/One. One of their patrols found what appears to be the Duster's staging location for their assault on Camp Zion. It's got some interesting images."

"Show me. And have someone get me some coffee, please."

"Aye aye, Sir." Upshur handed Bauer another crystal before returning to the outer office to get a cup of coffee for his commanding general.

Bauer studied the report from I/3/1's patrol and compared it with the MI report. After a couple of minutes' contemplation, he ordered, "Have General Porter assemble my primary staff and their seconds, if you please. Army, too. If he's here, I'd like General Purvis to attend as well. And link in Admiral Avery."

Of course, what a lieutenant general pleases, he gets.

Briefing room, NAU Forces, Troy HQ

"A-ten-Hut!" Brigadier General David Porter, the acting NAU Chief of Staff barked as Bauer strode into the room. The assembled generals and colonels broke off their conversations and stood.

"Seats!" Bauer said, as he reached the podium in the back of the room. There was a minor clatter as the staff heads and their seconds resumed their seats. He looked at the vid connection that showed Rear Admiral Avery, attending remotely from his office on the NAUS *Durango*, Task Force 8's flagship.

Bauer acknowledged Avery with a nod. "Admiral."

"General," Avery said back after a few seconds delay for the greetings to go to orbit and back.

Bauer looked out at his staff. "I had Colonel Neville prepare materials on recent findings by both Marines and Army reconnaissance patrols for each of you to study. The Dusters appear to have vanished. I don't believe for a moment that they've all been wiped out. And they certainly haven't quit Troy, we would have seen them leave, and the Navy would have attacked their shipping.

They're still here, most likely preparing a counter-attack. We need to find out where they are hiding, and neutralize them. To that end, I want patrolling, both ground and aerial, stepped up.

"When the Dusters launched their missile attack on ARG 17 they did it from underground installations on Minnie Mouse. When they counter-attacked us in Jordan, they entered structures from the basements, which they had reached via previously undetected caves and tunnels. I think it's likely, particularly in light of their evident absence from the surface, that they're hiding underground. So our main focus will be on locating caves and tunnel systems. Admiral Avery will use his orbital resources to locate gravitational anomalies. We will coordinate with Navy on that, and investigate whatever they find.

Brigadier General Shoup will be the center man in this. I want preliminary plans tomorrow early afternoon.

Questions?"

Major General Julius Stahel stood up; the commander of the 9th Infantry Division was the ranking Army officer present. "Sir?"

"Yes, General."

"Your orders include the Army, don't they?"

"Absolutely, General. The Army units, whether they are planetside or still in space, are integral parts of NAU Forces, Troy. I want your staff who have reached planetside, and the surviving staff of your 10th Brigade who are here, to work with my staffs. As units of VII Corps reach planetside, the Marine elements on Shapland will relocate to Eastern Shapland. General, this is your area." Bauer looked at the few ranking Army officers who had managed thus far to reach Troy. "Do what you can with what you've got. General Shoup will include you in his plans the same as he will the 1st Marine Division and 2nd Marine Air Wing."

"Thank you, Sir."

"If there are no more questions, you've got work to do. Get it done."

There was a minor clatter of chairs as the assembled officers stood while Bauer stepped off the small stage and marched out of the briefing room.

Briefing room, NAU Forces, Troy HQ, the next day

"Gentlemen," Bauer said to the Marine and Army division commanders, the commanding general of the 2nd Marine Air Wing, the operations officer of the 1st MCF, and the Navy Construction regiment commander. "We have preliminary reports from the increasing number of Marine and Army patrols that have been prowling about since yesterday. While most of our initial contacts with the enemy were in cities, towns, and other human settlements, it appears that they have abandoned built-up areas in favor of more remote locations, albeit in proximity to human settled locations. We are going to take the battle to them, not wait in cities and towns for them to come to us.

"To that end, I want the divisions to establish platoon and company-size firebases throughout your respective areas of operation, from which you will conduct aggressive patrolling. 2nd Marine Air Wing will position squadrons in locations where its aircraft can give rapid support to the ground elements—General Bearss, the MAW will be reinforced by three Navy Kestrel squadrons and a Navy Search and Rescue squadron.

"Captain Rooks, I know that you and your construction regiment will do a stellar job of building defensible firebases, bearing in mind that our foe is fond of attacking *en masse*, in the alien version of human wave attacks. Except that we can't assume that the leading waves will be either well defined or armed with dummy weapons as have some human forces in the past.

"The Navy, meanwhile, will continue its search for enemy bases and gravitational anomalies that could indicate underground installations.

"A salient point to keep in mind is that the human population is no longer here. We can hope that some day they will return, or that other humans will repopulate Troy. With that in mind, destruction of the infrastructure should be kept to a minimum when possible. Otherwise, the entire planet of Troy is a free fire zone.

"Again, Brugadier General Shoup will be your main contact person to coordinate your activities.

"Questions?"

Nobody had any. The commander's intent was clear.

"You know what to do. Good hunting, gentlemen."

Dismissed, the commanders took their leave, leaving Bauer alone with his operations chief, Brigadier General Shoup, and his aide, Captain Upshur.

"See what you can do about pulling Whiskey companies out of every regiment or higher," Bauer said. "I have a dreadful feeling that we're going to need them."

A "whiskey company" was a unit consisting of cooks, bakers, clerks, mechanics, and other non-trigger-pullers, for the purpose of providing replacements to trigger-puller units when their casualties reduced their ability to function.

Near Jordan, Eastern Shapland,
Semi-Autonomous World Troy

"KEEP YOUR EYES OPEN, HORTON," CORPORAL JOHN MACKIE CALLED TO HIS NEWEST man. Despite having been in combat, PFC William Horton still wasn't used to the frequently short sleep hours infantrymen had.

"I'm awake," Horton called back. "Just blinking, that's all."

"Blink faster. You almost walked into that bush." Mackie shook his head. Horton required closer supervision than Mackie'd had to give the others thanks to his lack of experience. *It's a good thing Orndoff's wound was minor,* Mackie thought, *or he'd still be on light duty and I'd only have one man I could rely on.*

The close supervision was especially needed now; India Company had been on the move almost constantly with little chance for sleep for six days. Everyone was drowsy, everybody was having trouble staying awake even while walking. Mackie was glad he was acting fire team leader because his extra responsibilities, the need to pay attention to his men, helped him stay awake.

"Sorry, Mackie," Horton mumbled. *How the hell did he see me?* he wondered. He glanced down at himself; the Marines' utility uniform had a camouflage pattern that tricked the eye into sliding right past it, even here where the foliage was closer to grey and dark blue than it was to the green he was used to back on Earth. He looked toward where he'd heard Mackie's voice, but it took several seconds for his fire team leader to register in his vision. He shook his head. *At least he's not calling me "new guy."*

For his part, Mackie divided his attention between keeping an eye on his three men and searching his surroundings, looking for any sign of the alien enemy.

The Marines were investigating gravitational anomalies the Navy had discovered, anomalies that might or might not indicate the presence of underground spaces where the Dusters were hiding. But the Marines had had no contact with the Dusters since they'd beaten off attacks two weeks earlier. That was when Duster forces surged out of concealed underground bunkers and caverns to attack the Marines from inside their perimeters, and even inside buildings the Marines were occupying.

Third platoon was negotiating an area of scrubland. Sparsely-leafed, tree-like growths spread spindly branches over the shrub-like bushes that seldom reached chest high on a man and grew every place sunlight reached the ground.

"Watch your dress, people," Sergeant James Martin shouted, "keep it staggered." The constant refrain of squad leaders supervising their Marines on the move. First and Third squads were on line in an inverted "V" formation, with Second squad on line fifty meters to their rear, ready to move toward whatever squad might need assistance. A two-machinegun squad was in the middle of the delta formation.

On the squad level, the Marines were using ordinary voice communications, shouting orders, questions, and answers. If there were Dusters in the area, they probably knew the Marines were there. It was almost impossible for anyone to move about silently in this terrain, so there was no need to keep quiet. On platoon level and higher, the Marines were spread far enough that radio comm was necessary.

"Look alive, people," Second Lieutenant Henry Commiskey's voice came over the platoon's comm into every helmet. "We're just about on top of that anomaly. If anybody's home, they might..."

A sudden rattle of gunfire and a cacophany of shrill *caws* and *skrees* cut off the rest of what the platoon commander was saying.

"First squad, hit the deck!" Martin shouted. "They're to our left!"

"Orndoff, Horton, do you see anything?" Mackie called. He involuntarily ducked from the projectiles he heard cracking overhead.

"Only bushes and bees," Orndoff called back.

"Nothing," Horton answered. He sounded excited, his voice rose sharply on the one word.

Mackie didn't see where the fire was coming from, either. The bushes of the ground cover were just thick enough to block the Marines' view of anything more than fifty meters distant. "Fire at the bases of the bushes," he ordered. "Move your shots around." He made sure his rifle's selector switch was set to burst, and began putting three round bursts into the bases of the nearest bushes. A quick glance to his sides showed his men doing the same. All around, he heard other fire team leaders shouting commands at their men, and the shouted replies. Fire from the Marines grew in volume.

"Where are they, honcho?" Mackie called to Martin on the squad radio net. "We're firing blind here."

"When I find out, you'll be the first to know," Martin answered. "Keep doing what you're doing."

Commiskey spoke into the platoon comm: "Everybody, keep low! They're all around us. Like a circular firing squad. Maybe they'll shoot each other!" His voice cracked.

"Yeah, sure," Mackie muttered. A spray of leaves pattered his head and back, clipped off a branch above him by a too-close burst of alien fire. "Unless they're standing full up, they're firing too high to hit each other." He grinned grimly. "Too high to hit us, either."

"Heads up, First squad," Martin shouted into his comm. "My motion detector says they're coming at us. Two hundred and closing. Watch for movement, then fire waist high." Even though the Dusters massed about the same as a human, they carried their torsos almost parallel to the ground, so a waist-high shot would hit a Duster head on.

The machine guns began firing twenty-round bursts side to side over the heads of the riflemen, scything through the tops of the bushes.

Shrill caws and shrieks ripped through the foliage, dopplered as the aliens closed the distance.

Then Commiskey gave a command that had seldom been heard in centuries, "Fix bayonets!"

In far fewer seconds than it would have taken humans to cover the distance, the Dusters appeared, jinking and dodging side to side within fifty meters of the Marines who began firing at the attackers who were moving too rapidly for anyone to aim at. Instead of the disciplined fire on which the Marines had long prided themselves, it was spray and pray: throw out enough bullets and some are bound to find a target.

In an instant, Mackie saw that the aliens were crossing each other's paths. He picked a spot and began firing at one. The first shots missed the Duster he sighted on, but hit another that jinked through the same small area. He managed to knock down two more before the Dusters closed with the Marines.

Mackie jumped to his feet, too focused on the nearest Duster to see what was happening to his sides. If he'd spared any attention, he'd have seen that the rest of the squad had also surged upright to meet the aliens with the blades attached to the muzzles of their rifles.

Here, the Marines had a slight advantage over their much faster opponents; their arms and rifles were longer than the Dusters'; a human could skewer one of them before it got inside its own reach.

But there were three coming directly at Mackie.

He pivoted sharply to his right and swung the butt of his rifle low at the head of the right-most Duster. The alien was moving too fast, but its neck followed its head into the path of Mackie's rifle butt. The Marine felt a satisfying *crack* of breaking bones. The Duster he'd struck was tossed aside, into the feet of the middle of the trio, sending that one tumbling. The third skidded to a stop and spun toward Mackie, stretching its head on its long neck to bite at him. Mackie stepped back to get out of the way of the toothed beak, and tripped on an exposed root. That saved him, as the Duster tripped by the first one had regained its feet and was lunging with its weapon at the Marine from his side, and its thrust went over him.

Mackie turned his fall into a backward somersault to increase his distance from the one coming from his front. The two Dusters collided in the space he'd just occupied, and staggered, dazed from the impact. Mackie leaped to his feet and plunged his bayonet into the side of the nearer alien. The third *cawed* loudly and kicked with one of its taloned feet before the Marine could wrench his bayonet free. Claws ripped at Mackie, tearing through his shirt and gouging his rib muscles. He let go of his rifle and, grabbing the alien's leg, yanked with all his strength.

The Duster let out a shriek and tried to wrest its leg from Mackie's grip, but only succeeded in throwing itself off balance. Mackie wrenched the leg upward, twisting the knee joint far enough to disjoint it. The alien let out a shrill cry, and thudded to the ground when Mackie let go of its leg.

With all three of his opponents down, Mackie took a few seconds to look around for his men.

On his right, Orndoff had a Duster by its head and was spinning it around. To his left, Horton was stomping a downed alien. Farther away Cafferata was swinging the butt of his rifle at another's head and neck. All three Marines had red staining their uniforms, but Mackie couldn't tell if the red was the blood of humans, or the slightly different red of the aliens' blood. Beyond his men, he saw other Marines grappling with Dusters, some against more than one. Approaching shouts sounded like more Marines were on their way to aid First squad.

He didn't have time to analyze the situation; another Duster was almost on him, its bayoneted rifle probing straight at him at groin level. And Mackie's was still stuck in the ribs of one that he'd already fought. Mackie bounded upward, legs spread. Not high, but enough to clear the rifle, which went between his thighs. He came down on the alien's forearms, his belly slammed into the Duster's beak, jamming its head back on its long neck. The impact hurt, but Mackie didn't have time to consider what injury he might have suffered. His hands reflexively snapped up, under the alien's jaw, knocking its head back. The thing began to fall forward from its momentum, but Mackie's body blocked its motion, and his weight bore its front down. Mackie swiveled, swinging his left leg up and over to disengage from his foe. With one hand he grasped the alien's weapon, and with the other slugged it in the side of the face. In an instant, he had the unfamiliar rifle in his hands, and used it like a club to knock the Duster down and pummel its head into the ground.

The Duster that had Mackie's bayonet sticking out of its side was still alive, writhing in agony, flopping the Marine's rifle side to side. Mackie stomped on its neck as he bent to grab his rifle. The alien spasmed. Mackie got a good grip on his rifle, twisted, yanked, pulled it free.

Crouching, he looked around for another enemy to fight. While he'd been engaged,Second squad and some of the machine gunners had arrived to reinforce First squad. Dead and wounded Dusters littered the ground around the Marines. Some of the Marines were down as well. But Mackie couldn't take it all in right away; he was faint from loss of blood and collapsed.

"It's about time you woke up, Mackie."

Mackie turned his head toward the side and saw Hospitalman Third Class David E. Hayden kneeling next to him where he lay on the ground.

"Hey..." Corporal Mackie started, then had to work some saliva into his mouth and swallow. "Hey, Doc, what are you doing there?"

"Patching you up, what do you think?"

"Patching...?" Mackie started to pat his belly and ribs, but flinched at the pain and stopped.

"Don't worry," Hayden said. "You'll live. And you'll be back to full duty before Sergeant Martin decides to give your fire team to Cafferata."

"How about Orndoff and Horton? They're mine, I need to know."

"Horton's wounded about as bad as you. Orndoff wasn't as dumb, he barely got scratched."

Mackie nodded, satisfied; all of the Marines he was responsible for were alive. That was important. "But we won?" he asked.

"The standard definition of victory is whoever holds the ground when the shooting stops is the winner. We're still here, the Dusters aren't. So, yeah, we won."

Mackie looked around and saw spindly-branched trees with bushes growing where sunlight reached the ground. "This is where we fought?"

"Yeah. We're waiting for transportation back to Jordan. Before you ask, I don't know when it'll get here."

Mackie fell back, and grimaced at the pain that lanced through his rib wounds from the impact.

"Now rest easy," Hayden said, patting Mackie's shoulder. "I'll check on you later." The corpsman stood and continued his rounds.

Mackie's eyelids suddenly felt heavy. He closed them, thinking *Doc must have slapped me with a sedative.* In seconds, he was sound asleep.

Orndoff was there when Mackie woke up again. This time he recognized the ground cover he was laying on, keeping him off the dirt, weeds, and pebbles.

"How ya feeling, honcho?" Orndoff asked.

"I've been better. How're you?"

Orndoff shrugged. "A damn sight better'n you." He raised his left arm to display the field dressing wrapped around it. "Just a scratch. Nothing serious."

"That's your second wound." Mackie shook his head. "How's Horton? Doc didn't tell me much."

"He got a leg wound, a bad one. A Duster kicked him hard, gouged deep into his thigh. He damn near bled out before I got a tourniquet on him. Doc's pumping him full of plasma and whole blood." He took a deep breath, nodded. "He'll pull through all right."

"And the rest of the squad?"

"Pretty much everybody got hurt." Orndoff looked unfocused into the distance. "I heard someone say the platoon had better'n fifty percent casualties, with most of 'em in First squad."

"How many dead?" Mackie choked on the word.

Orndoff shook his head. "Lieutenant Commiskey made us stay in our squads and fire teams when the Dusters broke and ran. I haven't been able to get around to see how anybody else is doing. Staff Sergeant Guillen chased me back when I tried. Told me my ass was his if I didn't stick with you." He shrugged. "That's why my pretty face was the first thing you saw when you came to."

"How's Martin?"

"Dinged. Worse than me, not as bad as you."

"Where's Horton?"

Orndoff pointed with his chin. "On your other side. Doc's keeping him under until he's sure he's got enough blood in him." He cocked his head. "Sounds like transport's on its way."

Mackie listened and heard the drone of approaching air-cushioned vehicles. In minutes, five "Eighters" hove into sight. They were air cushioned, amphibious vehicles, each capable of carrying a reinforced rifle platoon. Four were enough to carry an entire company, three if they squeezed in. But the casualties required more space, so regiment had sent five.

"All right, people, let's get the wounded aboard first," Captain Carl Sitter's voice came over the company freq.

"Platoon sergeants," First Sergeant Robert G. Robinson followed up, "you know your platoon's assignments. Get it done."

Platoon sergeants barked orders over their platoon freqs. Squad and fire team leaders raised their voices, repeating the platoon sergeants' orders. There weren't as many raised voices as there should have been; too many of India Company's squad leaders and fire team leaders were casualties. Still, the boarding of the casualties, followed by the able, went smoothly enough, and quickly. It wasn't long before India Company was on its way back to Jordan.

Field Hospital, Jordan, Eastern Shapland,
Semi-Autonomous World Troy

On the second day after its fire fight against the Dusters, India Company held a formation. They formed up outside the battalion's field hospital rather than on the battalion parade ground, because several of the wounded, even though out of intensive care, were still bed-ridden. Lieutenant Colonel Ray Davis, the battalion commander, spoke first.

"Marines, I know you suffered in close combat against the Dusters. Some of you are still suffering. Some, absent comrades, will suffer no more. But I assure you, the Dusters suffered more than you did. They left more of their own dead in Third platoon's area alone than India Company had Marines in the entire engagement. Their losses were horrendous. Whatever their unit strength was to begin with, they are no longer capable of functioning as a unit of that size. India, Three/One, however, is.

"But you won't have to. India Company is going into battalion reserve until your wounds are healed, and your absent comrades are replaced and integrated into the company.

"Thanks to you, we now know the location of a major Duster underground base and how to identify their entrances. The 6th Marines are in the process of reducing the base you found.

"Marines, you did an outstanding job. In this action you acquitted yourselves in the highest tradition of the Marine Corps, and you will again and again. Every time the Dusters have come up against you, they have been severely bloodied and thrown back with devastating losses. Ultimate victory will be yours."

Davis bowed his head for a moment, then raised it high and said forcefully, in a pride-filled voice, "3rd Battalion, 1st Marines has a long and proud history. You carry on in the best tradition of that history. Three/One is the best battalion in the Marine Corps, and I am proud and humbled to be your commander.

"Now, many of you received wounds in this recent action. For some of you it was a second wound suffered against the Dusters. I wish I had the Purple Hearts medals to award to you now, but we will have to wait until medals come from Earth. But I do have the printed citations, and your company commander will hand them out to you in an appropriate ceremony.

"Marines, I salute you." He raised his right hand in a salute.

"COMP-ney, a-ten-SHUN!" battalion Sergeant Major Harry L. Hulbert bellowed.

Every one standing snapped to attention. The bed-ridden did as well as they could.

"PRE-sent ARMS!" Hulbert called out, and everyone who could saluted, and held his salute.

Davis looked over the company before cutting his salute and about-facing to march away.

Hulbert let the battalion commander get twenty meters away before shouting, "OR-der ARMS!" the command for the Marines to cut their salutes. He saluted the company commander, Captain Carl Sitter, then followed the colonel.

Sitter waited for Davis and Hulbert to reach their vehicle and leave before facing his company. "Platoons, report absent comrades."

First Lieutenant Christian F. Schilt saluted Sitter and sounded off. "Sir, First platoon, three absent comrades."

Second Lieutenant Herman H. Hanneken then reported, "Sir, Second platoon, five absent comrades."

Second Lieutenant Commiskey reported, "Sir, Third platoon, seven absent comrades."

Finally, First Lieutenant Ralph Talbot reported, "Sir, weapons platoon, three absent comrades."

Twenty-five "absent comrades." Nearly one out of seven members of the company. Far too many, far too heavy a loss. But not all of the twenty-five had been killed. A few, pitifully few, were too badly wounded to be returned to full duty in the forseeable future, if ever. Twenty-five billets in the company to fill.

"The platoons need to be reorganized and some Marines will be promoted to give you rank commensurate with your positions. Some replacements, but only fifteen or so, not more than twenty, will come from the division's shore party and various headquarters units. When they arrive and are assigned, you will need to integrate them as quickly as possible.

Platoon commanders and platoon sergeants, I want your recommendations for reorganization and promotions in two hours.

Gunnery Sergeant, the company is yours."

Gunnery Sergeant Charles F. Hoffman stepped forward and saluted. "Sir, the company is mine. Aye aye, Sir." He watched while Sitter led the company's officers and first sergeant away, then about faced.

"Platoon sergeants," he ordered, "when I dismiss you, take your platoons and keep them together, ready to reassemble." He looked from one end of the formation to the other, noting without expression how many of the Marines were laying on beds or leaning on crutches instead of standing at attention, then said, *"COMP-ney, dis-MISSED!"*

The company was reassembled in less than an hour. The platoon commanders and sergeants had already decided how to reorganize their platoons, and which of their Marines needed promotions, so most of that hour had been taken up with getting approval from Lieutenant Colonel Davis and the promotion warrants printed.

Captain Sitter held a brief ceremony to award the Purple Heart citations to the wounded Marines, followed by the promotions.

The first replacements arrived the next day.

THE NAVY IN ORBIT SEARCHED THE SURFACE OF TROY FOR GRAVITATIONAL ANOMALIES which could indicate the presence of caves or tunnel systems that the Dusters were believed to use to hide in and to move about undetected. Infrequently, when the Navy found such an anomaly, the Navy also found Dusters on the surface. On those few instances a Marine or Army battalion was sent to do battle. More often, there was no sign of the aliens visible on the surface. On those occasions, Marine Force Recon was sent to investigate, to discover whether or not the aliens were using the caves or tunnels. Usually, they didn't find any sign of Dusters.

But they always had to check. Just in case.

"Attention on deck!" Gunnery Sergeant Ernest A. Janson bellowed.

"At ease, Marines!" Captain Walter Newell Hill, commanding officer, First platoon, First Force Recon Company boomed as he strode into the company classroom where two squads waited. First Lieutenant George H. Cannon, First section commander, accompanied him.

The ten Marines of Third and Fourth squads resumed their seats in the two rows of folding chairs near the small stage that Captain Hill jumped on to.

"We have a mission," Hill began.

No shit, most of the enlisted men thought, but none said out loud. *There's no other reason we would be here now.*

"The Navy found has another anomaly with no visible sign of Dusters on the surface."

Which is what we are for, most of them thought. *To find out if any bad guys are there.*

"Here is the satellite view of the area of the anomaly." Hill pressed a button on the lectern he stood next to, and a screen behind him lit up with an overhead view of several square kilometers of scrubland. "This is the area of the anomaly." A dashed line appeared overlaying the landscape. A narrow, many-doglegged section appeared on the south side, with several alcoves of various sizes sticking off its sides. The farther it went, the larger the alcoves became. It terminated in what must be a large cavern, or amphitheater. Three short legs led off the cavern to the northwest in different directions,

"N-1 suspects those legs are entrances to a cave-tunnel complex. Your mission is to determine whether they are indeed entrances, and whether there is any sign of Dusters using them. You are not to enter the tunnels, if that is in fact what they are. You are to avoid contact with the enemy if they prove to be there. Remember, your mission is to snoop and poop and gather intelligence, not to fight.

"Transportation into and out of the area will be provided by Eagles from MMH-628, cover will be provided by AH-5 Cobras, from MAH-115.

"Third squad, your call sign is 'Raider,' Fourth squad is 'CAP.' Control is 'Big Two.'

"Are there any questions? If not, your platoon sergeant will provide you with maps, detectors, water, rations, and anything else the mission requires.

"Good hunting." He stepped off the stage and headed for the classroom exit.

"Ah-ten-HUT!" Jenson bellowed, and the ten Marines of the two Force Recon squads stood and came to relaxed positions of attention.

Cannon followed the company commander. As he passed his men he said just loudly enough for them to hear, "Go get 'em, tigers!"

Jenson waited until the officers were gone, then stepped to the front of the stage and waved a come-here gesture. "Gather around," he said. The ten joined him. "Here's your maps. Test them now." He handed each squad leader what looked like a thin roll of fabric.

The squad leaders accepted them, unrolled them, snapped them to rigidity, and pressed various controls that appeared on the edge of each.

"Full power," Third squad's Staff Sergeant William J. Bordelon said.

"Full power," Sergeant Joseph R. Julian of Fourth squad said.

They pressed other controls and each pad displayed a matte map of the Force Recon area, centered on them. More controls enlarged the area shown, or gave a tighter view. Another brought up blue dots and rectangles, showing the location of people and vehicles.

"My map seems to be working fine," Bordelon said.

"Mine too," Julian said.

"You will go in here and here," Janson said, pressing buttons that brought up an X on each map. "These are your primary extraction points." He brought up a Z on each map.

"Here's motion and scent," Jenson said, handing over detectors. "We'll test them outside. I'll issue water and rations later."

The squads spent the next two hours studying their maps and making their plan of maneuver.

Later, fully equipped, they gathered at the compound's vertical takeoff and landing pad where two T-43 Eagles waited for them.

Captain Hill and First Lieutenant Cannon joined them. The officers looked them over.

"If there are any Dusters where you're going," Hill said, "they'll have a damn hard time seeing you."

"Yes, Sir," Bordelon said, not necessarily believing the company commander. He and the other Marines going on this mission knew what had happened to the First platoon of Second Force Recon Company before VII Corps was assembled and left Earth to retake Troy. The Force Recon field uniform was patterned in such a way as to make the eye slide past it, rendering the wearer nearly invisible to the naked eye. The Dusters had almost wiped out the entire platoon, so they knew the aliens must have some way of seeing them no matter how nearly invisible they were to human eyes. But they weren't about to gainsay their company commander, so neither Bordelon nor any of the others said anything other than, "Yes, Sir," when he said the Dusters wouldn't be able to see them.

"Good hunting, Marines," Hill said. He and Cannon shook each of their hands before they boarded the aircraft.

Scrubland, fifty kilometers from Jordan,
Eastern Shapland

The Eagles flew zigzag routes, touching down frequently on high grounds and hollows, until the Marines jumped off five kilometers from the anomaly; Third squad to its east, Fourth to its west. The Eagles made several more touch-and-goes away from the anomaly before turning back to their squadrons' airfields. The multiple touchdowns were to prevent watchers from knowing exactly where the squads were dropped off.

"Get ready, we're approaching your drop point," a voice buzzed in Staff Sergeant Bordelon's headset.

Bordeon took off the headset and hung it on a hook in the cabin. That was the signal for the squad to prepare to jump. He turned on his shoulder-mounted camera and looked to see that his men did as well.

Where Third squad dropped off was the sunny side of a defile. Knee-high bushes grew among the rocks and small boulders that speckled the ground, evidence of an ancient rock slide. Spindly trees popped up, mostly in the bottom of the defile. Fourth squad came down in a north-south oriented defile, with ground less rocky. Bushes here frequently rose to waist high, and trees were more frequent and not as spindly, although none of the Marines would characterize them as shade trees. In both areas, insectoids flitted and buzzed around the bushes once the interruption of the Eagle and disgorgement of the Marines had settled. Avians swooped among the insectoids, seeking a meal. High above, other avians glided on rising thermals. Occasionally one dove at a swooper, and sometimes caught its own dinner.

Bordelon looked all around, moving his torso so the camera picked up all directions.

Third squad went to ground on the shady side of its defile, a hundred meters from where they'd exited the Eagle. They formed a five-pointed star, with their feet touching in the middle. Lance Corporal Kraus, the best shot in the squad, carried its only rifle. The others were armed with sidearms; Force Recon's job was intelligence gathering, they believed that their mission was a failure if they got into a fire fight, so they went lightly armed.

They waited, watching for anybody coming to investigate the touchdown of the aircraft.

After a half hour's wait without seeing or hearing any sign of someone coming to investigate, Staff Sergeant Bordelon checked his map to verify that the squad was where it expected to be. The Marines were in the right place. He got onto his comm and sent a two word message: "Raider, moving," then tapped Corporal Stein and pointed. He didn't get an answer to his message, and hadn't expected one.

Stein rose to his feet and started along the defile. Bordelon followed, then came Lance Corporals Kraus and Roan. Sergeant Vaughn brought up the rear.

Stein followed the defile for a kilometer before stopping and looking back to his squad leader for instruction.

Bordelon pointed to the left, where the top of the defile had crumbled into a V-shaped notch. Stein headed for the notch, stepping carefully so as to not dislodge any of the stones on the slope. He stopped just below the notch and eased to the side before cautiously rising up to where he could see through it. Seeing no threat on the land beyond, he darted through the notch, keeping bent low enough to not show above the notch's side and dropped twenty meters beyond it. The other four Marines followed rapidly, all staying below the top of the notch. They took the same five-point circle they had when they first went to ground.

This time they only waited and watched for fifteen minutes before Bordelon signaled Stein to move out again.

They went bent low on a tangent to their objective, keeping out of the sightline of anyone who might have come straight out of the suspected tunnel entrance. The ground here was less rocky than in the defile, and more trees grew, providing limited concealment from potential hostile viewers. Along the way they zigged and zagged, sometimes heading more directly toward their objective, sometimes away from it. Moving slowly and never straight, it took three hours to get within three hundred meters of the possible tunnel mouth. The ground steadily rose.

Again, they went to ground in a five-point star. Bordelon deployed his motion and scent detectors for the first time. He spoke into his comm, "Raider in place." Again, he expected no reply, and didn't get one.

The motion detector was set to show only movement of something half the size of a man or larger, so the flitting insectoids and swooping birds didn't register on it. For the half hour they waited, neither did anything else. The scent detector didn't note any wafting chemicals that would indicate the possible nearby presence of a Duster.

Bordelon kicked into the cluster of feet in the center of the star—the signa thers and no farther. It was the first word any of them had said out loud except for Bordeon's comm messages since they boarded the Eagles back at the Force Recon compound.

Everyone stopped and went to a knee, looking in different directions. Except for Bordelon, who went to Vaughn's side. There, crossing Vaughn's path left rear to right front, were the distinctive taloned footprints of several Dusters.

Bordelon followed the tracks with his eyes—they went directly to the so-far unseen location of the suspected tunnel mouth. He signaled Vaughn to come with him. Along the way they gathered Roan. When they reached Kraus, Bordelon signaled Stein to join them. All five lowered to a knee and put their heads together.

"Tracks, leading there," Bordelon said softly, and pointed where they led. "We go. Be ready."

While the squad began an oblique approach to the suspected entrance, the squad leader sent another terse message, "Sign found. Investigating."

The tracks disappeared into a meter-wide gouge in the sloping ground. Bordelon stopped his squad and advanced alone, with his detectors held before him. The motion detector didn't register anything, but the display of the scent detector started jumping as soon as he extended it toward the opening. Carefully, he continued up the slope to where he could lie above the entrance. He stretched both detectors to aim into the tunnel. The motion detector didn't register anything but the scent was strong.

Found 'em! he thought, and shot a thumbs up at his men. Back on his feet, stepping softly with the scent detector extended, he walked along the ground in the direction of the tunnel, and onto the roofs of some of the side caverns shown in the Navy scans. He was looking for scents rising from ventilaiton shafts. He thought there must be some, but either there weren't any or the shafts had baffles that absorbed scents.

Deciding that further search would be futile, he returned to his squad. A few meters from the tunnel entrance, he pulled what appeared to be a large pebble out of his pocket and dropped it on the ground. The pebble wasn't as innocent as it looked. When activated by a given radio signal, it would radiate a pulse, that guided on, allowing Marines to home directly on it, and to the tunnel entrance.

He pointed the direction for Corporal Stein and sent another message as the squad began its movement, "Raider leaving objective. Success."

It took Third squad two hours to reach its extraction point, where they waited twenty minutes for an Eagle to respond to Bordelon's signal that they were there.

Force Recon compound,
Headquarters NAU Forces Troy

Fourth squad returned to base nearly an hour after Third; they'd had to investigate three possible tunnel or cave entrances.

Captain Hall delayed the debriefing of Third squad until Fourth squad returned. When both squads were assembled in the company classroom, he handed the debriefing to First Lieutenant Robert M. Hanson, First Force Recon Company's S-2—intelligence—officer.

Staff Sergeant Bordelon went first. Hanson's eyes glowed at the finding of strong Duster scent emanating from the cave entrance. Captain Hall grinned a predatory grin. Lieutenant Cannon looked at Third squad with obvious approval. They eagerly watched the vids the Marines had taken, especially of the tracks leading to the tunnel's entrance. They were mildly disappointed that Bordelon hadn't found any ventilation shafts.

Then it was Third squad's turn.

"Sirs," Sergeant Julian began, "The landscape on the northwest of the subject area isn't as rocky as what Staff Sergeant Bordelon described in his sector. It's still scrub forest, but with more trees and fewer bushes.

"We found no sign of Dusters until we approached the suspected entrances. There were a few footsteps, but not from as many individuals as Third squad discovered." The vids he showed made that clear. "These entrances, it's pretty clear, are smaller than the one to the south. My best guess is only one of these entrances is in use, and that simply as a way into open air when Dusters feel the need to get out of the cave." He shrugged. "At least that's what I'd think if the enemy was human instead of alien. One of the other two gave no detectable scent, it probably wasn't broken all the way through."

He had more to say, but nothing of significance. Neither did any of his squad mates, they thought he had covered everything they'd discovered.

"Outstanding, Marines," Captain Hall said at the end of the debriefing. "I'm sure whatever unit is sent to clear out that nest will find your intelligence immensely valuable.

"That is all. Gunny Janson, take charge. After they've showered and changed uniforms, you may sound the liberty call." He left the classroom with the other officers in tow.

"You heard the man," Janson said when the officers were gone. "Get yourselves cleaned up and take off on liberty. Base liberty, of course."

The ten Marines headed for their quarters and a shower. Liberty call didn't mean much, there wasn't really anywhere to go.

The next day the two squad leaders met with the officers and platoon sergeants of Company I, Third Battalion, First Marines to plan the company's approach to the cave-tunnel complex. The following day, the two squads went out again, to prepare to guide India Company to the cave-tunnel complex—and to assure that the Dusters were still there.

Ward 3, Field Hospital 4, near Pikestown,
West Shapland

"Up and at 'em, Mackie. The doctor tells me he needs this bed."

Corporal John Mackie, dressed in a hospital gown and thin robe, looked up from the book he was reading to see his squad leader, Sergeant James Martin standing at the foot of his hospital bed. Then he looked around the ward where eight of the twelve beds were already empty, and back at his squad leader. "Sure he does, Sergeant Martin. What do you think he's going to do with it?"

"He's a doctor," Martin answered, stepping around the bed to Mackie's side and lowering his voice. "How do I know what he's got planned? Maybe he's got something on with one of the nurses and needs a horizontal surface. Have you *seen* them, the nurses? Some of them are pretty choice." He looked toward the nurses' station, beyond one end of the ward. The station was the pivot point for this ward and two others. The fourth side opened into a corridor that led to the main entrance of the field hospital.

Mackie snorted. "No shit, I've seen them. What do you think I've been doing here? Can't spend all of my time sleeping and reading."

Martin laughed at that. "If almost anybody else in the squad said that I'd think he was joking. But you actually read a lot." He clapped Mackie's shoulder. "How's your gut?"

Mackie patted his abdomen. "I've got a scar, but that's about it. I heard you got wounded, too. How are you doing?"

"I'm a Marine sergeant. I heal faster than mere corporals."

"Yeah, sure. But you're okay?"

"I was released a couple of days ago. You're the last man from First squad who hasn't returned to duty yet. Even Horton's back, and his leg was hurt worse than your tummy."

"Then let's go." Mackie stood and opened the slender locker that stood next to the head of his bed. It held two field uniforms, his pack, and gear harness. The pack was empty and nothing hung on the harness. In seconds, he had his miniscule collection of toiletries swept from the bedside stand into a carrying case, which he put in the pack along with his book and library crystal. Another minute and he was out of the hospital gown and in uniform.

"Follow me," Martin said, and stepped out, toward the nursing station and the exit. Mackie fell in a pace to his left and rear.

"Corporal Mackie," the nurse at the station, a lieutenant junior grade, said sternly, "I don't want to see you back here. Understand?"

"Yes, Ma'am, I understand." Mackie said with a grin at her as he passed.

She smiled at the "Ma'am," as she was only a couple of years older than he was.

Out of her hearing Mackie said to Martin, "The Navy sure makes good nurses."

"Oh, yeah, the best." Martin agreed, remembering a night back in Riverside when he'd met an off duty nurse, and the night had turned into a weekend.

Firebase Zion, near Jordan,
West Shapland

Firebase Zion was a barren place, as such advance positions usually were. The vegetation had been removed inside the base's combat-wire perimeter, and fields of fire had been cleared some four hundred meters beyond the wire, making a rough circle nearly a kilometer in diameter of denuded ground. Holes, the beginnings of bunkers, had been dug a few meters inside the wire, with narrow zigzag trenches connecting them. Inboard from the bunkers were square tents, each capable of housing six men. Most of them had their sides rolled up, exposing cots that stood on plasteel pallets. A discarded packing crate squatted by each cot. A larger tent more or less centered in the compound served as kitchen and mess hall. A road cut through the field of fire from the north and terminated in a gate wide enough to admit an Eighter in the wire fence.

The Eighter that transported the now-recovered casualties from the hospital to the firebase rolled through the opened gate and pulled up in front of the command bunker, an unfinished hole with a roof that did little more than provide shade. Captain Carl Sitter heard the vehicle coming and stepped into the open as the Marines were jumping out of the vehicle. The platoon sergeants had also heard the Eighter coming and headed for the CP, where they stood off to the side.

"Detail, fall in at attention!" Gunnery Sergeant Robert Robinson ordered.

In seconds, the seven Marines who'd just been released from the hospital and the four squad leaders who escorted them on the Eighter were in line facing their company commander.

"Welcome back, Marines," Sitter said. "I'm very glad to see you. Not only because you are well again, but because the company needs you." He paused to look each of them in the eye. "There are still Dusters out there, and indications are they plan to hit us again.

Before they do, we have work to do. We need to finish making this firebase a strong defensive position, and we have to go out there," he gestured toward the landscape beyond the perimeter of the firebase, "and locate and neutralize any Dusters that are still in the area, break up any assembly points they're making."

He turned to face Robinson. "Gunnery Sergeant, the detachment is yours."

"Aye aye, Sir." Robinson didn't salute, not here where an enemy sniper might be watching for such a sign. As soon as Sitter ducked into the CP bunker, Robinson turned to the platoon sergeants. "Take your Marines to your areas and get them settled in. But do it quickly. You have your orders, brief your men and get ready.

"Do it."

Staff Sergeant Guillen pointed a finger at Martin and Mackie and crooked it in a "follow me" gesture. The two stepped out briskly to join their platoon sergeant who was already heading for Third platoon's part of the perimeter.

"We haven't had any contact since you got hit," Guillen said, looking at Mackie, when they caught up. "But we keep finding signs of them being out there."

"What kind of signs, Staff Sergeant?" Mackie asked. He and Martin hadn't discussed what was happening on the trip from the hospital, other than who the new men were and how they were fitting in.

"Fresh scratch marks in the ground, like from claws. Fresh scat. The kinds of thing that we'd think were made by a bear, or a big cat on a different world." He shook his head. "But nobody's seen a big predator here. Or any kind of animal much bigger than a middle size dog."

Martin listened as intently as Mackie did to the explanation; he hadn't heard any of that during the two days he'd been back. But then, Third platoon hadn't put out any patrols during that time.

"Has there been a lot of sign?" Mackie asked.

"Not much. Just enough to make me pretty sure there are still Dusters in the area, just like the Skipper said. And they aren't staying underground."

When they reached the squad area, Guillen told Martin, "Get him settled in, then take him to Sergeant Adams for his weapons and other gear." That was the end of talking about what they'd seen on patrols.

"Aye aye," Martin said. To Mackie, "Right here, all the comforts of home."

The comforts of home didn't amount to much. They consisted of a pair of two-man tents with their sides raised for ventilation, and a couple of boards laid across two stacks of sandbags at a tabletop-height for a man sitting on the ground. A field-expedient stove squatted a few meters from one end of the table and a water-dispensing camel was an equal distance from the other.

"We don't get the squad tents?" Mackie asked when he saw the tent he was assigned to.

Martin shook his head. "Squad leaders and up."

Then they were with Mackie's men.

Mackie was pleased with himself because he remembered his new man and was able to greet him by name."How's everything going, Horton? How's your leg? Any problems fitting in? Everybody treating you all right?"

"No, Corporal," PFC Horton answered. "Ah, I mean, yes, Mackie." He stood from where he'd been lounging in the shade of one of the tents and shifted foot-to-foot.

Mackie knuckled Horton's shoulder. "You mean you've got problems fitting in, and everybody's treating you like shit?"

Horton flushed. "N-No, Mackie. I mean, I mean…"

Mackie laughed. "I know what you mean, Horton. Relax. I'm I'm easy to get along with, just busting your chops a bit. Cafferata's the one you have to worry about."

"Say what?" yelped Lance Corporal Cafferata, who'd been sitting cross-legged in the other tent's shade.

"I didn't stutter, Hector. New guys have to watch out for you. Every one of them, and all the time." To Horton in a conspiratorial tone, "You should have seen him when he was in Second fire team and Porter joined us. Hector rode him mercilessly. The Skipper had to threaten him with a court martial to make him stop. At that, poor Porter almost got locked up in a psych ward."

"You're so full of it, John," Cafferata snorted.

"That's 'Corporal John' to you, Lance Corporal."

"That's enough you two," Martin finally interjected with a chuckle. "Mackie, let's go to Sergeant Adams, get your weapons and gear."

"Good to see you, Orndoff." Mackie waved at the other man in his fire team as he started off with the squad leader. "How's the arm?"

"Welcome back, Honcho," Orndoff said, and returned the wave, showing that his wounded arm was fully recovered.

The company supply room was another roughly dug and covered bunker in the central area of the firebase. Unlike the command bunker, the supply bunker could be locked to prevent theft. Sergeant Adams was in it, shifting containers about to find the ones belonging to the just-returned Marines. He already had their weapons stacked by the entrance.

"Sergeant Adams, I've got Mackie here," Martin said when they reached the entrance.

"And I'm getting everything ready," Adams shouted from the depths of the bunker. "Just a sec." In a moment he was at the entrance, dusting his hands against each other.

"Mackie, Mackie, Mackie. Corporal. Right. I think this one is yours. Check the serial number." Adams snatched an M23 rifle from the rifle rack, glanced quickly at its serial number, then handed it to Mackie. While Mackie verified that it was the right rifle, Adams laid out magazines, a bayonet, a water camelback, and a first aid kit. "Put these on your belt," Adams said, and turned to make a pile of body armor. "We finally got armor, would have prevented a lot of wounds." He glanced at Mackie's midsection. Helmet with integral comm, night vision glasses, foul weather gear, field bedding, and other miscellany. He even tossed in an extra pair of boots. Finally he handed Mackie a pad and said, "Sign these."

Mackie looked at the weapons and gear he was given, compared them to the listings, one for the rifle and one for everything else, and signed.

As Mackie and Martin turned to leave, the supply sergeant called after them, "I don't want to hear any shit about combat losses. You got that, Mackie?"

"You hear that, Sergeant Martin?" Mackie said loudly enough for Adams to hear. "Sergeant Adams says I have to stay out of combat."

"Sergeant Adams isn't your squad leader, Mackie," Martin said. "I am. I say that when the shooting starts, you head into it."

"You're the boss."

"Damn skippy, I am."

In front of the India Company CP

"At ease," Captain Sitter ordered, and his men relaxed their stance. Most of the Marines of the company were in formation in front of him. Only the few on perimeter duty, watching the surrounding landscape for approaching enemy, weren't present.

"We have just returned from a briefing on the current situation," Sitter said after a moment. "Here is our mission for today.

"We are going out to check out another anomaly the Navy found. The Navy didn't see any positive signs of Dusters, just an anomaly that probably indicates the presence of underground spaces. So Force Recon went in. They found entrances to a tunnel or cave system, and indications of Duster activity going in and out. They couldn't tell if the Dusters are still in there or if they vacated recently. Our job is to find out if the Dusters are still there and kill any alien bastards that we find.

"The Force Recon squads that went there yesterday will meet us at our drop off points and guide us to the entrances.

"Are there any questions?" That was a question not normally asked of an entire company.

"Yes, Sir," somebody from Second platoon called out.

Sitter looked at him. "Ask."

"If the Dusters are at this anomaly, how many can we expect to find?"

"I don't know. Nobody knows. For that matter, if the Navy knows how many Dusters might be there, they haven't told us."

Sitter ignored the *sotto voce*, "Typical squids, not telling the Marines what we need to know."

The captain's gaze swept the company, but nobody else seemed about to ask anything. He said, "If that's everything, platoon sergeants, take your platoons. Officers, with me. Dismissed!" He about faced and marched into the CP bunker. Only after the company's officers followed him did the platoon sergeants move their Marines back to their areas.

"Third platoon, on me!" shouted Second Lieutenant Commiskey as he neared the platoon's area following the officers' meeting in the company CP. "Gather around, semi-circle."

In moments, forty-six of the platoon's Marines stood in an arch to the front of their platoon commander; the platoon sergeant and right guide flanked the officer.

"Listen up!" Commiskey said. "This anomaly is in the same area where we fought them the last time. This time we will thoroughly search what might be a tunnel complex at the anomaly. Yes, I know, the 6th Marines cleaned up after our fight. But they didn't go underground. Third platoon will go

into the tunnels, if any are there. Second platoon will set security outside the complex, they'll be the anvil on which our hammer hits the Dusters.
We will kill or capture any Dusters we find, and destroy any equipment or
supplies. On leaving, we will collapse the tunnel system. First platoon will be
company reserve.

"Our order of march will be First squad, me, one gun team, Second
squad, Staff Sergeant Guillen, the other gun team, Sergeant Binder, Third
squad.

"We move out in thirty. Squad leaders will issue ammunition and tunnel
visions—your regular night vision glasses probably won't do enough in the
tunnels.

"Questions?"

There were, but "Why do we have to do this?" wasn't an acceptable
question, so nobody asked anything.

Camp Zion, near Jordan,
Eastern Shapland

"WHAT DO YOU THINK, MACKIE?" LANCE CORPORAL CAFFERATA ASKED AS THE TWO Marines lounged on top of their bunker, waiting for the orders to move out. First squad's other two fire team leaders sat leaning against the bunker's front.

"I think a lot of things, Hector," Corporal Mackie replied. "What do you want to know?"

Cafferata made a face. "You know. The only damn thing we need to know about. Are the Dusters in the cave we're going to? What are they doing there? Or did they leave, have we beaten them? Have they shot their wad?"

Mackie mulled over the questions for a moment before answering. During the pause, Corporals Vittori and Button pulled away from the bunker's front and looked up at the junior fire team leader to hear what he'd say.

"The last one first," Mackie finally said. "I don't think they've shot their wad. If we start thinking we beat them, things could go very badly for us the next time we run into them. As for your other questions, how the hell do I know? I don't have a pipeline into G-2 or N-2. And they sure as shit aren't telling me what they know." He shrugged. "What I think beyond that is, we need to stay sharp and be ready to do some serious ass-whomping on the Dusters." He shuddered. "Especially if we meet them in caves."

Cafferata screwed up his eyes and peered hard at the trees. He muttered under his breath.

"What's that?" Mackie asked. "I couldn't make it out."

"I said something like I don't understand why some people don't just give up when they know they're facing Marines."

"Dusters aren't people, they're aliens. That's why."

"You think about these things, Mackie," said Sergeant Martin from the back of the bunker. "That's why I keep you around."

Mackie and Cafferata spun about, bringing their rifles to bear at the unexpected voice. In front of the bunker, Vittori and Button ducked down and grabbed their rifles, ready to fire around the bunker's corners.

"Goddam it, Sergeant Martin!" Mackie shouted when he saw the squad leader. "You've got to stop sneaking up on us like that."

"I keep telling you, you need to have three-sixty awareness. Remember the house on Sugar Cover Place? You don't know that the Dusters can't come up inside the bunkers and hit you from behind when you're sitting like this.

"Now get your fire team leaders ready. It's time for us to go spelunking."

For the first time, First squad's fire team leaders became aware of the other squad leaders, the platoon sergeants, and Gunnery Sergeant Hoffman yelling for the company to assemble.

Scrubland, near Jordan, Eastern Shapland,
Semi-Autonomous World Troy

A squadron of T-43 Eagles airlifted India Company's First and Third platoons six kilometers from the main entrance of the cave-tunnel complex that First Force Recon's Third squad had confirmed was a Duster location. Second platoon was dropped seven klicks from the rear entrance to serve as a blocking force if any Dusters tried to escape that way. They also had a squad of sappers, who would endeavor to blow the tunnel mouths once the platoons going in through the main enterance made contact with the aliens, thereby preventing the Dusters from using them as bolt holes. Divisions of AV16 C Kestrels rotated in a holding orbit five minutes flight from the cave-tunnel complex, in case India Company found itself in a fight on the surface.

A nearly invisible Marine stood up from the scrub and walked to the company command unit.

"Captain Sitter," Staff Sergeant Bordelon said, greeting the company commander.

"Staff Sergeant," Sitter said.

"We got close enough to the tunnel mouth to pick up strong scents, Sir. I went over the top with my sniffer, and didn't find any ventilation holes. Still, I have no doubt the Dusters are still there."

"What about the rear entrance?" Sitter asked.

"The bolt hole is the same as before. Individual tracks coming and going from one mouth, no scents from another. The third still seems unused."

"Outstanding. Let's go dust some aliens."

"Aye aye, Sir." Bordelon turned from Sitter and signaled his squad. The other four Force Recon Marines stood from where they'd been effectively invisible, and started heading along the route they'd already planned. Bordelon took his place as the second man in the short column.

"Third platoon, follow our guides," Sitter ordered on his comm.

Third platoon hastened to get close enough for their point to easily make out the hard-to-see trailing Force Recon Marine. Sitter came with the company's heavy machine gun and mortar section. First platoon brought up the rear. They went slow and easy, and took three hours to cover the six kilometers. They moved as silently as they could, but two hundred men can't move as quietly as five, so they were much noisier than the earlier recon patrol had been.

Not that there were any Duster observation posts or patrols out to hear them.

Outside the cave-tunnel complex

Captain Sitter went with First platoon and had Third platoon station fire teams along the way to relay messages from the depths to the weapons platoon and sappers left on the surface.

Lieutenant Commiskey listened to the company command circuit on his helmet comm, said an "Aye aye" acknowledgement, then toggled his comm to the platoon freq.

"Listen up, Third platoon." he said. "The company's in place. We're going in. Sergeant Martin, move out."

"Aye aye," Martin answered on his comm. Using naked voice he said, "You heard the man, Vittori, go."

"Roger," Corporal Joseph Vittori said. "Harvey, lead off. I'm right behind you."

PFC Harry Harvey didn't say anything, he just ducked into the opening in front of him, and started into the tunnel. It went down at a steep angle and quickly dropped below the level of the flat ground above, where it turned sharply, cutting off most the light that filtered in from the outside, Then turned again, plunging the tunnel into darkness deep enough that normal night-vision glasses couldn't penetrate. Harvey slid his "tunnel vision" goggles over his eyes. Vittori followed about two meters behind, and like-wise slid his tunnel vision goggles into place. The rest of First fire team trailed him, with each man putting on his goggles as he turned the corner. Then came Martin and Third fire team.

Mackie wanted to be next after Martin, but knew that he had to be in a position to control his men, so he put Horton behind the squad leader and positioned himself in front of Cafferata. Orndoff connected with Second fire team.

The tunnel had a flat floor and smooth sides. Even though it was almost wide enough for two men to walk side by side, the ceiling was so low that the Marines had to walk slightly hunched over. There were no lights, at least none that were on. The tunnel vision goggles didn't show colors, but the walls shimmered with a slight gloss. The gloss didn't translate into a slickness to the touch. Mackie wondered, not for the first time, whether the Dusters had some form of echo-location or other sense that allowed them to "see" in reduced or non-existent light.

About fifty meters in, the smoothness of the wall on the right was broken by a doorway. Martin reported it to Commiskey, who came forward while Martin set security.

"What do you think, Sergeant?" Commiskey asked after he examined the door.

A lever-like handle was recessed into one side of the door. Other than that, there was no visible slot or other knob that looked like a locking device. The top of the door was low enough that a man would have to bend almost double to go through it.

Martin shook his head. "Doesn't look like there's anything important in there. But then, we don't know how they secure things."

"So the only thing to do is take a look."

"That's right, Sir. So if you'll step back—"

"A good commander never asks his men to do something he won't do himself. *You* step back, Sergeant."

Martin gave Commiskey a penetrating look, then made a curt nod and said, "First fire team, move forward twenty meters. Third, move forward and follow us in." To Commiskey, "I'm with you, Lieutenant." He pressed his back against the wall to the side of the door opposite the handle.

Commiskey faced the wall next to the door and reached for the handle. It didn't move when he pressed down on it. He lifted, and the door popped open into the space beyond it.

Martin was ready, and dove through the open doorway. He rolled away from it and came up in a crouch, pointing his rifle into the chamber; his eyes swept the room, the muzzle of his rifle tracked with his eyes. He saw Commiskey follow him the same way on the other side of the door. The officer held his handgun ready.

"Mackie," Martin shouted, "get in here!"

In seconds, Mackie and his men were spreading out inside the room.

To the Marines, it was a modest-size room, no more than fifteen meters deep, less than that in width, about double the height of the tunnel outside it. Pillars dotted the chamber, holding up cross beams that supported the ceiling. It looked to have been a storeroom, although whatever had been stored in it was now gone, leaving only a few racks and some shelving. It only took a minute to check behind the pillars to make sure nothing was hiding there. They didn't take the time to check the walls for hidden doors.

Commiskey reported the room to Captain Sitter, then told Martin, "The Skipper's going to have the sappers prepare it to blow on our way out," Commiskey said. "Let's continue."

In a moment, First squad was back in the tunnel, heading deeper into the complex. Every fifty to a hundred meters they found another room on one side of the tunnel or the other. The chambers varied in size from the smallish first one to the size of a small auditorium. Six rooms were as empty as the first one. The sappers prepared each of their entrances to blow once the Marines passed on their way out.

The seventh, compared to the other six, was mid-sized. And that wasn't the only difference.

Forty pairs of bowl-shaped objects—the Marines could only compare them to nests—were spaced through the chamber. One nest in each pair was larger, large enough to act as a bed for a Duster. The other, much smaller, was divided into segments; perhaps the Duster equivalent of a locker.

There was a long moment of silence before Mackie broke it. "I suddenly have an image of Dusters hunkering down on these things, with their heads tucked under a wing."

"Just like nesting birds," Martin said.

"Or dinosaurs," Mackie said softly.

All of First squad filtered into the... "It's a squadbay!" Cafferata exclaimed.

"Damn," somebody muttered, his voice muffled by the material of the nests.

"Look at the spacing," Mackie said.

"What about it?" Vittori asked.

"They're far enough apart that a Duster can stand next to one and his tail won't overlap any of the others."

"I do believe you're right," Martin said when he looked at the distance between nests.

"This is just like the Cretaceous nesting colonies paleontologists found back in the twentieth century."

"Mackie," Corporal Button said, wandering among the nests, searching, "sometimes I think you read too much. If you put that effort into being a Marine, you'll make Commandant one day."

Mackie snorted. Before he could make any other reply, Commiskey entered the squadbay.

"How recently was this occupied?" he wanted to know.

"Are they warm-blooded?" Martin asked.

"Don't know."

Martin removed a glove and bent over to feel the middle of a nest. "If they are, it's been long enough for the bedding to drop to room temperature. If not..." His camouflaged shrug went mostly unseen.

"Has anybody seen anything of interest in here," Commiskey asked, "other than these nest-things? No hidden doors? Nothing?"

Nobody spoke up.

"All right then, let's move out. We need to go through this whole complex until we find the Dusters. Time's wasting."

"Mackie, you know so damn much about the Dusters," Martin said, "third fire team has point. Lead the way."

"Got it," Mackie said. "Orndoff, point."

Orndoff grunted, and led the way out of the apparent squadbay and turned deeper into the tunnel.

An hour into the tunnel complex

The tunnel had long since stopped being straight lines and ninety-degree turns, with a ceiling constantly low enough that a man had to stoop to avoid banging his head. Neither were the walls and floor as uniform as they had been for the first few hundred meters. The floors and walls of the rooms became more uneven, and showed signs of having been worked to even them out a bit. And it always went down. Sometimes the slope was barely perceptible, occasionally it was acute.

"It looks like they cut a tunnel into an existing cave network," Corporal Mackie observed over the squad freq.

"No shit, Sherlock," Sergeant Martin said sardonically. "Just keep looking for bad guys."

There were more empty rooms, and chambers that showed signs of occupancy. There was no way the Marines could tell how recently the chambers had been occupied; perhaps their denizens had all been killed during the earlier fights. That was something everyone could hope for. It wasn't something that many believed.

"Got a big one here," Mackie said when he followed PFC Orndoff into a huge, oval-shaped chamber, maybe two hundred meters deep and nearly as wide at its widest point. Its back wall sloped away from the entrance in two terraces. Very little of the chamber had been worked; a few stalagmites jutted up from rubble on the floor, which looked as though it was in the process of being cleared. Stalactites hung from overhead. The walls were drapperied with flowstone. It was more properly called a cavern.

"Damn, I wish tunnel vision let us see colors," Corporal Vittori said when he entered the chamber. "I'll bet this place is gor—"

A bullet hit him square in the chest, knocking him backward.

"Down!" Mackie shouted at the same time as Martin. The eight Marines other than Vittori who were in the chamber dove for the floor and took cover behind stalagmites, some stubs, some still standing. They threw their rifles into their shoulders and began blasting into the depths of the cavern.

Martin didn't shoot, he looked for where the fire was coming from. He couldn't see the Dusters themselves because they were too well hidden, but he could see their muzzle flashes above the upper terrace.

"First fire team," he shouted, his voice rising over the cacophony of echoing gunfire; the *cracks* of bullets zinging past, the *pings* of ricocheting and shattering slugs. "Upper terrace, ten o'clock high to twelve. I think there are four in that area. Second fire team, noon to two. Third fire team, some of them are below the upper terrace. Look for their muzzle flashes."

The Marines' fire evened out, became more regular and more disciplined. Sparks thrown by bullets impacting stone showed where bullets were striking, hitting ever closer to the muzzle flashes of the Dusters' weapons.

Only once he saw that his men were hitting near where he knew the enemy had positions did Martin finally call, "Vittori, sound off!"

"Here," Vittori croaked.

"Are you okay?"

"Hurts, but—" Vittori paused while a cough blasted through his body. "—but I'll live." He gasped, but his body armor had stopped the bullet.

"See to it that you do, Marine." Martin looked to see where his men's rounds were hitting. He didn't need to adjust anybody's fire.

During the few seconds Martin took to give his men orders and check on Vittori, Lieutenant Commiskey darted into the cavern and dove for cover behind a thick stalagmite stump. He quickly assessed the situation, and ordered over the platoon freq, "Adriance, get your squad in here! Intersperse with First squad! First gun, let Third squad get in, then move in to lay down covering fire, right to left. The bad guys're mostly high."

"Third squad, move!" Sergeant Adriance shouted. "Keep low. Move, move, move! Spread out, spread out!"

There was more shouting and crashing of pounding boots as second squad scrambled into the chamber, and thuds as diving bodies hit the room's floor.

"Fancy meeting you here," Adriance said when he hit the deck next to Mackie. "Where are they?"

"They're on the upper terrace. Watch my tracers, they'll guide you." Mackie switched his rifle to short bursts and cranked off a couple.

"Got it," Adriance said. "Glowen," he shouted at his First fire team leader, who was to his right, "See where my bullets are going?"

"That's an affirmative," Corporal Glowen shouted back. "First fire team, put them where I'm hitting." He started pouring short bursts into the same area.

Mackie snorted. "We gotta stop meeting like this, Harry," he said between trigger pulls. "It could get dangerous."

Adriance's response was drowned out by the sudden staccato of the machine gun firing over their heads.

A few meters to Mackie's left, Commiskey got out his infrared scope and began scanning above the terrace—he had to ignore flashes from the speeding projectiles. *There!* He saw a greenish glow, the heat thrown off by bodies. "Gun, look for my mark! Five meters to the right of where you're hitting now."

"Ready," Corporal Andrew Tomlin called back.

Commiskey sighted on the infrared glow and pressed the button on the side of his scope that sent a brief pulse of laser light at the green. He saw red through the scope; the gun saw white in tunnel vision. Almost instantly, a long burst of machine gun fire blanketed the marked area. Fire from there ceased.

Martin had followed the verbal exchanges and the shifting of fire. "Third fire team," he said on his squad freq, "shift your fire to your right."

Mackie repeated the order to his men, even though they'd already heard it. "We're shifting right," he told Adriance.

"Got it." Adriance told his First fire team to also shift their aim to the right. Then he looked to see what the rest of his squad was doing.

The fire of two squads and a machine gun reverberating and echoing off the walls of the cavern was deafening, so much so that the Marines couldn't hear the Dusters' return fire. The sparks and flashes of ricocheting bullets added to a sense of visual confusion, as did bits of stone chipped off the flowstone and other rocky structures.

Suddenly, with a crash so loud it stunned the Marines in the cavern, a large section of ceiling above the rear wall collapsed onto the top terrace and avalanched down the rear wall. Dust billowed out, obscuring everything in its path. All shooting stopped.

Mackie gasped for breath; he felt like he'd been kicked in the chest and his lungs needed to be restarted. His ears rang so loudly he didn't think he could hear anything. He shook his head to clear it, blinked rapidly and repeatedly. He fish-mouthed, trying to squeak out sounds that might be words. His eyes finally focused on the mountain of dust and debris coming toward him, and he knew in a flash the danger the Marines were in.

"Pull back!" he croaked into his comm. He hawked to clear his throat and managed more clarity, "Pull back!" He slapped Adriance on the shoulder and jerked a thumb back, giving him the same message.

Adriance nodded, he was already on his comm odering his squad out of the cavern.

Dimly, Mackie heard indistinct sounds coming over his helmet comm; he thought it was Commiskey and Martin ordering everybody out. Looking to his flanks, he could barely make out the forms of Marines withdrawing. He scuttled to his right, then to his left to make sure his men were getting out. He was turning to exit himself when he bumped into Martin, who was checking that his squad was moving out.

"Third fire team, on the move," he managed to say. He used hand signals to repeat the message in case Martin's ears were still too numb to hear him.

Back in the tunnel, Commiskey moved Third squad back the way they'd come, where it would be out of the way of the Marines coming out of the cavern. He quickly considered what to do next.

Captain Sitter came forward to see what was happening. He thought the only viable option was a withdrawal. It was likely the tunnel would get blocked here, and he didn't know of any way out other than the way they'd come in—or farther forward.

"Pull back," Commiskey ordered, both over his comm and with hand signals. The Marines reversed their order of march and began heading out.

Corporal Vittori was the only casualty—unless loss of hearing and a few nicks and scrapes from flying rock chips counted—but was able to walk unaided.

Rumbles and crashes of more roof collapses followed the Marines as they withdrew. A few well-placed explosive charges collapsed tunnel sections and chamber entrances behind them. Pausing only to cover the sappers as they set off the charges they'd earlier set in rooms off the tunnel, it took less time for the platoon to reach open air than it had to reach the cavern where they'd had the fight.

Outside, the Marines gathered at a safe distance and watched dust and tiny rock chips billowing out of the tunnel, while constantly looking at their surroundings, watching for Dusters.

Outside

The sappers with Second platoon had blown the rear entrances as soon as they felt through the rocks the fire fight in the unfinished cavern. As soon as the Marines who had gone in were all out, Sitter had the sappers blow the main entrance.

The company stayed in place until the next day, in case any Dusters managed to get out. None did. Neither did other Dusters come to investigate. After twenty-four hours of waiting, a squadron of Eagles came to carry India Company back to its roost.

Advance Firebase One, under construction

THE DAY AFTER ALPHA COMPANY'S SECOND PLATOON SHOWED UP, THE FIREBASE WAS even more active than when the mobile infantrymen arrived. The soldiers immediately took over all security duties, and all of the engineers of the CB company set to on the base's construction.

First Lieutenant Miller, nominally subordinate to Second Lieutenant Greig, simply said he was taking his platoon out for a longer range patrol than the infantrymen could go on. The Mobile Intel platoon boarded their P-43 Eagles and took off.

Greig put two of his squads on perimeter duty.

"Sergeant O'Connor," he said to his Third squad leader, looking beyond the wire at the landscape rather than at the sergeant, "I want you to take your squad out a klick and a half, and do a circumnavigation of the firebase. Take a GPS, a map, and a motion detector. Go out the south gate and come back the same way."

Staff Sergeant Albert O'Connor looked to the south gate and the three hundred meters of scorched ground from it to the surrounding forest. "I sure wish we had our Growlers," he said. Growler, the M-117 armored vehicle used primarily by Mobile Infantry units.

"So do I, Sergeant. But we don't. That's why I only want you to go a klick and a half."

O'Connor nodded. He didn't like it, but he understood.

"Go slow and easy. I don't want you blundering into a Duster unit."

"You and me both, LT."

"Keep your eyes open for any sign of Duster activity. The Marines are still conducting mop-up operations and making kills, so we know they're still out there." Greig chewed on his lip for a moment. "We just don't know where. Try to avoid contact if you do see any Dusters. But I want you to be fully armed, five hundred rounds per man, so in case you can't avoid contact you can properly defend yourselves."

"Right, LT. Avoid if possible, kill the sonsabitches if we have to." He shook his head. "I wish we had body armor."

Greig hung his head and didn't answer that. Then, "Equip every man with a medkit and four liters of water. No rations, you won't be gone that long. Be back in three and a half, four hours.

"Run a comm check now. Run another when you reach the trees, and another at a klick and a half. Your call sign is Rover one."

"Wilco." O'Connor turned away and put on his helmet. "Third squad, comm check. Sound off." In two minutes all three of his fire team leaders responded, and he'd heard the men answering the fire team leaders call for a comm check.

While he was doing that, Greig walked off a hundred meters. "Rover one, Two Actual. Comm check. Over."

"Two Actual, Rover one. I hear you five-by. Three's comm check is successful. Over."

"Two Actual out."

The two looked at each other across the length of a football pitch, satisfied that they had communications at this distance. O'Connor headed for his platoon commander to get the extra equipment he would need for the patrol.

"Third squad, on me," O'Connor called when he reached his squad area, laden with ammunition and other gear.

In a moment his nine men stood before him in a tight group. Briefly, he told them what they were going to do, and dismissed them to get their weapons. When they reassembled, he had them fill their camelbacks with four liters of water. He gave their rifles a quick check and issued each of them what they needed to get up to the required five hundred rounds.

Satisfied, he gave the order to move out. "Sergeant Gasson, you've got point. South gate. Move fifty meters into the trees, stop, and set in a semicircle defense."

"Allen, move out," Sergeant Richard Gasson ordered his most experienced pointman.

Corporal Abner Allen spat to the side and headed for the south gate.

In the forest

Three hundred meters later, the squad moved under the trees. The ground at the edge of the forest was speckled with fast growing weeds and tiny saplings, growing in profusion now that more light was reaching the ground after the destruction of the trees in the burned area. Fifty meters in, half a dozen or more different varieties of tree were fairly close to each other and the cover was much thicker, dimming the light. Some of them grew arrow-straight with thinnish trunks, others were gnarly with thicker boles. Some lacked branches until they were close to ten meters tall, others began branching as close as a meter above the ground. At least one variety had buttress roots. The canopy gave almost total cover, nearly blanking out direct sunlight. Less undergrowth grew under the trees.

"Hold up," O'Connor ordered. "Positions."

The nine soldiers quickly moved into a semicircle and lowered themselves to the ground, facing outward with their rifles at their shoulders, ready to fight.

O'Connor looked around, and his lips twisted in something that wasn't quite a grimace. The forest was denser than he'd expected, and he wasn't comfortable in all these trees—it was entirely too possible for a foe to come close without being detected. If there'd been avians flitting about, sounding their cries and singing their songs, they could present an advantage to the soldiers. They'd likely go quiet if a large group of animals, think aliens or human, began moving through. Even the insectoids made precious little noise scrambling over and through the detritus. The flying insectoids left them alone; O'Connor suspected they'd already tried to dine off the Sea Bees and decided humans weren't to their taste.

Well, they'd really have to pussyfoot to walk quietly—there was too much detritus cruching and crackling under foot. He'd been disappointed by how much noise his men made moving through the forest. Still, it could be worse. After all, he had the motion detector. When he swept it in a circle it didn't show anything larger than a squirrel moving in the trees. He wondered what kind of animal was the Troy analog of squirrels. Or if the colonists had imported squirrels. Nonetheless, it felt spooky.

Time for the comm check.

"Two Actual, this is Rover one," he said into his helmet comm. "Comm check. How do you hear me? Over."

It was only a few seconds before Lieutenant Greig's voice came back. "Rover one, this is Two Actual. I hear you five by. You me? Over."

"Two Actual, Rover one. Five by. Over."

"Sitrep. Over."

O'Connor took a deep breath. How could he describe how the forest felt? He decided on just the basic facts. "Two Actual, Rover one. The trees are dense, less than ten meters between trunks, mostly about five meters, often closer. There's a lot of noisy ground cover that makes silent movement difficult if not impossible. Motion detector shows nothing bigger than a mid-size rodent nearby. Over."

"Rover one, continue your mission. Two Actual out."

O'Connor kept his face blank. It didn't sound like he'd gotten any of his misgivings across to the LT. Not that he'd made any real attempt to do so.

"Third squad, get up. Move out, same order as before." He checked his GPS and pointed the direction for Allen.

Allen spat to the side and started walking. His eyes pierced every shadow, looked at every possible hiding place, checked for booby-trap triggers. The muzzle of his rifle was in constant motion, always pointing where his eyes looked.

O'Connor called for another halt twelve hundred meters deeper into the forest and made his second comm check. He was surprised that, despite the trees between his current location and the firebase, that Greig's voice came through as clearly as it had when he made his first check. He finished his sitrep with, "We're going widershins."

After signing off, he called to the pointman. "Allen, go left."

Allen spat to the side and did as he was instructed.

"Widershins?" Sergeant Gasson asked.

O'Connor shrugged. "It's remotely possible that the Dusters are listening to our comm and able to break our encryption. If they understand English, maybe they know that counter-clockwise means go to the left. Widershins is archaic enough that they'll probably have no idea what it means. And, you'll note, I didn't say we were turning. A listener might think it's a code name for a location."

Gasson gave his squad leader a speculative look. "Smart. I guess that's why you make the big bucks."

"You got that right. Except for the big bucks."

O'Connor frequently checked his GPS, and corrected Allen's route when necessary to keep him going in a circle.

About three kilometers around the circle

Corporal Allen, on point, froze in place and lowered himself to one knee . He lifted his head and turned his face side to side. From behind, he looked like he was trying to locate the direction of a smell. Sergeant O'Connor padded to his side and squatted.

"Tell me," he said.

"Something. Maybe ammonia. There." He swung the muzzle of his rifle in an arc of about twenty degrees to his right front.

"How far?"

"Can't tell. Faint."

O'Connor sniffed. He wasn't sure, but he might have picked up a hint of ammonia in the air. "Not close," he murmured.

Allen shook his head, agreeing that it was not close.

"Let's check it out," O'Connor said. He turned to Sergeant Gasson, who had come up to find out why they'd stopped. "Allen and I are going to check it. You take the squad."

"Right. Be careful."

"I didn't last long enough to become a staff sergeant by being careless." To Allen, "Let's go."

The corporal led the way, stepping carefully to avoid making noise as much as possible, sniffing all they way. O'Connor watched sharply for any visible sign of Dusters.

"Getting stronger," Allen whispered after they'd gone a hundred meters deeper into the forest.

O'Connor nodded, he smelled it more sharply now as well. They slowed their pace, flowing from shadow to shadow, from the cover of one tree bole to another.

A casual *cooing* brought them up short.

Allen stretched his arm back and held up a finger at O'Connor, signaling *wait a minute*, then lowered himself to his knees and elbows to crawl forward. He only went ten meters before stopping and going flat to the ground. Moving slowly, he shifted his rifle to his shoulder and took aim.

Don't shoot unless you're spotted, O'Connor thought at Allen. *Please, don't shoot!* He had no way of knowing how many Dusters were nearby, but he was sure there had to be more of them than his squad had soldiers.

Allen watched carefully, and didn't pull the trigger. After a couple of minutes, he started easing backward until he reached O'Connor. He didn't speak, but signaled with a head nod for the two of them to withdraw farther. O'Connor nodded understanding and began a reverse elbows-and-knees crawl.

When they had gone beyond the point where they'd first heard the *coo*, Allen stopped.

"It's a latrine," he whispered with his lips near O'Connor's ear. "A Duster was relieving itself." He shook his head, marveling at what he'd seen. "It's a strange arrangement. There are two sticks poking up at each end of a short trench, with two poles going from one end to the other. The Duster is perched on the poles, one foot on each. It looked like it had a cloaca, with black-streaked white shit coming out of a slit."

O'Connor nodded, and signaled for them to go around the latrine. They went crouched low. It wasn't long before they saw the edge of a forest encampment. Leafy, tent-like structures were laid out in rows. Thin whisps of smoke rose from what the humans thought must be cook fires. The leafy overhead was just as thick as any other place O'Connor had seen—maybe even thicker. He wondered if the added denseness would block the infrared signals from live animals from getting out, whether the Mobile Intel platoon could spot this encampment from the air.

Some Dusters went about in purposeful-looking marches. Others lounged near the presumed tents, doing things to their weapons and gear. Cleaning them? Probably. O'Connor took images, 2-D and vid both, of the encampment, and used his GPS to record its location.

It wasn't possible to get an accurate estimate of the number of Dusters in the encampment, the two weren't at a good angle to see deep into it; the nearer tent-things obstructed their view. Still, going by the sounds of *cooing*, and *gobbling*, and the occasional *caw*, he estimated that there were the equivalent of a human battalion of the aliens in the camp. He thought they must feel very secure that they didn't have security out. Or had he and Allen lucked out and simply slipped between observation posts?

After a few minutes O'Connor decided they had gotten all the intelligence they could and were risking discovery. He signaled Allen and they withdrew. The first thing he did when they rejoined the squad was call in a report on what they'd found.

Lieutenant Greig didn't take time to look at the images before saying, "Continue your circuit. But be very careful. Now we know they're nearby."

"You got that right," O'Connor said, ignoring proper radio procedure.

"Two three," Greig said, "I'll be in touch with any change in orders. Until then, continue your mission. Over"

"Two Actual, two three. Roger, wilco. Over."

"Two Actual, out."

O'Connor signaled for the squad to gather close. "Keep watching outboard," he cautioned his men when they did. "Listen up, and listen good. There's a Duster camp less than half a klick in that direction." He pointed. "We are going to continue on our assigned route. I don't know if the Dusters have any patrols moving that could intercept us. When we move out, be as quiet as you can, be the most alert you've ever been in your life. We might have to fight our way back to the firebase.

"Same order of march. Five meter intervals. Move out."

Allen didn't hesitate. He spat to the side—away from the direction of the Duster camp—and began walking in the direction in which O'Connor pointed. In a minute, eleven very tense soldiers were continuing their circuit.

Lieutenant Greig was nervous about having the squad continue on the same route knowing that the aliens were so close, but they needed the intelligence. He notified the CB boss, Lieutenant Commander Harrison, of the discovery, and sent a report to Captain Meyer, who was still high above on the elevator station.

"Get that Mobile Intel platoon back to reinforce you," Meyer said when he found out that the MI platoon was out on its own. "At least one other platoon from the battalion is planetside. I'll ask to have them diverted to your location. Alpha Six Actual, out."

"Roger," Greig said to himself. Another platoon. Great. Even if he got the MI platoon back and got another platoon from the battalion, they weren't nearly enough to fight off so many Dusters. He knew from his briefings that nobody, Army or Marines, had artillery in place to support this firebase. The only fire assets that could be called on was a Marine AV 16C squadron. Maybe Meyer would ask Battalion to request that Brigade ask the Marines to sortie. The best would be for the Marines to strike the Duster camp before the aliens made a move.

But he couldn't ask for that in the open. Not as long as the possibility, no matter how remote, existed that the aliens could intercept and understand human transmissions. All he could do was make sure his men were ready to account well for themselves if the time came.

Not for the first time, he wished the Army had its own fast-flyers and didn't have to rely on the Marines and the Navy. The Army's aircraft were transports of various kinds, and the slow moving aircraft that provided support for the ground forces.

Allen stopped and knelt, looking at something on the ground.

Gasson joined him. "What'cha got?"

Allen pointed at marks that crossed their route. They resembled the tracks of a large bird, or perhaps lizard, with long claws. They were moving in a direction that would, if continued in a straight line, pass half a kilometer southwest of the firebase.

"I'll tell O'Connor," Gasson said. Allen didn't answer, just peered into the surrounding forest.

In a moment the squad leader had joined them. "How many are there?" he asked when he saw the tracks. Allen shook his head. "Could be lots hidden under the leaves."

"So maybe a fire team, but it could be a battalion?"

Allen shook his head again. "Not a battalion. Maybe fire team, maybe company." He shrugged.

O'Connor didn't ask any more questions, just took images and transmitted them to Greig. He listened to the lieutenant's answer, then ordered, "Follow that track."

Allen spat to the side and changed direction to follow the tracks.

Tension mounted as the men of the squad realized they were trailing an unknown number of Dusters. The tension would have been greater if they hadn't known they were getting closer to their firebase and help.

Broken circuit, tangental to Advance Firebase One

"KEEP IT STAGGERED," STAFF SERGEANT O'CONNOR CALLED TO HIS SQUAD. They were moving away from where he and Corporal Allen had observed the Duster camp, so he wasn't as concerned about maintaining quiet. "Let's not all get taken out by one burst." Ever since the mid-nineteenth-century development of the Gatling gun, infantry officers and non-commissioned officers have been concerned about the possibility of their men being wiped out by a head-on burst of automatic fire, and constantly told them not to stand directly behind one another. That, of course, did not apply on the parade ground where officers can indulge in their fantasies of commanding troops in the tactics of the Napoleonic Wars. So O'Connor admonished his squad to keep it staggered, and not walk directly one behind the other.

He himself wanted to be staggered more than the others to get the least obstructed view to the front. But they were still in the forest, and he couldn't see very far ahead even if he did walk farther to the side. Better to rely on Allen to spot trouble ahead before that trouble spotted the squad. O'Connor wasn't enough of a tracker to tell how old the tracks they were following were. They could have been less than an hour, or they could have been several hours old. But not so old that if whoever left them had set in an ambush, as they would have likely left the ambush position by now.

O'Connor thought walking into an ambush was a greater possibility than catching up with whoever they were trailing and being spotted by their rear guard before Allen spotted them.

He saw that the light was increasing ahead of the squad indicating that they were nearing the edge of the cleared area around the firebase when Allen stopped, lowered himself to a knee and looked back. O'Connor followed Gasson to the pointman.

Wordlessly, Allen pointed; the tracks he'd been following split, some continued straight, some bent to the right.

O'Connor looked in both directions but didn't see anything to tell him what the Dusters were up to. He called Greig, requesting instructions.

It took the better part of a minute for Greig to provide any. "Go left half a klick and then come directly in."

After acknowledging the new orders, O'Connor turned to Allen. "Stay far enough inside the trees to be behind someone lining up for an assault, but close enough to see into the open. When we get out, head straight for the main gate at a brisk walk. Got it?"

Allen nodded, spat to the side, and moved out on the new route. They didn't encounter anyone or any problems in the half-klick movement through the trees, then turned toward the firebase.

They were in the open, still more than a hundred meters from the firebase's wire, when shrill cries from the edge of the forest shattered the quiet of the day, and heavy fire began coming at them.

"Run!" O'Connor shouted, and began sprinting toward the open gate. The caws and shrieks behind him rapidly grew in volume, and the bullets whizzing and zinging past them felt closer.

"Third squad, *down!*" Lieutenant Greig shouted over the platoon freq.

O'Connor repeated the order. He dove to the ground and twisted around to face the forest. He began firing at Dusters, hundreds of them who boiled out of the forest, racing, jinking and jiving in a chaotic mass, at his squad. "Everybody, fire!" he shouted. To his sides, he heard the fire team leaders turning their men to face fire on the Dusters.

Then with a *r-i-i-i-p-p!* the M-69 Scatterer opened up, raining bullets over the heads of the soldiers of Third squad. One of the M-5C machine guns joined the Scatterer, and the two M-40 mortars began lobbing their bombs into the mass of Dusters. The rifles of a squad added to the death flying at the Dusters. Blood spurted and geysered from hit Dusters, feathers flew, and chunks of flesh and bone were flung about.

But there were so many of the aliens that it seemed to O'Connor that the monstrous casualties they were taking hardly seemed to dent their numbers. Already in the few seconds since O'Connor had first heard the cries of the Dusters they had halved the distance from the forest's edge to the humans. And there seemed to be as many as there were to begin with.

"Kill them!" O'Connor bellowed, firing as fast as he could at the charging enemy. The mass of Dusters was so dense that nearly half of his unaimed bullets found a target, and many of the hit Dusters tumbled to the ground. His men were striking almost as often as he did. He could see that the Dusters' speed was so great that they would have caught his squad if the men had kept running instead of stopping to allow the platoon's weapons squad to fire over them. He looked at the rapidly closing enemy and realized his only satisfaction now would be how many Dusters died with him and his men in the next few minutes.

"What's wrong with you?" he screamed, when he realized the mortar had stopped firing.

Before the words were fully out of his mouth a blur flashed through his field of view. He was buffeted, almost rolled over by the shock wave that accompanied the most deafening *boom* he'd ever heard.

Marine air had come!

The first strike was by two AV 16C Kestrels, which used the shockwave from their sonic boom to break up the Duster mass and cause casualties.

O'Connor raised his head and saw far greater disruption among the Dusters than at first. The aliens' chaotic movement was intended to confuse their enemy; this chaos was Dusters staggering about in confusion and disorientation, and tripping over their comrades who'd been injured by the sonic concussion.

A second pair of Kestrels swooped down at subsonic speed, firing their weapons along the long axis of the mass of Dusters. Blood, feathers, flesh, and bone fountained into the air. He realized that the aliens were no longer shooting at his men, and the rest of Second platoon had stopped firing.

"Third squad, on your feet!" he shouted. "Head for the gate." He looked around to make sure everyone heard and was obeying his order, and saw two limping soldiers being assisted by others. Before he could make a satisfied grunt about his men taking care of each other without being told to, he noticed an unmoving lump.

"Ah, shit." He sprinted to the downed soldier and found PFC George Buchanan staring lifelessly in a puddle of blood; an enemy projectile had hit him where his neck and shoulder met. O'Connor suspected the shot had hit Buchanan's heart, killing him instantly. He hoped it was instantaneous, that the soldier hadn't suffered.

He quickly glanced toward the Dusters. Noticeably fewer of them were milling about now, and none were charging or firing, not even at the Marine aircraft that were coming in for another strike. Those who could were staggering toward the cover of the trees. He hoisted Buchanan over his shoulders in a fireman's carry. No help for it, he carried his own rifle in his free hand but left Buchanan's to be retrieved later.

Speeding toward the gate, he almost felt like cheering when he heard the Marines' continuing fire on the Dusters.

Aftermath

They held a brief memorial service for PFC Buchanan, the first member of Alpha Troop to die in action.

"Brief" was all they had time for. Brigadier General Rufus Saxon, 10th Brigade's commander, and the battalion commander, Lieutenant Colonel Douglas Hapeman, flew in as soon as the battle was over to assess the situation.

"You need to get this cleaned up, Lieutenant," Saxon said to Greig as the three strode through the chewed up ground where the Marine Kestrels had slaughtered so many Dusters. "These bodies are going to start stinking something fierce in a very few hours. You don't have any heavy equipment to dig a trench-grave, so you're going to have to burn them. Put your boys to work gathering the bodies in one spot. I'll get you enough fuel to bonfire them. Got it?"

Greig had hoped Saxon would send in some engineers with equipment to dig a trench and bulldoze the corpses into it, but that wasn't to be. "Yes, Sir," was all he could say.

Saxon gave him a look. "I know you'd rather do it with heavy equipment. That'd be faster, certainly, but after the action you just had, and losing your first soldier, I think your boys need something other than their loss to keep their minds occupied."

"Yes, Sir, the general is right," Greig said. He wanted to say something very different, something that would get a mere second lieutenant in deep trouble if he said it to a brigadier general. So he simply said, "Yes, Sir, the general is right."

Saxon gave the field of carnage a long, penetrating look. "The Marines estimate that between their air and your ground fire, we killed about a quarter of the Dusters that attacked. What's your assessment of their casualties?"

"Sir, a quarter sounds about right," Greig said.

"You must have been hit by something more than a regiment."

"At the time, it looked more like a divsion, Sir."

Saxon barked a curt laugh. "And you only lost one man." He grinned fiercely. "These beasts may have made a quick hash of the colonial guard that was here when they first attacked, but now they're up against professionals. They don't have a chance."

"Begging the general's pardon, Sir, but they pretty much wiped out a Force Recon platoon. That sounds pretty tough to me." Greig swallowed at his own temerity; it didn't do for a second lieutenant to gainsay a brigadier general.

Saxon barked another laugh, and clapped a hand on Greig's shoulder. "Force Recon. Marines," he said dismissively.

Greig stayed quiet. Unlike many officers in the Army, he held the fighting ability of the Marines in high regard.

Soon after, Saxon said, "Carry on" and headed for his aircraft.

"I'll get you some protective gear," Hapeman told Greig, wrinkling his nose at the smell that was already beginning to rise from the scattered corpses and body parts. He followed Saxon.

Graves detail

"This is bullshit, Mr. Greig," Sergeant First Class Quinn groused.

Second Lieutenant Greig shook his head without saying anything. He agreed with his platoon sergeant, but couldn't complain to the sergeant about the inadequacy of the protective gear that the battalion commander had provided them with. The breathing filters cut down on the mounting stench of decomposition, and the long-cuffed disposable gloves kept the men's hands off the alien flesh and bones, but did nothing to keep them from trodding in the offal, or prevent anything from splashing on their uniforms, or any exposed skin.

"We should have full-cover hazard suits," Quinn continued.

"Should, would, could," Greig said impatiently. "That won't get us anywhere. We'll make do with what we have. Do you understand me, Sergeant?"

"Ah, yeah, sure, uh, Sir. We do what we can with what we got." Then in a low voice that might not even reach Greig's ears, "And hope none'a them creatures got anything that can kill us from simple contact."

But his words did carry.

"Sarge, if the Dusters were carrying any pathogens that could harm us, I'm sure the Navy scientists would have told us."

"I'm sure." To himself Quinn added, *They would'a told our brass, but would the brass have passed the word to us?*

All but a few soldiers assigned to picket duty to watch for another attack were set to clearing the field of corpses and body parts. The area was extensive enough that they didn't make one big pile, but made several, more than fifty meters apart. It took almost an entire day to assemble the piles. Then they were doused with fuel and set ablaze.

"Goddam!" Sergeant Gasson complained. "The fire stinks almost worse than the bodies did when we were collecting them."

"Could be worse," Staff Sergeant O'Connor said calmly. "We're upwind from the fires." He nodded toward the forest beyond the burning piles. "The wind is blowing the stink away from us, into the forest. If the rest of the Dusters, the ones that got away, are still in there, if they didn't go far, far away, how do you think they feel smelling their buddies burning like that?"

Gasson chewed on his lip, looking beyond the flames. After a long moment he said, "Yeah."

Advance Firebase One

"HEADS UP!" CORPORAL ALLEN SHOUTED AS HE GRABBED HIS RIFLE AND FIRED A SHOT toward the smoke-shrouded treeline.

"What's up?" Sergeant Gasson called.

"Dusters!" Allen shouted again and fired another round.

"Back, get back to the line!" Staff Sergeant O'Connor bellowed to his squad. They were gathering and burning corpses of the Dusters who had fallen outside the wire- and spike-studded trench.

Lieutenant Greig and SFC Quinn took up the cry, even though neither of them had seen any Dusters through the smoke from the burning alien corpses.

"To your positions!" Greig ordered on his all-hands freq.

It took little more than a minute for the graves detail to pick up their weapons and make it back through the opening in the wire wire stacked pyramid-like, four rolls high, over the board-bridge over the trench, and scramble into their defensive positions.

Greig picked up his infra scope and looked into the slowly thinning cloud of smoke. "Damn," he swore under his breath. In infra he saw Dusters jinking and darting toward the firebase. "They're coming," he said into the all-hands freq. "Wait for my order." *Where the hell is that Mobile Intel platoon?* He'd contacted them more than an hour ago and told them to come back, that he needed them at the firebase because the Dusters were here. He lowered the scope and peered at the slowly thinning smoke, scanning from side to side. Then he dimly saw hunched over shapes flitting through the smoke he shouted, "Fire!" Hundreds more shapes quickly became visible close behind.

All the weapons of the reinforced platoon opened up. The CBs had also taken up weapons and added their fire to the soldiers'. The answering *caws* of the Dusters couldn't be heard over the din of the outgoing gunfire—but the *cracks* of the Dusters' fire *could* be heard, and the *thuds* from the impacts of their bullets as random shots struck the faces of the bunkers. Some of the flitting forms fell or tumbled under the withering fire from Second platoon and the CBs. Then the Dusters started dashing through the smoke, darting here and there, going sideways more than forward, but always closing the distance to the wire. Dusters flipped, flopped, crashed to the ground. Some of them got up again and resumed their charge, although most of the fallen either stayed down or began crawling between the burning pyres, back toward the trees. But most of them kept coming.

The first dozen Dusters to reach the wire flung themselves onto it and writhed, bleeding from multiple punctures, pinning their bodies tighter and tighter to it until they couldn't move any more. Their shrill *caws* and agonized shrieks sent chills through some of the soldiers and inspired them to shoot at the pinioned aliens, to kill them, to put them out of their misery, to still their cries of pain.

"Ignore the ones on the wire," Greig commanded. "Shoot the ones still coming!"

The next dozen Dusters to reach the wire clambered up the bodies of their comrades already there and threw their own bodies onto the top tier of wire, pinning themselves to it, adding their caws and shrieks to the cacophony. The third wave scrambled over the first two and dove onto the downslope of the wire, completing a bridge over it that the following aliens used to cross the obstacle unharmed.

The first of the Dusters who crossed the wire on the living bridges jumped into the studded trench and collapsed when spikes impaled their feet. Screaming in agony, they fell onto more spikes. The initial Dusters had intentionally sacrificed themselves to make bridges, but none of them knew about the spikes in the shallow trench until their feet got impaled. The first to reach the shallow trench became unintended bridges over the spikes.

Hundreds thudded across their fallen mates, driving them deeper onto the spikes, snapping their bones, killing them. Those hundreds raced across the remaining killing ground at the bunkers that continued to blast death at them. More and more Dusters fell to the fire from the soldiers and CBs. And still they came on, shrieking caws and shrill battle cries.

In their bunker, Gasson and Allen kept up a steady fire of three-round bursts at the charging Dusters. PFCs Charles F. Sancrainte and Denis

Buckley joined them at the embrasure, firing at the charging aliens. The zigging and zagging of the attackers made it impossible to properly aim at them, but their sheer numbers made accurate aim unnecessary. If you picked a spot and kept shooting at it, sooner rather than later a darting, dodging body would cross through that space at the same time a bullet did, and a Duster would bite the dust.

But the Dusters weren't jinking directly at the fronts of the bunkers, mostly they angled and re-angled to the spaces between bunkers, to get between and behind them, where they knew the entrances were. As many as fell in the open ground between the wire and the studded trench, even more made it between the bunkers to attack them from the rear.

"Allen, cover the rear!" Gasson shouted.

The corporal scooted to the dog-legged entrance of the bunker and lay prone with his chest and shoulders in the tunnel section that emptied into it. He pointed his rifle around the corner just in time to see a Duster's head poke around from the outer section. He pulled the trigger of his rifle, sending three rounds at the beaked head. The alien was fast and jerked back just in time for Allen's shot to miss. The Duster stuck its rifle around the corner and let off a long burst, but its projectiles went high. Allen fired another burst, hitting the weapon and knocking it out of the alien's hands. The shriek that came told Allen he must have hit the Duster's hand or wrist as well as its weapon. Scrabbling noises said the wounded alien was backing out. or was being dragged out of the way.

Excited chittering came from outside, and a dark object crashed into the tunnel, and caromed around the corner to roll toward Allen.

"Grenade!" he shouted, and scooted back and flattened against the side of the bunker next to the entrance.

The grenade exploded with a deafening roar before it reached the corner to the final leg. Shrapnel ripped into the tunnel walls, but none entered the bunker itself.

Instantly, Allen went prone, shoving his chest and shoulders back into the tunnel, rifle first. The muzzle slammed into the beak of a Duster who was already reaching the inner bend. Allen pulled his rifle back far enough to get off a burst, and the Duster's head exploded from the impact of three bullets hitting from only a couple of centimeters distance. Allen pushed his rifle around the corner and quickly cranked off three more three-round bursts. Screams answered him, along with fire from alien weapons. He heard the movement of bodies withdrawing, and waited a few seconds before taking a quick look around the corner. He saw the twitching corpse of the first one he'd killed, and the sprawled body of another halfway around the next corner.

After waiting a few more seconds before looking again, he saw the second body being dragged back. He scrambled over the body of the first one to the corner onto the one being dragged and stuck his rifle around it to fire another three bursts. A scream met his fire, and the tension he'd felt in the body of the Duster he was on fell away; whoever had been pulling it was out of the fight. He fired again, but didn't hear any cry or other sound to indicate he'd hit another Duster. He scrambled back.

While Allen had been fighting off the Dusters trying to enter the bunker, Gasson and the rest of the fire team were at the embrasure, still shooting at the charging aliens, but not hitting as many as before—most of the surviving enemy had reached the area between the bunkers where they were safe from the continuing fire.

But not all had reached that momentary safety. One, shrieking madly, zigging and zagging manically, reached the bunker and jammed its weapon into the embrasure. It fired a burst into the face and chest of Sancrainte, making him Second platoon's second fatality. Gasson and Buckley each fired two bursts into the alien, killing it and tossing its blood-spewing corpse away to land in a broken heap.

And then there were no more Dusters in front of the bunkers.

"Buckley, stay, guard," Gasson snapped. He spun about and in three steps went prone, on top of Allen, to peer around the corner. Seeing only the two Duster corpses, he scooted back and off Allen.

"Let's get these things out of the way," he said.

Allen put his rifle down and reached around the corner with both hands to grasp the Duster by its upper arms. He pulled it none too gently as he crawled backward into the bunker. As soon as he had the body far enough, Gasson reached over him to grab the Duster and unceremoniously yank it the rest of the way in, where he flung it into a corner.

As soon as the first body was out of the way, Allen took up his rifle again and crawled to the second body. "Cover me," he said over his shoulder. A quick glance showed Gasson on one knee, aiming his rifle past him. Allen reached the body and pulled it by the arms, just as he had the other. It was tight, but he squeezed past Gasson who had tucked himself into the angle of the corner and kept aiming down the short length of the tunnel. In the bunker he tossed the body onto the other, and took a quick look through the embrasure at the vacant landscape visible through it.

"Stay sharp, Buckley," he said, clapping the PFC's shoulder. "When they figure out we've got them blocked at the entrance they might come around front again."

"Sure thing, Corporal," Buckley said, glancing nervously at Sancrainte's body where it lay on the pallet the dead soldier had used as a bed.

Allen scrambled back to Gasson, who was waiting for him inside the entrance tunnel.

"I'm bigger than you," Gasson said, "so I'll go first. At the entrance you either kneel over me, or lay on me. Between us, we can cover almost a hundred and eighty degrees. Got it?"

"Got it, Sarge. Any time you're ready."

Without another word, Gasson scooted into the long leg of the tunnel and fired around the next corner before looking down it. When he did he saw sky and ground and running, scaled legs that ended in taloned feet. And some crumpled bodies, a couple of which he thought must have been Dusters Allen had killed.

He bent himself around the corner far enough to see farther to the sides of the entrance, about a ninety degree field of vision. Almost immediately he saw a Duster looking in his direction and skittering toward him. He snapped off two quick bursts and was satisfied to see the Duster drop his weapon as he fell face down. He put another burst into the Duster when he saw it scrabbling toward its rifle.

Then Allen was leaning over him and looking farther out.

"Damn, but there's a shitload of 'em," the corporal said, putting his rifle to his shoulder and cranking off a few three-round bursts.

Gasson skooched forward until he could see almost a one-hundred-and-eighty-degree arc. "They've got no discipline! They're just running around."

"If they slowed down so's we could hit 'em, this'd be a goddamn turkey shoot!" Ignoring the fact that the Dusters weren't slowing down, that they were running as fast, firing as wildly, and jinking as unpredictably as during their charge, he began putting bursts out at randomly selected targets. Beneath him, Gasson did the same. They fired again and again, and some of their bursts hit.

But not all of the Dusters were as undisciplined as the ones the two soldiers were shooting at.

"They're on top of the bunker!" Buckley twisted around and shouted the warning at the entrance. If he could have, he would have squeezed through the embrasure to shoot at the aliens he heard on top of the bunker. But the opening was too narrow, he could barely sitck his head through it, and then only if he first removed his helmet.

"Look up!" Buckley shouted.

But Gasson and Allen couldn't hear Buckley's shouts over the din of firing, their own and the Dusters'. Allen was leaning out, completely exposing his head and shoulders, when a burst from above slammed into him and knocked him onto Gasson, driving the fire team leader flat. Two Dusters dropped off the top of the bunker and fired under Allen, into Gasson. With the two soldiers out of the way, the two Dusters darted into the entry tunnel determined to kill its last defender.

Unfortunately for them, Buckley had heard the shooting at the mouth of the tunnel, and its sudden cessation, and knew what it had to mean. He was ready when the Dusters came in, and—in the tunnel that was too narrow for them to jink—killed both of the attackers.

Buckley waited, dry-mouthed, for more Dusters to appear, either through the tunnel or outside the embrasure.

Command post, Advance Firebase One

Lieutenant Greig watched appalled as the Dusters overran his platoon's defenses, and the positions manned by the CBs. He knew his men had slaughtered many, many of the attackers before they reached the line of bunkers. But there were so damn *many* of the alien soldiers that it was only a matter of time, and not a very long time, before they completely wiped out the small human force. He'd put in a request for Marine air support, but was told none was immediately available, that all the Marine Kestrels and Eagles were on other missions, but the first available would be sortied to his aid.

At least his men had acquitted themselves well.

Then the manic running about of the Dusters took on a different tone, and many of them looked to the sky beyond the perimeter.

Greig grabbed his glasses and looked where the Dusters were looking. There! Coming fast, were four aircraft. They were still too far away for him to make out, but whatever kind they were they were going to save his platoon and the CBs!

The Dusters started to break and run. Only a few at first, but more and more as they saw the first ones fleeing. Soon, before the aircraft reached close enough to the firebase to lay effective air-to-ground fire on them, the Dusters were in full rout, being pursued by fire from the de-fenders. By the time the first aliens reached the trees, the aircraft were above them, raining fire. They were MH 15 Alphonses—the MI platoon had finally arrived!

The Butcher's Bill

Second platoon, Alpha Company, First of the Seventh Mounted Infantry had lost eight men killed and another seven wounded badly enough to re-quire evacuation to a field hospital—or even to orbital facilities. Close to half of the platoon required replacements. And from where were they going to come? The CBs had lost seven, dead or severely wounded. Where were their replacements going to come from?

Lieutenant Greig decided then that the Troy operation was even more of a royal cockup than he'd already thought—which, after the beating that ARG 17 had taken upon arrival in the Troy system, was saying a lot.

What next?? the lieutenant wanted to know. But there was nobody who could—or would—tell him.

VMA 214, Marine Corps Aviation Facility, near Jordan,
Semi-Autonomous World Troy

LIEUTENANT GENERAL BAUER WANTED COMBAT AIR CLOSE TO JORDAN, BECAUSE there
had been so much Duster activity in the area. Major General Hiram I. Bearss,
Commanding General of Marine Air Wing 2, selected an area that was many
square kilometers of level ground. The Dusters were known for using cave
and tunnel complexes as staging areas and to move about undetected. The
Navy in orbit was still conducting its search for gravitational anomalies
and hadn't covered all the Jordan region, but Myers concluded that a level
landscape wouldn't have caves or tunnels. Myers tasked Marine Air Group
14 with establishing an expeditionary air field and assigning a ground-
attack squadron to it.

The air facility was quickly constructed and Marine Attack Squadron
214 assigned to operate out of the newly established MCAF Jordan. Except
for one mission flown by a four-aircraft division in support of the Army's
Alpha Troop, First of the Seventh Mounted Infantry, life was quiet for the
first week and a half that VMA 214 was at Jordan, with nothing more
than routine patrols looking for possible Duster movement. So no one was
unduly concerned about the airfield not having any security beyond its own
personnel, most of whom were occupied with maintaining and operating
the squadron's AV16C Kestrel attack aircraft.

"Ah, shit!" Gunnery Sergeant Robert G. Robinson swore from his position
supervising the control tower. He got on the horn to the ready room. "Sir,

better scramble," he said when Major John L. Smith, VMA 214's executive officer and the senior pilot in the ready room, answered his call. "Got a shit-load of Dusters coming our way. On foot, from the east." Before Smith could ask for details, he continued, "Maybe six hundred of 'em, hard to tell, the way they're jinking. I don't see anything but small arms, but who knows what kind a shit they got outta sight." *Where the hell did they come from?* he wondered. *Ain't supposed to be no goddam tunnels or caves nowhere around here*

While Robinson was reporting, a *whooga whooga* alarm began sounding throughout the MCAF. On the ground, he saw pilots racing from the ready room to the flight line where a dozen AV16C Kestrels were lined up with their canopies standing open. Ground crew bustled around the aircraft, checking their armament and fuel levels, pulling the safeties on their missiles, pulling the chocks that kept them from moving when buffeted by gusts of wind. Half a dozen additional pilots ran from the mess and the barracks to the ready room to prepare themselves to fly. More ground crew trundled six more Kestrels from the hangars alongside the taxiway and began checking their ordnance and topping off their fuel tanks, preparatory to moving them onto the flight line.

And the speeding alien soldiers were fast closing on the runway.

"Tower, have them launch when ready," Lieutenant Colonel Merritt Edson, the squadron commander, snapped on his comm—he was one of the pilots running from quarters to the ready room.

"Aye aye, Skipper," Robinson replied. "Yo, who's ready to go?" he asked on the squadron freq.

"I am," Captain Jefferson J. DeBlanc was the first to answer.

"Then fly away little birdie. Next?" As the pilots answered their readiness, Robinson sent them off, until five were airborne and diving, guns blazing, at the Dusters.

But five Kestrels were all that made it into the sky before the aliens reached the runway to block the aircraft lining up to take off, and shooting at them from close range.

The next Kestrel, sixth in line, attempted to take off into the charging Dusters. It didn't have enough speed when it lifted, and tumbled into the end of the runway, bursting into a flaming ball.

Captain Henry T. Elrod, the next in line, fired his guns into the charging enemy, and tried to take off through the hole his cannon rounds made in the mass of Dusters. But the hole filled in before he reached it, and three of the aliens got sucked into his Kestrel's engines. The aircraft spun about uncontrollably with its guns still firing. The cannon fire knocked out two more Kestrels that were taxiing toward the runway.

First Lieutenant Kenneth A. Walsh was starting to turn onto the runway when he saw Elrod spin and fire at the Kestrels coming behind him. Almost instinctively, he twisted his stick in the opposite direction, pointing his aircraft away from the Dusters. He checked his rear-view and saw the nearest aliens were a hundred meters distant. He put on his wheel locks and air brakes, then hit his afterburner, sending exhaust flame gouting nearly two hundred meters rearward. Fifty or more Dusters were immolated by the torch-like flame. He released his locks and brakes, and sped the wrong way, going with the wind rather into it. Cutting the afterburner, he spun about to face the Dusters from half a kilometer distance. No other air-craft had turned onto the runway; Dusters were flooding off it to surround the Kestrels and mob the ground crews. But many were still on the runway. Walsh began firing his guns and launching his missiles at them.

Walsh saw explosions on the taxiway, and fireballs bloomed where three of the Kestrels waiting to turn onto the runway maneuvered—making it obvious that some of the Dusters had carried demolitions.

In the tower, Robinson looked on aghast as the aircraft of VMA 214 were destroyed on the ground, and as the ground-crew Marines were being shot down or torn apart by the vicious claws of the Dusters. He patted his hip where he should have been carrying a holstered sidearm, but no weapon was there. Neither were the two controllers with him armed. *Shit,* he swore, *why don't we have a grunt company for security?* But he knew why—and saw just how wrong the decision had been.

"Marines," he said to his controllers, "I hope to shit you remember your hand-to-hand combat training, because I believe we're about to be in a fight."

Rapid footsteps on the stairs leading to the control room gave proof to his words.

Robinson and the two controllers managed to kill four of the Dusters before they were overwhelmed.

"Now what do we do?" First Lieutenant James E. Swett asked as he circled over the air facility and the aircraft burning on it. Dusters still milled about on the ground, but Swett's plane, like the other four airborne Kestrels, was out of ordnance.

"We roll them, then head for Puller," Major Smith answered. "On me, echelon left!" The Kestrels lined up, angling back to Smith's left. They followed their XO down to thirty meters above the ground, and flashed past the enemy soldiers at just below mach speed, knocking them down with the concussion of their passage. Some Dusters were injured or even killed by debris thrown up by the zooming aircraft. A few were thrown bodily into burning hulks and burned to death. All suffered injuries from the concussion.

Then, running low on fuel, the five surviving aircraft of VMA 214 headed for Camp Puller, outside Millerton.

Camp Zion, near Jordan

"Third Platoon, saddle up!" Second Lieutenant Commiskey shouted as he scrambled out of the company headquarters bunker.

"Move, move, move, move, move!" Staff Sergeant Guillen bellowed, following Commiskey out of the bunker."

"What's happening, Honcho?" Corporal Mackie shouted, buckling on his harness and running out of his fire team's bunker, rifle slung over his shoulder, helmet perched on his head.

"When I find out, you'll be the first to know," Sergeant Martin shouted back. He held his rifle and helmet in one hand and his harness in the other. He was rapidly striding to the open area behind the platoon's section of perimeter, where the Marines would soon assemble. "First squad, get your asses out here!" he roared

The Marines of Third platoon were boiling out of their bunkers, strapping on gear, checking the action of their weapons, patting pouches to make sure they were fully armed and had everything else they were sure they'd soon need. As they lined up in formation the squad leaders quickly went along their lines, inspecting their men, double checking that they had all their gear and ammunition.

"'Toon, A-ten-HUT!" Guillen bellowed as he ran to face the formation. He looked to the side where he saw Commiskey racing to the platoon, then beyond where he saw three armored Scooters and a Hog warming up.

Commiskey took his position before his men. "Third platoon, the Air Facility is under attack, and we're going to relieve them. Vehicles are readying for us now." He turned to Guillen. "Platoon Sergeant, is the platoon ready?"

Guillen looked at the squad leaders. "Inspected and ready," they said, almost in unison.

"Where's guns?" Commiskey asked, noticing that the machine gun squad that often accompanied Third platoon wasn't there.

"Coming up, Sir," Sergeant Matej Kocak shouted. His voice was accompanied by the jangling of weapons and unsecured gear.

Commiskey looked and saw the seven men of the gun squad running to join the platoon. He nodded approval.

"Platoon Sergeant, move the platoon to the vehicles."

"Aye aye, Sir." Guillen snapped the orders that got the platoon, with its attached gun squad, marching in formation to the Hog and the Scooters that were now turned face away from the platoon and lowering their ramps to allow the Marines to board them. HM3 David E. Hadyen with his medkit, clambered aboard.

In little more than another minute, the armored vehicles closed up and sped out of the Marine firebase.

MCAF Jordan

The airfield had been put together so rapidly it only had a few sections of barrier fencing around it, allowing the vehicles to roar in unimpeded. They stopped near a Kestrel that hunkered alone, half a kilometer from the control tower and the burned and smoking hulks of other aircraft.

"What happened here?" Commiskey asked the pilot who stood in his Kestrel's open cockpit.

"First Lieutenant Walsh, Sir," the dazed-looking pilot answered. "We got flat mobbed by Dusters." He shook his head. "I think they're all gone now."

"Where are the rest of your people?"

Walsh waved a hand at the devastation visible in the middle distance. "I'm not sure anybody's left."

"Hang tight, Lieutenant," Commiskey said. "We'll check it out." He told the armored vehicle platoon commander to advance on line to a hundred meters from the nearest smoking hulk.

Wind blew lightly across the runway when the Marines raced off the Scooters and Hog, and formed up on line, the smell of scorched metal and electronics and charred flesh wafting up at them.

"Advance at a trot," Commiskey ordered. "Stagger it and watch your dress."

The Marines of Third platoon stepped up their pace and a minute later, with bodies clearly in view, they slowed to a walk. There were Duster bodies, some bloodied, some charred. The human bodies were all blood smeared. The charred remains were immediately recognized as alien because even in death, the Dusters were bent at the hip, their thighs bulged, and their faces jutted in muzzles over elongated necks. A shift in the breeze sent the odor of burnt fuel at the Marines, but the smell wasn't strong enough to disguise the stench of dead flesh.

"Check for live ones," Commiskey ordered.

"Is anybody alive?" Guillen bellowed. But nobody answered.

"Hey, this one's breathing!" Corporal Mackie shouted, bending over a Marine laying prone, with blood pooled next to his hip. "Corpsman up!"

Doc Hayden pounded up and dropped to his knees next to the wounded Marine and visually examined him. "Are you awake, can you hear me?"

The Marine moved his lips, trying to say something, but his voice was far too faint for Hayden to have any hope of understanding him.

"Stay with me, Marine. I'm gonna patch you up. You'll be running around before you know it." Having seen no injury, and only the blood by the wounded man's hip, Hayden carefully slipped his hands under the casualty to find the exact location of the wound and feel for others. Satisfied, he said to Mackie, "Help me roll him over. You do his shoulders. Nice and easy, we don't want to aggravate his wounds."

"Right. Say when." Mackie took a grip on the wounded Marine's shoulders and waited for Hayden to say when to move.

The corpsman carefully took hold both above and below where he'd felt the wound and nodded at Mackie. "Now."

The Marine groaned when they moved him, but didn't cry out. Working rapidly, Hayden used scissors to cut the casualty's uniform away from the wound and packed a dressing into it, even though the bleeding had slowed enough that there was only a small amount still seeping. He didn't see any other wounds.

"That's going to take some cleaning," Hayden said, mostly to himself. "It's a good thing you landed on your belly the way you did," he told the Marine. "It shouldn't have, but the way you lay applied enough pressure to allow the blood to start coagulating."

He got a stasis bag from his medkit. "Give me a hand with this." Together, Hayden and Mackie put the Marine, whose name they didn't know, into the stasis bag, which would hold him in a state of virtual suspended animation until he could be moved to a hospital for treatment.

While Hayden was working on the hip-wounded Marine, Guillen supervised other members of the platoon in locating other still-living casualties and assembling them near the corpsman.

There had been nearly two hundred and fifty members of VMA 214 on the ground at MCAF Jordan when the Dusters attacked. Only seven of them survived the one-sided fight.

FIVE OF VMA 214'S SEVEN SURVIVORS WERE IN STASIS BAGS. DOC HAYDEN had doped up the two least badly injured. The seven were loaded onto one of the Scooters, a lightly armed but heavily armored amphibious vehicle, which Lieutenant Commiskey dispatched back to Camp Zion. The more-heavily armed Hog amphib went along as escort.

"Secure that facility," Captain Sitter told Commiskey. "A division of Eagles is on its way to your location. When it arrives, battalion wants you to track the Dusters that attacked MCAF Jordan. Find out where they went, but do not engage. You are a recon in force. Understood?"

Commiskey acknowledged the order, although he didn't like it. If he had to run a reconnaissance, he'd prefer to do it with only a fire team rather than with a full platoon. Four or five men could move much more stealthily than the forty of a platoon, would be much less likely to be detected, and were less likely to get into a fight against heavy odds.

When the P-43 Eagles arrived one landed while the other three orbited.

"You Commiskey? I'm Captain Fleming, MMH 628. Me and my birds are here to assist you," said the gangly pilot who disembarked from the P-43 that landed. He stuck out his hand to shake. Looking around at the carnage he continued, "I understand there's a combat engineer detachment on its way to clean up this mess. Now, what do you have in mind for me an' my birds to do?"

"Good to meet you, Captain," Commiskey said, now that Fleming had stopped talking long enough for him to speak. "You can see what the

Dusters did here. Our intelligence is that several hundred of them headed west after this fire fight." He almost choked on the last two words. What had happened on the ground here was far too one-sided to be called a fight.

Fleming nodded vigorously. "I saw the raw vid of it from the fast flyers. It looked like four, maybe five hundred of the things took off after the Kestrels rolled them."

"We're following them. I want you to scout for us."

Fleming cocked an eyebrow. "You got what here, one platoon? You plan on taking on four, maybe five hundred Dusters with only one platoon?"

"No, Sir, not at all," Commiskey said with a vigorous shake of his head. "My orders are to conduct a reconnaissance in force. My platoon's job is to find out where they went, not to fight them."

"Uh-huh. A whole platoon for a recon patrol." It was obvious that Fleming had the same misgivings about the mission that Commiskey did. "Well, we'll be a lot of help. The Dusters'll hear us coming before they spot you. With any luck, or skill—I'd rather it was skill you know—we'll spot them in time to tell you where they are so you don't get into a fight you can't win."

"Sir," Corporal John Pruitt, the platoon's communications man, interrupted them, "just got a call. Two Hogs and a Scooter are on their way. They're three klicks out."

"That'll give you what," Fleming asked, looking around to see the armored assets already on the airfield, "three Scooters and two Hogs? Here's hoping you don't need the fire power, but it's a damn good thing you got it if you need it." He looked skyward. "I think I'll go up now and start scouting. We'll look a klick or two to your front when you move out, and frequently sweep your flanks. Sound good to you?"

"Yes it does, Captain. Thank you."

"My call sign is Farsight," Fleming said, "yours is Nearsight."

"You're Farsight, I'm Nearsight. Got it."

Fleming gave a wry smile. "If you hear me using the call sign 'Classroom,' that's me talkin' to my squadron operations."

A moment later, Fleming's Eagle was airborne.

Commiskey still wasn't happy about the recon in force, but the four Eagles and two Hogs made the recon seem less suicidal.

He told Guillen how he wanted the platoon organized into the armored vehicles when the rest of them arrived.

Twenty-seven kilometers west of MCAF Jordan

Farsight One, currently flying about two-and-a-half klicks ahead of the ground patrol, suddenly shot sharply up and twisted to the left, heading back in the direction of the armored vehicles. Flashes of brilliant light shot up from inside the trees at the space the aircraft had just vacated, and tried to track the bird as it jinked, twisted, and bobbed up and down in evasive action. In seconds the other three Eagles dove to treetop level and headed toward the area Farsight One had been flying over when it lofted. The three aircraft began firing their guns and rockets into the area the flashes had come from. Farsight One dropped low and spun about to join the other Eagle in their attack. After a moment's firing, the four Eagles backed, spun, and withdrew at speed.

Few of the Marines of Third platoon were in positions to see what was happening in the sky. Commiskey, on a periscope, was one of the few.

"Farsight, this is Nearsight," Commiskey said on the ground-air freq. "What's happening? Over."

"Nearsight, Farsight," Fleming's voice came back, "lots of bad guys moving on foot in your direction. We slowed them down and probably weakened them a bit. But there's still a lot more of them than there are of you. I advise you to hit reverse. Over."

"Far, Near. You say on foot. They don't have vehicles? Over."

"Nearsight, Farsight, they've got gun carts, you might have seen them taking pot shots at me. I didn't see any troop vehicles. But those suckers run fast. Over."

Yes, the Dusters were very fast on their feet, much faster than a human could run. But were they faster than the Marines' armored vehicles? Commiskey didn't think so.

"Far, Near, you said 'lots.' How many is 'lots'? Over."

"Nearsight, Farsight, I didn't have time to take a count, and the trees obstructed my view. But I'd say half a battalion. Could be more."

Half a battalion. Half the size of a Marine battalion could be the four or five hundred that fled from the air facility. Far too many for Commiskey's platoon of Marines to take on, even with the added fire power of the armored vehicles. And the Dusters had antiaircraft weapons. Did they also have antiarmor, or could their AA be used against armor? Commiskey remembered from his studies of history that AA artillery was sometimes used very effectively against armor.

Before Commiskey could respond to the size of the approaching enemy force, Fleming said, "We're making another run on them. I'll let you know what else we learn about their strength. Out."

Commiskey ordered the armored vehicles to halt and get on line facing toward the Dusters, to give maximum firepower if the aliens came at them.

The four aircraft maneuvered at low altitude to strike the Dusters from different directions, crossing them in a narrow "X" to hit the widest possible number. Commiskey watched through the periscope.

The first two Eagles flashed toward each other on parallel courses, firing their guns and launching rockets as they flew. The Dusters' return fire was late, and missed by wide margins. The second two followed quickly, cutting across the path of the first pair. This time the AA artillery was ready, and began firing even before the two birds were overhead.

Farsight Three was hit, and pirouetted like a top before staggering away, trailing smoke, in the direction of the air facility. An explosion erupted in the trees, large enough to rock the Scooters, still several hundred meters distant.

The remaining two aircraft orbited to the rear of Third platoon's vehicles.

"Nearsight, Farsight," Fleming said after a moment. "If you're going back, you may have to pick up Farsight Three. I'm not sure he can make it all the way. Can you do it? Over."

"Farsight, Nearsight. I will if possible." *If we're still alive,* was what he meant.

"Nearsight, Farsight, we need to rearm, so we're disengaging now. Good hunting. See you soon. Out."

"Right," Commiskey said to himself. He got on the comm to Captain Sitter to ask for instructions.

"Dismount," he ordered after he got orders from the company commander. "On line between the vehicles."

"What is this happy horseshit?" Mackie demanded as he shuffled his men into line along with the rest of the squad between two of the Scooters. "There's bad guys up ahead, and we don't have any cover here."

"You got trees for cover, Mackie," Martin snapped. "You're a Marine non-commissioned officer, now act like one and knock off the bitching."

Mackie flinched, like he'd just been slapped in the face. But he knew Martin was right; as a corporal and a fire team leader, he had to set the example for his men. Complaining the way he just had was a bad example; it could have a negative effect on his men's morale.

"Sorry," Mackie said. "So what are we doing, honcho?"

Martin held up a finger, signaling for quiet. Commiskey's voice came over the all-hands freq.

"Listen up," the platoon commander said. "The airedales say there are at least four hundred Dusters a third of a klick to our front, and coming this way. It could be the same ones that made the mess at the MCAF. The airedales put a hurting on them, but couldn't stop them. I talked to the Skipper. When the Dusters get inside two hundred meters, we're going to hit them with everything we've got, then mount up and get the hell out of Dodge. Wait for my signal before you fire.

"Does everybody understand?"

"You got that?" Mackie asked his men. All three replied in the affirmative, and he reported to Martin that Third fire team was ready.

Seconds later, the roar of an Eagle's rotors sounded above the platoon. Mackie looked up and saw one hovering several hundred meters up and slightly ahead of the platoon's line. A moment later, two more joined it and they began raining fire into the forest beyond the platoon's front.

Then came the order:

"Fire, fire, fire!"

The command was repeated by Guillen, Sergeant Binder, and the squad leaders.

Mackie screamed, *"Fire, fire, fire!" at his men.*

Along the line, forty-two rifles, two sidearms, two machine guns, and the cannons and guns of three Scooters and two Hogs blasted death into the forest.

Shrieks and *caws* and *skrees* cut faintly through the sounds of gunfire from the depths of the forest. Immediately, fire came back at the Marines. But it was wild, unaimed—point and jerk fire—most of which went too high to be any danger.

After thirty seconds of blazing fire, Commiskey shouted on the all-hands, "Mount up, mount up!" and the Marines of Third platoon jumped up and scrambled to reboard the armored vehicles.

"By squads!" Guillen bellowed.

"By fire teams!" the squad leaders shouted.

"Cafferata, Orndoff, Horton, with me!" Mackie cried, looking side to side to make sure his men were with him.

In the air, Eagle Two got hit, and spun toward the rear, dropping rapidly. The fire from the remaining two converged on one location, and an explosion erupted where their impacts joined—they killed the Duster weapon that had wounded Eagle Two.

"There they are!" Orndoff shrilled as he reached the rear of the Scooter right behind Horton, and scrambled aboard.

Mackie, standing slightly aside to follow his men, looked into the forest and saw the maniacally skittering Dusters coming through the trees. He grabbed Cafferata's arm and almost threw him aboard before jumping in himself. He turned around to give Martin a hand just in time to see the squad leader struck in the chest by a shot from a Duster's rifle. Martin fell backward, but Mackie managed to grasp his wrist and pulled him forward, into the Scooter.

Corporal Vittori, now the senior uninjured man in the squad, grabbed the intercom and told the Scooter commander to button up, that everyone assigned to the vehicle was aboard. The rear gate *clanked* shut and the Scooter twisted around on its center, then headed away from the charging Dusters.

Mackie, having pulled Martin aboard, and being the closest to him, shoved his rifle aside and clamped his hands on the wound where the Duster's projectile had found its way through a chink in Martin's body armor. Mackie was sickened by the feel of blood pulsing against his palms, trying to spurt out. "Stay with me, honcho! Don't you dare go into shock, you hear me?"

"Here's a field dressing," someone said, and shoved one at him. Mackie didn't look to see who it was, but the dressing was already open. He pulled a hand off Martin's chest to grab the dressing, then the other while he slapped the bandage onto the wound. "Another!" Then: "Talk to me, Sergeant," and reached for another dressing.

It took four field dressings, one stacked on another, to staunch the bleeding from Martin's chest.

"Is he still alive?" Corporal Button asked in a hushed voice.

"Yeah," Mackie said, feeling the side of Martin's neck for a pulse. "He lost a lot of blood, but he's still alive. Now we've got to keep him warm so he doesn't go into shock."

The Scooter jerked to a stop, and its ramp dropped down.

"Make room," a voice from outside called. "Four more coming aboard."

"Watch your step!" Mackie shouted, hunching over Martin to protect him from the four Marines in flight suits and helmets with side arms holstered on their hips who piled into the Scooter. They were the crew of Farsight Two; one had a bandaged arm.

"We're lucky, he's our only casualty," one of them said, pointing at the red-stained dressing. He looked down at Martin and the puddle of blood he lay in, and saw how much worse things could have been. They crammed in, giving Martin enough room.

The Scooter's ramp slammed shut and the vehicle lurched forward. Bullets from the pursuing Dusters *pinged* off the closed ramp. The Scooter didn't return fire; its guns couldn't reverse. But the Hogs' turrets could and did, sending streams of explosive twenty-millimeter rounds into the pursuing aliens.

The Marine vehicles gradually increased the distance between themselves and the enemy. After a few kilometers, the Dusters stopped chasing them.

DURING THE SHORT TIME THIRD PLATOON HAD BEEN ON ITS RECON IN FORCE, THE REST of India Company moved forward and occupied the minimal defensive positions that had been constructed on the west side of the air facility. They didn't only sit in place once they arrived, they engaged in building up the defenses. Combat engineers who came to bury the Duster corpses also brought wire and erected a barrier fence along the west side of the facility, and dug a broad but shallow trench on the inboard side of the fence. The wire was stacked three meters high, and the bottom of the trench was studded with short spikes intended to trip up and impale any Dusters who made it across the wire. And they dug a waist-deep trench fifty meters back from the barrier, a trench for the Marines to fight from. The company brought along a two-gun squad of M-69 Scatterers.

The armored amphibious convoy carrying Third platoon flowed through a section of the barrier fence that had been left unfinished awaiting their arrival, and the Marines immediately disembarked. Doc Hayden supervised moving Sergeant Martin and the platoon's other wounded to the hastily-repaired field dispensary where a flight surgeon who had come with India Company waited with a nurse and two more corpsmen.

"Mr. Commiskey, put your platoon in the trench, on the right flank," Captain Sitter ordered on his comm. "First platoon's in the middle, link with them. Then join me in the CP."

"Aye aye," Commiskey answered. He turned to Guillen and told him to put the squads in place, then headed for the command post.

"Vittori," Guillen shouted to the acting leader of first squad, "link up with First platoon on the left, and guns on your right. Two-man positions, five-meter intervals." After seeing that Vittori was positioning his men, he continued to the gun squad leader, "Kocak, put a gun to First squad's right. Linked with Third squad on its right. You hear that, Mausert? Your squad is in the middle. Same as First, two-man positions, five-meter intervals, with a gun team on each flank. Adriance, you've got the corner. Hold on to it, don't let the Dusters turn it."

In hardly more than a minute, Third platoon had taken position in the fighting trench. The engineers were busily closing the gap in the fence the convoy had come through, and completing the shallow trench inside it. Finished with the barrier to the front, the engineers began laying wire along the defensive flanks, enclosing the CP and medical dispensary.

Then they waited.

India Company's Command Post

"We lost contact with them twenty-two klicks back," Lieutenant Commiskey reported. "I don't know whether or not they continued following us after we broke off."

Captain Sitter nodded. "When they overran this facility they destroyed the satellite link. So until the link gets reestablished, which means a new antenna installed, we don't have the satellite view. Which means we need air. Colonel Chambers and Lieutenant Colonel Davis have convinced Major General Purvis to lean on Major General Bearss get us continuing air cover from MAG 14. Comments?" The question was directed at Commiskey.

"Sir, those Eagles from HMM 628 did justice by us," Commiskey said. "If we'd had an entire squadron, we could have put a serious hurting on the Dusters."

First Lieutenant Edward Ostermann, the company executive officer, snorted.

"A *more* serious hurting on them," Commiskey corrected himself.

"Sir, a message just came in," Sergeant Richard Binder interrupted excitedly as he turned from his comm unit.

"Tell me," Sitter said.

"Sir, MAG 14 is sending an AV 16 (E) from VMO 251 to give us some eyes." The AV 16 (E) was the electronic warfare version of the AV 16 Kestrel.

"Good!" Sitter said.

"I hope it has a shooter with it," Commiskey said. "The Dusters had anti-aircraft guns, and knocked two of the Eagles with us out of the fight. The Eagles tried, but they might not have killed all of the AA guns."

Sitter looked at Binder, who shook his head. "Sir, 14 didn't say anything about a shooter, just the Echo unit."

"Get their ops for me."

It took a few minutes, but Sitter was connected to the operations center at MAG 14.

"We really appreciate the Echo, it will be a tremendous help here," he told the operations officer. "But I'm concerned about its safety. The Dusters have triple-A. Without a shooter to give cover, the Echo will be a sitting duck."

The operations officer chuckled. "You must not be fully aware of the capabilities of the AV 16 (E). That baby's jamming set will screw up the Dusters' trip-A controller so badly it just might shoot itself. The latest 16 Echo doesn't need an escort to protect it against ground troops. And the bird on its way to scout for you has a primo driver. If anybody needs to be worried about this aircraft, it's any bad guys coming at you."

"You sound awfully confident."

"I am, I am. Now, if that's all, I've got other missions to run."

Sitter thanked the operations officer and signed off. The look he gave his officers and top NCOs gave no indication of what he was thinking. "You all heard the man, we don't have to worry about the Echo not having an escort."

Nobody else said anything, they didn't even look at each other. But every one of them had doubts.

AV 16 (E), call sign Troubadour, over MCAF Jordan

First Lieutenant Christine A. Schilt turned her Echo Kestrel in a lazy circle at one thousand five hundred meters above the air facility. Using her visual mags, she eyeballed the situation. What she saw made her whistle between tightly held lips and teeth. She'd seen the vids, of course, but pictures, even moving pictures, couldn't convey the enormity of the damage to the airfield. Everything was wrecked; aircraft were visibly damaged and unflyable, buildings were holed and partly collapsed, the runways were pocked with holes too big and close to each other to allow a fixed wing aircraft to taxi, much less land or take off. Debris choked the passages. And there was blood staining everything.

"India, India, this is Troubadour, above you at one-five hundred," she said into her local comm. "Do you copy? Over."

"Troubadour, this is India," said Sergeant Bender. "I hear you five by. Over."

"India, Troubadour, are you Six Actual? Over."

"Negative, Troubadour. Wait one."

A moment later, Captain Sitter was on the comm. "Troubadour, this is India Six Actual. Over."

"Six Actual, Troubadour. I'm at your disposal. What do you want me to do?"

"Troubadour, India Six Actual. We've got some bad guys out there. Last seen twenty-two klicks to our west. First thing is I need to know where they are now. Over."

"Six Actual, Troubadour, your wish is my command. On my way toward the setting sun. I'll let you know as soon as I see anything. Over."

"Roger, Troubadour. I await your report with bated breath. India Six Actual, out."

Troubadour, heading west from MCAF Jordan

First Lieutenant Schilt climbed to an altitude of three thousand meters and went thirty klicks west of the damaged air facility and the company of Marine infantry guarding it before she began her search for the Dusters. Her first step after turning on her ground-searching sensors was a leisurely, ten-kilometer-diameter, counter-clockwise circle back toward the MCAF. Her first sweep picked up nothing, so she did it a second time ten klicks farther east. Again no results, so she tightened the circle to seven klicks diameter and moved it ten klicks east, overlapping her first circle. At the easternmost arc of the circle she picked up something, but couldn't tell exactly what as it was at the very edge of her sensor range. She considered that it could be a small heard of ungulates, or a pack of wolf-like hunters.

Did Troy have such animals? She couldn't remember what the briefings had said about native lifeforms, or what Earth-animals might have gone feral. More likely, she thought, the traces she picked up were the Dusters she was looking for.

She tightened her circle to five klicks, moved it four more klicks east, and dropped to a thousand meters. At that altitude she might be able to get visual as well as instrumental identification of the trace.

The side-scanning radar showed several hundred man-size forms moving toward the MCAF. Schilt knew the Marines on the ground would need more information than that, so she had her comp make the necessary calculations and called in a report.

"India Six, Troubadour. Do you hear me? Over."

"Troubadour, India Six Actual, go," the reply came immediately.

"Six, Troub. I have approximately eight hundred, I say again, eight-zero-zero probable Dusters coming your way. They are twenty klicks to your west. At their current rate of movement, they should reach you in about seventy-five minutes. I say again, seven-five minutes. Over."

"Troubadour, India Six Actual. You say 'probable' Dusters. Can you confirm? Over."

"Six Actual, Troubadour. Wait one while I get a visual." Until now, Schilt had only used her instruments to check the movement on the ground. Now she used her VisMag.

The magnified visual image showed the distinctive bent-at-the-hip posture of the aliens, who seemed to be skittering more than trotting. She clearly made out the multi-pouched, leather-like straps that seemed to be their only garments, and the feathery structures that adorned their bodies and tails.

Tails and feathers on sentient creatures? Schilt shook her head in wonderment. But then, she only had humans for comparison. For all she knew, feathers and tails were more common on sentient creatures through-out the galaxy than were hair and sweat glands. What she did know was that sentience must have been fairly common in the universe. After all, in the small part of the galaxy so far explored by *Homo sap*, seventeen other sentiences had been found. Or the remains of their civilizations had, she wasn't very clear on the details. Hey, she wasn't an exobiologist or xeno-anthropologist to know such things.

She didn't notice that some of the Dusters looked up and pointed as she passed over them.

"Six Actual, Troub. I have made visual confirmation. They are Dusters. Over."

"Troubadour, Six, how are they armed? Over."

"Wait one, Actual. I'll swing over them again." She goosed her Echo to quickly circle back around to the mob of Dusters, checking her instruments as she went. "Six, Troub. I'm not picking up any electro-mag radiation. Going in for visual." After a moment she said in a low voice that probably wasn't meant for the Marines on the ground, "Ain't that cute. They see me." More loudly, she said, "Actual, Troub. I see small arms and some crew-served weapons including artillery pieces—maybe similar to pocket howitzers." She let out a short, delighted laugh. "It looks like they're aiming at me! No sweat. My jammers will send their missiles anyplace but at me. It's odd, though. I'm still not picking up any electro-mag. How the hell are they aiming?"

Puffs of black smoke appeared in the sky in front of her, and the AV 16 (E) shuddered as it ran into shrapnel thrown out by bursting aerial artillery— the dumb kind that humans hadn't used in centuries. Throw a bomb up in the air without guidance and let it explode. Maybe it'll hit something. The first one hit, peppering the skin of the Echo. That was really little more than cosmetic damage. What hurt the aircraft was the chunks of jagged metal that got sucked into its engines and tore them apart, screaming like lost souls.

First Lieutenant Christine F. Schilt would have screamed in the few seconds of her life that remained, but she couldn't believe that she was really being shot down.

The AV 16 (E) flown by Troubadour exploded in a fireball when it impacted with the ground. The impact was far enough away from the Dusters that none of them were injured by the flames or flying debris.

At their current speed, the Dusters were now little more than an hour away from MCAF Jordan. They picked up their pace. They had India Company outnumbered by four to one, if not more.

Observation post, three kilometers west of MCAF Jordan

"SHIT, SHIT, SHIT, I DON'T LIKE THIS," PFC HARRY ORNDOFF MUTTERED.

"None of us do, Harry," Corporal John Mackie said. "But this is what we're doing. Now shut up before you scare the new guy."

Mackie didn't have to worry about scaring the new guy, PFC Bill Horton was already scared. And with good reason. The fire team was in a four-man observation post in thin forest three kilometers away from the defenses at the air facility. They'd gotten there by way of a narrow farm road that hadn't been used in long enough that the forest was beginning to reclaim it. Their job was to provide early warning of the approach of the Dusters.

"Anyway, we've got a bug-out buggy," Mackie added.

The Major Mite they were given wasn't much of a bug-out buggy: a quarter-ton truck that strained when called on to carry four fully combat-loaded Marines. But it was a lot faster than running, and had a much better chance of letting the four Marines out-distance approaching Dusters.

Lance Corporal Cafferata leaned toward Horton and said *sotto voce*, "Ignore Orndoff, he's a chronic worrier. Don't mean nothing." He kept his eyes on the display of the motion detector console the fire team had been supplied with. Four individual detectors planted ahead swept the area to the OP's front, covering a width of half a kilometer. Cafferata had to watch the display carefully, as it was filled with static caused by leaves fluttering in the light breeze that wafted through the trees. Cafferata thought that, with a little bit of luck, they'd hear the Dusters before they were close enough for the detector display to pick up their motion.

"Luck is the final determinant in combat," Mackie had said when Cafferata earlier voiced his hope. "In the final analysis luck is more important than skill. But any Marine who relies on luck to accomplish his mission is a dead Marine."

Cafferata had sighed. He knew that, he just didn't like being reminded. He was on a mission that didn't require a tremendous amount of skill, and figured that made luck all that much more important.

Horton gave his fire team leader a worried look. He'd also heard what Mackie had said about luck. It didn't reassure him. He was entirely too conscious of the fact that there might be hundreds of Dusters closer to him than other Marines were. He'd also heard that the Dusters held a significant numerical advantage over the Marines at the MCAF, which also did nothing to reassure him.

Avians flittered and darted about in the trees, snapping up flying insectoids just like forest birds on Earth did. Somewhere a bark-boring avian *rat-a-tat-tat-ed* a tree, digging out insectoids that burrowed into tree trunks.

"That sounds just like the woodpeckers I saw back home when I was growing up," Mackie said. "How about you, Horton? Did you ever see woodpeckers?" He spoke softly, but kept his eyes front in case a Duster scout managed to slip past the motion detectors, and listened to the forest more than to Horton's answer.

"I—I don't know," Horton replied. He was too nervous to think about Earthly birds.

They sat quietly for a few minutes, Cafferata watching the display, the others looking into the forest, Mackie listening as well as looking.

Time drags when all you're doing is waiting. But wait was all they had to do—that and watch. The mind will drift after awhile. So it wasn't until the *rat-a-tat-tat* suddenly stopped that Mackie abruptly noticed the faint drumming of feet he'd been hearing for several minutes.

"Heads up," he called out, just loudly enough for his men to hear.

At the same time, Cafferata snapped, "Movement."

Mackie jumped up and ran to the movement detector monitor and studied the screen.

"They're coming," he said. He studied the display for a moment, read the numbers scrawling down one side of the screen, and said, "Two hundred meters and closing. Time for us to get out of here."

Mackie helped Cafferata close the control station and run with it to the Major Mite. The other two were all ready in it. Orndoff was at the controls, ready to go. As soon as Mackie and Cafferata were in, Orndoff gunned it. The Major Mite took off with a muted roar.

They'd barely started when wild *caws* and *skrees* echoed through the trees, and a few shots whizzed past, some thunking into tree trunks.

"Go!" Mackie shouted.

"I'm going, I'm going!" Orndoff shouted back. The smallish vehicle slowly picked up speed.

Mackie twisted around to look back and saw Dusters darting through the trees little more than a hundred meters to the rear. He took the most stable position he could in the moving, jouncing vehicle and raised his rifle to his shoulder. If any Duster got close, Mackie would attempt to shoot it. But his position wasn't steady enough to take the kind of shots he had when he'd faced them before.

More Dusters became visible, some running on the faint track the Major Mite followed. The vehicle hit a relatively smooth stretch of road and Mackie fired a three-round burst. A Duster tumbled, spraying red.

Cafferata was looking back and whooped. "Way to go, honcho! Got that bastard."

"Lucky shot," Mackie said back. "Just dumb luck."

Cafferata said dryly, "Right. I forgot. You only qualified as Expert." Expert, the Marines' highest level of marksmanship.

Belatedly, Mackie remembered he was supposed to notify the company when he saw the Dusters. He got on his comm and reported.

Defensive works, Marine Corps Air Facility, Jordan

"They're about two minutes behind us," Corporal Mackie shouted as PFC Orndoff skidded the Major Mite through an opening in the wire.

Corporal Vittori came up and grabbed Mackie's arm. "Get your men into the trench there." He pointed in the direction he was pulling Mackie.

Second Lieutenant Commiskey pounded to them. "How many are there?"he demanded.

Mackie didn't look at his platoon commander when he answered, but kept looking at the treeline where he expected to see Dusters bursting into the open at any second. "Sorry, Sir. They were shooting at us, I didn't get a head count."

"But you shot one of 'em in the head," Lance Corporal Cafferata said from his position a couple of meters away.

"You killed one?" Commiskey asked.

Mackie nodded. "He was getting too close."

"One burst, Lieutenant," Cafferata said. "Right in the head. You should a seen it, that head burst like a melon, spraying blood all over the damn place."

"Did any get on you?" Commiskey asked, looking at Mackie's uniform.

Mackie shot a glare at Cafferata. "He wasn't *that* close, Sir."

"Sixty, seventy meters," Cafferata said.

Commiskey glanced at the Major Mite. He'd ridden in them and knew how much they could bounce. "Damn good shooting at that range," he commented.

Mackie shrugged. "That was just one. There are hundreds more on their way. How much ammo do we have?"

Before Commiskey could answer, a Siren sounded. A line of Dusters had appeared at the edge of the trees, five hundred meters distant. They jittered side to side, fore and back, but didn't advance.

"Lock and load!" the platoon sergeants called. "Lock and load!" It was an unnecessary command, as all the Marines on the line already had their rifles loaded and most were pointing them at the distant treeline. The better command at the moment was one taken up by some of the squad leaders, and repeated by many fire team leaders: "Hold your fire, wait for the command!"

"Get ready," Commiskey said to Mackie and slapped his shoulder. He stood and shouted out the same command to the rest of the platoon as he trotted back to his position. "Everybody, get ready." His voice didn't crack when he saw the number of Dusters appearing on the far side of the cleared area. But his throat tightened.

"Third fire team, take aim but hold your fire!" Mackie shouted. First platoon was on the company's right flank. Mackie couldn't see it from where he was, but the twenty Marines of the combat engineer platoon had also picked up their rifles and took positions on the trench's left flank, ready to fight off the attackers.

Captain Sitter came up on the all-hands freq. "Guns, strafe that line. Mortars, lob some into the trees behind the line. One gun on each flank, crossfire at the Dusters' flank. Everybody else, hold your fire until I say otherwise. Do it now."

From points along the defensive line, the M5-C machine guns of the company opened fire. Their tracers flew on a flat arc and danced side to side along the ends of the Dusters' line. Behind the Marines line came the distinctive cough of mortars firing. Arching high overhead, there was a noticeable time lag before the mortar bombs burst in the trees.

"Why aren't they charging?" Horton asked. "Why are they just standing there?"

"I don't know. Maybe they're dumb?" Orndoff said.

"They're sacrificing some soldiers to see what kind of weapons we have," Mackie said.

"Say what?" Horton squawked. "What kind of crazy man would do that?"

"First off, they aren't men," Orndoff said.

"There have been human armies that did that," Mackie explained, "as you'd know if you'd studied military history like I have."

"But that's crazy," Horton objected.

"I didn't say it wasn't."

"They aren't learning what kind of weapons we have, the Scatterers aren't firing. Why not?" Horton could see that the distant Dusters were taking casualties.

"Maybe the Skipper doesn't want them to know we've got Scatterers."

That was when the aliens charged.

"Hold your fire," Sitter again ordered on the all-hands freq. "Wait for my command."

The Dusters ran fast, but they jinked and dodged, running more side to side than forward, so they weren't closing the distance much faster than running men would. They fired as they ran, but nearly all of their shots were wild and went high or hit the dirt between them and the barrier wire—few struck near the fighting trench the Marines were in. The width of the charging mass was double the width of the Marines' defensive line.

Mackie picked a spot in the mass and aimed at it, gently caressing the trigger of his rifle while waiting for the command to fire. "Damn," he said. "That looks like a lot more than the eight hundred that jet jockey estimated."

"What's he waiting for?" Horton nervously asked.

"Be patient," Mackie said. "He wants more of them to come out of the trees so we've got a denser mass to shoot at.

When the leading Dusters were four hundred meters distant, Sitter called on the all hands, "*Fire!*" and everyone opened up. The two Scatterers threw their two thousand rounds per minute at the Dusters. Aliens started dropping in increasing numbers. Some of the fallen stayed down, others began crawling back toward the cover of the trees. A few rose and staggered after the charging mass.

Horton shook his head. "They're getting slaughtered!" he shouted. "How can they charge like that?"

While reloading, Mackie said, "There have been human armies that did that. They called it 'human wave' attacks."

"There's a difference," Cafferata added. "The first lines in human wave attacks often carried dummy weapons. These guys are *all* armed."

The leading line of Dusters reached three hundred meters from the wire barrier and dropped into prone positions to put aimed fire at the Marines. Bullets started striking the dirt close to the trench; some audibly *whizzed* past. The rest of the mass charged past them, still flipping backward or falling to the side when they were hit. Some flopped forward when their jinking carried them into the path of bullets from their comrades.

The first cry of, "Corpsman up!" was shouted.

At two hundred meters the leading aliens dropped to put aimed fire at the Marines. The first shooters leapt to their feet and rejoined the charge. The mass of attacking Dusters was thinner than it had been, and the Marines' fire wasn't knocking down as many.

Next to him, Mackie heard Cafferata yelp, and turned to the sound. Cafferata was slumped against the front wall of the trench. Pain made a rictus of his face, and he clutched his right arm above the elbow. Blood flowed from around it.

"Corpsman up! How bad is it?" Mackie asked Cafferata.

"Hurts like hell," Cafferata said through gritted teeth.

"Doc's on his way, he'll take care of that." Mackie pulled the field dressing from Cafferata's first aid pouch and ripped it open.

"Gimme that," Cafferata gasped, and let go of his wound to grab the dressing. "I'll hold it on until Doc gets here. Get back to killing Dusters."

Mackie gave him a searching look. The other's face was beading with sweat, but his complexion wasn't turning waxy. He pressed the dressing on Cafferata's wound and withdrew his hand so the lance corporal could hold it in place. He turned back to see the Dusters were closer.

"What do you have here?" Hayden asked as he dropped into the trench. His eyes took in the blood-stained bandage Cafferata pressed to his arm. "Let me put another one on that." He got another dressing out of his medkit to tie around the one Cafferata was holding. "Does it hurt?"

"No shit."

"I've got something for that." Hayden dipped back into his medkit for a pain killer and injected it into Cafferata's shoulder. "That'll hold you until I can get you to the med station."

The Duster leaders at one hundred meters dropped in turn and the others got up to resume their charge. There were still fewer of them, and fewer were falling to Marine bullets.

Then the leaders leaped onto the wire and the following Dusters clambered up them to pin themselves higher up on the wire.

Captain Sitter shouted on the all-hands freq, "Fix bayonets!" All along the line, rifles stopped firing for the seconds it took to attach the blades around the muzzles of the rifles, turning them into clumsy spears.

The third Dusters flung themselves onto the top of the wire, bending over it. The rest of the mass clambered over their bodies to the top and jumped to the ground. They'd been warned about the spikes in the bottom of the shallow trench inside the defensive wire, and didn't jump blindly into it. Most of them stepped around the spikes, although a few weren't as agile and shrieked when a foot was pierced. Some of them fell onto more spikes, and the Dusters who came behind used them as stepping stones.

"Remember, their necks are a weak spot!" Mackie shouted at his men.

Mackie fired three more bursts and saw a Duster tumble from one of them. Then they were in bayonet range. One ran straight at him. He stood and jabbed forward with his rifle, under the reaching claws of the alien, which had dropped its rifle in favor of using its talons and toothed beak on Earthly flesh. The man's arms were longer, and the bayonet impaled the Duster in its shoulder near where its long neck stuck out. The blade went deep, and Mackie rolled back, using the alien's momentum to swing it up and over. The Duster flew off the bayonet and fell to the ground behind the trench, with a bone-snapping thud.

Another Duster was almost on him, and he slammed the butt of his rifle into its beak, shattering it. The Duster fell back, shrieking in pain and clutching at its face.

Next to him, he heard the banging of Doc Hayden's handgun. A quick glance showed him Cafferata firing his rifle one-handed. Another Duster came at Mackie, too close for him to use his rifle. He used the same advice he'd shouted to his men—he used his rifle to bat away the Duster's reaching hands and grabbed its neck behind its head with his free hand. Again, he used the alien's momentum to swing it around, dropping his rifle in the process. He slammed the Duster to the ground, where its legs landed on the corpse of the one he'd bayoneted, leaped out of the trench to straddle it and gripped its neck with both hands. He wrenched the neck and twisted it, feeling bones snap. The Duster bucked with its head flopping on the end of its broken neck. He spun back to the trench and surged to his feet just as a speeding Duster reached him, aiming low with outstretched talons, expecting him to still be down. They collided, and Mackie was thrown back. He rolled to the side and jumped to his feet. The Duster was staggering backward and fell into the trench. Mackie jumped in after him and landed one foot on the Duster's chest, the other on its neck. The snapping of bones was clearly audible. Then the Marine had to toss the writhing alien aside to get to his rifle.

Once again armed, Mackie faced the front to fight more Dusters, but the only ones he saw were laying on the ground, either still or trying to crawl away from the fight. He turned around to see the Dusters who had gotten past the line of Marines racing deeper into the ruins of the air facility.

"What are they doing?" Horton yelped. "Where are they going?"

Mackie could only shake his head. He'd read about battles where a force had broken through a line and didn't know what to do next, because their commanders hadn't told them what to do beyond charge and keep going. It seemed that was what was happening here.

"I don't know, and I don't care," he shouted. "Kill them!" He added his fire to the fire of other Marines who were already putting bursts into the backs of the speeding Dusters.

A couple of hundred meters from the trench, the Dusters started milling about aimlessly in the debris from the original attack on the air facility. When they realized they were being shot at from behind, many of them ducked behind piles of debris, or larger chunks of wreckage.

"India Company!" Sitter shouted on his all hands, "Up! Get on line. We're going after them."

The Marines who were able climbed out of the trench and got in line, their rifles ready to shoot at any Duster that showed itself.

Mackie became aware of more cries of, "Corpsman up!" coming from the trench.

"Watch your dress and stagger it!" the platoon sergeants shouted, the command echoed by the squad leaders.

"India Company, fast step, move out!" the company commander ordered.

As one, the able-bodied Marines started at a brisk walk toward the debris the Dusters were covering behind.

Mackie glanced at his sides to see that Orndoff and Horton were keeping pace, and weren't directly lined up with him or the Marines on their other sides. He blinked in surprise at what he saw.

"Hector, what are you doing here? You're wounded."

Cafferata grinned at him. "Doc patched me up and put my arm in a sling. I can still shoot."

Mackie shook his head. Cafferata had his rifle stuck through his sling, resting its forestock on his arm. *Doc must have given him a pain blocker*, he thought, *or that would hurt too damn much*. He returned his attention to the front, looking for any Duster foolish enough to expose itself. Here and there along the line he heard the sound of a three-round burst as another Marine saw—or thought he saw—a Duster poking its head out. He heard a shriek follow some of the bursts, indicating that not only had a Duster exposed itself, but the burst had hit home.

Fifty meters from the first debris pile the Dusters had taken cover behind, Captain Sitter gave a new command: "Slow fire bursts, keep their heads down." At ten meters he gave another: "Flush them out!"

The Marines sprinted to the piles of debris and bigger chunks of wreckage.

Mackie and his men dashed to what might have been the corner of a revetment roof, and turned to face it as they ran past. Mackie fired at the three startled Dusters hunkered down behind it. So did his men. The impact of the bullets threw two of the aliens back, blood spurting from sudden holes in their torsos and thighs. Missed, the third whipped around and raised its rifle. Before it could fire, Cafferata put a burst into it and it toppled backward, flinging its rifle up and to the rear as it fell dying.

More gunfire crackled, and more Dusters shrieked in deadly pain. Deeper cries told of Marines being shot by the aliens.

Then India Company was beyond the area where the Dusters had taken cover, but they kept going, making sure none had escaped farther.

"India Company, back to the trench," Sitter ordered. "Stay alert in case we missed anyone, or anybody's faking. Fast march. Watch your dress and keep it staggered."

"Hey, Mackie," Sergeant Martin said when they reached the trench, "you're bleeding."

"What? Where?" Mackie looked at his front, turned his arms to examine them. "Where am I bleeding?"

"On your left side."

Mackie raised his left arm and looked. Sure enough, he saw blood staining his side, and a tear near his armpit. He poked the fingers of his right hand inside the tear and flinched when they touched a gouge in the muscle. "No shit. I got hit and didn't even realize it." He looked at his squad leader. "You're bleeding, too. Your leg."

"Why the hell did you think I was limping?"

"Orndoff," Mackie said. "Hold your arms out and turn around."

"Why for?" Orndoff asked, but did as he was told. He didn't show any blood stains.

"Horton, you too," Mackie said, and looked the other way.

Horton didn't raise his arms and turn around; he was leaning forward on the lip of the trench. "I think I got hit, too," he gasped.

"Corpsman up!" Mackie shouted at the same time Martin did.

The Butcher's Bill

Except for the wounded Dusters who had crawled back to the safety of the trees while they were charging across the half-kilometer of open land in front of the defensive line, the entire attack force had been killed.

The Marines suffered seven dead, one from first squad. Besides Martin, Mackie, Cafferata, and Horton, six other men from the platoon were wounded.

LIEUTENANT GENERAL BAUER STUDIED THE AFTER ACTION REPORTS NOT ONLY FROM the division commands, but from the battalion and company commands as well. The various units of VII Corps, both Marine and Army, had acquitted themselves well in combat against the alien enemy. In almost all instances, the humans had severely damaged their foes. But their own casualties had mounted, and he had too few support troops that he could feed into the rifle companies to replace the dead or seriously wounded. And he had no knowledge of the number of aliens—or "Dusters" as the troops called them.

He looked again at the report from India/Three/One. In their latest action they had killed seven or eight hundred Dusters against only seven of their own kia and another eleven wounded.

But twenty casualties was ten percent of the company's strength.

In another action, the second platoon of Alpha, First of the Seventh Mounted Infantry had lost nearly half its strength. And the Construction Battalion detachment that was building their firebase was also severely injured. This against hundreds of Dusters killed.

How much did that damage the Dusters? Without knowing what the Duster strength was to begin with, he had no way of telling how badly his forces were hurting the enemy. For all he knew, the Dusters had the equivalent of two field armies on Troy—at least eight times as many troops as VII Corps had left Earth with. He reminded himself that not all of VII Corps had made it planetside; huge chunks of it were lost when the Dusters attacked ARG 17 after it exited the wormhole.

Task Force 8 was limited in the assistance it could provide the planet-side forces; it too had been seriously wounded in the attack on ARG 17.

What could he do? He hoped his message to the Joint Chiefs made it through and that the President and the Secretary of Defense decided to act on it. He knew Marine Commandant Talbot would push to send a relief force, and was pretty sure Chairman Welborn would as well. He desperately needed the additional troops, and the shotguns and artillery canister rounds he'd requested would be extremely valuable in defeating the "human wave" attacks of the Dusters, if the Dusters were dumb enough to continue making them.

He called for his aide.

"Sir." Captain Upshur appeared in Bauer's office door in seconds.

"Captain, I want to conference my division commanders immediately. They don't have to come in, a vid conference will do. Pipe them in to my comp."

"Aye aye, Sir." Talbot about faced and went to do his commander's bidding.

In moments, Major Generals Purvis, Noll, and Bearss appeared in windows on his comp's display.

"Gentlemen, thank you for attending me so promptly. I trust the infantry divisions, Marine and Army both, have designated regiment- and brigade-level Whiskey Companies. Start distributing the troops. I want the line companies up as close as possible to full strength quickly, as quickly as possible.

Let me assure you, I have noted that your people have acquitted themselves in the highest tradition of the NAU military forces. But they are likely to face the enemy Dusters again and again before a relief force arrives.

With that in mind, I don't want any more company- or platoon-size outposts. You can use them, but only if they are in locations where they can support each other. My preference at this time is for battalion-size outposts.

"The Navy is still scanning for Duster concentrations, and looking for gravitational anomalies that could indicate underground spaces the Dusters might be using.

"Questions?"

"Sir," Purvis said. Bauer nodded for him to continue. "I just want to make sure that we should begin pulling our farthest outposts back, tighten up our lines."

"That is correct, General."

"Sir," 9th Division's General Noll said. When Bauer indicated he should speak, he asked, "Have you received a reply yet from Earth on your request for reinforces and additional weapons?"

"I'm sorry, General, but there hasn't been enough time for my message to reach Earth and a reply to come back. Rest assured, I will inform you as soon as I receive a reply.

"If there are no other questions, distribute your Whiskey Company people now.

"Bauer out." He broke his conference connection. *Ass*, he thought. *He should know that I wouldn't hold that information back.*

Ten days earlier

The War Room, Supreme Military Headquarters,
Bellevue, Sarpy County, Federal Zone,
North American Union

Secretary of War Richmond Hobson sat centered at the end of the wide conference table closest to the door. To his right was Fleet Admiral Ira Welborn, Chairman of the Joint Chiefs of Staff. General John C. Robinson, Army Chief of Staff, sat at Hobson's left. Arrayed along the sides of the table were sixteen Army Generals, eight to a side. A Marine general, a Navy Admiral, and a civilian were seated at the far end of the table. Other generals and admirals occupied chairs that lined the long walls of the room.

"As of fifteen minutes ago," Hobson growled, "we still don't know how much of Amphibious Ready Group 17 and VII Corps survived the enemy attack, or how far along the survivors are in reaching planetfall on Troy. We can only assume, and you all know what 'assume' does, that the Marines have the situation well in hand.

"You have a question, Mr. Gresser?" he asked when the civilian at the foot of the table cleared his throat.

"Ah, yes Sir," Ignatz Gresser, the Special Assistant to President Albert Mills, "sort of, Sir. I didn't mean to interrupt—" An imperious *spit it out* gesture from Hobson made him clear his throat again. "Sir, what does 'assume' do, that evidently everybody here but me knows?"

Hobson laughed, his first genuine laugh since Welborn and the Joint Chiefs' head of intelligence, Major General Joseph de Castro, brought him word of the alien invasion of Troy. Still laughing, he gestured to Commandant of the Marine Corps Ralph Talbot, who sat next to Gresser.

"Mr. Gresser," Talbot said with no trace of condescension in his voice, "of course, you never served in uniform. What we say is, 'Assume makes an ass of you and me.' It's an admonition that making assumptions is rarely a good idea. But in this instance," he glanced at Hobson for permission to continue and got a keep-going hand-wave in reply, "we lack the intelligence to do anything *but* make assumptions."

"Thank you, Sir," Gresser said.

"If that's all the questions for the moment," Hobson finally said as his laughter died down, "our next assumption is that the aliens will soon send another invasion fleet to counterattack our limited forces on Troy. We must defend our colony, and save our people, both military and—if we can find them—civilian. To that end, Second Army will begin to mount out as soon as units and their equipment can board Navy shipping. Who's ready to go in the first wave?"

"Sir," Commandant Talbot said before anybody else could speak, "2nd and 3rd Marine Combat Forces are on two-hour standby and can be on the way to their assigned elevators as soon as orders to move are issued."

"Might have known the Marines would jump to the head of the line," Army Chief of Staff Robinson groused.

"The Marines *are* the door-kicker-inners," Fleet Admiral Welborn said calmly. "The NAU's force in readiness."

The corner of Robinson's mouth twitched, but he didn't say anything else.

"Which Army units can follow close behind the Marines?" Hobson asked, getting the discussion back on topic.

"I believe IV Corps is the most ready," said General George P. Hays, Second Army's commander, with a nod to Lieutenant General David S. Stanley.

"Yes, Sir," Stanley said. "Each of my divisions has at least one brigade on twenty-four hour standby. Fifteenth Division is fully on standby. I can have the equivalent of two divisions ready to mount out in two days time. Give me a week, and I believe my entire Corps will be ready."

"Very good," Hobson said. "What about transportation?" He looked at Chief of Naval Operations Fleet Admiral James Madison.

Madison sighed the sigh of a man being put upon. "As you will recall, Mr. Secretary, much of ARG 17 was killed in the alien ambush en route to Troy. The surviving vessels haven't yet returned to Earth."

"We know that, Madison," Hobson snapped. "The question is, what *do* we have?"

"Well, in Navy shipping, I have enough transports immediately available to transport one MCF."

Hobson gave Madison less than two seconds to continue, then said sharply, "What about the civilian shipping you were to commandeer?"

"That's not all available yet."

"Well, how much of it is available?" The impatience was evident in Hobson's voice.

Madison shrugged. "Almost enough to transport an Army corps, but not quite enough for an MCF."

"And when will there be more civilian shipping ready for us?"

"I'm getting it in as fast as I can, Mr. Secretary. But understand, I am short on fighting ships to escort the transports."

"Most of Task Force 8 is still in fighting trim," Hobson said sourly. "Unless you don't believe the last dispatch?"

"Do you mean the one in which Avery said, 'Issue in doubt'?" Madison asked.

Hobson stared at Madison for a moment before replying. "I'm referring to the message from Lieutenant General Bauer." To himself he added, *I've had enough of this baffoon. There will be a new CNO by the time the Navy launches with another MCF for Troy.*

"Oh, yes, the *ground* commander's assessment of Navy status in Troy space," Madison said dismissively.

Talbot lifted a hand a few inches from the table top.

"Yes, Commandant?" Hobson said, giving the Marine permission to speak.

"Admiral," Talbot addressed Madison, "I have known General Bauer since he was a platoon commander in Lima Three/Four when I was executive officer there. It wouldn't surprise me in the least if he knew more about the strength and disposition of the task force supporting his efforts planetside than the admiral commanding the task force."

"That's preposterous!" Madison sputtered.

"It may be hyperbole, but it's not too far off the mark," Hobson said. "While you may disagree with the details, I think we can accept that TF 8 is still in fighting form, and needs reinforcement more than it needs replacing."

"Another assumption," Madison muttered, but softly enough that only those sitting next to him heard.

Ignoring Madison's mutter, Hobson said, "This is the problem we always have dealing with interstellar distances. Our most recent intelligence on Troy is nearly two weeks behind. We have no way of knowing what the true situation is. But we must act on the assumption—I know, there it is again—that our forces on Troy have the situation in hand and can use our help.

So, Admiral," addressing Madison again, how soon can the Navy board the Marines and launch to Troy? It seems that everybody is ready except you."

"Sir, if I may?" said an admiral seated against the wall behind Madison.

"I don't believe everybody here knows you, so state your name, rank, and command first," Hobson said.

"Rear Admiral William Moffett, Sir. I'm commander, ARG 28. Sir, my ships have already begun moving to the elevator heads in anticipation of boarding the lead elements of Second Army, and can be ready to board them in three days."

"Excellent, Admiral!" Hobson said.

"Sir, by your leave," another admiral against the wall said.

"Speak."

"Sir, Rear Admiral Herman Stickney, commander Task Force 7. TF 7 is, as the CNO indicated, not yet fully up to snuff. However, it does have three dreadnaughts, three King class carriers, and seven other ships of the line. The lead elements of TF 7 can be in position to escort ARG 28 by the time it is ready to launch."

"That's thirteen warships," Hobson said. "TF 8 had thirteen warships. How does this make TF 7 less ready to launch than TF 8?"

"Sir, TF 7 has to escort an entire army, not simply a reinforced corps. It needs to be larger than TF 8."

"I see. Well, Admiral Stickney, coordinate with Admiral Moffett to escort ARG 28, and with General Talbot to get at least one Marine Combat Force on its way to Troy as soon as possible." He paused, looking at Madison, then said to Stickney and Moffett, "For purpose of this movement, you will report directly to Fleet Admiral Welborn."

Madison opened his mouth to protest, but shut it when he saw the glare Hobson gave him.

"That is all. Everybody, do it now." Hobson stood. In a moment, he was the only one left in the War Room. He headed for his office.

Command Post, Advance Firebase One,
Semi-Autonomous World of Troy

"SIR," CORPORAL OWEN MCGOUGH, SECOND PLATOON'S COMMUNICATIONS MAN SAID, holding the comm out to Second Lieutenant Theodore Greig, "it's Six. Wants the Actual."

Greig took the offered unit and said into it, "Two-Six Actual. Over."

"Two Actual, wait one for Six Actual."

Greig held the comm, waiting impatiently. He had to reorganize his squads into something that could at least marginally function as a platoon. And where was that transportation he'd requested?

"Two Actual, This is Alpha Six Actual," Captain Harry Meyer's voice came over the comm. He and the rest of 10th Brigade had finally made planetfall. "Transportation for you and your boys is on the way. ETA, thirty minutes. I say again, three zero minutes. Can you hold out that long? Over."

"Six Actual, Two Actual. We are not currently under attack. What do you mean, 'transportation for me and my boys'? Over."

"Two, you are being withdrawn. I'll explain when you get here. Be ready to board when your transportation arrives. Bring your dead and the CBs. Alpha Six Actual out." With that, the transmission went dead.

"Platoon sergeant, to me," Greig shouted.

Sergeant First Class Alexander Quinn came pounding up to Greig from where he'd been checking the disposition of the remaining soldiers in the bunkers.

"Yes, Sir," he said, panting slightly.

"Get the boys ready, we're pulling out," Greig said with a grimace.

"Really? Hot damn! I'll be glad to see the last of this place."

Greig looked at him grimly. "We paid for this patch of ground with a lot of blood, Sarge. It belongs to us. I don't like leaving."

Quinn looked back at his platoon commander just as grimly. "That's right, Sir. We paid with a lot of blood. And if we stay here, we're liable to pay a lot more blood. Maybe all of our blood."

Greig had no reply to that. Instead he said, "Get me the CB boss. Then start getting our boys ready. Make sure our dead are ready for tranport."

"Yes, Sir." Quinn ran off.

"What do you need, Mr. Greig?" Lieutenant Commander William Kelly Harrison asked when he reached the CP. "I don't have much time, my people have a lot of work to do."

"Sir, I have orders. Transportation is on the way. We're all pulling out."

Harrison looked around at the body bags that were lined up near the CP, and the bodies that hadn't yet been bagged.

"Probably a good idea. I don't think they'll give up with just the one assault."

"Instead of repairing and strengthening our defenses, I want you to prepare them to be blown as soon as we're out of here. I don't want any defenses left for the Dusters to use when we come back. Can do?"

Harrison nodded. "Yeah, we can. How much time do we have?"

"Less than half an hour."

"We can blow the bunkers in that time. What about the wire?"

Greig looked at the wire barrier, festooned with the bodies of the Dusters who'd sacrificed themselves to make bridges, and others who were killed trying to cross the once- living bridges.

"Leave it. The Dusters will be able to see the bodies hanging there from a long way off. It might give them pause about attacking humans again."

Harrison looked at the wire with the alien bodies hanging from it, and at the forest beyond. He nodded. "Either that or make them attack even more ferociously the next time." He took his leave and went to put his men to work arming the bunkers to be blown.

It only took a few more minutes for the soldiers to finish collecting and bagging the dead.

Quinn put them to work staging all of their gear and supplies to be put aboard vehicles when their transportation arrived. He hoped it wasn't those Marine Scooters again, although he did like the Hogs with their firepower.

All was ready when a convoy of six M117 Growler armored personnel carriers, the vehicles the platoon should have had to begin with, two five ton trucks, and two Marine Hogs as armed escort, arrived.

The soldiers and CBs tossed their gear and supplies into one truck, and hurriedly but reverently stacked the bodies in the other. Then the surviving soldiers and CBs piled into the Growlers. The convoy was moving five minutes after it arrived.

Firebase 17/10, under construction,
a few kilometers from Millerton

The temporary base for the First of the Seventh Mounted Infantry was bustling, with squad tents and larger being erected. Sergeants shouted orders, troops moved from place to place in groups or marching formations. Vehicles drove around raising dust. Heavy equipment was digging trenches and holes, and piling up berms, wire was being emplaced. Officers and senior noncoms moved about looking like they had important places to go and important things to do.

Captain Meyer greeted his Second platoon commander when Greig reported to the tent that temporarily served as the company command post. "Good to see you made it through, Greig. And damn sorry about your losses. First Sergeant Beaty is putting together a memorial service for them."

"Thank you, Sir," Greig said, somewhat stiffly. He was thinking about how Meyer, Beaty, and the rest of the company were just arriving planet-side when he and his platoon were fighting off hundreds of Dusters. He thought his platoon would have lost many fewer men if the entire company had been there. *Whose idea was it anyway,* he wondered, *to stick a lone platoon out in the middle of nowhere, with no more support than a Mobile Intelligence platoon that was somewhere else most of the time?*

"The Top is situating your boys. You've got a few days rest while you integrate new men from the Brigade's Whiskey Company." Meyer smiled crookedly "You hadn't heard about that, had you? The top jarhead ordered every division and brigade to assemble a Whiskey Company to provide replacements for combat losses. Anyway, I think you'll get enough cooks and bakers to reconstitute your platoon. In a few days, the battalion will be moving into a new firebase.

"Top Beaty will show your boys the chow tent, the latrines, and the shower point.

"If you have no questions, that is all for now."

Greig could think of many questions, but none of them were ones Meyer could answer to his satisfaction. So he said, "No questions, Sir," saluted, and left the CP tent. Off to his left he saw the company first sergeant supervising the placement of a rank of bayonetted rifles being stuck in the ground, a helmet perched on each and a pair of boots below.

He told himself that dust thrown out by the vehicles and heavy equipment got in his eyes and made them water, that he wasn't really crying.

Marine Corps Air Facility Jordan, Eastern Shapland

When the call from battalion came in for India Company to pull back, Captain Sitter wasn't surprised, he'd expected as much.

"We'll blow our fighting works," he told his assembled platoon commanders and platoon sergeants at an officers' call. "We've already got our vehicles, so we won't have to wait for any to arrive when we're ready.

"How long will it take your engineers to ready the fighting trench to blow?" he asked First Lieutenant Alexander Bonnyman, Jr.

"We can have the trenches, wire, and the major debris piles ready within two hours, Sir."

Sitter shook his head. "Leave the barrier wire and trench up. Only blow the fighting trench and the biggest piles and bigger pieces of wreckage. I don't want them to have much to block our fields of fire when we come back."

"In that case, maybe an hour."

"Good. The rest of you, put details to work moving our casualties and any equipment we aren't leaving behind into the vehicles. Have the rest of your Marines ready to fight off another assault, should the Dusters come at us again. And leave the alien bodies where they lay. Show those sonsabitches what happens when they tangle with Marines.

"Questions?"

There were none, Sitter's orders were clear.

"Then do it."

The platoon commanders and platoon sergeants left the command post to carry out the orders. Sitter turned to his executive officer, First Lieutenant Edward Osterman.

"Go to the dispensary and ask the surgeon which casualties are most ready to be moved. Ask if we need a triage to board them for removal."

"Aye aye, Sir." Osterman headed for the makeshift dispensary.

Sitter called battalion and requested medevac for the most seriously wounded. Battalion made no promises, but promised to try. Two Pegasus SAR birds arrived to take out the worst wounded. They were escorted by two AT-5 Cobras.

The Dusters didn't come back

Firebase Zion, near Jordan

During India Company's absence, a platoon from Kilo Company had moved in to hold it. Battalion commander Lieutenant Colonel Davis was at Zion waiting for India Company's return.

"Well done, Captain," Davis said and shook Sitter's hand. He saw the company's other officers and NCOs moving the platoons into their assigned areas and nodded his approval. "I want your Marines to know that I think they did an outstanding job at the MCAF. I've seen vid. The Dusters' tactics are astonishing. I guess they just don't understand."

"No, Sir, I don't think they have any idea of what they're up against."

"The question is, are they few enough for us to stand against until relief comes?"

Sitter perked up at that. "Has word come that a relief force is on its way?"

"Not yet. But I'm sure it will come shortly." Davis turned to the west. "Look over there. See the construction going on? That's a new firebase. Kilo Company's going into it. Then we'll do another to the east for Lima Company. The new firebases are each half a kilometer from FB Zion, close enough to provide mutual support. Another firebase will be to your rear. That'll have the headquarters and support company and an artillery battery."

He looked in the direction of the destroyed MCAF Jordan. "For all we know, the Dusters have shot their wad. But there's no way to know for sure. The Navy is still searching for Dusters, and any anomalies that could signal a cave where they're holing up. Word hasn't come down yet, but I strongly suspect that we'll be running search and destroy patrols.

"In the meanwhile, First Marines now has a Whiskey Company. Over there," Davis indicated a smll formation of Marines standing nervously some meters to his rear, "are your replacements. Get them integrated as quickly as possible. There's no telling how soon you'll be going on patrol, and I want them to at least begin feeling comfortable in their new squads. With any luck, you won't have to go before your lesser wounded are well enough to go with you."

Sitter looked beyond the battalion commander at a dozen Marines standing at ease, if not with ease, in two ranks. They were all armed, and each had a ditty bag at his feet and a pack on his back.

"I see their weapons. Do they have all their gear?"

Davis nodded. "All you have to do is provide them with platoon assignments. They've got everything they need."

"Thank you, Sir. I'll get right on it."

"Once more, Captain, you and your Marines did an outstanding job at the MCAF. It's just too bad we had to abandon it."

"It was."

"Carry on. And remember to tell your Marines I know what an outstanding job they did." With that, he headed for his vehicle and back to where his headquarters firebase was under construction.

The platoon from Kilo Company piled into its vehicles and returned to the rest of their company.

Sitter looked for his first sergeant, and saw him heading in his direction.

"Well, Top," he said, "we've got replacements from Whiskey Company. Let's meet them."

"Sounds like an excellent idea, Sir," the Top said. He followed Sitter a pace to his left and rear as they walked the few paces to the dozen new men, who came to attention, uncertainty on all of their faces.

"Marines, I'm Captain Carl Sitter. This is First Sergeant Robert Robinson. I'm sure you know why you are here. But in case any of you didn't get the word, India Company has just returned from a substantial engagement with the Dusters. They had overrun MCAF Jordan, and we went to fight them. The aliens used human wave tactics to attack us. They weren't successful, we killed hundreds of them. We don't believe they've given up. You are here to replace the seven Marines we lost, and five of our worst wounded. The first sergeant will assign you to platoons, and the platoon commanders and platoon sergeants will put you in squads.

"Don't worry about what you're going to do. No matter what your MOS is, you've all had training as infantrymen, and you've fired your rifles for qualification—more than once if you've been in the Corps for longer than a year. When you're in your squads and fire teams, pay close attention to what your NCOs tell you. They've all gone up against the Dusters several times and beaten them every time.

"I'm sure you will do well. We are Marines. Marines always win their battles."

He turned to face Robinson. "First Sergeant, the detachment is yours," and walked off.

As he left he heard Robinson barking at the new men, putting a little fear of god into them. As if they needed more fear. *Damn, I hope we don't have to fight again very soon. If we do these cooks and bakers and clerks are liable to get killed.*

A WEEK AFTER INDIA COMPANY FOUGHT THE DUSTERS AT MCAF JORDAN, Sergeant Martin, Corporal Mackie, Lance Corporal Cafferata, and PFC Horton were recovering from their wounds. Cafferata was back with the squad, although on light duty. The others were mostly recovered. The only member of First squad to be killed in the action had been Lance Corporal John Dahlgren from first fire team. Lance Corporal Edwin Appleton, a clerk from the battalion's S-1, personnel section, who had been assigned to Whiskey Company, replaced him.

None of the Marines would admit it, but the lack of action—or threat of action—was making them bored.

"You're lucky John," Corporal Joseph Vittori said when the squad's fire team leaders had a chance to relax, sitting against the face of a bunker, looking out over the surrounding landscape. They weren't doing it consciously, but they were watching for anything out of the ordinary, anything that could signal the approach of danger from the front. Their rifles looked like they'd been placed without a care, but all three could grab their weapons and have them in fighting positions at an instant's notice.

"What do you mean, lucky?" Mackie asked. "Me and two of my men were wounded at the air facility. How's that lucky?"

"For one, you didn't get anyone wasted. I lost Dahlgren."

"You say 'For one.' That implies a 'For two.' Spit it out."

"My newbie? He's a pogue. He was a clerk in S-1." Vittori grimaced and shook his head. "A goddam pogue."

"Hey, man, I got a pogue to replace Zion." Mackie shrugged. "No big deal, you just have to supervise him more closely than anybody else in your fire team, that's all."

"More closely," Corporal Bill Button said. "You know what that means, don't you? It means more than your other men combined. It means so closely that you maybe don't pay enough attention to what you're doing yourself and get *your* young ass blown away." He ducked away from the slow round-house punch Vittori threw at him.

Mackie laughed and Vittori glared at him.

"Horton's a fucking PFC. He's your bottom man. Appleton's a goddam lance corporal. That makes him my number two. I can't afford to spend all of my time supervising him, I have to rely on him to help me with my other men." He spat at his feet and scuffed some dirt over it. "And I almost had Dahlgren up to where he wasn't a liability."

"Better you than me," Mackie said.

"Come on," Button said, ignoring what he'd said about Vittori's new man needing more supervision. "The man's a lance corporal, he's gotta know something. How much supervision can he need?"

"I had to show him where to put his bayonet so he could get to it in a hurry if he ever needs it, that's how much."

"*Jesu gott*," Button swore. "I feel for you, brother."

"Hey, Joe," Mackie said, "you're senior fire team leader. You've been a corporal longer than either Bill or me. Hell, you're next in line in the platoon to make squad leader. You can deal with it."

Button slowly shook his head. "I hate to say it, Joe, but it sounds like you've been screwed, blued, and tattooed."

Their subconscious minds were so intent on watching for danger from the front that none of them noticed Sergeant Martin approaching from behind. The squad leader listened for a while before interjecting himself.

"You're all corporals," Martin said. They all jumped at the unexpected voice. "You're all fire team leaders."

"Oh, hi there, boss," Vittori said, looking up.

"Skootch over, let me get in there," Martin said. The others made room for him and he joined them sitting against the bunker's front, favoring his right leg which was still mending.

"See anything out there?"

"A few avians," Vittori said.

"I saw a dust devil," Button added.

"There's no cover for a Duster within three hundred meters," Mackie said. After a few seconds he added, "Of course, that didn't stop them from coming up underneath us in that house on Clover Sugar Place."

"You sure know how to make a man feel good about where he is," Button said.

"He's right, though," Martin said. "We're in a combat situation here. You can't assume anyplace is safe. You know, I ought to smack each of you upside the head for the way you let me come up behind you."

"We knew you were there," Vittori protested.

"We heard you coming," Button said.

Mackie stayed quiet, he remembered how all of them reacted to Martin's first words.

"Sure you were," Martin said dryly. "Then tell me, how long was I there?"

They didn't say anything at first, but Vittori finally said, "Long enough to hear what we were talking about."

"That's right," Martin said. "And about that, all three of you are corporals, fire team leaders. The Marine Corps has entrusted each of you with the lives of three valuable assets, the lives of three Marines. The Marine Corps believes you can do the job. Corporal Vittori, are you going to make a liar of the Marine Corps by not giving Appleton the supervision and training he needs if you get taken out tomorrow and he has to take over the fire team?"

"Uh, no, Sergeant," Vittori said sheepishly.

"I can't hear you, Corporal."

"No, Sergeant," Vittori said in a normal speaking volume.

"I still can't hear you, Corporal!" Martin said just short of a bellow.

"No, Sergeant!" Vittori shouted.

"That's better." Martin put a hand on Vittori's shoulder and used it to push himself up. On his feet, he looked down at his three fire team leaders. "Now figure out how you're going to deal with pogues who don't have experience or recent training. If I didn't think you could do it, I wouldn't tell you to." He paused and gave them a firm look. "I'd replace you." He cast another look at the landscape, then turned and walked away.

Shocked, the three didn't say anything, either to Martin or to each other. They knew he didn't have the authority to replace them on his own. But they knew his word carried enough weight that he *could* have any of them replaced if he thought they couldn't do the job. And the only way any of them was willing to give up being a fire team leader was to be moved up to squad leader. Not that any of them thought he was particularly ready for the added responsibility of squad leader. Still....

They put their heads together to figure out a way to bring Appleton up to speed, so he could take over the fire team if necessary.

The next day

Mackie was standing in front of the bunkers that had been built to defend Firebase Zion. Vittori stood next to him. The two of them were taking a break from giving Appleton the training he needed to get up to speed, ready to take over the fire team if necessary.

Slowly, Mackie shook his head. "Three hundred meters. That's all we've got between us and the trees."

Vittori spat into the dirt by his feet, and scuffed dirt over the sputum. "I wish we had five hundred meters cleared, like at the air facility. Hell, a full klick would be better."

"Yeah. Think of how many Dusters we could waste before they reached the three hundred we can see now."

"A shitload."

"And that's why I've got a job for you," Martin said from behind them. They both spun about with their rifles at the ready on hearing the unexpected voice.

"Boss," Vittori said, turning to look at the squad leader, "you've got to stop sneaking up on us like that. One of these times somebody's reaction will be too fast and your ass will get blown away."

"And you need to be more aware of your surroundings, not just your front. I've told you that before. Then I wouldn't be able to catch you sleeping like this." He joined them, looking over the open ground.

"So what's the job you've got for us?" Vittori asked warily.

"Not just you, it's for the whole squad. We're going out there and plant motion detectors."

"How far out there?" Vittori asked.

"Who's going with us for security?" Mackie wanted to know.

Martin shook his head. "Just First squad. Nobody's going with us." He glanced at the two fire team leaders. "We're going a half klick into the trees. I've already briefed Button."

"How many detectors are we humping?" Vittori asked.

"Forty. But we aren't humping them. A Scooter is going along to carry them for us, along with repeater stations for us to plant. We'll be able to ride on the way out."

"You said 'on the way out'," Mackie said. "Does that mean we'll be humping back?"

Martin shrugged. "Depends."

"Depends on what?" Vittori asked.

"Depends on the situation when we come back. The Scooter will return to base after it disembarks us and offloads the equipment. If we've got

Dusters coming at us, a Scooter will meet us on the way back in. No Dusters, no Scooter. Is that clear enough to you?"

"Yes, Sergeant," Mackie reluctantly said.

"Our call sign is Purple People. Get your people saddled up. Full ammo allotment. Make sure your people's camelbacks are full. I'll issue one meal ration before the Scooter arrives for us. Do it."

"Yes, Sergeant," Mackie and Vittori said.

A half kilometer into the trees

"You know, you didn't have to come," Martin said to Cafferata. "You're still on light duty."

"You already told me that, Sergeant," Cafferata replied. "Twice. But, dammit, I'm bored. I've already read everything in my library at least twice. And just about everything in the battalion library. Hell, I believe I've read more than Mackie has! So until Regiment sends down more books, going out with the squad is the only thing I can do, short of going totally bugfuck."

"I hear you, Hector, I hear you." He turned to his Third fire team leader. "Mackie, Cafferata doesn't hump any of the detectors. The battalion surgeon said he's not supposed to do any heavy lifting. Got it?"

Mackie looked at the stack of detectors and rolled his eyes, he estimated they each weighed half a kilo. "No heavy lifting. Got it."

Cafferata looked away, trying not to smile.

"All right, everybody," Martin said. "I've got the location for every detector programmed into my GPS. We start here and go west. Vittori, place the first one. The rest of you, come with me." He looked at his GPS and began following its directions.

The Scooter had gone back after dropping them off. Along the way it had stopped two hundred meters in to drop off the repeater units.

"Look sharp," Mackie told his men, all except PFC Orndoff, who was troweling out a shallow hole to plant a detector in. The lower part of the detector was bulb-shaped, and had several thin spines protruding fifteen centimeters around its greatest circumference. The spines had to be placed carefully, parallel to the surface of the ground. They would pick up the vibrations from footsteps. The neck of the detector stuck two centimeters above the surface and could detect the heat radiating from the body of any lifeform larger than an Earth rabbit. An aerial out of the rear of the neck sent its data back to a repeater, which in turn would send it to the master unit at Firebase Zion.

"Ready," Orndoff said, sitting back on his knees.

Mackie knelt next to him and examined the detector's placement. "That's why I have you doing the digging, Harry. You do it right. Now cover it."

Orndoff carefully scooped dirt back into the hole, covering everything except the neck. Then he scattered fallen leaves and twigs over it to conceal it from view.

"Let's go," Mackie said. He and his men rose to their feet and headed toward the rest of the squad. They passed First fire team and continued to Second, where Martin waited.

"Follow me," the sergeant said, and looked at his GPS for direction.

It took the better part of three hours to emplace all of the detectors.

"Now we hump," Martin said. "First fire team, Third, Second. I'll be between Third and Second." Cafferata was still on light duty, Martin didn't want him at either of the most exposed positions. He put himself near the rear of the short column because that was the direction he thought any trouble was most likely to come from; normally he'd be closer to the front of his squad.

Even moving cautiously, it took little more than half an hour for the squad to reach the cache of repeaters. They repeated the earlier exercise, leapfrogging as the fire teams individually planted repeater units.

They were just starting to put in the last of the ten units when the call none of them wanted came over the comm: "Purple People, Purple People. This is Homebase. Over,"

Martin put his comm to his mouth. "Homebase, this is Purple People. Over."

"Purple People, Homebase. Repeaters one through six are showing massive movement in this direction. You are hereby instructed to come home. Over."

"Homebase, we will begin movement as soon as we finish planting the last repeater, it's almost in. Over."

"Purple, that could be too late. Strongly advise you leave now." There was a brief pause during which Martin heard indistinct voices in the background. "Purple People, a Scooter and two Hogs are being dispatched to your location. Meet them. Do you understand? Over."

Martin looked at Vittori, who was inspecting the placement job PFC Simanek had just finished. "Homebase, I understand. We are moving now. Over."

"Purple People, Homebase. We will see you soon. Out."

"We gotta go," Martin told his squad. "Somebody's coming this way, and we're going to be picked up along the way. Same order as before. Move out."

Vittori kicked some leaves over the repeater's antennas and said, "Harvey, point. Let's go at a trot. Move now."

The squad formed into a column as they ran, Martin took a place near the rear. They'd only gone a few meters before they heard the muted roar of the vehicles coming for them. In the distance, to their left rear, they heard the first *caws* of the Dusters.

Camp Zion, near Jordan

"INTO YOUR BUNKERS, MOVE, MOVE, MOVE, MOVE!" STAFF SERGEANT GUILLEN ROARED as soon as the Scooter carrying First squad dropped its rear ramp and the Marines started rushing out with Sergeant Martin and the fire team leaders echoing him. Guillen was the only Marine standing in the open.

The Scooter and both Hogs took position to fire on the aliens when they came into sight.

As Sergeant Martin ran to his bunker, he looked at his men to make sure they were all headed to the right bunkers. Before he ducked into Third fire team's bunker he paused to look out across the open ground. He didn't see any Dusters.

Inside the bunker, he took a position at the aperture and got on the sound-powered phone and called the command group. "Where are they? I don't see them."

"Company says they stopped a hundred meters inside the trees," Sergeant Binder replied. "The Skipper's called for artillery. Maybe we'll wipe them out before they begin their charge."

"Yeah, maybe." But Martin didn't believe it. He told Third fire team what Binder had said, and got on his comm to pass the word to the rest of the squad.

"What the hell are they waiting for?" Lance Corporal Cafferata asked.

"That's something new for them," PFC Orndoff said.

Corporal Mackie shook his head. "We don't know that. For all we know, when they attacked before they held a prayer meeting inside the trees to psych themselves up."

Horton snorted. "A prayer meeting. Yeah, sure."

"Mackie could be right," Martin said. "Sort of. We don't have any audio pickups in the trees. Their CO could be giving them a pep talk, telling them they've only got a short run and they'll be able to overrun us. All we can do now is wait."

"And hope nobody gets the idea that we should go out there and see for ourselves," Mackie said softly.

"Wait a minute, how do we know where they are?" Horton suddenly asked. "The motion detectors are farther out and shouldn't be able to see them."

"It's the seismo detectors," Martin answered. "They pick up vibrations three-sixty through the ground."

"Oh. Right."

To the rear, muffled by the walls of the bunker, they heard the *booms* of artillery rounds being fired.

The Marines all looked at the trees, and barely heard the rearward *booms* that told of another artillery salvo being fired. Seconds later, six explosions blossomed in the trees. The explosions themselves weren't visible through the trees, but the sudden swaying of foliage and thrown up debris was. All along India Company's line, the Marines cheered. They just knew that the Dusters had lost a chunk of their power, and were probably thrown into disarray. Hey, they might even be running away.

No such luck.

Word came down from the company CP. As soon as the first salvo was fired, the Dusters moved two hundred meters to their right.

The second salvo hit in the same place as the first, and must have done as much damage to the enemy as the first. Which is to say, little or none.

A third salvo was fired after an aiming adjustment.

This time word of the Duster's movement came sooner.

"Damn, they're just inside the trees," Martin swore. Then he muttered to himself, "Where the hell's our aircraft?"

Another salvo came in, once more hitting the place the Dusters had just vacated.

There wasn't a fifth salvo.

The Dusters burst from the trees in their by-now expected jinking and jiving, more side-to-side than to the front charge. Constant unexpected movement to confuse the foe and throw off aim.

"Open fire!" Captain Sitter shouted into his all-hands freq. "Everybody, blow them away!"

Along the line, every Marine began shooting. Not only with rifles, but the machine guns and Scatterers as well. The Scooters and Hogs added their fire. The mortars were silent.

"Why aren't the mortars firing?" Mackie shouted.

His answer came seconds later when a division of AV16 C Kestrels zoomed across the mass of Dusters, from one flank to the other, dropping Scatter-Blast cluster bombs. The Scatter-Blasts flew open fifty meters above the ground flinging their hundreds of bomblets in a pattern that covered the length and width of nearly the entire Duster formation. The bomblets erupted individually, looking like nothing so much as popcorn on a griddle. Chunks of flesh and bone and feathers were tossed into the air. Too far away for the Marines in the bunkers or manning the crew weapons, to see how bloody the pieces were.

The Kestrels turned around and swooped low, less than fifty meters above the Duster mass. The powerful wind of their near-mach passage roiled the bits and pieces of what had moments before been living, charging, alien fighters. The Kestrels gained altitude and orbited, their pilots and instruments searching the carnage for movement. They didn't see anything that couldn't be accounted for by random air movement. They turned again and overflew Camp Zion, wagging their wings in salute.

The killing ground in front of Camp Zion

"Goddamn shit!" Mackie swore. He tried to be careful where he put his feet, but he'd just stepped with both feet in offal. He breathed through his mouth to cut down on the stink.

"Shit is what it is," Cafferata said, laughing. He made no attempt at fastidiousness, yet his boots weren't any more befouled than Mackie's. He also breathed through his mouth.

The killing ground smelled as badly as the words Mackie and Cafferata used to describe it. Third platoon was prowling through the area seeking Dusters who had survived the bombing and low-level, high-speed passage. Nobody expected to find any living aliens. Most wondered why they'd been given this shit job, what genius thought looking for life in a cesspool was a good idea.

"I hope S-4 has boots in store," Mackie said. "We're going to need new ones after this. I don't believe this stench will ever come out."

"You just might be right," Martin said, coming up behind them. "And if you are, you'll need new utilities, too."

Mackie flinched at the unexpected voice. "I hope not," he said with a grimace that was partly directed at his squad leader for sneaking up behind him again. "But why?"

"You haven't seen the back of your legs." His lips were closed, though not sealed.

"What?" Mackie twisted around to look down behind himself. He swore again; the backs of his trouser legs were spattered with Duster blood and offal.

"I suggest you shitcan your gloves before you return to your bunker."

All of the Marines were wearing gloves to protect their hands from anything that might contaminate them in this search for survivors.

Cleanliness no longer mattered to Mackie. Now he kicked through piles of flesh and bones and feathers, no matter how splashed with blood they were, no matter how covered with the contents of erupted guts.

"I'm taking this one home," he said, bending down to pry a Duster rifle from the disembodied hands that still gripped it.

"Don't you dare take that into the bunker!" Orndoff yelped. "You'll stink us out if you do."

Mackie snarled at him.

After half an hour of fruitless searching for survivors, Third platoon was called back in. As soon as First Sergeant Robinson got a whiff of them, he ordered the entire platoon into the showers.

"Don't take off your uniforms and boots," he ordered. "Scrub them down on your bodies. *After* you've cleaned the crud and corrosion off them, strip down and scrub it off your scuzzy-ass bodies."

They did their best to follow the Top's orders without too much objection.

Mackie managed to get enough of the stink off the rifle he'd claimed as a souvenir that nobody seriously insisted he not take it into the bunker.

Firebase Gasson, under construction,
a few kilometers from Millerton

A week had passed since Alpha Troop's First platoon had been pulled from Advance Firebase One. New personnel had been brought in from Whiskey Company to replace its losses. One of the toughest for Second Lieutenant Greig to take was Sergeant Gasson. So, with the agreement of the other survivors, he named the new firebase after the late fire team leader. He'd been a brave and steady small unit leader, he'd be difficult to replace. But he would have to work with what was available. Fortunately, none of the replacements were sergeants. Sergeant First Class Quinn agreed with him that Specialist Abner Haynes was the best man best to replace Gasson. Greig put in a request to promote Haynes to sergeant. He expected the request to be granted promptly; the Army wanted its junior leaders to hold the rank their positions called for.

Firebase Gasson was called "under construction," and indeed there was building going on. But the little that remained to be done wasn't much more than cosmetic. Heavier construction was taking place at the two firebases to the left of Gasson, which the troop's other platoons would occupy. Temporarily, Captain Meyer had his command post co-located with First platoon.

And Meyer wanted the new men to get fully integrated into the platoon quickly.

Alpha Troop's temporary HQ

"Ted," Captain Meyer said when Greig reported to him, "your new boys need to get up to speed as quickly as possible."

"Yes, Sir," Second Lieutenant Greig fully agreed. "Yes, Sir."

"Short of coming under fire, which I sincerely hope doesn't happen any time soon, I think the best way of doing that is for your new boys to go on patrol out there." He waved a hand at the farmland outside the firebase, and distant forest beyond. "The Navy hasn't reported spotting Dusters in this area, so I suspect it's clear. I want you to take your platoon out on a ten-hour patrol tomorrow. One of the other platoons can hold Gasson during your absence. I'll come up with a proper patrol order for you by evening chow. You can brief your platoon after morning chow tomorrow.

Any questions?"

"No, Sir. That seems clear enough."

Meyer smiled wryly. "Any doubts?"

"If it's as quiet as the Navy says, there shouldn't be anything to cause a doubt."

"Of course, we all know the Navy sometimes misses something."

Greig didn't say anything to that.

"Then that's all until this evening."

"Thank you, Sir." Greig saluted and left the HQ tent.

Farmland and into the forest

Second platoon followed a dirt tractor-track. The farmland was checkerboarded with different crops. First was a broad field of something that looked like knee high grass, turned brown and gone to seed. It may have been Earth's wheat for all the soldiers knew. Beyond it was something much lower and leafy, perhaps soybeans. Then something stalkier, which might have been the greens of potato plants. None of the soldiers of Alpha Troop's First platoon had been farmers and didn't know. But this had been farmland used by the human colonists of Troy, so whatever the crops were, they were likely Earth-evolved food plants, perhaps genetically engineered to grow healthy in this alien soil. At its edge, the forest was already beginning to reclaim the farmland; saplings and other forest undergrowth were sprouting among the probable potato plants.

Just inside the trees, the undergrowth grew thick and was reclaiming the roadway. It thinned out as the tree cover became denser, blocking more and more sunlight. Avians chirped and sang in the canopy, swooped among the branches. Insectoids buzzed and clicked all around. They all ignored the column of humans passing in their midst, even the insectoids, some of which had been actual Earthling insects imported as pollinators, left the men alone. Again, none of the men in Second platoon knew or cared. Although Greig saw an avian that looked like a blue jay and an insectoid that might have been a bee buzzing about looking for a a patch of nectar-bearing flora.

And none of the soldiers were comfortable about taking a walk in the woods.

Particularly not the new men from Whiskey Company, soldiers who days before had been manning comps or comms in headquarters units, or maintaining vehicles, or issuing stores, or moving the materials the heavy equipment operators needed to build up firebases. One had been working in a medical station in Millerton, treating the minor scrapes and bruises that afflicted rear area personnel. He was particularly uncomfortable humping the field medical kit he'd been issued when he reported to Whiskey Company.

The order of march was Third squad, Greig, Second squad, SFC Alexander Quinn with the medic, First squad.

"Make a comm check," Lieutenant Greig said when the platoon was fully under the trees.

PFC Charles H. Marsh spoke into the comm he carried. "Goal Line, this is Red Rover. How do you read me? Over."

The answer came immediately, "Red Rover, Goal Line. I read you five-by. You me? Over."

"Goal Line, Red Rover. I read you five-by. Over."

"Roger, Red Rover. Goal Line out."

"Sir, comms read five-by," Marsh reported.

"Good." Greig turned on his map and studied it for a moment. It was linked into the orbiting warships; his position showed up as a glowing blue dot on the barely noted track through the forest. His assigned patrol route was a purple dotted line. Clearings were hashmarked green, and water courses were blue lines. Dusters, if the warships picked any up, would show up flashing red.

He saw all the colors except red.

Greig went to the head of the column where he found Staff Sergeant O'Connor behind his point fire team.

"Sergeant O'Connor"

"Yes, Sir."

Greig showed him the map. "I want you to go fifty meters off the right side of the trail, and proceed to this blue line," he pointed at a thin line that indicated a stream cutting across the direction in which the platoon was headed.

O'Connor studied the map for a moment, then nodded. "What do you want me to do then?"

"Hang a right and go far enough for the entire platoon to be along the water course.

Again, O'Connor nodded, and he asked, "Do you want us on the bank or back from it?"

"Stay inside the trees. I don't want to get surprised on the bank."

"Got it."

"Go."

O'Connor nodded and headed for the point, he'd lead the squad until it was time to make the turn.

This had all been covered in the squad leaders' briefing before the platoon left the firebase, but repetition was always helpful.

The blue line on the map was only a few hundred meters away, but it took the platoon most of an hour to get there. Part of the slowness was due to the frequent times the more experienced squad and fire team leaders had to spend instructing their Whiskey Company replacement on silent movement. The avians and insectoids gave proof of their noisiness by falling silent as the platoon passed; the noise disturbed them in a way their more quiet passage on the dirt road hadn't.

The platoon stopped when all its members were in the trees parallel to the stream that showed on the map. Greig called for a squad leaders' meeting. They edged through the trees to where they could see the waterway. It was a stream only two or three meters wide, that softly gurgled over a pebbly bed. The trees on the other side looked as quiet and empty as the woods they were in.

"How are they doing?" Greig asked *sotto voce.*

"They're learning," O'Connor said. "Slowly, but my squad isn't making as much noise as it did when we first got into the trees."

"I wish we had time in the rear to drill them," First squad's Staff Sergeant Alphonso Lunt said.

"We don't," Platoon Sergeant Quinn snarled, equally unhappy about taking out a patrol with so many untested men into possible enemy held territory. "So let it go."

Lunt looked across the stream and didn't reply.

"They'll get there," said Second squad's Sergeant Charles Breyer with a shrug. "At least there aren't any Dusters near us."

"Listen," Greig said, holding up a finger and looking up into the canopy. The avians and insectoids on their side of the stream were resuming their calls.

"If the birds and bees start talking again this quickly after we stopped moving, any ambush set over there has been in place long enough for them to start up again. We need to stay alert. I don't want to totally rely on the Navy for intelligence."

"The LT's right," Quinn said in a lower voice than he'd used before.

"Look." Greig held out his map. "We're only a couple of hundred meters from the nearest part of the road we came out on. We'll sit here in ambush for a couple of hours. Then we'll go beyond it maybe three hundred meters farther, then head back in, using a different track through the fields." The map showed the stream made a slight turn to the left, so the way back in would be a bit longer than the way out had been. "When we start out again, keep instructing your boys on silent movement. Let's see if we can move without causing undue distress to the fauna. Order of march will be First squad on the point, Third, tail end. Now see to your boys, and take a rest."

The squad leaders acknowledged the orders with nothing more than grunts, and headed back to their squads.

Two hours later, Second platoon was once more on the move. Enough of the soldiers whispered among themselves about how relieved they were to be on the move out of the forest that the avians and insectoids went silent once more.

When they pulled out of the ambush, Quinn kept Second squad in the middle because Breyer was his least experienced squad leader, and he wanted as much experience as possible front and back.

The return to the firebase was as uneventful as the trip out.

Almost.

Halfway across the fields Greig glanced at his map again, then did a double-take. He thought he saw a brief flicker of red at the far edge of the map. He turned to look back the way they'd come, but didn't see any pursuers. He gave the entire treeline a quick scan and still didn't see any sign of Dusters. Nonetheless, his map had shown that faint flicker of red. He resisted the urge to have the platoon pick up speed.

He didn't know how many Dusters might be in the forest, or whether they would attack. But the flicker of red told him positively that Dusters were still in the area, despite their heavy losses.

As was usual, the lighting in the CAC was dim, the only illumination coming from the display screens at the workstations scattered about the compartment, spaced and angled so that their lights didn't interfere with each other. The only sounds were the muted sussurus of air circulation and occasional reports from the techs at the stations.

"Chief, I'm picking up something odd," Radarman 3 John F. Bickford suddenly said, a bit louder than anybody else's reports.

"What kind of odd?" Chief Petty Officer James W. Verney asked, taking the two steps from his station to Bickford's. He looked over the radarman's shoulder to see what was so odd. "That's not odd, son," he said when he saw it, "that's downright anomalous." He turned toward the station where the division head oversaw the entire operation. "Mr. Hudner, we got us a problem."

Lieutenant Thomas J. Hudner, the radar division head, glanced at the chief to see which display he was looking at, dialed his screen to show the same image, and quickly saw what Bickford had spotted. He swore softly, then said only loudly enough for Verney to hear, "We've been expecting something like this."

Verney nodded. "Yes, Sir, we have."

Hudner picked up the comm and pressed the sensor that connected to the bridge. "Bridge, CAC."

"CAC, Bridge. Go," replied Lieutenant Commander Allen Buchanan, the bridge watch officer.

"Bridge, it looks like a fleet is approaching from the scattered disc. Roughly four AU out. Two-seventeen, three degrees above ecliptic."

"Show me," Buchanan said, all business. He peered at the display that popped up on the bridge's main board. "I will inform the captain," he said as soon as he saw the display of approaching bogies. He toggled his comm to the captain's quarters. "Captain, Bridge."

Captain Harry Huse answered immediately, but sounded groggy as though suddenly awakened from a deep sleep. "Captain. Speak."

"Sir, CAC has spotted what appears to be an unknown fleet approaching. Range, four AU."

"I will be there momentarily. Notify the admiral's CAC."

"Aye aye, Sir," Buchanan said, but Huse had already signed off.

Bridge, NAUS Durango

"Captain on deck!" Petty Officer 2 Henry Nickerson shouted as the *Durango's* commanding officer stepped into the bridge.

"Carry on," Captain Huse snapped, ignoring the fact that nobody had stood to attention at the announcement that he had entered the bridge. He took the command chair and strapped himself in. Buchanan, who had vacated the seat as soon as Huse said he was coming, stood by its side. "Details," Huse said as he began studying the big board.

Buchanan gave his report. "Sir, the bogeys were first spotted as an anomalous smudge coming from the scattered disc during a sweep for any missed survival capsules."

During an attempt to intercept and destroy a swarm of enemy missiles aimed at Amphibious Ready Group 17, many of the SF6 Meteors off the fast attack carrier *Issac C. Kidd* were killed. The fighter craft were built around a "survival capsule" intended to keep the pilot alive in the event the craft was severely damaged or destroyed. The surviving starships of ARG 17 had been conducting a rescue mission for them and survivors of the starships that had been killed by the missiles that had gotten past the Meteors and defensive fire from the ARG's escort of warships. The *Durango's* radar had been aiding in the search for survivors.

"CAC estimates there are at least forty spacecraft in the approaching fleet. ETA at current velocity, ninety-seven hours. Composition of fleet not yet determined. CAC thinks that determination will be possible in approximately twenty-four hours."

"Thank you." Huse toggled his comm to the admiral. "Sir, did you get that?"

"Yes I did," replied Rear Admiral James Avery, commander of Task Force 8. "I have ordered the remaining ships from ARG 17 and the escort to move at flank speed to Troy orbit. And I am notifying the forces planetside to prepare for company."

Huse thought about the report. The scattered disc was exactly that; scattered. The wormhole the fleet came from must have been in line with a clump of the icy dwarf planets and cometary objects that made up the scattered disc.

Not that it mattered. More of the aliens were on their way.

Headquarters, NAU Forces, Troy, near Millerton

"Sir," Captain William P. Upshur stood in the doorway of Lieutenant General Harold W. Bauer's spartain office. He held the control of a surface-orbit comm in his hand.

"Yes, Bill?" the commanding general of the human ground and air forces on Troy said, looking up from the reports he'd been going over, showing where the elements of the 1st Marine Combat Force and those elements of the VII Corps that had made it to planetside were deployed.

"Admiral Avery wishes to speak with you at your earliest convenience."

Bauer cocked an eyebrow at his aide. The last time he'd talked directly with Avery, it had been face to face. On that occasion, he'd had to talk the commander of Task Force 8 out of resigning on the spot; falling on his sword, as it were. "Make the connection." He gestured for Upshur to stay, but be out of sight.

"Aye aye, Sir." Upshur manipulated the control in his hand and a display on the office's side wall came to life, showing the interior of the Admiral's Bridge on the NAUS *Durango*, in orbit above Troy. Avery was centered in the image.

"General, thank you for replying so rapidly," Avery said.

"Of course, Admiral. When the Navy shield wants to speak to the planetside commander, the wise ground commander complies as rapidly as possible. What can I do for you?"

"You can get ready. We have detected an unidentified, forty-plus spacecraft fleet approaching Troy. Estimated arrival, slightly more than ninety-six hours." He paused before adding, "The fleet's vector makes it being from Earth unlikely."

Neither felt it necessary to mention communication—or the lack thereof—between the approaching fleet and the humans in orbit around Troy. Had there been contact, Avery would have said so. Attempts to make contact were standard operating procedure.

"How firm is that ninety-six hours?" Bauer asked.

"It's at current velocity. We have no way of knowing at what point they will begin to decelerate, or whether they will overshoot before braking.

More, we cannot yet determine how many are combat ships, or how many are transports or other support vessels."

"What is the disposition of the outlying ships of ARG 17?" Bauer asked.

"Not good. Four wounded transports plus the *Kidd* have resumed their voyage to Troy orbit. They're all limping badly, but they should arrive in orbit within two hours of the soonest arrival of the unidentified fleet."

"A wormhole is out of the question?" Bauer's question was almost a statement, and Avery didn't bother replying to it. They both knew that a wormhole from Earth wouldn't open in that direction.

"I am drawing plans to counter any hostile action by the unknowns," Avery said.

"The Army brought limited surface-to-orbit defensive weapons. I will make sure they're all operational by the time the unknowns arrive. Do you have anything else?"

"No, Sir, that's everything for now. I will keep you appraised of developments as they arise."

"And I will inform you. Thank you, Admiral. Bauer out."

Upshur touched a sensor on his control and the display blinked out.

"Notify my staff and component commanders. A vid conference will do. Meet in thirty minutes."

"Aye aye, Sir." Upshur left to do his commander's bidding.

Upshur had a conference screen set up in Bauer's small office. It took up a side wall of the room, from front to back, and gave the small office a claustrophobic feel. Bauer's desk had to be moved to make room for it. The screen was divided into twelve windows, one for each of the MCF's primary staff, and the commanders of the NAU Force's major components. Two of the windows were for Admiral Avery and Captain Huse, or their representatives.

Thirty minutes after Bauer called for the meeting, Brigadier General Porter, 1MCF's Chief of Staff, standing in the doorway for lack of space inside the office, turned on the screen. All twelve remote attendees expectantly looked out of their windows.

"Gentlemen," Bauer began, "thank you for appearing so promptly, I'm sure you've all come from important duties. Many of you are going to have to change your planning as result of what I have to tell you.

"The day we've all been expecting is upon us. Two hours ago, TF 8 detected a large fleet approaching Troy from a direction that disallows it being from Earth. At its current estimated velocity, it will arrive in ninety-four hours." He looked at the admiral and captain for confirmation. They nodded. "At this time we don't know the composition of the fleet, except it's likely a mix of warships, transports, and support vessels. We have to be prepared for a hostile assault within days. Possibly simultaneous on TF 8 and a landing.

"Task Force 8 is down to nine warships, one of which is severely damaged. The Navy will need as much help as we can provide. Marine artillery and aircraft will be essentially worthless in the space battle. General Noll, Colonel Ames, what about your artillery?"

Major General Conrad Noll, commanding general of the 9th Infantry Division, said, "Colonel Ames, kindly take the question."

Colonel Adelbert Ames, commander of the 104th Artillery Regiment cleared his throat before answering. "General, Sir, my regiment is fortunate enough to have all four of its battalions on Troy, none were lost in the attack on Amphibious Ready Group 17."

Bauer made an impatient *get to it* gesture.

"Ah, yes, Sir. Each battalion has a laser battery, consisting of four companies of twelve lasers that are capable of striking orbital targets."

"Are they currently deployed for planetary defense?"

"Ah, no, Sir."

"Well, get them so deployed. You have less than four days to have your lasers positioned to support TF 8 in its battle. Deploy the other batteries to do maximum damage to a landing force, and then support infantry and armor once the hostiles make planetfall.

"General Purvis, have your artillery regiment do the same once the enemy commences planetfall.

"Admiral Avery, can you put TF 8 in geosync so that we can concentrate our fire to assist you?"

"Yes, Sir. Most of TF 8 is already in geosync over the locations held by NAU forces. I can quickly have the rest of the task force join up. It's better for the Navy anyway to be together, so we can concentrate our fire on the enemy."

"General Purvis, General Noll, I want you to locate your forces where they can support each other, I doubt that when the Dusters make planetfall that they will ever attack in numbers small enough for a company to defeat. General Bearss, liaise with the ground commanders to provide air support. Colonel Reid, have your Force Recon company ready to conduct recon missions, and to fill gaps in our defenses.

"Brigadier General Porter is your primary point of contact.

"If there are no questions, gentlemen, you have your orders."

None of the generals or admirals had any questions, they all understood the commander's intent. One by one over a few seconds, all the windows closed until Bauer was alone in his office with Porter.

"This may be what we expected to find when we first made planetfall," Porter said.

"Except then we expected to have an entire Army corps at our back, not a reinforced division."

Combat Action Center, NAUS Durango,
Flagship of Task Force 8, in geosync orbit around Troy

THE DIMLY LIT QUIET OF THE CAC WAS BARELY DISTURBED BY RADARMAN 3 JOHN F. Bickford's murmured, "Chief, they're decelerating."

Chief Petty Officer James W. Verney took the two steps from his station to Bickford's and looked over the junior man's shoulder at his display.

"So they are," he affirmed. "I wonder what kind of couches they have." That was a reasonable query; the apparent deceleration of the alien spacecraft was greater than human ships ever achieved—fast enough to injure human passengers. "They aren't going to fly past us after all," he murmured as he turned toward Lieutenant Thomas J. Hudner, the radar division head. "Mr. Hudner, they're slowng down—fast."

Hudner glanced at Varney to see which station he was at, and dialed his monitor to display Bickford's view, examined it for a few seconds, made a couple of mental calculations, and whistled under his breath at the result of his calculations. He toggled his comm and signaled the bridge.

"Bridge, CAC."

"CAC, Bridge. Go," Lieutenant Commander Allen Buchanan answered.

"It looks like they're slamming on the brakes. Here's the data." Hudner sent the data from Bickford's display.

"Is that accurate?" Buchanan asked after studying it briefly.

"Yes, Sir. I make it twelve Gs." At twelve gravities of deceleration, it wouldn't take long at all for a human to be rendered unconscious. And not much longer to burst enough blood vessels in the brain to bring about death.

"I will notify the captain," Buchanan said. He switched his comm to buzz Captain Huse, *Durango's* captain.

Huse had been napping, but woke and sat erect immediately on hearing the beep of his comm. "Huse."

"Sir, the bogeys are making their move," Buchanan reported. "They should reach high orbit within fifteen hours."

"Not flying past," Huse said. It was merely an observation, so Buchanan didn't reply. "Notify the Admiral. I will be on the bridge in a moment."

"Aye aye, Sir."

Huse was in his combat quarters, a small cabin directly adjacent to the bridge. He slipped his feet into shoes, tugged his uniform straight, and was through the door to the bridge before Buchanan finished notifying Rear Admiral James Avery of the development.

Task Force 8, deployment around Troy

The fast attack carrier *Rear Admiral Isaac C. Kidd* was still limping in when Rear Admiral Avery began issuing orders for the screening formation. In total, Avery had one carrier, an injured fast attack carrier, three destroyers, three frigates, and one battleship to combat twenty or more enemy warships of unknown capability, and impede the planetfall of a similar number of transports—if their guess about the enemy fleet was right.

The situation might not be that dire; some of the approaching spacecraft could be support ships rather than combatants or transports. Still, there were forty-plus enemy vessels to the nine of TF 8.

The frigates were the fastest warships in Avery's task force. He placed them high to the port of the oncoming fleet's vector, ready to strike at its flank. The three destroyers made a thin screen ahead of the *Durango* and the carrier *Rear Admiral Norman Scott*—and the *Kidd*, if she arrived in time. The *Scott* prepared to launch her four space-combat squadrons; her atmospheric combat squadrons, which wouldn't be of use in the coming fight, were already planetside.

As soon as Avery issued his preliminary orders, he had Lieutenant Julias Townsend, his aide, contact the planetside headquarters of the 1st Marine Combat Force—he needed to talk with the planetside commander.

Camp Puller, Headquarters of NAU Forces, Troy

"Sir," Captain William P. Upshur said, standing at attention in the doorway of Lieuteant General Bauer's tiny office.

"Yes, Bill?" Bauer, looking up from the map display he was studying, waved Upshur in.

The captain took a step inside and stood relaxed. "A message from geosync, Sir. 'Rear Admiral Avery would like to speak to the General at his earliest pleasure.'" He restrained the smile he felt coming.

"That was Townsend?"

"His words verbatim."

Bauer nodded. "Tell him it's my pleasure now," and went back to his map display.

"Aye aye, Sir." Upshur left, and was back a moment later. "Sir, the admiral is on." He handed Bauer a surface-orbit comm unit.

Bauer waited for Upshur to leave and close the door before he picked up the handset of the comm.

"Jim, Harry here. Good to hear from you. How's orbit treating you?"

"Not as well as one might like, Harry. We're about to get very busy."

Bauer straightened, this was the report he'd been waiting for. "Tell me."

"The alien fleet is decelerating, very rapidly. We anticipate their arrival in high orbit in less than fifteen hours."

"Any change in their composition?"

"Not that we can tell. Forty-plus spacecraft, probably half and half combatants and transports, perhaps a few support ships in the mix."

"How much damage will TF 8 be able to do to them?"

"We'll try to stop their transports, but my main effort will be killing their combatants."

"Understood. How much damage can you do to them?"

Bauer could hear Avery swallow; the man hadn't been quite the same since he'd lost a significant part of TF 8 and an even larger part of ARG 17, when Bauer had needed to talk him out of relinquishing command of the Navy forces.

"Sir, we still have no idea of the strength of the combatant vessels. All we know of their weaponry is the leviathan that attacked Troy to begin with had a laser."

"So do you, Jim. And your gunners are better. I know my Marines and soldiers are better shots than the Duster infantry." Bauer had deliberately used Avery's first name, to draw him back from the formality of calling him "sir." As the higher ranking officer, Bauer was in overall command of the operation, but he needed Avery to be in top form when he fought the alien spacecraft. "You know where the Army's laser batteries are. Their primary targets will be the transports once they start to make planetfall, but you know I'll give you as much support as I can against the warships before then. Between us, we can handle them."

Avery audibly took a deep breath. "You're right, Harry," he said, sounding more confident. "We can do this."

"You know it. Now, let me get my troops ready to do some serious ass kicking. Bauer out."

He'd considered asking Avery to copy him on the orders to his fleet, but decided against it out of concern that Avery might misinterpret the request, might think it indicated that Bauer lacked confidence in his abilities. Anyway, he knew that Captain Edwin Anderson, TF 8's operations officer, would keep him appraised.

"Bill," Avery said loudly enough for his voice to carry into the outer office, "get my staff and component commanders on the horn."

"Aye aye, Sir."

Ten days earlier

The War Room, Supreme Military Headquarters,
Bellevue, Sarpy County, Federal Zone, North American Union

"Admiral Stickney," Secretary of War Richmond Hobson growled, "how soon can Task Force 7 launch for Troy?" His tone suggested the only acceptable answer was *immediately.*

"Sir," Rear Admiral Herman Osman Stickney answered, "we will finish provisioning tomorrow morning, Omaha time, and TF 7 can launch immediately thereafter." A thin smile cracked his face. "Or I can begin sending my ships piecemeal to the wormhole now."

"Begin moving them." Hobson turned his attention to Rear Admiral William A. Moffett. "How soon can Amphibious Ready Group 28 launch?"

"Sir, ARG 28's ships are already positioned at the elevators. We can leave as soon as the Marines board."

It was Lieutenant General Edward A. Ostermann's turn. "How soon can Third Marine Combat Force board the ARG?"

"Sir, the elements of 3 MCF are prepositioned at Jarvis Island, waiting for the order to embark." His mouth curved slightly in a grim smile. "I've already given orders for them to begin staging at the elevator lobby."

"Sir." Moffett raised his hand.

"Yes, Admiral?"

"Sir, I request that ARG 28 begin launching as soon as the first two starships are loaded."

"No, I can't authorize unarmed transports leaving before the entire TF 7 has launched."

Moffett grinned. "But, Sir, the first two transports I want to launch are the *Enterprise* and the *Tripoli.*" Seeing a lack of understanding on the faces of a couple of the Army generals, Moffett explained, "The *Enterprise* and *Tripoli* are amphibious battle cruisers—troopships with combat capability equivalent to a light cruiser. Between them they can carry an entire Marine division."

Hobson stared at Moffett for a moment, then looked at Osterman. "Can do, General?"

"With pleasure, Sir."

"Outstanding. Get those Marines aboard immediately. Now all of you, you have your orders. Go."

The three component commanders rose and left the War Room, on their way to fight a war.

Briefing room, Headquarters 1st Marine Combat Force,
Camp Puller, Semi-Autonomous World Troy

"Attention on deck!" Brigadier General David Porter, the 1st MCF chief of staff, boomed out. The sudden silence in the largest interior space in the 1st MCF HQ as conversation abruptly stopped was punctuated by the scraping of chair legs on the floor, and the clicking of buttons on commanders' comps as the assembled staff and commanders rose to their feet.

"Seats, gentlemen," Lieutenant General Bauer said as he strode into the room. The assembled senior officers took their seats, facing the small stage set at the front of the room. Bauer stepped onto the stage and turned to face his staff and major subordinate commanders—the Marine commanders on Eastern Shapland attended by conference vid.

"You all know Major General Noll of the 9th Infantry Division, but you may not know the man with the oversized stars on his collars. He is Brigadier General Rufus Saxon. He runs the Army's 10th Brigade, and is a welcome addition to our force. His soldiers, as you know, have already taken on the Dusters many times—and just as often defeated them."

Heads turned to look at the Army general. Many of the Marines nodded at him. A few said, "Welcome aboard." None followed up on Bauer's remark about the size of Saxon's rank insignia, they simply accepted that Army officer rank insignia, for unknown reasons, was larger than the insignia worn by Marine and Navy officers.

"More survivors of the attack on ARG 17 are on their way and will be joining us in defense of Troy," Bauer said. "And they can't get here too soon. The Duster fleet approaching Troy's orbit is decelerating. It has been coming at speed, and declerating more rapidly than human spacecraft can. The fleet should be overhead engaging TF 8 in little more than twelve hours. Navy's best estimate at this time remains the same, the alien fleet is half combatants, half transports. If they operate anything like we do, we can anticipate that they will bombard the surface prior to making planetfall with their ground troops. But, they're alien, so we can't safely make that assumption. We must be prepared to be in a fight by this time tomorrow. In the meanwhile, we won't be sitting on our thumbs playing switch. We will work on improving our defensive positions. The Cee Bees are busy on that, right?" He looked at Captain Mervyn S. Bennion, commander of the 44th Construction Regiment.

"Yes, Sir," Bennion answered. "My engineers are working with army engineers at ten different locations, mostly on Shapland. A couple of the platoons are working with Marine combat engineers on Eastern Shapland."

"Outstanding. We all know what excellent work your people do." Bauer looked around the room. "Revise your plans, and be prepared to revise them again as we get more intelligence about enemy action. Lieutenant Colonel Neville—" the 1st MCF intelligence chief—"will keep you updated with developments. I want all of you to keep Brigadier General Shoup appraised of all changes in your plans.

"We have an invasion to defeat. Let's do it."

With that, he stepped off the stage and marched out of the room to Porter's shouted, "A-ten-*hut!*"

Firebase Gasson, near Millerton, Shapland,
Semi-Autonomous World Troy

CAPTAIN PATRICIA H. PENTZER, THE COMMANDING OFFICER OF FOURTH PLATOON, H
Battery, 1045 Artillery Battalion (Laser), stood on the mount of laser 2 and
looked around with disapproval. *Firebase Gasson is just too damn small,*
she thought. *It won't take much at all for a counter-laser attack from orbit
to take out all three of my guns. Even one gunboat can do the dirty deed in
minutes.*

Such an attack would wipe out that Leg platoon that was there to
protect her guns as well. As if a Leg platoon could defend a position from an
orbital attack. She shook her head and made a face. And assigning a
Mobile Intelligence platoon to Gasson made as much sense as tits on a bull.
What were they thinking?

It was that Jarhead three-star who did this, no Army general could be
dumb enough to order a cock-up like this. Hell, she needed a base the
size of Gasson for each of her lasers—and they should be separated by a
minimum of a klick, better yet three klicks. One gunboat would have a hell
of a time taking them all out before it got killed itself. Even a lone destroyer
couldn't survive trying to get all three if they were properly spread.

Damn dumb Jarhead. Has to *be his fault.*

She craned her neck, looking at the sky overhead. A futile motion, she
knew. But, damn, she had to take a look after the sitrep that sent her
climbing the laser's mount. A presumably hostile fleet rapidly approaching
Troy. She had to have her battery ready to aid TF 8 in combating the enemy
warships, or to blast landing craft if they attempted to make planetfall.

Now, where was that Leg lieutenant—what was his name, Cragg or something—in command of her security? She looked around until she saw him walking the perimeter.

"Hey you, Leg LT!" Her shout was loud enough to be heard all through the small base, even if not understood at its farthest reaches.

Lieutenant Greig didn't even turn his head.

She glared at his back and filled her lungs to shout again.

"You, Leg LT!"

Again, he didn't react to her, even though a soldier poked his head out of the bunker the Leg lieutenant was standing next to and up looked at her.

"Him!" she shouted, and pointed at the Leg. The soldier said something to the Leg, and pointed at Pentzer.

The Leg turned to look at her and mimed, "Are you talking to me?"

"Yes, you!" She pointed emphatically at the base of the laser mount, and hopped to the ground. The Leg ambled over to her.

"Yes, Ma'am," he said when he reached her. "What can I do for the captain?"

"Mister, I should put you on report," she snapped. "You deliberately ignored me when I called."

Greig blinked innocently. "Ma'am? I'm sorry, but I didn't hear you call me. I did hear you call some Leg LT, but I didn't realize you meant me—I'm not a Leg."

Her face turned red and she shoved her face up into his. "You're infantry, right? That means you're a Leg."

He sauntered to her, shaking his head. "*Mounted* infantry, Ma'am. There's a difference."

"Is that a fact, now?"

"Yes, Ma'am. It's a distinction we take very seriously."

She ostensibly looked around, "I don't see any vehicles. If you're mounted infantry, where are your vehicles?"

Greig went rigid. "Ma'am, most of Alpha Troop's vehicles were lost when the Dusters almost killed the *Juno Beach*. The few that survived are with a platoon that is conducting patrols."

Pentzer flinched and the red in her face washed out. The 1045 Artillery Battalion (Laser) had been on the Wanderjahr, which had not been hit during the Duster attack on ARG 27. The battalion had suffered no losses, but she knew that many of the soldiers on the *Juno Beach* had been killed.

"I'm sorry, Lieutenant. Did you lose many people?"

"No, Ma'am. I managed to get my entire platoon into a stasis station in time to save everybody."

"Outstanding. Now," she reddened again, but with embarrassment this time, "I'm sorry, but what's your name? I know we exchanged names when I arrived, but I had other things on my mind then."

"That's all right, I sometimes have trouble remembering names myself. I'm Theodore Greig."

She extended her hand. "Patricia Pentzer." They shook, all business now, "Have you heard the latest? A fleet, probably alien, is approaching Troy. It'll reach orbit in a matter of hours. My lasers are going to be involved perhaps as soon as they're in range. I strongly suggest that you move your people at least a kilometer away from my guns before then."

He blinked. "Why?"

"Counter-battery fire will take out this entire base, that's why. Where's that MI platoon that's supposed to be here?"

"They're out running recon patrols. If you're concerned about counter-battery fire, why don't you spread your lasers out more?"

"Because we're assigned to Firebase Gasson, and we're spread out as far as its dimensions allow, that's why."

Greig hesitated before speaking again; what he was about to say could be insulting. "You've never fired your guns in anger, have you? You haven't come under fire yet."

If Pentzer was insulted, she managed to control it. "That's right. Both counts. You have?"

He nodded. "Not only on the *Juno Beach*. We've had plenty of action." He turned in a circle, looking over the landscape beyond the perimeter. "You know, if you keep one gun here and move the other two to the other platoon firebases, you won't have to worry about counter-battery fire taking you all out at once."

"But that's outside where I'm supposed to be."

He looked down and nodded, as though thinking, then back at her. "Ma'am, your CO didn't come here, did he? He doesn't know how confined you are in this firebase. You're the commander on the scene. The placement of your guns is your tactical decision to make. I'll talk to my company commander. I'm sure he'll agree."

She studied him for a moment, then said, "I do believe you're right, Mr. Greig. We just have time to move my guns before they'll probably have to fire." She looked for her platoon sergeant, and began giving orders to move two of the lasers.

Captain Meyer's only reaction to Greig's request was an astonished, "Hell yes! Move those things."

NAUS Durango, Fleet Combat Action Center;
in geosync orbit around Troy

In the dimness of the CAC, Lieutenant Commander Rufus Z. Johnston scowled at the images on his status board. "Get me the Admiral's Bridge." His voice cracked like a whip over the soft pings emitted by the comps, and the muted voices of the techs manning the stations..

"The Admiral's Bridge, aye," said Radioman 2 Edward A. Gisburne. Then into the fleet comm, "Bridge, CAC."

"CAC, Bridge," Radioman 3 Matthew Arther immediately answered.

Gisburne saw Johnston adjust his speaker and told Arther, "CAC wants to speak to the admiral."

"CAC wants to speak to the admiral, aye," Arther said.

Seconds later Johnston heard, "Avery, CAC. What do you have for me?"

"Sir, the leading elements of the unidentified fleet are now within extreme range of the *Durango*."

"Let me know when they are within range of the *Scott's* Meteors." The fast attack carrier had almost closed to range; the slowing down of the Duster fleet had given her time to get close.

"Let the admiral know when the bogeys are within range of the *Scott's* Meteors. Aye."

"Avery out."

Johnston went back to peering at the board. How many of these vessels were warships? How many were transports? Or support ships? Those were the questions he most needed to answer. But the North American Union Navy had no information on the alien spacecraft. Even if they were close enough to make out details, he had no way to know for certain.

But, if the Dusters' navy was organized along lines similar to human, then he could assume—and, yes, he knew what "assume" did—that the ten ships in the front were similar to human frigates and destroyers, forming a screen for the eight ships following them, possible cruisers and battleships, even carriers. He wasn't about to assume that none of them were carriers—just because the Dusters didn't use any aircraft planetside, that didn't mean they had no space fighters, analogs to the NAU Navy's SF 6 Meteors. If he was right, that meant that the score-plus ships farther back were transports and, possibly, support ships.

Although as profligate as the Dusters had been with the lives of their troops planetside, he wasn't going to assume that they were any more concerned about the repair and rescue of their own damaged ships. He was willing to go only so far to risk making an ass of himself.

He changed the board's scale to close up on the bogey fleet, enlarged the view again to include the warships of TF 8. He wondered how much good the *Kidd's* remaining Meteors could do when they launched a flank attack on the bogeys.

An hour later Johnston contacted Avery again.

"Sir, I have tentative identification of the bogey ship types."

"Give me," Avery said.

Johnston's earlier estimate hadn't changed; ten frigate/destroyer types, eight cruiser/battleship types, one or more of which might or might not be a carrier, twenty-four transports and/or support ships.

"Range?"

"Sir, they will be in range of the *Scott's* Meteors in fifteen minutes. Ten minutes after that they will be in range of the *Durango's* lasers, and in five minutes more the destroyers will be able to strike them. The *Kidd* should be close enough for her Meteors to strike their rear."

"Avery out."

Admiral's Bridge, NAUS Durango

"If it pleases Captain Huse, I would like to speak with him," Avery said into his comm. Task Force 8 belonged to Avery, but the *Durango* belonged to Huse, and his position must be acknowledged.

"Huse here, Admiral," the captain's voice came back seconds later.

"Captain, I am shortly going to have the *Scott* launch her meteors to strike at the bogey fleet. When the Meteors are halfway there, I want the *Durango* to give the fighters covering fire."

"Give the Meteors covering fire when they are halfway to the bogeys, aye."

"Avery out." He turned to Lieutenant Commander George Davis, his communications officer. "Get me Captain Rush on the *Scott*."

"Captain Rush on the *Scott*, aye aye," Davis said, and got on the ship-to-ship radio.

It took twenty seconds for the message to go from the *Durango* to the carrier *Rear Admiral Norman Scott* and a reply to come back.

"*Scott* Actual," Rush's voice came came over the ship-to-ship.

"*Scott*, how soon can your SF 6 squadrons launch?"

"The crews of two squadrons are in the ready room now. How soon they can head for the flight deck depends on the length of time it takes to prepare and deliver the operation order. Once they get the 'go' order, they can begin launching within ten minutes."

"The op order is brief. The bogey fleet is five hours from Troy orbit. The front row is a screen of frigate and destroyer analogs. Kill them. *Durango* and the destroyers will provide covering fire. Send all four of your SF 6 squadrons."

The pause before Rush replied to the operation order was longer than before. When he spoke again there was a thickness in his voice. The operation sounded to him like a suicide mission for his space fighter group. "Aye aye, Sir. The *Scott's* entire space fighter group will launch and attack the screening ships of the bogey fleet."

"Good hunting, *Scott*. Avery out."

Avery studied the big board, which covered most of the forward bulkhead and displayed all the elements on both sides. He watched the tiny flecks that indicated the SF 6 Meteors launching from the *Scott* and forming up, then heading for their targets.

Distance between the bogey fleet and TF 8 was closing rapidly. But the Dusters hadn't begun firing. *Don't they see the small fighter craft yet?* Avery wondered. *Or maybe they don't see such small things as a threat. They're alien, and we don't have a grasp on how they think.* He didn't see any specks that would indicate Duster fighter craft. *Maybe they don't have any carriers.*

Time seemed to drag as Avery watched the fighters getting closer to the bogeys.

Finally, the four squadrons were halfway to their targets, and the *Durango* opened fire with her lasers. A moment later, TF 8's three destroyers did as well. They didn't aim at where they *saw* the bogey fleet, but where they expected the ships to be in several seconds; what they saw when they fired was not where the ships were *now*, but where they had been a few seconds later.

Lasers suddenly lashed out from the second rank of bogeys, the rank Johnston had tentatively identified as cruisers and battleships. The front rank didn't fire.

Avery looked to where his three frigates were stationed, high and to the left of his main formation, and ordered them to move in and attack the flank of the second rank.

Glowing red began to appear on the bogey ships—hits from TF 8!

Enemy lasers converged on the destroyer *First Lieutenant George H. Cannon*, and she erupted, her spine split through and her missile magazine exploded. Debris scattered everywhere.

Avery felt the *Durango* shudder as she suffered multiple laser hits. Horns sounded throughout the warship, calling damage control crews to action.

The Meteors finally got close enough to the first rank of bogeys to fire their missiles. A squadron concentrated its fire on one, and it burst open. The rest of the screening warships seemed to suddenly notice the small craft, and began flinging missiles at them. Avery watched stone-faced as six of the dots representing the SF 6's blinked out, killed by enemy fire. He doubted that any of their pilots survived.

"Bridge, CAC," the call came.

"CAC, bridge," Davis answered.

"Kindly inform the admiral the bogey fleet is accelerating."

"The bogey fleet is accelerating, aye." Davis turned to Avery. "Sir—."

"I heard." *Why did they do that*, Avery wondered. He watched as lasers and missiles killed another destroyer, the *Rear Admiral Herald F. Stout* and a frigate, the *Sergeant Major Daniel Daly*. The first rank blinked out another dozen Meteor dots, but the only significant damage to them was one that lost acceleration, and drifted, evidently powerless. The remaining frigates scored a kill on the left-most ships in the second rank.

Firebase Gasson, near Millerton, Troy

The lasers of fourth platoon, 1045 Artillery Battalion (Laser) had begun attempting to lock onto the approaching enemy fleet as soon as they were emplaced in all three of Alpha Troop's platoon firebases. Finally, the warships were close enough to fix on a target; they all locked on one craft in the front row. Had it been a human warship, Captain Patricia Pentzer would have identified it as a frigate. Her three lasers should be able to kill it, even at this extreme range, a distance that would spread their beams.

"Fourth platoon," Pentzer ordered, "commence countdown to fire in five seconds."

Five seconds later, the air above the three lasers flashed with the heat of the beams they shot heavenward. Watching through her glasses, Pentzer saw three lines of light converging on the designated target. When they struck the warship she saw a red glow sprout in its center, and spread outward. Before the edges of the red could begin to dull, a second salvo hit, and the warship split in two.

A cheer went up from everybody in Firebase Gasson who was looking up and saw the distant death.

"New target," Pentzer ordered, and gave the coordinates to what she tentatively identified as a destroyer.

H Battery fired.

Admiral's Bridge, on the Durango

"Sir, another message from CAC," Lieutenant Commander Davis said. Avery turned his head to face his comm officer.

"Twenty-two of the trailing starships are falling behind. They appear to be going into low orbit around Troy."

Transports, Avery thought. *Planetfall will commence shortly.* "Notify Commander NAU Forces, Troy."

"Notify Commander NAU Forces, Troy, aye," Davis said, and got on the orbit-to-surface comm.

The bogey warships were almost on TF 8 when lasers blasted up from Troy. Another of the enemy's first rank died, and a second, larger warship staggered and lost weigh.

All the warships on both sides were firing; lasers, missiles, and guns, as well as the remaining Meteors off the *Scott*. The *Kidd's* Meteors launched and joined the frigates attacking the left-most ship in the Dusters' second line.

The planetside lasers ceased fire as the Duster fleet zoomed past TF 8, but picked up again as soon as there was space between the front rank and TF 8.

The frigate *Gunnery Sergeant John Basilone* died in the close up exchange, and the *Durango*, the *Scott,* and the destroyer *Hospitalman 3 Edward C. Benfold* were injured. Half of *Scott's* Meteors were gone. Two warships from the Dusters' second rank died as well, and three others appeared to be damaged.

The Duster fleet was losing more warships than TF 8, but the odds were still heavily in the aliens' favor.

"Bridge, CAC," another report came in. "The bogeys are beginning to decelerate and are arching in an evident attempt to begin a parabolic orbit around the planet."

"How long before they come back?" Avery asked.

"Best estimate at this time, six hours."

Avery looked at the big board. By then, the *Kidd* would link into the task force's formation.

"Instruct the *Scott* to retrieve her SF group and the *Stout* to begin retrieval rescue and operations," Avery said ordered. "*Durango, Butler,* and *Benfold*, knock out those transports that are moving into low orbit."

Camp Zion, West Shapland, near Jordan,
Eastern Shapland, Troy

"LOOK ALIVE, MARINES!" STAFF SERGEANT GUILLEN BELLOWED. "WE DON'T KNOW when or where or how many, but we know they're coming, and we had best be ready when they get here. Or be ready to go out and find, fix, and fuck them, whichever comes first."

The other platoon sergeants were shouting similar orders at their Marines throughout the firebase. So was Gunnery Sergeant Hoffman, while First Sergeant Robert G. Robinson stood watching, crossed-armed.

There wasn't the hustle and bustle one might normally expect in a Marine company when its senior NCOs, under the watchful eye of the company's top sergeant were shouting orders. They'd known for a few days that a counter-counter-invasion was coming. It was only a question of when, where, and how many. So when they weren't out running patrols in search of Dusters who might or might not—but often were—out there someplace, they'd been busily engaged in building up Camp Zion's defenses. By this time, there wasn't really all that much that still needed doing. Marines on the perimeter looked through the sights of their weapons, making sure they had clear views of their fields of fire. Fire team leaders checked their men's positions. Squad leaders oversaw the fire team leaders and inspected their men's equipment and weapons, making sure they all had everything they might need and all was in proper working order. The machine gun and mortar crews checked and rechecked their weapons.

Being expeditionary, the Marines didn't have the same heavy-lift capability that the Army did. One thing that meant in practical terms was the biggest artillery pieces, including laser guns able to fire on orbiting targets, belonged to the Army. Where the Army had lasers powerful enough to augment the Navy's "shore batteries" in attacking enemy ships in orbit from the planetary surface, the Marine lasers couldn't. The Marine lasers were most useful against ground armor, as anti-aircraft guns, and to shoot down enemy shuttles on their way planetside from orbit. A four-gun laser platoon from 2nd Marine Air Wing's base defense squadron had joined India Company in Fire Camp Zion.

Captain Carl Sitter came out of the command bunker and joined Robinson, looking over the company. "What do you think, Top?" he asked.

"They look ready right now, Sir," Robinson answered. "But if something doesn't happen soon, I think they'll get over-wound."

Sitter nodded. A high level of readiness couldn't be maintained for a long period of time without the readiness falling off drastically. "Suggestions?"

"An inspection never hurt."

Sitter chuckled. He'd been an enlisted man before he got his commission, and remembered how he hated company commanders' inspections in the field. "You know, that'll piss them off."

Robinson nodded. "Yes, Sir, it will. And they'll take it out on the next Dusters they see."

"One platoon at a time. Have First platoon in formation here in fifteen minutes. Shift everybody else to cover their section of the perimeter. I think twenty minutes per platoon will be enough."

"Will you flunk anybody, Sir?"

"Not unless somebody has a weapon fouled badly enough it's liable to misfire. I'll have an officers' call to inform the platoon commanders. You tell the platoon sergeants. Do it."

"Aye aye, Sir," Robinson said to Sitter's back as the CO returned to the CP bunker. Then at the top of his lungs, "Platoon sergeants up!"

Nobody in First platoon was happy about having to stand in a parade ground formation for a company commander's inspection, not even the platoon's top people, who knew and understood the reason for it. But nobody complained. Not out loud, anyway.

"Are your people ready, Mackie?" Sergeant Martin asked while Second platoon was being inspected, when there were only a few minutes left before Third platoon had its turn.

Corporal Mackie grimaced. "Shit, ready. Look at this." He gestured at the bare ground of the firebase, at the thin clouds thrown up by gusts of wind. "You can't do spit-and-polish in this. No matter how clean you wipe something down, half an hour later it's coated with dust again."

"At least it's not raining," Martin said. "Spit-and-polish would be impossible then."

"Maybe not the spit part," Mackie said with an ironic laugh.

Martin had to laugh. "Got that right. But that doesn't answer my question."

Mackie grimaced again. "Depends on how hard-ass the Skipper's going to be."

Martin looked toward the Marines of First platoon. None of them seemed upset at the results of their inspection. "I believe the inspection is nothing more than ass-busting make-work. Something to take our minds off of when are the Dusters going to make planetfall."

"You're probably right. But there are other things we could be doing if all he's looking for is make-work."

"Could be. But he's the boss, so it's his decision. Besides, it gives him something to do to take *his* mind off the waiting."

Then Sitter finished his inspection of Second platoon and Third was called to stand in ranks in front of the CP bunker to be inspected.

The company commander wasn't hardass at all.

Second Lieutenant Commiskey stood at attention in front of Mackie, but looked through rather than at him, while Captain Sitter inspected Private Frank Preston, on Mackie's right. Sitter's only comment to Hill was, "Keep it that clean, Preston," when he returned his rifle after giving it a visual once-over.

Mackie sharply raised his rifle to port arms as soon as Commiskey stepped away. Out of boredom as much as anything else, Mackie let go of his rifle as soon as his peripheral vision showed Sitter's hand moving to take it.

Sitter had to move fast to catch the weapon before it fell to the ground. He leaned close and whispered, "Corporal, we've both been around too long for you to pull that kind of crap."

"Sorry, Sir," Mackie whispered back. But he didn't sound apologetic.

Sitter gave the rifle more of an inspection than he had Preston's. He wiped a finger along the barrel guard, picking up a faint smudge of dust. "Clean it again, Mackie," he said as he returned the rifle. To Commiskey, "Inspect him again after he's cleaned it."

"Aye aye, Sir," Commiskey said, and gave Mackie a disgusted look.

They moved on, which put Guillen directly in front of Mackie. The platoon sergeant gave Mackie a barely perceptible headshake and mouthed, *Later*, at him.

Later came and Guillen wanted to know, "What was that about, Mackie?" Martin stood at Guillen's left side, arms folded across his chest, glaring at Mackie.

Mackie stood at his tallest and defiantly looked Guillen in the eye. "An inspection in the field, when we're expecting the bad guys to make planet-fall at any minute, is mickey mouse, that's what it was about."

Martin snorted and looked away.

Guilllen snarled. "Junk-on-the-bunk in garrison is mickey mouse. In the field, when we expect a fight soon, is maybe the best time for an inspection. An inspection is necessary then, to make sure everybody's weapons and gear are ready for the fight. Now, you've got fifteen minutes to clean your rifle before Lieutenant Commiskey comes to inspect it.

You know, I really do expect better from you, Mackie." Guillen spun about and stalked away.

Martin stayed and watched to make sure Mackie was cleaning his rifle instead of sulking.

After Mackie's rifle passed Commiskey's inspection, the lieutenant marched him to the company HQ bunker, where Captain Sitter inspected it again. This time, Mackie didn't let go of his rifle until Sitter's hand touched it. He passed.

Watching the sky

The battle above began on the night side of Troy, which also happened to be during Camp Zion's night. The first thing the Marines of India Company saw were three lights moving across the sky; the impulse engines of the three frigates as they crawled into higher orbits to intercept the lights of the Duster fleet, which had been visible close to the horizon, and rising toward the zenith since sundown. The frigates' movement was followed moments later by the larger lights of the *Durango's* and *Scott's* engines as the battleship and carrier followed them. The ground observers couldn't see any lights showing that the *Scott* had launched her fighters—they didn't flare brightly enough.

There were abrupt flashes in the night sky, as the warships launched missiles and fired lasers at each other and each other's missiles. Larger flashes erupted as lasers slashed through missiles, igniting their warheads.

"It's like a far away fireworks display," PFC William Horton murmured, awed. "I wonder what it sounds like up close." He was sitting cross-legged on top of the fire team's bunker.

"It doesn't sound like anything, Horton," Corporal Mackie said. His voice had a trace of fear instead of awe. He understood better than the younger man what the lights in the sky foretold. This was merely the preliminary, the

Duster fleet would soon enough turn its attention to the ground. Followed by alien ground forces making planetfall. "They're in vacuum up there. There's no sound." He was laying supine on the bunker's top.

Horton looked at the shadow that was his fire team leader and considered. "Right," he said, remembering his nearly-forgotten basic science studies. "You need air for sound waves to propagate." After a further moment's reflection he added, "I think I'm glad I can't hear it."

Mackie's nod went unseen in the night dark. "When a missile hits a ship, everybody onboard will hear it. And for many of them, it'll be the last thing they hear."

There was another moment of silence before Horton whispered, "Right."

Throughout Camp Zion, the Marines watched the battle in the sky. For the most part, they didn't say anything as the warships continued moving closer to one another. They watched and some cheered as the three frigates made their move, coming in on the flank of the Duster formation and sending missiles and laser beams flying at the enemy. The sharper-eyed of the Marines picked out tiny flashes of Navy fighters being hit by Duster weapons. The Marines cheered again when lasers from Shapland struck a Duster warship and broke it in half. The cheering didn't last long, not once it became clear that there were only three ships hitting the Duster flank. They could see the NAU ships were badly outnumbered.

"What are they doing now?" Lance Corporal Cafferata suddenly asked, sitting bolt upright.

It looked like the human task force and the Duster fleet were merging.

"Whadafug?" was all Mackie could say.

Then the Dusters were through the task force and seemed to be gaining velocity. Another of their warships tumbled from being hit by Army laser fire.

Laser fire from orbit and Shapland chased the Duster fleet for a short while before stopping.

"Why aren't they chasing them?" PFC Orndoff asked.

"Maybe because they're waiting for more Duster ships to come," Sergeant Martin said from behind them.

"Goddam it, Sergeant Martin!" Mackie snapped. "You've got to stop sneaking up on us like that."

"And you've got to—" Martin started.

"Yeah, yeah, I know," Mackie said, interrupting him. "We've got to have all around awareness. But, man, you're a Marine, you're quiet."

Martin crained his neck looking up. He pointed toward the sky above the eastern horizon. "That's why they aren't pursuing."

The others looked where he pointed in time to see lines of light from TF 8 zipping at large, barely seen shadows in the sky. Small flashes of light shot out from from the shadows and began dropping, plunging planetward.

"That's the invasion fleet," Martin murmured.

Shadow-ship after shadow-ship rolled past the horizon. Half of them dropped shuttles and altered their trajectories, maneuvering out of the way of the lasers from TF 8. The others headed onward, aiming for Shapland, to drop their invaders on the elevator, and the Army positions near Millerton. Here a shadow-ship spun as laser bolts slashed through its hull and vented its atmosphere. There a shadow-ship broke in half when lasers sliced its spine in twain. Another burst apart when lasers penetrated to its power core. A shadow-ship began limping with its power reduced, another staggered and lost way.

The diving Duster shuttles glowed red as Troy's atmosphere ablated their heat shields.

"They aren't making planetfall near us," Mackie observed.

"Over the horizon," Martin agreed. "Be ready to move out, we might go out to meet them."

"Shit," Cafferata said. "That'll leave us without defensive works."

Marine anti-air laser artillery began lancing beams at the distant, plummeting shuttles, too far away for explosive artillery. Some beams hit the shuttles, some beams missed. And some were too diffuse to kill by the time they struck their targets.

A few shuttles were broken open by hits. A few more were tossed so their heat shields no longer protected them from burning up. Most passed through the barrage of killing-light lances to drop below the horizon.

Headquarters, NAU Forces, Troy,
near Millerton, Shapland

"If their shuttles carry the same numbers as ours, we can expect the equivalent of a reinforced corps to make planetfall. More on Eastern Shapland than here, because the transports coming west are subject to more fire from TF 8 and the Army's laser artillery," was the gist of Brigadier Shoup's operational assessment. "That's opposed to a battle-weary Marine division and wing on Eastern Shapland, and an even more battle-weary Army division here. Navy air assets are here to give the Army support, as well as two AV16C squadrons."

"Do you want to go after them, Sir?"

Lieutenant General Bauer hardly had to think about his answer. "The best defense, and all the other clichés aside, they can overwhelm our ground forces if they catch us in the open. Make sure all our defensive positions are as strong as possible—especially the Army's."

He turned to Captain Upshur, standing ready in the doorway of Bauer's office.

"Get me Admiral Avery, if you please."

Upshur was back a moment later. "Sir, the admiral is on the surface-to-orbit."

Bauer took the comm. "Admiral, I see TF 8 acquitted itself well against the Duster warships."

"Thank you, General," Avery replied after a few seconds lag for the surface-orbit transmission. "What can the Navy do for the ground forces?"

"We have large numbers of Dusters making planetfall in locations remote from our positions. I don't believe they'll stay at a distance. It would be very helpful if you could keep us appraised of their locations, directions, and speed of movement, as well as their formations and armor, if any."

"General, I will bend every asset the Navy has to that task, provided it doesn't reduce TF 8's ability to defend itself."

"That is understood. Jim, the Marines and the Army thank you. We also offer our sympathies for your losses. TF 8's actions here will go down in Navy lore."

There was an audible lump in Avery's throat when he said, "Thanks, Hal. I appreciate that. I will pass it on to my task force."

"Bauer out." He set the comm aside and looked at Upshur, who still stood ready to do his commander's bidding.

"Bill, we have a fight on our hands. A big one."

Camp Zion, West Shapland,
near Jordan, Eastern Shapland

FIRST LIEUTENANT BONNYMAN CAME BACK WITH HIS PLATOON OF COMBAT ENGINEERS.
"Not good news, is it Captain?"

"It could be worse," Captain Sitter said. He looked eastward, toward where the Duster shuttles had touched down beyond the horizon. "It's still pretty bad. The Navy says they cram more than twice the number of soldiers in a shuttle than we would in the same similar size vessel." He shook his head.

"Two corps coming at the First Marine Division," Bonnyman said. "Eight to one odds."

"Marines have faced worse odds in the past and won. I don't see why we can't win again. They throw their soldiers' lives away."

"Yeah, they do. And we're here to help them throw away more. My people are enlarging the spiked trench inside your platoons' wire and adding another outside it. They've already done that for Kilo Company. Lima is next."

"It'll help."

"I better see how progress is going. By your leave, Sir?"

"I'll go with you." Sitter donned his helmet and led the way out of his command bunker.

"Hey, Skipper!" Corporal Mackie called when the two officers were parallel to his fire team's bunker. "Does this mean we aren't going hunting?"

Sitter paused to look at him. "We've got beaters out there, driving them toward us. Turkey shoot, Marine!"

Mackie threw a thumbs-up at his company commander.

Firebase Gasson, near Millerton, Shapland

"A corps and a half?" Sergeant First Class Quinn yelped. "Are you kidding?"

Second Lieutenant Greig shook his head. "I could only wish." He'd just returned to his platoon's area from a battalion officers' call, where battalion commander Lieutenant Colonel Hapeman had delivered the latest intelligence from Navy surveillance. The majority of the alien transports and shuttles had made it through the gauntlet of orbital and surface missiles and lasers to land their counter-invasion force. The Dusters had landed the equivalent of seven human infantry divisions.

"But all we have is a single division," Quinn said. "And it's worse than that—the division was assembled from bits and pieces of other units!"

Greig smiled crookedly. "It's more like a reinforced division. Besides, it could be worse."

"How could it possibly be worse?" Quinn demanded.

"The Marines don't have as many troops or armor as we do, and they're facing two full corps."

Captain Patricia Pentzer and her platoon sergeant, James H. Bronson, joined Greig and Quinn after giving her own noncoms basic information.

"I can depress my guns," she said. "They can knock out armor if it comes here. But they won't be a lot of use against infantry."

"The foot soldiers present targets that are too small for you to hit?" Greig asked. "I can always use more riflemen on the line if that's the case."

"They aren't too small, it's just that a laser beam will only hit one at a time, unless they're lined up."

"You can't sweep the beam side to side?"

"Very little. Just so you know, I'm not putting my crews on the line until I know the Dusters aren't bringing armor at us."

"We'll do what we can with what we have."

Surveilance and radar section, NAUS Durango, in orbit

"Chief," Radarman 2 Peter Howard said over the susurration of soft voices and gentle pings that were the only sounds in the darkened compartment.

"What do you think you see, Howard?" Chief Petty Officer William Densmore answered.

"I *know* I see maneuvering," Howard said.

Densmore stepped close to bend and lean in to study Howard's screen over his shoulder. The screen showed a view from the side-looking radar of a section of the surface of Eastern Shapland east of the positions of the 1st Marine Division. After a moment he sucked on his teeth and stood straight.

"Sir," the chief called to Lieutenant George McCall Courts, "we've got something for the Jarheads, or for CAC. Your choice."

"Zero it in for me," Courts ordered.

Densmore bent back to Howard's station and reached for the controls. In seconds, an enlarged image of Howard's screen appeared at Courts's command station.

"Oh, my," the lieutenant whispered. He got on the comm to the bridge.

"Bridge," Lieutenant Commander Buchanan replied.

"I'm sending you coordinates. It looks like the Dusters are making a move at the Marines."

Buchanan only took a couple of seconds to study the display before whistling. "Keep an eye on it," he told Courts, "and have somebody take a close look at the Dusters west of Millerton. I'll notify the Skipper."

"Keep watching, and put someone on the Dusters west of Millerton, aye," Courts said.

As soon as he was off the comm to S&R, Buchanan called the captain.

"Huse," the *Durango's* skipper answered immediately.

"Sir, Bridge. It looks like the Dusters are maneuvering. The Marines should know."

"I'll be right there. Notify the Admiral."

Huse was on the Bridge before Buchanan could finish notifying TF 8's commander.

Admiral's Bridge, NAUS Durango

Rear Admiral James Avery took almost no time at all to understand import of the side-looking radar images he was sent.

"Get me General Bauer," he told Lieutenant Commander George Davis.

"Get General Bauer, aye," Davis said, and made contact with Head-quarters, NAU Forces, Troy. "Sir, General Bauer's office," he said, and handed the comm to Avery.

Avery waited a few seconds before he heard Lieutenant General Harold Bauer's voice.

"Jim, it's good to hear your voice," Bauer said.

"And yours as well, General." Avery used Bauer's title to make it was clear this was an important call.

"What do you have, Admiral?" Bauer asked, taking the hint.

"Sir, the Dusters are moving on Eastern Shapland. We are tracking them, and will feed you our intelligence as we get it. Your G-2 can expect the first data burst in fifteen minutes."

"What about the Dusters on Shapland?"

"We are checking on them now."

"How is your situation?"

"The majority of the alien transports managed to get away, although many of them were damaged. We estimate eight hours before their warships return. Good hunting, General."

"Good hunting to you as well, Admiral. Bauer out."

Surveillance and Radar Section, NAUS Durango

"Chief, I have movement," Radarman 3 Michael McCormIck said in the quiet of the *Durango's* Surveillance and Radar Section.

"Show me," Chief Densmore said. He leaned over McCormick's shoulder to study his screen. "Sir," he called to Lieutenant Courts, "we've got them. I'm dialing you in."

Courts looked at the data and saw the alien army's movement toward Millerton and the Army division surrounding it. He notified the Bridge, where Captain Huse was still in his command chair.

Fifteen minutes later, Headquarters, NAU Forces, Troy had all the available information on Duster movement on both continents.

The staff began to change the plans based on this new intelligence.

Headquarters, 9th Infantry Division, near Millerton, Shapland, Troy

Major General Noll, commanding general of the 9th Infantry Division, which he was beginning to think of as the Frankenstein Division, as it was pieced together from those elements of the 9th that had survived the missile attack and other units that had made planetfall, looked wonderingly at the situation board hanging on the wall behind him. Red smudges moved on it, showing the movement of the alien army as they moved at the white dots, rectangles, and circles that represented the NAU forces.

They've got to be crazy, he thought. *I don't care how badly they have us outnumbered. This is insane, they won't be able to concentrate their forces enough to break through our lines.*

His G-3, Lieutenant Colonel Henry Merriam, had worked closely with Brigadier General Shoup, the acting NAU G-3, to arrange defenses around Millerton and the McKinzie elevator station. *But this?*

He looked from his sitboard to his assembled staff and major element commanders. "When they get in range, our artillery will begin to shred their formations. We have," he said proudly, "the artillery with the greatest range and power of all human armies. So far the aliens haven't shown that they have any artilllery other than dumb anti-air artillery. Don't discount that, even dumb anti-air artillery can be highly effective against armor and hardened defensive positions. Past wars have clearly demonstrated that.

"They're going to hurt us badly, I have no doubt of that. But if we fight our best, I have absolute confidence that we will defeat the alien army.

"You all know what to do. Now do it."

There was a clattering of chairs as the assembled generals and other senior officers rose to their feet. Someone, Noll didn't see who, gave out a *huzzah!* In seconds, so did the rest of them. Some pumped their fists in the air.

Camp Zion, 3rd Marine Regiment complex, near Jordan

Major General Purvis, commanding general of 1st Marine Division, put the 6th Marine Regiment in a triangle of mutually supporting battalion fire-bases five kilometers northeast of Jordan, and the 7th Marine Regiment, also in mutually supporting firebases, an equal distance to the city's west. The 1st Marine Regiment, similarly placed, went three kilometers north of Jordan. He divided his artillery regiment, the 12th Marines, among the three firebases. He based his headquarters battalion, along with the division's armor, reconnaissance and other units, just outside the small city, adjacent to the 1st Marines.

When the Navy's latest intelligence reports were passed on to the regimental headquarters, and from there to the companies, platoons, and squads, it caused surprise, and not a little consternation among the junior officers and the enlisted men.

"Say what?" Corporal Mackie yelped when he heard. "Are they out of their ever-loving minds?"

"They're aliens, Mackie," Sergeant Martin said patiently. "Who knows what goes on in their minds? I sure don't. And if anybody higher-higher knows, they aren't telling me."

Mackie shook his head and looked at his men. They were staring at him and their squad leader as though they were crazy. Or at least like the Navy intel report was.

"We're Marines," Martin said. "When we're surrounded, all that means is, now we can shoot in all directions." He left, headed for the platoon CP bunker. He hadn't said it, but he agreed with Mackie; the aliens had to be out of their fucking minds.

Not long after, the Dusters for the first time made a coordinated attack. Their combat fleet completed its circuit of Troy and fell on Task Force 8. At the same time, their ground forces, having completed their encirclement of the NAU forces on both Shapland and Eastern Shapland attacked.

Combat Action Center, NAUS Durango

"Chief," Radarman 3 John Bickford said, "I'm picking up another anomaly from the same direction that Duster fleet came from."

Chief Petty Officer Verney rushed to Bickford's station and looked over his shoulder.

"Damn," he swore, "they've got more coming!"

NAUS Durango, Fleet Combat Action Center

Lieutenant Commander Rufus Z. Johnston sat in his command chair, peering at the display on the big board, showing the warships of Task Force 8 maneuvering into position to take on the invaders. The display's scale was small enough to show the slow approach of the wounded Fast Attack Carrier Kidd, and the far faster approach of the enemy fleet. It was clear that the enemy would arrive first. The display also showed the remnants of Amphibious Group 17 in its ongoing rescue and recovery operation for survivors—and the remains of those who didn't survive—from the missile attack that had devastated the ARG.

And there, on the far edge of the display, beyond ARG 17's operation.,..

Johnston toggled his headset to signal Rear Admiral Avery. "Sir," he said after Avery's gruff, "Speak," acknowledged him, "Sir, someone else is coming into range from beyond ARG 17."

"Identification?" Avery demanded.

"Not yet, Sir." Johnston's fingers danced over the keypad on the right armrest of his chair, signaling the comm shack, ordering it to attempt to contact the newly detected spacecraft. "Comm is working on it."

Lieutenant Commander Davis's excited voice intruded. "CAC, comm."

"Comm, go. The admiral is on," Johnston answered.

"Sir, we just received a message from Earth via drone. Task Force 7 is en route. It should reach the Troy wormhole terminus within a day."

Within a day. The new arrival CAC detected beyond ARG 17 must have been the lead elements of TF 7. At flank speed, the warships were still more than two days out.

"Comm, attempt to contact TF 7 and extend my compliments on their timely arrival. Tell them I request they come to Troy high orbit at flank speed. I will instruct Captain Anderson to prepare a brief for you to transmit to TF 7 so they will know what to expect when they get here. Do it."

"Aye aye, Sir," Davis said, and dropped out of the communication link to obey Avery's orders.

"Avery out."

"CAC," Avery said, sounding much stronger and more confident than he had at any time since the attack from Minnie Mouse, "I anticipate two days for TF 7 to reach us. Stand by for revised orders. Perhaps we will still be here to greet them when they arrive." That last sentence was said so softly that Johnston wasn't sure Avery intended him to hear it. He told Davis to contact the ground commander, so he could give him the news about the relief force.

An hour later

The Admiral's Bridge, NAUS Durango

"Sir, a message," Lieutenant Commander Davis said excitedly.

"Speak."

"Sir, the unidentified starships are the van of TF 7 and ARG 28! The warships are the battleship *Nebraska*, cruisers *Grandar Bay* and *Suvla Bay*, the carrier *Vice Admiral Theodore S. Wilkinson*, and the amphibious battle cruisers *Enterprise*, and *Tripoli* with the Second Marine Division on board."

"Outstanding!" Avery said. "If we survive the next day and a half, we may live through this war. Notify the commander, NAU Forces, Troy."

Ends Book II

In All Directions

— So (Not) — Like Dogs

An 18th Race Short Story

DAVID SHERMAN

THE HANDLER ROSE SLIGHTLY FROM HIS HIP-BENT STALKING POSTURE AND SNIFFED, seeking the scent that had brought his charges to point. His head twitched side to side, frequently pausing for an instant to peer through the spindly foliage of the scrub forest. The fact that he smelled nothing other than the greenery of the flora and the dust of the rich earth, or saw nothing other than thin trunks, spiky leaves, and dense undergrowth meant nothing—he knew that although his eyes were sharper than those of his charges, his nose was nowhere near as sensitive. It would soon be night, when scent told more than vision could. He would rely on the beasts. He lowered himself back to his normal hunting posture, his back parallel to the ground, his tail feathers jutting straight back in counterbalance to his head on the end of its long neck.

Intelligence knew that the main line of the alien game was a quarter day's march ahead of where the Handler now was, and that the game had placed a guardian line of outposts well in advance of their main line. His mission, his pack's mission, was to destroy one of the outposts, to create a hole through which a large force could charge to assault the game's main line. He squealed a happy squeal, his wasn't the only patrol sent to wipe out an outpost in this area. The hole they would make in the guardian line would be huge.

The ninety members of his pack, half the Handler's height though otherwise looking very like him, hissed softly as they looked up at him expectantly, bouncing up and down in their excitement for action. He returned their looks, and his mouth opened in a tooth-exposing grin. He patted the air, telling them to be patient...that their time would come soon enough. Then they could slash and rend and eat to their hearts' content. He would gleefully join them in the eating. But first he needed to discover exactly where the furless and scaleless prey was, and how many were there. He wasn't concerned about how they were armed—he knew his charges moved too fast for the aliens to track and aim at them.

The Sixth Marine Regiment had made planetfall on Semi-Autonomous World Troy on D Plus 4. The following day its second battalion had its first engagement with the ferocious aliens who had evidently wiped out the entire population of the planet. Second battalion's Echo Company suffered the least heavily of the battalion's companies in that engagement, which was why Echo was tasked with putting out a platoon-size observation post five kilometers ahead of the battalion's line. Captain Eli Fryer, Echo's commanding officer, only had to transfer four Marines from other platoons to bring first platoon up to full strength. Second Lieutenant John Leims, first platoon commander, wasn't fully happy with getting four Marines he didn't know under these circumstances.

"I know them, Sir," Staff Sergeant Mitchell Paige, the platoon sergeant, told Leims. "And so do most members of the platoon. These're all good Marines. They'll fit in with no problem." Paige had been with Echo, 2/6 for more than two years, where Leims had only joined the company a couple of weeks before the deployment.

"If you say so," Leims said. He didn't sound convinced.

A squad of Combat Engineers and one of sappers went with first platoon. The Engineers' heavy equipment took most of a day to construct defensive works and living bunkers on both the forward and reverse slopes of a four-hundred-meter-high ridgeline that overlooked a road junction in a forest of middling-height, spindly trees; they camouflaged the works as they went. The sappers took a little less time to seed the approaches to the ridge with sensors; visual, audio, motion, scent.

Before they left, the engineers and sappers gave the infantry Marines all the shotgun shells they had. Two men in each fire team carried an M7 shotgun instead of the standard-issue M-82 rifle. Most of the Marines had done little more than orient on the M7—learned how to load and aim, but not well enough to gain any proficiency. Corporal Truesdale took one of his fire team's shotguns as he'd done more firing with it.

As soon as the sappers were out of the way, Leims and Paige registered artillery and rockets, and directed a practice run of AV16C Kestrels.

"No sweat, Lieutenant," Paige told him. "You've got a whole platoon of Marines to keep you company."

"Yeah," Leims answered. In his mind he saw the speedy, herky-jerky rushes of the alien soldiers and their smaller attack. . .dogs, for want of a better word. A platoon of Marines didn't seem like enough company.

Second Lieutenant Leims had never felt so lonely.

The Handler crouched down, facing his pack Alpha, and leaned in, shoulder to shoulder. He stroked the Alpha, from the feathery top of its head, down its long neck, and its longer back, all the way to its twitching tail. He murmured nonsense words into the Alpha's ear hole, calming it. Satisfied that the Alpha was no longer too excited to listen to commands, he instructed it to stay in this place, and to keep the rest of the pack there, until he returned.

The Alpha hissed its understanding, and gave the side of the Handler's muzzle a long lick with its raspy tongue.

The Handler gave the Alpha a last, long stroke, then stood and headed in the direction where he knew the aliens must be putting their outposts. He would locate and observe the nearest outpost, then make his plan and fetch his pack. He looked forward to the panic the aliens would experience before they died.

"Look alive, second squad," Sergeant Alexander Foley said into his helmet comm's squad circuit during the day's brief dusk. "We're all alive and I want us to stay that way. Anyone who gets himself killed will have to answer to me."

Lance Corporal Harry Fisher snorted. "What's he going to do, follow us to heaven to kick our asses?"

Fisher's fire team leader, Corporal Don Truesdale, leaned over inside the bunker his fire team was in and smacked the back of Fisher's helmet. "No, dummy. He'll follow you to hell to kick your ass. Now pay attention to that visual pickup."

Fisher curled his lip, but bent his attention to the visual sensor receiver that was the fire team's responsibility.

"Everybody else, watch sharp," Truesdale ordered his other men. "Memorize the shadows."

"Right, memorize," PFC Oscar Upham murmured softly enough that Truesdale could ignore it.

A moonless night. Black on black. Experienced infantrymen watched the shadows deepen and merge as dusk turned to night, memorized their shapes so that if they later saw a shadow that hadn't been there before, they knew it might be an approaching enemy. But the downward slope that was second squad's front held only knee-high scrub, no trees or boulders or anything else that would protrude above the scrub. And the forest beyond the roads below the ridge was too uniform to show anything. But maybe that uniformity was the point of memorizing the shadows; any anomaly would clearly show up.

First squad was on second's left and third was on the reverse slope, held in reserve. One of the two scatterer gun teams attached to the platoon was between the two front squads, the other was with third. One fire team per bunker, Foley with the scatterer team in the middle. Fifty meters between bunkers. Seven bunkers covering a front three hundred meters wide. The command group was with the reserve on the opposite slope.

The Handler found a spot from where he could observe the ridgeline without being seen himself by a foe with vision as poor as the aliens' was known to be. Moving slowly so as to not disturb any of the foliage around him, he withdrew a magnifier from one of the pouches on his chest strap. That and a few other straps were his sole garments. The magnifier showed him the line of bunkers the aliens had constructed. He didn't know how many of them occupied a bunker, but seeing their size and knowing the size of the aliens—close to his own when he stood erect—he estimated that only three or four of them were in each structure. Fewer than thirty alien soldiers. Maybe many fewer. He tucked his muzzle under an arm to muffle his chuckle. His pack would make quick work of them. The packs to his flanks would do likewise with the stretches of ridge they were to clear. Then the main attack force would charge through, to attack and destroy the alien army.

"Hey Corporal Truesdale, take a look at this," Lance Corporal Fisher said as dusk deepened. He leaned out of the way so his fire team leader could look at the visual sensor display.

"What am I looking at?" Truesdale asked, ducking his head into the display's hood.

"Maybe something, maybe nothing. I'm not sure. That's why I want you to take a look."

"Are you focused on a spot?"

"Yeah."

Truesdale peered at the display, wishing he had a heat or infrared sensor to compliment the visual display. But the engineers and sappers hadn't brought any heat or infra sensors. Dammit.

"What do you think?" Fisher asked after a moment of stillness from his team leader.

"Wait for it," Truesdale murmured. Then, abruptly, "Got it!" He withdrew from the hood. "There's a Duster out there." "Duster," short for "feather-duster" so called because of the feather-like structures that trailed from the aliens' arms and jutted from the base of their torsos. "I think he's a scout, anyway he just pulled back." He looked at where he knew Fisher was and nodded. "Looking good, Marine. Even knowing there was something to see, I had a hard time spotting him. Take over." He withdrew to the bunker's entrance and picked up the comm to the squad leader.

"What do you have for me, Don," Sergeant Foley asked. Truesdale briefly told him what he and Fisher had seen.

"Thanks, I'll pass it up. Let me know if you see anything else."

"Roger that, honcho," Truesdale answered.

Having seen what he needed to see, the Handler stealthily withdrew, returning to his pack. That was when he noticed something that looked wrong. He surreptitiously examined it, without pausing in his movement. Yes, it appeared to be some sort of visual pickup. No matter. Even if the aliens had seen him, which they might well not have, the dashing and darting of his pack was too fast for the aliens to kill more than a few of his beasts. Yes, let the visual pickup let them know he was there, let their fear increase. Their foreknowledge wouldn't change the outcome once he attacked.

The pack was still where he'd left it, all members accounted for. Even though one was too badly injured to participate in the coming fight. and another was partly lamed. The Handler stroked the Alpha and murmured into its ear hole, praising it for keeping the pack together and in place. That only two of the beasts were injured was good; the Alpha hadn't had to kill any of them to keep them in line.

The Handler sent the agreed-upon message, informing his commander that he'd scouted the alien defenses and he and his pack were ready to advance to the assault line.

He settled back to wait for the command to strike.

All along the outpost line in front of the Sixth Marines, reports came in of sightings of individual alien scouts. Something was up, but nobody knew what. Whoever this enemy on Troy was, the Marines—any humans for that matter—hadn't had enough contact with them to have any understanding of their tactics. The word went down from Regiment; "Prepare to repel boarders."

"'Repel boarders,' I guess that's as good a way of putting it as anything else," Corporal Truesdale said when Sergeant Fryer passed the instruction to him over the squad comm.

Truesdale heard the shrug in Fryer's voice when the squad leader said, "Just think of your bunker as a ship's rigging and you'll be fine."

"Right." Truesdale got off the comm and told his men, "We're in simulated ship's rigging. You better not be simulated sharpshooters when the bad guys come." One of the duties of the original US Marines, centuries earlier, was sharpshooters in ships' rigging, shooting down on the officers and crew on the decks of enemy vessels.

"We gonna be able to see 'em coming?" PFC Campbell asked.

"We can hope. Cop some Zs, Campbell. Everybody else, look sharp. Got anything on the display, Fisher?"

"Negative," Fisher answered. Minutes later, "Belay my last, I've got a lot of movement."

The Handler lowered his torso between his legs, his thighs and lower legs formed triangles along his sides, his feet angled toward the ground, his toes relaxed with his entire weight well distributed on them. He resisted the urge to tuck his head under his arm—it wouldn't do to be asleep when the order to attack came.

He didn't have to wait long for the order to advance to the assault line. With a few, sharp commands he got his pack into movement formation and began the short march to the assault line. The Alpha trotted here, there, and around the pack, keeping the beasts in proper formation. The Handler smiled; this was the best Alpha he'd ever worked with, its intelligence was well above that of its mates. It was almost like having another Handler with him.

When they reached the assault line, the Handler went from beast to beast, stroking each and murmuring to them. The beasts gazed up at him adoringly, hopping from clawed foot to clawed foot in their excitement at the anticipated charge into mayhem and bloody food.

"Get ready!" Sergeant Foley ordered over the squad comm.

"Get ready!" the fire team leaders needlessly echoed. "Infras," most of them added.

Corporal Truesdale looked at his men through his infrared goggles and was gratified to see that PFC Upham had his shotgun in hand, and looked like he knew how to use it. "Keep your eyes on your display," he told Fisher.

"It looks like they're starting to move forward," Fisher reported.

"How many are there?"

"It's hard to tell without infra. Best guess, more than twenty right in front of us. Could be a whole lot more, though."

Truesdale repeated Fisher's report to Foley.

"Put him on the squad comm," Foley ordered. "I want everybody to get his reports without delay.

"Aye-aye, Sergeant." Truesdale reached over to Fisher's comm unit and, working mostly by feel, switched his transmissions from fire team to squad comm. The he peered out through the embrasure, straining to see the alien enemy.

The Handler got his pack on line facing the alien positions that he knew were on the ridgeline, even though he couldn't see them in the night's darkness. Not being able to see them from this distance wouldn't be a handicap; his charges could smell them well enough at this range. A little closer, and he'd be able to smell them as well. The smell of the aliens would be enough to guide the Handler and his pack almost as well as vision would.

Second Lieutenant Leims, in his command post, watched the platoon's display feeds. He'd already called for a standby illumination mission from the regiment's attached artillery battery.

"All hands, listen up," he said into the full platoon comm. "Nobody fire until the illume pops. Then hit 'em with everything you've got." He glanced at his platoon sergeant, then back at the displays. "Do they even know we're in front of them?" he asked.

"Is that a rhetorical question?" Staff Sergeant Paige asked.

"I guess it is," Leims said after a moment. Nobody knew when the aliens might attack, how close they would approach before they attacked.

"I hate this waiting," Leims muttered.

"No more than the Marines up front," Paige said softly.

Leims swallowed. "You're right."

The Handler looked side to side and allowed himself a smile. His pack was maintaining good order, keeping their line straight. He wondered how close they would get to the prey before he could release them to the attack. He wondered how long he and his Alpha could keep the pack in good order.

The orderliness of the line was starting to break when the command finally came. The Handler shrilled out a hunting caw, and his pack broke formation, charging forward, jinking and jiving, dashing here, darting there, making themselves impossible for a larger predator to focus on for the kill.

"They're too damn close" Second Lieutenant Leims said when the aliens were almost to the road at the foot of the ridge. "If they begin their charge now, the illum won't get here until they're on us." He turned to his communications man. "Call that light mission now!"

Seconds later, flares began popping open above the ridge's side and the beginning of the scrub forest on the other side of the road junction, bathing the area in a cold, eerie, blue-tinged light.

The Handler squawked outrage. He hadn't anticipated illumination—at least not this soon, his pack had barely begun clambering up the side of the ridge. Then he saw the alien fire coming, and missing almost every member of his jinking and jiving, dashing and darting pack, and crowed out a cry of victory.

He joined the manic scramble toward the alien positions. Now this way, now that, now in a third direction. A beat this way, two beats that way, a beat and a half in another. Mixing up directions and intervals between. Never going in any one direction long enough for anyone to adjust aim sufficient to make a lucky hit on him

He cawed out another jubilant cry; there weren't as many of the aliens in the bunkers as he'd thought, and they didn't have any truly rapid-fire weapons, weapons that from sheer volume could create casualties in his pack. This line would be very easy to burst through.

"Scatterers and shot guns, hold your fire," Second Lieutenant Leims ordered on his all hands comm. He could clearly see the aliens on his displays now. They were running fast, but their zigzagging slowed their advance up the ridge—they were running two or three meters for every meter they climbed. The shotguns were relatively short-range weapons; they wouldn't be effective much farther than halfway down the slope. The scatterers were also shorter-range than normal machine guns.

"Mitch," Leims said, "get the other gun team in place, toward the right flank." At least they aren't shooting at us, he thought.

"Aye aye, Sir," Staff Sergeant Paige said, and ducked out of the command post, already talking to Corporal Robert O'Malley, giving him orders.

In less than a minute, Paige was shifting second squad's first fire team into the other squad bunkers to make room for the scatter gun team in its bunker.

The aliens were now halfway up the side of the ridge.

Close enough, Leims thought. "Everyone, open fire!" he shouted into his comm.

More fire suddenly erupted along the alien line. It took the Handler a couple of heart beats to realize that the fire wasn't the same discrete slugs that had been all the fire coming from the aliens, the slugs that almost always missed.

There was a ripping fire from the center, one that threw out too many slugs too fast to be always dodged. And a similar ripping came from the left side. These tore through the pack, and many of the beasts were flung backward, gouting blood and chunks of flesh and bone from the impacts.

Most of the aliens' fire missed the beasts of the pack, but some sprays of pellets were wide enough for some them to hit a beast before it could dash and dart out of the way.

The Handler shrilled out in fury at the loss of so many in his pack. He and the Alpha urged the pack on.

Corporal Truesdale was proud of the fact that he was a Marine Rifle Expert. That meant he was a better shot than nine out of ten of all human marksmen. But, damn, these creatures were hard to hit! The pellets from the shotgun's shells spread out, but not wide enough to always hit a dodging target before it jinked out of the way.

The aliens zigzagged so fast Truesdale couldn't take aim and fire before his target was off in a different direction. After a few wasted shots, he decided to simply fire without aiming, directing his shotgun blasts into wherever the mass seemed densest. He was satisfied to see an occasional alien drop. A few more fell, shot by bullets from Marines' rifles. Others from slugs thrown by the whirring barrels of the two scatterers, putting out more than two thousand tiny pellets per minute in a widening spray.

But there were so many of them, and they were rapidly clambering up the side of the ridge. There was no chance the Marines could kill all of them before the charging enemy reached them, and the bunkers all had open entrances in their rear.

If only Truesdale could shoot the one that was twice the size of the others; he knew it must be the leader. But it moved just as fast as the smaller ones, and was equally hard to hit.

The surviving pack members—most of the original ninety were still alive and in fighting form—ran straighter, with fewer changes of direction, as they closed on the line of defensive positions. That gave the prey more time to aim, but the Handler cackled with pleasure when he saw that the longer time the prey had to aim wasn't enough to make much of a difference—he though he lost no more than two additional beasts because of it.

He crowed with increased pleasure when he saw the foremost of the pack reach the bunkers and run between them. Soon, very soon, all of the prey would be dead, and the feasting would begin.

"Fisher, Upham," Corporal Truesdale shouted, "turn around, stop them from coming through the hatch!"

An instant later, both Fisher and Upham fired at three of the small aliens trying to jam their way into the bunker at the same time. One was blown backward by the force of a shotgun blast from Upham, a second crumpled when three rapid shots from Fisher slammed into it. Freed of its mates, the third pounced at Fisher, extending the claws on its feet and snapping with the teeth in its long muzzle.

Fisher didn't have time to scream before his throat was shredded. Scarlet blood spurted from his carotid arteries. Intestines boiled out of deep gashes in his abdomen. He thudded to the floor of the bunker.

Truesdale heard Fisher's corpse hit the floor, and spun in time to see the third alien shudder from a blast from Upham's shotgun. He spared Fisher a quick look; it was obvious the lance corporal was dead. He had to deal with the living.

"Campbell, turn around and help Upham keep them out!" Truesdale shouted. Without waiting to see if Campbell obeyed, he turned back to the embrasure and fired four quick shots at two aliens that were trying to squeeze through it. Both fell back, their feathers tattered and flesh shredded. He fired three more times and saw two more aliens die and two others run screaming down the hill.

The Handler cawed, appalled at the undisciplined way his beasts milled about, some trying to squeeze through embrasures clearly too small for them to fit in, others jamming themselves at the rear entrances to the defensive positions. He saw them being killed in far greater numbers than they were killing the foe. For the first time he wished he had some soldiers with him instead of only the pack. Soldiers would have rifles, and could shoot the alien defenders without having to enter the positions.

But he didn't. And his rifle and knife were the only weapons his force had. It was up to him to turn the tide.

He dashed to the side and around to the rear of the nearest bunker.

Where did the big Duster go? Truesdale demanded of himself. He knew he hadn't shot it and was sure no one else had, either. He must have made it between the bunkers, and was behind the positions.

Few of the aliens were still on the side of the ridge below the defensive line. Truesdale fired three more times and saw one of them go down, crumpled. Another reached his bunker and tried to climb through the embrasure. Truesdale reversed his grip on his shotgun and slammed its butt down hard on the alien's thrusting, snapping muzzle. He heard bones shatter, and the alien jerked backward, weakly cawing in pain. Truesdale shot it, then looked for more. He didn't see any, so he turned his attention to the bunker's entrance.

The Handler stepped around the corner of the defensive position and watched pained as two more of his beasts died in its entrance. They didn't fall all the way down, there were too many bodies already laying there, stacking up. He stepped forward and stuck his rifle though the entrance, moving its muzzle around so his fire would go to every corner as he pulled the trigger as rapidly as he could.

But before he got off more than a few shots, someone grabbed his rifle and jerked it out of his hands. He staggered.

Truesdale flung the alien's weapon into a corner of the bunker and sucked air between his teeth at the pain in his hand from grasping the hot barrel. But he had no time to worry about it; the aliens were still attacking even though there were far fewer of them.

"Give me a hand clearing this," he ordered, and grabbed the neck of the alien on top of the pile. A quick yank pulled the thing inside. Upham and Campbell lent themselves to the job, and in fifteen seconds enough bodies were cleared out of the way for Truesdale to scramble over them to see outside.

He saw dead and dying aliens scattered on the ground near the entrances of the bunkers. Others were screeching and scrabbling at the entrances, trying to get at the Marines inside them.

And Truesdale saw the big one, standing bent at its hips, torso parallel to the ground, tail-feather-like structure jutting out behind, head on its long neck twisted toward him. A saw-bladed knife was in the alien's hand. It opened its maw wide at sight of the Marine, exposing glistening, rending teeth. The alien shrieked and charged, bending its arm back to the side to swing its knife in a disemboweling slice.

Truesdale dove to the side, under the swinging blade. He rolled and sprang to his feet, facing the alien which had already recovered and was charging again. It was close and coming too fast, Truesdale didn't have time to bring his weapon to bear and fire. He fell back to avoid the alien's knife. This time the alien was prepared for tbe movement, and twisted its stroke to swoop downward rather than across.

The Marine cried out at the sudden pain in his right wrist. He rolled and swung out with his good arm, catching the alien's foot. He yanked, and it crashed to the ground.

Ignoring the pain in his right wrist, Truesdale pounced onto the alien's back and grabbed its neck just below its head. He leaned all his weight onto his left hand and jumped up, to crash back down, landing his knees on the alien's back. He felt bones break.

Then Upham and Campbell were at his side. Campbell shot the alien in the side of its head with his rifle, and ordered Campbell, "Guard us!"

"Its dead, Honcho," Upham shouted at Truesdale, who was shaking the alien's neck. "And you're going to be dead if you don't let go of that and let me take care of you."

Dazed, and weakening from loss of blood, Truesdale let himself be pulled off the big alien. He watched dumbly as Upham tied a tourniquet around his right wrist. "Where's my hand?" he mumbled. "I don't see my hand."

"Corpsman up!" Upham called out.

The rest of the platoon was topping the ridge, and the last of the alien attackers were falling to their bullets.

"They were like a pack of rabid dogs," Truesdale said when the Corpsman asked what happened to him.

Echo, 2/6 only lost one man killed in the battle with the "dogs" of war. Only one Marine other than Corporal Donald Truesdale was badly wounded in the action. The planned assault against Second battalion, Sixth Marines never happened.

Corporal Truesdale returned to full duty three months later, with a newly regenerated hand at the end of his right wrist.

TO HELL
AND
REGROUP

DAVID SHERMAN
KEITH R.A. DeCANDIDO

"Marines don't die—they go to hell and regroup."
—old Marine Corps aphorism

This book is dedicated to the memory of:

Sergeant Alvin York

*328th Infantry Regiment
Awarded the Medal of Honor
for action in the Argonne Forest
October 8, 1918*

—David Sherman

*To Master Sergeant Charles Keane, U.S. Army Special Forces (ret.),
or, as I call him, Senpai Charles. My fellow student of karate, as well
as a fellow teacher in our dojo, Senpai Charles and I went for our
second-degree and third-degree black-belt promotions together in
2013 and 2017. It's been an honor to train with you, my friend.*

—Keith R.A. DeCandido

*Dedicated to the memory of Jeff (Thorir) Scott, super-fan.
Ever patient, ever loyal, and ever missed.
(6/26/56 - 4/29/20)*

—All of us at eSpec Books

ACKNOWLEDGEMENTS

The authors would like to thank eSpec Books publishers Danielle Ackley-McPhail, Mike McPhail, and Greg Schauer for rescuing this trilogy, republishing *Issue in Doubt* and *In All Directions*, and publishing this final book.

Thanks also to Dayton Ward—Marine and author extraordinaire—for casting a watchful eye over the manuscript.

The Prairie Palace, Omaha,
Douglas County, Federal Zone,
North American Union

DOCTOR JULIA GAUJOT SAT, WAITING AND NERVOUS, OUTSIDE THE OFFICE OF THE NORTH American Union President. While Gaujot had done a significant amount of work for the government, from internships while at graduate school all the way to various government projects on other worlds, she'd never actually been to the Federal Zone before. A New Yorker born and bred, she spent most of her time these days either in the lab at Stony Brook University or on other worlds studying the ruins and fossils of alien civilizations.

"You okay?" the tall, wiry dark-skinned man sitting next to her asked.

Gaujot shook her head. "Not really. I mean, I'm having a meeting with the *president*. It's a very strange ending to a very strange month."

"I getcha." He held out a hand. "Doctor Travis Atkins."

"Doctor Julia Gaujot." She returned the handshake.

Gaujot and Atkins were seated on a bench opposite a large desk occupied by a small woman. That woman touched her ear, then said, "Yes, Sir." She looked over at the two doctors. "The president will be ready for you shortly."

"Um, okay," Gaujot said nervously.

Atkins smiled. "Deadly, t'anks."

The double doors to the Round Office opened and an unfamiliar face poked out between the doors. This was probably the Secretary of War, Richmond P. Hobson. Gaujot had been dealing exclusively with Hobson's chief of staff, Joseph Gion, up until today.

"Doctor Gaujot, Doctor Atkins, I'm Secretary Hobson," he said, confirming his identity, "come in please."

They both rose and followed Hobson into a place that was previously seen by Gaujot only on vid screens.

While the president's desk was on the far side of the room, it remained unoccupied at present, with several people seated nearby around a rectangular table.

One of the curved walls of the room had a large screen, which included several images that Gaujot recognized, as she had forwarded them to the Prairie Palace before she left Stony Brook.

At the table itself sat seven people. On one side were four men in uniform. One woman and one man in suits faced them. Hobson moved to sit next to the man. At the foot of the table stood two empty chairs, which were obviously meant for Atkins and Gaujot.

At the head, of course, was President Albert Leopold Mills, who stood up as they entered.

Everyone around the table did likewise.

"Mr. President," Hobson said, "this is Doctor Julie Gaujot of Stony Brook University in New York and Doctor Travis Atkins of Memorial University in St. John's."

Gaujot cast her gaze downward, frightened to look the president in the eye, equally frightened to correct Hobson's mispronunciation of her family name. He'd been saying "GAW-jot" when it was actually pronounced "GOW-joh." But she'd already heard every conceivable pronunciation of her family name over the course of her life and had grown weary of correcting it in any event. And she certainly wasn't going to correct one of the most powerful people on the planet.

"Welcome to the Prairie Palace, Doctors," Mills said with the congenial smile that Gaujot knew full well from the man's presidential addresses.

"Thank you, Sir," Gaujot muttered.

"T'anks," Atkins said more loudly, with a broad smile. "It's an honor to be here."

Hobson then performed the introductions, starting with the three military men. "This is Admiral Ira Clinton Welborn, Chairman of the Joint Chiefs of Staff, General John C. Robinson, the Army Chief of Staff, General Ralph Talbot, Commandant of the Marine Corps."

All three nodded to the two doctors. Gaujot gave a quick nod back, while Atkins's smile grew even broader.

To the civilian side of the table, Hobson said, "Jose Nisperos, the President's Chief of Staff, and Secretary of State Mary Walker. I, of course, am Secretary of War Richmond Hobson."

Unlike the others, Hobson put out a hand, and first Gaujot, then Atkins shook it.

Mills took his seat, and then everyone else did likewise. Hobson took the seat next to Walker. Gaujot hesitated before taking the seat next to Atkins at the foot of the table.

"You haven't met Secretary Hobson before?" Mills asked Gaujot. There was an undertone of menace to the president's voice, as though he'd been under the impression that Hobson had been the one to bring these two in on the Duster problem.

"No, Sir," Gaujot said, "I've only spoken to the secretary's chief of staff, Mr. Gion?"

Seemingly satisfied, Mills nodded. "Of course. Now I know that Mr. Hobson's office has told you all of this already, and I know that you signed non-disclosure agreements, but I'm going to repeat what you probably know from both of those—the work you have done on our behalf is classified at the highest level. You are to speak to no one of any of this outside this room, and all reports that you have made and will make will remain encrypted and eyes-only. Is that understood?"

"Yes, Sir," Atkins said quickly, his smile having modulated into a more serious expression.

Gaujot simply nodded.

"Good. Now, I understand, Doctor Gaujot, that you are a xenobiologist and that you have been studying the alien bodies that were sent back from Troy?"

"Yes, Sir," Gaujot said.

"These lovely pictures on my wall are from your analyses, yes?"

Again, Gaujot said, "Yes, Sir."

The screen on the wall showed one of the aliens who had invaded Troy. The so-called "Dusters" had heads that were angled down and forward, with long jaws filled with sharp teeth, sitting atop long, sinuous necks. At a resting position, the aliens' torsos tended to run parallel to the ground, bent at the neck above and the hips below, a crest of feathers running from the top of the head down to the hips. Their legs were thick and ended in taloned feet, knees bending backward.

"What is it you have to tell us about our enemy, Doctor?"

"It's about how they reproduce, Sir." Gaujot blew out a breath and started the speech she'd been mentally rehearsing since she got on the plane that took her from Long Island to Omaha this morning. "Based on the tests we've run and the autopsies we've performed on the alien bodies, we have come to the preliminary conclusion that they are hermaphrodites and that they reproduce asexually."

Welborn leaned forward. "You're saying they don't mate?"

"Yes, Sir, I am saying that. They appear to be fertile instantly and can produce a plenitude of eggs. Each of the bodies had blastocysts developing, and one had an egg nearly complete."

"How many eggs in a plenitude, exactly?" Walker asked.

"It's impossible to know without observing a living specimen in their native habitat. I don't suppose any of the reports from Troy have mentioned eggs?"

Welborn shook his head. "Negative, but the Marines and soldiers on the ground haven't been looking for that in particular—nor, I might add, is there any reason for them to do so now."

"Agreed, Sir, my apologies," Gaujot said quickly, "I was merely asking in the hopes of confirmation."

"So your theory," Hobson said, "is that they reproduce at will?"

"It's more of a hypothesis than a theory, Mr. Secretary, given how little data we have to go on. But I think it's a viable one. It also indicates a massive population, one far greater than humans can create, especially since they're also tool users and creators of technology, which will enable them to enhance that reproductive process. In fact, one of the corpses had a device implanted inside it that seems designed to inject hormones into the body. I saw no such device on any other alien, which leads me to think that this particular being had a need for artificial medical enhancement in order to reproduce."

"I see," Mills said. "Thank you, Doctor. There's an old saying that says you should know your enemy, and you've given us more of that knowledge. The NAU appreciates your efforts."

"Those efforts are still ongoing, Sir," Gaujot said.

The President frowned, and Gaujot belatedly realized that his words were a subtle way of saying she was done talking now.

"My apologies, Sir," she said quickly, "I merely wished to state that we will know more as time goes on."

"Of course, Doctor." Mills gave those three words a new undercurrent of menace. "Now then, Doctor Atkins, you're one of our foremost experts in xenopsychology, and I'm told you have a report based on Doctor Gaujot's findings."

"Yessir," Atkins said. "Based on both the doctor's findings and on the reports we've gotten back from Troy about the enemy tactics."

Welborn bridled. "Are you an expert on military tactics, Doctor Atkins?"

He grinned again. "Expert? No, but I did serve in the NAU Navy for a six-year bit. Growin' up in Newfoundland, bein' on the water was always a part'a my life." Atkins cleared his throat, as his Newfie accent had gotten thicker with that last sentence.

Welborn was placated by knowing that Atkins had served. "Carry on."

"One common theme in the reports we've gotten so far is that the Dusters have been attacking without any regard to their personal safety. They've sacrificed hundreds in order to achieve their goals in combat. And I think that Doctor Gaujot's hypothesis indicates a cultural bias. See, us humans, we try to live. Even sailors, soldiers, airmen, and Marines do their best to stay alive. We're willin' to sacrifice ourselves if we have to, but it's a last resort for us, even people who're servin'.

"I don't think that's the case for the Dusters. They don't have the same self-preservation instinct that we got. An' I think that the fact that they breed like bunnies is part of it. They're not the type to care much about individual lives, long as the greater good's achieved."

Nisperos folded his hands on the table. "So what you're saying is that the Dusters have a much different notion of acceptable losses in terms of casualties than we do?"

"Pretty much, b'y. Uhm, Sir," he added quickly. "The Dusters'll die in the hundreds, even thousands, just to achieve an objective. Their attitude is prob'ly that they can just make a whole lot more."

"Obviously," Nisperos said slowly, "this is not a tactic that we can adapt. And it does go some way toward explaining how the other seventeen races we've found got wiped out by these guys."

"Perhaps, Jose," Welborn said, "but they also never had to face the NAU Navy, Army, and Marines before. We've held our own against them, and even they can't reproduce forever."

"For all we know," Gaujot said, "they have people selected specifically for breeding back on their homeworld to birth more soldiers. Without any idea of their population—"

Hobson held up a hand. "It doesn't matter. This is useful information, but I don't see how it changes anything. Hell, it's information that the people on site already have. We know how they fight—we just have to fight back."

"They'll know they were in a fight, that's for damn sure," Welborn said.

Mills stood up, and so did everyone else a second later. "Doctor Atkins, Doctor Gaujot, thank you both."

"It's our honor, Mr. President," Gaujot said quietly, while Atkins just smiled.

Hobson led the two of them to the door and then left them in the care of the president's secretary.

Mills sat back down, and everyone else took their seats. Hobson did so once he was sure that the two scientists were taken care of.

"Is there any other business?" Mills asked the question in a manner that indicated that he didn't want there to be any other business.

Which explained why Admiral Welborn sounded pained when he replied with: "I'm sorry to say there is, Mr. President. I've got a reporter from the Omaha World-Herald cooling her heels in my office."

The president sighed. "Which one?"

"Florence Groberg."

Another sigh, but it was less resigned. "That's something. She generally knows her ass from her elbow. Didn't she serve?"

Welborn nodded. "Yes, Mr. President, she captained a SEAL boat for two tours before she took her honorable discharge and became a reporter. She's always been savvy to the military POV, which puts her one up on most World-Herald word jockeys."

That impressed Mills. She may not have been a SEAL, but she still would have had to go through the training to qualify to run a boat for the SEALs.

Which was good, because the World-Herald was mostly a pain in his ass. He had always respected the paper—which had become the premier source for political reporting ever since the NAU formed and established its capital in Omaha—right up until he was elected.

Welborn said, "Unfortunately, she knows everything."

"We have a leak?" Nisperos asked. The chief of staff sounded more than a little concerned.

Sounding much less concerned, Welborn replied, "I'd say we've got several. Groberg's got a *lot* of good sources."

"Honestly," Walker said, "I'm stunned we've kept a lid on for this long. An operation the size of this is incredibly difficult to keep secret, especially out in space. I figured if it did get out, it would be from some kid with a telescope."

Mills gave the secretary of state a derisive look, but then General Talbot said, "She's right. There's no cover out in space—it's why we call it 'space.' And we had to take the most direct route to the wormhole terminus, and you *know* there are civilians out there who look at that route regularly from their back yards. Even a cheap store-bought telescope might see something, and most of these hobbyists have the fancy ones. We could hardly stop them. We were very lucky that it didn't leak that way."

"Is she running the story?" Hobson asked.

"She's playing her cards pretty close to the vest," Welborn said. "I got called into this meeting before we could really get into it. She's a smart cookie. I'm willing to bet dollars to donuts that she's gonna make a very compelling constitutional argument as to why she should run the story."

With another sigh, Mills asked, "I don't suppose we can muzzle her?"

Nisperos shook his head. "Not legally. And truly, not sensibly, either. All we'll do is make an enemy of one of the best and friendliest reporters who cover the Prairie Palace beat. There's no upside, and if Groberg has the story now, the lesser reporters will have it in three or four days, and they *won't* be considerate enough to check in with Admiral Welborn first."

Walker nodded in agreement. "We should get out in front of this. Do a press conference, tell the public everything we can."

Talbot said, "We knew this day was going to come eventually, and Secretary Walker is right, it'll be disastrous if the press tells the public before we do."

"Agreed." Mills turned to Welborn. "Admiral, give her whatever she needs to hold off on the story until after that press conference."

"Yes, Mr. President."

"I assume our esteemed communications director and press secretary have a strategy?" he asked, referring to, respectively, David Bellavia and Clinton Romesha.

"David's had a speech ready for a month now," Nisperos said. "He's been updating it, but it's ready to go, just needs your okay to lock it. And Clint can have the press room ready to go in a matter of minutes."

"Good. Have David send me the speech, and we'll do the press conference first thing tomorrow."

"Mr. President," Walker said hesitantly.

"Yes, Mary?"

"We should inform the families of the citizens of Troy tonight. They shouldn't find out their loved ones are dead from a press conference."

Mills nodded. "Agreed. Let's get it done."

Admiral Welborn entered his office to see the tall, athletic form of Florence Groberg. She may not have been with the SEALs any longer, but she still looked like she kept herself in shape. Welborn respected that—most journalists lived sedentary lives and were significantly rounder around the middle by the time they reached Groberg's age.

She was staring at the east wall of Welborn's office, covered with images of warships from the eighteenth century forward. The wall included drawings, photographs, lithographs, paintings, and holograms from colonial frigates to the latest spaceships and everything in between.

At present, Groberg was studying a black-and-white photograph of two submarine chasers from the early twentieth century.

"SC-43 and SC-44," she said. "Commissioned during the war to end all wars, and then used extensively in the war after that one."

Welborn snorted. He also was not that impressed. The boats were clearly labeled with their designations in large white characters, and the quality of the photograph indicated that it was the early twentieth century.

Groberg went on. "Submarine chasers, designed to go after German U-boats in both wars, and Japanese ones, too, in the latter war. Based on British designs, but significantly improved on them." She finally turned to face Welborn. "They didn't look like much, certainly not something that could take on a behemoth like a German sub, but they were fast, and they were efficient, and they got the job done."

Now Welborn was impressed—both with her knowledge of military history and her not-so-subtle metaphor. "Sorry to keep you waiting, Ms. Groberg. Have a seat."

Even as Groberg sat back down in the guest chair, Welborn sat in the plush leather chair behind his large desk.

"So, before you were called away, you were about to give me the national security speech, right?" Groberg said with a grin.

"You do understand that this mission is classified, yes?"

"The Semi-Autonomous World of Troy has been wiped out by an alien invasion force, and the NAU has responded with a massive tactical response the likes of which has not been seen since SC-43 and SC-44 up there were decommissioned." Groberg waved a hand at the photograph she'd been admiring. "Do the families of the people killed even know what has happened?"

"It's being dealt with," Welborn said neutrally.

Groberg's face hardened. "That would be no, then."

"I can't divulge—"

"Admiral, before you dig yourself deeper, I've spoken to several relatives of people who live on Troy—don't worry, I didn't give anything away. I spoke to them on the pretense of a story about having family living on other worlds. Every single one of them thinks their family member is alive and well and living on Troy. Now I understand why you kept a lid on this to start—you didn't know what was going on, and you didn't want to tell people that a colony world was wiped out without knowing who or what did it.

"But we're past the point where that even makes sense anymore. I know we've engaged an alien species on Troy and that the fighting has been brutal. And I know how easy it is to fall into the cycle of secrecy."

"Excuse me?" Welborn said angrily, not liking the way the conversation was going.

"It starts with keeping it a secret because we don't know anything and don't want people to speculate. But that feeds on itself, and you keep it a secret because you've already kept mum about it so long and people will ask why you've kept it quiet, and on and on and on. It has to stop sometime."

"Can the palaver, Ms. Groberg, and kindly tell me what you want in exchange for sitting on this story until the president's press conference tomorrow morning."

Groberg grinned. "Oh, so there will be a press conference?"

"Yes. And the families will be notified before that, rest assured. So—what do you want?"

"Ten minutes with the president."

Welborn snorted. "No chance. I can give you the first question tomorrow morning, and I'll even talk on the record about the operation after the conference, but—"

"I'll take both those things, but I still want ten minutes with the president. I'll send my questions ahead of time, and you'll have full veto power over them, but this is not negotiable. If my editor knows I sat on this for a week—"

"You've had it for a *week*?" Welborn sputtered.

"Bits of it—it didn't come completely together until yesterday, and I spent last night drinking a significant amount of bourbon while trying to figure out whether or not to run it or come to you first."

For the first time since he came into the office, Welborn smiled. "Always admired the magical properties of a good glass of bourbon."

Groberg snorted. "Five good glasses, but yes. In either case, the only way I keep my job after not telling my boss about this is if I get an exclusive with President Mills. So that's my price, and it's *not* negotiable."

Welborn sighed. The president *did* say to give her whatever she needed. He stood up and held out a hand. "Done."

Groberg also rose and returned the handshake. "Excellent." Her face softened. "I understand that you lost Task Force 7. I'm sorry."

"Thank you, but you can rest assured that all our losses will be avenged. Troy will be ours again, you can count on that."

Admiral's Bridge, Battleship NAUS Durango,
in geosync orbit around Semi-Autonomous World Troy

REAR ADMIRAL JAMES AVERY, COMMANDER OF THE NORTH AMERICAN UNION NAVY'S
Task Force 8, studied the big board, which covered most of the bridge's
forward bulkhead and displayed all the elements on both sides. He watched
the tiny flecks that indicated the SF 6 Meteor space-fighters as they
launched from the carrier *Rear Admiral Norman Scott*, formed up, then
headed for their targets: the leading ships of the approaching alien fleet,
forty enemy vessels to TF 8's eight warships.

When the Meteors were a third of the way to the enemy, Avery said,
"Laser batteries, fire on my mark."

Avery didn't see Captain Harry M.P. Huse standing behind him as he
replied, "Laser batteries, stand by." The admiral was completely focused on
the tactical display on the big board.

Lieutenant Commander George F. Davis spoke sotto voce into his
headset, transmitting Avery's orders to the three destroyers in TF 8.

"Laser batteries standing by," said the voice of Chief Petty Officer Henry
Finkenbiner.

When the Meteors were halfway to their destination, Avery said, simply,
"Fire."

"Laser batteries, fire," Huse said much louder, enough to echo off the
bulkheads.

Finkenbiner said, "Laser batteries firing."

Beams of coherent light burst forth from the *Durango*. A moment later, TF 8's three destroyers fired their lasers as well, carrying out the same fire order, relayed by Davis.

Lasers lanced out from the second rank of the enemy fleet, the alien equivalent of battleships and cruisers.

Avery ordered his three frigates, stationed above and to the left of the enemy, to attack the second rank.

TF 8 achieved several hits on the bogeys, which appeared on the board as glowing red splotches.

Avery looked on stoically as enemy lasers converged on the destroyer *First Lieutenant George H. Cannon*, and she erupted, her spine split through and her missile magazine exploded. Debris scattered everywhere.

Multiple laser hits struck the Durango's hull. Horns sounded, signaling damage control teams into action.

The Scott's four Meteor squadrons closed to range and opened fire on the leading rank of alien warships, their version of frigates and destroyers.

The enemy fleet opened fire on the fighters, killing many of them. The only evident damage the Meteors had done was one warship in the leading rank lost weight.

Another of TF 8's destroyers was killed, as was one of the frigates.

"Sir," Davis said, "the bogey fleet seems to be accelerating."

The fast attack carrier Rear Admiral Isaac C. Kidd,
approaching the flank of the alien fleet

"This shouldn't be any more difficult than when we acted as a screen for ARG 17," Captain John P. Cromwell, the *Kidd's* Commander Air Group, said at the end of his mission briefing. "Now get out there and kick some alien ass. Catfish first, followed by Lionfish."

He strode from the briefing room, trying very hard not to think about how few of his pilots remained after the fight to save Amphibious Ready Group 17. They had what they had, and they would fight to the end, regardless.

"Catfish, let's go!" Lieutenant Adolphus Staton, the commander of VSF 114 Catfish squadron snapped. He led his pilots to the launch bay. Only twelve of the squadron's original sixteen pilots remained, and only ten of them had usable fighter craft.

In the launch bay, the pilots, heading out on what they feared might be a suicide mission, quickly ran pre-flight checks on their SF 6 Meteors and mounted up. By the time the Meteors of VSF 114 began trundling to the launch tube, the remaining pilots of VSF 218 Lionfish were engaged in their pre-flights.

In minutes the two truncated squadrons were linked together in echelon left formation, with Catfish in the lead. They blasted toward the flank of the rear rank of alien warcraft.

"They're dropping back," Lieutenant Abraham DeSomer, Lionfish's commander, said into the joint squadron freq.

"Stand by for new vector," Staton replied, his fingers dancing over his tac-comp's controls. In seconds, he transmitted a course adjustment to the two dozen Meteors, putting them on a firing line for the closest ships in the enemy's rear rank. He watched his tactical display as the two squadrons closed on their targets.

"On my mark," he said when the comp showed the space closing to effective range, "Lionfish, lead the nearer ship with Beanbags. Catfish, fire Zappers at the second."

He began a countdown.

"Ten."

Staton found his mind going back to when he first signed up.

"Nine."

In particular, he remembered something Sergeant Frank Fratanellico told him during training.

"Eight."

"You're not you anymore," Sergeant Fratanellico had said back then.

"Seven."

"Once you climb into the cockpit, you're not Adolphus Staton, you're the fighter."

"Six."

"You're the brain, and the fighter's the body that does what you tell it to do."

"Five."

Fratanellico had pointed a thick finger right at Staton's face at the next part.

"Four."

"You'll know you're a *real* pilot the moment you and the fighter react as fast as your body does to your brain's commands."

"Three."

Staton had found that Fratanellico was right—by the time he had become CAG, the Meteor and he were in perfect sync.

"Two."

He hoped that was enough today against the Dusters.

"One. *Mark!*"

Staton's Meteor lurched when a missile shot out from its bay on its underside. He effortlessly keyed in commands for his tac-comp to calculate a vector to a different target, and the Meteor responded instantly, just like Sergeant Fratanellico said it would.

A moment later, glittering puffs appeared in front of the nearest alien ship. The vessel staggered and began tumbling when it slammed into the sand and gravel the Beanbags scattered in its path. The particulates blocked visual and also got into the machinery, causing the Dusters' craft to seize up and crash. Seconds later, another ship shuddered and spun out of formation when the Zappers from Lionfish squadron blasted out powerful bursts of electromagnetic energy, frying its electronics.

"Two down," Staton murmured to himself. "Twenty to go?" He thought the starships next in line, which appeared to be dropping into planetfall trajectories, must be transports.

He also knew the math was never going to work here. The air group could take down some of the Duster ships, but a mess of them were going to get through to land on Troy.

But they kept fighting. Something else Fratanellico had said back then: "You don't stop fighting until ten minutes after you're dead. And maybe not even then."

Admiral's Bridge, NAUS Durango

Rear Admiral Avery, watching his big board, saw the trailing ranks of alien ships falling back and heading planetward, and came to the same conclusion as Staton about the math not working.

"Comm," he said to Lieutenant Commander Davis, "notify Commander, NAU Forces, Troy that twenty or more enemy transports are preparing to make planetfall."

"Notify Commander, NAU Forces, Troy that twenty or more enemy transports are preparing to make planetfall, aye," Davis said, and made the call.

Headquarters, North American Union Forces,
near Millerton, Shapland
Semi-Autonomous World Troy

"Sir."

Lieutenant General Harold Bauer, commander of the 1st Marine Combat Force and acting commander of NAU Forces, Troy, looked away from the display he was studying of the battle going on in orbit.

"Yes, Bill?" he asked, seeing his aide, Captain William Upshur, standing in the doorway of his office.

"A message from orbit, Sir." When Bauer nodded, Upshur continued. "The rear echelons of the Duster fleet have dropped into planetfall orbits. It appears that half of them are headed for Shapland, and the rest to Eastern Shapland."

"Get my major element commanders on conference."

"Aye aye, Sir." Upshur about-faced and went to do his commander's bidding.

In moments, images of the commanding generals of the 1st Marine Division, the 2nd Marine Air Wing, the Army's 9th Infantry Division, and the independent commands under NAUF-T came up on Bauer's display.

"Gentlemen," Bauer said brusquely, "the moment is upon us. Twenty-odd Duster ships are dropping into planetfall orbit. We should expect them to begin launching landing craft at any time. Make sure you are linked into the Navy's tracking feed so you can follow the shuttles' movements once they launch, and when they make planetfall.

"One-oh-fourth Arty, as soon as the ships come into your laser batteries' range, start taking them out. Marine artillery, kill the landing craft with your lasers.

"Force Recon, I want eyeballs on the lead Duster elements.

"Second Marine Air Wing, get Kestrels aloft, ready to strike targets of opportunity as identified by NavInt and FR eyes.

"Everybody, stand by to kick some Duster ass. Bauer out."

Headquarters, 1st Marine Division,
near Jordan, Eastern Shapland

Major General Hugh Purvis turned from the blanked display of the just-ended conference call to look at his staff and major subordinate commanders. Before the call with Bauer, they had either been watching the tactical display from space coming in or just looking up into the sky. There had been flashes and blossoms of actinic light speckling and freckling the night sky over the past few hours as TF 8 and the alien warships went at it. It might have made an impressive display under better circumstances.

"Gentlemen," Purvis said, "if any of you had any residual uncertainty, now you know what the light show we've been admiring was all about. The fight is about to pass to us."

His gaze fixed on First Lieutenant John A. Hughes, commander of the first section of the Force Recon platoon.

"Go find 'em, Lieutenant."

"Aye aye, *Sir*," Hughes said, and turned to gather his Marines.

Nobody asked why Force Recon had to go find the Dusters when Navy intelligence was watching them from orbit. They all understood that a Marine with his boots on the ground might see and understand details that the Navy eye-in-the-sky might miss. Besides, the Navy had its own fight above, and comm with planetside could be broken.

Firebase Westermark, Eastern Shapland

Corporal Denise Conlan sat tensely at the controls for the long-range laser batteries that had been emplaced in Eastern Shapland.

Next to her, Corporal Horace Carswell regarded the scanners, waiting for the Dusters to come into range.

The pair of them had trained together and worked together for several months now, and they had achieved an impressive reputation for accuracy and speed. The rest of the unit called them "C&C," though the brass objected to the nickname's similarity to the abbreviation for Command and Control.

The brass, typically, missed the point. The nickname stuck *because* of the homonym, not despite it.

"Think the Marines'll be able to take them out?" Carswell asked Conlan.

"They can try," Conlan said. "But those wussy-ass guns they're firing couldn't light a firecracker, much less dust a Duster. Don't worry, though, when those jarheads screw the pooch, we'll be there to show 'em how it's done."

Carswell smiled. "Damn right."

Then the smile fell as his scanners started to beep several alarms. "Bogeys coming in!"

The voice of Marine Sergeant William Doolen sounded over both of C&C's comms. "Preparing to fire batteries. We got these—"

Doolen cut himself off, and Carswell saw why immediately: the Dusters' course was taking them a hundred klicks from Eastern Shapland, completely out of the batteries' range.

"No firing solution," Doolen said quickly, "I say again, Marines have no firing solution."

Carswell grinned. "Wussy-ass is right. Their lasers'll be flashlights by the time they reach the bad guys."

"Line 'em up," Conlan said. "Let's show them how we do things in the Army."

"Acquiring target now," Carswell said with a grin.

Then, for the second time in five minutes, he lost his grin. "Enemy changing course! Dammit! Out of range!"

"Sonofabitch!"

Doolen's voice came over the comms. "Looks like the Dusters made monkeys out of all of us."

Conlan and Carswell watched as the Dusters landed well out of everyone's range.

"What the hell're they planning?" Carswell asked.

"Staying out of range of our batteries, forcing us to engage them on the ground. I guess they figure they have a better shot at hand-to-hand, even after moving on dirt for an hour to get to where the fight is instead of just landing right here."

"Well, we would've taken them out if they landed closer."

"Exactly. Probably cost 'em some casualties, and then there's the effort of hauling ass all the way here from where they're landing."

Carswell frowned. "You think it's a smart strategy, Corporal?"

Shrugging, Conlan said, "The only smart strategy is the one that works. And we ain't gonna find that out until it's all over."

Firebase Gasson,
near Millerton, Shapland,
Semi-Autonomous World Troy

SECOND LIEUTENANT THEODORE W. GREIG AND SERGEANT FIRST CLASS ALEXANDER M. Quinn, commander and platoon sergeant of second platoon, Alpha Company, First of the Seventh Mounted Infantry, left the command bunker and headed for an open area in the firebase. First Lieutenant Archie Miller of the Ninth Mobile Intel Company trailed them.

"Second platoon, gather around," Quinn shouted.

In moments, the forty men of the second were grouped in front of their commander and sergeant.

"Troops," Greig began, "we're about to begin earning our pay—again. It looks like Duster troop ships are shortly going to drop landing craft near the Marines on Eastern Shapland. It also appears that another flotilla of troop ships will head toward us. Very shortly," he waved a hand toward the laser in the center of the firebase, "the arty will be getting ready. Maybe they can kill some of the ships before they drop their landing craft on us. Certainly, they can kill some of the landing craft before they land their troops. We need to be ready to fight them and defeat them once they land and we are in the thick of things. We fought them before, and we beat their asses when we did. We'll do it again.

"But!" He paused and gave his men a hard look. "That doesn't mean it's going to be easy. Don't think that these Dusters don't know what's already happened here. Don't think that, because they're new, they're dumb. There's a damn good chance they learned from the mistakes made by the ones we already beat. We have to be ready in case this new alien army uses different, less suicidal tactics." He took a deep breath. "We know they can kill us. That's how our firebases got their names."

Several of the troops lowered their heads. Gasson, Cart, and Garrett were all soldiers from Alpha Troop who had been killed by the Dusters.

Greig continued: "Once the Dusters make planetfall, I'm sure our friends in Mobile Intel will let us know where they're coming from, and what their strength is." That last was said with a glance at Miller.

In response, Miller gave the platoon a confident thumb's up.

"In the meanwhile, squad leaders see the platoon sergeant. He'll make sure your squads have enough ammunition to defeat a Duster battalion."

Someone in the platoon muttered loudly enough for everyone to hear, "One platoon against a battalion? Mamas, don't let your sons grow up to be soldiers." At least a few soldiers developed quick coughing fits to cover their laughter.

Greig studiously ignored it, which stopped even the coughing. He turned to Quinn. "Sergeant, the platoon is yours."

"Yes, Sir." Quinn faced him and saluted. Greig returned the salute and headed back to the command bunker.

"All right," Quinn said as soon as the officer was far enough away, "squad leaders, check your men's ammo and report back to me how much they have so I can get you up to snuff. Dismissed."

Even as he said the words, he thought, *Enough ammo to defeat a battalion? If we have to fight that many, we won't live long enough to use it all.*

The squad leaders took their soldiers to their bunkers to inspect their ammunition supplies, and returned with their reports in just a few minutes.

"First squad has fifteen thousand rounds," Staff Sergeant Albert O'Connor said.

Quinn grimaced. If everybody had a similar amount of ammunition, they didn't have nearly enough to beat off a battalion—even if the new Dusters used the same suicidal tactics as the ones already on Troy used.

Staff Sergeant Alphonso Lunt reported, "Two has fourteen-five." He didn't look any happier than O'Connor did.

"Third's got a bit more than fifteen," Staff Sergeant Charles Breyer said. He looked and sounded more stoic than the other two, but Quinn figured he was just as displeased.

Staff Sergeant Sydney Gumpertz, the machine gun squad leader, muttered, "Guns never have enough."

Quinn looked at the three rifle squad leaders. "Sounds like some of your boys have been hoarding. I'll try to get you up to twenty each. Twenty-five if I can. As for you," he looked at Gumpertz, "that tells me squat about how much you *do* have. Try again."

Gumpertz shrugged. "At rapid-fire, we can keep going for not much more than twenty minutes. A couple of hours at slow-fire. But the way those bastards jink and jive, we need rapid-fire most of the time. Oh, and extra barrels, 'cause we'll be melting them like butter if we have to shoot that much that fast."

"You're right, you don't have enough. If we go up against a battalion, we'll be fighting all day, all night, and maybe into the next day." *If we live that long.* He repressed a shiver. "What about grenades?"

Each staff sergeant reported their supply, which wound up to an average of six per soldier.

Quinn nodded. "I'll double that. Now, I need a work detail to go with me to pick up the ammo. Squad leaders, assign one man each. I'll tell the LT what we need, and see about getting a truck. Anything else?"

Gumpertz raised a hand. "Yeah, how do we get outta this chicken outfit?"

Several soldiers chuckled, but Quinn's face hardened. "Feet first. Anything else that isn't nonsense?"

The chucklers clammed up, and everyone else remained quiet. "Good. Dismissed."

Inside the Command Bunker,
Firebase Gasson

Captain Patricia H. Pentzer, commander of fourth platoon, H Company, 1045 Artillery Battalion (Laser), watched the reports coming in from her battalion headquarters and the HQ of First of the Seventh with keen attention. She wanted to know the moment the alien fleet started dropping landing shuttles.

Across the way, Quinn was telling Grieg what he needed.

"How much do we have in the platoon's ammo bunker?" Greig asked. "Just in case they won't give us as much as we ask for."

"We're down to seventy-five thousand rifle rounds and the same number for the guns, along with a couple hundred grenades."

"'Down'?" Greig frowned.

Quinn nodded. "I was concerned that some of the troops were hoarding. Some of them probably raided the ammo bunker to beef up what they had. That seventy-five is about twenty-five percent less than what we had on my last inspection."

Pentzer snorted. Soldiers were *always* sneaking off with extra ammo, like a junkie going for a fix. She knew because she'd done it plenty in her time in service.

"All right, Sergeant," Greig said. "I'll also get you that truck."

"Thank you, Sir."

"Dismissed."

Quinn retreated from the command bunker to summon the M117 Growler armored personnel carriers.

Greig walked over to where Pentzer was watching the display.

"They're coming," she said.

One hour later

The first shuttle craft started dropping in the area of the Marines on Eastern Shapland. In another moment, it became evident that the Dusters were dropping half of their forces there, and sending the rest to Shapland—and Pentzer's platoon.

"Fourth platoon, man guns!" Pentzer cried as she raced out of the bunker. Greig and Quinn were right behind her, calling for second platoon.

First Sergeant James Llewellyn P. Norton, the H Battery platoon's top dog, stepped outside the bunker and bellowed the same command as he dashed to a nearby Major Mite quarter-ton truck.

Throughout the firebase, artillerymen stopped whatever they were doing and scrambled to their guns.

"Man guns, man guns, man guns!" Pentzer snapped into her comm on the platoon freq.

"Where to, Top?" Corporal Joseph Fisher asked as he hopped into the Major Mite.

"Cart first, then Garrett," Norton answered as he climbed in and grabbed the dash-bar—he knew how manically Fisher drove when he was in a hurry. The way the platoon commander and top sergeant had shouted their orders, the driver knew he had to go fast.

"Cart, then Garrett," Fisher repeated. "On the way!"

The small truck lurched as he slammed the accelerator, the vehicle raised a rooster tail of dust and debris as it headed out the gate and turned right to Firebase Cart, a kilometer distant.

When they arrived, they found the ten-strong laser crew already in place, and the gun captain, First Lieutenant William H. Newman, on his comm being briefed by Pentzer. Norton gave the laser and its crew a quick inspection with Master Sergeant David Ayers, the assistant gun captain. Satisfied that all was in readiness, he gave Newman a quick glance to determine that the gun captain was still being briefed, then climbed back into the Major Mite and grabbed hold.

Fisher spun out, heading for Garrett.

There, they found First Lieutenant Abram P. Haring just finished with Pentzer's briefing.

Norton snapped a quick salute. "Everything ready, Mr. Haring?"

"As ready as we can be, Top," Haring said. He turned to his assistant, Master Sergeant Henry Fox. "Right, Sergeant?"

"You got it," Fox replied. "All we need is targets."

"You'll have targets soon enough," Norton said. He looked toward the eastern horizon, half expecting to see Duster troop ships appearing. He accompanied Haring and Fox in an inspection of the laser and its crew. All was ready.

"Home, James," Norton said when he was again seated in the small truck.

"Sure thing, Boss," Fisher replied with a wide grin. He drove slightly more sedately this time.

Captain Pentzer was back in the bunker, giving fire directions to her guns when they returned. Before ducking in, Norton looked toward the eastern horizon, where he could see the glints of reflected sunlight off enemy spacecraft as they moved into view. The screech of tortured air jabbed at his ears, and he saw a spear of coherent air lance toward the troop ships, joined by spears from the guns at Cart and Garrett. A ragged cheer raised inside Gasson from the soldiers who saw the targeted spacecraft spout atmosphere and begin to lose weight. More cheers rose when small dots of reflected light began dropping off the ship.

Norton didn't cheer; he knew that the smaller dots were probably landing craft being launched from the wounded troop ship. He doubted that they were going to make planetfall at the same place as the rest of the landing force. The soldiers were going to be facing the enemy from two directions.

Camp Jimmie E. Howard,
Home of 1st Section, 1st Force Recon Platoon
Near Jordan, Eastern Shapland

"ALL RIGHT, MARINES," FIRST LIEUTENANT JOHN A. HUGHES SAID AT THE END OF HIS briefing, "you know what to do. Now do it!"

The twenty Marines of the section roared as one: "*Oo-rah, Force Recon!*"

"On me," Gunnery Sergeant Ernest Janson ordered as Hughes marched toward the section's command bunker.

The Force Recon Marines gathered around their top NCO. "You've got your maps, your comms, water and rations, and weapons. Squad leaders, you have your Squad Pod assignments. Now get out there, find 'em and fix 'em so air can fuck 'em before they get here. Anybody got any dumb questions?"

Nobody asked why Gunny Janson said air instead of Navy gunfire—they all knew Marine air would probably have to lay the first fire on the alien enemy because the Navy had its own battle in space and might not be able to launch a planetside bombardment. Nobody asked why Hughes and Janson weren't going, either—they all knew that an officer or senior NCO on patrol with an FR squad would more likely than not be in the way. There weren't any other questions, dumb or otherwise.

"Squad leaders, go to it." Janson came to attention and popped a sharp salute at the men heading into enemy territory.

"First squad, with me!" Staff Sergeant J. Henry Denig shouted, and began moving to the right-most of the four Squad Pods that sat waiting a hundred meters distant. His four men followed briskly.

"Two, let's go!" called Staff Sergeant Andrew Miller, and led his men at a trot to the next Squad Pod in line.

"Third squad, let's beat them!" Staff Sergeant William Bordelon shouted, and began sprinting.

"Ho-ho, Four, go!" Sergeant Joseph Julian roared, and sprinted at the head of his squad, trying to get ahead of the others.

In a minute, the twenty Marines were in their Squad Pods, small anti-grav vehicles capable of flying a Force Recon squad or half an infantry squad in nape-of-the-earth flying, and the vehicles' ramps were closing in preparation for launch.

In Sierra Papa One, Denig pulled out his rolled-up map, snapped it to rigidity, and plugged it into the pod's navigation comp. "Count off," he ordered his men.

Behind him, Sergeant Edward Walker barked, "One, tucked in, J. Henry."

Almost everyone in the section called the staff sergeant "J. Henry." It dated back to Denig's time in Boot Camp when the other Marines kept calling him "Denigrate." Finally, Sergeant Jon Cavaiani, who referred to everyone he trained as "motherfuckers" up until they finished Boot Camp, barked, "You will call him J. Henry, motherfuckers!"

From that moment forward, *everyone* called him "J. Henry."

"Two's beddie-bye," came from Corporal John Rannahan.

Corporal Charles Brown answered, "Three's in, J. Henry."

"Four, bringing up the rear, J. Henry—as usual," Lance Corporal Erwin Boydson said with a trace of ironic sourness.

Walker carried the only rifle in the squad—everyone else had sidearms and knives. He adjusted the rifle's position, only to poke Rannahan in the side with it.

Rannahan yelped. "Watch it, Walker!"

"Sorry 'bout that." Walker didn't sound in the least bit sorry.

Rannahan glared at the sergeant.

Denig glanced at Walker and Rannahan both. "You've got the only offensive weapon in this pod, Sergeant. Use it to poke Dusters, not Marines."

"Sorry, J. Henry." This time, Walker sounded like he meant it.

Satisfied that Walker was sufficiently chastised, the staff sergeant checked the pod's nav display, confirming that the route was programmed in, and switched to his comm's control frequency. "Sierra Papa One, zeroed in and ready to launch."

In another moment, the other three squads reported ready to launch.

Hughes's voice came back, "Foxtrot Romeo One, one through four, launch in sequence."

"Sierra Papa One, launching."

Denig's fingers tapped the launch sequence on the Squad Pod's control panel, and the craft's anti-grav engine came to life, lifting it from the launch pad. At ten meters, high enough to clear the surrounding berm and defensive wire beyond, the transport began moving forward, gaining velocity as it went. A hundred meters farther and it banked shallowly to the right and slowly rose to just above the tops of the tree-like forest growths that began at the edge of the kilometer-wide cleared area that surrounded Howard—the killing zone.

A small screen next to the main control panel showed the other three pods launching in sequence, and turning onto their own courses.

Once over the trees, the Squad Pod began wending its way, keeping as much as possible to the lower areas of the gently undulating landscape. After a flight of little more than half an hour and two hundred kilometers, the pod eased itself into a small clearing created when a bolt of lightning had split a forest giant; the large tree had toppled smaller trees when it fell. The pod's ramp dropped, and the five Marines scrambled off. They dashed in different directions and went to ground facing outward fifty meters from the Squad Pod, each of them making one point of a five-pointed star. They didn't exactly blend into the foliage; their uniforms' camouflage was patterned so as to fool the eye into looking past them, rendering them effectively invisible to any but the most intense gaze. Even the faceplates of their helmets had the eye-tricking pattern on their outer sides, although they allowed unobstructed vision from the inside.

The surrounding forest held of a variety of flora, some spindly, some gnarled and twisty, some bush-like. The foliage wasn't packed as tightly as most that the Marines had seen on other worlds; some of them were basically trees, much taller than the rest, raising more than fifty meters into the air. These had branches that began a couple of meters above the ground, and large leaves that blocked most of the sunlight from reaching the surface. Most of the saplings that managed to sprout between the trees looked weak. There was a light speckling of fern-like fronds amid the fallen leaves and other detritus on the ground.

As soon as he dropped, Denig sent a five-word burst transmission on a tight beam to orbit, where it would be retransmitted to the Force Recon headquarters at Camp Howard, "Foxtrot Romeo One, in place."

"Roger, Foxtrot Romeo One," was the four-word burst reply from Force Recon command.

From that point on, nobody in the squad would say anything else unless the enemy was detected, or until it was time for the squad to move out.

All five of the Marines had motion detectors, set to register anything larger than a mid-sized Earth dog moving within two hundred meters. All five of them also had infrared filters for their helmet plates, allowing them to see heat signatures. Sergeant Walker and Corporal Rannahan also had "sniffers," devices that analyzed organic molecules wafting through the air—in the time the Marines and Army had been on Troy, the Navy science team had isolated the airborne tells that would signal the presence of the Dusters and their smaller companions.

Denig's helmet comm also drew in a feed from orbit, showing the current location of the enemy forces his squad awaited. The feed showed the outliers of the main Duster formation, if the skittery mob advancing toward the Marines could be called a formation.

The forest noises returned to normal after a few minutes. Some daring avians swooped at the Squad Pod, investigating this strange object that had manifested in their territory. More hopped or flitted about, dining on the buzzing and crawling insectoids expressing an interest in colonizing this abruptly new environment.

After twenty minutes, with the nearest Dusters closing to ten kilometers, Denig made his next transmissions. The first was five words to Camp Howard: "Foxtrot One, moving to intercept." The second was one word to his squad: "Online." The message to the squad was over a freq that fizzled to less than a whisper within two hundred and fifty meters. On his command, the five Marines rose from their prone positions and spread out to seventy-five-meter intervals, facing toward where they knew the Dusters were. Denig *beeped* a command to the Squad Pod to close its ramp, which had remained down in case the squad had to leave in a hurry, and launch to a holding position three kilometers above. They moved carefully enough that they didn't disturb the fauna back into silence.

The Marines began advancing until they could hear the approaching Dusters. Then Denig sent another one-word message. "Trees." Each of them went to the nearest forest giant and scrambled up it.

The squad leader scooted halfway up the tree he climbed. The first thing he noticed as he settled onto a branch sturdy enough to support his weight without bending, was the sudden silence from the avians, all of whom seemed to have ceased their flitting and swooping.

Odd, he thought, looking at the feed from orbit. *These Dusters aren't close enough to disturb them.*

A flicker of motion on the ground caught his attention. He peered at it, and saw the form of a Duster, padding softly through the thin undergrowth. Its torso was bent parallel to the ground, the feather-like structures that usually fanned out from its tail were stuck straight behind. In front, its beaked head swung side to side on its long neck. The feathery crest that ran from the aliens' heads to the fan at their tails was invisible, covered by something a low glossy deep brown. *Body armor? That's new.*

Denig thought the thing carried a rifle in its short arms, almost hidden from above by its body. It moved straight ahead at about the speed of a rapidly walking man.

Now Denig checked his motion detector; it showed movement about twenty meters to either side of the alien. A quick visual check confirmed that there were more of the aliens.

Strange, he thought. *They seem to be a skirmish line in advance of their main force. They haven't done that before.* He nodded when he saw that the feed from orbit didn't show the thin line of Dusters passing beneath the trees. *Not enough of a mass for orbit to pick up.*

To make sure, he brought his infra into play and scanned the entire ground area visible from his position. Nothing showed up, other than the Dusters he'd already spotted. These had been quiet, unlike the Dusters he'd heard moments earlier, Dusters that sounded closer now.

He turned all his sensors to the sounds; the muted *caws*, ripping of claws through the detritus on the ground, snapping of treelings, shrill *yelps* and *thuds* from aliens who had tripped and fallen.

And then he saw them.

This was the kind of disorderly mass he'd previously seen. Individual Dusters skittered side to side, dashed ahead, darted backward. Somehow kept moving forward. Their movement too fast for him to aim at, even if he'd been on an interdiction mission rather than reconnaissance. He began seeing small packs of the half-size aliens among the Dusters. These didn't wear the suspected body armor or carry weapons. Their stubby arms stuck out forward and displayed the vicious talons at the ends of their hands.

He hoped the scuttlebutt going around was true—that Lieutenant General Bauer had requested shotguns. Weapons that threw out a spray instead of single bullets would make shooting the manically moving aliens easier for individual riflemen to hit when the shooting began.

Self-propelled carts lumbered among the Dusters, barrels sticking up from them at a forty-five-degree angle. Denig thought they must be the anti-air artillery the aliens had used a few times. He saw nothing that resembled an electronic control unit, which made him suspect the AA was dumb artillery like the guns that had killed an AV 16 (E) aerial reconnaissance plane earlier. The guns looked like their barrels could depress far enough for them to be used as surface-to-surface artillery. Mechanical noises began to clank from behind the mob of Dusters and AA artillery.

Denig gritted his teeth; whatever was coming was too far back for him to make out, even in infrared. He was going to have to wait to see whatever additional new equipment the aliens were bringing to bear on the Marines around Jordan.

He took a deep breath and got his nerves under control. Patience was a virtue that Force Recon Marines had in abundance. It was the first thing that Sergeant Cavaiani had taught them—not how to field-strip a weapon, not how to climb a wall, not the art of hand-to-hand combat. Instead, the first day, Cavaiani had them all stand stock still for an hour in the middle of a field on a hundred-degree day in San Diego. Anyone who moved had to do fifty pushups, and the time it took to do those pushups was added to their time standing still.

"When the bell rings, motherfuckers," Cavaiani had said afterward, "you need to be the best fighters in the damn galaxy. But most of the time you're going to be not moving, not fighting, not doing a goddamn thing. A Marine's life is one part fighting, and ninety-nine parts sitting on your ass waiting to fight. Which means you motherfuckers need to be patient about not doing jackshit."

You'd be proud of us today, Sergeant, Denig thought as he watched the mass of Dusters and trundling carts pass below without noticing the five Marines watching them overhead. Denig recorded them and mentally estimated their numbers.

Hundreds.

Thousands.

Yeah, Lieutenant Hughes's briefing had said that Navy intel estimated the Dusters landed at least a corps-size number of soldiers. The intel didn't say what size corps, but that meant the 1st Marine Regiment was outnumbered at least two to one, probably by more than that. And the Navy hadn't said anything about the AA or whatever it was that clanked ever closer. He didn't dare send a burst of data to orbit; nobody knew what kind of electronic capabilities the Dusters had, or whether they could detect transmissions from nearby, even transmissions directed away from them. If they had that capability and he sent a burst to orbit, Denig and his squad were dead.

He estimated that, if they were more or less uniformly spread or bunched in his squad's area, five thousand Dusters passed below them, along with at least four hundred AA carts and a thousand or more of the dog-sized raveners, before the clanking machines got close enough to appear in infrared. What showed made him blink in surprise.

Tanks?

The Dusters hadn't had armored vehicles of any sort before—certainly not that he'd heard of.

It wasn't long before they were close enough for Denig to see them with his unaided eyes. If the tubes protruding from their fronts were the guns they resembled, the vehicles were tanks, but of a strange design. They didn't appear to have turrets, so the entire vehicle would have to point at its target rather than swivel from side to side as human armor did.

They didn't stay in a disciplined formation, but rather went forward in spurts and jinked side to side, mimicking the movement of the foot soldiers. Some of the soldiers lagged behind the mass of Dusters and Denig thought they were in danger of being run over by their own tanks.

The Marine gave an internal headshake. Artillery mixed in with infantry, followed by armor. That was so counter to how humans would move: put the armor up front supported by infantry, with the artillery bringing up the rear where it could fire over the heads of the infantry and armor.

I guess we call them alien for a reason, he thought.

When the last of the armored vehicles finally clanked past, Denig allowed another ten minutes for any stragglers to come along before he was satisfied they were all gone. Then he sent burst messages to his men, asking what they'd seen. Their reports confirmed the numbers he'd already estimated. It was only the work of another minute to prepare a transmission to orbit, to be forwarded to the Force Recon command group at Camp Howard. He included the vids from all of his men. Then one more message to his men:

"Dismount." As he began climbing down the tree, he beeped another message to the loitering Squad Pod, for it to descend to pick them up.

As soon as his boots hit the ground, he saw something half-buried in the dirt.

Picking it up, he saw that it was a snow globe, with a small crack in it. Inside was an image of the North Pole, with a building that said "Santa's Workshop" on it. On the bottom, someone had scrawled a note in dark ink. The letters were slightly smudged, but still legible: "Merry Christmas, see you when I join you in a year, love, Day."

Denig sighed and shoved the snow globe into a pocket. *Someone's back home's gonna have a shitty day when they find out about this.*

The Squad Pod arrived, and he jumped in, along with the rest of the First. Once all five of them were tucked into the pod, they headed farther east. They needed to take a look at the Dusters' landing zone.

MAJOR TERRY KAWAMURA LOOKED AT THE LARGE MONITOR IN FRONT OF HIM. They included reports that came in from Force Recon, as well as the data from the Navy ships in orbit.

His CO, the Head of Operations Colonel José Jiminez, looked over the lieutenant's shoulder. "That is a shit-ton of aliens."

Kawamura pointed at the section of the screen that included the report from Staff Sergeant Denig. "And they brought along some SUVs."

Jiminez snorted at Kawamura's joking reference to the Dusters now having tanks. It didn't warrant more, as the Dusters' new toys were no laughing matter.

Realizing his joke had fallen flat, Kawamura went back to his computer. "I think I've got me a plan of attack."

"Good. Hurry it up over to the 121st. Courtney's waiting for it."

"Okay, but—"

Kawamura hesitated, and so Jiminez prompted him. "But what, Major?"

"It's not a very good plan of attack."

"Mind telling me what's wrong with it, Marine?" Jiminez asked with a bit of menace.

"It needs about a hundred more Marines, Sir." Kawamura was not intimidated by the colonel's tone.

And Jiminez was grateful for that. He preferred his subordinates to be honest.

"Well, unless you have a squadron in your hip pocket, you're stuck with what we've got. We've been outnumbered before, and you know what? The Corps is still here."

"Yes, Sir." Kawamura did not say what he was thinking, which was that the Corps would still be "here" even if every Marine on Troy died—they'd just all be back on Earth and the other colonies. Wouldn't do the dead ones much good.

But he knew better than to say that out loud. Instead, he just said, "All right, I'm uploading it to the Hell Raisers."

"All right, Hell Raisers," Lieutenant Colonel Henry A. Courtney, CO of Marine Attack Squadron 121, shouted as soon as he finished giving the mission order to his pilots, "the bug eaters of Force Recon found us some targets and Ops has given us a battle plan. Now let's get out there and raise some hell on their sorry asses!"

Flight helmet in one hand and comp in the other, Courtney sprinted for the exit. The other fifteen pilots of VMA 121 followed right on his heels.

Sixteen AV16C Kestrels were lined up, cockpits open, ground crew standing around their aircraft.

"Is she ready for me, Ike?" Courtney asked his crew chief, Staff Sergeant Isaac N. Fry.

"All lubed up, wide open, and waiting for ya, Sir," Fry answered with a wink. "It's all I could do to keep her from bucking. She's going to cream all over them Dusters when you get her there."

"I ought to transfer you to Army artillery, Ike," Courtney said, shoving his helmet into Fry's waiting hands so he could use both of his while he went over his pre-flight checklist. "They've got women over there. Then you could stop having wet dreams about killer aircraft."

"No thankee, Sir, I've seen them doggie dames. Half of 'em look like they got teeth behind the wrong set of lips."

"And the rest have razor blades down there, I guess. Right?"

"You must'a seen 'em, too, Boss."

"Must have," Courtney said, with most of his attention on his checklist.

"You could transfer me t' the VMO, ya know. They got splittails over there, too, Sir."

"Uh-huh. *Officer* splittails. Do you really think they'd go for a grease monkey like you?"

"Hell, ain't all a them dollies ossifers. Some's NCOs like me."

"They're probably too refined for you, Ike."

Fry snorted.

Satisfied that his Kestrel was fully armed with its six five-hundred-pound scatter-blast cluster bombs and 10,000 rounds of 30mm depleted uranium rounds for its Hades guns, fully fueled, and prepped for the mission, Courtney tucked his comp into its pocket in his flight vest and took his helmet back from Fry.

Settled, plugged in, and ready for launch, Courtney called his pilots on the squadron freq. "Hell Raisers, are you ready?"

Eight reports came in, seven from the other flight leaders, and one from 1st Lieutenant John Power, his wingman. Everybody was ready.

"Schilt Tower," he said on the ground control freq, "VMA 121 requests permission to launch."

"VMA 121, permission granted," the control tower replied. "No incoming to watch for. You are clear on ninety degrees."

"Let's go!" Courtney shouted into his squadron freq. He gave Fry a thumb's up, returned the salute his crew chief popped at him, then taxied for takeoff.

Two by two, the sixteen Kestrels flashed down the runway and launched into the sky. At two thousand meters altitude, some twenty kilometers east of the airfield, they shifted into four divisions and began to spread widely—when they reached their target, they'd be attacking along a fifty kilometer-wide front.

A Hundred and Fifty Kilometers East of MCAF Schilt

"Hell Raisers, Hell Raisers, I have the target on my forward-ground," Lieutenant Colonel Courtney called on his squadron freq.

A rapid-fire series of squelches and broken words told him that all of his pilots also saw the Duster formation on their ground-searching radars. The jerkily advancing aliens formed a rough rectangle about fifty kilometers wide and twenty deep.

"Full spread," Courtney said. "We'll hit them front to back with scatter-blasts, spin about, and hit them back to front with Hades. Acknowledge."

Another series of squelches and broken words told him everyone understood the order. A glance at his sideways radar showed him the sixteen aircraft spreading out online; they'd be three kilometers apart when they began their bombing run.

"Remember, their trip-A is dumb artillery. No seekers, so just watch out for objects to dodge." Courtney didn't really need to remind his squadron, they'd all been thoroughly briefed on the fire-and-forget anti-air artillery that had killed First Lieutenant Schilt. But a reminder never hurt, just in case it slipped someone's mind in the heat of battle.

While the Kestrels were spreading and Courtney was giving his reminder, they dropped from the two thousand meters at which they'd been flying to a hundred and fifty meters for their bombing and strafing runs.

They didn't see the thin picket line that led the mass of Dusters, but the pickets had seen them when they began dropping, and signaled the maneuver to their commanders.

The Duster AA artillery began firing just as the Kestrels began dropping their scatter-blasts. Not all of the alien guns were ready to fire, and none of them had the range yet. Most of the AA guns turned rearward, to fire at the aircraft once they passed. They still didn't have the range, and their shells were too high when they burst, showering their shrapnel harmlessly groundward.

Harmlessly to the humans, that is. The plummeting shrapnel added to the mayhem and murder flung out by the scatter-blasts' cluster bombs, ripping huge holes in the mass of Duster infantry that followed the AA guns.

VMA 121 flew twenty-five kilometers past the aliens' and spun about for its reverse run. Taking advantage of the small amount of time allowed by the maneuver, Courtney looked at his displays to make a quick damage assessment of the enemy formation.

He smiled grimly at what he saw, and muttered, "Take that, you sons-abitches." According to his displays, the squadron had damaged, destroyed, or killed about fifteen percent of the Dusters and their machines.

The Hell Raisers closed on the back of the formation, and their 30mm Hades guns began pouring destruction into the rear of the tanks, many of which exploded when the massive rounds slammed into their weapons lockers.

But this time, the triple-As had the range. Anti-aircraft artillery shells burst their deadly blossoms in a wall in front of the squadron.

"Break!" Courtney screamed into his comm, and jerked his Kestrel into a vertical climb. The aircraft staggered when chunks of hot metal thudded into its underside.

"Seven is hit!" First Lieutenant Wilma Hawkins shouted. "I'm going down." Then only static.

Courtney barely heard her. He was too busy trying to wrestle his wounded Kestrel under control.

"Ten—" was all Captain Robert Dunlap got out before his Kestrel exploded, showering heated chunks of itself into the air, and pelting the ground.

There were more reports of damage from other pilots. Courtney barely registered them as he cried, "C'mon" to his controls, trying to keep the Kestrel steady and rising.

Another volley of anti-air artillery flew into the sky and burst into murderous flowers. But it wasn't as effective as the first; the Dusters didn't have ranging radar for the guns, they all had to be manually aimed. Some of the shells went too high, but most burst too low to hit the rapidly climbing Kestrel. Still, some found targets.

Courtney's speed slowed as he climbed. He was almost down to stall speed by the time he reached three thousand meters. Then he flipped his nose over and made a turn to the right, gaining speed and cutting across the front of the triple-A rather than resuming his flight into its front.

"Hell Raisers, Hell Raisers," he radioed, "get the hell out of here. See me, do the same, go your best angle to get free." He was still wrestling with his aircraft but had it well enough under control that he was able to change its angle of descent and turn away from the Dusters' fire.

Once he was clear, he took stock of his squadron. His displays only showed eight aircraft other than his own still aloft. Had VMA 121 really lost nearly half its strength in—he glanced at his chronometer—less than fifteen seconds? Who was still up?

"Hell Raisers, report!" he snapped. The command was unnecessary, one display told him which aircraft were flying and which were missing from the sky. Reporting gave his pilots something to do other than concentrate on how bad their situations were.

All eight reported in smartly, though Captain Daniela Bruce's voice sounded ragged and raspy when she said, "Two, in."

"Form on me," Courtney said once he heard from all his remaining pilots. In little more than a minute, nine Kestrels were lined up, hovering ten kilometers behind the aliens who had done so much damage to the squadron.

"Keep your distance," Courtney ordered. "On my command, fire your Hades at them until you run out of ammunition. Then follow me home."

He paused a beat, then shouted: "*Fire!*"

The Hades guns fired rapidly. Even in hundred-round bursts, it took little more than a minute for the nine Kestrels to expend their remaining ammunition. Other than a few blasts from destroyed tanks, they couldn't tell how much additional damage they did to the enemy.

Hands gripped tightly on the controls as he nursed his wounded aircraft, Courtney led his surviving pilots in a wide arc around the formation. Some wobbled, and Captain Bruce's Kestrel trailed a great deal of smoke.

But they all made it back to Schilt.

The nine surviving ones, anyhow.

Marine Corps Air Facility Schilt,
Near Jordan, Eastern Shapland

Major Kawamura's board lit up with a communiqué from Navy Intelligence in orbit of Troy.

"Sir," he said to Colonel Jiminez once he read through the report, "according to our birds in orbit, VMA 121 reduced the strength of the Dusters moving toward Jordan by twenty percent from its original numbers. They also report that the enemy has slowed its westward advance by half."

Jiminez nodded. "And what damage did the Hell Raisers take?"

"Seven Kestrels and pilots gone, two Kestrels badly damaged, including Colonel Courtney's."

Again, Jiminez nodded. It could've been better, but it could've been worse, too. Still, the Hell Raisers were now at half-strength, and all they did was slow the Dusters down...

One Hundred Kilometers West of Firebase Gasson

TWO FLIGHTS OF MH 15 ALPHONSE ATTACK-TRANSPORTS FROM THE 9TH INFANTRY Division's Mobile Intelligence squadron, each escorted by a two-aircraft flight of AV 16C Kestrels from Navy Attack Squadron 43, touched down in an area of open woodland and disgorged their passengers. Sixty kilometers to the north, a second pair of Alphonses touched down, and their passengers scrambled off. The Kestrels then escorted the Alphonses east, to a safe distance, closer to Millerton and the 9th ID's base.

Then the Kestrels flew back to take up loitering positions five thousand meters above the Mobile Intel squads. They were too high to hear from the ground, high enough to resemble raptor-like avians gliding on thermals. And far enough away from the enemy to be able to see and escape any anti-air artillery thrown their way if they were identified for what they were—the pilots of VA 43 had been briefed on what happened to VMA 121, and were in no hurry to reenact their Marine counterparts' fate.

Navy intel had reported the Duster force heading toward Millerton, and the headquarters at Camp Puller reported them advancing along a forty-kilometer front. Rather than observe the aliens head-on as the Force Recon Marines had, the soldiers of first platoon of the 9th Mobile Intel Company were going to recon its flanks.

The soldiers were more heavily armed than the Marines of Force Recon over on Eastern Shapland had been. They also had different orders: kill stragglers, and take prisoners if possible.

First and second squads were accompanied by First Lieutenant Miller on the south of the anticipated Duster route. Master Sergeant Bronson was with third and fourth to the north.

The ten soldiers of first and second squads quickly assembled around Miller, who wasted no time on repeating the orders he'd given the platoon at Gasson. Instead, all he said was, "If you need air, the Kestrels are 'Halo,' you're 'Snare.' You know what to do. Get it done. I'm with second squad."

Sergeant First Class Levi B. Gaylord gave his platoon commander a curt nod, signaled his four men with another nod, and headed slightly east of north at a rapid pace. His men unhesitatingly followed. To their left, Miller and second squad went north on an equal tangent to increase the distance between them and first squad.

Gaylord went fast, but not so fast that he couldn't observe his surroundings. The major trees didn't form a solid canopy and allowed considerable sunlight to penetrate to the ground. While the undergrowth grew in profusion, most of it was barely knee-high, and therefore did not provide a solid ground cover. A multiplicity of game trails traced through it, many easily wide enough for the soldiers to traverse only periodically touching the growth on either side. Gaylord frequently looked at the ground when he was on the trails, watching for the tell-tale tracks of Duster feet. He didn't see any gouges that could have been left by the aliens' talons. What he did see was dimples left by the feet—hooves?—of what he suspected were native ungulates and smaller footprints of other local fauna. Here and there was a pug mark of what he presumed was a carnivore. The carnivores seemed to be solo animals; he thought they were highly unlikely to attack the five-man group.

In less than an hour, the squads closed to half a kilometer short of the anticipated flank of the Duster formation. They were most likely to intercept outlying flankers or stragglers here. They set up in an echelon right formation, facing west, twenty meters between men, with Gaylord in the middle. The soldiers seemed to blend into the ground cover. Their camouflaged wardress was different from the Marines'; it tricked the eye into not seeing details, and fuzzed the edges of shapes, making them effectively invisible to the human eye. (It was anybody's guess what they looked like to Duster eyes.) A kilometer to their west, Miller and second squad went to ground in the same formation.

Gaylord didn't send a signal to Miller to inform the platoon commander that he and his men were in position. They were in a comm blackout unless a squad got into trouble and needed help.

He checked his sensors. Nothing even as large as a middle-sized dog showed up on his motion detector. In infrared, he saw only small splotches, the signatures of avians flitting among the trees. The smeller, set to pick up the air-born molecules emitted by the alien enemy, showed nothing. As far as Gaylord's sensors could tell, the Mobile Intel squad was alone with the local fauna, just a bunch of small creatures that presented no threat to the humans.

After about a quarter of an hour, Gaylord began to hear noises from the northwest, the din of thousands of Duster voices shrieking out their caws. Listening carefully, he thought he could make out the rumble and clanking of mechanical noises under the caws. Looking to his left and his right, he said in a voice that wouldn't carry much more than twenty meters, "Look alert, flankers might come now. Pass it."

PFC Cassius Peck on his right and Corporal Charles Hopkins on his left each turned and bared their faces to him, and nodded to let him know they heard the order, then looked away to pass the word.

With the enemy entering auditory range, Gaylord checked his comp for the feed from orbit. It showed first squad's position, not from "seeing" the squad, but from noting the location of his info request. That made him smile; his signal was sent by tight beam, undetectable by anything not along its path—there was no way the Dusters could intercept his call to orbit. The feed from orbit rode his tight-beam signal back down, making it equally undetectable by anything not along its path.

The nearest point of the Duster mass—formation felt like a too-disciplined word to describe the aliens' manner of grouping—clustered half a kilometer north and just over a kilometer west, or about level with where second squad should be. Too far away for a single voice to carry, but the massed caws and shrieks of the thousands of voices were growing steadily louder.

The resolution of the feed wasn't sharp enough to show individual aliens, only groupings. However, the vehicles near the front edge did stand out. If this formation was arranged the same as the ones the Marines on Eastern Shapland had observed, these were the Dusters' anti-air artillery.

He stopped watching the low-res orbital feed, as it couldn't pinpoint any Duster flankers or scouts in the vicinity. He and his men would have to rely on their eyes and ears, and the sensors they carried.

Distant gunfire suddenly broke out to the west, from the direction second squad's position. Seconds later, Gaylord heard second squad's leader, Sergeant Grace, break comm silence.

"Halo Two, Halo Two," Grace called, "Snare Two needs you. Many bad guys closing on us from the west. Help us out here. Over." There was a buzz of static, then Grace called again. "We need it *now*, Halo!" An increasing volume of gunfire was clearly audible under Grace's voice.

He's alerting all of us, Gaylord thought. *That's why he didn't use a tight beam to call for air.* He wondered if third or fourth squad was also under attack—they were too far away for him to hear a firefight from their locations north of the enemy mass.

Second squad's firefight told Gaylord the aliens probably knew more humans were nearby, so he broke radio silence. "Look sharp," he said into his squad's short-range freq. "They might already be on their way to us."

As he said that, he heard the scream of Halo Two's Kestrels diving toward the ground, and the yammer of their cannons firing in support of second squad.

"Snare One, Snare One, this is Halo One." Lieutenant Herbert Jones's laconic voice came over Gaylord's tight beam. "We're coming down to mezzanine level, just in case you need us in a hurry."

"Appreciate it, Halo One," Gaylord replied.

In seconds, he started to hear the drone of a Kestrel losing altitude.

Sergeant James Elision, on the squad's right flank, suddenly broke his comm silence. "Movement on the right flank!"

Gaylord looked at his motion detector. At its extreme limit, he discerned movement through the forest, three hundred meters to the squad's right front. "Stand tight," he sent to his men. As open as the woodland was, it wasn't open enough for him to see that far. The Dusters, if it was the aliens, had to be barely in view from Elision's position. Was it close enough for the flank man to see what was making the movement?

He continued looking at the motion detector's display. One, two, three, more. Jerky movement. Not good. If it was the aliens, he should be able to hear their calls at that distance. Or were their flankers moving silently?

"Halo One, Snare One," he sent. "Azimuth, three-one-zero. Range, three hundred. Movement. Say hello for me. Over."

"Snare One, Halo One," Jones said. "Three-One-Zero. Three hundred from you. I see it. Hiya, fellas."

The Kestrel's steady drone abruptly turned to a scream as it heeled over and dove. It cannons began yammering, firing explosive rounds at the ground and whatever was there. Then the timber of its engine changed again, shrieking as it twisted out of its dive and clawed for altitude. Its sound dopplered away, and now the caws of Dusters came through, coming closer and closer, rapidly.

"Get ready!" Gaylord yelled into his comm.

Faster than humans could have covered the distance, Dusters began flicking through the trees, coming straight at the right side of the soldiers' thin line.

"Oh, shit!" Gaylord swore as he took aim at a charging, shrieking alien. *Whoa! There's too many of them; more than five men can fight off. Even with air support.* He pulled the trigger and would have been astonished at hitting his target had he been conscious of the fact that the Duster he shot was running straight instead of jinking and dodging side to side the way he'd always seen the aliens charge before. They were cawing and shrieking, the way he had always heard them on the attack.

Situational awareness told him that his men were firing at the Dusters; a change in the pitch of the Kestrel above them told him it was returning for another strafing run. His training and duty as a squad leader made his actions automatic. He was able to function without thinking about what he should do.

Which was good, because this was a situation that didn't particularly bear thinking about.

He toggled his comm's command freq and called HQ.

"Snare One is being overrun," he reported in with a calmness he didn't feel. "Snare One requires additional air support and immediate extraction. Over." He kept shooting while making the request for assistance, help that he knew wasn't particularly likely to arrive in time.

Line sights on target. Pull the trigger. Shift aim. Repeat.

To his front, beyond the nearest enemy soldiers, the Kestrel's Hades gun tore up the ground, shrapnel from those rounds ripping gory chunks of flesh from the aliens' bodies, spraying thin red blood.

Gaylord was vaguely aware of new sounds entering the firefight—distant thumps, followed by closer, overhead cracks.

Ominous cracks.

The cracks of anti-aircraft artillery rounds exploding in the air.

Hot chunks of metal casing scythed down, mostly but not always behind the charging alien soldiers, shredding limbs from tree trunks, thunking into the ground, slicing into Duster bodies. Some jagged, razor-sharp fragments landed closer. Gaylord didn't hear the scream from PFC Charles Bieger, on the squad's left flank, when a piece of shrapnel knifed down and severed his left arm.

Lieutenant Jones's voice didn't register on him when the Kestrel pilot called out, "I'm hit! I can't make it back."

He didn't notice the tremor in the ground when the Kestrel slammed into the earth a few hundred meters to his rear. He couldn't, not with three Dusters on him, their talons slashing him to ribbons.

More Navy Kestrels arrived soon thereafter, but by that time, all that the pilots could see was scorched earth and dead bodies.

The human bodies far outnumbered the Duster ones, and the survivors among the latter had moved on. The pilots searched in vain for survivors among their own forces amidst the burning grasslands and bloody corpses.

Returning to base, the Kestrels reported this engagement lost.

Headquarters, North American Union Forces,
office of the Commanding General
Near Millerton, Shapland

"Sir, it's General Noll," Captain William Upshur said, standing in the doorway of Lieutenant General Harold Bauer's office.

Bauer looked up from the reports from Force Recon and VMA 121 on their actions against the Dusters on Eastern Shapland—reports that told of anti-air artillery and armored vehicles, things the Dusters hadn't had before.

"Thanks, Bill." He picked up his comm. "General, what can I do for you?"

Major General Conrad Noll, ranking Army officer on the planet, spoke in a flat tone. "General, it's my unhappy duty to inform you that the platoon of Mobile Intel scouting the flanks of the western Duster formation appears to have been wiped out. As were the AV 16Cs that were providing them with cover."

Bauer momentarily closed his eyes. Four Navy Kestrels in addition to the seven Marine Kestrels that had already been killed in the east. The human air assets were taking a severe beating.

"My sincerest sympathies for the loss of your brave soldiers," he said. "Let your staff do their jobs. Your platoon will be avenged. As soon as possible, we will recover all the bodies. Bauer out."

After closing the connection, he looked at Upshur. "I want to conference all major element commanders in thirty minutes."

"Aye aye, Sir," Upshur said, and backed away to set up the conference call.

Thirty minutes later

"We're ready, Sir," Brigadier General David Porter said. The Chief of Staff stood next to a bank of eleven monitors that had been set up inside Bauer's office. The three major element commanders and their operations chiefs looked out of six of the monitors. Bauer's operations chief and the commanders of the three independent commands out of the other five.

"Thank you, gentlemen," Bauer said. "You've read the reports."

It wasn't a question. He knew they had to have read them; part of the reason for giving them half an hour's warning for the meeting was to make sure they had time to read them.

"The Dusters have weapons they haven't used before. We must change our tactics to meet this new threat." He looked at the commander of the 2nd Marine Air Wing and the commander of the Navy's Air Group Five (and highest-ranking Navy officer planetside). "General Bearss, Captain McNair, continue slowing the enemy advance and degrading their capabilities. Use stand-off weapons, avoid putting more of your aircraft in situations where they might be killed. Your primary target at this time is the anti-air artillery."

To the commanders of the 1st Marine Division and the Army's 104th Artillery Regiment, he said, "General Purvis, Colonel Ames, deploy your laser and conventional artillery to strike the enemy as soon as they are in range. Your primary targets are the armored vehicles—and anything in the way.

"Colonel Reid, Lieutenant Colonel Grant, I want Force Recon and Mobile Intel to gather intelligence to the rear of the enemy formations, see if they have bases or weapons/supply caches behind we can strike against.

"I don't think we can expect any assistance from Task Force 8 for the foreseeable future. Let's defeat these Dusters before 2nd Army arrives. As before, Brigadier General Shoup will coordinate. That is all."

Bauer nodded to Porter, who turned off the monitors.

"You sounded awful confident there, Sir," Porter said.

"Marines have been in tighter spots before. So has the Army. We won it in the past, and we'll do it again."

"Let's just hope they don't come up with air assets."

"Yes, let's."

Two hundred and fifty kilometers east of
Jordan, Eastern Shapland

First section, 1st Force Recon Platoon retrieved its Squad Pods after the mass of Dusters passed, but before the Kestrels of VMA 121 engaged the enemy, and headed east, toward the enemy's landing site, a scorched area many square kilometers wide.

The Pods touched down at four different locations, all four kilometers from the landing site, so each squad could approach from a different direction; first and third from its flanks, second from its rear, fourth straight on.

Staff Sergeant Denig had his squad spread out at twenty-meter intervals. The Marines advanced slowly, watching carefully for any booby traps the Dusters may have left in their wake. They didn't find any. Along the way, they didn't see any earth-born birds or insects. Neither did they see any native avians or flying insectoids.

A small part of Denig's mind wondered how the crops were pollinated without insects or birds about. But he was easily able to compartmentalize that curiosity to the back of his mind, leaving the front of his mind free to focus on watching for alien surprises. That ability to concentrate on the important stuff while not completely forgetting the unimportant stuff was why he was promoted to sergeant, or so he had been told.

That was one of two things that his then-CO, Colonel Hector Santiago-Colon, had told him during the promotion ceremony.

"When you're up in the officer ranks," the colonel had said while placing the three-stripe patch on his arm, "it's all about the big picture. And when you're down in the lower ranks, it's all about what's right in front of you and that's it. But when you're a sergeant, you gotta think of the big picture *and* the little picture all at the same time. You're the bridge between the Leathernecks on the ground and the officers back at HQ. And you've proven, time and again, J. Henry, that you can do that. So go do it."

The other thing Santiago-Colon said was a truly terrible joke: "With the promotion, you also get a transfer: three stripes, and you're out."

Denig didn't even like baseball.

Three kilometers in, Denig's squad reached cropland. The first was a field of half-grown corn, its stalks shoulder high. Six hundred meters farther, they encountered lower growing crops, stalky legumes of some sort. Beyond them, a farmstead was visible, near the center of the area in which the Dusters had landed. The scorched area began at what was now the far edge of the legume field. Denig stopped his squad there to observe.

From here, he could see that the scorching wasn't solid, but was overlapping spots where the alien landing craft had touched down. Here and there, where the ground wasn't blackened, were broken and trampled beanstalks. They watched for twenty minutes without seeing anything moving; not a person, not an alien, not a bird, not a grazing or hunting animal.

Looks like the animals that weren't killed by the Dusters landing got outta Dodge while the getting was good. Smart critters.

On Denig's signal, the squad rose and moved on, stepping carefully so as not to raise puffs of dust.

The Dusters had made no such attempt when they landed. The ground was scarred with lines and gouges from their talons, running helter-skelter, overlapping and obliterating each other so it was impossible to estimate how many there had been. There were also the very distinctive tracks of the tank-like anti-aircraft vehicles, running westward in straighter lines.

Denig stopped his squad less than a hundred meters from the farmstead, and the Marines went to ground. Corporal John Rannahan faced the rear, watching for anyone approaching from that direction. They all used their motion detectors.

A whitewashed, two-story, gable-roofed structure with a wraparound veranda was center-most: the farmhouse. To its right and slightly behind was a barn-like structure, likely a garage for farm vehicles and storage. An open-sided forge stood twenty meters to the side of the barn. Denig could hear the chugging of a generator shed, though his view of it was blocked by the barn. Fencing from what he thought was probably an animal enclosure jutted from the far side of the house, though Denig didn't hear any animal sounds from it. A silo stood twenty meters tall beyond it.

Denig turned his helmet's ears all the way up, listening for any sounds other than the muffled generator noise and breeze-ruffled leaves. He heard none. He studied the farm buildings and yard with his eyes. There was no movement save for vagrant leaves gusting with the breeze, and curtains fluttering in three second-floor windows of the house. He turned on his Sniffer to sniff for the telltale airborne organic chemicals of Duster scent. It was faint, but the aliens' scent was stronger than it should have been if it was only the residue of the Dusters that had already left.

But was it current, telling of Dusters present now? Or was it residual, from the passage of the thousands who had gone beneath them under the trees?

Slowly, cautiously, he turned about, aiming the Sniffer in a circle. He found a scent moving westward, in the direction of Jordan. But the strongest scent was clearly to his front—from the farm buildings.

He prepared a burst transmission tight beam to the Navy in orbit, to be relayed by tight beam back to the other squads, and to Force Recon headquarters at Camp Howard: *Dusters are here, but out of sight, numbers unknown.*

In little more than a minute, replies came from the other squads: *Same here.*

Then a two-word reply from Camp Howard: *Continue mission.*

They needed more intelligence, more information.

Denig tight-beamed another message: *First squad, sending two in close.*

Staff Sergeant Bordelon, third squad leader to the north of the complex, sent back, *Three sending two.*

Denig tapped Corporal Charles Brown on the shoulder, and the two rose to crouches and started toward the forge. At a hundred meters, their camouflage made them extremely difficult to focus on. Still, they continued to move in a crouch. They didn't know whether or not the enemy had detection devices set out, or what kind they might be, so they moved in random patterns. The two Marines didn't maintain a constant distance between themselves, but drifted closer then farther apart. Neither ever took more than three consecutive steps, nor did they have a rhythm to their paces; the pauses between their steps were irregularly spaced. And some steps were normal weight. Others were very soft. Their objective was to keep any audio nor seismic detectors from picking up anything that would read as the gait of a walking man.

It took them nearly half an hour to reach the open-sided forge. Brown watched the other buildings from outside the forge, while Denig, knife in hand, examined its interior. A quick look around showed nobody present.

Denig investigated farther. The gas-fired hearth was cold, and the gauge on the tank that fed it registered empty. Tongs, hammers, rasps, and other tools were scattered about. The anvil had been overturned. The oil in the quenching bucket had filmed over, with a few leaves and other bits of debris floated on top. Scuff marks on the dirt floor and stains on a hammer and tongs looked like the farmer, or whoever did the blacksmithing, had been attacked and put up a fight before being overwhelmed. Whatever happened here had happened long before this wave of Dusters had made planetfall.

Satisfied that he'd learned everything he could here, Denig signaled Brown, and the two continued to the barn, angling to circle around it, putting it between themselves and the house.

When they reached the rear of the barn, they could see a small shed, which was the source of the generator's chugging. A large gas drum squatted behind it. The drum had markings and symbols that weren't in any language or culture Denig was familiar with. He suspected it was something the aliens had brought with them. Had they known they would find a generator? Or had they brought their own?

Denig and Brown returned to the side of the barn. Some of the boards that formed its side were warped, and a number of them had been recently broken. Denig stood next to one of the larger breaks and listened carefully. When he didn't hear any sounds of occupancy, he risked looking through the break.

It was dim inside the barn. Other than diffused light, all the illumination was through slants from the breaks in the walls. Large machines were vaguely visible. Denig recognized a tractor, a small truck, a harvester, and a couple of farm carts for hauling produce. There were things he couldn't identify, either because they were blocked by other equipment or because they were too deep in the shadows.

He put his helmet next to Brown's and gave orders. Then they parted, Brown to the front left corner of the barn, and Denig back to the rear right corner. There they lay, observing the house. After twenty minutes without seeing any motion through the windows, Denig dropped to all fours and painfully made his way to the generator shack.

There were no warped boards on the sides of the shack, and none of the boards were broken, although several showed signs of recent repair. Denig crept around the shack and found a broken generator and gas tank on its other side. He would have liked to see inside the shack, but when he briefly checked he found its door locked. Still, the broken machine and tank beyond confirmed his thought that the Dusters had brought their own power supply. He wondered what they needed it for besides powering the house.

He returned to the rear corner of the barn and watched the house. On three occasions during the next half hour, he saw a long-jawed face looking through the parted curtains that covered windows on the second floor. He recorded each appearance for transmission to Camp Howard. The light inside was too dim for him to tell if they were the same face or different ones. And he didn't know whether NAU Forces Troy had enough facial recognition capability to distinguish among Duster faces. Without that, there was no way of knowing how many of the aliens had looked out the windows.

After watching long enough, he went back around to where Brown had been watching and gathered him to return to the rest of the squad. There, he tight-beamed his report to orbit for relay to Camp Howard. They waited for further orders.

Camp Zion, near Jordan

"KILO COMPANY, FORM UP!" GUNNERY SERGEANT JOHN L. YOUNKER ROARED, BREAK-
ing the afternoon's quiet.

"Third platoon, up!" Staff Sergeant Douglas Haperman bellowed.

The camp became a riot of shouted voices, as the platoon sergeants,
squad leaders, and fire team leaders yelled out, harrying their men into
formation.

With a lot of yelling back and forth of, "What's up?" and jangling of
equipment, the Marines of third platoon, Kilo Company, Third Battalion, First
Marines scrambled into formation in front of their platoon sergeant. The
other platoons of the company assembled to their sides. In less than a
minute after Younker's command, all but a few stragglers were in company
formation in front of him. Every one of them carried his weapons and ammo
belt—it was a remote possibility, but if the camp got attacked so suddenly
that they didn't have time to get to their bunkers, they wanted to be able to
fight.

"'*Toon* sergeants, re-*port!*" Younker shouted.

The platoon sergeants had already gotten reports from their squad
leaders, and about-faced to give their reports to Younker.

When it was his turn, Haperman stated loudly, "Third platoon, all
present and accounted for!"

Younker turned to face the company's HQ bunker and waited.

Mere seconds passed before Captain Charles Ilgenfritz emerged,
followed by the company's other officers.

Ilgenfritz came to attention two meters in front of Younker, who sharply saluted and said, "Sir, Kilo Company all present and accounted for."

Ilgenfritz returned the salute and said "Thank you, Gunnery Sergeant. Take your post."

"Aye aye, Sir." Younker turned sharply to his right and marched to his position in front of the leading edge of first platoon.

Ilgenfritz took a brief moment to look over his company. Not quite as big as it had been when it formed before leaving Earth, and some of the faces were still strangers to him—recent replacements for combat losses. But Kilo was a good company, capable of fulfilling any mission assigned to it.

And this one was a doozy.

"Marines," he said in a voice that carried clearly to every man in his command, "you know about the Duster force heading toward Jordan. Force Recon has located their landing site and discovered a force of unknown size still there. We are moving out in one hour. The landing site is our objective. Aircraft are on their way to transport us. When we reach our objective, we are to engage and destroy all enemy forces present there and destroy any and all weapons, munitions, and supplies present. If I receive any additional intelligence on what we can expect when we get there, you will be informed. When you are dismissed from this formation, your platoon sergeants will see to it that you have sufficient ammunition and other equipment and supplies for the mission."

Third Platoon's area, Camp Zion

"Squad leaders, with me," Staff Sergeant Haperman ordered as soon as the platoon reached its bunkers. The four gathered in front of him immediately. The rest of the men loitered where they could overhear. "We don't know what we're going to find out there. The Dusters might have left nothing more than a single team as fire watch. Or there could be a reinforced battalion. We just don't know. Even if Force Recon can't detect more than a fire team in the buildings, if there's any kind of underground structure, well, we all know that they use tunnels and caves.

"So, I want every rifle to have five hundred rounds and four grenades, minimum. Guns, four thousand each. Every fire team humps an extra ammo can for the guns. Yeah, that's an extra nine thousand rounds for the guns. If there's a lot of those buggers, that might not be enough. Let's hope it is enough. We can't rely on air support, the airedales might be needed to help out Regiment. And the squids topside have their own fight and might not be able to help us.

"Inspect your men. Make sure their weapons are clean, they've got their night-vision goggles, three days' rations, and plenty of water. Give me your reports when I get back with the extra ammo. Do it." He turned about and headed for the company's ammunition point to collect as many bullets and grenades as he could get.

"Whoa-shit, luna," Lance Corporal Daniel Inouye said, using the Hawai'ian word for "boss." "I don't like the sound of that one little bit."

"Yeah, 'little bit' is right. That's what you are, Danny, just a little bit chicken," Corporal John Capodanno replied.

PFC Jay R. Vargas laughed. "Little bit chickenshit!"

"I've been in enough shit with these bad bastards to have the right to be a little bit chicken, Jay." Inouye swung the flat of his hand at Vargas's head.

Vargas ducked out of the way and clucked.

PFC James K. Okubo watched the two from close to the entrance of the fire team's bunker. He was a last-minute addition to the team right before they left Earth, replacing PFC Christopher Nugent, whose wife had given birth to triplets. He was granted hardship leave, and Okubo was brought in to replace him fresh out of Boot.

"Knock off the grab-ass and line up so I can inspect your weapons," Capodanno ordered. Nobody grumbled. The inspection didn't take long, his men all kept their rifles and bayonets in good condition. Capodanno even checked their magazines to make sure there weren't any blockages.

Sergeant Alejandro Ruiz watched as his fire team leaders inspected their men, then ordered, "First squad, get everything you're supposed to take, then line up on me."

The twelve Marines of first squad scrambled to their bunkers and were back in two minutes with packs on their backs. Ruiz didn't bother inspecting the weapons and ammunition belts. He had full confidence in his fire team leaders. Instead, he inspected the contents of their packs. Nobody had more than four hundred rounds of ammunition, and not all of them had three days rations. He made a mental note of who needed how much of what. Water was a different problem.

Haperman was back in twenty minutes, accompanied by a Major Mite quarter-ton truck over-loaded with ammunition and rations. He had the squad leaders collect enough ammo and rations to bring their squads up to the requisite amount, including the extra cans of machine gun ammunition. Then he distributed the rest equally through the platoon. The riflemen now averaged six hundred rounds and five or six grenades each, there were five extra thousand-round ammo cans for the guns.

"You did good, Boss," Ruiz said *sotto voce* when he saw how much extra the platoon sergeant had brought back.

Haperman nodded and said equally quietly, "I wish we could take the vehicle with us." More loudly to the entire platoon, he said, "Now for water. Fall in." He marched them to the water point.

They heard the drone of approaching VSTOL P 53 Eagles.

In twenty minutes more, Kilo Company was aboard the Eagles, heading east, escorted by a division of four AT 5 Cobra ground attack aircraft. Their call sign was Chiricahua. The aircraft made a wide circle around the approaching Duster formation.

After little more than an hour's flight, the Eagles touched down two kilometers from the farm buildings where Force Recon had confirmed Dusters were present. First platoon, with the company headquarters group, was to the east. Second and third platoons were north and south, respectively, of the building complex.

Captain Ilgenfritz checked his feed from orbit and noticed that the Force Recon squads weren't indicated. Which didn't surprise him at all; their uniforms were exceptionally good at avoiding detection throughout the entire range of the electronic and visual spectra.

Sergeant Timothy O'Donoghue, Ilgenfritz's communications officer, tight-beamed to orbit for relay to the FR squad leaders: "Leatherstocking, Leatherstocking. This is Chiricahua. Talk to me. Over."

As soon as the Force Recon squad leaders acknowledged that they were online, Bender nodded at Ilgenfritz, who turned on his relay comm.

"Chiricahua Six Actual. Update," Ilgenfritz said.

The four updates were brief, all variations on, "No change."

The Marines still didn't know whether they were up against a few aliens on fire watch, or a reinforced battalion.

"Leatherstocking, we are closing to five mikes. Will contact you again then. Chiricahua out." He issued orders for his platoons to advance to the edge of the scorched area. They went slowly, taking more than an hour to advance a kilometer and a half.

"Leatherstocking," Ilgenfritz sent when the company was in position. "Chiricahua Three is half a klick south of the built-ups. Can you send them a guide?"

A moment later, Staff Sergeant Denig sent back, "One Foxtrot Romeo on his way to your three."

"Chiricahua Three, Six Actual," Ilgenfritz said into his comm. "A guide is on his way to you. When he gets there, follow him and check out the buildings."

Denig didn't stutter-step his way to third platoon's location as he had when he first approached the buildings. If the Dusters had seismic sensors planted around the area, they already knew they were surrounded. He didn't rush, and reached third platoon twenty minutes after leaving the rest of his squad in place.

"Staff Sergeant Denig, 1st Force Recon," he reported when a sergeant escorted him to third platoon's commander. "I understand you're waiting for someone to show you the way through the barricades and deadfalls."

"Are there any?" Second Lieutenant Dan D. Schoonover asked.

"Not that we found. But you'll probably trip over my people if I don't stop you in time."

"Fair enough." Schoonover turned to Haperman. "In line. First squad, third, guns, second. I'm between first and third, you're with the guns. Line 'em up, and take Denig to Sergeant Ruiz so he can lead. Get online when we reach the Foxtrot Romeos."

"Aye aye." Haperman turned away, softly calling for the squad leaders so he could pass Schoonover's orders to them.

Battleship NAUS Durango,
in geosync orbit around Semi-Autonomous World Troy

CHIEF INTELLIGENCE OFFICER, LIEUTENANT COMMANDER FINN MCCLEERY, STUDIED the data that had been sent up from Troy. Her job was to examine all the images taken by ships in orbit, by Marines and soldiers on the ground since the first Force Recon teams that investigated the invasion of Troy, and whatever else they were able to find on comps and other devices that had been left behind.

She noticed one major difference in the latest batch of images: the distinctive tracks made by the Dusters' new vehicles.

Her aide, Ensign Fred Zabitosky, stood behind her, peering at the screen over her shoulder.

"Looking for something to hang over your couch, Commander?"

"Nah, I'm partial to abstracts," McCleery said, a tinge of her Irish accent peeking through. When she first signed up, she had a full-on brogue, cultivated by growing up in South Boston, but a career in the NAU had reduced it to the occasional odd vowel.

Zabitosky peered more closely at the central image on her screen, which was the tracks left on the ground by the Duster vehicle. "I've never seen anything like that."

McCleery whirled on the ensign. "Say that again, Fred."

"Say what again?"

She glared at him. "Say. That. Again. Ensign."

"Yes, *Ma'am*." Zabitosky cleared his throat. "I've never seen anything like that, Ma'am."

She waved him off. "I don't give a shit about protocol, it's what you said. That you've never seen anything like this."

"Um, okay." Zabitosky was confused.

"Neither have I. And I've been spending the last week doing nothing but looking at evidence of the Dusters."

This just confused Zabitosky more. "Sorry?"

She touched a few controls on her comp, calling up a whole bunch of less familiar visuals. After a moment, Zabitosky realized these showed other worlds where they'd found wreckage that, they now knew, were the result of Duster invasions.

McCleery scrolled through: a world with four moons, a world with purple foliage, a world with massive (badly damaged) structures of crystalline design, a world where all the buildings were constructed on mountaintops, a world where the people lived in trees but nonetheless had impressive technology.

"What are you looking for, Commander?" Zabitosky asked.

But McCleery didn't answer, as she started scrolling faster and faster through the images.

Then she turned to Zabitosky. "Ensign, get Commander Yntema over here."

That got Zabitosky's attention, as McCleery never referred to anybody by rank unless someone who outranked her was in the room—or it was really important.

"Aye aye, Ma'am," Zabitosky said.

Five minutes later, the Durango's executive officer, Gordon Yntema, entered.

"I was just on my way to the mess, Commander, and today's the last of the real eggs. I'm potentially missing my last omelet, so this better be good."

"They make awful omelets in the mess, Sir," McCleery said with a small smile, "and I think this is something worth mentioning."

"What's that?" Yntema folded his arms and waited for the intelligence officer to impress him.

"I've been looking at the damage the Dusters did to the other seventeen worlds where they seemed to have wiped out all life. And there's an obvious pattern to all of it."

"We already knew that, Commander, and I've got an omelet waiting."

Holding up one finger, McCleery said, "Hold on, Sir, I'm getting there. Now, everywhere we've got the same style of damage: chaotic, thorough. All the destruction is either minor single-impact—probably from ships landing—or from weapons fire at ground level. The damage is from the bottom up. There's also the Dusters' tracks. Not all the locations have the type of ground that shows tracks, but the ones that do match what we've seen on the ground here on Troy after the Dusters come through: back-and-forth tracks with their talons."

"Commander—"

"Here's the thing," McCleery said quickly, "you know what I see *no* evidence of on *any* of the other seventeen worlds?"

"You really think it's a good idea to keep me in suspense, Lieutenant Commander?"

McCleery winced, the use of her full rank reminding her that she needed to get to the point. "Sorry, Sir, but I needed to set this up properly." She touched controls and showed once again the image of the unique Duster tank tracks.

"The wheels on the Duster tank have a very distinctive tread. And it's *deep*, too—even the worlds where you can't make out Duster footprints, you'd be able to see evidence of the tanks. If not the tread, at least the damage they've done from running over things. But aside from here on Troy—and that only in the last couple of days—there's been *no* evidence of this."

Yntema just stared at the screen, his brow furrowed, for several seconds.

Finally, McCleery broke the silence. "Worth losing out on an omelet?"

The commander waved that off. "The cook'll hold my omelet for me, lest he get my foot in his ass. I was just busting your chops. But this—" He let out a long breath. "This is—what is this? In your opinion, Commander?"

McCleery blew out a breath through her teeth.

"One of the things they teach us in spook school, Sir, is that the discrepant part of a set is the most noteworthy. Troy is now a discrepant part of the set of the Duster invasions. We know of eighteen invasions they've engaged in, and this is the first time they've felt the need to whip out the SUV of doom they've got down there."

"And what are we supposed to do with that information?"

Unable to help herself, McCleery grinned. "That's not for me to say, Sir. My job is to provide the intel. It's the job of you and those above to you to decide what to do with it. But it is my considered opinion that NAU forces have given the Dusters more of a fight than they've ever gotten before. Which may mean they're desperate."

"Or it may mean that they love that they're getting a real challenge for a change." He put a hand on McCleery's shoulder. "Good catch, Finn. I'll bring this to the captain, and we'll take it to the rear admiral. Meanwhile, I want a *full* write-up on this."

"Aye aye, Sir, with twenty-seven eight-by-ten color glossy photographs and four-part harmony."

"Say again, Commander?" Yntema asked with a quizzical expression.

"Old folk song, Sir, sorry," McCleery said sheepishly. She pointedly did not add that it was about someone who avoided the draft in the late 20th century back on Earth.

"You may need to give that spiel to the captain, Admiral Avery, or any number of other brass—try to keep it shorter next time."

Nodding, McCleery said, "Aye aye, Sir."

"Good work, Commander."

Firebase Westermark, Eastern Shapland

STAFF SERGEANT WILLIAM ZUIDERVELD HAD JUST RETURNED TO THE MOTION DETECTOR station with his coffee, which he put down as quick as he could in the console's cup holder.

"Damn, that's hot," Zuiderveld muttered. "We can fly through space, we can go to other worlds, we can terraform planets, but we haven't figured out how to make a cup that doesn't burn your fingers when you put hot coffee into it."

"It's a mystery, Sarge," Corporal Victoria Vifquain said from the station next to his. "I don't know how you can drink that sludge, myself."

"I'm a traditionalist, Vic. I pour it down my gullet."

Vifquain snorted. "I wouldn't use that stuff to polish my weapon—it might eat through the metal."

"Not a coffee fan?"

Laughing, Vifquain said, "Oh, I *love* coffee. That's why I can't drink *that*. Back home, I buy unroasted Kona beans, roast them myself in my big-ass roaster, and grind them in my burr grinder. *That's* coffee. *This*," she pointed at Zuiderveld's cup, "is industrial waste."

Shaking his head, Zuiderveld took a sip of his coffee—

—and just as he did, an alarm went off.

"Picking up motion, ten klicks northeast."

Vifquain checked her readout next to him. "Confirmed, ten klicks, bearing— What the hell?"

Having heard the alarm, their CO, Captain Michael Crescenz, came over. "What've we got?"

"Movement, Sir," Zuiderveld said. "Ten klicks northeast."

"Not our people?" Crescenz asked his personnel officer, Sergeant Robert Modrzejewski.

The sergeant peered at the readouts on Zuiderveld's board. "We don't have that many people in one place, Cap. So unless the 104th, the 1st Marines, *and* the Leathernecks decided to have a marching party—"

"Got it," Crescenz said. "So they're Dusters. Heading?"

Vifquain said, "Sideways, Cap'n."

That was not the answer Crescenz was expecting, as he figured the aliens would be bearing right down on them. "Explain, Corporal."

"I swear to you, Cap'n, when I realized what heading they're on, I got flashbacks. My brothers and I used to play war games when we were kids. What the Dusters are doin' reminds me of when we used to do medieval games and someone decided to do a siege of a castle."

Zuiderveld looked over at Crescenz. "Sir, I've been running some numbers while Corporal Vifquain was telling her bedtime story." That last part was said with a look at the corporal, who had the decency to look a bit abashed. "And she's right—they're moving in an oval, like they're gonna surround."

"Can C&C take them out?" Crescenz asked Zuiderveld.

The staff sergeant shook his head. "No, Sir, too close."

"Dammit, we need the 104th to engage," Crescenz said.

Modrzejewski consulted his tablet. "They're way out of position. We were expecting something more direct."

"Who's closest?"

"Lieutenant Albanese's platoon is nearby—in fact, they've been reporting movement, which is probably what we're looking at here."

"All right, let's take this up the ladder." Crescenz pointed at Zuiderveld. "Updates every five, copy?"

"Yes, Sir," Zuiderveld and Vifquain said simultaneously.

While keeping a sharp eye on his readout, Zuiderveld asked Vifquain, "These brothers you played war games with—these are the same ones that washed out of Basic, right?"

Grinning, Vifquain said, "Yup."

"How often did they win?"

Vifquain shrugged. "Never."

"Really?"

"Well, okay, there was the time I let Alberto win because it was his birthday."

Zuiderveld snorted. "Figures." Then he peered more closely at the readout. "Raises the question, though..."

"What question?" Vifquain asked.

"Well, last time I checked, this wasn't a medieval castle, and the Dusters weren't knights in shining armor. So why the fuck are they setting up a siege?"

Outskirts of Eastern Shapland

After receiving instructions through his headset comms, 1st Lieutenant Lewis Albanese turned to face the sergeants in charge of the fire teams in the fifth platoon of the 104th Artillery Regiment.

"We gonna see some action, Lulu?" asked Sergeant Michael Estocin of Fire Team One.

Albanese had reluctantly gotten used to that nickname, which he'd acquired when he got promoted to second lieutenant and had kept on elevation to first lieutenant, as the merging of the abbreviations for his rank and first name proved impossible to resist. He didn't mind over-much because the alternative was for people to refer to him by his last name, which *everyone* mispronounced "al-ban-EES," rather than the proper "al-ban-AY-zee."

Answering Estocin's question, Albanese said, "Maybe yes, maybe no. HQ finally admitted that the Dusters're out there like we told them half-an-hour ago. Problem is, now we know why we ain't seen 'em yet—they're goin' around."

"Around what?" asked Fire Team Two's commander, Sergeant Leo Thorsness.

"The firebase."

"Takin' the scenic route?" Estocin queried.

Sergeant Dale Wayrynen, who commanded Fire Team Three, said, "Wait, what about all those booby traps we laid down?"

With a sigh, Albanese said, "It was good practice, but it ain't gonna do us much good if they're not coming at us."

The fifth had spent the entire morning laying down booby traps in preparation for the frontal assault that they were expecting. Now the brass wanted them to scout the Dusters, see what they were actually doing, but not to engage.

Which was fine with Albanese. He only had half a dozen fire teams out here. There was a whole fucking regiment of Dusters—they'd have their asses handed to them.

Then a thought niggled at the back of the lieutenant's mind. "Leo, I need the trap map."

Thorsness nodded and then cried out to the soldiers under his command who were in ready positions amidst the trees. "Corporal Fleek, front and center!"

The soldier in charge of keeping track of all the booby traps they'd laid, Corporal Charles Fleek, got up from underneath a bush and ran toward the sergeant. "Sir!"

Thorsness held out a hand and said, "Tablet, Corporal."

"Yes, Sir." Fleek pulled out a tablet from his pack and handed it to the sergeant.

Taking the tablet from Fleek, he said, "Thank you," and then activated it and handed it to Albanese.

After two seconds of looking at the layout of where they'd put the traps, the lieutenant muttered his grandmother's favorite curse, *"Faccim."*

"What's up, Lulu?" Thorsness asked.

Rather than answer directly, Albanese activated his comms. "Westermark, fifth, Westermark, fifth."

"Fifth, Westermark."

"Westermark, this is Lieutenant Albanese. We've got Dusters heading right toward one of our claymores. Estimate they kick it in twenty minutes."

There was a brief pause. "Say again, Lieutenant."

"I say again, the Dusters are going to set off one of our claymores in twenty minutes. Please advise."

Another pause, then another voice came on, which Albanese recognized as belonging to Colonel Adelbert Ames. "Lieutenant, this is Colonel Ames. Can you retreat without engaging the enemy?"

Because it was a bird colonel on the other end, Albanese didn't say what he wanted to say, which was *only if the enemy is blind and stupid, and we both know they're neither.* Instead, he blew out a breath and said, "Exceedingly unlikely, Sir."

Yet another pause. "Lieutenant, you are hereby ordered to prepare to engage the enemy, should they trip the claymore and engage you. Try to minimize casualties." It was to Ames's credit that he could obviously tell that last sentence sounded ridiculous even as he said it, but he had to give the order.

"Yes, *Sir.*"

"Give 'em hell, soldier."

"We absolutely will, Colonel. fifth out."

Albanese paused for one moment to cross himself and then turned his comms to address all the soldiers in the fifth.

"People, we've got Dusters about to get blown to hell by those claymores we laid down this morning over at grid 7B. They're probably gonna be a little cranky, so we're gonna need to calm them down a bit. Take positions— we do *not* engage until they do."

He paused and thought about the fact that he was likely never to eat his grandmother's pasta and sauce ever again. That pissed him off and made him even more determined to take down as many of them as he could.

"And if they do—*when* they do—we'll let 'em know that they fought the fifth!"

Firebase Westermark, Eastern Shapland

Colonel Ames listened to the reports coming in from the comms of all the members of fifth platoon.

He heard nothing until the claymores went off. It was to Lieutenant Albanese's credit that they didn't make a sound until they had to.

He heard the screams of the wounded Dusters and the noise as they jinked their way toward the fifth.

He heard the report of weapons fire from Army guns, as well as the return fire from the Dusters.

He heard the screams of the human wounded and the Duster wounded. There were far too many of the former and not enough of the latter.

When he heard nothing but the Dusters continuing on their merry way from the few comms that were still intact after the engagement, Ames quietly saluted to the air in front of him.

"We'll get them for you, Lieutenant, that's for goddamn sure." Then he turned to the comms officer. "Get me General Bauer, *now*."

"Yes, *Sir*."

Battleship NAUS Durango,
in geosync orbit around Semi-Autonomous World Troy

CAPTAIN HARRY M.P. HUSE FELT HEADACHE #4 COMING ON.

Ever since he'd taken command of *Durango*, Huse had started classifying his headaches. Number one usually came on when he had to deal with the brass, and was the one that felt like a needle was being driven through the bridge of his nose, while #2 was the throbbing at his temples that generally accompanied an argument with his husband. He hadn't had #3 in years—that ache in his forehead only showed when he had to bring an underling up on charges, and he hadn't had any underlings that fucked up in either of his last two postings. The *Durango* crew, in particular, had been exemplary, even now against as brutal an enemy as the human race had ever faced.

As for #4, that was a sharp pain behind the eyes that characterized reading a report he didn't like.

This particular report was from his chief intel officer, Lieutenant Commander McCleery, which stated that this was the first time in eighteen engagements that the Dusters had utilized tanks, as there was no evidence of any kind of large ground vehicle on the other seventeen worlds.

Huse was reading her report in advance of the lieutenant commander herself reporting along with his XO, Commander Yntema.

Just as he got to the end of it, the comms rang out with the voice of his adjutant, Lieutenant Rufus King Jr. "Sir, the XO and CIO are here, as ordered."

"Send 'em in."

The two officers entered.

Huse waved his right hand in the direction of the guest chair. He was grateful that Navy tradition was that you only saluted a senior officer once per day, and then only in duty areas. You didn't salute inside. Of course, a spaceship was entirely inside, but for these purposes, an office counted as inside. For his part, Huse didn't even like the daily saluting, and in fact, he'd been written up more than once for violating protocol by not saluting properly or at all. Everyone on *Durango* knew the hierarchy, and as long as they paid attention to their superiors, Huse didn't give a shit if they put their hands to their foreheads. It was like an oath of office: you only needed to swear it the once.

Yntema and McCleery sat down in the guest chairs, as requested.

"Sir," Yntema said, "I'm afraid Commander McCleery has a new report."

"I don't need another headache, Gordon."

"None of us do, Sir, but we've got one."

Huse looked at the intel officer. "Go ahead."

McCleery cleared her throat, glanced at Yntema, who nodded, and then said, "Sir, we've got confirmation that the Dusters are taking positions surrounding Firebases Westermark, Gasson, and Cart."

"Surrounding?"

"Yes, Sir."

"All the way around?"

"Yes, Sir."

Huse frowned. "On purpose?"

"Looks like, Sir," McCleery said. "They've moved into position completely surrounding each firebase."

Calling the report up on his screen, Huse stared at the report, which showed the images they'd taken from orbit.

"I'm not buying it," Huse finally said.

"Sir?" McCleery asked, confused.

"Oh, I believe your report," the captain said quickly. "But I'm not buying that the Dusters are this stupid. They've been tactically sound up until now. Why suddenly go all stupid on us?"

McCleery said, "If I may, Sir?"

Huse made a *go-ahead* gesture.

"This may relate to my original report about the ground vehicles. This may be new territory for them. After all, this is the first time in eighteen engagements that they've had to whip out the big guns. Maybe they're in tactically unfamiliar territory."

"Maybe." Huse stared at the report some more.

Then he got to his feet. The two junior officers did likewise.

"Either way, we gotta run this up the ladder so they can run it down to the surface. But we can't just assume the enemy is stupid. Nobody ever won a war assuming that." Then he smiled. "Of course, lots of people have won wars *because* the enemy is stupid. But that's for the enemy to deal with. We just need to fight them."

"Yes, Sir."

"Rufus!"

King stuck his head into Huse's office. "Sir?"

"Tell Admiral Avery I need to talk to him ASAP."

"Yes, Sir."

"You two are dismissed. Reports every fifteen from intel."

"Aye-aye, *Sir*," McCleery said.

A few minutes later, after Yntema and McCleery had returned to their stations, King made a slight yelping sound.

Frowning, Huse got up and went to the doorway to his office, only to see King standing at attention and Admiral Avery himself approaching.

"At ease, Lieutenant," Avery said.

King shifted to parade rest.

"Sir, I would've come to you," Huse said.

"I need to stretch my legs," Avery said. "What's the scoop?"

They both entered the office, and Huse filled him in on both reports he'd gotten from McCleery.

"We've been getting reports from the ground that indicate the same thing—good to get confirmation up here." Avery rubbed his jaw. "Interesting about the ground vehicles, but I don't see that that matters much in the here and now."

"Agreed, Sir, but it does show a pattern, as intel indicated. The Dusters may be in uncharted waters."

"That just may mean they'll fight harder. Then again, surrounding our Marines and soldiers down there may mean the same thing."

"Yes, Sir."

Avery got up from the guest chair and said, "Good work, Harry."

Huse rose and nodded. "Thank you, Admiral."

Turning toward the door, Avery said, "Tell King to contact Davis and have him be ready to send a squib to the surface."

"Aye-aye, Sir."

Camp Zion, Near Jordan, Western Shapland

"SAY WHAT?" CORPORAL JOHN MACKIE YELPED WHEN HE HEARD THE NAVY INTELLI-gence report. "Are they out of their ever-loving minds?"

"They're aliens, Mackie," Sergeant James Martin, his squad leader, said patiently. "Who knows what goes on in their minds? I sure don't. And if anybody higher-higher knows, they aren't telling me."

Mackie shook his head and looked at the men in his fire team. They were staring at him and Martin as though the two were crazy. Or at least like the Navy intel report was.

"We're Marines," Martin said. "When we're surrounded, all that means is we get to shoot in all directions." He left, headed for the platoon CP bunker. He hadn't said it, but he agreed with Mackie; the aliens had to be out of their fucking minds.

Mackie glared at his men. "You heard Sergeant Martin," he said. "All this means is we get to shoot in all directions." He shook his head in disgust. "Crazy fucking aliens," he muttered.

Lance Corporal Cafferata shook his head as he checked his weapon. "That's just nuts. I mean, completely surrounding a defensive position like that, they're all set up for a circular firing squad."

"Not if they hit us in front of them instead of their own people behind us," Orndoff said.

Horton shrugged. "We can duck."

"Damn right." Cafferata laughed and slapped the new PFC on the back. "Then we come up shooting. Got nowhere else to go, anyhow, since we're surrounded, so we fight those Dusters even harder."

"All right, people, let's get ready to rumble," Mackie said. "Sound off, 3/1/3."

"Here," Cafferata said.

"Present," said Ordnoff.

Horton just said, "Yo."

"Let's move out."

As they marched to position, Horton muttered to Ordnoff, "You know what I don't get?"

"Probably a lot," Ordnoff said.

Horton snorted. "Don't the Dusters realize that we set up the firebases to have mutually supporting fire? We should be able to hit the ones around Gasson from behind from Cart and Westermark."

"Pretty sure that's why Mackie said, 'fucking aliens'," Ordnoff said.

"Can the whispering," Mackie said. "Double time! Horton, take point."

They moved toward the firebase, having to reposition themselves because they were prepared for a frontal assault, not a weird-ass siege.

Horton was still the rookie in the squad, so he took point. He moved to take cover in one tree, then Ordnoff moved ahead while Horton covered him, then Cafferata moved past them both while they covered him, with Mackie the last to progress from the squad.

Each squad moved in the same formation, taking cover behind trees or rocks or bushes, depending on what the terrain presented.

For some reason, Horton's mind went to his best friend, Fred Phisterer. They had grown up together in Regina, Saskatchewan, living next door to each other. They went to school together, enlisted together, went through Boot Camp together.

But once they survived Boot, they got assigned to different units. Fred was sent off to a base in Europe, specifically an airbase in Budapest.

Horton got assigned to India Company, which got sent to this god-forsaken planet that had been overrun by aliens who had really dumb strategies.

"Whatcha gonna do?" Horton had said when Fred apologized for his billet. "We dance where they tell us. No big deal."

"Send me a postcard from Troy," was the last thing Fred had said to him.

The last thing he'd said back was, "The mail don't come that far."

Mackie having moved to the front, it was back to Horton, who went past his squadmates and took point once again.

As he did so, something caught Horton's eye as he once again moved forward, taking point.

Holding up a fist, he stopped moving, and then looked down.

Activating his local comms for the squad, he said, "Tripwire."

Mackie nodded. "3/1/3, hold position. Horton, check it out."

Shouldering his rifle around to his back, Horton knelt down and examined the tripwire.

Slowly moving to his left, he tracked it visually, being careful not to touch anything, finally finding a small device.

"Whatcha got, Horton?" Mackie asked.

"Could be a paperweight for all I could tell you, Corporal, but I'd bet real money that it's an explosive."

Mackie immediately activated company comms. "India Company, be advised, 3/1/3 found a booby trap, repeat, 3/1/3 found a booby trap. Eyes wide, everyone."

All the other squads acknowledged in short order.

Then a voice screamed, "Shit!"

"Back off, back—"

An explosion shook the ground, and everyone stood at the ready with their rifles.

Voices screamed over comms.

"Gaienne's down!"

"Burnes, move!"

"Corpsman!"

Sergeant Martin's voice bigfooted everyone. "3/2/1 down. Tripwire tripped. Everyone, stay frosty, we're gonna be up to our ass in Dusters in a minute."

"Confirm, Top," came the voice of Corporal Mausert. "We got movement bearing right on us."

"This is it, India Company," Martin said. "Stay frosty. *Oo-rah!*"

Around Horton, everyone cried out, "Oo-rah," but Horton himself couldn't bring himself to say it.

He'd only been with the squad a short time, having replaced PFC Zion. He wanted to fit in with the other guys, to become part of the group, but he didn't quite feel like he'd earned his place.

At least I found the tripwire, he thought as he aimed his weapon, waiting for the Dusters to come in sight.

"Here they come!"

Horton heard them first, the sound of several dozen Dusters jinking back and forth, the dirt and brush being kicked up by their movement.

And then they broke through, firing away.

Taking aim, Horton shot at them from behind his tree.

At that point, training took over. There were no thoughts of fitting in with the squad, of filling Zion's shoes, of his family back in Regina, or of Fred

Phisterer.

No, all he thought about now was the imperative of shooting Dusters and not getting shot by them.

His weapon became an extension of his own arm at that point. Aim, shoot; aim, shoot.

Three Dusters went down from his weapons fire, and three more were obviously wounded.

Aim, shoot.

He heard a scream behind him that sounded a lot like Ordnoff, but he wouldn't take his eye off the Dusters, as more of them were coming, and he had to keep shooting.

A dozen of them were headed right for him. There had been two score of them, but the other eighteen were taken down, but those dozen kept coming, and Horton was out of ammo.

Shit.

The Dusters kept firing. Horton huddled behind the tree to reload his weapon, hyperaware that the enemy drew closer each second it took.

He also saw that Ordnoff wasn't the only one who went down; he was just the only one who had time to scream. Mackie, Cafferata, and Ordnoff were all bleeding on the ground, and it didn't look like any of them were breathing.

His weapon reloaded, he fired at much closer range now, but to much less effect.

Aim, shoot.

Pain sliced through his bicep as one of the Dusters' weapons got his arm.

Eyes tearing, he blinked them away and kept firing.

Aim, shoot.

They were almost on top of him now, and he couldn't take them all out himself.

Or could he?

Looking down him, he saw the tripwire that he'd spotted, the very booby trap that the Dusters had so poorly lain for them. There were a mess of them, but only one went off.

Anyone for two?

The Dusters were almost on top of him now, and there was no way he was going to survive.

So he kicked the tripwire.

The world exploded, and Horton's last thought was he was glad Fred, at least, would survive. He did regret never sending that postcard...

CAPTAIN PATRICIA PENTZER BELLOWED TO HER GUNNERS, "I NEED FIRING SOLUTIONS, people!"

First Lieutenant Abram P. Haring reported from Gun 1, "Dusters are blocking the ground vehicle headed for us, but we've got a shot on the Dusters themselves that are closing in on Cart."

"Do it," Pentzer said. Since the Dusters were being kind enough to surround the firebases, Pentzer was happy to take whatever target presented itself.

From Gun 2, First Lieutenant William H. Newman reported, "We've got our own people blocking some of the shots on Westermark, but we've got a clear shot on the vehicle."

"Take it."

For her part, Pentzer watched as the battle unfolded, and her jaw dropped.

"Jesus," she muttered.

"What is it, Cap?" Sergeant Norton asked.

"The Dusters are taking shots without *any* regard to what they're hitting. They're taking out their own people as well as ours."

Norton shuddered as he peered over her shoulder at the display. "Takin' out a lot more of ours, though."

"Fire," Newman said.

His assistant gunnery captain, Master Sergeant David Ayers, said, "Charging," activating the laser battery, double-checking that it was aimed at the Dusters' ground vehicle, and once the indicator showed green, he fired.

The lasers weren't visible to the naked eye, but the heads-up display showed the arc of the beam in infra-red as it issued forth from the very large gun, right at its intended target.

The beam from Gun 2 was absorbed by the Duster vehicle, with absolutely no indication of any harm to the enemy target. No temperature changes, no dislocation of the metal surface, nothing.

"No damage," Ayers said, "say again, *no* damage."

"Shit," Newman said. "Fire again."

"Charging." Once again, Ayers went through the motions, and the weapon fired again, but nothing happened.

"Still no damage, LT."

Newman shook his head. "Hell with it, no point wasting good energy after bad. Switch to the Dusters themselves. Maybe we can clear a path."

Meanwhile, Gun 1 was already doing what Newman had realized was his best course of action.

"A dozen Dusters down," Master Sergeant Henry Fox said to Haring after Gun 1 fired upon the Dusters.

"Band-aid on a bullet wound," Haring muttered.

"Sir?"

"Just keep firing, Sergeant."

Pentzer was watching her own HUD when she saw the ground vehicle that was approaching their own firebase shot a wide-beam laser that was actually visible to the naked eye.

"Oh, Jesus," she muttered as the beam sliced through a dozen Marines, several pieces of artillery, and all the way through to the Dusters on the other side of the firebase.

The beam from the vehicle vaporized everything in its path.

"What the hell's wrong with them," Fox cried out, "they're taking out their own!"

"Yeah, we know, Sarge," Pentzer said, "but they're taking out ours, too. Keep firing on the support, and somebody get on the horn to Colonel Ames and tell him to get everyone the hell *out* of the line of fire of those tanks!"

Firebase Cart

Sergeant William Pelham lobbed three grenades at the ground vehicle, all of which exploded harmlessly as it lumbered toward him and his Marines.

"Keep firing!" he cried out unnecessarily.

On either side of him were the two Corporal Greenes. Corporal John Greene fired his automatic rifle on continuous burst on the tank, while

Corporal Oliver Greene went with explosive bursts on the Dusters themselves.

Only the latter was having any luck.

As soon as Pelham had both of them assigned to his squad, he knew that it was going to be a problem, especially since both corporals were dark-skinned with shaved heads and no facial hair. They were both within an inch of each other in height. They were not related.

No nickname stuck, so he finally just started calling them by first name. Even when he included rank, it was "Corporal John" and "Corporal Oliver."

"What the hell's that thing made of?" John asked as his weapons fire proved utterly ineffective.

"Fucked if I know, Corporal John, but keep firing." Pelham tossed another grenade. "Fire in the hole!"

The grenade did no more good than John's weapons fire.

"Wanna gimme a hand with these Dusters, Boss?" Oliver asked.

"That tank ain't stopping," John added.

Pelham sighed. "All right, fine. I was hoping if we kept hitting the wall enough times, sooner or later it'd crack, but that wall's tough and we ain't got that kinda time. Let's—"

The front of the tank then started to glow red.

"Shit, it's armed!" John said, even as he turned his weapons on the Dusters who were jinking back and forth toward them on the right-hand side of the tank.

"Hit the deck!" Pelham cried out.

But even as all three went down on the ground, the world suddenly got *extremely* hot.

Pelham and both Corporal Greenes didn't feel anything after that, and neither did anyone else in their platoon.

Elsewhere, Corporal Joseph Frantz was bellowing to his people, whether they outranked him or were subordinate to him, "Hit the sides! Stay away from that damn beam!"

Everyone started to get out of the way of the ground vehicles, instead going for the sides, where the Dusters were jinking back and forth and moving alongside their new toy.

Then the beam fired again, in the same direction—but there was nobody and nothing there.

Private First Class Henry Du Pont said to Frantz, "Hey, did they just fire at nothing?"

"Not just that, but that tank on steroids hasn't changed course, even after we got out of its way."

"Ain't there a saying about gift horses and mouths?" Du Pont asked.

Frantz snorted. "I grew up with horses, Private, and all's I can tell you is that horses have really bad breath. Either way, I ain't stickin' my head in one. Let's keep at it!"

Firebase Westermark

Captain Michael Crescenz saluted Colonel Adelbert Ames, the CO of the 104th as he approached.

"Report," Ames said, returning the salute.

Crescenz returned to parade rest and said, "Sir, those tanks of the Dusters are killers. But they're all front-firing, Sir. We've got to rearrange the troops so they're attacking from the side."

"That's where most of the Dusters are anyhow, aren't they, Captain?"

"Yes, Sir."

Ames nodded. "We need to take those vehicles out."

"Sir, none of the laser batteries have made a dent."

"Dammit."

"Captain Pentzer used stronger language, Sir."

"I'll bet she did. What are we looking at for casualties?"

"We're down thirty percent, Sir, and that's just KIA. Lot more wounded, but they're still fighting as best they can."

"And the enemy?"

Crescenz was reluctant to answer, and he hesitated.

"Out with it, man," Ames snapped.

"Ten percent, Sir. And that's with the Dusters themselves taking out some of their own people in the circular firing squad." Crescenz shook his head. "Sir, we just don't have the numbers."

Staff Sergeant William Zuiderveld stuck his head in Ames's office just then and saluted. "Excuse me, Sirs!"

"What is it, Sergeant?" Ames asked, returning the salute.

"I'm sorry to interrupt," Zuiderveld said, "but we seem to have hit on something. Duster casualties just skyrocketed."

"Show me."

Zuiderveld led Ames and Crescenz to the motion-detector room.

Corporal Victoria Vifquain stood at attention.

"As you were," Ames said. "Sergeant Zuiderveld says you have something to show us, Corporal?"

"Yes, Sir!"

She pointed at the motion detectors, the NAU forces in yellow, the Dusters in red, including their ground vehicle.

The Dusters were all closer to the firebases they had surrounded, but their formation was exactly the same. In particular, the devastating ground vehicles had not changed course or direction, even though there was nothing in their path anymore.

Meanwhile, the NAU soldiers and Marines had all changed position to hit the Dusters themselves. Casualties were still awful, but they'd been lessened since the NAU had adjusted.

"Sir, I don't think anyone's driving those things," Vifquain said. "They're on a preprogrammed course, and the Dusters are staying near it for cover, but—" She shrugged. "I mean, there can't be anyone at the wheel, can there? They'd have, y'know, *turned* by now."

To Crescenz, Ames said, "Ping all personnel on the ground at all three firebases. Keep it up. Ignore the ground vehicles, and just stay out of its way. Focus on the Dusters themselves and just treat the tanks like an obstacle."

"On it!"

"LET'S DO IT, HELL RAISERS," LIEUTENANT COLONEL COURTNEY SAID INTO THE COMmand freq for Marine Attack Squadron 121.

They only had the nine AV16C Kestrels left after their last engagement with the Dusters, but Courtney had been aching for a rematch.

Luckily, the orders came in. VMA 121 was to engage the Dusters that were surrounding the three firebases.

Courtney continued as the Kestrels took off: "Our targets are those RVs the Dusters have whipped out. Ground-based artillery isn't cutting it, so let's show those ground-pounders what we can do from the sky."

From the copilot seat in front of him, Lieutenant Power muted the freq and then said, "Uh, Sir? If Pentzer's lasers and the hand weapons can't do the trick, what makes higher-higher think our Hades guns can cut it?"

While Courtney saw where Power was coming from, and was glad he didn't say that on open comms, he also didn't appreciate the questioning. "Eyes forward, Marine."

"Aye-aye, Sir."

The truth was, they didn't have much of a chance, and they also ran the risk of losing the rest of VMA 121 after having almost half of them taken out in their last engagement.

But it made no sense for 121 to sit on their asses, either. In a war, you didn't keep your weapon holstered, and the nine remaining Kestrels were pretty damned effective weapons—too effective to be stuck in Schilt collecting dust.

Besides, Courtney wasn't the only one itching for a rematch with the Dusters. Despite cracked ribs, Captain Bruce insisted on going out, against the advice of the chief medical officer. ("It's going in your jacket that you went back on duty AMA," Dr. Frances Cunningham had said, and then she'd added, "It can go with all the other AMAs in pretty much every Marine's jacket on this planet." She'd rolled her eyes while she'd said it, too.) Captain Henry S. Huidekoper of Thirteen had gone through Boot Camp with Captain James R. O'Beirne of the destroyed Fourteen.

And while Courtney wasn't supposed to know that the pilot and copilot of Seven, Captain Emisire Shahan and First Lieutenant Wilma Hawkins, were sleeping with, respectively, the copilot and pilot of Eleven, the truth was that both Captain V.P. Twombly and First Lieutenant Alexandra S. Webb had revenge on their minds, too.

At least the planes were in tip-top shape. Staff Sergeant Fry and his grease monkeys did their jobs well, and everything was patched up and ready to go. He'd replaced a fuel line in Courtney's own Kestrel One, and all the other wounded birds were ready to fly again.

Having said that, Power was right about one thing: the Hades guns weren't going to cut it any more than anything else NAU forces had tried against the Duster vehicle.

The scatter-blast cluster-bombs, on the other hand…

They had nine Kestrels and three firebases to support, so it was easy enough to split them in threes.

"Sound off," Courtney said to make sure everyone was on the ball. "Team Beta."

Bruce's copilot, First Lieutenant Carla Ludwig, said, "Two on the way to Cart." Bruce herself had a sore throat from her wounds, so Ludwig was doing all the talking for Two.

Under other circumstances, Courtney would have told Bruce to listen to the doctor, but they couldn't spare anyone right now.

Besides, they were Marines. Cracked ribs were no different than a paper cut.

Three and Eight also reported that they were headed to Firebase Cart.

Courtney nodded, then said, "Team Gamma."

"Nine for Gasson," Captain Moses Luce said in his quiet drawl, while Captain Twombly was much more animated when he reported, "Eleven en route to Gasson." Captain Huidekoper likewise said, "Thirteen on the way to Gasson."

Fifteen and Sixteen were accompanying Courtney to Westermark. They were the only two Kestrels who didn't have at least a captain running things, as they'd taken too many casualties. Instead, both pilots were first lieutenants (with NCOs from Fry's ground crew serving as wingmen), and so they got to go along with the CO.

When Courtney said, "Team Alpha," both first looies, Bart Diggins and Louis P. Di Cesnola, acknowledged that they were following One.

Diggins simply replied, "Fifteen on the way to Westermark."

"Sixteen on Bart's tail, Sir," Di Cesnola said, and Courtney could hear the young officer's perpetual grin over comms. Nothing ever got that young man down, not even the casualties they'd suffered. Whenever someone asked why he was always in such a good mood, he always said the same thing: "I'm in the Corps, what the hell's there *not* to be happy about?"

"Give 'em hell, Hell Raisers," Courtney said. "*Oo-rah!*"

"*Oo-rah!*" came the response from all eight of the other planes.

Courtney flew his Kestrel toward Westermark, which was the farthest of the three from Schilt. Fifteen and Sixteen trailed behind.

"Shit," came Twombly's voice over the command freq. Gasson was closest to Schilt, so Nine, Ten, and Thirteen were already on site.

"Report, Gamma."

"Sir, we got friendlies in the blast zone."

Twombly sent his visual to Courtney's board, and the lieutenant colonel saw that the Marines on the ground were engaging the Dusters and were practically on top of the target vehicle.

"Power, get on the horn to someone at Gasson, tell them to back the hell off so we can do our jobs."

"Aye-aye, Sir," Power said, and he opened a discreet freq to Gasson.

"Holding pattern till you've got a drop, Gamma," Courtney said.

"Request permission to take out some of the Dusters while we wait?" Twombly asked.

Courtney hesitated for only a second, knowing that Twombly was particularly out for blood.

But so were they all. "Granted. Watch for friendlies."

Luce replied, "Don't you worry, Colonel, we'll just be hittin' the bad guys."

As revenge-obsessed as Twombly might have been, that's how calm under fire Luce would be. A veteran of a dozen campaigns, Luce was one of the most relaxed people Courtney had ever met, but he could navigate any flying vehicle through a fogbank blindfolded and still land right in the center of a runway.

So long as Luce's calmer head prevailed, the Gasson group would be fine.

Meanwhile, Courtney, along with Fifteen and Sixteen, did a recon run over Westermark. He saw that the Dusters' vehicle was surrounded by Dusters, but no Marines or soldiers were anywhere nearby.

Good.

Switching to local freq, Courtney said, "Alpha, ready drop, acknowledge."

"Fifteen ready," Diggins said.

Di Cesnola replied, "Rockin', rollin', and ready, Sir."

"One, two, three, on my mark," Courtney ordered.

The Kestrels flew up and around and made a second run over Westermark, flying in a straight line: One, then Fifteen, then Sixteen, about a thousand feet apart. Each would drop their load of bombs one at a time.

That last part had been suggested by Major Kawamura at Schilt. It was just a theory, but something as hard to get through as whatever the Dusters made that tank from was more likely to buckle from repeated smaller blasts rather than one big one.

Of course, "more likely" didn't mean much when they had no clue what the thing was made of or how to destroy it, but it was better than a poke in the eye with a sharp stick.

Courtney watched his HUD waiting for just the right moment to drop the cluster-bombs, and then said, "One, drop!"

Power let the bombs loose, activating the undercarriage doors that held the bombs in place.

"Break!" Courtney then said. The other part of the battle plan was to climb as high as possible as soon as the bombs dropped to give the Kestrels the best chance of not being blown out of the sky by Duster AA guns.

"Fifteen, drop!" came the voice of Diggins, and he dropped his load as well.

Diggins's copilot said, "Break!" and Fifteen started its climb.

"Sixteen, dr— Shit!" Di Cesnola cut himself off, and Courtney saw why a moment later.

Duster AA guns were firing right at him.

To Di Cesnola's credit, Sixteen dropped its load before it blew up, killed by the Dusters.

Power muttered, "Gonna miss that asshole's smile."

"Sir," Diggins said, "you seein' what I'm seein'?"

Courtney checked his HUD. It showed a huge hole in the roof of the ground vehicle.

Ludwig broadcast on the command freq. "Beta reporting success, Sir. Raised the roof, and the sucker's not moving."

"Good work, Beta."

Luce then said, "Marines on the ground have finally backed off. We remonstrated with a few aliens while we were loungin' around, though. About to begin—"

Then Luce was cut off.

Shit. "Gamma, report! Gamma! Luce, Twombly, Huidekoper, report!"

"Sir," Power said, "not picking up any of Gamma. Gasson's reporting that they've all been shot down."

Bruce's raspy voice then sounded over comms. "Sir, Beta just did a flyover of target—it's empty, Sir."

Diggins said, "Confirmed with Alpha target—no signs of *any* life in the Dusters' RV."

They'd already lost four more Kestrels, and they'd also completed their mission, so Courtney said, "Let the ground pounders worry about the cleanup. Back to base, double time!"

Firebase Cart

Corporal Joseph Frantz slowly moved toward the no-longer-moving ground vehicle, stepping over corpses of both Dusters and humans—though, he was happy to see, there were a lot more Duster bodies.

"Fuck!" came a voice from behind him, followed by the report of weapons fire.

Turning, Frantz saw PFC Du Pont had just discharged his weapon at one of the bodies.

"It twitched, Sir."

"Until it actually aims a weapon at you, save your ammo, Private. As it is, that's coming out of your allowance."

"Yes, Sir."

Normally Frantz would have been fine with Du Pont firing at an enemy who wasn't entirely dead yet. He remembered a very old movie that his mother loved, where a character referred to the difference between mostly dead and all dead—mostly dead meant partly alive and still able to be revived. The enemy needed to be all dead, otherwise, they were still targets.

But NAU forces were also depressingly low on ammunition, and if this kept up much longer before they got resupply, they were going to have to start throwing rocks at the Dusters.

Assuming they even got resupply. Frantz was genuinely concerned that the suits back on Earth would decide to just write off Troy as the 18th victims of the Dusters and not send any more good people to die.

What especially pissed Frantz off was that he could totally understand that theoretical point of view. If he had been one of the suits back on Earth, he might well consider the need just to cut their losses on Troy.

Let's hope I'm a bigger asshole than they are, he thought as he approached the vehicle.

The 121st had done a number on the roof, finally breaking through the seemingly impenetrable hull. His line to Du Pont before about looking a gift horse in the mouth still held, though. They had to clear the vehicle before they could declare it no longer a factor.

As soon as he reached the base of the tank, his soldiers right behind him, he confirmed that there were no hostiles still breathing around.

"Quinlan, Du Pont, Bourke, get up there."

The three privates got to work. PFC James Quinlan got a grappling hook out of his pack and attached it to a rope that Du Pont provided. He then handed it to John Gregory Bourke, who holstered his weapon and then twirled the rope and threw it up to the roof of the tank.

The hook caught on the big hole that the 121st had made with ease. Bourke tugged on it and smiled. "Easy as 3.14159."

"Say what, Greg?" Du Pont asked. Bourke hated being called "John."

"It's math humor," Quinlan said. "Easy as pi."

"That supposed to be funny?" Du Pont asked.

"Only to folks with more than one brain cell," Bourke said as he tugged one more time on the rope, then started to climb up.

"Du Pont left his brain cell on Earth," Quinlan said. "S'why he fired on that dead Duster."

"Fuck you, Jimmy," Du Pont said, but he was smiling ruefully.

Frantz knew that Du Pont wouldn't make that mistake twice, and his fellows razzing him reassured him that everyone still trusted him. After all, you didn't give shit to someone you didn't trust.

First Du Pont, then Quinlan climbed up the rope. Du Pont was halfway up when Bourke hit the roof, and he immediately unholstered his rifle and pointed it down into the gaping hole in the roof.

"Sonofa— Clear!"

Frantz looked up in surprise. He hadn't even gone down into the thing yet. "Say again, Bourke?"

"Clear—there's nothing here."

Du Pont had made it to the top and was also peering down with his weapon at the ready. "Wow, this— Corporal, you gotta see this."

Frantz had intended to wait until the privates completely cleared the vehicle before going in himself, but it seemed they already had.

Holstering his weapon and gripping the rope, he climbed up the side of the tank. The metal was unyielding under his boots, and he wondered just what the hell the Dusters made this damn thing out of.

He got to the top and peered down through the jagged hole that was pretty much all that was left of the vehicle's top.

Inside was a great deal of machinery of a design he'd never seen before.

And that was it. No bodies, no Dusters, not even any chairs or places for a living being to stand or sit or lay down or *anything*.

Just equipment.

"No wonder this thing was just firing straight ahead," Frantz muttered. "It's completely automated. Not even remote-controlled, they just pointed it at the firebase and had it shoot until it was done."

"Well, maybe it was being controlled," Du Pont said, "and the guy controlling it is one of those DBs down below."

"Maybe. Either way, let's secure this thing. The nerds at the Corps of Engineers are gonna want a gander at this sucker."

Combat Action Center, Battleship NAUS *Durango*

RADARMAN 2 MICHAEL MCCORMICK GULPED DOWN THE LAST OF HIS TEA AND STARED at the screen, which continued to show him the same nothing it had all along.

But he had to keep staring. At this stage of the action in and above Troy, the job of keeping an eye on the radar was at once the most boring and the most important.

Most boring because nothing had happened since the last batch of Dusters came through.

Most important, because something *could* happen, and if and when it did, they needed to know immediately.

When *Durango* first arrived at Troy, everyone had been caught off-guard by the Duster ships that appeared from behind Troy's moon, nicknamed Mini Mouse. But that was when they didn't know what to expect from their trip to Troy—their job was, after all, to find out what, exactly, had happened.

Now, though, they had to keep a sharp eye out.

The radar station that was pointed at the location through which the Dusters' wormhole had opened each time they'd arrived was staffed by two people at all times, though McCormick was alone for the moment because Radarman 3 John F. Bickford was in the head.

Making it more boring, but no less important, was that they had a twelve-hour duty shift.

All things being equal, *Durango* functioned on three eight-hour watches, but with some personnel killed in action, others rotated to the surface to replace personnel KIA down there, shortages forced some stations into two twelve-hour watches instead.

Since the physical requirements of staffing radar were minimal, it was one of those cut from three to two.

Bickford came back in from the head, nodding to Chief Petty Officer James W. Verney and taking his seat next to McCormick.

"Everything come out okay?" McCormick asked.

Shuddering, Bickford asked, "You gotta ask that *every* time, Mike?"

"I just don't want to slip on your piss when I go."

"Don't worry. I held it nice and steady just for you."

Behind them, Verney said, "Jesus H., you guys gotta do this comedy routine *every* time one of you goes to the head?"

McCormick shrugged. "It's our way of breaking up the monotony, Chief."

"What, with more monotony? Smart plan, Radarman."

"I never said it was a *good* way." McCormick turned to grin at the chief.

Bickford added, "That's why we're lowly radarmen."

"But why are we called that?" McCormick asked.

In a very slow, deliberate tone, as if speaking to a four-year-old, Bickford said, "Because we're the men who run the radar."

"Well, first of all, I think Davidson would object to the first part," McCormick said, referring to Radarman 3 Andrea Davidson, who had McCormick's spot on the other watch.

Verney said, "'Radarwoman' and 'radarperson' have too many syllables. And Davidson, I know for a fact, doesn't give a fuck."

"Right, but that brings us to the first half of the word." As he spoke, McCormick got up and walked over to the recycler and tossed the used teabag in his mug into it.

Holding his hands palms-up, Bickford asked, "What the hell's wrong with that? You work at the radar station. What else are we supposed to be called?"

"But it's not radar, really."

Verney rolled his eyes. "Oh, here we go again."

Bickford shot a look at the chief. "Again?"

"You used to be on second watch, Bickford, and McCormick here was on first, so you've been spared his stupid rants. Until now, that is."

McCormick wanted more tea, but he wasn't about to leave the CAC for the galley until he was done with his rant. Especially now that the chief had baited him.

"How," Bickford asked, his arms now folded, "is it not radar?"

"Radar's actually an acronym for radio detection and ranging."

"That's a pretty crappy acronym," Bickford said. "Shouldn't it be RDR?"

"Talk to the U.S. Navy circa World War II. The Royal Air Force went with radio azimuth direction and ranging, but that's worse 'cause most people don't know what an azimuth is."

"Most people don't know that radar's an acronym, either," Bickford said, "so what difference does it make what it stands for?"

"Because of what it stands for. We haven't used radio signals for detection in ages, certainly not since we went into space. Lasers are way more efficient because light's faster than sound, and space is so big that we need the speed so the info gets to us in a timely manner."

This time Bickford rolled his eyes. "Gee, it's a good thing you told me that, Pete, 'cause I was asleep during training."

"Well, that certainly explains your aptitude rating," Verney said with a cheeky grin.

"Thanks, Chief," Bickford drawled, then turned back to McCormick. "Besides, so what? Language adjusts—it always has. When you record something visually, you still say you film it, even though nobody's used film in ages. And what we do here is the same type of thing that the old radar systems in World War II did, only better and faster—but it does the same basic thing, so it has the same name. So what's the big deal?"

McCormick just stared at Bickford for several seconds, his mouth hanging open.

The brief silence was broken by Verney's laughter. "Damn, I shoulda put you on watch with McCormick sooner. You're the first person to shut him up this whole tour."

Both radarmen chuckled, and McCormick said, "Chief, request permission to hit Radarman Bickford on the head with my tea mug."

"Denied—you might break the mug, and a new one isn't in the budget, and if you don't have your tea, you're even *more* of a pain in the ass."

Grinning, McCormick then said, "In that case, permission to get more tea."

Before the chief could reply, Bickford said, "Got a reading!"

All thoughts of tea abandoned, McCormick scrambled into his seat next to Bickford. The radar—misnamed though it may have been—had picked up readings consistent with a wormhole opening. And it was in the same relative location as the last two Duster wormholes.

Verney tapped the intercom and said, "Mess hall, CAC. Lieutenant Hudner, you're needed."

Thomas J. Hudner, the head of the radar division, ran in a few moments later. Protocol kept Verney from pointing out that the lieutenant had a bit of mustard from the lunch the chief had interrupted on his chin.

"What's happening, Chief?" Hudner asked

"Radarman McCormick, report to the lieutenant," Verney said.

"Sir," McCormick said, "we've got a Duster wormhole, and now we're picking up indications of objects coming through. Based on previous data, we should have confirmation in six minutes."

Hudner wasted no time, but activated the intercom. While doing so, he wiped off the mustard with his wrist, which relieved Verney.

"Bridge, CAC."

The first time they encountered the Dusters, the watch officer on the bridge was Lieutenant Commander Allen Buchanan, who'd sounded almost bored.

Buchanan had been reassigned to the surface to administrate the field hospital, as his previous assignment was administration at the Saxton Naval Hospital on Luna. To Hudner's surprise, the watch officer was Captain Huse his own self, who said, "CAC, bridge. What's happening, Mr. Hudner?"

Not expecting to hear directly from the captain, Hudner swallowed and said, "Wormhole opening with more Dusters coming in, Sir. We should have numbers in five minutes."

"Sound general quarters," Huse said, "Meteors, get ready to launch, and someone wake up Admiral Avery."

Admiral's Bridge, Durango

Rear Admiral James Avery once again studied the big board. There were twenty-seven blips on the right-hand side, indicating the Dusters that had come through the wormhole.

On the left was what was left of Task Force 8.

Captain Huse said, "Radar room reporting that enemy vessels are all the same size."

That got Avery to turn and face the captain of the ship. "Say again, Captain?"

"This isn't a fleet, it's a battle group. They're all small craft, moving in a single formation."

"No support vessels, no motherships?"

"That's what they're telling me." Huse pointed at the big board. "And look at those blips—they're all the same size."

The tactical display on the big board generally had larger blips for bigger craft—as an example, the blip for the *Durango* was the largest on the board—but Huse was correct in that the Duster markers were the same size. Avery had assumed that to be due to a lack of data, as the Dusters were still several light-minutes away.

But no, they really were all the same size. "Just a bunch of fighters?"

"Looks like," Huse said.

The board showed several Meteors launching from the *Norman Scott*—many fewer than the last time they engaged the Dusters.

"Laser batteries, stand by," Avery said.

Lieutenant Commander George Davis relayed those orders to the *Scott*, the only capital ship they had left.

Chief Henry Finkenbiner said, "Laser batteries standing by."

Then two of the blips disappeared.

"What the hell was that?"

Finkenbiner peered at the display at the weapons console. "Sir, we no longer have a firing solution on enemy vessels designated seventeen and twenty-four."

"Did someone fire on them?" Avery asked angrily.

"Meteors not in range," Davis said, "and neither we nor the *Scott* have fired."

Huse added, "Radar room confirms heat signatures consistent with enemy ships exploding."

Avery shook his head. "What the hell just happened?"

"Meteors thirty seconds from optimum firing range," Finkenbiner said by way of reminding Avery that he still had to give the order to fire batteries.

"Thank you, Chief. Fire batteries."

The lasers fired from both *Durango* and *Scott* and struck four of the enemy targets.

Three of them went the same way as the two that had seemingly spontaneously exploded.

"Meteors engaging," Finkenbiner said at the same time that Lieutenant Julius Townsend said, "Enemy firing."

Two more Duster blips disappeared without warning.

"Bridge, CAC," came the voice of Lieutenant Hudner over the intercom.

Huse said, "CAC, bridge, report."

"Sir," Hudner said, "we're reading several of the Duster ships venting atmo—including the two that just went boom."

"Which ones?" Avery asked.

"Ah, two, nine, eleven, twenty, and twenty-seven."

Turning to Davis, Avery said, "Tell Cromwell to have the Meteors focus their fire on every ship *but* those five. We can turn on the wounded later, but let's focus on the ones that have a better shot at taking us down."

"Aye-aye, Sir," Davis said and relayed the order to the *Scott*'s CAG.

Even as he did so, three more enemy ships exploded.

That still left twenty-one Duster vessels, and they fired back.

Avery now focused entirely on the big board as he saw the Dusters fire their laser batteries on the irritatingly few remaining Meteors.

"Batteries recharged," Finkenbiner said.

"Fire," Avery ordered.

Avery was pleased to see that, while his side suffered some losses, the enemy suffered many more, and within a few minutes, there were only seven Duster fighters left intact, and two of them were drifting.

To Davis, Avery said, "Have Cromwell tow fifteen and nineteen in." Those were the two that were drifting.

"Aye-aye," Davis said, and relayed the order.

Townsend said, "Fifteen is firing!"

Before Avery could say anything, fifteen exploded without having fired.

"Bridge, CAC." It was Hudner again. "Sirs, the heat signature was much greater on fifteen. I think the weapons malfunctioned."

"We'll take what we can get," Huse muttered.

Avery shook his head. "What the hell are they throwing at us, their surplus ships? Boats that were in the repair yard? Rejected designs?"

"All of the above?" Huse asked.

One of the Meteors was now towing nineteen. The other Meteors exchanged fire with the remaining Duster ships.

In a few more minutes, it was over. The Dusters were all killed, save the one being towed, and the NAU losses were lighter than Avery had feared.

"Comm," he said to Davis, "get General Bauer on the horn. If this is the best the Dusters can do for reinforcements, we might have a shot at winning this thing."

Farmhouse near Jordan, Eastern Shapland

Lance Corporal Inouye led first team to their designated spot, having been given instructions by Sergeant Denig of Force Recon as to where the latter's people were, and then been given orders by Sergeant O'Donoghue as to where to set up.

Inouye's team was to enter the farmhouse first, followed by five more teams to secure the location.

They still didn't know if there were just a few Dusters in there or a whole battalion, but Inouye figured that they knew they were surrounded at this point.

Not that the Marines *actually* surrounded them. They were hardly going to make the same mistake the Dusters made around the firebases.

No, they were in a semicircle around the front entrance, with two teams in reserve around the rear in case the Dusters decided to try to sneak out the back door. Not that there was a back door, but they'd done enough tunneling that Lieutenant Commiskey didn't want to take any chances. They needed to be ready for anything, including a ton of Dusters firing at them all at once.

For his part, Inouye just didn't want to die.

He had lived his entire life in fear of him and his entire family dying. Service was in his blood—his mother was a sergeant in the Honolulu Police Department, and his father was a firefighter in the same Hawai'ian city. All four grandparents served as well: Tutu Mark and Tutu Anna were both in the Army, Tutu Tommy was a Marine, and Tutu Yvonne joined the Navy.

When he was eight years old, an HPD detective came to the house and informed him and his father that his mother had been wounded in the line of duty. She'd survived that, and went back to work a few months later, though she stayed in administrative duties from that point forward. But the gut-twisting fear that his mother was dying never left young Daniel.

From that day forward, he lived in constant fear of losing everyone he loved and of dying himself, that his mother would get shot again (never mind that she was on desk duty), that his father would die in a fire, or that any of his grandparents would be killed in combat. Even though, by the time he turned eighteen, his mother was comfortably riding a desk, and his father had retired after twenty years on the job, and all four tutus were no longer on active duty, the fear didn't go away.

He felt there were only two ways to confront those fears. One was music. Inouye had a great singing voice, and he loved to use it.

The other was to become a Marine himself.

It was, on the face of it, an insane notion. But he also did some research that revealed some very simple math: the vast majority of the people who signed up for the armed forces—or to be police officers or firefighters, for that matter—did not die on the job. Indeed, the chances of doing so were about one in a million, as long as the NAU wasn't in a declared state of war.

As a private in Third Platoon, he saw no action outside of training. There was plenty of it in training, of course, but none of it was life-threatening, though it did involve being *ready* for something life-threatening.

Then he got promoted to lance corporal.

Two days later, the NAU got sucked into a war against these crazy-ass aliens.

The whole idea was working up until then, he thought dolefully.

But he didn't let the rest of the team know that. They just knew him as the guy who liked to sing a lot. In fact, he spent most of the downtime on the trip to Troy and between engagements on the planet regaling the rest of third platoon with songs. He crooned lovely renditions of many popular songs from the past few years: "One Hour Too Far," "Planetfall," "Love Will Let You Down," and "Vitamin Star."

One time, Vargas asked him to sing, "Tiny Bubbles," and in response, Inouye did an off-key version of Vargas's favorite song, "Layla," and Vargas stopped making him sing stupid Hawai'ian songs after that. Though he did hit him with crap like the chickenshit joke...

Corporal Vincent Capodanno signaled for them to enter. Inouye went first, gun raised, entering the farmhouse's large vestibule. To the left was a dining room and kitchen, to the right a large living area, and directly in front was a staircase to the second level and a door that went to the basement.

Capodanno, Vargas, and the new guy, Okubo, all entered behind him, and they took up positions. Second team, fifth team, and eighth team followed right behind.

Eighth team then moved to secure the upstairs, as planned.

Just as the last private from eighth hit the stairs, the basement door flew open.

Inouye fired instinctively, as they'd already gotten the report from Force Recon that there were Dusters inside, possibly in the basement.

Hesitation got you someone visiting your parents' house to tell them you're dead.

The first Duster through the door went down immediately from Inouye's fire, but there were a dozen more behind that one, and they came *pouring* through the door all at once, weapons blazing.

On the one hand, it was a crazy stunt, and risky with this many Marines around.

On the other hand, even as Inouye was firing, he saw Vargas, Okubo, and Capodanno all get shot.

Then, after a few minutes, the shooting just stopped, as no more Dusters came through. Someone shouted for a corpsman as Inouye headed for the basement door.

His initial estimate of a dozen Dusters was wrong—he only counted seven Duster corpses on the floor. But the way they jinked about combined with the cramped space made it seem like there were more.

Sergeant Ruiz had entered at some point during the mêlée, along with several corpsmen to care for the wounded. Inouye noted that Okubo was still breathing, but he wasn't sure about Capodanno and Vargas.

Grieve later. At least he was still in one piece.

Ruiz spoke *sotto voce* into the discreet battalion freq. "Inouye, Bresnahan, Gurke, Kephart, check the basement. Eighth team, inform when you clear the top floor. Secure the ground floor."

Inouye wasn't sure why there was any need for Ruiz to be so quiet, given that there was plenty of noise, and stealth was pretty much out the window at this point.

Then again, shouting wasn't always heard, especially with eighth team upstairs. If it was on comms, everyone was guaranteed to hear it.

Inouye tried not to think about the fact that Bresnahan and Gurke were from second team and Kephart from fifth. Besides, they all had the same training.

Since the other three were PFCs, Inouye took point as the ranking Marine. He gingerly stepped over the Duster corpses and headed to the staircase.

He slowly padded down the stairs, weapon raised, casting his eyes back and forth. The basement was dimly lit by a far-away source.

Pointing to the night-vision visor on his helmet, he then pulled it down. He heard the other three do likewise a second later.

The entire basement became a much clearer, albeit entirely green-tinged, tableau, as the visor conveyed images via how much heat they gave off rather than how much light they reflected.

All he got for heat signatures, though were five ovoid shapes on one of the workbenches, which was along the far wall—no other signs of life.

No, wait, there was one thing—residual heat on the floor leading back—to a tunnel!

Hitting comms, Inouye said, "Hey, luna, we got no enemy contact, but we have some weird objects, and a tunnel leading north. Tunnel's been dug out of the basement wall."

Gurke muttered, "Regular buncha gophers, we got."

Ruiz's voice crackled over the speakers. "Roger that. Investigate tunnels."

Inouye pointed at Gurke and Bresnahan and then at the tunnel. Let *them* take point.

They nodded and moved forward.

PFC James Kephart said, "Uh, Danny?"

Inouye looked over at Kephart, who was inspecting the round shapes. "Yeah?"

"Um, I think these are eggs."

"Say what?"

"Eggs. And I ain't talkin' the kind you scramble, I'm talkin' the kind that turns into bouncing baby Dusters."

"Shit." He hit comms again. "Sergeant, I think we're looking at a creche here."

For a moment, there was no response, and Inouye was worried that comms were out.

"Say again, Corporal?"

"We've got what looks like five eggs down here." He looked more closely at the workbench and noticed that there were strips of cloth arranged around the shapes, like napkins next to plates on a dining room table. "It looks like a nest, Sarge. That's what they were setting up here. It's a goddamn nursery!"

Upstairs, Ruiz shook his head in amazement. *Middle of a goddamn war and they're making babies?*

He contacted Corporal Paul J. Wiedorfer of seventh team, which was one of the two out back. "Seventh team, any activity?"

Wiedorfer glanced over at PFC Pedro Cano, who held the scanner.

At first, Cano shook his head no, but then he said, "Hold up."

"Stand by," Wiedorfer said to Ruiz.

"Pickin' up movement," Cano said.

After Wiedorfer relayed that to Ruiz, the sergeant said, "We've got a tunnel in the basement leading away from the house. That's probably them. I want Seventh to follow and engage if you can."

"On it."

Once, Wiedorfer had made the mistake of saying, "Yes, Sir" to Ruiz. But only once. Ruiz made his displeasure felt in multiple ways. "Don't let these stripes fool you, Corporal, I fucking *work* for a living."

Wiedorfer had almost made the mistake of responding to *that* with "Yes, Sir," but stopped himself just in time, though he almost choked on it. Saying "Yes, Sir" to superior officers was second nature for a Marine who'd survived Boot.

But as far as Ruiz was concerned, he was a Leatherneck just like the rest of them, even with the three stripes on his sleeve.

Since both seventh team and ninth team were guarding the rear— seventh on the west side of the farmhouse, ninth on the east—Ruiz had specified that Wiedorfer's team was to go after the Dusters that were scampering underground, leaving Ninth to hold position in case something else happened behind the farmhouse.

There was nobody around aside from the Dusters Cano was picking up, but it still paid to be operationally secure, so Wiedorfer didn't raise his voice to shout across the way to where ninth team was positioned to the east of the farmhouse. Instead, he pointed at Corporal Britt Slabinski, then pointed to the ground, then pointed at himself and then at the way north.

Slabinski gave him a thumb's up in reply.

Secure in the knowledge that Slabinski would reposition his people for maximum coverage once seventh team moved out, Wiedorfer pointed at Cano, indicating he should take point, since he had the scanner.

Lance Corporal George W. Roosevelt followed close behind Cano. While the latter was good enough to switch from his scanner to his weapon in a second or two, that span could be an eternity when you were under fire yourself. So Roosevelt backed him up.

PFC Matthew S. Quay was the worst shot in the team, so he got the big shotgun and took up the rear to cover the team's six.

Cano, Wiedorfer noted, was heading straight toward a well.

Directly underneath seventh team, Inouye and his group followed down the tunnel. Inouye had no idea how the Dusters excavated this passage— there was no evidence of tool use to make these big burrows in the ground—

but however they did it, the tunnel was stable and smooth as possible given that it was made of compacted dirt.

The whole notion freaked Inouye out a little bit. Growing up in Hawai'i, he was used to open spaces. Nobody on the island of O'ahu had basements, and Inouye had never even been in an enclosed space until he went to Boot. That was another reason why he had Gurke and Bresnahan take point.

However, he followed them in due course, telling Kephart, "Stay here, guard these suckers."

"Okay, but—I mean, they're just eggs."

"No, they're these people's kids, and trust me, ain't nobody in this universe crankier than a mother protecting her young. Dusters may not be the same, but they may, and it ain't worth the risk. Guard those things with both eyes open."

"Don't wink, got it," Kephart said with a cheeky grin.

Rolling his eyes, Inouye jogged to catch up with Gurke and Bresnahan.

As soon as Inouye got to them, Gurke pointed ahead. "You hear that?" he whispered.

The weird brushing sound of the Dusters' jinking movements over dirt. Inouye had heard that way too much since they landed on Troy.

"Let's double-time it."

Top-side, Wiedorfer, Cano, Quay, and Roosevelt set up around the well. Sure enough, half a dozen Duster started to scamper up the sides. They saw the four Marines and turned tail and ran back the way they came.

"Did you see any weapons on them?" Wiedorfer asked.

All three PFCs shook their heads.

"Civilians, maybe?" Roosevelt asked. "Prob'ly why they were running."

Down below, Inouye raised his weapon when he saw six Dusters coming toward them, but they stopped short and ceased movement.

"They ain't armed," Gurke said.

"I noticed," Inouye replied.

He looked beyond the Dusters to see another hole in a wall that led to a place that was getting some sunlight.

"If I remember right," Bresnahan said, "that's the well over there."

A rope dropped from above just beyond the hole, and then Roosevelt landed with a squish. Inouye noted that the lance corporal was up to his ankles in water, which made sense if that was a well.

The Dusters continued not to move.

Roosevelt said, "They turned tail and ran just lookin' at us up top. Now they ain't movin'."

Inouye nodded. "Yeah." He activated comms and said, "Sergeant Ruiz, seventh team and the tunnel crew just captured us six unarmed Dusters. We, um, we think they're surrendering."

"Corporal, please confirm, unarmed Dusters surrendering?"

"Confirming unarmed—surrendering is a guess. I mean, they're not raising their arms or waving a white flag or anything, but they're aliens. They're just, y'know, *standing* there."

"All right, Corporal, secure them and bring them back to the farmhouse."

"Will do." Inouye also knew better than to "Sir" the sergeant. "Let's bundle us up some prisoners."

Inside the Command Bunker, Firebase Gasson

CAPTAIN PATRICIA PENTZER WATCHED HER STATUS BOARD IN HORROR AS SHE SAW THAT the Duster ground vehicle was heading straight for her front door, along with a large number of Dusters.

Opening her comms to a wide freq, she cried out, "Mayday, mayday, command bunker under attack!"

Even as she did so, she whipped out her sidearm.

Behind her, Sergeant Norton did likewise. "Been a while since I fired a gun this small."

Pentzer snorted.

There was no response to her mayday, which meant that no one was available to help her. They were too busy keeping their own asses intact to have time to come save Pentzer's.

To First Lieutenants Haring and Newman, she said, "Norton and I will cover you. Keep firing at the Dusters on the other firebases."

"Yes, Ma'am," they both said in unison.

Pentzer and Norton set up in position near the front door to the bunker, which was dented and scorched from being fired upon by the Dusters.

"Think it'll hold, Cap?" Norton asked, indicating the door with his head.

"Hell if I know," Pentzer answered. "Only thing that's even slowed the Dusters' little APC, or whatever it is, down is cluster bombs. Lasers and everything else is like spitting on it. This door's good, but it's taken a pounding already, and I'm not sure it's gonna be able to keep that damn thing back."

Haring called out, "Captain?"

"Go, Haring."

"I've got good news and bad news. Which do you want first?"

Again, Pentzer snorted. "Can't remember the last time I got good news, so hit me with that."

"The Dusters attacking Cart and Westermark are in full retreat."

Despite herself, Pentzer was impressed. Even factoring in their stupid surround-the-fire-base strategy, the Dusters had numbers and willingness not to let friendly fire get in the way of victory on their side.

However, she had a feeling she could guess the bad news.

Sure enough, Haring went on: "The bad news, though, is that they're retreating here."

"Of course, they are."

Her mayday had continued to go unanswered, and the firebase was now surrounded, the Kestrels that tried to blow up the tank were killed, and now they were about to be overrun.

"I don't fancy the idea of the Dusters getting their hands on all our big guns," she said.

"Me either," Norton said.

"They got enough of an advantage."

As Pentzer spoke, she could hear the fire on the bunker intensifying. It was only a matter of time.

"They do," Norton said.

"Can anyone get Colonel Ames or Lieutenant Grieg or *someone* on comms?"

Staff Sergeant Cleto Rodriguez had taken over at communications. "I can't raise anyone on Gasson, Cap'n. All I can get from Cart and Westermark is that they're still securing their positions."

Pentzer nodded, even as the Dusters continued to pound on the bunker's walls and door.

It would be at least a few minutes before any reinforcements would get the order to come to Gasson, and it would take many more minutes for them to arrive, if not longer.

Gasson didn't have that kind of time.

"Fuck it. Engage Plan Omega."

Norton nodded. "That's the right call, Cap."

Haring and Newman both again said, "Yes, Ma'am" in unison, and they, along with their crews, started the process by which the big guns would overload and explode.

To Rodriguez, she said, "Send our intentions to General Bauer at HQ."

Swallowing loudly, Rodriguez said, "Yes, Ma'am."

About seven seconds before the Dusters busted down the bunker door, the guns exploded in a fiery conflagration. The firebase had become a literal base on fire, with flames vaporizing everyone inside as well as everyone who was right outside—which was a large number of the Dusters.

Headquarters, North American Union Forces,
near Millerton, Shapland

Lieutenant General Bauer was starting to allow himself to think that they might pull this off.

Even though it would clearly be at a most terrible cost.

He'd been collecting reports for the last hour that were guardedly encouraging.

The first was from Admiral Avery in space.

"General, we had twenty-seven Duster ships come in as reinforcements, but they didn't really reinforce all that well. Just a collection of fighters, no support, no capital ships."

That surprised Bauer. "That's it?" When he'd gotten the word that another Duster wormhole had opened, he had assumed another fleet was going to come through. This was barely even a group, much less a fleet.

"That's it. We were able to take them out with minimal losses, thank Christ. And, Harold? I swear to God, half those ships blew up all on their own."

"What's your take, Jim?"

"It is my considered opinion that the Dusters have spent the first two major engagements throwing their best at us, and they're now scraping the bottom of the barrel."

Bauer nodded. That was his take, as well. "What's your status?"

"We've got one Duster ship in tow that's depowered."

"I'll contact Captain Otani and tell his nerd squad to expect another toy to play with," Bauer said. Kazuo Otani was the commanding officer of the team from the Army Corps of Engineers assigned to Troy.

"Another?"

"We've captured two of the Dusters' tanks."

"Excellent. I'll have Captain Huse coordinate delivery of the Duster ship."

Bauer's next reports were from Colonel Ames at the firebases.

"Cart and Westermark are secure," Ames said. "Not without significant losses, but we've got two of those vehicles for Captain Otani's nerds to play with."

"A pity about Gasson," Bauer said quietly.

Ames nodded. "We couldn't secure it. Forces there were overrun, and the enemy was two steps away from capturing the base *and* its weaponry. Captain Pentzer had no choice but to Plan Omega the base."

"It was absolutely the right call, but I suspect we're gonna miss those lasers before this is over."

"Better to have them slagged than in the Dusters' hands, Sir."

"Damn right. Good work, Colonel."

Bauer's final report was from Colonel Frances Cunningham, M.D., the chief medical officer.

"Colonel, what's the casualty report?"

"Appalling," she said, wiping sweat off her brow. "We lost fifty percent of our people assigned to the firebases before Pat Pentzer decided to channel the kamikazes. We're still crawling through the wreckage there for final numbers."

The general was about to say something, but the doctor held up her hand.

"I know, General, I know, get the wounded back on duty as fast as possible."

"I'm sure you will, Colonel. What's the supply situation like?"

"Also appalling. We're low on bandages, staples, salves, painkillers, antibiotics... Honestly, it'd be faster to tell you what we're *not* low on."

Bauer took the bait. "Fine, what are we *not* low on?"

"Casualties. Think you can do something about that?"

With a sigh, Bauer shook his head. "It's war, Frances, you know—"

"Oh, for the love of Christ, don't give me the 'in war, people die' speech. I get that, but what I'm worried about right now aren't the people dying in combat, it's the ones that'll die of an infection or from some post-op complication because I don't have the right meds to give them."

"I'll see what I can get from the Navy," Bauer said.

"Yeah, I tried that, but Pym's a hoarding little shit," Cunningham said, referring to Lieutenant Commander James Pym, her equivalent with the Navy. "I used all my charm on him, and he won't give me bupkus."

"I'll give it a shot anyhow." Bauer smirked. "My charm has three stars to back it up, not just a little bird."

Cunningham smiled for the first time in a long time. "Thank you, Harry."

"Keep up the good work, Frances."

After the CMO signed off, Bauer put in a call back to *Durango*. He needed to pry more supplies out of Pym, and then figure out what crazy-ass thing the Dusters were going to try next...

Corps of Engineers Bunker,
Headquarters, North American Union Forces,
near Millerton, Shapland

MOST OF WHAT THE NAU ARMY SENT TO TROY INCLUDED SOLDIERS UNDER THE
command of Major General Conrad Noll, clerical and support staff, under
the command of Lieutenant Colonel Ernest von Vegesack, and medical
personnel under the command of Colonel Frances Cunningham.

But there were also a hundred or so people under the auspices of the
Army Corps of Engineers, commanded by Captain Kazuo Otani.

The main job of the "Aces," as they'd been nicknamed, was to build
things. Upon making planetfall, the Aces—the vast majority of whom were
construction workers who put up buildings and bunkers, built bridges and
byways, and generally made something out of nothing under the watchful
eye of Chief Petty Officer Samantha Fuqua—built everything that the NAU
forces needed to run their campaign on Troy.

The main reason why it took so long for the Dusters to get through the
command bunker of Firebase Gasson—thus giving Captain Pentzer time to
enact Plan Omega—was because the Aces built their bunkers to *last*. Even
the Dusters' devastating weaponry couldn't get completely through on one
shot.

However, in addition to Fuqua's crack construction squad, the Aces also
included a team of specialists under the command of Otani's second-in-
command, Lieutenant Nicky Daniel Bacon, who had acquired the nickname
"Pork" at some point in his career and had yet to shake it. Where Fuqua's
scaffold monkeys were all privates, Pork's team of scientists, engineers,

and programmers all had the rank of specialist and were experts in their particular field.

They hadn't had much to do since making planetfall, aside from helping the Aces out in their construction work—nobody sat idle for long if they wanted to stay in the Army—and examining what little equipment they'd managed to take off the Dusters. Bacon had been genuinely concerned that they were going to go stir crazy without a proper project to occupy their time, and that usually led to a practical joke war among the group of them, which would later extend to the rest of the Aces.

Now, though, they had the mother lode, for which Bacon was grateful, as he really wasn't looking forward to waking up with an APC taken apart and reassembled in his bunk, which was what happened the last time his specialists were not given sufficiently diverting tasks to perform.

The Dusters' latest batch of reinforcements had also included their fancy new ground vehicles, and the two captured at Firebases Cart and Westermark had been brought to "the Pork Barrel," a shack that was the last item constructed by Fuqua's team on Troy as it had the lowest priority. But it was filled with all the equipment they needed to play with their toys, once they got their hands on some.

And this one was a doozy, one that would keep all thoughts of practical jokes far from the specialists' hearts and minds.

The morning after the battle at the firebases, Otani himself came out to the Pork Barrel to get a report.

Lieutenant Bacon nodded to his CO upon his entrance through the thick metal door. "Morning, Sir."

"It is that," Otani said wearily. "I'm really looking forward to this war being over so I can get a *good* night's sleep."

"Wouldn't know about that, Sir," Bacon said. "We've been up all night."

Otani blinked in surprise. "They haven't had any sack time?"

"Couldn't talk them into it, Sir. You know how they get when they've got a new toy to play with."

"And you haven't, either?"

Bacon shook his head. "When my boys and girls are left unsupervised, they get into mischief."

That prompted a snort from Otani, who also recalled the APC incident. "So, what do we have?"

"Quite a bit, actually. Romulus and Remus have told us a great deal."

Otani let out a sigh. Having been in charge of the Aces in general and Bacon's nerds in particular for so long, he knew that the Duster vehicles wouldn't escape the custody of the Aces without being nicknamed. And given some of the loopy names they'd come up with over the years, Otani had to admit to being relieved it was something as relatively straightforward as the mythological twins who were said to have founded the Roman Empire. He still remembered the embarrassment when Specialist Josephine Cicchetti had named a vehicle they were refurbishing after a famous male stripper she was fond of, which didn't sit well with the four-star general they were refurbishing it for when his aide informed him of the nickname's provenance.

Bacon led Otani through the corridors of the Pork Barrel to the large room in the back, which had been dubbed the garage. The wide-open space barely had room to fit the two Duster vehicles.

Otani couldn't help but think that right now, they looked like packages that had been ripped open. The tops were exposed, charred, and damaged from the bombings, but the sides, front, and back remained unscathed.

He also noticed that the one on the left had "ROM" painted on the side, while the one on the right said, "REM." One pair of legs stuck out from under Romulus, another from under Remus, and Otani could hear voices from inside one of them, possibly both.

Were this a standard Army unit, Bacon would have barked, "Ten-*hut!*" and then the various specialists would fall in and stand at attention.

But these were engineers and mechanics and programmers, and expecting standard discipline from them was just asking for trouble. So Bacon just said, "Kids, Daddy's home."

Specialist Willa Alchesay, the team's mechanical engineer, turned out to belong to the legs under Remus. She slid out from under the vehicle on a rolling flat cart, wiping a smudge of dirt off her small nose. "Morning, Captain Otani!"

"Good morning, Specialist."

The legs under Romulus belonged to the structural engineer, Specialist Demetri Corahogi, which Otani only knew because he recognized the voice that cried, "Ow," followed by a stream of Russian profanity.

As she clambered to her feet, Alchesay said, "Jesus W. Christ, Dema, when you gonna learn to stop dropping the wrenches on your head?"

The remaining three members of the team were inside Remus. Each popped up from the hole in the top in sequence. Otani assumed they were using a ladder or some such that he couldn't see. A metal staircase on wheels sat against the vehicle near the engineers.

First came Cicchetti, the team's electrical engineer, her dark hair flying out in all directions despite an attempt to hold it in place with a hair tie. She'd had short hair when they'd shipped out to Troy, but it had grown to neck length just in the time they'd been there. Unfortunately, the only ones who brought a barber to Troy were the Navy, and he was in space right now.

She started to climb down the stairs, followed by the scowling face of Specialist Rodney Yano, the tactical systems expert, and the smiling face of the head programmer, Specialist Joe Rodriguez Baldonado.

"Stumble in, please," Bacon said with a smirk, and Otani chuckled.

Back when he'd first taken command of the Aces, Bacon had warned him that they weren't exactly Regular Army, and in particular, right before Otani's first inspection, had urged him not to expect them to fall in regulation-style.

Sure enough, when they had assembled for inspection, they had sort of wandered into something vaguely resembling a straight line, and not even at attention—indeed, Cicchetti and Yano had been murmuring about a laser tracking system they had been in the midst of upgrading.

"You're right, Lieutenant," Otani had said then. "They don't fall in, they stumble in."

Everyone had laughed at that, and Bacon had breathed a sigh of relief. The worst thing the Army could have done was put a hardline baton-up-the-ass military stickler in charge of a team of engineers.

But Otani understood that these were original thinkers, people who needed a chance to cut loose and do what they did best so that the people using the equipment they worked on could do their best.

"So tell me," Otani said now, "what we have here."

While they were all the same rank, Alchesay had been with the Aces longest, so she tended to be the unofficial spokesperson for the team. "As far as we can tell, Sir, it's a souped-up APC."

Otani frowned. "There were no Dusters inside the vehicles when they were captured, isn't that correct?"

"Yes, Sir," Alchesay said, confused.

"Then how, Specialist, do you all come to the conclusion that this was an armored personnel carrier when it wasn't carrying any personnel?"

"It wasn't, but it could have," she said. Reaching into the pocket of her fatigues, she pulled out a minicomputer and called up something on its display, then showed it to the captain.

Otani saw the floor of the interior of one of the vehicles, which had indentations.

"What am I looking at, Specialist?"

"Seats, Sir. I believe, and Dema—er, Specialist Corahogi concurs, that these are seats for the Dusters."

Corahogi spoke up, out of turn, of course, but that, too, was par for the Ace course. "A human would not fit properly in such a place, but I believe the Dusters would easily be able to sit and spread out comfortably while being carried."

Yano added, "It's my guess that they weren't carrying personnel, as you say, Sir, because there was no need for that part of its function. We usually use APCs to get from one place to another, but that's for engagements that are all on the same planet—hell, on the same continent. But the Dusters came from space. They got here via spaceships."

"We're thinking," Alchesay said, "that they only brought them along now instead of in the earlier engagements because they're designed for terrestrial work. But they got enough of an ass-whooping from our soldiers that they had the need to bring in the big guns."

Bacon hid a smile. That was one way in which the Aces were just like everyone else in the Army. If the NAU forces won an engagement, it was *obviously* because of the hard work of the soldiers, and the Marines and sailors just helped out a little. It was all nonsense, of course, but try telling that to any soldier—or, for that matter, any Marine who felt the same disdain toward the Army and Navy or any sailor who felt that way about the Marines and Army. Bacon figured it kept everyone sharp, knowing that they had to maintain the standard of being better than the other two services.

"And a mighty big gun it is," Alchesay added with a look at Yano.

Taking the cue, the tactical systems specialist stepped forward a bit. "Romulus here uses a beam of coherent light that fires at ten thousand megawatts."

Otani's eyes widened. The laser batteries at the firebases were at one thousand, and the most powerful laser batteries in the Navy's arsenal were only at two thousand. "No wonder this was cutting down everything in its path."

"Yes, Sir." Yano pointed at Remus. "Remus has what looks like an older model."

"You think," Alchesay put in.

"Yes, Willa, I *think*, and since this is my area of expertise—"

"The gun on Remus is smaller, more compactly designed, and has less physical wear-and-tear on it."

"Probably because they haven't used it much," Yano said. "And anyhow, the main reason why I think it's older is that it only fires at nine thousand megawatts. The newer ones are usually the more powerful ones."

"Not always—sometimes, you sacrifice power for versatility and ease of use. Everything's more streamlined on Remus's gun, and besides—it's not that much of a difference."

"Willa's got a point," Baldonado said with his trademark grin. "I mean, if you're in a building on fire, it don't matter if it's eight hundred degrees or nine hundred degrees. You're dead either way."

"Right," Alchesay said, "in terms of raw damage, it's pretty much the same, and I think they cut down a thousand megawatts so they could use the smaller aperture, which gives them—"

Otani had been willing to let them go up to a point, but it was time to yank on the reins and haul them in. "The point is," and then they all quieted down, "that these weapons are devastating. My next question is more important: why weren't there any personnel in it?"

The specialists all exchanged confused glances.

Bacon came to their rescue. "The captain isn't referring to the empty divots in the floor, he's referring to the lack of any kind of driver for the vehicle."

"Nowhere to sit," Alchesay said. "We haven't been able to find any kind of manual steering controls—and that's accounting for the fact that the Dusters' ergonomics would be different from ours. But all the systems we've found look like they're designed to be preset."

Baldonado jumped in again. "I was able to break into their programming—even aliens are stuck with ones and zeros when it comes to computers—and it looks to me like it's all meant to be set up and then run. Kinda like a game. Lots of if-thens, where it's designed to respond to a particular way if something happens."

"That's why we think these are meant for terrestrial engagements," Alchesay added. "It's a lot easier to preprogram something that's on your homeworld in familiar territory."

Otani nodded. "Okay, here's the big question: can you operate it?"

Baldonado said, "Absolutely" at the exact same time that Yano said, "Not a chance in hell."

There was an awkward pause, and then Otani slowly said, "At least one of you two has to be wrong."

"He is," Baldonado said.

"It would take years to figure out how to reprogram the stupid thing." Yano's voice was climbing.

Baldonado kept his tone even. "We don't *have* to reprogram it." He glanced at Otani. "I'm assuming the captain wants to know if we can turn this into a weapon for our side?"

"Affirmative."

"Then all we really need to do is set it up to go in a direction and keep shooting until it gets there."

"And how do we make it do that?" Yano asked.

"We don't have to *make* it do that. It's already *programmed* to do that. That's what the Dusters did with it at the firebases. All we have to do is figure out how to hit 'go' on it, and we're golden."

"*Chyort*," Corahogi muttered. "He's right."

Otani turned to Baldonado. "Specialist, how long do you need to find the Duster equivalent of that 'go' button?"

"Couple hours? Maybe less if Rodney actually, y'know, *helps* instead of bitching and moaning."

Now turning to Yano, Otani said, "Specialist Yano your bitching-and-moaning privileges have hereby been revoked. Assist Specialist Baldonado in any way necessary to make these things operational."

Something occurred to Bacon as Otani was speaking. "Excuse me, Sir, but I have one other concern—what's this thing's power source?"

"We were saving that for last, Sir." Alchesay looked over at Cicchetti. "Floor's yours, Jo."

Cicchetti ran her hand through her tangled mop of hair. "I've been examining Remus's power structure, and I've found what looks like a battery. Here's the thing—it's covered in tiny little holes that, after futzing with them half the night, I've realized are absorption ports."

"What do they absorb?" Otani asked.

With a huge grin bisecting her face, Cicchetti said, "Everything. Sir, as far as I can tell. This sucker takes in anything in the vicinity and converts it to energy. Air, dust, dirt, spit, you name it—if it comes in any kind of contact with it, it gets sucked in and transformed into energy to keep it going. It's like some Duster genius figured out how to universalize a solar or wind converter. Sir, we take this back to Earth, we won't have any kind of energy problem ever again."

"And the good news there," Alchesay added, "is that we don't have to worry about Romulus or Remus losing power."

"Sir," Cicchetti said, "we've only had this thing for one night, and we've already found the most powerful semi-portable weapon in creation and a self-perpetuating battery. I get that this'll be a useful weapon to use against the Dusters, but I think I speak for all of us when I say that at least one of these guys should stay with us so we can learn more from it."

"Romulus has more powerful weaponry," Corahogi said. "Best to use it against Dusters, let us continue to learn from Remus—not just for science," he added quickly, "but to learn more about the enemy."

"Forewarned is forearmed, and all that," Alchesay put in.

"I'm fine with my two arms, thanks," Otani drawled, "but I see your point. That decision gets made over all our heads, but I'll recommend it very strongly higher-higher."

"Thank you, Sir."

"Meantime, priority is to put these monsters to our good use. So your assignment is to continue to be the wolves suckling Romulus and Remus so they can go found Rome."

All the Aces present chuckled, and Alchesay said, "You got it, Captain."

"Commencing howl-at-the-moon maneuver," Baldonado said, his grin widening.

Corahogi actually howled at that, and everyone laughed more.

"All right, enough," Otani said. "Get to work."

For a moment, he considered ordering them all to nap. They *had* been up all night, and they were obviously even punchier than usual.

But he also saw the glint in all their eyes. Even the usually downbeat Yano was obviously excited to get back to crawling around inside Romulus and Remus.

And they had gained incredibly valuable intel, both for the war effort and for Earth in general.

Having said that, sleep deprivation was a torture method for a reason. "Lieutenant Bacon, I want you to set up a rotation of naps for your team—make sure they at least get to reboot their brains a bit."

"Will do, Sir," Bacon said gratefully. Had he himself given the order, there was a better than even chance that the nerds would try to work around it, but coming from the captain, it would carry more weight.

For his part, Otani left the Pork Barrel trying to figure out how to convince the various majors, colonels, and generals above him to let the Aces keep one of their shiny new weapons to study longer and only give one of them back to the Army to use against their builders.

The Prairie Palace, Omaha,
Douglas County, Federal Zone, NAU

FLORENCE GROBERG ONCE AGAIN FOUND HERSELF SITTING IN ADMIRAL WELBORN'S
office.

She had expected to return to the Prairie Palace as soon as her interview
with the president was scheduled. However, she was not brought to the
Round Office when she arrived, as expected. Nor was she taken to the
Purple Room—on those rare occasions when Mills had granted a one-on-
one interview, he often had it in that violet-colored space.

Instead, she was back in Welborn's place of work, staring at his picto-
rial history of warships. At present, she was regarding SV-41869, the prosaic
designation given to the experimental military vessel that was the first to
be used in space successfully, and which wound up defending Earth during
the Lunar Uprising.

Public response to the Troy tragedy was mixed. President Mills had
explained that the distances involved made it difficult to have proper
information in a timely manner, and they didn't want to announce the
invasion and its response publicly until they knew for sure that there
was an invasion.

That, Groberg knew, was only half true, but humans had been in space
long enough—and dealt with the time lag inherent in such distances—that
most people bought it.

There was also significant outrage, of course, and tremendous support
for the troops being sent in to avenge Troy's loss.

Welborn finally entered his office from a back door. "Sorry to keep you waiting, Ms. Groberg. The president is still willing to give you those ten minutes, but we wanted to make you a better offer."

Groberg steamed. "Are you kidding me? Admiral, I made it quite clear in this very room that the interview with the president was non—"

"How'd you like to go to Troy?"

That brought Groberg up short. "Excuse me?"

"There's a long history of embedding reporters with military units. We've been assembling reinforcements for Troy, and they're shipping out first thing in the a.m. There's a berth for you on one of the transports, if you're up for it. Since you have combat experience, you're the only reporter we really trust not to get yourself killed over there."

Opening her mouth and then shutting it, Groberg then shook her head. That was *not* what she was expecting.

It was also a great opportunity. And a terribly risky one. As a former SEAL boat captain, she knew damn well how bad things got in open combat, and these so-called "Dusters" seemed like a nastier foe than anyone SEAL Team 9 faced back in the day.

But journalistic careers were made covering combat close in like this.

"I'd have full access?"

"Well, we can do it one of two ways. Everything you write has to be subject to approval by Secretary Hobson's office. If you agree to that, you'll have full access. If you don't agree to that, you'll only be interacting with NCOs and privates and ensigns."

"Um." Groberg chuckled. "The admiral may have forgotten this from being flag rank for so long, but all the really *good* stories come from the NCOs and privates and ensigns."

"Yes, but that's all you'll get if you don't agree to War Department approval."

Groberg was tempted to tell Welborn to take his War Department approval and shove it where the sun didn't shine, and if she was one of a pool of reporters being embedded, she'd have done so.

But she was going to be the only journalist on Troy, at least initially, and she had a responsibility to paint the *entire* picture for the people back here on Earth who were now desperate for information about how their colony was being avenged and defended.

Which meant she needed to be able to talk to everybody, from the generals and admirals who were making the plans to the colonels and captains who were giving the orders to the grunts who were doing the actual work.

She was correct in that the best stories would come from the latter group, but Welborn was right that it would limit her focus too much.

Besides, she was friends with Charles Abrell, the head of public information for the War Department. He wouldn't go crazy with the redactions, just limiting it to strictly classified material. And Groberg generally knew what subjects to avoid in that regard in any case.

"All right, Admiral." She rose to her feet and offered her hand. "I'm in—full access, and full approval by Secretary Hobson's office."

Welborn returned the handshake. "Excellent."

"But I still want my ten minutes with the president. I came all this way, and I don't have to leave for Troy until morning, you said."

At that, Welborn smiled. "That's fine, Ms. Groberg. In fact, it's more than fine, it's perfect, as it means I'm now ten bucks richer."

Groberg frowned. "Excuse me?"

"Secretary Hobson thought you'd take the embedding assignment in lieu of interviewing the president. I was fairly certain you'd stick to your guns on those ten minutes."

"Can't have been that certain, if you only bet ten bucks." Groberg chuckled. "The Purple Room?"

"Actually, the president has a lot of work today, so he can only give you his ten minutes in the Round Office. Let's go."

Headquarters, North American Union Forces,
near Millerton, Shapland

MAJOR GENERAL HUGH PURVIS STARED AT LIEUTENANT GENERAL HAROLD BAUER FROM the screen in the latter's office.

"What's your sitrep, Hugh?" Bauer asked.

"Holding firm, but I don't know how much longer that'll be the case. Some of the Dusters are engaged with our forces in Jordan, and we're holding our own, but a lot of the survivors from the firebase conflicts have retreated into the woods of Shapland, and I think they're regrouping and getting ready to hit us again."

"Orbital recon tells us they're just sitting there," Bauer said.

Purvis nodded. "The problem is, we don't have the manpower to go in after them. They picked a thick part of the woods. Prior to the engagements at the firebases, we'd have been all over it, but our losses were too great."

"Can you reinforce with personnel from Jordan?"

Shaking his head, Purvis said, "I don't believe it will be enough to make a difference, and we'll probably lose Jordan on top of that."

"Reinforcements from Earth are due in three days."

"I'm not sure we have that, Harold." Purvis sighed. "And if they come out guns a-blazing, we might be able to hold our own, we might even win, but I don't know how many'll be left to celebrate."

"The Aces say they can have one of the Dusters' vehicles ready for our use by tomorrow. Will that help?"

"It might." Purvis sounded tentative.

Reading that as his subordinate having another idea, but not wanting to speak out of turn, Bauer cleared his throat. "What's your recommendation, General Purvis?"

Taking the cue to be more formal, Purvis said, "Sir, I recommend we divert Navy resources for orbital bombardment. The last report from Admiral Avery is that the only forces the Dusters have left to send against us are clapped-out ships that can't even hold together. The likelihood of more Dusters coming through the wormhole is minimal at this point. Task Force 8 is holding the line against an enemy that isn't coming, in my opinion. And if TF 8 can drop some Rods from God on the Dusters' location, it'll take out a big chunk of their forces in one shot. Then we can divert everyone to Jordan, including the Duster tank we've commandeered."

Bauer rubbed his chin. "I'll talk to Admiral Avery and get back to you."

"Thank you, Sir. Meantime, Force Recon is going in to try to get a better idea of what the Dusters are doing in there."

"Good. Keep up the good work, Hugh."

"Thanks, Harold."

Purvis's face disappeared from the screen, and Bauer called his aide in.

Captain William Upshur entered the office. "Sir?"

"Get me Admiral Avery."

"Yes, Sir. Dr. Cunningham's waiting outside for you."

Referring to the chief medical officer by her title instead of her rank indicated that she specifically had something medical to discuss with him. "Bring her in."

Upshur nodded and went back to his office.

Moments later, he escorted the CMO into the general's office.

"What've you got for me, Frances?"

Cunningham was wearing a white lab coat over her fatigues, and her hands were in that coat's pockets. "You know those eggs they brought back from the farm?"

Bauer nodded.

"I think—I think they're hatching."

"That is what eggs generally do," Bauer drawled.

"Thanks for that, 'cause I wasn't paying attention when we did biology in med school."

"Your sarcasm is noted, Doctor," Bauer said a bit more tightly, "but I'm not clear why you felt the need to come all the way over here to tell me that eggs are hatching."

"For starters, the Aces never bothered to build me a maternity ward. Or a NICU."

Bauer sighed. "I was under the impression that you studied xenobiology, or is that another class you didn't pay attention during?"

"Your sarcasm is noted right back," Cunningham said. "But the entire field of xenobiology is primarily theoretical at this point. And given the Dusters' similarity to certain insectoid and avian creatures, a vet would probably be better qualified than I am."

"Do the best you can, Colonel. That's all any of us are doing."

Cunningham blew out a breath. "Fine. I've got the eggs in the quarantine unit, and they'll stay there even after they hatch. No goddamn clue what to feed the little monsters, but we'll figure something out."

"If you do," Bauer said, "let Army CID know. They've taken charge of the prisoners, and we don't know what to feed them, either."

Upshur stuck his head in the office. "Excuse me, General, Colonel, but I have Admiral Avery."

Bauer regarded the CMO. "Is there anything else, Colonel Cunningham?"

"I suppose not." The doctor sighed. "I was hoping you had a better idea of how to deal with these things."

"My job isn't to take care of them, Frances," Bauer said gently, "it's to stop them."

"Yeah. All right, I'll let you know when we have some bouncing baby whatevers in quarantine."

She left with Upshur, and Bauer then activated his comm to start the conversation with Avery, whose face appeared on his screen from his office on *Durango*.

Quickly and concisely, Bauer passed on Purvis's proposal.

"I'm assuming," Avery said after Bauer finished, "that you approve of this plan as well?"

"I think it's our best chance of putting a major dent in the Dusters' forces. We've mostly had the upper hand, but only by the skin of our teeth, and only after significant losses. I'd rather deal them a vicious blow before they have a chance to catch their breath. They may be able to take us down before our reinforcements get here." Bauer hesitated. "But I need your opinion, not as your CO, but as a fellow commander. Will this leave your ass hanging the breeze?"

"Oh, I can talk to you as my CO either way, General, because your call came to me about half an hour before I was going to call you with a proposal that is eerily similar to the one General Purvis gave you." Avery gave a half-smile. "It is my opinion, based on my own experiences—and, I might add, backed up by my intelligence personnel up here—that the fleet we engaged was the last-ditch attempt by an enemy who knows that the end is near and is making one last Hail Mary pass before they lose the game."

"So, you agree that it's unlikely that you will be needed to face more Dusters coming through the wormhole?"

"I do."

"Very well, Admiral. Glad to see we're all on the same page. Send me your battle plan when it's complete, and we'll bomb the shit out of those Dusters in the woods."

"Expect the report in twenty minutes."

Once Avery signed off, Bauer had Upshur get in touch with the Aces. "Tell Captain Otani," he said, "that the Duster combat vehicles are to be assigned to Colonel Chambers at Camp Howard."

"Yes, Sir, but, um—" Upshur hesitated.

"What is it, Bill?"

Blowing out a breath, Upshur said, "Sir, the Aces want to hang on to one of the vehicles for further study. They said the tactical benefits would be massive if the nerd squad can crawl through its insides some more."

Bauer suspected that the nerd squad in question just wanted to learn more, but he also had faith in Colonel Chambers's Marines only to need the assistance of one really big gun.

"Very well, but tell the captain that the second vehicle is on standby in case things in Jordan go pear-shaped."

"Understood."

Admiral's Bridge, Battleship NAUS Durango

THE NOTION OF ORBITAL BOMBARDMENT WITH SIMPLE PROJECTILES DATED BACK TO THE twentieth century. The theory was that, from a high enough orbit, you simply let go of an object and let it fall. As it plummeted planetward, the kinetic energy built up so that by the time it hit its target, it impacted with the force of a bomb.

The best part was that you didn't need any kind of special equipment. You could use rocks, and it would work just as well. No need to manufacture explosives or dangerous materials.

The most efficient projectile was quickly determined back in the day to be a twenty-foot metal rod that was about a foot in diameter. The length provided a wide surface area to absorb the kinetic energy that would then be discharged on impact. The small diameter minimized friction and maximized speed.

NAU Navy capital ships were all equipped with a complement of so-called "Rods from God" that could be used for bombardment. (Several military and civilian ship designers had tried to find a way to equip smaller fighter craft with them. Unfortunately, while most bombs could be dropped from a horizontal position, the Rods from God really needed to be fired vertically to be at their most effective. The only way to equip fighters properly would be either to give them a twenty-foot rod mounted vertically on the side of the craft, which was spectacularly awkward and complicated maneuvering, or to have the pilots only be able to fire the weapon while diving toward or climbing away from the target, neither of which was optimal.)

Avery watched the big board as *Durango* moved into geo-sync orbit over the forest where the Dusters were hunkered down.

"Verify position of Marines," Avery said.

Captain Huse immediately opened a channel. "Bridge, CAC, verify position of Marines."

A moment later, Chief Verney's voice came over comms. "Marines in position three miles from forest perimeter."

"The Dusters aren't at the perimeter, Chief."

"Radar can't penetrate the forest, Sir, perimeter's the best we can do."

Avery snarled. "Davis, call the Marines—they must've sent Force Recon in to get the Dusters' position. Find it."

"Aye-aye, Sir."

Minutes later, Davis reported back with specific coordinates.

Huse sighed. "Send that to CAC. Chief Verney, based on coordinates Lieutenant Commander Davis is sending you, position of Marines relative to the Dusters, please?"

"Stand by, bridge." Verney muttered something Avery couldn't make out, then: "Estimate Marines at four-point-seven miles from Duster position."

"Chief Finkenbiner," Avery said, "give us a firing solution for the Rod from God that will give us a blast radius of three miles or less, and send it to navigation."

"Aye-aye, Sir." Finkenbiner turned to consult with the weapons techs.

While waiting for the weapons techs to do the math on what orbital position *Durango* would need to take up to drop a rod that would provide a blast radius big enough to wipe out the Dusters in the forest but small enough so it wouldn't take the Marines with them, Avery stared at the big board.

The space around them was clear. There'd been no activity at the wormhole.

He was sure that he and his people were right, that the Dusters' last "fleet" had been a final bit of desperation. There was no way anyone else was coming

But every time there was a pause in the action, he stared at the readings of the wormhole.

Sure, he was ninety-nine percent certain that no more Duster ships were coming through the wormhole. So were his tactical people, so was General Bauer, so was General Purvis.

Still, there was that other one percent. *What if we're wrong?*

"Firing solution received," said the navigator, Lieutenant Henry Brutsche.

"Plot a course, Lieutenant," Huse said.

Avery nodded in approval.

"Aye-aye, Sir," Brutsche said. Seconds later: "Course plotted and laid in, Sir."

The helm officer, Lieutenant Junior Grade John Mihalowski, stifled a yawn. He was usually on the second shift, but he had traded shifts at Captain Huse's recommendation once it became clear the Rod from God was being used.

Mihalowski, according to Huse, was the best pilot he'd ever seen. "The lieutenant could land *Durango* on the head of a pin," the captain had claimed, never mind that *Durango* wasn't even designed to land on a planet's surface. But it also had the spatiodynamics of a brick—it wasn't meant for precision flying, but if you wanted the Rod from God to hit a particular target, as opposed to just a general pounding of the surface, you needed your ship to be in a specific spot in geo-sync orbit. That took a pilot with ice water for blood, and Huse believed Mihalowski was that pilot.

"Helm," Huse said, "put us into position."

"Aye-aye, Captain," Mihalowski said through another yawn.

"We keeping you awake, Lieutenant?" Huse asked.

Mihalowski grinned. "Just barely, Sir."

The helm officer manipulated the thrusters in tandem to get *Durango* into the position dictated by Brutsche's course.

"Too much, Mihalowski, you're gonna overshoot," Brutsche muttered at one point, and Mihalowski heard him.

"No, I won't, Hank," Mihalowski said, "it'll be fine."

"It better be," Avery said.

Mihalowski swallowed. "Yes, Sir, Admiral!"

Brutsche shook his head. "It'll only be okay if you go the way I told you to go—and don't call me 'Hank.'"

"Soon's you pronounce Mihalowski right," the pilot said with another grin. Avery noted that the helm officer said, "me-uh-LOV-skee," as opposed to Brutsche, who pronounced it, "me-ha-LAU-skee."

Another thruster blast, and then Mihalowski said, "In position."

Finkenbiner said, "Confirmed, *Durango* at optimal position for orbital bombardment."

"Ready projectile," Huse said.

With a nod, Finkenbiner said, "Readying projectile."

Avery glanced at a corner of his big board, which showed the external camera by the bay door that was now opening. The Rod from God levered out until it was pointing straight downward at the atmosphere below.

"You're drifting, me-ha-LAU-skee," Brutsche said.

"I see it, I see it," Mihalowski muttered, firing another thruster.

This type of drift was common for so large a vessel as *Durango*, and also typically wasn't any kind of cause for concern, except during a docking maneuver—or when trying to fire the Rod from God to a precise target. Half a degree off course, and the projectile would hit the Marines four miles away—or the clearing four miles east—or the farms four miles west.

So Mihalowski had to keep this large, ungainly ship from drifting even a little bit. No mean feat when micrometeors heading toward Troy struck the hull, or when the gravitational pull of the planet itself tugged you off course.

Finkenbiner said, "Firing solution *not* optimal."

"Hang on, Chief, just got hit by a micrometeor," Mihalowski said. "Compensating."

"That did it," Finkenbiner said. "Firing solution optimal."

Avery turned to nod at Huse, who nodded back. "Fire projectile."

"Projectile away," Finkenbiner said.

On the screen, the Rod from God disengaged from its mooring and started to fall toward the planet lazily.

Checking his console, Finkenbiner said, "Projectile is on course for target."

"What's the time to impact, Chief?" Huse asked.

"Three hours, forty-eight minutes, Sir."

"Projectile on main screen," Avery said. *They all should see this.*

"Putting projectile on main screen, aye," Davis said.

The cameras on *Durango*'s outer hull were able to follow the Rod from God as it fell toward the stratosphere.

"Good work, people," Avery said.

Huse added, "Lieutenant Brutsche, plot us an orbital course that will bring us back over target three-and-three-quarter hours from now."

Brutsche smiled. "Already done, Sir, and sent to me-uh-LOV-skee."

Mihalowski turned and stared at the navigator in shock. "We been serving together six months, you finally get it right?"

"You finally earned it."

"Thanks, Hank."

That made Brutsche's smile fall. "Excuse me, but as everyone on this bridge is a witness, you said you'd stop calling me Hank when I pronounced your name right."

Mihalowski shrugged. "I lied."

Chuckles went around the bridge.

Normally, Avery and Huse would shut down such side talk, but they'd just performed an intense maneuver successfully, the results of which wouldn't be known for almost four hours.

More to the point, it was a planetside engagement, one that helped all the Marines and soldiers on the ground. It had, Avery knew, been a source of frustration to many of the sailors under his command—and, when the admiral was willing to admit it, to Avery himself—that the losses his own forces had taken had combined with the need to be vigilant against more space-bound attacks from the Dusters to make the Navy a non-factor in the terrestrial parts of this engagement. The loss of Task Force 7 meant that naval resources were stretched thin.

But this last engagement with the dregs of the Duster fleet indicated that that had changed.

The ground-pounders may think they can do it all themselves, but it goes a lot better when you've got your guardian angels in orbit, and we've got your backs now, Avery thought toward the surface.

Brutsche and Mihalowski were still going at it. "Damn pilots. No respect at all for the people who tell you where you're supposed to go."

"I'm glad after six months you finally figured *that* out." The cheeky grin Mihalowski said that with fell as he added, "Sir, orbital position now eighteen hundred miles and holding steady. ETA back at this spot is three hours, forty-one minutes."

Huse nodded. "Excellent work, both of you, which is why I'm going to forgive you squabbling like teenagers on the bridge of a Navy ship."

Both lieutenants swallowed audibly.

"Yes, Sir," Brutsche said quietly.

"Thank you, Captain," Mihalowski said in a more subdued voice than Avery had ever heard him use.

Avery gave Huse an approving nod and then said, "Captain Huse, come with me to my office, please."

Getting up from the center chair, Huse nodded to the watch commander, Lieutenant Commander Rufus Z. Johnston, who replaced him in the chair.

Upon entering the admiral's office, Avery went straight for the drinks cabinet and pulled out a bottle of single-barrel Jack Daniel's.

"Sir?" Huse prompted.

"It's almost four hours before we know what'll happen dirtside, Captain, and after all that, I need a damn drink."

"I see, Sir."

Avery then smiled as he pulled out two thick-bottomed glasses. "Drinking alone is a sign of depravity. So you're drinking with me."

Huse wasn't about to turn down Avery's quality booze. "Understood, Sir."

The admiral poured the amber liquid into each of the glasses and then handed one to Huse.

"To the Rod from God."

"To the Rod from God," Huse repeated and waited for Avery to sip his drink before he did likewise.

The alcohol burned pleasantly in both men's throats.

"Hope to hell it works," Avery muttered.

Huse let out a sigh. "Amen."

Outside Jordan

SPECIALIST BALDONADO WAS STARTING TO WISH HE'D KEPT HIS MOUTH SHUT AND JUST agreed with Specialist Yano that they couldn't program Romulus and Remus to work for them.

Because if he hadn't been so goddamn cocksure that he could dope out how to run the Duster vehicles, they wouldn't have sent him to babysit Romulus while the Marines used it against the Duster forces outside Jordan.

"We're giving Romulus to the Marines," Bacon had told the nerd squad. "They're letting us keep Remus for now, but we have to be ready to hand it over at a moment's notice if they need another big-ass gun."

"Understood," Alchesay had said.

"Who's coming to pick it up?" Yano had asked.

"We're bringing it to them—specifically," Bacon had then looked right at Baldonado, "you are, Joe. And you're gonna operate it."

Baldonado had put a hand to his chest in abject shock. "Me?"

"You're the one who knows the programming, and we need an Ace on standby in case it goes tits-up."

And so Joe Rodriguez Baldonado, specialist first class in the NAU Army, whose only fieldwork was building things before or after combat occurred, and who otherwise spent most of his time in laboratories, was going into battle with the reinforcements being sent to Jordan.

At this point, it wasn't a single company or platoon that was going, but all the able-bodies who could be spared. The firebases were either secured or destroyed, ditto the farm where they'd captured the eggs, but the losses had been hefty. Major Yeiki Kobashigawa had been tasked with assembling an ad hoc company to reinforce the soldiers and Marines at Jordan. Someone had nicknamed them Improv Company, and it had stuck.

"This is *not* what I signed up for," Baldonado muttered to himself as he walked behind Romulus, which rolled slowly across the ground outside Jordan toward where the fighting was.

"Thought you joined the *Army*, soldier," said Corporal Nantaje. He was the leader of Baldonado's Marine escort. The corporal had been assigned to protect the engineer, along with three PFCs, Jose M. Lopez, Alexander Mack, and John J. Tominac.

"I joined the Army Corps of Engineers. We're a non-combat unit."

"What idiot told you that?" Nantaje asked.

Shaking his head, Baldonado said, "My recruiting officer."

"Ah, that explains it. They lie like cheap rugs."

"Yeah," Lopez said, "they told me it was a place to build character."

Nantaje chuckled. "Lopez already was a character, so that was bullshit."

Mack added, "They told me it was good pay and great benefits, and let me tell you, I'd make more money in my Mom's business and better benefits, too."

Tominac didn't say anything, so Baldonado prompted him. "What they tell you, Private?"

Shrugging, Tominac said, "Didn't tell me nothin'. Just signed my ass up."

"The point is," Nantaje said, "what they tell you in recruiting is bullshit. Kinda like how the battle plan never survives engagement with the enemy."

"Got *that* shit right," Lopez said. "These alien motherfuckers weren't supposed to be this crazy."

"Neither were we," Baldonado said.

"What do you mean?" Nantaje asked.

Pointing at Romulus, Baldonado said, "According to the metric shitloads of paperwork we got with this thing, this is the first time the Dusters have used these suckers in one of their invasions of other worlds."

"Really?" Nantaje stared at Romulus. "Not any of the other seventeen times?"

"*Seventeen times*?" Lopez asked. "They done this shit before?"

"At least," Nantaje said.

Tominac shook his head. "Fuck me backwards, Lopez, don't you read the reports?"

"He started 'em," Mack said, "but his lips got tired."

Lopez shrugged. "Don't need to read 'em, Johnny, I got you to quote 'em at me chapter and motherfuckin' verse."

With a sigh, Tominac said, "We found seventeen planets that've been wiped out the same way the Dusters wiped this place out. But none of them have had any sign of things like Romulus here."

Lopez winced. "C'mon, man, don't be usin' that stupid Ace name."

"What's wrong with calling Romulus by name?" Baldonado asked.

"Just call it a fucking attack vehicle."

Baldonado shook his head. "You jarheads got no poetry in you."

"Fuck you, Ace, I got plenty'a poetry."

"Yeah," Mack said, "but they're all dirty limericks."

"Wait," Lopez said, "there's *other* kinds of poems?"

Nantaje was about to say something when his earpiece crackled with a single word from Sergeant Arthur F. Defranzos: "Mark."

The Marines all clammed up at that point. They were now at the spot where they needed to be ready to engage, as they were almost on top of the fighting. Now that he wasn't bantering with the Marines, Baldonado could hear the reports of weapons fire from both sides.

Whatever pleasant distraction the Marines' bullshitting had accomplished for Baldonado went right out the window once they shut up, because now Baldonado could hear his own death.

He tried not to tense every time he heard the report of weapons fire, especially since it meant he was constantly tensing.

Besides, he had a job to do. He was the programmer, and his task when Defranzos said, "Mark," was to run the second of two programs. The first was a simple roll-along, but now that they were about to engage, he had to run the second program: where Romulus would fire the ten-thousand-megawatt weapon at regular intervals.

His original orders were to fire when instructed, but Baldonado had to admit to Major Kobashigawa that he couldn't.

"Explain yourself, Specialist," Kobashigawa had said in a tight voice.

"We've been able to figure out how to run the programs that are already in the system, but we haven't been able to reprogram them."

"So?"

Baldonado had sighed. He'd learned the hard way not to get too technical with non-engineers, especially ones not actually assigned to the Corps of Engineers. Marines, in particular, tended to get cranky when you over-explained. So he tamped down his lengthy diatribe about how it's easy to read the programs but not so much to rewrite them, and instead said, "Right now, the best we can do is do what the Dusters had it do: move and shoot occasionally."

"You can't control the weapons?" Kobashigawa had asked. "Then why do we even have this thing?"

"Uh, Sir, we can control it, but it's limited. We can tell it to fire every—" He had double-checked his control unit, then. "—forty-nine-point-four seconds because that's what the Dusters programmed it to do. I can't change the interval, I can just either have it at that interval or not fire at all."

Kobashigawa had sighed. "I repeat my question: if we can't control it that much, why have it?"

It was Sergeant Defranzos who had replied to that: "Sir, the weapon it fires is ten thousand megawatts. It wiped out most of our forces at the firebases."

The major had blinked several times, then had looked at Defranzos, then at Baldonado, then at Romulus. "All right, then," he had finally said before walking off.

Right now, the Marines of Improv Company were on either side of Romulus. Glancing around the side of the vehicle, Baldonado saw that the Marines whom they were reinforcing had adjusted position to the left and right so that they weren't in Romulus's line of fire.

The vehicle was going to fire in ten seconds.

The Dusters themselves were adjusting their fire, but also advancing through this unexpected hole in the Marines' line.

Oh, man, was that a stupid idea.

Nine seconds...

The Marines had made a V-shaped hole in the line, and were firing across the Dusters' flank.

Eight seconds...

In retaliation, the Dusters charged right forward, weapons blazing.

Seven seconds...

The Dusters' weapons fire bounced off Romulus the same way the NAU weaponry did at the firebases. If they were moved by the fact that their own weapon was being used against them, they didn't show it in any way that Baldonado could see.

Six seconds...

Mack was winged by Duster fire and fell to the ground.

Five seconds...

Baldonado swallowed audibly, realizing that the Dusters were getting very close now, and he suddenly wondered if the aliens were somehow immune to the weapon or if they had a way of controlling it that he and the rest of the Aces hadn't noticed.

Four seconds...

"Corpsman!" Mack was crying out.

Three seconds...

This was the first time Baldonado had seen the Dusters up close and personal. While he intellectually knew about their weird jinking motion when they traversed ground on foot, actually seeing it was a bizarre experience.

Two seconds...

He found he needed to look away before he got seasick.

One second...

The front of Romulus started to glow with a blinding luminescence. Looking down at his control unit, he saw the infrared scan that showed the giant arc of the ten-thousand-megawatt laser beam.

It stopped firing, and he peeked out from behind Romulus to see the result.

The Dusters that were still upright—which weren't many of them—were in total disarray. Some were still firing, but most were jinking back and forth in place and confused.

The ones that weren't dead, at least.

Thank Christ it worked, Baldonado thought.

"Move in!" came Defranzos's voice over general comms, and all the Marines moved forward, closing the hole once again, now with much greater numbers on their side.

On the discreet freq, Defranzo said, "Specialist Baldonado, discontinue firing and cease forward motion of Romulus."

"Um, okay. I mean, yeah."

He tapped several commands into his control unit. Seconds later, Romulus rumbled to a stop.

A Corpsman had arrived and knelt beside Mack, whipping out a pressure bandage.

"We gonna get in on the action?" Lopez asked Nantaje.

"Nice try, Private, but we stay here, make sure that nobody messes with our new truck. Our job is to protect it—and the specialist here—at all costs."

"Glad I made the cut," Baldonado muttered.

It only took a few minutes after that, but it was all over. The Dusters who survived Romulus's blast seemed to have been completely caught off-guard by the vehicle's attack.

Just as Baldonado was about to ask if he could turn Romulus around to bring it back to the Pork Barrel, he was stunned by a massive blast to the west.

Turning his head, he saw a huge explosion where the forest outside Shapland was supposed to be.

Admiral's Bridge, Durango

"Projectile has struck dead on target!" Chief Finkenbiner cried out as the Rod from God struck the forest with a massive impact.

Admiral Avery and Captain Huse nodded. Everyone else on board let out a single whoop of glee.

"Good work, sailors," Avery said. "Lieutenant Commander Davis, contact General Bauer and inform him that the Rod from God has done its job."

"Aye-aye, *Sir!*" Davis said with a grin.

"And ask for further orders. About time we got into the ground game."

Mathews Base Hospital, Millerton

COLONEL FRANCES CUNNINGHAM HAD STEPPED OUTSIDE FOR AIR. SHE STARED UP AT THE sign that was attached to the wall next to the doorway to the medical base. It was the second sign the base had had. The first had just read BASE HOSPITAL.

Then, during the earliest of the engagements with the Dusters after making planetfall, Georgia Mathews, one of Cunningham's medics, got shot while getting a comatose Marine to safety. She had refused treatment, insisting on getting the Marine to the ambulance, then going out and bandaging someone else's wounds instead of getting treatment for herself.

Eventually, she'd collapsed on the battlefield, but not until four soldiers and two more Marines were patched up and sent back to this very base hospital. And everyone she'd treated had made it back alive—unlike Mathews herself, who died from internal bleeding thanks to an untreated wound.

In the same tradition that led to the firebases being named after the fallen, Cunningham had had the base hospital renamed after Mathews, and the medic was for damn sure getting some kind of posthumous medal when this was all over. Hell, if I have to steal a medal from the Prairie Palace itself, I'll do that, she thought.

Cunningham hadn't been able to keep track of every single patient who had gone through the hospital, but she'd made sure to check on the status of the seven troops throughout the rest of the fighting. Two of the soldiers were wounded, but still at it, two of the Marines had been killed in later action—one in the field, one on the table in Cunningham's surgical unit—and the other two soldiers and one Marine had, so far, continued to survive.

Her gaze moved from the sign up to the sky. The sun had set, and it was a clear, cloudless night, so she saw tiny pricks of light that she figured were Navy vessels in orbit. Or maybe they were stars that were particularly bright—astronomy wasn't Cunningham's strong suit. Either way, they made for a pretty sky, whether or not they were faraway suns or close-by fighting ships.

Those fighting ships had, at least, provided a shipment of meds, which they sent down via the orbital elevator. She'd been two steps away from proscribing booze to ease her patients' pain for lack of anything better, and Cunningham really didn't want to be reduced to that. Besides the fact that it wasn't as effective, she didn't want to dip into her precious personal supply of single-malt Scotch.

An alarm sounded from inside the hospital, disturbing Cunningham's reverie. She went back inside to the main desk. "What's going on?" she asked Private Verna Baker, the clerk.

"Something's happening in quarantine, Ma'am."

"Shit." That meant the Dusters, since no humans had been admitted to the Quarantine Unit in the rear wing of Mathews since the armed forces had arrived at Troy.

She moved quickly through the halls of the hospital to the QU, which consisted of ten large rooms, each with its own observation chamber.

In addition to the five Duster eggs that had been confiscated on the farm outside Jordan, they had been forced to put five of the prisoners into quarantine. The Duster prisoners—designated PW0015, PW0016, PW0018, PW0020, and PW00022—had all started secreting some kind of fluid.

The lab was still trying to figure out what that fluid *was*.

The eggs and prisoners had all been placed in Room 8. Going into Room 8's observation chamber, Cunningham saw that two of her other physicians, Major Allan Jay Kellogg and Captain Georgia Nee, were already there.

"What've we got?" Cunningham asked.

Kellogg pointed at the eggs, which were on the far side of the quarantine unit, sitting on tables.

Which, Cunningham noticed, were shaking. And one of them was cracked.

"Oh, great," she muttered. "They're hatching."

Nee shrugged. "We knew that was going to happen eventually."

"Yeah, but I really didn't want it to happen while the prisoners were still in there."

"We could've put them in a separate room," Nee said. "In fact, I said from jump that—"

Interrupting Nee harshly, Cunningham snapped, "I know what you said, Georgia, I was there. I know I was there because I rejected your proposal."

"For no good reason!"

"For *very* good reason!" Cunningham shook her head. "We've only got ten rooms in the QU, and if we put Dusters in *another* room, that's *two* we can't use anymore for our people."

Nee was insistent. "We haven't needed *any* for our people, much less eight—or nine. And it means there's no risk of cross-contamination between the eggs and the adults."

"We haven't needed any for our people *yet*, but that could change in a heartbeat, and I don't want any soldiers, sailors, or Marines dying of some delightfully exotic new alien disease because we didn't have enough room in the QU because *two* of the rooms were occupied by the aliens who murdered every living being on this planet. Am I clear, *Captain*, or do I need to explain again?"

Letting out a long sigh, and not looking nearly abashed enough to suit Cunningham, Nee said, "Yes, Ma'am."

Turning her back on Nee, Cunningham regarded Kellogg, who had stood very quietly during that harangue. "Do we have any idea what that damn fluid is that they're spitting out?"

Shaking his head, Kellogg said, "We do not. Unfortunately, it's gotten worse since we put them in there. It's specifically coating their extremities."

"Yeah, but—" Then suddenly something occurred to Cunningham. "Where did those prisoners come from?"

"What do you mean?" Kellogg asked.

Even as he asked that Nee was reaching for a comm unit.

"I mean," Cunningham said, "we've got a batch of prisoners the Navy took from the last engagement in space, and we've got a batch that came along with these eggs from the farm near Jordan. Which batch did these prisoners come from?"

Nee scrolled through the display. "Here it is—PW0015 through PW0023 were all brought in by Sergeant Ruiz."

"The farm." Cunningham blew out a breath and looked back at the eggs, which had now started to crack. "It's very possible that these particular Dusters laid these particular eggs." She shot a look at Nee. "All the more reason why we shouldn't separate them."

"We don't know that," Nee said petulantly.

"No, but as a general rule, living beings tend to be present when they produce offspring. I think we can play the percentages here and keep the parents with the kids."

"If they are the parents," Nee said. "They could—"

Kellogg interrupted. "They're hatching!"

A bit of shell broke off one egg, and a larger bit broke off another.

Soon all five of them started to shed the shells.

Glancing to the side, Cunningham verified that the surveillance in Room 8 was functioning properly. This needed to be saved for evaluation.

"Can you believe this?" Nee asked. "We're seeing something no human has seen before. An actual alien birth."

"I'd be more impressed," Kellogg said, "if it was a nice alien birth."

"I make it a rule never to judge babies by their parents," Nee said.

Cunningham had to admit the woman had a point. Just because the Dusters they'd encountered were murdering bastards didn't mean they all were. And one of several reasons why she'd rejected the Catholic Church as a teenager—much to her parents' chagrin—was that she rejected as revolting the entire notion that all humans were born sinners.

For all that this was an alien birth, the process by which the eggs hatched was surprisingly mundane. The shell cracked and fell away to reveal a beige membrane, through which they could see indistinct shapes wriggling about.

One limb poked through the membrane of one egg, then another. Similar actions happened throughout the clutch.

The creature that came out looked nothing like the adult Dusters. They had light green skin, covered in a viscous fluid that probably had provided nutrients while inside the egg. The infants had no feathers, their limbs were comparatively stunted, and their bodies were quite skinny. They had the long necks of their adult counterparts, at least, and the long jaws that jutted forward from their heads.

As soon as they extricated themselves from the membranes, they jumped to the floor and immediately ran toward the adults.

For their parts, the five prisoners were sitting on the floor with their limbs all jutting forward, covered in the unidentified fluid.

And four of the infants started licking the fluid off the limbs. The fifth wandered around the room for a few minutes, then finally meandered toward the last remaining adult Duster, and also started licking the fluid off the limbs.

Cunningham glanced at Kellogg. "Allan, we have samples of that fluid, yes?"

"Yes, Ma'am."

"Get the lab to start trying to reproduce it. We may finally have something we can feed the prisoners."

"Colonel," Nee said, "with all due respect, that's like feeding mother's milk to a grownup."

"If it's the only food available, I'd do that in a heartbeat. At least we know it's something that will keep them from completely starving to death."

"I'll get right on that." Kellogg turned and left the observation room.

The five infants sat happily licking away. Meanwhile, the adults were making clicking noises.

Between gulps, the infants were making the same clicking noise back.

"Holy shit," Cunningham muttered.

"What is it, Ma'am?" Nee asked.

Ignoring her, Cunningham went to the intercom and contacted the front desk.

"Baker," the clerk said.

"Private, contact Durango, tell them they need to put their ship's linguist on the elevator down here ASAFP. Then get me General Bauer and tell him we've got Duster babies—and they're already talking."

PETTY OFFICER SECOND CLASS ISAAC L. FASSEUR RODE DOWN THE ORBITAL ELEVATOR
to Troy with his stomach doing flip-flops and his heart beating like a trip
hammer.

"You all right, Ike?" Chief Petty Officer George Francis Henrechon asked
him.

"No, I'm not all right! What the hell kinda question is that?"

Henrechon shrugged. "I woulda thought you'd be happy as a pig in shit,
m'self. I mean—you're a xenolinguist, right?"

Fasseur rolled his eyes. "No, Chief, I'm the ship's cook, but I talk real
good, so they assigned me to this duty."

That prompted a belly laugh from the chief, and a chuckle from
Lieutenant Commander Benjamin Levy, who sat on the other side of Fasseur
in the elevator.

"Well, frankly, Petty Officer Fasseur, I wouldn't put it past the great NAU
Navy brass to assign a cook to this particular duty."

"Actually, Chief, I can't even boil water."

"Fine, then you really are a xenolinguist. So why aren't you all happy and
stuff? I mean, school was a while ago, but I'm pretty sure they taught me
that if you put 'xeno' in front of a word, that means 'alien,' which means
that your specialty is alien languages, am I right?"

Fasseur nodded.

"So now you get to talk to an actual alien in its actual language. What's
the problem?"

"How much time before we land?"

"Twenty minutes," Levy said.

Nodding again, Fasseur said, "I might have enough time." He took a deep breath. "Look, it's one thing to *study* alien languages. You've got a margin for error, and it's all theoretical. You write papers, you compare stories, you look at the big picture, you check all the different sources. Hell, for the last six weeks, all I've done is read over every damn thing from all seventeen sites where we've found evidence of Duster invasions, trying to find some damn thing that will give me a hint as to what their language is.

"But, y'see, that's the *easy* part. Research is safe. If you fuck up, nobody cares—well, that's not true, all the *other* linguists care, and they rip you to pieces, but that's just 'cause we all ripped *them* to pieces when *they* fucked up. But even that's useful because when you fuck up, you learn stuff.

"That's back home, though. In the field? Ain't no damn margin for error. I fuck this up, and I could make the war go on longer. Or at the very least get people killed. There are *stakes* now, you know what I'm saying? That's why I was so glad that Jimmy Mestrovich got this gig initially, may he rest in peace."

Petty Officer Second Class James I. Mestrovich was, like Fasseur, a xenolinguist, and he'd been assigned to *Durango* when they shipped out to Troy initially. He was also rated as a pilot, and after the initial engagement, he was called upon to fill in as copilot in one of the Meteors—which was then destroyed.

However, it quickly became clear that there wasn't a need for a xenolinguist on this mission. The Dusters had shown no interest in negotiating, no interest in *talking*, and given their actions, nobody in the NAU military was all that interested in having a conversation, either.

Now, though, they were at the talking stage. As he'd said to the chief, Fasseur had been assigned to study everything he could about the Dusters once hostilities kicked in, and now he was assigned to the latest batch of reinforcements.

"Coulda been worse," Henrechon said. "We coulda got here and had to fight our way to Troy. But it looks like the Dusters are pretty much toast."

"So are our forces," said the woman sitting across from them.

Fasseur had actually forgotten that the reporter was there. Florence Groberg had been sent along to report on the war for the folks back home, and when she learned that Fasseur was being ordered to make contact with the aliens via the prisoners they'd taken, she bullied her way into going along. She'd been sufficiently unobtrusive in her observations on the trip out here that she had blended into the background, which probably helped her do her job better, though Fasseur found it unnerving.

He'd also heard a rumor that she was a former Navy boat captain, though he wasn't sure he believed that.

Groberg continued: "The difference is, we still have reinforcements in reserve, while they seem to have run out. I got to talk to someone on *Durango* after we arrived, and the ships the Dusters sent through were rejected surplus."

"Which means they're ready to talk," Fasseur said, "but what if I get it wrong? What if they misunderstand us? What if I misunderstand them?" He shook his head. "I call myself a xenolinguist, but honestly? There isn't any such thing, because the field is so new and unknown and we haven't encountered enough other languages even to have a proper database, and—" He made a strangled noise. "It's just a mess."

"Maybe," Groberg said, "but it's all we got. Diplomacy happens either because you can't fight anymore or you don't want to fight in the first place."

"The second one was never the case here," Levy muttered.

Nodding, Groberg said, "Right, but the first case is now."

"Oh, I dunno," Henrechon said, "I'd be happy to keep fighting until all those fuckers are dead. Don't," the chief added quickly, "quote me on that! But I had friends who lived here on Troy."

"Nothing we're saying right now is on the record," Groberg said softly.

"Good, then I can say this to you, Ike: don't worry about it. Best case, you talk to these alien assholes, and we get a treaty in place, or at least a cease-fire, and we go our separate ways. Worst case—well, like the reporter lady said, we got reinforcements, they don't. I like our odds if conversation don't work out so good."

Fasseur found he had nothing to say in response to that, and neither did anyone else.

And then the elevator started its deceleration, which would take up the final fifteen minutes. Fasseur's stomach went from flip-flops to out-and-out rebellion as the brakes were applied to the elevator. For a moment, he thought for sure he would throw up all over the deck.

Finally, the elevator came to a stop. Everyone undid their safety re-straints before waiting for the announcement that the elevator was secure, and they could disembark.

Awaiting them was a small group of people in uniform, but only two stepped forward to greet them: a Marine with captain's bars and a soldier wearing a lab coat and a colonel's bird.

"Welcome to Troy," the captain said. "I'm Captain Upshur, General Bauer's aide, this is Colonel Cunningham, our chief medical officer."

Levy nodded. "I'm Lieutenant Levy, this is Chief Henrechon. I'll be taking care of the first batch of reinforcements."

Indicating a major who was standing nearby with a group of Marines, Upshur said, "Major Metzger will take care of you, Lieutenant."

Again, Levy nodded, and then said, "The chief here will be escorting Petty Officer Fasseur."

"You're the linguist?" Cunningham asked.

Fasseur nodded. "Yes, Ma'am."

"Then who's she?" She indicated Groberg with her head.

"Florence Groberg, *Omaha World-Herald*. I've been sent to tell the folks back home what's happening here."

Upshur snorted. "Hope that tablet has a *lot* of memory on it. You're gonna have plenty to write about, Ms. Groberg." He turned to Fasseur. "Chief Henrechon, Petty Officer Fasseur, you're both to come with the colonel and me to the base hospital. That's where we're holding the aliens, and you can start your work."

Upshur and Cunnigham led Fasseur, accompanied by Henrechon and Groberg, away from the elevator station, while Levy met up with Major Metzger to organize the distribution of the other elevator passengers, who were there to replace some of those who'd been killed in action.

As they walked toward the hospital, Fasseur asked, "Why are they in the hospital? Are they sick?"

"In quarantine," Cunningham said. "We've got some baby Dusters that just hatched." She quickly gave a rundown of the Dusters who were secreting the fluid and also the hatched eggs. "But that's not the fun part," she added. "It's what the babies are saying."

"They're talking already?"

"Oh, yes. Quite the chatterboxes, are they. And they're growing quick, too. Only been a couple days, and they've doubled their size. At this rate, they'll be the same size as the adults inside a week."

"Wow." Fasseur hadn't expected that.

"But that's not the interesting part." Cunningham smiled strangely when she said that.

"What do you mean?"

"You'll see."

Mathews Base Hospital

Florence Groberg wasn't sure what surprised her more: that Lieutenant General Harold Bauer, commander of the 1st Marine Combat Force and acting commander of NAU Forces his own self was in the observation room of Quarantine Unit #8, or that she was hearing words in English through the speakers.

The latter went some way toward explaining the former, as the early stages of this sort of diplomatic event would normally be beneath a three-star's notice.

But the only beings inside the QU were Dusters. And yet Groberg definitely was hearing English words coming over the speaker.

Most of what came from the speakers were clicks of varying lengths, but they were mixed in with more familiar words. Groberg caught "fluid," something that sounded like either "feeding" or "heeding," and "growth" amidst the clicks.

Upshur said, "Lieutenant General Bauer, this is Chief Henrechon, who's escorting our xenolinguist, Petty Officer Second Class Fasseur. The civilian is Florence Groberg—she's reporting on the war for the *Omaha World-Herald*."

Henrechon saluted to Bauer, but Fasseur was completely captivated by the aliens he saw through the window.

Bauer returned the chief's salute, then said, "This is Captain Nee, one of Colonel Cunningham's staff." He offered a hand to Groberg. "Pleasure to meet you, Ms. Groberg. I've always admired your work."

"Thank you, General," she said.

Then Bauer turned to Fasseur, who was still staring, open-mouthed, at the Dusters. "Never seen an alien before, Petty Officer Fasseur?"

Without even looking at the general, Fasseur said, "No, Sir, I haven't. They're—they're amazing."

Groberg wondered how Fasseur had managed to become a xenolinguist without encountering any aliens but said nothing.

"So amazing that they make protocol fly right out of your head, eh?" The general's tone was reproving, but friendly.

Shaking his head several times, Fasseur whirled around and quickly stood at attention and saluted. "Sir! Sorry, Sir!"

Returning the salute, Bauer said, "At ease, Petty Officer."

"Thank you, Sir," Fasseur said, sounding incredibly relieved. Bauer would have been within his rights to discipline the young man severely, but he was here for a very specific purpose that they needed to commence. "Sir," Fasseur said hesitantly, "they, um, speak English?"

"Not quite," Cunningham said. "But they've been picking up words and using them when they talk to the adults."

"And the adults are sticking with their language?"

Cunningham nodded.

"How much of their language have you been able to dope out?" Bauer asked.

"Not that much," Fasseur admitted. "They speak in what sound like clicks and dashes. It has a certain structural similarity to Morse Code, but it's not a one-to-one analog, obviously. They also seem to convey a lot of information through minimal words—kind of the verbal equivalent of certain pictographic languages that convey lengthy multisyllabic words with a single image."

Fasseur then hesitated, listening to the sounds coming from the QU.

Groberg also listened, mostly hearing the Duster words, but with "nutrients," "growth," "mobility," and "development" mixed in. She also noticed that the pronunciation was a bit odd. "Development" in particular sounded odd—more like "develonent." It seemed like any sound involving lips was hard for them to manage. But glottals and sibilants didn't seem to be an issue.

"Right." Fasseur turned to look at the Dusters. "Everything they're saying is a word that you, Colonel Cunningham, and you, Captain Nee, and any other medical personnel who were in here would have been using multiple times to describe their progress in there." He turned to Bauer. "Sir, I believe that the newborns are able to assimilate language from what they hear around them—same way we do as infants, but it seems to happen at a greatly accelerated rate with them, especially given that they're obviously already conversing with the adult Dusters."

"So, you're saying they may learn English?"

"I'm saying we need to make sure there are lots of conversations here. Maybe even speeches that have concepts we need them to understand and be familiar with so they can serve as translators for the adults."

Bauer turned to the reporter. "Ms. Groberg, how'd you like to help the war effort? Or, more to the point, the peace effort?"

"How's that, General?" Groberg asked though she had an inkling.

"I want you to work on that speech the petty officer was talking about with Captain Upshur here. I want these alien babies to hear all about diplomacy and treaties and terms of surrender—and also strength of reinforcements, if you get my drift."

Groberg smiled. "I do, General."

"Sir," Fasseur said, "with your permission, I'd like to stay and observe the aliens further."

"That was going to be my order, Petty Officer," Bauer said. "I want you to get to know these prisoners as best you can, and I especially want you to trust the newborns, since you'll be communicating with them. Let's get to it, people."

Article by Florence Groberg
in the Omaha World-Herald

TODAY, THE GUNS ARE SILENT.

General Douglas MacArthur said those words at the end of the second World War on Earth in the twentieth century, and they also apply today on the Semi-Autonomous World of Troy, as the fighting that raged on this colony world has at last ceased.

The joint forces of the NAU military, including an Army division, two Navy task forces, and two Marine divisions, have fought a long and brutal battle here on Troy, though it is as nothing compared to the suffering of the people of Troy, which prompted the battle.

Without warning, without hesitation, the alien species that have come to be known as "Dusters" invaded Troy, leaving no one alive in the wake of their vicious assault.

This is not the first time that the so-called "Dusters," whose own name for themselves is unpronounceable by human tongues, have done this to a world. We have, in the years since we started colonizing space, found seventeen different worlds that showed the type of destruction and devastation wreaked upon Troy.

Unlike the other seventeen races that were demolished by the Dusters, however, the people of Troy had someone to avenge them.

The losses were devastating. Navy Task Force 7 was utterly wiped out, and Task Force 8 has suffered considerable losses in battles that took place in the space above Troy.

On Troy itself, thousands of Marines and soldiers have died, both on the ground and in the air. The Dusters have been relentless in their attacks, tunneling under the ground, engaging in brutal assaults across the terrain, and finally using a series of ground assault vehicles that fired lasers more powerful than anything seen on Earth or Troy.

But the Dusters reckoned without the fighting spirit of the NAU soldiers, sailors, and Marines.

They also reckoned without human ingenuity. According to several of the personnel interviewed by this reporter, one of the major turning points in the campaign was when NAU forces captured two of the Dusters' ground-assault vehicles and turned them over to the Army Corps of Engineers. The "Aces," as they're called, were able to reverse-engineer the vehicles and use them against the Dusters, helping to turn the tide of battle.

The forces here never forgot those who fell, but they also never lost sight of what they fell fighting for. Many of the structures here are named after the fallen—firebases renamed after Marines killed in action; the base hospital renamed after a medic who died saving the lives of multiple troops.

It was at the Mathews Base Hospital that the hostilities officially ended. By the time this reporter arrived on the scene with the second batch of reinforcements the NAU sent to Troy, there was very little fighting still going on—a few skirmishes here and there—but the Dusters seemed ready to surrender.

Dusters appear to be asexual, and they reproduce automatically. Several eggs laid at a farmhouse outside Jordan hatched to form a new set of Dusters. These, however, weren't fighters—at least not yet.

This reporter was privileged to observe these alien newborns in action. They quickly learned not only the Duster tongue of their forebears but also the human tongue that they heard while in the Quarantine Unit of the base hospital.

As it turns out, this was the method by which the Dusters intended to negotiate terms of surrender. They knew that their offspring would be able to learn our language and communicate with us, enabling us to draw up a treaty.

The Dusters ceded control of the Semi-Autonomous World of Troy back to the North American Union and also pledged to stay away from any world under Earth control. Any Duster ship seen approaching an Earth colony would be treated as hostile and fired upon. Unlike the invasion force that first attacked Troy, we now know what to look for, after all.

Normally, there would be some manner of reparations from the surrendering side. Either they would provide financial compensation for losses, or make an offer to assist in rebuilding. The Dusters seemed utterly baffled by this concept, and it soon became clear that this was not to be part of any negotiation.

This leaves the fate of the world of Troy up in the air. Only a fraction of the world's infrastructure is still in place, with most of it devastated, damaged, or destroyed. It's an open question whether or not the world will even *be* rebuilt, given the devastation. Especially with no help forthcoming from the Dusters.

It's not clear whether or not they have no concept of financial remuneration, no concept of finance at all, or if they do, but find the idea of reparations foreign. As much as the newborn Dusters were able to understand at least some of the English language, a lot of the concepts did not translate back and forth.

One of the unexpected bones of contention was over how the Dusters would retreat. Many of their space-faring vessels were damaged upon arrival by the Navy, and many more were shot down by NAU forces. Lieutenant General Harold Bauer, commander of the 1st Marine Combat Force and overall commander of the NAU Forces on Troy, felt that their casualties were high enough that their remaining vessels would be sufficient to the task. The Dusters, however, were insisting on having transport vessels brought in from their homeworld.

Negotiations on that particular point lasted the better part of a day and were in danger of growing contentious. It took considerable back-and-forth among the Dusters and with General Bauer and the Navy xenolinguist, Petty Officer Second Class Isaac Fasseur—who assisted in translating—before a compromise was *finally* reached. The Dusters will send one rescue vessel, to be escorted by a flotilla of NAU Navy ships from the wormhole to Troy and back to the wormhole, along with the remaining spaceworthy Duster ships.

In addition, the Dusters wished to gift approximately a hundred eggs containing soon-to-be-born Dusters to the NAU as tribute to do with as they would. This reporter got the impression that they intended to hand over their newborns as slaves for us to exploit—or, possibly, spies to learn more about us for potential future incursions.

General Bauer politely declined that offer, which seemed to confuse the Dusters greatly. The general did not wish to raise the security concerns specifically, and they did not seem to understand that slavery is very much against the law in the NAU. At Petty Officer Fasseur's suggestion, General Bauer explained to them that integrating their people into our society would cause more problems than it would solve.

Once the negotiations were concluded, official statements were made by both sides. Petty Officer Fasseur read the following statement, which he helped the Duster newborns put together on their behalf:

"We wish to express our admiration and respect for the human battlers who have fought us to defeat. Never in the history of our worlds have we fought a foe as valiant or as tenacious. In particular, we are impressed with the human battlers' ability to commandeer our battle vehicular conveyance for their own use against us."

After that, General Bauer made his official statement on behalf of the forces under his command:

"We have fought hard and paid a dear price, but in the end, we were victorious. We have shown that human ingenuity, stubbornness, pride, skill, and determination will win the day. We have shown that we will not tolerate an invasion of our homes, that we will not tolerate the wholesale slaughter of our people. We can be friendly and tolerant people, but we will not be abused, we will not be crossed, and we will not be victims. The fine Marines and sailors and soldiers—the fine human beings who make up my command here on Troy have excelled themselves against a vicious, brutal foe who gave no quarter. And we gave none back. Our losses were significant, but they did not give their lives in vain. An invader that would surely have turned their attention to another colony world next, or even to Earth itself, was instead shown the door. Our primary mandate is to protect the people of the NAU and the people of the human race, and when we can't protect them—as, sadly, we could not protect the people of Troy—then our secondary mandate is to avenge the fallen, which we have done here. The Dusters will think twice before crossing the people of Earth again."

EPILOGUE

William F. Lukes Memorial Park, Shapland,
Semi-Autonomous World Troy

Staff Sergeant J. Henry Denig stood with most of the able-bodied soldiers, sailors, and Marines left on Troy. They had assembled in the large park in the center of Shapland that had been hastily renamed after the late President of Troy, who had died in the Dusters' initial invasion.

Right next to him were the rest of Force Recon first squad: Sergeant Edward Walker, Corporal John Rannahan, Corporal Charles Brown, and Lance Corporal Erwin Boydson.

They watched as Lieutenant General Bauer, Admiral Avery, and Major General Conrad Noll, the commanders of the Marines, Navy, and Army, respectively, on Troy took their places facing them all. Avery held some kind of control in his left hand.

Between the three commanders and the troops stood a brazier.

Bauer stepped forward. "I'm not one for long speeches—the lengthy harangue that was in the *World-Herald* notwithstanding."

Denig chuckled, as did several of the personnel gathered.

"But I do want to say this: We lost a lot of good people in this war. I won't insult your intelligence by saying I knew every Marine who died, and Admiral Avery and General Noll can't say the same about the sailors and soldiers they commanded. For that matter, few if any of us really knew the people of Troy personally. We can't stand here and eulogize all of them, much as we would wish to. The sheer numbers are overwhelming—but so were the odds that we would win this war.

"And so, rather than try to memorialize everyone individually, we choose instead to memorialize everyone collectively."

General Noll stepped forward. "Specialist?"

Willa Alchesay from the Army Corps of Engineers stepped out of the crowd and walked up to the brazier. She touched a control on the side, and then a huge flame bloomed from within. The flames licked high toward the sky.

Noll looked out at the assembled multitudes. "The Army Corps of Engineers has put together this eternal flame that will burn in this park forever. We don't know yet what the future holds for the world of Troy—that's for the folks back home to decide. But no matter what will be on this world in the future, this flame will continue to burn in memory of those who fell, both the civilians and military personnel who died in the initial invasion and the people under our command who died in response to that invasion." Noll reached into a pocket and pulled out a metal plate. "We will now affix this plaque so future generations will know what happened here—what we lost and what we gained."

The general placed the plaque on the side of the brazier.

He then stood at attention.

Off to the side—Denig couldn't tell who—cried out, "*Comp*-ney, ten-*HUT!*"

Everyone came to attention.

Bauer, Avery, and Noll all looked at the brazier and saluted.

The entire complement assembled saluted as well.

"Rest in peace." Bauer whispered the words, but everyone heard them.

The three commanders finished their salutes, as did everyone else a moment later.

Avery held up the control in his left hand and pressed a button.

Moments later, fireworks blazed in the sky above.

A susurrus of "ooh" and "aahhh!" spread through the personnel gathered as the colored lights burst through the twilight sky.

"Courtesy of *Durango*," Avery said with a proud smile.

"Excuse me, Staff Sergeant Denig?"

Turning, Denig saw a woman in civilian clothing. She must have come with the latest wave of reinforcements, and he wondered what a civvie was doing here. "Yes?"

She held out a hand. "Florence Groberg, *Omaha World-Herald*. I've been sent to cover the war and its aftermath."

"Um, okay." Denig returned the handshake out of politeness, but he had very little use for journalists. Still, he wasn't about to be rude. "What can I do for you?"

"I've actually been looking for you for a while. Sergeant Ruiz says you were part of the team that first scouted out the farm where the eggs came from?"

Frowning, Denig said, "Among other things. Why?"

"I've been talking to everyone who was on or near that farm. It was owned by a man named George B. Turner. He came here to start up his own farm, along with his family. There was one family member, though, who wasn't able to come out with them initially, as she had obligations back on Earth, working on a project. But that project was almost finished, and she was getting ready to head to Troy to join the farm. Obviously, that's not going to happen."

"Okay." Denig really hoped the reporter would get to the point soon.

"I talked to Day Turner before I came here, and she mentioned a snow globe that she'd sent to George last Christmas."

And now it all came together. "Holy shit."

Groberg tensed, and spoke with a hopeful lilt in her voice. "You know what I'm talking about?"

Nodding, Denig reached into the pocket where he'd placed the damaged snow globe. "It's not in the best shape. I found it on the ground near the farm. Honestly, not sure why I kept it, I guess—" He glanced at the eternal flame. "I guess I wanted to memorialize the people here." He turned to face Groberg. "I suppose you want to bring it back to her?"

"It would mean a great deal," Groberg said emphatically. "She honestly didn't expect anyone to find it, and I didn't think anyone would. I was just asking on the off-chance. You found it on the ground?"

Denig nodded. "Under a tree. Here." He handed it to her. "And—and tell her I'm sorry, and—and Merry Christmas."

Groberg smiled and wrapped the snowglobe in a cloth before placing it in her pack. "Thank you, Sergeant. You've done a good deed today. Now, if you'll excuse me, I have to talk to Specialist Alchesay. I've been promised a detailed description of how they reverse-engineered the Dusters' tanks."

"Hope you budgeted an hour," Denig said with a snort. "The Aces tend to get a little long-winded."

"That's what editing is for, Sergeant. Thanks again." She offered another handshake.

This time, Denig returned it with more enthusiasm.

As Groberg went to talk to Alchesday, Rannahan clapped Denig on the back. "Jesus, J. Henry, you really are a softie, ain'tcha?"

"Kiss my entire ass, Corporal."

First Lieutenant John A. Hughes walked up to them and said, "All right, Marines, playtime's over. We've still got a shit-ton of work to do. There are some Dusters *and* our own people and equipment that are unaccounted for, and nobody sniffs out what needs sniffing better than Force Recon. So let's get back to work!"

Denig said, "Oo-rah, Force Recon!"

All the Marines standing before Hughes repeated, *"Oo-rah, Force Recon!"*

And then they got back to work.

THE END

ABOUT THE AUTHORS

DAVID SHERMAN IS THE AUTHOR OR CO-AUTHOR OF SOME THREE DOZEN BOOKS, most of which are, like this trilogy, about Marines in combat. He has written about U.S. Marines in Vietnam (the *Night Fighters* series and three other novels), and the *DemonTech* series about Marines in a fantasy world.

Other than military, he wrote a non-conventional vampire novel, *The Hunt*, and a mystery, *Dead Man's Chest*. He has also released a collection of short fiction and nonfiction from early in his writing career, *Sherman's Shorts; the Beginnings*.

With Dan Cragg, he wrote the popular *Starfist* series and its spin-off series, *Starfist: Force Recon*—all about Marines in the twenty-fifth century—and a *Star Wars* novel, *Jedi Trial*. His books have been translated into Czech, Polish, German, and Japanese.

After going to war as a U.S. Marine infantryman, and spending decades writing about young men at war, he's burnt out on the subject and has finally come home. Today he's writing short fiction, mostly steampunk, and farcical fantastic Westerns.

He lives in sunny South Florida, where he doesn't have to worry about hypothermia or snow-shoveling-induced heart attacks. He invites readers to visit his website, novelier.com.

Keith R.A. DeCandido is a writer and editor of more than three decades' standing (though he usually does them sitting down). He is the author of more than 50 novels, more than 100 short stories, around 75 comic books, and more nonfiction than he is really willing to count. Included in those credits is fiction in the worlds of *Star Trek, Alien, Farscape, Doctor Who, Andromeda, BattleTech,* and many other science fiction milieus, as well as in universes of his own creation (such as the "Precinct" series of fantasy police procedurals, also published by the fine folks at eSpec). As an editor, he has worked with dozens of authors, among them Mike W. Barr, Alfred Bester, Margaret Wander Bonanno, Adam-Troy Castro, Peter David, Diane Duane, Harlan Ellison, Tony Isabella, Stan Lee, Tanith Lee, David Mack, David Michelinie, Andre Norton, Robert Silverberg, Dean Wesley Smith, S.P. Somtow, Harry Turtledove, Chelsea Quinn Yarbro, and Roger Zelazny.

Having edited David Sherman's first two 18th Race books, *Issue in Doubt* and *In All Directions*, he is honored to assist in finishing the trilogy by coauthoring *To Hell and Regroup* with him. Keith is also a martial artist (he got his third-degree black belt in karate in 2017), a musician (currently with the parody band Boogie Knights), and a baseball fan (having avidly followed the New York Yankees since 1976). Find out less about Keith as his cheerfully retro web site at DeCandido.net.

PATRIOTIC SUPPORTERS

A. Parsons
Allyn Gibson
Amy Laurens
Andrew Corvin
Andrew Glazier
Andrew Timson
Andy Hunter
Ashli Tingle
Barb and Carl Kesner
beardedzilla
Bradij
Brenda Cooper
Brendan Lonehawk
Brian D Lambert
Brian Griffin
C. Frost
C.A. Rowland
Caleb Monroe
Carol Gyzander
Carol Jones
Carol Mammano
Charname
Chelsea Provencher
Cheri Kannarr
Chris Matthews
Christopher D. Abbott
Christopher J. Burke
Christopher J. Ford
Christopher Thompson
Chuck Wilson

Cody Steinman
Craig "Stevo" Stephenson
Dale A. Russell
Daniel Lin
Danielle Ackley-McPhail
Danny Chamberlin
David Holden
Dawfydd Kelly
Diánna Martin
Dominic
Donald J. Bingle
Dr Douglas Vaughan
Dr. Karen
Eli Berg-Maas
Eli Mellen
Emily Weed Baisch
Eron Wyngarde
Evan Ladouceur
Frankie B
Gary Vandegrift
Gavin
GraceAnne DeCandido
Håkon Gaut
Hiram G Wells
Howard J. Bampton
Ian Harvey
Idran
Isaac 'Will It Work' Dansicker
J Paulus
J. B. Burbidge

Jakub Narębski
James Flux
James Goetsch
Jaq Greenspon
Jeff Metzner
Jeff Singer
Jennifer L. Pierce
Jeremy Bottroff
Johanna Rothman
John Green
John Idlor
Joseph Charpak
Josh Vidmar
Josh Ward
Judith Waidlich
Keith West, Future Potentate
    of the Solar System
Kelly Pierce
Kerry aka Trouble
Kierin Fox
Kyle Franklin
Lark Cunningham
Larry
Leon W. Fairley
Lewis Phillips
Lisa Hawkridge
Lisa Kruse
Lorraine J. Anderson
MaGnUs
Malcolm Eckel
Margaret M. St. John
Maria T
Mark Beaulieu
Mary Catelynn Cunningham
mdtommyd
me@edmondkoo.com
Michael Brooker
Michael Doyle
Mike M.
Ms. Dyane Stillman
Nathan Turner
Norman Jaffe

Pam DeLuca
Patrick Foster
Paul van Oven
Peter D Engebos
Phillip Thorne
PJ Kimbell
Pulse Publishing
Ralph M.Seibel
Richard P Clark
Richard Todd
RKBookman
Robert C Flipse
Robert Claney
Robert M. Sutton
Samara N. Lipman
Scott Crick
Scott DeRuby
Scott Mantooth
Scott Schaper
Serge Broom
Shane "Asharon" Sylvia
Sharon Abdel-Malek
Shervyn
Sheryl R. Hayes
Stacy Butcher
Stephanie Souders
Stephen Ballentine
Stephen Lesnik
Steven Callen
Stoney
The Amazing Maurice
The Creative Fund
Thierry Millié
Tim DuBois
Tom B.
ToniAnn Marini
Tony Hernandez
V Hartman DiSanto
Vince Kindfuller
Wayne Garmil
William C. Tracy
Zeb Berryman

2 1982 03